EVA'S CHILD

Whitney Buggey

ISBN: 1530065577
ISBN 13: 9781530065578

ACKNOWLEDGEMENTS

I owe a debt of thanks to many others who played important roles in helping me write this novel.

David Arnason, Head, Department of English, Film and Theatre at the University of Manitoba, now retired, has encouraged me literally for decades to write. His guidance has been an inspiration. John Lent, Professor of Creative Writing, Okanagan University College and a valued colleague, also encouraged and inspired me to write fiction.

Shelly Singer and my fellow students at "writers.com" led me to discover that there were a whole host of very talented other people out there doing the same thing that I was and who were most generous with their time and energy in helping me through the revision process.

Louise Donnelly, a truly fine writer, was a valued mentor, critic and friend over the several years that the writing of this work entailed.

My Mother was an unintentional motivator for the idea behind this novel when she gave me a sealed envelope about a decade before she died and told me not to open it until after she was gone. So I wondered for years what secret she was passing on to me posthumously. Of course, this led me to speculate on what my origins or someone else's might have been. Did I have a twin somewhere? Had I been adopted? Hmmm!

My Father taught me patience, wisdom and always to ask "Why?" These are valuable gifts for a writer of fiction.

Being married to someone with a hobby like fiction writing can be a bit trying. The walls of our home have been covered in small yellow sticky notes at times. I have been distracted, still listening to the conversations in my head when my beloved wife, Patricia, has been trying to talk reality to me. The gift of her patience and understanding, her skill as a proof reader and her unfaltering love over the decades of our marriage have given me a rich and fulfilled life.

In spite of the encouragement, inspiration and guidance by those who helped me there will remain the inevitable errors. These are my responsibility. But so is the good stuff!

There are a zillion books in the world to read. Thank you for choosing mine.

Whitney Buggey
October 30, 2015

PART ONE

January 1939 - November 1940

PROLOGUE

Thursday, February 2, 1939 The Berghof, Southern Germany

She stood in front of the large picture window and stared out at the distant mountain peaks, frosted with snow and so clear and perfect they scarcely looked real. In the foreground on the hillside below were other buildings, some houses, Martin Bormann's house obvious by its size and opulence, a hotel, a military barracks, a maze of sharp geometric lines and shadows in the light of the almost full moon. The small village in the distance was a jumble of softer shapes, with the spire of the local church poking up in the middle. A few street lights glittered. The headlights of a single vehicle moved cautiously around the village square and disappeared down a side street. The village doctor on an evening errand of mercy, perhaps, no one else would be out at this time of night. Thin plumes of smoke from the small stone chimneys floated straight up in the frigid night air like columns of sentries guarding the village.

Two soldiers by the small guard house on the road below moved back and forth behind the barrier, stamping their feet on the hard packed snow, small clouds of mist forming from their breath. She knew they weren't smoking. That was not allowed anywhere inside the compound they were guarding. The other soldiers were staying inside, their presence revealed by occasional shadows on the windows and the white smoke rising from the small chimney. They would likely be huddled around the stove. They might as well be comfortable since the road wound its way steeply up to the gate and any vehicle approaching had to weave its way through a series of concrete barriers alternately blocking one then the other side of the narrow road. There would be plenty of warning if anyone was driving up here.

As she heard the door open behind her, she glanced over her shoulder and half turned to put herself in profile against the moonlight streaming through the window. She lifted the champagne glass to her lips and took the chilled sparkling wine into her mouth. She knew she wouldn't be drinking much more of it. Turning back to the view, she felt the thin blue silk night gown move sensually against her naked breasts. She heard the man move across the room and felt his presence behind her but he didn't touch her.

"I first came here in 1924 and fell in love with the place." His voice was husky, tinged with lust. "We bought the Grand Hotel in 1936 and began renovating the Haus Wachenfeld the same year. Now we have a southern headquarters here. "

The woman said nothing. She had learned that responding in a conversation was rarely required and he did not have a romantic phrase in his entire vocabulary. She sometimes thought of him as the Little Professor, always teaching, always explaining, always in detail, rarely interesting. He moved beside her and pointed at the mountains. "See the cleft in those mountains?"

She leaned slightly to her left, brushing her breast against his pointing arm.

"That is Austria." He dropped his arm, then took the champagne glass from her hand and set it on a small table beside the window. As he straightened, she cupped his face in her hands and softly kissed him, biting his lower lip, at first gently then harder and more insistently. The bristles of his short mustache briefly irritated the skin of her upper lip and then he pulled away from her. Grasping her shoulders roughly, he pulled her awkwardly against him. She pushed her breasts into his chest and ran her fingers up the back of his neck and into his hair.

"Come," he said, pulling her toward the bed. He stumbled slightly as he turned her. His German was rough and guttural when he was aroused, the working class accent strangely at odds with the opulence of their surroundings.

She had lit a candle on each of the heavy oak bedside tables and their flickering light made the huge canopied bed, with the ornate damask curtains tied tightly to the large carved posts at each corner, look like something out of a fairy tale. The pillows were in shadows. The dark wood panelled walls absorbed the light from the candles leaving the rest of the room in darkness except the area near the window bathed in the white light of the moon. The door to the adjoining living room was open and she could see the large chesterfield, its bright blue and gold pattern looking like shades of grey and black in the moonlight that filtered through the gossamer curtains at the far end of the room. The painting above the chesterfield, a reclining model, was only another shadow in the room.

She knew he normally slept in a single bed, his room as sparse as a monastic cell, the bed hard and covered with a couple of coarse grey woolen blankets. But she had enticed him into this suite to ensure that he appreciated the finer arts that she could bring to him.

She undid the sash on his burgundy silk dressing gown and slipped her arms inside of it. She suppressed a smile as she encountered his undershorts, the usual standard military issue that he wore, even on occasions like this. She pushed them down and brushed his erection as they slid down his thighs. Then she slipped the silk gown off his shoulders, sliding it sensually down his back, dragging her manicured fingernails down to his buttocks before letting the gown fall to the floor.

He reached for her hungrily but she stepped back and took his hand, leading him, almost demurely to the edge of the bed. She stepped close to him and pushed him lightly back onto the satin sheets. She had pulled the duvet down to the bottom of the bed since the room was quite warm. Earlier in the day she had arranged for one of the orderlies to light a fire in the Bavarian tile Kachelofen.

"Up there," she said softly, indicating the down pillows at the head of the bed.

He moved obediently and lay quietly on his back. She sat on the bed and picked up a heavy velvet cord, slipping the loop over his right wrist and tightening it. He closed his eyes but she knew he was still watching her. Then she stood up and moved to the foot of the bed. She let her silk peignoir slide off her shoulders and fall to the floor. She caressed her full breasts and pouted, then moved to the far side of the bed to secure his other wrist.

She stood there, her smile sensual and provocative but with a trace of amusement evident if he had the sensitivity to notice. She was sure he did not. She was clad in a flimsy pair of silk panties, the kind he normally hated, they came from France but passion erased political borders. She stroked her smooth flat stomach and let her hand steal down into the top of her panties. Moving to the foot of the bed she secured each of his ankles with velvet cords and tightened them pulling his legs apart.

Slowly she slipped her panties down and stepped out of them, standing naked beside the bed. From a drawer in the end table she took out a blind fold and sat beside him again.

"What is this?" he asked sharply.

"A surprise, my darling." She leaned forward to tie it around his head, dragging her breasts across his chest.

He turned his head to one side, then the other to avoid the blindfold.

She sat up and slapped him hard on the face. "Lie still, my love," she whispered. "Lie still."

She tied the blindfold securely over his eyes and sat back to look at him. He was a small man, thin arms, scrawny almost hairless legs, an unimposing cock.

"This is not necessary." His voice was strident.

"None of this is necessary, my love," she whispered, running her fingers across his chest. "But you will enjoy it." She stroked his thighs and ran her fingers into his pubic hair grasping his cock lightly. She stroked him gently at first, then more insistently. He began to squirm, driving himself upward into her hand. She stopped and stood up, moving to the sideboard near the Kachelofen. She glanced up at the rich tapestry that hung above it. In the darkness she could see the faint outlines of some long forgotten Roman legion, their swords raised against ferocious barbarians. From a large bowl filled with warm water, she retrieved an open bottle of champagne.

"Where are you?" he snapped imperiously. "Remove this blindfold immediately," he ordered, turning his head back and forth to loosen it, but she had secured it quite firmly.

She sat down on the bed again and began to caress him. "In a moment my love, trust me for a moment." She felt him relax as she stroked his cock again. She crawled on to the bed and straddled him, sitting on his thighs at first and then moving up. She guided his cock into her and sat down on him. He squirmed beneath her, struggling for a moment to withdraw from her. As she poured the warm champagne onto his stomach he moaned and arched upward, crying out as he slammed into her and climaxed.

CHAPTER ONE

Monday, October 30, 1939 Bavaria, Germany

The woman screamed again and then gasping for breath, settled back to a quiet sobbing.

"Just one more time," the midwife whispered. "Just a little more." She stood between the stirrups of the delivery table watching intently. The woman was fully dilated and ready. The midwife did not like using a bed and stirrups and would have used a birthing chair if that damned doctor wasn't here, insisting they use "modern" methods of childbirth. What did a man know about childbirth? He treated her like she was some primitive witch doctor and he was indulging local superstition. The woman moaned softly as the midwife gently massaged her swollen stomach.

A young dark haired nurse stood silently, almost anxiously, beside the patient's head. She wiped the woman's forehead gently with a damp cloth.

The midwife was aware of the doctor behind her again. He had left the room a few minutes earlier. She glanced over her shoulder. He now wore a long white apron, reminding her of a butcher, the sleeves of his white shirt rolled up past the elbows, ready to carve some chops off a pork loin. He was fat and officious, but although she was annoyed with him, she knew he was an excellent doctor. Women who went into labour prematurely were often unpredictable and she had to admit that she took some comfort in his presence. She felt his hand on her shoulder.

"I think I will take over now," he said softly. "This doesn't seem to be going anywhere."

"As you wish, Herr Doctor," she replied and stepped around him. She hadn't seen the forceps until she moved beside the woman on the table. "Surely that is not necessary yet."

The doctor glanced at her with an indulgent smile. "This is a city girl, not one of your wide-hipped country girls made for breeding. She needs a little help or we will be here all night."

"Is everything going to be all right?" the woman whispered through her gritted teeth, glancing from the midwife to the doctor, but the doctor was concentrating and ignored her.

The midwife recovered her composure and stroked the woman's hand. "Of course," she murmured. "The Doctor and I have delivered thousands of babies. Yours will be just fine. Any moment now."

A few minutes later the doctor handed the newborn to the midwife. "Clean him up," he said and walked out of the dispensary. It was a large brightly lit room, its upper walls lined with glass fronted cabinets containing an array of labelled bottles and small boxes. A white enameled counter top ran below the cabinets with drawers underneath. The centre of the room was occupied by an examination table that also served as a delivery table and a site for minor surgeries.

The midwife turned to the dark-haired nurse and smiled at her reassuringly. She was young and she had only attended a few deliveries. "You clean up the mother and I will clean up the child. Then we will see if they like each other." The midwife was grateful to have the young nurse present. If she had her way there would be only women present at a birth. The dark-haired nurse was built like a city girl, too, slim, elegant in a way, with a pretty wide-eyed innocence about her and although she walked with a certain clumsiness, her hands moved with quick precision. City boys would find her beautiful, country boys would be intimidated. There was a time when she would have envied the young nurse but now, approaching fifty, she knew that her role in life had not been to look beautiful. She wondered if the doctor had been thinking of her when he made his wide-hipped country girl remark. A friend had told her once that all she lacked to become an opera singer was the voice. She was full breasted, had hair the colour and texture of straw and her squat stature made her look rooted to the ground like Mother Earth. Her face was what people described as wholesome.

The midwife laid the tiny infant on a pile of soft towels on the counter by the small sink and began cleaning him up. He had screamed for a moment when the doctor had held him up but now he seemed calm. His big dark blue eyes looked straight at her although she knew he could only distinguish light and dark and movement. She hummed an old Bavarian folk tune to him as she systematically cleaned him. "What's this?" she murmured, as she discovered a small brown birthmark, circular and about a centimetre in diameter, on the right side of the baby's head just on the edge of his thatch of downy dark blonde hair. "You'll have a little mark there, my sweet one," she whispered. "But no one will ever know about it until you are an old man and lose your hair."

In the distance, she heard a door bang closed as someone came into the maternity wing. She looked at the clock on the filing cabinet in the corner and wondered who would be coming to the clinic at four in the morning. Perhaps it was some emergency, a car accident perhaps, although since the war had started, there were all sorts of strange things going on. She put a diaper on the baby and wrapped him in a small white flannel crib sheet. The dispensary door opened as she started across the room toward the mother.

"We have a visitor," the doctor said, standing in the doorway. "Can we receive him?"

The midwife handed the baby to the mother who was now propped up on pillows. "Not yet, I think, Herr Doctor," she said. "We need to move her to a regular bed in the annex to rest." She saw the doctor frown.

"Unless it is the father, of course," she added. Then she saw a familiar silhouette behind the doctor. It was the army officer who had arrived a week ago, the day the first child had been born, but in the dimness of the hallway all she could make out was his shadowed face under the brim of a peaked military cap. He had come and gone over the intervening time, but had returned after the birth of the second child. And here he was again. She wondered what was so special about these three births but when she had asked the Doctor, he had brushed off her questions, although she suspected from his demeanor that he didn't know either.

"Good evening, Captain Brandt," she said with a smile. "You are back to see us again." She saw the doctor frown at her informality, but she had come to know the officer slightly from his previous visits since he always checked with her on the health and general condition of the infants.

"Good morning," he said, touching the brim of his cap. The mother looked up expectantly for a moment and then back at her newborn son.

"Not the father," the doctor announced unnecessarily. "Nonetheless, I think we should cooperate."

She had seen this happen before with the doctor. He was all officiousness when he was in charge of some medical procedure, but faced with anyone in authority, his officiousness was transformed to obsequiousness. "All right," she said. "But only for a minute."

The tall uniformed officer moved around the doctor and walked toward the maternity bed. His dove grey uniform was immaculate, not a wrinkle. Had he just put it on or did he sleep standing up? He glanced at the mother and then stared intently at the child. He nodded, seemingly satisfied, then came rigidly to attention and banged the heels of his knee high glossy black leather boots together. The child seemed startled by the sound but the mother ignored it and murmured softly to the baby.

"I have other babies to deliver," the midwife said firmly. She was in the doctor's office with the military officer. In contrast to the dispensary, the office was all dark wood, one wall lined with medical books on dark oak shelving, the wall behind the desk contained more dark shelving with photographs, a couple of beer steins, and two small trophies from the doctor's youth when he had been a competitive skier. It reeked of tobacco smoke from the foul smelling pipe the doctor used. "Frau Schmidt no longer needs my care. The nurse is perfectly capable of caring for her and the child is now three days old and doing well."

"Thank you," the tall officer said softly from behind the doctor's desk, a large solid piece of unadorned furniture with a dark green leather top. "However, we will require your assistance here for another day or two or until you feel Frau Schmidt can travel."

"Captain Brandt, you can't keep me a prisoner here," she said, unconsciously standing with her hands on her hips. Frau Schmidt had been the third pregnant woman to come to the clinic in the last ten days and the last to deliver. The other two births had gone more smoothly than the last with the doctor only arriving in the delivery room after the birth had occurred. The other two women had already been released with their children, driven off in an official military convoy with Captain Brandt accompanying them.

"You are not a prisoner here," Brandt assured her in that soft persuasive voice. "You are carrying out the business of the Reich, very important business, too. We have explained to your husband that your services are required here and we have made arrangements with other midwives to look after your patients. We have cared well for you, fed you, brought clothes from your home. Is there anything else we can do to help you?"

"Just let me out of here so I can get on with my work."

"But that is not possible," he replied quietly, shaking his head. "Besides, your work here is not yet finished."

"But of course it is," she said. "I have delivered three babies. Only Frau Schmidt's child posed any problems and the Doctor resolved those. If there are complications now, it is a job for the Doctor not for a mid-wife."

Brandt smiled at her. He was really quite handsome when his face relaxed that way. "We have had three children to care for and I would feel much more confident that they had all been well looked after if you remained here until the last one was released." He held her eyes with his. There was a genuine warmth in him that had surprised her the few times she had seen it. Perhaps he had children of his own. "Besides, we both know that you can provide better care to mothers and new born children than the Doctor, even with all his formal education and medical skills."

She knew she was being manipulated, nonetheless, she was flattered. He spoke the truth, regardless of his motivation. A thought suddenly occurred to her as she rose from her chair to leave. "I didn't realize there was any connection among the three mothers and their babies."

"They are all important to the Reich. If they were not, I would not be here."

"Very well," she said. "I understand staying here until all three children were born, but now I would appreciate being released from here as soon as possible so I can deal with my other patients.

"And so you shall be." The officer stood, indicating that the interview was over. "Thank you for your patience."

The midwife turned and left the doctor's office which she now thought of as Captain Brandt's office and walked down the hallway to the annex where Frau Schmidt's room was located. The other two women had been housed in two other wings of the clinic. She wondered what the connection was and why they had been separated this way. It was customary to keep all the post-natal patients in the same wing. She wondered how Frau Hofner and her little son were doing. The mother was fine but she had some concerns about the child. He was a little underweight and frail with a wisp of black hair. He had little of the baby fat that was a normal part of a new born child. However, Frau Hofner doted on the child already and her breast milk was ample so he would likely do quite well.

The other child was a big robust boy with traces of white blonde hair beginning to appear on his handsome little head by the time he and his mother, Frau Moser, had been released. Frau Moser, was another city girl, they all were, but she seemed almost indifferent to her child. Her first request the morning after the birth had been to have a manicure and to enquire whether the clinic had provisions for having her hair done. A vain woman who didn't appear at all ready or even interested in bringing a child into her life.

She passed the two armed soldiers in the hallway of the annex. She didn't recognize them so she knew they were not local. The soldiers guarding the other two children had also been unknown to her. She didn't recognize the insignia on their field grey uniforms either but there were so many different parts of the army these days. They nodded at her, acknowledging her passage. She had noticed the younger one's interest in her nurse. He was a nice looking lad, blonde and wholesome.

As she entered the nursery she saw Frau Schmidt was still sleeping. The baby, also asleep, was in the tiny crib beside the bed. He had acquired some shape and colour now. She stared down at the mother and child and wondered again who they were to cause all this trouble. The mother had arrived by car about eight o'clock in the evening, near her time, although she claimed it wasn't due until November 12. Still, she had often seen births come a little sooner or a little later. The child was certainly healthy enough and his entry into the world a couple of weeks early hadn't seemed to bother him much. She looked at the mother again. Her left hand hung off the edge of the bed, the long elegant fingers still showing the care of expensive manicures. The mid wife had noted the absence of a wedding ring but pregnant women often removed them if their fingers swelled. Although the mother had spoken little, the mid-wife felt a kindness and compassion in her. She would be a good mother.

The dark-haired young nurse stood up.

"All is well?" the midwife asked.

The nurse nodded and walked past her to close the door. "How much longer are we going to be kept here?"

"Not long. As soon as our patients are stabilized and able to be moved they will leave the clinic and we will be on our way. Another couple of days I should think."

The third ambulance arrived nine days after Frau Schmidt's child was born. This ambulance was a large Daimler Benz, the same as the previous vehicles that had taken the other two mothers and their children away. Frau Schmidt was taken out in a wheel chair with the child. She smiled at the midwife and motioned her closer.

"Thank you for everything," she said softly in the gentle lilting voice the midwife had come to know. Frau Schmidt had been a pleasure to have as a patient. Never complaining, always smiling, focussing on her child. She was also quite a beautiful young woman, her dark blonde hair thick and waved with natural curls. She was young and resilient and she would soon regain her slim figure. There was both an elegance and a simplicity about her that was quite charming. She had been the sole highlight of their incarceration.

"It has been our pleasure to have you here, Frau Schmidt. Your child is beautiful."

"Thank you," she said.

A motorcycle with a side car and two soldiers was parked in front of the ambulance. Behind it there was small army truck with several armed soldiers in the back. After the door closed on Frau Schmidt, the midwife watched as the small cavalcade drove off down the winding road toward the little village and onto the main street, disappearing around the corner by the church. She nodded to herself, glad the ordeal was over. She shivered in the crisp clean air. The sky was clear and the pale November sun already cast long thin shadows across the town square. It would probably snow tonight or tomorrow, the first of the season, and turn the village into a Christmas card, the old stone houses and the church steeple, frosted like a cake.

Inside the clinic it was warm and comforting. In the room that she and the nurse had shared for the last few days she gathered her things together and packed them in the small suitcase she used to travel about when she was working in rural areas. She saw the nurse had left her packed bag on the bed. She heard the door open behind her.

"Are you ready?" Captain Brandt asked.

The midwife snapped the latch shut on her suitcase and turned to face him. He looked particularly handsome today, tall, slim and formal in his pressed grey uniform. He always looked as though he was dressed for a gala ball and lacked only a beautiful woman in an elegant evening gown on his arm. But he looked tired today, perhaps tense was a better word. Maybe he had enjoyed an extra glass of schnapps last night and was feeling the effects. She had resented him at first but had come to rather like him as the days had unfolded. He was unfailingly polite and courteous and had been honestly interested in the welfare of their patients. Other than keeping she and her nurse here virtually as prisoners, he had arranged for everything they needed. "Yes, thank you," she replied.

"I will have one of my men bring your suitcase," he said. He smiled at her warmly. "Thank you for everything. It has been a pleasure to have you serve the Reich."

The midwife liked his smile. It transformed his face from a rather threatening visage to one of warmth. "You're welcome," she replied, smiling back. "I am free to go now?"

"I will deliver you home in my staff car," he said. "Your nurse is already waiting."

The staff car was a large, black, prewar model. The officer ushered her into the back seat beside the nurse and slid into the front with the driver. He turned to them and smiled again. "We have one stop on the way and then your duties will be over."

The car followed the same route out of town as the ambulance had and after a few kilometres, they turned onto a main road and headed toward a range of low hills, a shadowy purple line in the distance. "Where are we going?" the midwife asked. She glanced out the rear window of the staff car and saw a small army truck following them. The two soldiers who had been stationed at the clinic were in the front with the younger one driving.

"It will just be a brief stop," Captain Brandt said, turning to face them and smiling again. "You will receive the thanks of the Reich for your services."

Half an hour later the staff car turned off the main road and a couple of kilometres down the secondary road, stopped at a high iron gate set in a long stone wall. Two guards stationed at the gate swung it slowly open. The officer waved a casual salute at them. They responded by banging their heels together and raising their right arms. The long gravel driveway was lined with tall fir trees and the grounds were also well treed. The driveway ended in a circle in front of a large old stone manor house, with a broad set of matching stone stairs leading up to large studded double doors flanked by two small stone lions. Above the door was the only sign of the new age, a large flag, a black swastika on a blood red background. The driver halted the car.

"We've arrived, ladies," the officer said. He got out and opened the midwife's door. She and the nurse got out and looked around. It was cooler here and the air was crisp and scented with pine and fir. It was silent and peaceful, the afternoon sunlight filtering down through the branches of the tall trees. The midwife looked at the house. It appeared to be closed up for the season. "Our host is in the back garden. He is pruning some of his rose bushes for the winter."

They heard another vehicle labouring up the driveway and a moment later the small army truck pulled into the circle and stopped behind the staff car. The two soldiers from the clinic got out of the cab and saluted the officer. He returned the salute with a casual wave. "We are just going to find our host," he said to them. "Come along."

They started off on a cobblestoned path around one end of the manor house and a few moments later entered a large garden area. "Just down this path toward the small greenhouse," the officer said, pointing the way. "My men will take you there and I'll join you in a minute."

As they walked down the path, the midwife noted that the garden had been put to rest for the winter, the rose bushes already pruned and mounded, and a variety of other perennials covered. It would be a lovely garden in the spring and it would be in flower all summer and well into the fall. A small gazebo off to the left with a fountain, now drained, would provide a peaceful spot to view the garden. The younger soldier followed a narrow path around one side of the greenhouse and called to them. At the back of the greenhouse there was a large pile of topsoil and beside it another large pile of what looked like peat moss, covered by a tarpaulin. "Just over here," the young soldier said, motioning them toward the pile of topsoil.

The midwife turned to him just as he raised his machine pistol and fired a short burst. The shells tore into her chest, hurling her back onto the pile of dirt. The dark haired nurse's scream was cut off by a second burst of fire from the older soldier's weapon. The two soldiers looked at the bodies lying half upright against the topsoil. "A pity to waste the dark haired one," the older soldier said with a rueful grin.

"You can take her now," the younger one said laughing. "She's still warm."

The older soldier looked at his companion and then spit on the ground near the midwife's foot. He grinned sardonically. "If I wanted to fuck a corpse, I'd go home to my wife."

Captain Brandt walked around the corner of the greenhouse and up to his men. "Well done," he said. "The Reich will see you rewarded." He raised his luger and fired it point blank into the head of the older soldier. The younger one gasped in astonishment as the second shot exploded into his face.

CHAPTER TWO

Tuesday, September 3, 1940 Berlin, Germany

Martin Bormann was in a foul mood. His early morning meeting with the Fuehrer and Rudolph Hess, had infuriated him. Hess was the Deputy Fuehrer and in theory, the second most powerful man in Germany. He, Martin Bormann, was Hess's Chief of Staff, with the rank of "Reichsleiter", one of the highest ranks in the country. While Hess was only six years older than he was, Hess had been born in Egypt, in Cairo, and had been a pilot in the last war. Hess was given to mysticism, studied astrology and could not organize his own breakfast, never mind the administration of the Third Reich. He would have long since vanished from Hitler's hierarchy if Bormann had not done his job for him. In fact, Hess often failed to attend important meetings, significant decisions were taken in his absence, and if Bormann had not intervened by getting himself invited to the Fuehrer's meetings to represent Hess, neither Hess, nor, more importantly, Bormann himself, would have retained any vestige of power in the Reich. And still he had to put up with meetings where Hess mumbled on, wasting the Fuehrer's time, confused and naive as always on every matter, political or military, economic or social, that he presumed to raise with Hitler.

It remained a mystery to Bormann how Hess could continue to be a close confidant to Hitler and perhaps as close to a personal friend as the Fuehrer had. Perhaps Hitler enjoyed him because Hess hung on his every word, parroted the party line and was a slavish sycophant. The sycophant part he could understand. No one who hoped to survive near the Fuehrer could be anything else. Hess also had a personal closeness to the Fuehrer, perhaps born of a shared past, perhaps the result of some personality quirk that he had missed, but strangely irritating since Hitler had no close personal friends. Bormann's relationship with the Fuehrer, by contrast, remained distant, and very clearly a master servant one. Perhaps that was too strong, Bormann reflected, but it certainly lacked the closeness that Hess's relationship enjoyed. However, these personal musings aside, the real problem was that as Hess's Chief of Staff, he had to be present when Hess had nothing to say and took an hour of his time to say it. The Fuehrer always had plenty to say.

There was a light knock on his office door. Captain Lausbeck, his assistant, stepped inside, closed the door, and walked across the office to stand in front of Bormann's desk. "The Braun woman is here," he announced quietly, his voice carefully neutral as he referred to Hitler's mistress. "I told her she would require an appointment but she is insistent."

Bormann drummed his fingers on the top of his large ornate cherry wood desk, staring vacantly at Lausbeck for a moment. All he needed was Eva Braun to ruin the rest of his morning. Still, he knew he had to see her again soon, so why not this morning. "Send her in, Lausbeck," he snapped. "And bring us some coffee." Bormann leaned back in the leather chair, took a deep breath and relaxed, deliberately composing himself for the ordeal ahead.

Lausbeck came rigidly to attention, banged his heels together, nodded curtly, executed an about turn and marched across the office.

Bormann smiled and shook his head slightly. He had never quite gotten used to this presumptuous military formality for even the most trivial of occasions. He looked around his large, well-appointed office. It was a functional workplace with a small round table and four chairs in one corner for short working meetings with his staff, an area with two chesterfields and a coffee table in another corner. This served a multitude of uses including regular trysts with some of the more attractive and cooperative secretaries who worked in his area. The windows from this corner looked out over the Chancellery gardens. He often opened the windows in the summer and enjoyed their peaceful beauty. Occasionally he even went outside and walked among the roses. It reminded him of simpler and more peaceful times. One wall was covered in dark, leather bound books which he had never read, indeed had never touched, they were purely decorative. The wall behind his desk was hung with two huge red banners emblazoned with black swastikas which framed a huge portrait of Adolf Hitler so that anyone entering his high ceilinged office through the doors opposite his desk could not avoid the piercing eyes of the Fuehrer and would be instantly reminded of the obvious importance of the man seated below. He had a smaller portrait of Hess on an adjoining wall.

Lausbeck knocked sharply and opened the door, ushering Eva Braun into the office. Bormann watched her walk across the office and felt the stirrings of lust as he always did when he saw her. She was a beautiful woman, elegant and self-assured.

She was wearing a gold cashmere suit. The full shouldered jacket with several buttons undone revealed a simple white silk blouse with French cuffs showing at her wrists. The skirt hugged her shapely hips, accentuating their sensual swing as she came toward him. The straight skirt ended just below her knees. He looked up at her face and saw the trace of a smile flitting across her luscious lips as she slid smoothly into the leather armchair on the other side of the desk and with a feline movement settled herself comfortably. What a shame to waste a woman like her on the Fuehrer, who didn't even like women very much.

Bormann had chosen the armchair because it forced visitors to his office to look up at him. It also had the added advantage that when someone like Eva Braun sat in it, and crossed her legs as she had just done, the view was quite tantalizing. He looked at her and smiled. She smiled back, knowingly, fully aware of the effect she was having on him.

"Thank you for seeing me without an appointment, Martin," she said, her voice soft and husky, caressing his ears. "That was gracious of you."

"I am always available for you," Bormann replied, keeping his eyes firmly fixed on her face. He smiled at his unintended flirtatious remark and watched while she opened her handbag, took out a slim gold case and extracted a cigarette. She rummaged for a moment and then looked up at Bormann with a helpless shrug.

"Do you have a light, Martin?"

"Of course." Bormann stood up and walked around the front of the desk, aware of his short stature and stocky figure, aware, too, that Eva Braun had just shifted the control of their meeting to herself. He pulled a lighter from the pocket of his jacket and leaned forward snapping it under the end of her cigarette. He watched her breasts rise as she inhaled.

As an afterthought she held the closed cigarette case up to him. "Thank you, no," he said, shaking his head. Eva knew he didn't smoke but often offered him a cigarette, a gracious but empty gesture. The Fuehrer despised smoking, something he regarded as a personal weakness, and he despised all forms of personal weakness. Bormann was surprised that Hitler tolerated Eva Braun's smoking, but he tolerated her dancing and even her choice of contemporary music. The Fuehrer preferred Wagner. Bormann considered the Fuehrer's infatuation with Eva Braun a personal weakness, although given her obvious charms, an understandable one. Still, better Eva Braun than someone else, not that Eva Braun was the only woman that Hitler consorted with, but she was the only one that he acknowledged and that he had an ongoing relationship with. At least Bormann had come to an accommodation with her.

There was a knock at his office door and Lausbeck entered with a tray bearing a silver coffee pot and service. He paused for moment uncertain where to put it. Bormann motioned him to the corner by the windows and Lausbeck obediently set the tray on the low coffee table between the two chesterfields. He hovered above the table for a moment waiting to learn whether Bormann wished him to serve the coffee. He knew his superior was angry as he always was after a meeting involving Hess, and he wished for nothing more than to see him calm down. He had personally born the brunt of Bormann's foul moods often enough.

"That will be all, Lausbeck," Bormann said curtly. He turned back to Eva Braun, still sitting in the low chair, her legs crossed, lightly swinging one elegant ankle. "Coffee?" he said formally, waving his hand in the direction of the chesterfields.

"Thank you," Eva replied. She leaned forward in the low soft chair, smiled up at Bormann, and then held out one slim hand. "Could you help me out of your chair, Martin?"

Bormann held out his hand and felt her strong grip and the surprising softness of her hand as she pulled herself up. She gave his hand a short squeeze and released it. "How delightful," she murmured, walking past him to the chesterfield in the corner. She stared out the window for a moment. "I always love the view from this side of the Reich Chancellery. The gardens are so beautiful." She turned abruptly and sat down, placing her cigarette in a small crystal ashtray and picking up the heavy silver coffee pot. She poured two cups. "Cream and sugar, Martin?" she asked.

Bormann nodded and smiled in spite of himself, knowing that she had come to him, a supplicant, and had now taken charge. In their early relationship, he had assumed, like most people, that Eva Braun was a simple, very attractive young woman with whom the Fuehrer amused himself. As he had come to know her, however, he had discovered an iron will and a determination that was quite surprising. He had also discovered that she was very smart, politically adept and quite capable of using her beauty and charm to achieve what she wanted, although carefully maintaining her subservient status in the eyes of Hitler. He sat down opposite her and took a sip of his coffee.

"Martin, I need to talk to you," Eva said. "Our last discussion was very upsetting."

"I'm sure it was, Eva," Bormann replied. "But I don't see any other solution."

"Why can't I just talk to Adolf and explain things?"

Bormann felt a flash of fear. "I think you know why we can't do that," he said carefully. "You knew the answer to that when you first came to me with the news that you were pregnant. The Fuehrer has the welfare of the Reich and the conduct of the war to deal with. You and I have the welfare of the Fuehrer to consider and you knew that he could not be burdened with the responsibilities of fatherhood to say nothing of the complications of having an illegitimate child."

"I came to you for advice on when to tell him," Eva said, staring angrily at Bormann. "You were the one who convinced me not to tell him at all. I think he would have rejoiced in the knowledge that he had an heir."

"I think not, Eva," Bormann said, deliberately keeping his voice quiet and even, hoping to diffuse her growing anger. "I think he would have insisted on an abortion and if you recall our conversation, you agreed that that was precisely what he would have done."

"Women are emotional when they are pregnant. I couldn't think properly. I was too open to suggestion."

"I was not pregnant and I see the Fuehrer almost every day, Eva. I know that is what he would have done. You did not have the choice of telling him about your pregnancy, getting married, having the child and living happily ever after. Your choice was to tell him and have an abortion, or to not tell him and have the child. You made a truly great decision, Eva. You protected the Fuehrer from distraction and at the same time provided him with an heir. You could have done no better. But now we must protect the heir."

"All right, all right, let's not go over this for the hundredth time. The question is, what do I do now."

"Let me give you some simple facts, Eva. The Fuehrer is a brilliant political leader and a fine soldier. We love and admire him above . . ."

"Martin, your loyalty is not in question," Eva snapped.

Bormann paused and sat quietly for a moment, suppressing a sudden fury that anyone but Hitler himself would address him in this condescending fashion. However, the stakes here were simply too high to indulge his personal temper. Eva's Braun's time would come. He thought about how best to bend her to his will. "To put it bluntly," Bormann began, pausing again on the precipice of what he was about to say. "Germany is probably going to lose the war."

"You're mad, Martin," Eva said, setting her cup down. "Adolf would never let that happen. You just called him a brilliant soldier . . ."

"A brilliant political leader," Bormann corrected her. He watched her reaction, wondering how much to tell her. He had to tell her enough to convince her but not enough to incriminate himself through her pillow talk, although he knew from his previous dealings with her that she was remarkably discreet. He also knew that Hitler considered women little more than attractive ornaments, art objects useful for charm or seduction, but essentially brainless. "And a fine soldier," he added.

"Then how is this possible?" She took another cigarette from her case and leaned forward over the table. Bormann snapped his lighter again, peering down the front of her blouse as she drew in the smoke.

Bormann sighed, a melancholy sound calculated to set a tone of sombre reality. "The truth is that we started the war three years too soon. Our military production figures are rising but there are limits. The Fuehrer is now intent on the invasion of the Soviet Union although that could be a year away. If he could be content with the liberation of Russia and the other Soviet Republics from the yoke of Stalin, rather than enslavement of the population in a way which will make Stalin's rule look like English democracy, there might be some hope, but that is not what he plans. We cannot sustain a war of the magnitude that he envisions on two fronts. I know the production figures we are capable of. To be blunt, we will simply run out of munitions, supplies and replacements, even with the Fuehrer's most optimistic assumptions."

"But surely the Fuehrer knows this," Eva said incredulously. "You must have told him this if you are telling me?"

Bormann shook his head ruefully. "I dared to do that, Eva," Bormann said softly, remembering the scene. "He was not taken with the idea of liberating the Slavs." Bormann stared past Eva Braun at the large portrait behind his desk. He recalled the Fuehrer's screams of outrage. "We will not liberate those sub-humans, Bormann, we will enslave them, we will exploit them for the greater good of the Reich. Do not presume to lecture me on strategy, Bormann. You are a simple bureaucrat." After that his voice had softened and his tone had become conciliatory, although the condescension remained.

"Then he must know what he is doing," Eva said confidently.

"Of course he does, Eva," Bormann said. "But when Germany invades the Soviet Union, if we could be seen as liberators, govern the republics and isolate Russia, we could starve them into submission and fight the final battles on our terms."

"I don't understand all this military strategy, Martin," Eva said. "In any case, it has nothing to do with my son."

"If we lose the war, Eva, or rather, when we lose the war, the Fuehrer will not survive it, nor will those close to him."

"What do you mean? There is the Geneva Convention."

"Yes there is, but it will not protect him, nor your son, nor you and I for that matter. It only protects soldiers."

"I still want my son with me here," Eva said with finality. "He is safer in Germany than anywhere else."

"I understand your wishes but I disagree. We must protect the heir to the Reich at all costs, Eva, even at the cost of our personal comfort and desires. He cannot be allowed to perish."

"No one is going to perish, Martin. This is just nonsense."

Bormann got angrily to his feet and strode over to his desk. He snatched up a newspaper, glanced at the front page and with his back to Eva Braun, took several deep, calming breaths.

Then he turned and walked slowly back to thc chesterfields. He sat down and set the paper on the coffee table in front of her. "Please be good enough to read aloud the headline, Eva."

She picked up the paper. "British Air Pirates Over Berlin." She looked up at Bormann, puzzled. "But we are at war with the British, Martin . . ."

"The British have bombed Berlin three times in the last week and those bombs weren't nonsense," Bormann snapped. "They are hard evidence that the Reich is not invulnerable. The fact that the British could penetrate our air defences and bomb Berlin, even if it was not a major bombing raid, should tell you that your son will not remain safe for long." He leaned back on the chesterfield and sighed. "Please, Eva, consider the situation rationally. You have the Fuehrer's child, the heir to the Reich, the future of National Socialism and of Germany. He is relatively safe for the moment but that will not continue. You cannot tell the Fuehrer. He will feel betrayed, he will banish you." Bormann paused again, wary of his next comment and the reaction he knew it would produce. "He may even claim the child is not his."

"What are you talking about?" Eva screamed, slamming the china coffee cup down. The saucer shattered, the delicate handle of the cup snapped off and the cup rolled over.

Bormann ignored the cup and the coffee slowly spreading over his table. He leaned forward and spoke softly and firmly, his voice without expression. "I am only trying to consider the reactions that the Fuehrer might have if he learned that his mistress became pregnant over a year and a half ago, arranged to go to a private sanitarium in Bavaria to have the child secretly, and that she has deliberately deceived him about the existence of his child, who is now ten months old. He might reasonably wonder why all these precautions were necessary if he were the father and why you hid everything from him. He might reasonably conclude that the identity of the father was not at all clear. You were not as emotionally stable at the time as you obviously are now, Fraulein."

"I was distraught, Martin," Eva whispered, her eyes full of tears. "You know that."

"I know that, Eva," Bormann said softly. "And I was here to help you. Remember that I was the one whom you called."

"I know, Martin," she said, dabbing her eyes with a silk handkerchief. "I know you only want to help."

"I was the one who arranged for you to spend the last months of your pregnancy away from Berlin, away from the Fuehrer, and I was the one who arranged for the birth of your son and for ensuring that everything was handled with discretion."

"I am grateful, Martin. Truly, I am. But the thought of not seeing my child for years is just too awful to consider. It is bad enough now when I can only see him every few weeks." She watched some of her coffee trickle over the edge of the table onto the thick dark carpet. She pulled a small white silk handkerchief from the sleeve of her jacket and set it like a small dam to stop the flow of coffee.

Bormann watched the coffee soak into the silk and then continue its course over the edge of the table and onto his carpet. "I don't want to frighten you, Eva, but it is better to give him up for a time and have him for the rest of your life than to lose him altogether. We can't hide him much longer and do it safely."

"I know, Martin, but will I never be able to tell Adolf?"

"Yes, you will," Bormann replied carefully. "If we are able to win the war, and, of course, the Fuehrer may yet produce a miracle, he has certainly achieved that before. Then you will be able to tell him. It is also possible that the Allied Forces may falter or may make fatal strategic mistakes. If they do, then that will be the time. I will tell you the time, Eva."

"All right, Martin. Make the arrangements. But he must be safe."

"He will be, Eva," Bormann said with obvious relief. "He will be. I will ensure that everything is taken care of."

"Who will go with him?"

"I think a doctor and a nurse, as well as one of our security people."

Eva stood up and walked over to the window, staring out into the sunny garden for a moment. She turned to Bormann. "That nurse who helped with my delivery. Could she be the nurse?"

"Of course, Eva," Bormann said. "I'll look after it."

Martin Bormann leaned back in his chair, satisfied with his morning's work. Eva Braun had been easier to convince than he had anticipated. He was relieved but he knew he would have to watch her carefully. She was unpredictable at times. At least she was the only one he had to contend with. The other two had already been disposed of, their children placed with carefully chosen foster families, essentially the same arrangements as he had made for Eva's child. Now he would arrange for their transport out of Germany to safety. He had initially considered Spain but had rejected it as too unstable, even under Franco's new government. North America was where he would send them, although the logistical problems of getting them there were considerably greater than with the Spanish option. Perhaps he would place one in Canada and two in America. Canada was at war with Germany already and the US soon would be if his assessment was accurate, so placing Hitler's children in the middle of a peaceful enemy country would be something no one would ever think of. The planning and logistics were already well advanced.

He thought about Eva Braun again. He would have to remain very reassuring with her. In spite of her evident resilience she was quite fragile in some ways. Her two suicide attempts, ineffectual as they had been, confirmed an emotional instability, even if they had been aimed more at securing the Fuehrer's attention than at ending her life.Still, she was a lot better than the last one. He shuddered as he thought of Geli. That had started over a dozen years ago in Obersalzberg, a small alpine village near the Austrian border.

Bormann recalled his first visit there to see Adolf Hitler. It had been in 1927 and Hitler had been happier than he had ever seen him. He soon discovered the source of this elation. It was Geli Raubal, a beautiful young woman, who, with her mother, was living with Hitler. Bormann recalled that he had rather liked Geli, her brightness, her irrepressible good humour. He was pleased that his leader had found a woman at last. His pleasure was tempered when he learned that Geli was only nineteen compared to Hitler's thirty seven, but his pleasure turned to furious condemnation when he discovered that Geli was Hitler's niece, the daughter of his half-sister, Angela Raubal. He was appalled. The future leader of Germany was fucking his niece like some incestuous pervert. It was intolerable. He and others in the party had tried to approach the subject with Hitler but he was adamant. His personal life was simply not a subject for discussion. Bormann and the others had tried to interest him in other women, something Hitler had periodically enjoyed, indeed still enjoyed. At times he would use them but always he returned to Geli. In the fall of 1929 he had arranged for Hitler to meet Eva Braun and although he was obviously quite taken with her, he still stuck with Geli.

He had surveillance put on Geli and discovered that she was quite generous with her favours, sleeping with several senior party people, some of them married. However, when he discovered that she was sleeping with her art teacher in Vienna, a lascivious Jew, he knew he had to deal with the problem. He discussed it with no one, and as he had done so often, acted in the best interests of the Party and the Reich.

He had gone to the flat in Bogenhausen, ostensibly to see Hitler, although he knew he was not there. He had entered Hitler's suite, surprised as he always was at the Spartan, almost monastic nature of his accommodations. From the top right drawer of the small desk that Hitler used, Bormann had removed Hitler's pistol, checked it and slipped it into the pocket of his jacket. Then he had gone down the hall to meet with Geli. His intention was to persuade her to break off her liaison with Hitler, but failing that, to simply solve the problem.

He opened a bottom drawer in his desk and pulled out a folder. It contained a single newspaper clipping. He read it over carefully once again. It was dated September 21, 1931 and had been taken from the Munchener Neueste Nachrichten

> According to a police communique, a twenty-three-old student fired a pistol aimed at the heart in a room of her flat in the Bogenhausen district. The unfortunate young woman, Angela Raubal, was the daughter of Adolf Hitler's half-sister, and she and her uncle lived on the same floor of a block of flats on Prinzregentenplatz. On Friday afternoon the owners of the flat heard a cry but it did not occur to them that it came from their tenant's room. When there was no sign of life from this room in the course of the evening, the door was forced. Angela Raubal was found lying face down on the floor, dead. Near her on the sofa was a small-calibre Walther pistol.

Bormann had had no other option but to leave the gun beside her but he experienced the feeling of relief he always did when he noted that the paper had not dared to print the fact that the Walther was Adolf Hitler's service pistol.

CHAPTER THREE

Monday, October 28, 1940 Berlin, Germany

Captain Albert Brandt sat on a hard wooden chair in the waiting room. He had not been in this particular SS facility before, but he recognized the style, plain, utilitarian and uncomfortable, a large framed portrait of the Fuehrer flanked by a slightly smaller one of Himmler, the head of the SS, were the only decorations on the wall. Four straight backed wooden chairs with a small table were arranged in one corner with a coffee table in front them. No one had offered him coffee, but perhaps at four o'clock in the afternoon there was none left. The only window in the room was in the entry door and it looked into a hallway. A cold drizzling rain had been falling when Brandt had arrived half an hour ago. He had removed his trench coat and hung it on a tree stand in the opposite corner. His forage cap rested on the empty coffee table.

A female secretary glanced at him periodically and smiled. He nodded and returned the smile. She was in her mid-twenties, blonde, slim and attractive and wore a wedding ring, not that her marital status would protect her from the lechers that usually worked in offices like these, but perhaps her smile revealed a willingness to overlook the implications of the ring. She stood up, gathered some papers from her desk and walked to a file cabinet a few steps from her desk. She was tall and moved with elegance. Brandt wondered what she was doing here. She likely hadn't been discovered by more senior officers in other locations or she would have been transferred. He smiled in spite of himself. All SS officers weren't lechers. He certainly wasn't but he was not an administrative officer with nothing to do and all day to do it, he was a field officer, in charge of a Sonderkommando unit.

Sonderkommando units were formed to undertake particular tasks or to implement and oversee a particular program and then were often dissolved when the tasks were accomplished. A year ago his present unit was formed and had been assigned to oversee the births of three children in Bavaria and their transport and settlement into foster homes. After that they had been reformed and assigned to the Heuaktion Program, which essentially involved kidnapping Germanic looking children from the occupied countries and taking them to "Lebensborn" institutions in Germany. He wondered at the choice of name, 'Lebensborn', 'source of life'. Brandt had been surprised that the Nazi hierarchy, who clearly considered Poles inferior, nonetheless transported a large number of Polish children with "Aryan" characteristics to Germany to be raised as Germans. The youngest were placed with foster families. He was beginning to feel that his unit was in charge of children and one of his subordinates had even coined the term "kinderkommandos" to describe what they were doing. He had been ordered off the Heuaktion Program about two weeks ago. Further tasks would likely emerge as soon as the self-important people in the inner office deigned to call him in.

The secretary returned and resumed her seat. The telephone on her desk rang shrilly and she picked it up. Her voice was soft and husky but the words and manner were smooth and professional. She jotted something on a pad on her desk, her long dark blonde hair swinging rhythmically as she nodded in agreement with whatever was being said. As she hung up, she smiled again at Brandt as though apologizing for the interruption.

Brandt saw a small pile of brochures on the corner table beside his chair. He picked one up and glanced at the title. "The SS as an Anti-Bolshevist Fighting Organization". He read on.

> "We shall unremittingly fulfill our task, the guaranty of the security of Germany from the interior, just as the Wehrmacht guarantees the safety, the honour, the greatness, and the peace of the Reich from the exterior. We shall take care that never again in Germany, the heart of Europe, will the Jewish-Bolshevistic revolution of subhumans be able to be kindled either from within or through emissaries from without. Without pity we shall be a merciless sword of justice for all those forces whose existence and activity we know, on the day of the slightest attempt, may it be today, may it be in decades or may it be in centuries."

Brandt set the brochure back on the table without bothering to read the rest. So that was what he was doing. He smiled at the rhetoric, another example of an administrative officer without much to do; however, he did note that the quote was attributed to Himmler, himself.

The door beside him opened and a uniformed officer, a major, stepped into the reception area. "Captain Brandt?"

"Yes, Sir," Brandt said rising and coming to attention. He picked up his forage cap and as he entered the office, the door was closed behind him. He stood at attention, always a good move when facing an important civilian.

"Sit down, please, Captain Brandt." Martin Bormann sat behind a small desk and motioned him to a chair in front of it. Brandt had met Bormann on two previous occasions, the first in October 1939 when he had been called upon to "supervise" the births of three children. The second had been a week ago when he received orders to retrieve one of the children from his foster home and deliver the child to a medical care centre in Berlin. Then yesterday he had carried out the second phase of his orders. He had collected the child from the medical centre and delivered him to an office near the Friedrichstrasse Station. From the location of the office, he assumed the little lad was going for train ride somewhere. The nurse who had taken him was an attractive woman, probably a little younger than he was and seemed pleasant and competent. He was mostly relieved to pass the child over to her. He knew better than to enquire where they were going. In any case, it was unlikely that the nurse knew. All actions and information seemed to be quite compartmentalized as far as this operation was concerned.

Brandt sat down. The major took a second chair beside and slightly behind his. He did not expect to be introduced to the major and he wasn't disappointed. The major was wearing the black uniform that the SS had worn until 1938 when they had been called in and replaced by the current dove grey issue. Some officers had not turned in the old uniforms and still wore them from time to time, usually when they were trying to impress or intimidate someone. Brandt preferred the dove grey, especially in the summer.

"I trust you have been enjoying your assigned duties since last we met, Captain?"

"I have, Sir." Brandt was uncertain whether Bormann was being polite or sarcastic.

"I was impressed with your performance on the previous occasions where we required your services."

"Thank you, Sir."

Bormann consulted a file on his desk and looked up again. "We have need of your services again, Captain. It will involve you in the same project."

"Yes, Sir."

Bormann's voice took on an impatient edge. "Do you have any questions, Captain?"

"No, Sir."

"Good," Bormann said. He closed the file and slid it across the desk toward Brandt. "The details are in there. It will require you to retrieve the remaining two children from their foster care families and transport them to another site. The destination and the dates of delivery are specified. However, as usual, you may choose your own personnel, equipment and procedures. You will act with your usual efficiency."

"Yes, Sir."

In the back seat of the staff car that was returning him to his office, Brandt opened the file. It contained three sheets of paper, the first with the names and addresses of the two other couples who had served as foster parents, although he already had that information. The second sheet contained instructions. They were simple and straightforward. By November 5, pay a visit to each couple, collect a child from each and deliver the children to the same medical care facility where their arrival was expected. The third sheet said that on November 16 he was to collect the children again from the medical care centre and deliver them to another site. A street address and office number were given. Brandt knew Berlin fairly well and guessed the address would be near the Templehof Aerodrome. The last instruction read, "You will ensure the discretion of the foster parents."

Brandt closed the file and leaned his head back on the seat. He took a deep breath and closed his eyes. He had delivered the children to these same couples about a year ago. They were neither Jews nor communists, just citizens of the Reich, prepared, as he was, to do their duty to build a greater Germany. It was a shame he would have to ensure their discretion, which could involve having them executed.

He had joined the Schutzstaffel in 1930, when he was twenty, about a year after Himmler had taken over the small palace guard of a few hundred members whose function it was to provide personal protection to the Fuehrer, and expanded it over the following three years into a force numbering in the tens of thousands. Brandt was smart, ambitious and ruthless, but he had been promoted, he suspected, because he was also well organized and got things done, and done correctly and discreetly. How he had come to Bormann's attention, he had no idea. Bormann was a shadowy figure in the Reich, but was close to Hitler and wielded immense power. Why Bormann had bothered to meet with him personally to hand over three sheets of paper was a mystery. Whatever this project was, knowledge of it must be very tightly controlled.

CHAPTER FOUR

Tuesday, October 29, 1940, A Train, Berlin, Germany to Lorient, France

Katherine Shore sat alone in the darkened compartment staring out the window at the countryside, a muted tableau of light and shadows rushing by in the moonlight. The steady clicking of the wheels and the slight swaying of the train was becoming hypnotic. She pulled her small nurse's watch from her handbag and held it up to the window to read it. It was a little after ten. She decided she would check the baby's diaper one more time and then get ready for bed. She switched on the reading lamp on the small end table beside her comfortable arm chair. Then she stood up and stepped carefully over to the crib.

She realized that she was getting accustomed to the motion of the train. She had never been on an overnight train before and had certainly never seen a private coach as luxurious as this one, or indeed any private railway coach, for that matter. It was a bit ornate for her taste with the compartment walls paneled in dark wood, the embossed ceiling a soft ivory hue and with rich dark blue velour curtains on the windows. However, it was certainly a pleasant way to travel. The crib was placed beside the full sized bed and had been fixed to the floor, as was all the furniture in the compartment including the pair of armchairs behind her. She had been sitting in one earlier when she had fed the baby and he had quickly fallen asleep with the gentle rocking rhythm of the train. Quite a travelling nursery she was in charge of, and all for one little child. She moved over to the crib and checked him, slipping her hand deftly under the small body and finding it still dry. She smiled. "You're such a good little boy, Erich."

She had only been in charge of the child for a few hours. In the afternoon, a tall good-looking SS Captain had met her in an office near the train station and had passed the child into to her care. He had been alone in the office when she arrived and had said very little. She sensed that he was relieved to hand the child over. "His name is Erich," he had said. "Have a safe journey." He had touched the peak of his cap, looked at her carefully and smiled. With that, he had left the room.

There was a knock on the compartment door behind her and as she turned, the door opened. It was the doctor. She corrected herself. It was Gilford, her "husband" for the next few weeks. And she was Katherine Shore, wife of Dr. Gilford Shore, not Fleta Kraus as she had been just a few days ago. There was so much to remember.

"How is our little one, Katherine?" Gilford asked quietly, peering over her shoulder into the crib. She moved aside so he could get closer. He was a handsome man, tall and slim, with a touch of elegance about him, strong features, a straight nose, high forehead and a sensual mouth. He didn't seem particularly aware of his good looks, which was unusual in most of the attractive men she had met. So far he had treated her with respect and reserve. She watched his pale grey-blue eyes twinkle as he stared down at Erich. She wondered about him and where he had learned his upper class English accent and mannerisms. She had heard his cultured German a couple of times when he had lost patience with their Gestapo companion, Klaus Schultz, but otherwise he had spoken only English.

"He's fine," Katherine replied. "I fed him about an hour ago and I was just checking his nappy when you came in."

Gilford nodded. "Let's chat for a moment, Katherine."

She noticed that he was carrying his small black leather doctor's satchel. He moved over to the armchairs and sat down heavily in one of them, setting his bag on the small table between them. He opened the bag and removed a liquor bottle, setting it carefully on the table, and then took out two small glasses. He leaned back in the chair and stared out the window into the passing night. Katherine tucked the small blanket around Erich and joined him in the other chair. He sat up and handed her the two glasses, pulled the stopper from the bottle and poured each glass about half full.

"Bristol Cream," Gilford said. "The best sherry in England." He replaced the stopper, set the bottle back down on the small table between the armchairs and took a glass from her. She noticed the table had a raised edge, presumably to prevent things from sliding off with the vibration of the train. Gilford raised his glass in a toast and they touched the rims together with a faint clink. "Cheers," Gilford said.

Katherine took a sip. She remembered having sherry when she was in England and wondering how the British could seriously enjoy it. This was scarcely the same drink. It was rich and smooth, not harsh and sickly sweet like the sherry she recalled. She nodded her head in appreciation.

Gilford leaned back in the chair again, took a large sip of the sherry, and tilting his head to one side, he looked at her. "I don't know how much you have been informed about what we are doing, Katherine," he began. "I thought it would be useful if I knew what you have been told." He loosened his tie and undid the top button of his shirt. She noticed for the first time that he looked tired. He pushed a lock of his sandy brown hair off his forehead. "Tell me a bit about yourself as well."

"I was working in a hospital in Muenchen . . ."

"Munich," he corrected her.

"I'm sorry, Munich," she said. "And some man from the local Gestapo office came to see me. He chatted to me in English for a few minutes and then took me to his office. My supervisor was furious. You know how short-staffed we are everywhere. The Gestapo officer asked about my training in England and how long I had lived there and so on. He carried on for about half an hour and then he brought in another man and I had to repeat the whole thing all over again in German. He seemed to approve of what I told him. Then he informed me that I would not be returning to the hospital, nor to my apartment for some time and that my services were required elsewhere. He showed me a letter which told me to cooperate. It had 'By Order of the Fuehrer' and someone's signature at the bottom of the letter." She paused and thought for a moment. "They appeared to know a lot about me."

Gilford smiled grimly. "They know a lot about everyone, it seems," he said. "At the risk of having you repeat it all one more time, can you tell me about your time in England?"

"Of course," Katherine replied. "My father was German and my mother was English. As a child, I lived in Munich but spent most of my summers in England visiting my grandparents. My grandmother died in a motor accident in 1925 and we moved to England to live with my grandfather. I was ten at the time." She smiled at Gilford. "So now you know I'm twenty-five."

"Since we're telling secrets, I'm thirty," Gilford said with a chuckle.

"In 1932 my grandfather died and we came back to Germany. I was only here a year and then returned to England for my nurse's training. My mother died three years ago so I came back to Germany again to live with my father but he remarried a year ago and seems quite settled now. I can't go back to England, of course, with the war on, but I rather prefer it there. I might even like it better now that I am Katherine Shore. When I left the last time, the English were getting a bit suspicious of people with names like mine."

"An understandable sensitivity," Gilford said dryly. He reached for the bottle on the table and poured himself a second sherry, holding the bottle toward Katherine and raising his eyebrows in a silent question.

"No more for me, thanks," Katherine said, holding up her glass. "How about you? Your English is flawless."

"A story not unlike yours," he began. He sat back in the chair and took a sip of the sherry. "My parents were both German. My father was a diplomat who had been posted to England for a number of years so I went to English public schools as a child, spent holidays in Germany and returned to England for some of my university years. I came back to Germany about five years ago because I was excited about how it was being rebuilt. It seemed to be rising from its ashes like a Phoenix while England just seemed to be sinking further into a quagmire." He paused and took another drink. "In retrospect, it was a mistake. You can't rebuild a country on hate."

Katherine was silent, realizing the trust he had shown by uttering such a remark.

"Do you know where we're going and what we're up to?" Gilford asked.

"Only that I won't be back for a little while."

"Quite right," he said. "Here is what I know. We are going to Lorient on the west coast of France on this train and then by submarine across the Atlantic Ocean to Canada. You may have noticed that some of the other coaches are common day coaches full of sailors. There are also a number of cars carrying torpedoes, munitions and other supplies. It is a regularly scheduled train running from Berlin to Lorient. I believe they call it the 'submarine train'."

"Really?" Katherine said in astonishment. The Gestapo man had implied a few weeks away from Munich, not months, and had not mentioned anything about leaving Europe. She felt a rising anxiety as she recalled her Gestapo interview and the few questions about whether she had ever suffered from claustrophobia.

"We will remain there until the end of the war," Gilford continued. "Perhaps a few months, more likely a few years," he added sardonically.

"My God, what will we do?" Katherine gasped, as the thought of 'years' sank in.

"We'll work it out," he said quietly, his face relaxing into a gentle smile. "But first we have to get our young man there."

CHAPTER FIVE

Tuesday, October 29, 1940 Berlin, Germany

The staff car and driver arrived at Captain Brandt's office at 10:00am. He had debated phoning the family to let them know of his imminent arrival. He had done that with the first family and had arrived to discover the foster mother distraught to the point of hysteria at the prospect of losing the child, the foster father, surly and withdrawn. Perhaps just showing up was a more effective and humane method. He would know shortly.

He had requisitioned Fritz, the same driver he had used on the previous occasions. He was a fat jolly Sergeant who had told him he liked being fat because he had nearly starved to death as a child at the end of the last war and had promised himself he would never be hungry again. He had passed on this information with a laugh, but Brandt had sensed an undercurrent of seriousness beneath the humour.

Forty minutes later, they stopped in front of a small brown brick house, one of a number of similar houses on the same street.

The front yard was enclosed by a low stone wall. A small grass area and some now empty flower beds near the house made it look a bit like an English cottage, or at least his memory of one from his only visit to England as a nine year old child. Fritz stayed in the car with the engine running and the heater on while Brandt went to the front door. It was a bright sunny day for the end of October but there was little warmth in the sunshine. Brandt knocked on the door and stepped back.

A moment later, the door opened and a woman stood there. As she recognized Brandt, she gasped and covered her mouth. She was tall and slim, dressed in a simple black woolen skirt and grey cardigan sweater, a red flowered blouse visible where the cardigan was open.

"Good morning," Brandt said politely. "I'm sorry if I startled you."

She put her hand down and let out a long sigh. She shook her head and stepped back. "Please come in."

"Thank you," Brandt said. He stepped into the front room, closing the door behind him. It was a small room but cozily furnished. A plump sofa covered in a bright blue and yellow print material sat against one wall, a blue upholstered chair with a lamp behind it and a wooden rocking chair were arranged around a low dark wooden coffee table. He could smell a cake baking or recently out of the oven, perhaps a plum cake but given the state of rationing, it was likely something else.

"You have come for the child?"

"I'm afraid so," Brandt said. "I am sure you have become attached to him."

"I have, of course," she replied. "But I knew this day would come so I have tried to keep myself ready for it." She stepped back and sat down in the carved wooden rocking chair. "He likes to be rocked in this chair."

Brandt noticed her use of the first person. "Your husband is well?" he asked.

She nodded. "He was called up four months ago and sent to Poland."

"So you have been raising the child on your own," he said. "That must have been more than you expected."

She looked thoughtful. "Yes, but he has been a great comfort. I think I would have been quite lonely if I had not had him here."

Brandt moved to the upholstered chair and sat down. "And how is your charge getting along?"

"He is a wonderful child, rarely cries, sleeps well . . ." She pulled a handkerchief from the sleeve of her sweater and dabbed at her eyes. "He is having his morning nap."

"I'm afraid we will have to wake him."

She stood up. "Yes," she said. "What about his toys and clothes, his blankets and things?"

"I will leave them with you. Just dress him and wrap him in a blanket," Brandt said. "He will not be going far."

"Could I come with you?"

Brandt looked at her carefully. If she came along it would make the transfer much easier, but she would learn where the children were being taken. However, they would not be there for more than a few days.

"Very well," Brandt said. "I can count on your discretion?"

"Oh, yes," she said. "I won't tell a soul."

Brandt watched her as she left the room. He hadn't really noticed her before. A year ago he had been focused on delivering the children. She was about his age, perhaps a year or so younger, her long golden hair was pulled back severely and pinned at the back of her head. The long skirt clung to her, swaying sensually as she walked out of the room. He shook his head. He had been too long without a woman and with little to do in the last week, he should have taken care of that.

He stood up and walked about the room. There were a couple of framed photographs on the wall showing two stern looking people posed in a studio with a backdrop of clouds and some Greek-looking ruins behind them. The second photograph was of a farm yard with a smiling woman standing in the foreground, clearly her mother, judging by the features.

"I think he is ready," she said.

Brandt turned to her. "Your mother?"

She glanced past him to the picture on the wall. "Yes," she said. "I don't have a photograph of my father. He died in the war."

"I'm sorry," Brandt said. "Was the farm your home?"

She stood with the child in her arms, rocking him back and forth gently. "Yes," she replied. "Until I was sixteen." She stepped forward. "Could you take the baby while I get my coat, please?"

Brandt held out his arms as she stepped close to him and placed the baby in his hands. She moved the child and put her hand on one of his pushing it upward slightly. Her hand was soft and warm. Brandt felt uncomfortable and perhaps the child sensed it. He recalled the last time he had held a child was when he had taken the child to the station. That had seemed to work.

"Just rock him a little and he'll be fine," she said. She smiled up at him and then turned away. She was back a moment later slipping her arms into a black woolen coat. She held out her hands and Brandt gratefully handed the child back.

She had been quite stoic as they passed the child over to a nurse at the medical care centre but then had wiped a few tears from her eyes as she walked out to the staff car with Brandt. She was silent on the return trip until they were nearing her home.

"Are you married, Captain?" she asked. "Do you have children of your own?"

Brandt shook his head. "I have not found a woman who will put up with me." He smiled at her.

"You probably haven't looked hard enough," she said. "Do you have nieces or nephews?"

"I am an only child," Brandt replied. The car stopped in front of her house, the engine running, Fritz staring steadily ahead.

"I am too," she said. "We wanted children of our own but we have not been blessed so this child has been a great gift."

"I'm sure you have been a fine mother to him."

She studied Brandt for a moment. "Could I offer you coffee, Captain? I have a fresh baked cake to go with it."

"That is very kind of you, Fraulein, but I should be getting on with my other duties."

She smiled. "I would enjoy the company but I understand. I know I will be lonely for a little while."

Brandt really had no other pressing duties, he wasn't going to retrieve the second child until tomorrow. "In that case, I accept," he said formally. "Do you have a telephone?"

"Yes," she replied. "It was installed when you delivered the child. I will miss that, too."

Brandt leaned forward and touched Fritz on the shoulder. "Sergeant, I will call you when I need to be picked up."

"Very good, Sir."

She took Brandt's trench coat and hung it in a small closet behind the front door, then disappeared into the kitchen. Brandt looked around the room again. It had a warmth and a personal feel to it that he had not encountered since he had left his own home.

"How do you take your coffee?" she called from the kitchen.

"A little milk, please, if you have it." He walked to the doorway leading to the kitchen and leaned against the frame. She was boiling water on a small electric hot plate and had two large cups set on the counter beside it. An electric refrigerator occupied one corner of the small room, next to the sink.

"Come in," she said, catching sight of him in the doorway. "What will happen now to the refrigerator?"

Brandt recalled that it had been installed as part of the equipment assigned to the household when the child had been delivered. "If you wish to keep it, I will arrange that."

"I would appreciate it, if that is possible."

"The coffee is nice, too," she added.

Brandt had ensured that a number of rationed items were also supplied to the foster households as small rewards for caring for the children. He reasoned that happy parents would be better parents. Unless he took steps to cancel these deliveries, they would continue. "I think you can count on the coffee ration to continue."

She poured some milk into a small pot, took the kettle off the electric hotplate and placed the pot on it. She poured the boiling water into a coffee maker and turned her attention to a small cake on the counter. She cut two pieces and placed them on small plates.

As Brandt watched her carefully perform each task, he was glad he had accepted her invitation. It had been a long time since he had been inside a real home and experienced the comfort of simple domestic rituals.

She turned off the hot plate and put the cake on a small dining table set against a wall. "Please, Captain, sit down," she said. "The coffee will be ready in a moment."

Brandt sat down. "Thank you."

"Call me Trudi, please," she said.

"Thank you, Trudi," Brandt repeated. "Please call me Albert, at least when we are not around others."

"Very well." She poured steaming milk into the two cups and added dark, strong coffee.

An hour later Brandt phoned Fritz, who said he would be there in about twenty minutes if that would suit the Captain. Brandt had enjoyed the interlude. It had been a long time since he had just relaxed and chatted with someone. He spent his days in a highly charged political atmosphere where a wrong word, an improper association or a failed task could be grounds for a reassignment to less pleasant duties. Of course, the fact that Trudi was an attractive woman and somewhat beholden to him certainly increased his satisfaction.

He slipped on his trench coat, retrieved his forage cap from the coffee table and stood by the front door. "Thank you for the cake and coffee," Brandt said. "I will scarcely need to eat for the rest of the day."

"I am pleased you enjoyed them," Trudi said. "Thank you for joining me."

"If there is anything else that you require," Brandt said. "Please call me." He took a pen and a small note book from the pocket of his jacket and wrote his phone number on a page. He tore out the page and handed it to her.

"You are very kind, Captain."

Brandt smiled down at her. "Albert," he said. "Remember?"

"Albert," she repeated.

Brandt looked out the window as Fritz pulled up in front of the house. He held out his hand to Trudi in a formal handshake. "Thank you for your service to the Reich." Her hand was small and soft and he held it for a moment longer than was necessary. He knew he would be back.

"It was an honour," Trudi said.

As Brandt released her hand, she looked up at him with a frown on her face. "Am I permitted to know where the child is going?"

Brandt shook his head. "I'm sorry you are not," he replied. "I don't know either," he added. "And it is best that neither of us pursue the matter. The child will be well cared for."

"That is all the assurance I could wish for."

CHAPTER SIX

Tuesday, October 29, 1940, Henley Page Airfield, Southern England

Sergeant Ronald Willis stood in the grass beside his Spitfire, listening to the quiet sounds of the early night, a few crickets that hadn't gone to sleep for the winter, the faint rustle of the few remaining leaves on a couple of trees by the small armoury shed behind him. It would be his last silence for a while. He walked slowly around the Spitfire, making a final leisurely inspection, although he knew it was just a ritual. His ground crew would have checked every hose and every rivet. Someday he wouldn't be flying Spits anymore, he would have a job. He would miss the flying but not the fear driven adrenaline that burst into his body every time he saw an enemy aircraft bent on his destruction. He'd been lucky so far.

He inhaled the scent of the Spitfire, powerful and intoxicating, a heady mixture of petrol, oil and glycol from the engine. All aircraft had that, but his had the exotic addition of gun oil and burned explosives. He had once tried to explain it to a woman, a Canadian nurse he had been seeing briefly before she was transferred somewhere else, and she had listened with patient sympathy but no comprehension. She had asked, with a quizzical smile, if she should use gunpowder instead of perfume. He wondered where she was now.

He stared up at the few high clouds scudding across the full moon. The sky had cleared as the met report had predicted and the earlier icy drizzle was gone but the air was still thick with moisture. "The Merlins will love it," he murmured, referring to the Rolls Royce Merlin engine that powered his Spitfire.

"Say again?" Sergeant Michael Downs said as he walked up to Willis. He tossed his cigarette onto the sodden grass.

"Good night to fly," Willis said. "The Merlins will like the air."

"Right," Downs replied. "They'd bloody better and no misfires or we're gone for."

Willis laughed. "That's probably why they're sending two of us, old man."

They stood together in silence staring into the high, frosty sky. "A hunter's moon, that one," Willis said softly.

They turned as they heard the chatter of the ground crews coming toward them. "See you up there," Downs said and walked away toward his plane.

Willis felt the Spitfire shake as the Merlin fired and then smoothed out into a steady roar. It almost felt fragile when it was on the ground. He glanced over at Downs but could only see the silhouette of his head through the cockpit cowling. He watched him for a moment, then ran his eyes over the gauges and squirmed to get himself more comfortable in the tiny cockpit. At five foot eleven, he was big for a Spitfire pilot and he always felt cramped and crowded when he first got settled in. He knew it would pass. He throttled up the engine, felt the plane begin to pull at the ground, anxious to get into the air. He released the brakes and it rolled forward. He turned it into the wind, opened the throttle and was pressed back into the seat as it shot down the short grass runway and lifted into the night sky. He glanced off his starboard wing and saw Downs a hundred feet or so away.

A few minutes later they were streaking across the English Channel towards the coast of France, skimming the wave tops.

Katherine awoke with a start but everything seemed all right. The train was still moving smoothly but she sensed it had slowed down a bit. Perhaps now that they were deep in the occupied French countryside they feared the partisans might sabotage the rail lines. She had heard the rumours. Just as Gilford was leaving, a conductor had come by to tell them that all lights were to be turned off and were to remain off as they were entering a blackout region. She glanced toward the window and saw that the moon was still high, lighting the outside world an ethereal white. There was something wrong with the silhouette of the chair by the window. She sat up and then she smelled it, stale cigarette smoke and the stench of cheap schnapps.

"Good evening," Klaus Schultz said, rising from the chair. He moved like an unsteady shadow toward the bed. "It is time we got to know each other a little better."

Katherine pulled the eiderdown up around her. "Get out of here, Herr Schultz," she said quietly, the steadiness of her voice surprising her. "You'll waken the child." Schultz was squat, solid and coarse featured. He had tried to make it clear that he was in charge but Gilford had simply ignored him. Katherine had been courteous but cool.

"Here, here," Schultz said, his words slurring slightly from the schnapps. "You got to know the Doctor earlier, now it's my turn."

"Get out or I'll scream."

Schultz leaned against the door frame and snapped on the lights. They were both blinded momentarily.

Katherine glanced at the crib as Erich began to whimper softly, waving his small arms in the air.

"You won't scream if you want to stay beautiful," Schultz snarled, a short but vicious looking knife in his right hand. The train lurched slightly and Schultz stumbled into the corner of the bed, falling heavily across Katherine's legs. She recoiled and then lashed out smashing both feet into his shoulder. He rolled off the bed to the floor but was on his feet again immediately. He grasped a corner of the eiderdown and ripped it off the bed. He stared at her as she huddled against the end of the bed. A slow smile spread across his face as he moved toward her again.

"Shultz," Katherine said sharply. "I am on the Fuhrer's business. How dare you treat me like this."

Erich began to cry, reaching out toward the bed and then rolling toward the side of the crib.

Schultz sat down on the bed and held the knife point against the side of her leg. "I am also a servant of the Fuhrer and he does not like his servants to be kicked." He stroked her knee roughly. "So I will give you a chance to redeem yourself. If you do not I will report your lack of cooperation and have you transferred to an army field hospital."

"Nonsense," Katherine snapped with a great deal more confidence than she felt. "Now get out of here. The child is awake. You're frightening him."

"Relax," Schultz murmured pushing her nightgown up and digging his fingers into her thigh.

Willis watched the French countryside flash by, barely fifty feet below him and then pulled the Spitfire into a gentle climb, levelling off at a thousand feet. A fast glance off his starboard wing confirmed that Downs was still with him. The land was flat here with an occasional low hill and the Germans seemed to have enforced the blackout a lot better than the French had. They picked up the de Roussey road off to their left just where it should be and moved over it. Another couple of minutes and the target should be in sight.

Katherine Shore was an attractive woman and had learned long ago how to fend off advances she didn't want but she had never been faced with the prospect of rape. An occasional drugged patient had tried to grope her and she knew how to avoid those, too, and still preserve her patient's dignity. She stared at Schultz with a calmness that surprised her. Suddenly she leaned toward him and gently put her hand on top of his knife hand. Startled, Schultz glanced down at his hand and as he did so, Katherine swung her clenched fist as hard as she could, slamming it into his nose just as he looked up. He dropped the knife and recoiled from her, blood streaming out of his left nostril. Then with a guttural moan, threw himself at her, grabbing her by the throat and tearing her fragile nightgown open. His face flushed as he stared down at her nakedness.

Erich screamed.

Then Willis saw it, moving like a snake around a curve, a single lighted window like a beacon guiding them onto the target. He swung his Spitfire to starboard, eased it up to 1500 feet and then pushed the nose over gently as he began his strafing run. He listened as the Merlin skipped a heartbeat, fuel-starved for a second by the centrifugal force on the carburetors. He would come down the length of the train from the right side with Downs coming in from the left a few seconds later. He snatched a quick glance at his fuel gauge and knew they would have only one run. The last coach in the train, the one with the lighted window, came into his gunsight and he squeezed the trigger on the column. He felt the Spitfire shudder and felt its speed drop slightly as the 30 calibre Brownings poured out their streams of tracer shells converging like strings of small glittering stars onto the coaches below.

Katherine felt his knee slam between her legs forcing them apart and then his fingers digging painfully into her. She raked her fingernails across Schultz' face, searching for his eyes. Schultz grabbed at her hand and she sank her teeth into his wrist. He screamed and leaped up, his face a mask of fury. Suddenly Shultz' chest exploded in a mass of blood and shattered bone as he was hurled backwards across the compartment. A thunderous roar followed and the compartment was plunged into darkness. She rolled off the bed onto the floor as another roar and a second series of explosions tore through the car. For a moment she was deafened and then as her hearing returned she felt the train slowing. She dragged herself up by the bars on the crib and felt for Erich. He had rolled into a corner. He grasped a finger of her hand, crying softly.

Willis glanced back as he pulled the Spitfire around in a tight arc climbing away from the train. It was grinding to a halt and two cars behind the engine were on fire. The last coach was in darkness. "As the chaps in bomber command say," he murmured softly to himself. "Milk run."

CHAPTER SEVEN

Wednesday, October 30, 1940 Berlin

Fritz arrived promptly at 10:00am to collect Brandt from his office. They walked out together to the staff car, a black Daimler Benz, polished to a lustrous shine by the staff at the SS motor pool. That could change shortly. It had been overcast and threatening rain when he had arrived at his office at 6:00am. He liked the quiet time when no one else was around other than a couple of night duty officers, and as a rule, they were sleepy enough after an all night stint that they didn't bother him. He accomplished a lot in the first couple of working hours of the day.

As Brandt looked up at the trees on the boulevard outside his office, a morning breeze moved the branches gently back and forth and a few reluctant brown leaves drifted down. He pulled the collar of his trench coat up around his neck. He would soon be wearing his woolen great coat. Fritz was about to open a rear door for him but he shook his head and slipped into the front seat.

"This will be the last one, Captain?" Fritz asked.

"Yes," Brandt answered. "Then we'll only have a few details to clean up."

Following the success of yesterday's transfer, Brandt had not bothered to telephone ahead. The traffic was light but steady, much improved since fuel rationing had been introduced for the civilian population.

Half an hour later they arrived, this time in front of an older frame house. There were weeds in the small front yard and paint peeling around the eaves. Brandt frowned. The paint could be the result of rationing but there was little excuse for the yard. The low wooden gate was partially open. He tried to close it after he passed through but one hinge was loose and it groaned in protest as he tried to pull it shut.

He mounted the three steps to the front door and knocked. He heard a woman's voice call something out and a moment later the door was opened. A man stood there, looking tired and dishevelled, a frown on his unshaven face. He took in Brandt's uniform, then called over his shoulder. "Gretchen, someone is here for you." He made no move to invite Brandt in.

Brandt looked at him closely. He didn't recognize the man. It had been a year since he had seen him, but he was certain this was not the husband of the woman he had left the child with. As he waited, he detected the smell of schnapps on the man's breath.

A moment later the foster mother peered past the man, saw Brandt and burst into tears. She shoved the man aside and tried to close the door but Brandt was tall and muscular and easily pushed the door open and stepped inside. The man turned away and walked into the next room.

"I am sorry to upset you, but I have come for the child."

"No!" she shouted as she tried to shove him back against the door.

Brandt grasped her wrists and waited patiently for a few moments hoping she would calm down. He gently guided her to a chair. "Sit down. Please calm down. You knew this was going to happen and I am sure you have done your duty for the Reich." As he looked around the living room he was not at all certain of this but he judged now was not the time to talk about it. The front room was a bit bigger than Trudi's but it was messy, filthy really, with bits of food on a table, old newspapers strewn on the sofa and the floor beside it, and a light layer of dust on a china cabinet in one corner of the room. It smelled musty, the air was stale.

"You can't have the child," she wailed.

"You can't take him."

Brandt walked into the kitchen and saw a short narrow hallway off to one side. He moved into the hallway, opened the door at the end of it and was hit by the stench of vomit and dirty diapers. He walked over to the crib and looked down on the child. He was thin and pale, almost emaciated. He lay unmoving and naked save for a soiled diaper that he had pushed down around his knees. He had vomited and the dried remains were on his cheeks and around his mouth. Brandt leaned forward and peered closely. The child was not breathing. He placed his finger tips on the child's neck but there was no pulse and the skin was cold to the touch. He was dead. He must have choked to death while the foster parents were drinking. How long ago? An hour perhaps? He realized it didn't really matter. The problem was what to do now.

He walked slowly down the hall. As he passed through the small kitchen, he saw the man sitting morosely at a small table, a glass of schnapps in front of him, a half empty bottle beside it and a second glass, partially full on the other side of the table. He glanced indifferently at Brandt. Brandt continued back into the living room. The woman was sobbing quietly in the same chair he had put her in.

"What happened to the child?"

The woman looked away, shaking her head slowly.

Brandt repeated the question.

"He got sick."

Brandt leaned forward and lifted her out of the chair, shaking her like a rag doll. "You are lying. The child was neglected. You have starved him and allowed him to choke to death."

The woman stared wide-eyed at him, her face inches from his. Her breath reeked of alcohol. He threw her back into the chair.

"Where is your husband?"

The woman looked at him blankly.

Brandt knelt by her chair and repeated the question.

"In the kitchen," she replied.

"That man is not your husband."

The woman shook her head. "Gone."

"Gone where?"

She continued shaking her head. "It doesn't matter."

Brandt leaned forward, grasped her shoulders and shook her violently, slamming her back into the chair. "Answer my questions," he snapped.

She stared at him, terrified. "He was called up a month ago."

"So you have failed in your duty to care for a child whose life and welfare you were entrusted with and you have been unfaithful to a soldier of the Reich?" Brandt felt his temper rising. "A man who is defending the honour of our country? And you are treating him like a common slut would?"

"I thought the child needed a father."

Brandt slapped her hard across the face. "You are an incompetent mother. You have murdered a little boy and are a whore as well." He heard a noise behind him and turned to see the man standing with a short iron bar, raised menacingly and poised to strike. Brandt straightened up and took a step back. He would not get his luger out of the holster in time if the man swung at him. He stepped forward, his face inches from the man's face. "Put that down," he ordered.

Confusion clouded the man's eyes for a moment and then he stepped back and swung.

Brandt raised his left arm, grabbed the bar wrenching it back and out of the man's grip. He smashed it across the bridge of the man's nose, blood spurted out his nostrils as he staggered backward. Brandt raised the bar again and smashed it down on the top of the man's skull with a satisfying crack. He crumpled to the floor.

Still holding the iron bar, he turned back to the woman, "Who is this man?" he asked, pointing at him with the bar.

"A friend," she whimpered. "He moved in after Conrad left." She started to cry again.

Brandt knelt and placed his fingers lightly on the man's neck to check for a pulse. It was faint. He knew he could not leave the man here while he dealt with the problem. He pushed the iron bar across his throat and jammed it down. He glanced up at the woman who watched him in terror. He held the bar in place until the man went limp. When he was certain the man was dead, he stood up. "Where is your bedroom?" he asked quietly.

Brandt saw a mixture of panic and relief in her eyes. He wondered if she thought he could be bought off with sex. She pointed to a doorway off the living room.

"Get up," he snapped.

She stood and shuffled into the bedroom. The bed was unmade and the room smelled of dirty linens. "Lie down," Brandt ordered.

The woman lay down on her back.

"On your stomach," Brandt said.

She obediently rolled over. Brandt picked up a pillow and held it close to her, drew his luger and fired a single muffled shot into the back of her head. She twitched and lay still. He sighed. He did not mind the killing, but in a case like this it was messy and unnecessary. Why couldn't people just do as they were told? There was a regular program in place to check on the welfare of the three children. Presumably the child was fine three months ago when the last check would have been made.

In the kitchen he picked up the phone and made a call, then went out to the car. "I need to post the house," he said to Fritz. "Do we have signs in the trunk?"

Fritz got the signs out and while Brandt went back into the house, Fritz tacked them prominently on the front door. They were quite simple. They had a large SS insignia at the top and identified the house as the scene of criminal activity, warning anyone who read it not to enter on penalty of imprisonment.

In the nursery Brandt looked about for something to wrap the child in. He saw a blanket crumpled in the corner and picked it up. He moved it gingerly toward his face and smelled it. It seemed fairly clean compared to the other smells in the room. He laid the blanket in the crib beside the child, pulled up the diaper, then wrapped him up in the blanket. Holding him carefully, he returned to the living room, looked at the body on the floor and went out the front door, closing it behind him.

He slipped into the back seat of the car, still holding the child. "The Disposal Squad should be here shortly," he said. "I don't think we need to wait."

In Brandt's experience, the first question that would be asked in a situation like this was not, 'How can we solve this problem?' but rather, 'Who is to blame for it?' Brandt knew precisely where the blamc would fall. It would fall squarely and entirely on him. Part of his success was his ability to solve problems rather than be blamed for them. But how could he resurrect a dead child? He couldn't. What was his second choice?

The first problem to be solved was to dispose of the body of the child. He could have left it in the house, but the disposal squad would file a report and it would show three bodies. He would have to dispose of the child's body separately.

The second problem was how to deliver a child to the medical care centre. He thought he might have a solution to this in his office files, or more accurately in the files of his former Sonderkommando unit.

Brandt thought about the three children. He had kept them clear in his mind by remembering their hair colour. The dark haired child was Lienhard and he had been thin and sickly, clearly the fragile one. Trudi had been caring for him and he had collected him yesterday. Erich was a quiet infant with dark blonde hair and he was the first child he had picked up and transferred. Johann was the healthy, robust one with white blonde hair whose small body he now had wrapped carefully in a blanket.

By the time Fritz had returned Brandt to his office, he had the outlines of a solution. He dismissed Fritz, took the small bundle that had been Johann into his office and instructed his secretary that he was not to be disturbed.

In the Heuaktion program a few of the children being moved to Germany had gotten ill and died. He scanned the files until he found one. The cause of death was simply listed as "Died in transit" and was signed by the officer in charge, not a medical officer. That simplified things.

Next he searched the Heuaktion files for a male child, about a year old with blonde hair. There were several and he chose one at random. On a small desk in the corner of his office he kept a typewriter. He often found it useful when he needed to produce documents or orders that he did not want his secretary to see. He also did reports on it sometimes as he could type about three times as fast as he could write them out by hand. He turned to the typewriter and began to type up the necessary orders.

CHAPTER EIGHT

Wednesday, October 30, 1940 Kerneval, France

Gilford Shore came reluctantly out of a deep sleep, drifting up toward chaos, rolled roughly about in his bed, a rising noise in his consciousness. Then suddenly he was totally awake. The noise became a roar, splintered by the blast of machine gun fire. His railway coach rocked as he felt the train slowing, then grinding to a halt. In the darkness he scrambled into his clothes, years of practice with emergency calls making it a reflex. A series of massive explosions erupted from the front of the train. Munitions cars? The pale white light of the moon was eclipsed by brilliant orange and yellow flashes. As he shoved his feet into his shoes, the coach shuddered, tilted dangerously, dumping him back on the bed, and then spun slowly sideways and landed upright in the ditch beside the roadbed. As suddenly as it had begun it was over.

He stood up, grasped the door handle of his compartment and wrenched the door open. As he stepped into the narrow hallway that ran the length of the coach, he could see flames on the roadbed above him and the silhouettes of a few running figures. The door to the next compartment hung open. He stepped inside and found Katherine crumpled in a heap between the bed and the crib. The child was in her arms, awake and tugging at a curl of her soft blonde hair, watching the flickering patterns of light on the walls of the compartment. His small cheeks were streaked with tears but he had stopped crying.

Gilford lifted Katherine to a sitting position. "Katherine," he said. Then he leaned close to her and spoke directly into her ear. "Katherine. Are you all right?"

She was dazed and unresponsive for a few moments. Then he took the child from her arms as she struggled to stand. When she was on her feet she looked about the compartment and walked unsteadily to a cabinet in the corner and pulled out a small suitcase. The front of her night gown was torn open but she seemed unaware of it. She slipped out of the remnants of it, rummaged in her suitcase for a moment and began to dress. Gilford watched her, a stripper-in-reverse, feeling somewhere between a voyeur and an art critic. My God she had a beautiful body, slim, shapely, and skin that shimmered white in the moonlight.

The baby began to squirm and snuffle, getting cold perhaps, as a chill breeze drifted through the shattered windows of the coach. He took a small blanket from the crib and wrapped it around Erich cuddling him against his shoulder. For a few moments he walked slowly back and forth in the narrow confines of the compartment and then. he noticed something jammed into a corner behind one of the arm chairs. He looked down at the remains of Klaus Schultz, his body torn open by machine gun fire. Odd, he thought, that it should have ended up in Katherine's compartment but explosions sometimes had a random way of distributing their victims.

When Katherine finished dressing she turned to him with a look akin to surprise on her face, as though she was coming out of a trance. He handed the baby to her and looked at her carefully. She seemed back to normal, business-like and efficient, but still quiet and withdrawn, understandable given the traumatic events of the previous few minutes.

"Katherine," he said. "We have been attacked by aircraft." He paused and looked at her. "Do you understand what I am saying?"

She stared at him for a moment and then nodded. "Yes," she said. "That was what all the noise was."

"I am going outside to see if I can help. There will be injuries, I am sure." He put his hand on her shoulder. "Will you be all right if I do that?"

She stared at him for a moment longer, then looked down at Erich. When she looked up again her eyes were clear and comprehending. "We'll be fine," she said. "I want to check Erich and get him settled."

"Okay", Gilford said. "I will come back in a few minutes to see how you are doing." He walked the few steps to his own compartment and slipped on his greatcoat and retrieved his forage cap and his medical bag. Then he walked gingerly out onto the platform at the back of the coach but it seemed stable enough. A short distance away some flares were burning. He could hear orders being shouted as he climbed down the steps. The grass was long and brittle, covered in frost. He made his way to the area where the flares were burning and discovered that a small field hospital was being set up. Armed sentries had been dispatched to form a cordon around the area and to cover the approaches to it. Half a dozen stretchers were on the ground already. A couple of navy medics were tending to the wounded.

An officer saw him approaching and waved him to a halt. "We are only tending to the wounded here," he said.

"I'm a doctor," Gilford said. "How can I help?"

"Right now there are more wounded than we have medics to deal with so just move in and do what you can."

"Are there medical supplies on the train?" Gilford asked.

"Yes," the officer replied. "We are locating them and will get them here as soon as we can."

An hour later Gilford was suturing a leg wound when Katherine knelt beside him. "I can finish that for you," she said. "There are others more in need of your help."

Gilford looked at her. "Erich?"

"I settled him back in his crib, covered it with some blankets from the bed and have a sailor posted as a sentry in the coach with orders to fetch me if Erich needs me. I thought I could do more good out here."

The rescue team arrived in mid-morning. All but the walking wounded had been treated and many of those on stretchers had been moved back into the shelter of the coaches. Several ambulances, motorcycles with side cars and mounted light machine guns, as well as three light armoured vehicles and a large black Mercedes staff car, had accompanied the rescue team and their trucks.

The ambulances were loaded with the seriously injured and they set off immediately. Another group set up a small field kitchen and served food, a rich and hearty vegetable soup with bread, cheese and hot coffee, to those remaining.

By mid-afternoon everything seemed under control and Gilford, Katherine and Erich were ushered into the staff car. With one of the light armoured vehicles and two of the motorcycles they set off in a small convoy.

"It's a cold day to ride a motorcycle," Gilford said, looking ahead at the two motorcycle outriders muffled against the chill October air in their army great coats. He leaned his head back on the seat, tilted his forage cap forward and closed his eyes.

After the tension of the last few days he had been looking forward to the train trip from Berlin to the west coast of France and he had been well into his first decent night's sleep in a week when those bloody Spitfires had shot the train all to hell and he had spent the rest of the night putting sailors back together.

He felt a hand on his shoulder, squeezing gently, and then heard a woman's voice.

"Gilford," it said softly. "Gilford, we have arrived."

He opened his eyes. The staff car was stopped and the driver and the other soldier in the front seat were opening their doors. He looked at Katherine and smiled. "Thank you. I must have been asleep."

She laughed. "You have been sound asleep since you got in the car three hours ago."

"I guess I was tired," he said sheepishly. "I certainly feel rested now."

The driver opened the rear door and stood to one side. "We are at Admiral Donitz' headquarters Sir." He saluted as Gilford climbed out of the car.

Gilford returned the salute. "Thank you, Corporal."

Admiral Donitz' headquarters was an elegant old chateau. Katherine and Erich were taken upstairs somewhere and he was shown into Admiral Donitz' office by his Adjutant.

Now, in the dusky light of the late afternoon, he stared out the window of the Admiral's office quarters, across the lawns and through the fine old trees as though his vision was creeping from the window out into the world. The small panes of glass created a series of miniature landscape paintings.

Beyond the lawns he could see Port Louis and the entrance to the harbour at Lorient. In the distance a ship was anchored and he could discern the outline of a submarine tied up to it. It looked like an old wooden ship but he couldn't be sure. He took a sip of the cognac and examined the delicate crystal goblet that Admiral Donitz' first officer had given him before excusing himself and leaving Shore alone in Donitz' office.

Thinking back on the events of the previous night, Gilford was struck again by the stunning beauty of Katherine, disheveled, in torn night clothes, but still somehow elegant. Gilford took another large sip of the cognac, felt the warmth spreading through his stomach and wondered how much was the cognac and how much was the vision of Katherine.

He heard the door open behind him and Admiral Donitz strode into the room, tall and slim, looking every inch the naval commander. Gilford knew little about Donitz other than that he was in charge of all German U-boat operations and was apparently beloved by those he commanded. A good sign, he reflected, since Donitz would look after the next stage of their journey.

"How are you feeling, Dr. Shore," Donitz asked. He placed his forage cap carefully on one corner of the huge oak table that served as his desk.

"Please call me Gil, and I'm feeling much better, thank you. Cognac is a much underestimated medicine."

Donitz laughed, his face transformed from the seriousness of moments ago. "Glad to hear it," he said. "Karl Donitz," he added shaking hands with Gilford. His grip was strong and firm. "Please come and sit down. Tell me about your journey or adventure I should say." He led him to a sitting area in a corner of the office and pointed to a large dark leather arm chair. At an ornately carved sideboard he picked up the heavy crystal decanter of cognac and poured a generous measure into a glass. He topped up Gilford's glass before he sat down opposite him. He raised his glass in a toast. "Cheers, I think is the English toast?"

Gilford nodded and they drank together. "Thank you for your hospitality, Admiral . . ." he began.

"Karl, please," Donitz interrupted him. "So few people around here get to call me by my name that I sometimes think my Christian name is 'Admiral'."

"Thank you, Karl," Gilford resumed. "It is gracious of you to offer your hospitality and to devote one of your ships to our service."

Donitz laughed again. "Don't let my men hear you call one of their beautiful U-boats a ship. Submarines are referred to as 'boats'." He sipped at his cognac and resumed his serious expression. "To be frank with you, I was quite angry when I first heard of this operation. We started the war a year ago on September 1. At that time we had fifty seven U-boats of which thirty nine were operational and assigned to war patrol duty. By September 1, 1940, a year later, we had commissioned an additional twenty eight boats and increased our training and recruitment levels substantially but that meant assigning more boats as training vessels." He paused to take another sip and his face darkened. "We also lost twenty eight boats in our first year so we still have a fleet of only fifty seven and with the added training requirements we are down to 27 boats available for war patrols, eleven fewer than we had a year ago." He took another sip of the cognac. "And now we have twenty six."

"That is quite surprising," Gilford said. "From the reports of your successes I would have thought there were many more submarines out there."

"We are hopeful that the Allies think the same but, unfortunately, our resources are stretched very thinly," Donitz replied. "So I'm sure you can understand my reluctance to see one of our boats diverted to other duties."

"I'm sorry," Gilford said quietly. "But thank you nonetheless."

"A soldier serves by following orders," Donitz said. "But I should be the one thanking you after your night of service to my men. It is a rare situation that we have a full-fledged Doctor in circumstances like that."

"Thank you. I suppose it is, but your medics performed with great distinction."

"Glad to hear it," Donitz said, leaning back in his chair. "And I understand that we have a birthday to celebrate today. Your young charge is one year old. Quite an exciting time he has had so far."

"Indeed he has," Gilford said.

"These are important occasions and I thought we could have a small dinner this evening in his honour. I have arranged for a few of my staff officers and the commander of the U-boat you will be travelling on to join us. I trust the little lad can eat some chocolate torte?"

"I'm sure he can," Gilford said. "He seems able to cope with most things pretty well."

"Good," Donitz said, rising from his chair. "We'll meet again at eight." He glanced at his watch. "That will give you about three hours to rest and freshen up."

As Gilford, Katherine and Erich entered the dining room, a small wooden clock on the mantle over a stone fireplace struck eight. Gilford looked around the long and elaborately set table. This was his first visit to a naval officers' mess but it was much like the army messes he had been in, elegant china, ornate silverware, glittering crystal.

Donitz crossed the room to greet them. "I apologize for the clock,' he said. "It is a French civilian clock and we have so far been unable to teach it to ring properly in four hour watches like a naval clock should."

"You will see the old Isere close up tomorrow afternoon when we leave the harbour," Captain Rolf Echart said, responding to Gilford's question about the old wooden ship he had seen from Donitz' office window. Echart was the commander of the U64, the U-boat that would take them across the Atlantic and Donitz had seated Gilford between himself and Echart. "It is an interesting bit of local history. It was a French prison ship used to transport convicts to French Guiana. We use it now as our first and last mooring point."

"A somewhat more humane use it would appear," Gilford said. Captain Echart seemed surprisingly young to be in command of a U-boat, perhaps in his late twenties but he certainly exuded an air of confidence.

"I take it you have not been on a submarine before?" Echart asked.

"I've never even seen one."

"You're in for a treat," Echart said with a quick laugh. "You will find it rolls around a lot when we are on the surface, which will be most of the time, it is extremely crowded and you will learn to love the smell of diesel oil and humanity."

"It sounds bearable," Gilford said. He glanced across the table at Katherine, seated on the other side of Donitz with Erich in a high chair between them. Someone had found a small sailor cap and Erich wore it, perched at a jaunty angle. He kept looking about the table, taking in the laughter and conversation with his big hazel grey eyes as though he knew what was going on.

"Thanks to you, Doctor Shore," Echart continued. "I am now in command of the only U-boat in the fleet that has two heads."

"Two what?"

"Two toilets."

Shore looked at him, puzzled. "And how did that happen?"

"The Type 7 U-boat normally carries a crew of forty four ratings and four officers and to serve their needs we have one toilet. To accommodate the four of you, we had a second one installed and our crew reduced by four ratings. That will work fine since this is not a combat patrol. We will also be carrying only four extra torpedoes instead of the usual fourteen and that will give you a decent bit of room."

"That's very kind of you, Captain," Gilford said. "But there are only three of us, my wife and son and I."

Echart's face tightened into a sneer. "You'll have a new Gestapo agent with you. I gather you managed to rid yourself of the last one."

"Klaus Schultz. He was a victim of the RAF."

"And good riddance," Echart said, but offered no further explanation.

"I apologize for our company, Captain, but I assure you it is not my idea," Gilford said.

"In any case, you can thank Admiral Donitz for your private head," Echart replied. "I just have to convince him to leave it in the boat after we deliver you. That would be a real luxury."

Admiral Donitz picked up a small silver bell beside his plate and rang it once. The table fell silent. "I would like to propose a toast to our young guest," he said. "As you know, it is his first birthday today and tomorrow he will set out in U64 on his first submarine patrol. I thought it fitting that he have some small souvenir of his time here with us." He produced a small box tied with a red ribbon and gravely handed it to Erich.

Erich took the box and looked at it for a moment and then with great concentration, put one corner of it into his mouth. Donitz laughed. "Perhaps your mother could assist."

Katherine reached over and gently pulled the box from Erich's mouth. While he held tight to it, she tugged on the red ribbon. The bow came undone and she handed the ribbon to Erich. He released the box and she slipped the small lid off it, revealing a polished brass U-boat commander's hat badge, set on dark blue velvet. Erich looked solemnly into the small box and then grasped the badge in his tiny hand and pulled. The badge and velvet lining came out and he laughed gleefully.

As a wave of laughter spread around the table, Donitz turned to Gilford. "Your young son seems to be taking well to naval life. Perhaps he will wear that badge someday."

"Perhaps, he will."

Gilford was slipping out of his jacket when there was a light knock on his bedroom door. He glanced across the large room, past the enormous four-poster bed to the ornately carved wood door. "Come in."

The door swung open and Katherine entered. She was still dressed from the dinner party in an emerald green calf-length dress that clung to her, moving sensually when she walked, outlining her figure when she was still. The naval officers had been formally polite but none of them, including Donitz, had been able to take their eyes off her for long. She had handled their attentiveness with grace and charm. Now she stopped and looked about the room. From the heavy antique oak desk in one corner she swept her eyes past the fireplace where a couple of small logs still burned, to the seating arrangement in front of it, two large armchairs, a love seat and a couple of low ornately carved tables. Her eyes paused briefly on the bed and then came to rest on Gilford. She smiled, then giggled and shrugged. She walked across the thick carpet toward him, the dress swinging suggestively with each step. He wondered where she had found it.

"How did I do?" she asked stopping in front of him. He caught a whiff of her perfume, light, delicate and fresh.

"Marvellously," Gilford replied, still holding his jacket, uncertain whether to put it back on or hang it up. He laid it over the back of a small chair next to a French provincial dressing table beside the bed. "I think we were both convincing this evening. At least the officers referred to us as Erich's parents."

"They did, didn't they?" she said and then her face clouded over. "I heard Captain Echart say something about another Gestapo agent coming with us."

"Apparently they have replaced Schultz."

Katherine turned away from him and walked dejectedly over to the fireplace. Turning to face him again, she looked fragile and frightened. She shook her head silently.

Gilford walked over to her, took her hand and guided her to the love seat in front of the fire. He sat down beside her. "Something's wrong, Katherine," he said gently. "We can't keep secrets about this."

"I know," she said softly, still holding on to his hand. "Schultz . . ."

Gilford was intensely aware of her hand, small, soft and delicate. "What about Schultz?"

Katherine started to cry and he slipped his arms around her. She snuggled into his shoulder and he held her against him, stroking her back. He held her reassuringly and thought back to the evening before. He stiffened suddenly as he remembered the crumpled body of the Gestapo agent in Katherine's compartment and her night gown ripped open. "Did Schultz come to your compartment last night?"

She nodded against his shoulder and took a deep breath. She sighed and sat up straight, taking his hand again. She looked at him tearfully and told him briefly what had happened.

"Are you all right now?" he asked, realizing even as he said it how inane it sounded. Gilford silently thanked the Spitfire pilot, wherever he was, for his intervention but was infuriated by Schultz' actions. Quite aside from the brutal sexual attack on Katherine, Schultz had been drunk while on duty, attacked one of his team members, acted with complete irresponsibility and threatened the success of the entire mission.

She nodded. "A few bruises but I might have gotten those in the aeroplane attack."

"Are you certain you feel up to leaving tomorrow?" Gilford asked.

She nodded again. "I think so, but I am a bit worried about Schultz' replacement."

"Don't be," Gilford grimly assured her. "I will have a chat with him about the consequences if he comes near you. Schultz knew we weren't husband and wife only because I told him. I won't tell the next one and he may be a bit more circumspect. I don't know where they recruit these swine from."

"Why do we need a Gestapo agent with us?" Katherine asked. She pulled a white lace handkerchief from the pocket of her dress and dabbed at her eyes.

"We don't, of course," Gilford answered. "But our masters in Berlin apparently don't trust anyone to do as they say. I met with a man who said he was working with the authority of the Fuhrer, a man named Bormann, and he said the Gestapo would have to be involved, although he didn't seem terribly confident that they would do any good."

"Bormann was the name on the documents the Gestapo showed me," Katherine said. "When they took me from the hospital and interviewed me the paper they showed me had that name signed below the phrase 'By Order of the Fuehrer'."

"I'm glad you only had to see his signature," Gilford said. "Bormann is an unpleasant, officious little man, but he has a lot of power and he is the one responsible for our mission. We are to report to no one else."

Katherine stood up. "Thank you, Gilford," she said. "I feel much better now. I think I'll go back to my room and check on Erich." She stood on her tiptoes and kissed Gilford lightly on the cheek, turned and walked to the door.

CHAPTER NINE

Wednesday, October 30, 1940 Berlin, Germany

That morning Brandt requisitioned a staff car, had it delivered to his office and dismissed the driver. He took the small bundle that had been Johann out to the car and set it on the front seat. He then drove to an SS facility that dispatched Disposal Squads and delivered the remains of Johann along with the necessary signed orders that he had fabricated on his typewriter the previous afternoon. SS Disposal Squads undertook a variety of duties required to ensure the smooth functioning of the organization. Often such duties involved disposing of live persons rather than dead ones, but they were capable of many things.

He had called Trudi the previous evening to enlist her assistance and she had readily agreed. He had told her only that they would be picking up a child and that she would be caring for him for a couple of days before delivering him to the medical care facility they had been at previously.

Brandt mounted the steps to the front door of Trudi's house but before he could knock, the door opened and she stood smiling up at him. Her hair which had been pulled tightly to the back of her head yesterday, now framed her face in a golden halo. He smiled back at her.

"Please come in," she said.

He stepped into the living room, again feeling the sense of peace, almost tranquillity, he had experienced on his previous visit. He held her coat as she slipped it on and they went out to the car together. He smiled at the image of himself as domesticated, with a woman and a child in his life, if only for a short time.

The Lebensborn institution occupied the facilities of a former private Jewish elementary school. A Star of David was carved into the stone over the front doors, and two points of the Star were visible at the edge of the large swastika that hung above the entrance. As they were led down the hall by the matron who had met them at the front door, they passed a number of small classrooms occupied by older children, Brandt guessed they ranged from preschool to perhaps eight or nine years old.

"So you are going to adopt one of our children?" the matron asked as they entered the nursery. She arched her eyebrows coyly.

"We are relocating one of them," Brandt replied. "As my orders will explain.

"A pity," the matron said, smiling up at him. "You two look like you would make good parents for one of our little children." She was short and full bodied and the creases around her eyes suggested she smiled and laughed a lot.

Trudi looked up at Brandt. "It is a pity," she murmured.

Brandt responded with a startled glance.

There were about a dozen cribs along one wall and she led them to one of them. "Here is the young man you have come for."

Brandt looked down at the sleeping child, white blonde hair, well fed and healthy, and according to his file, about fifteen months old. His facial features were somewhat different than those of Johann, but still regular and perhaps a little more handsome, if that term could describe a child.

Half an hour later, they entered Trudi's house and she handed the bundled child to Brandt as she removed her coat and hung it in the closet. Then she took the child back and cooed at him, nuzzling him against her shoulder. "What is his name?"

"Johann," Brandt replied.

The child squirmed and stared up at her. He had cried for some of the journey but for the last while had been content to snuffle and had actually fallen asleep shortly before they had arrived.

Brandt hung his coat in the closet and took off his forage cap, setting it on the coffee table in front of the small sofa. The living room was warm and smelled fresh and clean. He watched Trudi carry the child into the nursery and followed her. She laid him gently into the crib and carefully loosened the blanket. His eyes opened for a moment and then he closed them again.

As he watched Trudi settle Johann, he thought of the first family. They had taken care of the child and had done what was required but both foster mother and foster father were seriously distraught at losing the child. How seriously was difficult to judge. While his orders did not specify any particular action to be taken, he knew that the phrase ""Ensure the discretion of the foster parents", provided him with whatever latitude he needed in dealing with them. So he had gone back to see them two days after he had removed the child. He shook his head at the memory.

He had been greeted by a string of abuse from the mother in spite of her husband's attempts to silence her. She had demanded to know where the child had been taken, and "demanded" was not something civilians did with an SS officer. Finally she had threatened him. She would get to bottom of this whole business, she had said.

Brandt had tried to rationalize their distress at losing the child. Certainly they had cared for him in an exemplary manner and there was no doubt about the genuine love that they had developed for the child. He could understand them being distraught. Still, getting the child had been in the nature of a contract, with clearly specified terms, and one of those terms was that at some point they would be required to return the child. It was a sad situation.

So Brandt had been conciliatory, reassuring them that the child was being well cared for and had offered to arrange a visit for both of them so they could see for themselves. He pointed out that on such short notice he would not be able to accompany them, but would have SS personnel pick them up that afternoon and transport them to the medical care centre where the child had been taken so they could satisfy any concerns they had. They were mollified by this and actually thanked him when he left.

Later that day he had received confirmation from a Disposal Squad that the foster parents had been picked up. They would simply disappear and their neighbours would be visited and given a plausible story, although given the degree of intimidation that the SS inspired these days, that was largely unnecessary.

Brandt returned to the living room and removed a small package from the pocket of his coat, a gift for Trudi, a token of his thanks for assisting him with the second child. In truth hc also hoped it would impress her in other ways. He was not really experienced in the niceties of dealing with women, other than being polite and respectful. When he wanted sex, he usually just took it without affection, occasionally paying for it, and with the only objective being his own satisfaction, so his finding Trudi attractive was a relatively new experience. Brandt walked into the kitchen and found her busy preparing coffee for them.

She looked up and smiled at him.

He handed her the gift. He had had one of the girls in the office pool wrap it for him.

Trudi looked surprised. "What is this?"

"A small gift to thank you," Brandt replied.

She took the package and looked at it carefully, then back at Brandt. Her eyes were wet. "This in not necessary but thank you. I am not used to this."

"You're welcome," Brandt said, looking at her carefully, hoping the tears in her eyes were not tears of sadness or anger.

"You can stay and have coffee with me?"

"I would enjoy that," Brandt replied.

"The child is sleeping," Trudi said. "probably finishing his morning nap."

They stood looking at each other for a moment and then Trudi set the gift on the kitchen table and turned her attention back to the stove. Brandt stood in the doorway watching as she got cups and plates from the cupboard.

She turned and saw him. "Please, sit down. I am not used to someone watching me."

Brandt smiled, moved to the table and sat down.

Trudi reenacted the ritual of making coffee and as he watched, he again found them profoundly satisfying, a peaceful interlude in his busy and often brutal world. His life was ordered, structured and contained little room for personal pleasures. Trudi poured the coffee, added the milk and set two cups on the table. “May I open this now?” she asked, picking up the small gift.

“Of course.”

She pulled at the slim white ribbon that held the paper, then slipped off the paper revealing a small box of Belgian chocolates. She put her hand to her mouth and stifled a laugh. “How did you know that I loved chocolate?”

Brandt laughed with her, enjoying her happiness. “Just a lucky guess.”

She reached across the table and squeezed his hand, still smiling with pleasure. “We must have one with our coffee.”

Brandt glanced at his watch and was surprised to see that almost two hours had passed since his arrival. As he stood to leave, Johann began to cry in the nursery. Trudi arose and quickly crossed to the doorway. The crying ceased and a moment later she returned with the child.

“If you can wait a moment, I will change him and get him settled.”

Brandt followed her into the nursery and watched as she deftly changed his diaper.

He had not intended to kiss her, but as they were standing at the front door, he slipped his arms around her and held her. When she turned her face up to him, it seemed so natural. While he had been with many women, he couldn’t recall ever really wanting one in the intensely personal way he wanted Trudi. He released her slowly and she rested her head on his chest, her arms still lightly around him. After a few moments she let go of him and stepped back.

“You will be here on the fifth to pick up the child?”

“Yes, I will,” Brandt said. “If there is anything you require in the mean time, please call me. You have my number.”

CHAPTER TEN

Friday, November 1, 1940 U64

Katherine Shore huddled in the frigid early morning rain and watched the U boat crew in their olive green sea kits, mustering in front of the Prefecture in Lorient. She and Gilford were dressed in the same drab olive green but were off to one side and had a little protection from a battered old umbrella. The wind blustered across the square, threatening to tear it from her hand. She could feel small icy rivulets of water trickling down her neck.

Erich was dressed in a pair of heavy cotton coveralls, wrapped in a blanket and covered in a small rubber sheet. Gilford was holding him and he watched the proceedings quietly from under the peak of a small woolen bonnet. She held the umbrella to shelter the space between them and it kept most of the rain off Erich.

Despite the rain, a small coterie of French children were playing around an old wooden bandstand and chattered and shouted at each other until one of the older ones had them all line up like a caricature of the U boat crew. Admiral Donitz, standing on a small podium, addressed the crew and wished them well but the wind snatched many of his words.

The U boat crew marched down to the wharf and across the narrow gangplank onto the deck of the U boat. She watched as some of them disappeared down a hatch in the fore deck and others mounted the conning tower.

She and Gilford followed an officer who guided them across the gangplank. Gilford passed Erich to one of the sailors who scrambled up the iron ladder on the outside of the conning tower and down a small circular staircase into the control room. They followed closely behind and she retrieved Erich from the sailor. A number of the crew were seated in front of various banks of dials, gauges and controls. She felt the faint vibration and steady rhythm of the diesel engines. As she looked around the crowded room and then down the impossibly narrow corridors she felt herself breathing more rapidly, shallowly, on the verge of hyperventilating. She passed Erich to Gilford who seemed quite comfortable in their new environment. She closed her eyes and leaned against the staircase railing, willing herself to be calm. After several deep breaths her pulse slowed and she felt in control again.

The U boat cast off and she became aware of the motion of the boat moving through the water, rhythmic and comforting. Captain Echart said something to the first officer and turned to her. "I will take you to your quarters now, Mrs. Shore."

"Where are Erich and Gilford?"

"One of my crew has shown them there already," he replied. He smiled at her. "You looked like you could use a few moments to adjust your bearings."

"Thank you."

"If you will follow me . . ."

They left the control room and entered a narrow passage. It was scarcely a passage at all. As they moved forward she crawled around things, stepped over them, ducked under them or squeezed by them. Captain Echart laughed good-naturedly.

"We typically carry rations for seven weeks," he said, pointing out the mesh bags of Kommissbrot, the hard navy bread, sacks of potatoes and other fresh vegetables that seemed to hang everywhere, in every passage and compartment, nook and cranny where they would fit. "Some of it will get moldy after a while but you and your family will likely be gone before much of that happens. By the end of a successful patrol when all the torpedoes have been fired and all the fresh food has been eaten or has gone bad and been tossed overboard, the U boat is really quite roomy."

"Impossible!" Katherine declared.

And now, a few hours later, Katherine Shore wondered grimly if the kind of nausea she was enduring was what morning sickness was like. Thankfully, Gilford was caring for Erich. She had been vomiting forever, it seemed, and her stomach had nothing left, had really had nothing left after the first few minutes. Gilford brought some small hard biscuits from the galley. He encouraged her to eat some and she tried but they just didn't help. Sipping water didn't seem to help either. The brandy she had tried an hour ago just made her dizzy and triggered another bout of nausea. Captain Echart had assured her it would pass. The only thing good about throwing up was that it kept her mind off the claustrophobia she had felt as she had crawled through the submarine. Even though it seemed much larger inside than it had appeared floating beside the pier, it was still awfully close. She had noticed in the last short while that her heaving was getting less severe and that she could actually sit up on the narrow steel bunk for a few minutes without doubling over in a spasm.

Gilford parted the curtain and peered in at her. "How's my patient?" he asked, gripping the edge of the upper bunk to keep his balance. Erich stood beside Gilford, gripping his leg tightly and looking up at her. She envied Gilford the ease with which he seemed to adapt. He had told her something about spending a lot of time on the water while he was in England but she hadn't paid much attention between bouts with the small galvanized pail on the floor beside her bunk. It kept sliding around as the boat pitched and rolled and yawed and corkscrewed in the Atlantic swells, she wasn't sure how many words there were for being tossed about like this. Or were they still in the Bay of Biscay? She didn't care. Gilford had tried to explain the various motions of the boat to her until she had stopped him. Knowing one from the other did surprisingly little to calm her tortured stomach.

"I think I am improving but very slowly," she said and then doubled over as another spasm hit her. Gilford swung in beside her and sat down, picking Erich up and sitting him on the bunk beside him. Gilford hunched over on the narrow bunk, his head bent forward to stay clear of the bunk above hers, then wiped the back of her neck with a cool damp cloth and put his arm around her shaking shoulders.

"Another few hours and it will pass."

"My God, I hope so," she said, gingerly sitting up again.

Gilford kept his arm around her and drew her gently against him. "Quite the bridal suite they have for us, isn't it?"

Katherine nodded. Their bridal suite consisted of two very narrow steel bunks, one above the other, closed off from the central companionway by a thin grey curtain, so they certainly weren't going to have much of a honeymoon. So far Gilford had not seemed much interested in that side of things and right now she didn't feel in much of a bridal mood either, whatever that was. She just wanted to sleep.

She looked past Gilford's shoulder to check on Erich. He was standing up on the bunk, hanging onto the edge of a small bassinette that had been installed in a hammock and fitted diagonally across the foot of her bed. It swung steadily back and forth with the movement of the boat. She leaned her head against Gilford's shoulder. "Perhaps Erich would like to rest in his bed."

Gilford turned to the child and gently hoisted him into the bassinet. "He seems to be adjusting well so far," he said, turning back to Katherine.

A bell rang somewhere and she heard sailors moving down the narrow companionway between their bunks and the lockers on the other side. They tried to do it quietly but their boisterous good humour made it difficult.

"They're changing the watch," Gilford said. "It happens every four hours."

"What's a watch?" Katherine murmured, not really caring.

"Like a shift of workers in a factory," Gilford explained. "They work for four hours and then have four hours off to sleep or relax."

"Relax?"

"You'll get used to it," Gilford said and snuggled her against him again.

"I doubt that," Katherine said. She thought about what the next couple of weeks held in store for her. She had found out that all her clothes had been packed and sealed tightly to make sure they didn't come out smelling of diesel fumes and that she would wear what she had on for the entire voyage, without changing anything, without a bath, without washing her hair. She was appalled. How could people live like this? She had imagined life at sea as a glamorous adventure spiced with danger and intrigue but had just never thought about how personal hygiene fitted into it all. Little Erich was the only one who was going to be bathed throughout the entire journey. When she had lived in England her habit of bathing daily had been regarded as some Teutonic eccentricity and she had been quite surprised to discover that most of her English friends considered one bath a week to be quite adequate. Well, let them try life on a U boat for a while.

Captain Echart had told her the journey itself was some 4600 kilometres, if they could go directly and that it would be a bit longer if they had to divert to avoid convoys or enemy ships. Gilford had told her to forget that number and remember 2500 nautical miles if she remembered anything. She didn't give a damn about kilometres or nautical miles, she just wanted to know how long this ordeal was going to last. About eleven or twelve days had been the awful answer, if they didn't have to divert. Two weeks without a bath was absurd.

There was a knock on the bulkhead outside their small compartment. The curtain was pulled aside and Ernst Klassen, their new Gestapo companion, peered in at them. He was younger than Schultz had been, blonde, good looking and in his early thirties. He had a friendly smile but his eyes always stayed the same flat, lifeless blue, and they never seemed the slightest bit friendly. They had met on board the U boat and Katherine's fears about having to deal with another attack were quickly allayed. Klassen had shaken her hand with little more than a glance at her.

"How are you feeling, Mrs. Shore?" he asked politely.

"A little better, thank you," Katherine said. She tried to sit up straight but Gilford held his arm around her.

Klassen glanced at Erich's little hammock and then turned back to Gilford. "I need to talk to you about our arrangements."

Gilford squeezed her shoulder lightly. "Will you be all right for a while?"

"I'll be fine," she said. "I think I'll try to sleep."

Katherine came awake slowly, confused and disoriented. In the dim light, she looked up at the grey painted steel of the bunk above her and remembered she was still on the wretched U boat. She wondered how long she had been sleeping. How did you keep track of time when you lived in a steel tube? She closed her eyes again. She was exhausted and weak. Then she noticed the silence. The engines had stopped and the boat was almost still. She wondered if they were under water. Surely she would have heard them dive.

The curtain was parted and Gilford peered in at her. "Feeling better?" he whispered.

"Yes, but weak," she replied. "What's happening?"

"You've been asleep for about four hours. We're now in heavy fog," Gilford replied. He pulled out one of the safety boards and sat down on the bunk beside her. "Apparently we have accidentally sailed into a British convoy, likely one that has come out of the Mediterranean through the Straits of Gibraltar. Captain Echart is trying to figure out whether we are in the middle of it or just on the edge. I think he is going to dive the boat." He leaned over and looked into the bassinet. "Erich is still asleep."

She heard a hum as the electric motors started and then the noise and hiss of the compressors as the ballast tanks were flooded. The boat tilted forward at an alarming angle as it slid under the water and she found herself leaning comfortably on Gilford. Some ominous sounding creaks and groans occurred as the submarine adjusted to the pressure. After a few minutes the boat levelled, the motors stopped and there was silence again.

"What's happening?" Katherine whispered. "Why have we stopped?"

"I think the Captain is waiting for the convoy to sail over us before we continue on."

"What's that noise?" Katherine asked sharply as she heard a faint gurgling mechanical sound.

Gilford listened carefully. "The propeller of a ship passing near us or over us I should think."

As the sound grew louder and more intense, the hum of the electric motors started again and she felt the boat move forward. The hum stopped as the sound of the ship above them slowly faded away. "This is much better than bouncing all over the Atlantic," Katherine said. "Why don't we stay under the water all the way across?"

"The electric motors run on batteries and we can only go about eighty miles before we run out of power. Also, we can only go about half the speed and we will run out of air after about twenty four hours."

"How do you know all this?"

"I've been spending time with Captain Echart."

"What did Klassen want?" Katherine asked.

"He wanted to explain to me who is in charge of things," Gilford said. "Like Schultz, he thinks he is."

"I hope you set him straight?"

"I certainly tried," Gilford said shaking his head. "But he was quite insistent. Captain Echart overheard part of our conversation and told Klassen that as long as we were on his boat that he was in charge, Gestapo or not."

"How did Klassen react to that?"

"He quoted his orders, supposedly authorized by the Fuehrer himself, and shouted about serving the Reich, but Captain Echart was having none of his nonsense. He laughed and asked him if had ever considered burial at sea," Gilford said, smiling as he recalled the incident. "Klassen blustered something about reporting him and Echart told him to keep his filthy Gestapo hands off his crew members."

"I wondered," Katherine said.

"Yes, so did I," Gilford said. "Well, apparently Echart believes he is homosexual and is not at all pleased about it."

"I'm kind of relieved," Katherine said.

"His sexual choices are likely to be the least of our worries," Gilford said grimly. "Once we are off the boat, he will try to take over again."

"What exactly is he trying to take over?"

They were interrupted by the gurgling mechanical sound of a ship's propeller although this time it was a high pitched pulsing sound. They listened as it drew closer and louder. It had to be passing directly over them. As it began to fade slightly they both exhaled and then smiled as they realized they had been holding their breath.

They turned toward the bassinet as Erich made a mumbled sound. Gilford slid over and lifted him gently out and rested him on his knee. Erich reached toward Katherine and Gilford passed him over to her. She smiled at Gilford. "Sometimes only a mother will do," she said softly, cuddling him against her shoulder.

"Herr Docktor," a voice in German came quietly from the other side of the curtain. "The Captain would like you to join him for a moment in the command centre."

"Can I come, too?" Katherine asked.

Gilford stood up. "Are you sure you're feeling up to it?" He slipped his hand under her elbow and helped her stand up.

She nodded. "I think so."

"Herr Doctor?" The voice was more urgent this time.

"We're coming," Gilford replied, pushing the curtain aside and holding it for her.

As they proceeded carefully down the narrow companionway, Katherine was impressed again at how the young rating in front of them seemed to skip gracefully through the obstacles. As they entered the command centre the pulsing sound of the ships propellers began to rise again.

"How are you feeling, Mrs. Shore?" Captain Echart asked in almost a whisper as he looked over the shoulder of one of the sailors seated in front of some kind of control panel. He was staring intently at a bank of gauges in front of the sailor. Without waiting for her reply he went on. "We are submerged at sixty metres and that noise you hear above us is a British destroyer hunting for us. He knows we are down here somewhere so he may drop some depth charges to see if he can find us. A secondary tactic will be to force us to stay submerged until his convoy is safely past and out of our range."

"What if he finds us?" Katherine asked. She shifted Erich to her other arm.

Echart glanced at her with a grim smile. "Then we shall have to lose him, won't we. However, if that happens we may get rather badly shaken about. I just wanted to warn you in advance. If they depth charge us it will be noisy and frightening.

Erich squirmed around and straightened his small body, a sure sign that he wanted to be set down. Katherine knelt and set him carefully on the floor, holding on to his hand tightly. With his other arm, he held firmly to her leg and looked around wide-eyed at the scene before him.

"What is going on, Captain?" Ernst Klassen asked sharply as he entered the command centre.

"I was explaining to Doctor Shore and his wife that there is a British destroyer hunting for us and that we may be depth-charged."

"This is ridiculous, Echart," Klassen stormed. "Your orders are clear. You are to avoid all hostile engagements until we are delivered."

Echart turned to Klassen and stared at him for a moment. A sarcastic grin spread across his face. "You are quite correct, Klassen. I shall surface immediately so you may swim over to the British destroyer and inform her captain of your orders. I am sure he will immediately break off and let us pass." He turned back to his gauges and winked at Katherine and Gilford. "If you have any other suggestions, Klassen, pass them on to the first officer. Now get out of my command centre, go back to your berth and let me run my boat."

"I'll report you, Echart," Klassen fumed. He glared around, his cold blue eyes taking in everyone. Then he turned abruptly and left the command centre.

"Where do they recruit these idiots?" Echart said with a sigh. "Now, my guests, please return to your bunks and brace yourselves. We will be fine and they likely won't find us."

Katherine picked up Erich and followed Gilford back to their quarters. She lay down on her bunk and placed Erich on her bunk next to the bulkhead. Now that she was feeling better she realized she was hungry. She felt in the pocket of her shirt and found a couple of the hard little biscuits that Gilford had gotten for her earlier. She bit off a tiny piece and gave it to Erich. He put it in his mouth and sucked on it. She munched on the remainder. Erich grinned at her with small pieces of sticky biscuit in his mouth, then reached out and pulled gently at her hair. She cuddled him against her and pulled the coarse woolen blanket up around her shoulders. The thin pad that served as a mattress didn't provide much protection from the cold steel of the bunk. Two weeks of this and she would be crippled.

Half an hour later the first depth charge exploded. The muffled roar was clearly some distance away. The U boat shook slightly and the electric motors came on for a few seconds. They felt the boat canting forward as Echart took them deeper.

Then it levelled and there was silence. Katherine lying in her narrow bunk wondered where the destroyer was. She closed her eyes.

The second depth charge knocked her out of her bunk. She felt the cold steel of the floor against her face and realized that she was still in the same position that she had fallen asleep in. Erich was crying in the berth above her. As she crawled back into the bunk and folded her arms around Erich's tiny body, the lights flickered and went out. She stroked his head and held him tightly and his crying subsided. A moment later some emergency system cut in and a dim light crept in under the curtain. There was a hissing sound from somewhere in the direction of the command centre and then silence again. She heard the noise of the destroyer above them and gripped the edge of her bunk.

"Katherine, are you all right?" Gilford whispered from the bunk above her.

"So far," she whispered back.

"Hang on," he said quietly. "The destroyer is circling above us so there will be more."

Katherine tasted something salty and realized it was her own blood. In the faint glow of the emergency lights she wiped her hand across her face and looked at the long red smear on the back of her hand. She held Erich tightly, gripped the edge of her bunk and softly began to cry.

CHAPTER ELEVEN

Saturday, November 16, 1940 Berlin, Germany

Fritz drove the large Daimler Benz sedan steadily through the mid-morning traffic, the windshield wipers slapping out a steady rhythm. It had been raining lightly for the last two days, but a few broken clouds in the west suggested that the rain would end sometime later in the day. Brandt was in the front seat with Frtiz and they were on their way to the medical care centre to pick up thc two children, the new Johann and Lienhard, the child that Trudi had previously cared for.

He had received a phone call from the Major that he had met at his recent meeting with Bormann. He was confirming that he was to pick up the two children and deliver them to the address in the city where they would be turned over to a nurse. It was not a long trip, but Brandt had decided again that he would utilize Trudi to assist him, rather than requisitioning a nurse although he knew that this was merely an excuse to see her again.

When he had taken the child to the medical care centre on November 5, he had requisitioned a car on his own and driven to Trudi's home. He had arrived about 11:00am and Trudi had invited him to share lunch with her before they took Johann to the centre. It had been a bit awkward when he arrived but that soon passed and they had chatted amiably over a light lunch of bread, sausage, cheese and coffee. As she had organized the food, he had held Johann on his knee. He set him on the floor and the child was able to stand alone and take a few tentative steps before sitting down. Then he crawled across the kitchen floor toward Trudi before Brandt retrieved him.

"He is developing well and soon will be walking around on his own," Trudi said.

"Really?"

"Yes," Trudi said, smiling at his surprise. "Most children become mobile somewhere around a year old. I don't know his exact age, but that must be close."

"Yes," Brandt said. "He is just over a year old."

During lunch Trudi had held Johann on her lap. He laughed and reached gleefully for the edge of the table, grabbing the small table cloth. Trudi and Brandt had laughed with him and saved lunch from landing on the floor.

"He seems like a happy little lad," Brandt said. "When we picked him up he seemed a bit subdued."

"A bit of love and care will do wonders for a child," Trudi said. She ruffled his white blond hair. "I have enjoyed having him and I will miss him."

Brandt was silent, enjoying the moment. "A bit of love and care will do wonders for most people," he said.

Trudi looked at him directly and smiled. Then she looked down at Johann again. She stood up with the child. "I will get him ready." She turned and walked into the nursery.

Brandt sat at the table and watched her go. Then he stood and gathered the dishes from the table, placing them on the counter by the sink. As he turned back, Trudi emerged from the nursery with Johann wrapped securely in a blanket. She handed the child to Brandt.

"If you can hold him I will get my coat."

Brandt found he was getting comfortable holding Johann, the awkwardness was gone. Perhaps it was being around Trudi, who seemed so naturally at ease with children.

She returned a moment later buttoning her coat. Brandt handed her the child, retrieved his coat from the small closet behind the front door, his forage cap from the coffee table and they walked out to the car.

An hour later they had arrived back at her home. She had invited him in as he had hoped she would. They had sat in the living room for an hour talking about life before the war, growing up in small towns, his in the northeast, hers in the south. Brandt had an appointment in the later afternoon and a few minutes before 3:00 he rose to leave. Trudi got his coat from the closet and Brandt slipped it on as they stood by the door. She was standing close to him and he slipped his arms around her, holding her tightly. She pressed herself against him and they kissed, deeply and longingly. Finally, she stopped and pressed her head against the chest of his tunic. "I'm sorry," she murmured. "You must think I am a desperate woman."

"No," Brandt replied softly. "Only a lonely one, as I am a lonely man." He released her and stepped back. "If anyone should be apologizing it should be me."

Trudi shook her head. "No," she said. "I thought the child you brought was a blessing. My husband thought it was an affront to him. We had not been able to have a child of our own and somehow the child you brought came to symbolize his failure."

"I'm sorry to hear that," Brandt said.

"I was too, but by the time he was called up, he was very angry and resentful. It was quite sad." She had stared up at him intently. "I didn't mean to talk like this. You have many important things to be concerned about without listening to my problems."

Brandt brought his mind back to the present as Fritz stopped the car in front of Trudi's house. He got out of the car, walked up to the front door and knocked. A moment later Trudi opened the door with a smile and he stepped inside. This time there was no awkwardness as they embraced. She kissed him lightly.

"I don't want to leave lipstick on you," she said, quickly pulling back.

"Not yet," Brandt replied, smiling down at her.

She had her coat on and took a moment to button it up. She looked carefully at Brandt's mouth. "I think we are ready."

Brandt ushered her into the back seat of the car. "We are getting both Johann and Lienhard," Brandt said. "I hope that seeing Lienhard again will not be difficult."

"Quite the contrary," Trudi said. "I came to love the child and want the best for him, not to own him."

At the care centre, Brandt and Trudi waited in a reception area for a few minutes. A doctor arrived with some forms for Brandt to sign and then left. A few moments later, two nurses arrived with the children. Both the children were dressed in navy blue pants and pale blue sweaters, small white shoes on their feet.

Trudi held out her arms for Lienhard and hugged him gently. The second nurse handed Johann to Brandt. They wrapped the children in blankets and returned to the car.

Fritz held the back doors open while they entered and settled themselves with the children. Fritz had been oddly quiet this morning. Brandt wondered if he was disapproving of involving a civilian in their small enterprise, or if he realized that things between Brandt and Trudi had progressed beyond the purely professional. Perhaps he was just being quiet around someone he didn't know.

Half an hour later they arrived at a low brick building near the Templehof Aerodrome. As they got out of the car, Brandt watched two Messerschmidt Bf 109's roar up into the sky, and disappear into the low clouds.

Fritz held the car doors open for them again, and went with them to the entrance, a large wooden door, embossed with a coat of arms. Beside it was a small sign announcing that this was the headquarters of the Berlin Trading Company. Brandt doubted that. It was likely an SS sign intended to cover a security detail. Fritz opened the door and stood aside as Brandt and Trudi entered.

A woman behind a long dark wooden counter stood up as they entered. "Captain Brandt?" she asked.

"Yes," Brandt replied. "We are here with the two children."

The woman nodded and picked up a telephone. "They are here," she said.

A door to their left opened and two women entered, dressed in white nurses uniforms. They smiled at the sight of the children. The shorter of the two approached Brandt and took Johann. The other one, a bit taller and darkly attractive, smiled at Trudi and waited for moment while Trudi bestowed a final kiss on Lienhard's small cheek.

This time there were no forms to sign or to hand over so they returned to the car, Fritz once again performing his chauffeur's duty by holding the door for them.

As they drove back, Trudi slipped her hand into Brandt's and squeezed gently. Brandt looked at her as she silently mouthed the word "Lunch?" and raised her eyebrows. Brandt nodded, then leaned back in the seat. He felt oddly relieved. This had not been a difficult assignment, but it must have been extremely important to have involved Bormann and his minions. In any case it was successfully concluded, or at any rate, his part in it was.

When they arrived at Trudi's house, Brandt told Fritz that he would call him when he was ready to be picked up. Trudi hung their coats carefully in the closet and then turned to Brandt and embraced him.

"The children are gone," she said, holding him tightly. "Are you going, too?"

"I hope not," Brandt said. "I am based in Berlin so whatever my next assignment is, it should be here or nearby."

"So perhaps I may see you again after today?"

"You will if you want to."

"You know I do." She looked up at him and slipped into his arms.

They were in the bedroom and Brandt had taken off his belt and holster and was unbuttoning his tunic. Trudi had slipped off her sweater and skirt and stood before him wearing only her bra and panties. She stepped forward and began unbuttoning the lower buttons on his tunic but Brandt pulled her hungrily against him and kissed her deeply, slipping his hand into her bra and enclosing her breast. They both heard the loud knock on the front door and quickly stepped apart.

"Were you expecting someone?" Brandt asked as he began doing up his tunic.

"No," Trudi said. "Other than you, no one has come to the house in months." Trudi was pulling the sweater over her head when the knock was repeated.

"I'll answer the door," Brandt said. He looked at his belt and holster on the bedside table and left them there. He opened the bedroom door and crossed quickly to the front door, pulling it open.

"Good afternoon, Captain Brandt," the Major said politely. He was flanked by two SS guards holding Schmiesser machine pistols.

Brandt automatically came to attention. "The children were safely delivered to the Berlin Trading Company this morning, Major."

"Yes," the Major said. "I know. May we come in?"

Brandt stepped back and they entered, closing the door behind them. Trudi opened the bedroom door and entered the living room.

"Good afternoon," the Major said. "You and Captain Brandt will be coming with us."

Brandt recognized the process of the SS Disposal Squad although it was unusual for a Major to be involved. There might be some bureaucratic error somewhere but he seriously doubted it. They were here to make sure that he and Trudi disappeared. He had cleaned up details of this sort on numerous operations including this one.

"Very well, Major," Brandt said. He turned to enter the bedroom.

"Where are you going, Captain?" The Major's voice was a command not a question.

"My forage cap," Brandt snapped back.

"I'll come with you. I don't want any surprises."

Brandt nodded and entered the bedroom. His forage cap lay on the bedside table beside his belt and holster. As he picked up his forage cap he snapped open the holster and pulled the luger out. As he spun toward the Major, snapping back the slide to chamber a round, he knew he was too late.

The Major stood with his own Luger drawn and pointed at Brandt. Perhaps the Major had been behind a desk too long and hesitated. Perhaps Brandt had shot enough people without the slightest hesitation. Brandt squeezed the trigger. The sound of two shots was deafening in the small room. Brandt knew he was hit even as the Luger bucked in his hand. He felt a searing pain in his left shoulder and stumbled back against the bedside table and into the wall. The Major staggered against the door frame and then fell forward. Brandt stepped into the doorway. His second shot took down one of the guards before the other one fired a burst from his Schmeisser hurling Brandt back into the bedroom. He didn't hear Trudi's scream of anguish, or witness the burst of gun fire that killed her.

CHAPTER TWELVE

Sunday, November 17, 1940 Berlin, Germany

Captain Kurt von Niessen strode across the tarmac toward the Focke-Wulf Fw 200A Condor. It was parked on a runway some distance from the half dozen other civilian aircraft that were scattered about. They had been deliberately staggered to prevent a bombing or strafing run from destroying more than one or two at a time. He wondered at the effectiveness of the strategy since all the British had to do was bomb the runways and the aircraft would be unable to take off until the runways were repaired.

As he approached the aircraft he looked at it more critically. It was the civilian version of the long range bomber he was now flying on routine patrols out over the North Atlantic in search of Allied shipping. He hadn't seen one of these in over a year. The Fw 200A had been built originally for Deutsche Luft Hansa, the German airline where he had worked before being conscripted into the Luftwaffe as a bomber pilot. It had been designed as a four engine, long range passenger and transport aircraft but had been modified and armed for its military role. Von Niessen had flown the civilian version for two years, making the second trans-Atlantic non-stop flight from Berlin to New York in September 1938, little more than a year after the first production aircraft rolled out of the Focke-Wulf factory in July 1937. It had been a long, grueling twenty five and a half hour flight although the return trip, a week later had been closer to twenty three hours.

He preferred flying the civilian version as it was faster, more maneuverable and responsive than the heavier military version, especially when the latter was laden with a cargo of bombs, torpedoes or mines. That didn't take into account the running machine gun duels that he and his crew fought over the Bay of Biscay with the British in their Short Sunderland Flying Boats.

He looked up to see the broken high cloud cover still partially obscuring the stars and the light from a thin crescent moon glistening across the asphalt runways, still wet from the early evening rains. The air was calm and cold. He heard laughter behind him and light spilled out of the small terminal building as the door opened and his crew started across the tarmac. His co-pilot and good friend, Max, plus their navigator and Frieda, their attendant, made up his crew.

He examined the markings, newly painted on the Condor, "Syndicato Condor, Brazil", one of the few airlines that had been able to acquire the Condor before the Luftwaffe had taken over the production facility complete with all the aircraft in whatever stage of completion, regardless of who had ordered them.

The boarding stairway was in place and he made his way into the aircraft, a much simpler procedure than hauling himself up through a hatch in the belly of the 200C version he currently flew. He made his way forward into the pilot's compartment and was joined shortly by the rest of his crew. He and his co-pilot, Maximilian Krause, began running through the pre-flight checklist. He had been able to pick his crew for this assignment and he and Max had a lot of hours together. His navigator, Renfred Seidel, was a replacement for the man he had chosen. His choice had been shot down over the English Channel a week ago. He had lost many friends in the last year. He knew Seidel more by reputation than personally but had approved the replacement.

He glanced out the window of the cockpit as light spilled again from the terminal door. Two armed soldiers stepped outside, followed by a civilian in an overcoat who closed the door behind him. They looked about for a moment, then the man in the overcoat opened the terminal door again and a small procession moved out toward the aircraft. There were several more soldiers carrying suitcases, a couple carrying bassinets, presumably containing the children he was transporting, two women and two other civilians, probably the medical staff that would be accompanying the children.

He heard them settling into the passenger cabin behind him. The Condor had been developed to carry twenty-six passengers but the interior of this aircraft had been designed specifically for the German high command. The passenger compartment had been modified so that seats could be added or removed, a small conference table could be installed when required, the food service section had been enhanced and the decor was much more lavish. For this mission, the passenger cabin had eight seats, although there were only five passengers. A couple of small cribs equipped with restraint belts had been installed, bolted to the floor against the likelihood of air turbulence. The regular passenger seats had been replaced by reclining seats that would more easily permit sleeping.

He and Max completed their checks as he heard the firm thump of the boarding door closing, and saw the red light on the console go out. Moments later he started the first engine.

Von Niessen climbed slowly out over Berlin, enveloped in darkness below them, the blackout broken only by an occasional flicker here and there. He levelled the Condor at 3000 metres and turned the controls over to Max. Their fighter escorts would be joining them in a few minutes for the first part of the journey although why they had been assigned escorts while flying southwest over Germany was a mystery to him. Still, the British had sent out a few night sorties deep into Germany and although they were of little more than nuisance value militarily and of propaganda value to the Allies, it would be unfortunate to encounter them on their current mission.

Their first destination was Lisbon on the west coast of Portugal, about a seven hour flight if they travelled in a straight line, but tonight they were flying southwest, avoiding much of France and would turn on a more westerly course when they reached the southern coast of France. They would stay east and south of the Pyrenees Mountains flying across Spain to Lisbon. This would add about 250 kilometres to their flight, about an hour's flying time, assuming they didn't encounter any serious headwinds. They would refuel in Lisbon and head west across the Atlantic to the United States, landing in Philadelphia. The distance from Lisbon would suggest a flight of seventeen hours or so but, given the weather, von Niessen guessed it would be at least an hour longer.

He took a clip board from a small compartment beside his seat, opened the cover and began reading. It was a list of weather reports sent in from German U-boats operating in the Atlantic, with a map indicating the locations of the boats so he could track the weather for their route across the ocean. These reports were several hours old and new ones should be waiting for him in Lisbon. To the north of their Atlantic flight path a cold front was moving south from Greenland. He was familiar with North Atlantic storms and did not relish the prospect of trying to manoeuver through or around one with his current cargo. Trans-Atlantic flying was a fairly recent phenomenon and storms would add a further element of uncertainty to an already uncertain endeavour.

To the south of their flight path the weather descriptions sounded like the beginning of a small tropical storm but those were common this time of year. They should miss both weather systems. It should be a straightforward flight.

He glanced out the cockpit window and saw the shadowy forms of two fighter aircraft, Messerschmitt Bf 109E's. He assumed there were two more on the starboard side of the Condor. He leaned back in his seat and closed his eyes. He would rest a while and then relieve Max when they reached the Mediterranean.

As soon as they took off from Lisbon Emil Altwasser had tried to get comfortable in the aircraft seat. It reclined but not flat, so all it really did was allow him to lean far back. He had tried to lie on his right side but his back quickly let him know this was not going to be comfortable. The seat was well upholstered and the light grey fabric had been soft against the side of his face. He had certainly slept in far more uncomfortable spots but this time it was not going to work.

He adjusted his seat to the upright position and looked out the window. In the fading moonlight he could make out the tops of a few fluffy clouds below them. He glanced at his watch and saw it was a little after 7:00am and although there was no sign of dawn yet, it would not be long in coming. He would have to figure out a good time to reset his watch since their destination was five hours earlier than Lisbon time. They had been airborne for about five hours out of Lisbon although it seemed longer.

He looked around the dimly lit cabin listening to the steady drone of the four engines and feeling the vibration that they transmitted through the fuselage. It had seemed loud at first but now it was merely irritating. Perhaps he was going deaf. The two children were asleep in their cribs, the two nurses asleep in their reclined seats, one of them snoring softly, and their Gestapo escort appeared to be sleeping with his seat upright. Periodically his head would fall forward, he would snort loudly, squirm around in his seat for a moment and put his head back, beginning the cycle over again. The female cabin attendant sat in a seat in the rear of the aircraft near the small galley and in the light from the counter was reading a magazine.

The other doctor, Schwartz, had never been on an aircraft before and had suffered so severely from air sickness that he had been left behind in Lisbon. Altwasser had wondered why even one physician was on this flight let alone two. Both children were healthy, both nurses were competent and it was unlikely in the hours that they were airborne that a physician would be required. Once they were in Philadelphia they would have access to all the medical care they could need.

He wondered if he would have any free time in Philadelphia in the three days they were scheduled to be there. Perhaps he could look up a couple of old friends. He doubted that their Gestapo guide would like this idea but a telephone call could surely be arranged. He had spent four years at the Hospital of the University of Pennsylvania in graduate medical studies and on his return to Berlin in the summer of 1929 it had been a sad parting. He had enjoyed his time in America, made a lot of friends there and had received some interesting job offers. However, he was committed to return to work in his father's practice. As it turned out, America changed quite dramatically a couple of months after he left. The stock market crash in October had devastated the fortunes of many of his friends and their families and the resulting economic depression had put many of their careers on hold, at least financially.

He had prospered in Germany in the 1930's and life had been good until this wretched war began. Along with hundreds of other physicians all over Germany, he had been drafted into the army and sent to wherever his services were most needed. Fortunately, he was stationed in Berlin in what was essentially a trauma hospital where the most severely wounded were sent from the front. He quickly realized that many of their wounds were far more than physical and sometimes wondered what future the young men had, even if he could physically patch them together again. He had seen veterans from the previous war who had never recovered their ability to live anything close to normal lives, their sleep disrupted by horrendous nightmares, their days filled with torturous memories, their lives moving predictably from one crisis to another, unable to hold a job, incapable of keeping a marriage together, barely able to attend to their own personal hygiene. They often suffered from severe depression and terrible anxieties and he could see the patterns developing all over again in the young men he was treating.

The door to the pilot's cabin opened and a tall, blonde haired man stepped through. He was dressed in the uniform of the Brazilian airline that their plane was disguised as. For a moment he looked around the cabin, then saw the doctor awake and came over to sit beside him.

"Kurt von Niessen," he said, offering his hand. "I am your pilot," he added, speaking English.

"Emil Altwasser," he replied with a smile. "I am your doctor."

Von Niessen laughed. "How are things back here, Doctor?" He paused and looked up at the cabin attendant who had come forward and was standing by their seats. Van Niessen looked at Altwasser. "Coffee, Doctor?"

Altwasser nodded.

"Two cups of coffee, please."

"Thank you, Captain," the attendant said. It was the first time Altwasser had heard her speak and her voice was soft. Her English sounded like east coast American, much like his own.

He turned his attention back to von Niessen. "So far everyone is fine," he replied. "The children have been fed and are sleeping. So are the others. I don't sleep well in moving vehicles including aircraft as I have recently discovered."

"You will get used to it." Von Niessen looked up as the cabin attendant leaned forward with a tray containing two steaming mugs of rich smelling coffee. She offered cream and sugar but both declined. "This is much better than the Luftwaffe serves on its flights," he mused.

"Better than the Wehrmacht serves, too."

"It is part of our disguise," von Niessen said. "We could hardly arrive in America with ersatz coffee on a Brazilian aircraft, now could we?"

Atlwasser laughed. "I must try to recall what else Brazil produces that we have been doing without." He took a sip of the rich dark brew and nodded in appreciation. "How is it that we are flying in a plane with Brazilian markings?"

"Brazil actually owns a couple of Condors but does not have the facilities to train pilots to fly larger aircraft. So, like many airlines in the world, they have hired German pilots to fly them. Our disguise is excellent."

"Why not just arrive in the United States as Luft Hansa? We aren't at war with them." Altwasser took another sip of the coffee. It was wonderful.

"It's true that we aren't at war with the United States," Von Niessen replied. "At least, not yet," he added ominously. "But there is considerable suspicion about Germany's intentions and if Roosevelt can convince the American congress to support Churchill and the British, then we soon will be."

Altwasser shook his head. "I think that is unlikely," he said. "When I studied there in the late 1920's there was a tremendous sense of isolation in their political thinking. Their view of European politics was quite simple although quite naive as well. Let the old world have their wars and butcher each other into oblivion. Our ancestors left Europe, settled in America and established democracy to avoid this recurrent political stupidity."

"But they had their civil war," Von Niessen said.

"Ah, but that was different, " Altwasser replied with a smile. "That was their own war."

They were silent for a moment, enjoying the luxury of the coffee. Von Niessen leaned forward. "I was hoping not to have this chat," he continued, his voice suddenly serious. "However, the cold front that was supposed to stay to the north of us has decided to move south. If this pattern continues it will cause us some serious turbulence in a few hours as we divert south to get around it."

"Why will it be turbulent then?"

"Unfortunately, a storm is developing to the south of us."

"I see," Atlwasser said. He took the last sip of his coffee and looked hopefully over his shoulder toward the back of the aircraft. The attendant caught his eye and smiled.

"We had information from our U boats in the Atlantic when we left Lisbon but have had no updates since then. We will avoid as much of it as we can but we may encounter its fringes."

"Are you familiar with hurricanes, Doctor?"

Altwasser shook his head.

"We don't know a great deal about them but they are huge storms originating in the tropics and can be hundreds of kilometres in diameter. They can have winds of well over a hundred kilometres an hour. The storms are circular, the weather system is basically a huge unstable mass of rising warm air, full of moisture and turbulence."

"Are we in any danger?"

The attendant appeared beside them and hovered with a carafe of coffee. Altwasser gratefully held out his cup, von Niessen shook his head.

"I hope not," von Niessen replied. "But things could get a little rough back here. The primary concern is to make sure that everyone is securely fastened into their seats and the children strapped into their cribs. If it gets turbulent, no one will be able to leave their seats."

"When are we likely to encounter this?"

"We are about seventeen hundred kilometres west of Lisbon, approximately over the Azores Islands at the moment. If it happens, the worst of it will be about five hours ahead of us, but you'll begin experiencing some turbulence within the next two to three hours. You'll feel it coming." Von Niessen rose from his seat. "I will leave you in charge of the aft cabin here."

Altwasser glanced over his shoulder at the sleeping Gestapo agent.

Von Neissen shook his head. "This is a military aircraft regardless of the markings." He was staring at the Gestapo agent with undisguised contempt. "He is not a soldier."

CHAPTER THIRTEEN

Sunday, November 17, 1940 U64

Gilford Shore relaxed against the cold steel cowling of the conning tower, his arms cushioned by the heavy pea jacket he wore. As they glided through the long ocean swells the steady sound of the twin diesel engines was muffled by the close fitting knitted seaman's cap and the hood of his jacket, tightened against the steady wind. The blackness of the night was relieved by a quarter moon glittering off the water behind them and rippling lightly off the swells ahead. It exaggerated the illusion of forward speed so that they seemed to be flying through the water, the moonlight on their bow waves making them phosphorescent.

A pair of binoculars hung around his neck, passed to him by a lookout who had explained that with the moon behind them they could be silhouetted to anyone in front of them. An additional set of eyes was always welcome. He raised the binoculars and peered through them, amazed as usual by the clarity of the optics, the tops of the long black waves ahead of the submarine standing out stark and clear, highlighted by the rays of the moon. As the boat rose on the crest he could see far ahead and as it slipped into the trough he found himself looking up at the back of the next swell.

Katherine and Erich were sleeping soundly in the small curtained compartment they had called home for the last couple of weeks. He had been restless and had walked down to the command centre, chatted to Captain Echart and asked permission to go up on the conning tower for some fresh air.

While he was not finding this duty unpleasant, he found he was getting bored. There wasn't much to engage him. Erich was a healthy and exuberant child and any needs he had were easily attended to by Katherine. He had dressed a couple of scrapes and cuts, but the navy medics could easily have handled them. He had become friends with Captain Echart and discovered that they shared an enjoyment of chess, and although Echart routinely beat him, he felt his game was improving.

Gilford had always been an active man and he found that the restrictions and limited space on a submarine provided little opportunity for physical activity. Nonetheless, he had started a daily routine of deep knee bends, pushups and situps, and found a bar to do chin-ups. Even though the conning tower swayed about more than the hull of the submarine, he took every opportunity to spend time in the fresh air despite the cold and occasional freezing spray.

He swept his binoculars across the tops of the swells again. Just as the submarine slid into the next trough he caught a glimpse of a shadow far off the starboard bow. Then it was gone. Perhaps he had imagined it. Perhaps it was nothing. As the boat rose on the next swell he fixed his binoculars on the position where he had spotted the shadow. Whatever it had been, it was no longer there. He realized he was holding his breath and that his hands were clenching the binoculars. He smiled at himself as he released his breath. The boat slipped down into a trough again and as it rose on the next swell he heard the rating beside him draw his breath in quickly and grab the speaking tube.

"Vessel off the starboard bow."

"Range and bearing." The answer was immediate.

"Two thousand metres, perhaps a bit more. 310 degrees."

The boat slid into the next trough and the engines were throttled back to an idle.

"Confirm sighting."

The boat rose on the next swell. "Confirmed," the rating replied.

Gilford could see it as well. When he lost it the first time it likely had been in a trough when they were on crest.

"Prepare to dive." Echart's voice was quiet, almost casual.

The rating stepped past Gilford and opened the hatch that led down from the conning tower into the submarine. "After you, Sir," he said to Gilford, indicating the hatch.

Gilford swung himself down the ladder and descended quickly. The diesels had gone silent and the hum of the electric motors had taken over.

The last lookout came down the ladder. "All secure," he said to Echart.

"Take us down to periscope depth," Echart said quietly. The bow of the submarine tilted downward as it slipped under the water and then levelled. As the periscope rose he gripped the handles, read the bearing off the bezel and peered through the eyepiece. He held it steady and after a few moments, snapped up the handles. As it slid smoothly down, he turned to his second in command. "Take us down to sixty metres, as quietly as you can." Immediately the bow of the submarine began canting downward again.

"Did you see our friends up there?" Echart asked.

"I saw a shadow and it was moving so I assume it was a ship," Gilford replied.

"Quite correct. And given our position it can only be an enemy ship, likely coming out of the estuary of the St. Lawrence River. That is where the Canadian convoys bound for England leave from."

"What next?"

"Now we sit quietly and wait for them to pass."

Forty minutes later Gilford Shore lay in his bunk and listened. The electric motors had shut down some time ago and the boat had levelled. Somewhere another motor hummed for a moment and then stopped, likely a bilge pump. The ventilation fans had slowed and shut down a while ago and the U boat was silent. The air seemed fetid although he knew this was his mind playing games. The only thing he could hear was the destroyer, or at least that was what he assumed it was, somewhere out ahead of them from the sound of it, circling relentlessly, stopping, listening with their asdic and moving on again. He heard Katherine take a deep breath and sigh. She was probably finding the air hard to breath like he was. It seemed thick and moist and difficult to draw into the lungs.

At least this time he had some sense of what to expect. They had encountered a British convoy on their first day and been forced to dive. The depth charge attack had been terrifying but they had survived it and escaped. Now it seemed they had run into another convoy. Hopefully the destroyer would be content to keep them down while they passed.

He wondered if this was what fighting a war on a submarine was like, days or even weeks of inactivity and boredom, followed by minutes or hours of fear and terror. He had spoken to Captain Echart about this. Echart had laughed and said he was half correct. There were bouts of fear, but not much inactivity and boredom. On this voyage they were doing everything they could to avoid encounters with the enemy while on a normal patrol they would be actively hunting for enemy convoys, attacking them and then disappearing.

So for the last two and a half weeks they had been motoring across the Atlantic Ocean, rolling in the swells, tossing in the storms and on a couple of occasions, diving when they sighted another vessel on the horizon.

This time the destroyer above them had dropped one pattern of depth charges but it was some considerable distance away. Perhaps they didn't know whether there was a submarine in the vicinity or not and were just making sure. Erich awakened and he heard Katherine gather him out of his bassinette to comfort him. Erich was a fine little lad and Katherine seemed such a natural mother with him. He almost hoped that the war would last a while and perhaps they could live like a real family. He smiled at the wholesome image and admitted to himself that a large part of that appeal was Katherine. He knew he was attracted to her, she was so beautiful that men would easily find her appealing, but he had been careful to avoid dwelling on it.

However, out of the experiences they had gone through, he was developing a deep respect and affection for her. He even felt a twinge of jealousy a couple of times as he watched her at Lorient, being charming and laughing with some of the younger officers on Donitz' staff. She had enjoyed the same effect on the submarine, but the officers and crew had been consistently polite but reserved. He wondered if this had anything to do with the old superstition about women on war ships being bad luck. More likely it was a response to Echart's orders on the treatment of their guests. Whatever the case, his feelings for Katherine, or for that matter, her feelings about him, would simply have to wait until they were safely in Canada and had delivered Erich to his new family. Oddly, the thought of doing that saddened him.

He heard the destroyer turning toward them again, the sound of the engines and propellers rising far above them and the pinging sound of the asdic stroked the hull of the U boat. He listened as it passed overhead and the sound slowly receded. Either the destroyer had found them or it was just making a lucky pass. He wedged himself more tightly into the narrow bunk, his knees pressed against the padded wall, his back braced against the safety board on the edge of the bunk. "Hang on tightly, Katherine," he whispered.

The roar of the explosions seemed to be right on top of them. The boat heaved and shuddered and the lights went out. For a few moments he was deafened but as his hearing returned he heard the sound of glass shattering from the direction of the command centre and then a sudden hiss, although he couldn't tell if it was water or the compressed air they used to blow the ballast tanks when they surfaced. Below him Erich shrieked in terror and he heard Katherine whispering words of comfort. His crying quickly subsided.

"We're fine, Gilford," Katherine said. "Erich is just frightened."

The bow of the boat began tilting downward and he heard one of the bilge pumps start up, then the sound of the destroyer returning. It seemed like a more confident sound as it passed over them more slowly this time.

The next explosion was near the bow and the front of the boat heaved upwards. Three more followed so quickly that Gilford had no idea where they were. As his hearing cleared he heard someone shouting in the command centre and then silence except for Erich's muffled sobs.

"Captain Echart needs you in the command centre, Doctor." The voice was quiet and calm from the other side of the curtain. "He asks that you bring your medical bag with you."

"Of course," Gilford said, clambering down out of the top bunk and grabbing the small bag from a hook on the wall. The emergency lights flickered back on as he pushed the curtain aside. He stepped into an inch of water as he moved to the companion way. The rating had a flashlight and guided them forward to the command centre.

"There's glass on the floor, sir," the rating warned him as they entered the crowded centre. "Over here, sir," he said, indicating a body crumpled in a heap next to another of the crew seated in front of a battery of gauges. Gilford could see that some of them had no glass, some appeared to be entirely shattered and others were still working.

He knelt by the body in the dim light and realized it was Ernst Klassen, their Gestapo guard. "What's Klassen doing here?"

"Sleeping for the moment," Echart answered curtly. "He barged in here and ordered me to surface." A tired smile flitted across his face. "He was clearly hysterical and one of my officers provided the standard treatment."

Gilford turned his attention back to Klassen. He had been struck on the side of the head and was bleeding from a small cut. Swelling had started.

"I want you to give that swine something so he won't wake up for the next several hours. You may also treat his wound if you wish."

Their eyes met and Gilford nodded. He took a syringe from his bag, carefully filled it from a small vial and slipped the needle deftly into Klassen's arm, slowly depressing the plunger.

"Hang on again, Doctor Shore," Echart said softly. "Our friends are back."

Gilford heard the destroyer pass over them again and grabbed a railing on the ladder leading up to the conning tower. It vibrated under the impact of the explosion and the boat rocked violently to port, swinging Gilford around like a child on a Maypole. The lights flickered but stayed on. He glanced down to see that Klassen had been thrown across the command centre into a bulkhead on the other side. He lay there like a broken rag doll. As two more explosions shook the boat again and put out the lights, Gilford wondered if the injection he had given Klassen might not be a good idea for him and Katherine and Erich. He could hear water spraying in the direction of his bunk. Two of the sailors in the command centre turned on flashlights.

"I will have one of my men show you back to your quarters, Dr. Shore," Echart said softly, the slightly sarcastic grin passing over his countenance again. "We will provide what additional care Herr Klassen requires. Thank you."

Gilford nodded and walked unsteadily down the narrow passageway, bracing himself on the bunks and bulkheads. The passage was cluttered with debris from the bunks and with loaves of bread and vegetables sloshing about in the water that now seemed almost up to his ankles. In front of the curtain to his bunk he turned to the rating. "Thank you for bringing me back."

"You might like to keep the flashlight, sir," the rating said, handing it to Gilford. "You never know about the lights around here." He grinned and with a wink went off down the dark passage.

Gilford pushed the curtains apart and knelt by Katherine's bunk. "How are you and Erich doing?"

"About as well as the rest of the crew, I guess," Katherine answered. She was holding Erich between her body and the padded wall. The little boy's eyes were huge and tearful, and he was snuffling, recovering from his crying, holding tightly to Katherine.

"Good," Gilford said. "It seems our friend Klassen got hysterical and someone knocked him unconscious. Echart wanted him put to sleep for a while so I obliged. We don't need some Gestapo officer ranting about the place."

"Did Captain Echart tell you how long this might last?"

"No, I'm sorry he didn't, but it can't be too much longer since the destroyer is supposed to be guarding the convoy. I don't think they have enough destroyer escorts that they can have one out here hunting for submarines." He leaned over Katherine and ruffled Erich's thatch of dark blonde hair. The large brown eyes stared up at him and then the little face broke into a grin. Gilford found himself smiling back. He glanced at Katherine and found she was watching him. She reached out and touched his hand.

"Don't worry about us, Gilford," she whispered. "We'll be fine."

He squeezed her hand briefly. "I know." He hauled himself wearily up into his bunk and braced himself again. The sound of the spraying water had stopped and he heard several ratings moving quickly down the companionway. He felt helpless and it was not a familiar emotion to him. He was used to being in control of life around him, not being dependent on people he didn't know, although in this case he certainly trusted their competence.

He thought back to their departure at dusk, two and a half weeks ago. It had been late afternoon, the sun was setting and the clouds, dark and brooding along the horizon, had lifted for a moment like a curtain, and sunlight had streamed across the bay lighting up the low coastline near the entrance to the inner harbour and silhouetting the old church on the cliffs above Larmor Plage. While Gilford was not religious, he had been raised a Lutheran and the image of the church, haloed in the sun, had seemed like an omen. He had stayed on the bridge for a while, the chill damp air slowly seeping into him. He had felt the steady throbbing of the twin diesel engines and the gradually rising swells of the ocean. It was dark when they passed the island of Le Groix. Their small escort had flashed a light signal at the conning tower and then turned back to Lorient leaving them alone on the open sea. Everything had seemed so safe and solid.

He had gone below and found that the cook was preparing dinner in the small galley. Fried eggs, bread, coffee and sweetened tea were being distributed down the narrow crowded passages. Crew members were jammed into bunks, corners and anywhere else they could find that was stable enough to hold their food. They were in high spirits, laughing and joking among themselves and the hydrophone operator had begun to play popular songs on the gramophone and pipe them through the boat's address system.

Don't let it get you down!
Why take life with a frown?
Bad times will pass
And nothing can last
So please sugar, don't let it get you down.

Gilford suddenly realized that the sound of the destroyer was gone. Had it broken off or was it lying in wait on the surface guessing that sooner or later the U boat would make a noise or attempt to surface. Then faintly he heard the sound of a second ship but far in the distance, then other engine and propeller noises. This must be the convoy the destroyer escorting and it was keeping them down so they couldn't attack. The noise increased and as the first ship passed nearby he heard the ventilation fans come on and then the sound of the electric motors. They were underway again, creeping forward, the noise of the convoy above them covering their escape.

CHAPTER FOURTEEN

Monday, November 18, 1940, Over the Atlantic Ocean

Emil Altwasser was jolted from sleep. The aircraft had suddenly dropped, tightening his lap belt as he was lifted in his seat and then slamming him down as the aircraft felt like it hit bottom. He realized that in spite of his own predictions he must have fallen asleep. He glanced at his watch. It was a few minutes past 11:00am. He must have slept the better part of four hours.

After Altwasser had finished the rich dark Brazilian coffee, the flight attendant had brought him a tray with breakfast, hard boiled eggs, two kinds of sausage, which Americans would have called "cold cuts", a small block of creamy rich butter cheese and a couple of buns and butter. The others had awakened and had also been served. After the breakfast trays had been cleared away, the last thing he remembered was reclining his seat slightly and leaning back to relax. Recalling von Niessen's forecast, he smiled in grim appreciation at its accuracy. He squirmed around in his seat trying to get comfortable again.

He stretched his legs out, moved his arms above his shoulders and slowly rolled his head from side to side.

After a moment he realized that he was not going to get into a position where he could easily fall asleep again. His back hurt, and the seat cushions that had initially felt quite soft were now feeling hard. He adjusted his seat to the upright position and looked about the interior of the aircraft. The cabin lights were glowing softly reflecting slightly on the pale metal sheathing of the ceiling. A brighter light behind him caught his attention and he glanced over his shoulder to see the attendant strapped into a seat near the small kitchen still reading a magazine. She glanced up from her reading and smiled at him, reassuringly. The others appeared to have slept through the first bump in the storm. The babies were asleep, too, or at least quiet.

He had hoped for a beautiful sunrise to light up the clouds as they crossed the Atlantic but if there had been one he had certainly slept through it. During the time he had been asleep, the sky had changed from black and clear and was now an ominous dark grey. Rain was streaking off the windows. Visibility was no more than a few metres so he could barely see the wing tips. How did a pilot navigate in this? A compass he supposed, like ships had been doing for several hundred years. Perhaps there were other more sophisticated devices that aircraft used. He would ask von Niessen when they got to Philly. "Philly", an American slang term for Philadelphia. He hadn't thought of it in years.

One of the nurses, Francine, as he recalled her English name, "Frannie" she had asked him to call her, stirred in her sleep, then opened her eyes and fumbled for a moment for the small lever on the side of her seat. She found it and the seat back moved to the upright position. She glanced around, looking startled for a moment. Catching his eye, she smiled sleepily and then looked over at the crib near her chair. Unfastening her seat belt, she rose and walked over to stand beside it. She leaned over the crib and moved the small child, apparently checking his diaper. As Altwasser started to stand up to join her, the aircraft suddenly took a small bounce upward, pushing him back into his seat. He smiled at the sensation, waited a moment and attempted standing up again, this time successfully.

"Good morning, Doctor," Frannie said, gripping the edge of the crib as Altwasser came up beside her. Her English had a trace of a British accent. The crib was a solid metal piece of furniture, covered with dark brown enamel, no drop down sides, and it was bolted onto a steel frame which was in turn bolted into the fixtures that normally would have held the seats in place.

"Good morning, Frannie," he replied. "Please call me Emil. In America we are much less formal." She had soft dark brown hair with small waves formed across the top and was probably in her late twenties, slim, small boned, with a bright happy smile. Her large, long lashed eyes were a deep brown. Perhaps there would be some time to get to know her better when they were in the United States. He had noticed she wasn't wearing a wedding band. "How is our charge this morning? This is Johann, is it not?"

"This is him." She laughed, her eyes sparkling mischievously. "He's soiled and hungry, like most babies."

As the aircraft lurched again, Emil grasped the edge of the crib as Frannie lost her balance and fell against him. He caught her and held her leaning against the edge of the crib to steady himself. He kept his arm around her for a moment longer than necessary but she didn't pull away. "Captain von Niessen, our pilot, told me a few hours ago that we could be encountering some air turbulence, so as soon as you get the child comfortable, fix his safety harness securely. Then go back to your seat and fasten your own safety belt."

Frannie looked up at him, frowning. "How long is this likely to last?"

"I don't know. It could be an hour or so, hopefully less, but I'm not really sure."

He saw the second nurse, at the crib near her seat, leaning over the other child.

He moved across the cabin and stood beside her. Her English name was Nancy. She was shorter than Frannie and the word "sturdy" came to mind as he looked down at her. Her features were plain but pleasant, her hair a nondescript pale brown. The child was Lienhard, an unAmerican name if he had ever heard one. Perhaps they would change it to something that would fit into America better. "Lincoln" would be a good choice. As he looked down into the crib, the child began to cry, softly at first and then more stridently.

Nancy glanced up at him, gripping the edge of the crib to keep her balance. She looked decidedly nauseous as she turned back to changing the diaper.

"Troubles?" Altwasser asked.

She shook her head. "Just a small diaper rash. It will be fine."

The plane dropped quite suddenly, and almost before he could lose his balance he had regained it.

"It is getting a bit rough, isn't it?"

Altwasser turned to find their Gestapo companion standing behind him. They had met briefly before they boarded the plane. His last name was Stahl, first name still unknown,

Stahl moved to the other side of the crib, and gripping the side rail, smiled down at Lienhard. He looked up at Atlwasser. "You slept well?"

"Apparently I did, although I hadn't expected to," Atlwasser answered. He was surprised at Stahl's civility. In his very limited experience with Gestapo personnel he had found them to be unfailingly rude and unpleasant.

"And how is the child," Stahl asked quietly. "Nothing serious I trust?"

"No, Herr Stahl," she replied. "He will be fine.

Altwasser made a note to talk to her about the use of "Herr". It would not do once they were on US soil. They would use first names.

Stahl turned to Atlwasser. "I believe the pilot was out here chatting to you earlier. Did he indicate how long this might last?"

Altwasser shook his head. "There is an arctic weather system moving south from Greenland so the Captain has changed our flight path further south to avoid it. However, there is tropical storm there and we are likely skirting the edge of it."

"Then before it becomes too rough I will prevail on our attendant to bring me some coffee," Stahl said. "Perhaps you would join me?"

Altwasser was surprised but nodded his assent. "Thank you."

Stahl turned to the attendant and mimicked drinking from a cup, then followed Altwasser to his seat, taking the one beside him.

A moment later the attendant appeared beside them with two empty cups. "I will be back in a moment with the coffee. Do either of you take cream or sugar?"

"Cream, please," Stahl said. The attendant took Stahl's cup and moved toward the rear of the aircraft. Stahl watched her for a moment and then turned to Altwasser. "Since we are going to be spending some time together, Doctor, I thought we should get to know each other a little better. Please call me Heinrich." He held out his hand. "I should say 'Henry'", he added with a smile.

"Emil," he said. "I should have thought you would already know quite a lot about me?"

Stahl laughed merrily. "Ah, you mean our famous dossiers on everyone from the famous to the trivial," he said. "We are by no means as thorough as our reputation suggests."

The attendant returned with Stahl's cup and the coffee. She braced herself against the edge of Stahl's seat back and held out a carafe. The smell of fresh brewed coffee enveloped them. "If you will hold your cups out, away from yourselves, I will try to pour you some coffee without spilling it. However, don't linger over it too long. The turbulence will likely get worse before it gets better." She poured Stahl's first without incident but as she was about to pour Altwasser's the plane lurched sideways and a small stream of brown fluid poured onto the carpet between them.

"Hold mine for a moment," said Stahl, handing his cup to Altwasser and taking his. "It will be easier to pour from this side."

"Thank you," the attendant said, bracing herself against the back of Stahl's seat and filling the second cup without spilling any.

"Thank you," Stahl said. "This is very kind of you."

"It is my pleasure," the attendant said. She waited a moment, still leaning lightly on the seat and then scurried to the back of the plane.

"Now, Doctor, I know that you are currently an army physician, working in Berlin in one of our trauma hospitals, trained in Germany and following that, for some time in Philadelphia. You are an excellent surgeon, you are single and you speak fluent English. Prior to being conscripted, you had a large private practice with your father, primarily among the wealthy and aristocratic folks of Berlin. You see, that is not really a great deal of knowledge."

"But quite accurate," Altwasser replied. "How about you? How did you come to be working for the Gestapo?"

"This is truly fine coffee," Stahl said, taking another sip and leaning back in his seat. "I was a policeman in Munich in the early 1930's, working mostly on homicides and other serious crimes. As the National Socialist Party gained influence and took over the governance of Germany, I sometimes found it quite difficult to conduct my investigations. I often ran into the Gestapo who would take over my investigations and usually mess them up. I fought against this but eventually decided that it was more effective to join them. I was rather surprised that they took me because, although I had joined the NAZI party some years prior to that, I was never a particularly dedicated or involved party member. I merely joined because it was apparent that only party members had any hope of promotion."

The flight attendant appeared beside them again and handed them a couple of small paper sacks. "These are for air sickness," she said, bracing herself once more on Stahl's seat as the aircraft experienced another bump. "When the turbulence is past, I will bring you some more coffee, if you wish."

"That would be lovely," Altwasser said. "But there's no hurry."

She moved quickly forward and handed two of the bags to each of the nurses.

Altwasser thought about what Stahl had just told him. "So how did you get assigned to this duty?" he asked.

"I'm not sure," Stahl said thoughtfully. "But I think it may be a form of banishment. I was working on a case that had some political implications and my boss decided that I was not taking an appropriately sensitive approach to it. So I was reassigned."

"Interesting," Altwasser said. "You are rather different than other members of your organization that I have met."

"So I am told," Stahl replied with a slight smile. "Too sensitive, perhaps."The aircraft bounced upward for a moment before steadying again. "I checked with some friends in the Luftwafe when I discovered what aircraft we would be flying in and apparently there have been some problems with military versions of this aircraft. It seems that when fully loaded with fuel and munitions and subjected to significant stress loads, the wings have literally fallen off in a few cases. Apparently, this has not occurred on the civilian version."

Altwasser looked at him carefully, wondering if he was serious. It appeared he was. "You are a sensitive soul, aren't you?" he said.

Stahl laughed. "I suppose I am."

Francine Brown, or "Frannie", as she had decided to call herself in her new English identity, quite enjoyed the early hours of her first ride in an aircraft. The segment from Berlin to Lisbon had been smooth, although the noise of the engines took some getting used to. She had also been a little nervous as the plane rolled down the runway, engines roaring, the nose lifting up as the aircraft left the ground and began to climb into the sky. The unaccustomed sense of being pressed back into her seat by the acceleration and the sudden smoothness of the ride as the aircraft left the ground had all been novel experiences. And now she was nearing the end of her first trans-Atlantic flight and the novelty had worn off entirely.

She slept intermittently during the first few hours after they left Lisbon in the middle of the night, about 2:00am, as she recalled. She had come awake in the early morning, and enjoyed the breakfast served by the attendant. She hadn't really thought about life on an aircraft but was pleased to discover that there was food, a small but quite adequate and well-appointed bathroom, although the toilet was smaller than normal, and while it was a small thing, that the coffee was excellent.

The severe turbulence they had encountered as the aircraft skirted the tropical storm had been terrifying but she didn't have any clear idea whether this was a normal part of flying or something quite out of the ordinary. When the plane had begun bouncing around, it moved as though it was being struck by something, dropping precipitously, then rising again, before shuddering with the next blow. She had no idea that air could sound and feel so hard. She wondered if the aircraft could withstand the abuse. She had been alternately frightened as the aircraft was tossed about and then relieved as it had passed through relatively calm patches, then frightened again as it slammed into the storm once more.

It had been an immense relief to leave the storm behind. The whole process left her emotionally drained and mildly nauseous for a while but finally they flew into stable air and she gradually recovered.

After they passed the storm, the attendant brought them trays of food, a beef broth with some vegetables and a sandwich, followed by coffee again. She was surprised at how hungry she had been. As a treat, she had added a dollop of cream to her coffee, although she usually didn't indulge herself that way. The late afternoon sky was clear, the sun was shining and far below them the ocean sparkled, a deep beautiful blue.

Johann had been remarkably subdued during the flight. He required changing a few times, and she had taken him out of his crib a short time ago and walked with him up and down the length of the aircraft cabin. She allowed him to play on the floor with a couple of his toys for a while. Now he was back in his crib for an afternoon nap. He was used to some solid food and she wondered how he would adjust to having only bottles for their trip but he seemed fine.

However, Lienhard had been another matter. Earlier in the day, he fussed a lot, and during the turbulence of the storm he had become very agitated, crying and rolling about, waving his arms and kicking his small legs as far as the limits of his safety harness would permit. Nancy had been quite ill and Lienhard had been left to his own devices. As the aircraft gradually flew out of the storm, Frannie went back and cleaned him up, changing his diaper, and the sheets in his crib that had also become soiled. Nancy was weak and pale from the long bout of vomiting that she had gone through during the turbulence.

Frannie glanced over her shoulder at the doctor, Emil, he had told her to call him. He seemed relaxed in his seat with his eyes closed although she suspected that he wasn't sleeping. She liked him so far. He treated her with respect, Nancy too, and had left the care of the children to them. He told her he was there for any emergency that they couldn't handle, but then added that he didn't really think there was an emergency that they couldn't handle. He was gracious and handsome, too. Perhaps they would get to know each other a bit better before this assignment was over. Whatever happened, this was certainly better than the war wounded hospital she had been in for the last year.

She could see that Nancy was sleeping now, still looking pale and exhausted. Herr Stahl had been clearly nauseous, too, but seemed fine now. The only Gestapo agent Frannie had met before Stahl was the one who had informed her that her services were required elsewhere. He had been rude and officious and had leered at her menacingly although it had stopped there. A second interview followed with another man who was pleasant enough but seemed quite cold and aloof. So Stahl had been a welcome surprise, warm, friendly and interested in the welfare of the children.

Johann awakened and was standing up, gripping the railing of the crib and waving a small wooden rattle. He banged it against the bars of the crib and laughed gleefully, probably at the sound it made, although the noise from the aircraft engines drowned out anything that she might have heard from a couple of metres away.

She looked over her shoulder at Emil who smiled back at her and then arose and came forward. He took the seat beside her. "Will we be much longer?" she asked.

"No," Emil replied. "If Von Neissen's earlier estimates still hold, we should be a couple of hours out from Philadelphia. Apparently we will be landing at a new airfield, the Philadelphia Municipal Airport. It has only been open since June."

"Have you been to Philadelphia before?"

"I lived there for four years, from 1925 to 1929," he replied. "I was studying at the hospital at the University of Pennsylvania."

"So you know your way around the city?"

"Well I did eleven years ago, so if it hasn't changed too much I'll be fine. However, I don't think we will have much opportunity to wander around."

What will happen when we get there?" Frannie asked.

"As I understand it, we will be in the United States for three to five days before we fly back to Germany," Altwasser replied. "I don't think we will be in Philadelphia for more than a few hours, if that."

"Where are we going?"

"I'm not sure, but I believe it is to a smaller town outside of the Philadelphia area. We will turn the children over to a foster family who will care for them. We will stay for a couple of days to make sure the children are fine. Then we will return to Philadelphia and thence back to Germany."

Frannie frowned. She had been looking forward to doing some shopping in America, to buying some new clothes. "So you don't think that we will have any time to go shopping?"

"Not much time, I shouldn't think," Altwasser said. "But in any case, what would you use for money?"

"I brought some with me," Frannie replied.

"German money?"

"It's the only kind I have," she said. And then it dawned on her that she would need American money to spend in America. Stupid that she hadn't thought of it. She had used English money in England when she lived there, so of course, she would need US money in America.

Emil smiled at her. "I wouldn't worry about it, Frannie," he said. He had a nice smile. "Stahl will have US money and we won't have to pay for anything anyway."

CHAPTER FIFTEEN

Monday, November 18, 1940 U64, Marsland Cove, Nova Scotia, Canada

The U64 had been running submerged for about four hours, creeping slowly in toward the shore of the Canadian mainland. According to Captain Echart, their rendezvous point was a small cove on the coast of Nova Scotia, deep enough to take the U boat into and sheltered from the open sea by a small island so that unloading their passengers would not be hampered by high seas.

Gilford carried Erich as he and Katherine moved carefully down the crowded passages saying their farewells. They had become used to the peculiar smells of diesel fuel, humanity and stale air and as they chatted with crew members, Gilford reflected that they now looked like a bunch of buccaneers, unshaven, unkempt, naval haircuts getting shaggy with their clothes wrinkled and dirty.

Erich had quickly become a kind of mascot for the boat, toddling along the passages until one of the sailors picked him up, found a bit of sweet biscuit or a piece of chocolate. They had made him a small hat one day and a couple of days later had delivered him back to Katherine in a complete miniature uniform. The cook had always found some little treat for Erich and even Captain Echart had gotten used to having him wander about the command centre. Only Klassen had remained aloof for the entire voyage. Since his hysteria the previous day during the British destroyer attack he had kept to himself, staying in his bunk, appearing at meals, sullen and uncommunicative, and then retiring again. He had refused any further treatment for the cut on his head and had taped a small bandage over it himself.

"Sir." One of the ratings touched Gilford's arm. "I'm one of the boat's machinists and we've made a small toy for young Erich. We'd like him to have it as a souvenir." He handed Gilford a package, wrapped in a soft white cloth.

Gilford handed the package to Katherine. "Thank you very much," he said to the rating. "Erich is a very lucky young man."

Katherine unfolded the cloth to reveal a perfect miniature, about nine inches long, of a U boat, machined steel and painted grey with tiny lettering on the conning tower, U64. She looked carefully at the delicate workmanship and held it up for Gilford and Erich to see. "It's beautiful," she said. "This is a work of art, not a toy."

"Erich will treasure this," Gilford said, peering at it closely, amazed by the detail of the conning tower with a small steel rod protruding to represent the periscope, and the rudders and diving planes and even a miniature 88 millimetre deck gun.

"Thank you sir," the rating said grinning broadly. "He's a fine young lad."

"Finished your last tour?" Captain Echart asked, as they entered the command centre. Except for the sigh of the ventilation fans and the soft hum of the electric motors, the U boat was strangely quiet. A group of ratings stood by the conning tower ladder, ready to run aloft when the boat surfaced. Bundled up in a small parka, Erich toddled awkwardly over to the ladder and one of the ratings put him up on the third rung and braced him there.

"Yes, we have, Captain," Gilford said. "Thank you for your hospitality."

"It's been our pleasure to have you aboard," Echart replied. Then he drew Gilford into his berth and pulled the curtain. "But I have a word of caution for you. We have gone through Klassen's gear. That Gestapo swine has a Luger, a dagger, incendiary devices, pills that look like cyanide and some other vials of drugs as well. I don't know anything about your mission and I don't want to know anything, but these Gestapo bastards just can't be trusted. To them, everyone is expendable but themselves. If you are stopped by the authorities and any of that is found, he will be arrested immediately and we have already witnessed how he reacts under pressure."

"I'm quite aware that Klassen is dangerous," Gilford said softly. "But I didn't think that he was stupid too. His English is functional but by no means passable to anyone who questioned him closely. I can't say I'm surprised that he is armed. Were these things just in his kit?"

"Exactly," Echart said. "No attempt at concealment. I took the liberty of having the boat's armourer check the Luger and disable it". Echart turned and pulled open a small drawer in a chest beneath his bunk. "I presume you can use one of these if you have to?"

Gilford looked down as Echart put a small pistol into his hand. He looked closely. "Berretta?"

"Yes, and here is an extra clip. Do you have a place to conceal it?"

"The bottom of my medical bag has a compartment about an inch deep. That should do it."

"Captain to the bridge," the voice came softly from the other side of the curtain. As they stood up the electric motors stopped.

"Sounds like we've arrived, Dr. Shore," Echart said.

"Have a look at your new home," Captain Echart said, standing aside and motioning Gilford to look through the periscope.

Gilford pressed his face against the soft rubber housing and looked out on a calm sea. In the distance, perhaps a kilometre away, he could see the outline of the shore, low, dark and solid against a blue black sky. He swung the periscope slowly around as he had just seen Echart do. Nothing moved on the tranquil sea except for a long gentle swell that seemed to roll up in front of the periscope lens and then recede. Close by the starboard side of the boat a low island loomed out of the darkness, the swells breaking gently against the steep rocky shore. He swept along the island but it seemed to be deserted or else all the houses were inland. It ended suddenly and he realized it was quite small, perhaps a kilometre long, a little more than half a mile, he corrected himself, beyond it, open gently undulating water.

"Interesting, Captain, thank you. What now?"

"Now we get you ashore." He turned to his first officer. "Stand by to surface. Signal the shore."

The first officer took over the periscope just as Ernst Klassen came into the command centre. He walked over to Echart and Gilford.

"We have arrived?" he demanded imperiously.

"We have indeed," Echart replied.

"Then what are we waiting for, Captain Echart? Bring us to the surface and we will be on our way."

"I thought you might like to wait for your pick up, Herr Klassen, but if you wish to swim ashore, I will be pleased to arrange it."

"A dory approaching off the port bow, Captain," the first officer said. "She's replied to our signal."

"Very well, take us up, without a ripple, if you please ." Echart turned away from Klassen, looked at Gilford and rolled his eyes. The first officer's voice was quiet as he issued his orders and Gilford listened to the hiss of compressed air rushing into the ballast tanks. The U boat rose slowly, the bow tilting up slightly, and then the hatches were opened and the waiting crew members scrambled up, with Echart behind.

"You'd better take Erich now," one of the heavily dressed ratings said, gently handing the child to Gilford. He turned and followed his comrades up the ladder of the conning tower. Fresh cold air came pouring down into the command centre. Gilford breathed it in gratefully, but felt its chill through the heavy jacket and seaman's cap he was wearing.

"Are we ready to go?" Katherine asked.

"As ready as we are going to be," Gilford replied. He saw her hair was neatly pushed up under a knitted cap. The wool jacket and trousers she wore were too big for her, but rather than making her look clumsy, Gilford thought they made her look cuddly and cute, even kind of vulnerable. "You go up first and I'll follow with Erich."

"If you please Dr. Shore," Klassen interrupted. "I will go first and make sure it is safe."

"As you wish, Klassen," Gilford said with a sigh, wondering how he was going to stomach Klassen for the next weeks. He turned to Katherine with a smile and shrug. She touched his arm reassuringly.

The air was bitterly cold and Gilford snuggled Erich against him. He looked down over the fore deck. The gun crew had uncovered and manned the 88 millimetre deck gun. It was pointed toward the small dory that was approaching, its one cylinder engine popping rhythmically on the still night air. Suddenly the motor stopped and the dark shadows of a couple of men in the dory disappeared below the gunwales. Seconds later one of the lookouts quietly announced, "Boat in sight off the starboard bow."

Gilford turned quickly and saw a small ship appearing around the headland of the little island he had seen through the periscope. It was faintly silhouetted but carried no lights. It was moving slowly in their direction about half a mile in front of them. The crew on the deck gun had seen it too and swivelled the 88 to cover it.

"Open fire, Echart," Klassen snapped. "Sink it."

"Do shut up, Klassen," Echart snapped. "If we fired our deck gun we would wake up half of Nova Scotia."

"I order you to fire, Echart, in the name of the Reich."

"We are not firing on innocent fishermen, you idiot," Echart said, completely exasperated. "He hasn't seen us, he is fishing illegally which is why he has no running lights, and even if he did see us, he couldn't report us without getting into serious trouble with the authorities."

"The boat is turning back," the lookout announced in the same quiet voice.

Gilford saw the boat turning away from them in a large circle and heading back around the headland. A moment later the motor on the small dory resumed its steady popping.

Echart turned to Gilford. "Time to go," he said, shaking his hand firmly. "Good luck, Doctor. Mrs. Shore."

"I'll take the little boy down the ladder for you, sir," one of the ratings said. He took Erich from Gilford, hugged him close to his shoulder and swung easily down the ladder.

CHAPTER SIXTEEN

Monday, November 18, 1940 Philadelphia, Pennsylvania, USA

Altwasser looked out the small window as the Condor lazily circled the airport to line up for the runway. In the distance he spotted the City Hall Tower, the peculiarly adorned landmark and, at 495 feet, the tallest building in Philadelphia. Looking down at the airport, he could see it had been expanded significantly since his last visit there in 1927, almost exactly thirteen years ago. At the time there had been talk of expansion and of the growing role that the city fathers hoped Philadelphia would play in the developing field of air transport and travel. It had been a period of such euphoria in America that any dream could be turned into a viable project, but the stock market crash of October 1929 and the ensuing depression of the early 1930's had shattered a lot of dreams and halted a lot of projects.

Until the last couple of years he had maintained a periodic correspondence with a few of his former colleagues from the University Hospital and had found their tales of life in a depressed America quite astonishing. They had related stories of tens of thousands of migrant workers drifting through the dust bowls of the middle and south western United States, of suicides on Wall Street, of massive unemployment and bread lines in the industrial heartland, of the rich becoming poor and of the poor moving to destitution. It had sounded like the entire social, cultural and economic fabric of the nation had been torn apart. In many ways, it reminded him of the conditions that existed in Germany in the aftermath of the Great War, as the Americans had called it, minus the destruction, of course. But then the stories had slowly changed. The irrepressible American optimism slowly reasserted itself as things bottomed out and began their slow climb back. They were still a long way from the euphoria of the 1920's but things were better.

As the Condor made its final approach he realized where the airport had expanded. Evidently, the old shipbuilding yards on Hog Island, originally developed as an emergency shipbuilding facility during the Great War, had been redeveloped as part of the Municipal Airport. He smiled at the irony of a small contingent of German military personnel landing on the site.

He thought of his last visit to the airport, recalling the crisp October day in 1927 when he and a number of friends from the hospital had driven out to the airport in Northrop Granger's open touring car to see and hear Charles Lindbergh, fresh from his epic flight from New York to Paris. Lindbergh had landed in the Spirit of St. Louis, the plane he had flown across the Atlantic, and had given a short speech on the future of aviation in America and of the role the city of Philadelphia could play. He had raised an American flag to officially dedicate the Philadelphia Municipal Airport.

Altwasser felt his ears pop again as the plane descended further, and then saw the tarmac rushing by when the wheels thumped down on the runway. As the aircraft slowed, the tail gradually settled. Von Niessen taxied the plane toward the new terminal building and brought it gently to a halt. The engines slowed and shut down and in the sudden silence that followed Altwasser wondered for a moment if he had gone deaf. The small sounds of others moving in the aircraft, the opening of the door to the flight deck and a happy laugh from Johann assured him that his hearing was still intact. They had arrived.

Captain von Niessen emerged from the flight deck and surveyed the passenger cabin. He smiled at Atwasser as he walked across the sloping floor of the aircraft to take a seat beside him.

"I trust you enjoyed your first trans-Atlantic flight, Doctor?"

"I did," Altwasser replied. He undid the buckle on his seat belt. "Although it may be some time until my hearing recovers. I will likely shout at everyone for a day or two."

Von Niessen laughed. "It will pass in a short while." He leaned toward Altwasser. "I will expect you back here in three days, Doctor. I have two days of grace so if you require extra time, I can wait for you and the nurses." He handed Atlwasser a card. "We are staying at the Biltmore Hotel. Here is the telephone number. The local operator can connect you. Just leave a message at the desk."

"Thank you for delivering us safely, Captain." Altwasser looked up to see their Gestapo minder, Stahl, hovering above them, smiling amiably.

Von Niessen rose. "I was explaining to Doctor Atlwasser our arrangements for leaving America."

Ah, yes," Stahl said. "In three days as I recall?"

"That is correct," von Niessen replied stiffly. "With a two day period of grace. I have provided Doctor Altwasser with contact information to confirm our departure."

Stahl nodded, still smiling. "You are staying at the Biltmore Hotel and we can contact you through the front desk."

"You are well informed," von Niessen said curtly.

"It is my job to be well informed, Captain," Stahl replied pleasantly. "Once we leave the haven of your aircraft, it is my responsibility to ensure the safe conduct of our charges."

Altwasser got to his feet. He extended his hand. "Thank you, Captain, and please extend our thanks to your crew as well."

Von Niessen shook his hand firmly. "It has been a pleasure to have your group with us."

Stahl extended his hand and von Niessen shook it briefly. "Thank you, Captain," Stahl said. "I shall look forward to more of your excellent Brazilian coffee on the return flight."

Stahl turned to Altwasser. "Doctor?" he said, indicating the open door. Frannie and Nancy were waiting by the companionway, holding Johann and Lienhard, two small bundles wrapped warmly against the coolness of the late afternoon.

Altwasser moved to the companionway with Stahl, who excused himself and stepped in front of the two women. He looked out across the tarmac toward the terminal building for a moment before descending the moveable staircase that had been wheeled up to the doorway. As the two nurses started down the companion way, von Niessen put his hand on Altwasser's arm as he handed him his black leather medical bag. He leaned close to Altwasser and in little more than a whisper said, "I have taken the liberty of adding a Luger to your medical supplies. I trust you will not require it but America can be a dangerous country." He touched him lightly on the back, guiding him forward.

As they walked across the pavement to the brightly lit terminal building, with the three airport officials who had met them at the foot of the stairway, Altwasser pulled his overcoat collar up against the light but chilly wind. Someone had arranged for their arrival as he, the nurses, the children and their Gestapo companion were quickly led through the building and out the front door. The uniformed airport personnel led them to two large black Packard sedans, opened the doors and ushered them in, he, with Frannie and Johann in one, Stahl, with Nancy and Lienhard in the other.

Altwasser received only a nod when he thanked the uniformed official holding open the door of the Packard. He heard the trunk lid open and then close, presumably to accommodate their luggage, and then the car moved smoothly away from the curb. Moments later it swung onto a new four lane road, new at least since he had been there, and headed north in the late afternoon traffic.

Northrop Granger had been the driver of the beautiful Lincoln touring car that he had driven away in from the airport the last time he had been here. Northrop was so bright, so talented, so warm, so friendly and amusing and so very rich. He and Northrop had roomed together for his last two years at the hospital and they had become good friends. The Granger wealth, it seemed, had survived the depression rather well, as had Northrop. However, Altwasser had detected a growing strain in their correspondence of the last couple of years. The growing power of Nazi Germany had been a concern to Granger and when in the previous fall, Hitler had invaded Poland and Britain had declared war on Germany, Granger's letters had simply stopped. Altwasser had written a couple of times but his letters had gone unanswered. Perhaps he would phone Northrop while he was here. What harm could a phone call do? Their presence here was certainly not in violation of any American law. Diplomatic relations with Germany continued. To the north, of course, Canada was at war with Germany as part of the British Empire and had been since September 1939.

The driver slowed the car and they swung left off the highway and headed west into the dark countryside. Altwasser looked at his watch and was surprised to discover they had been driving for almost an hour. He tried to remember the geography of the area but couldn't really place where they were. Perhaps sixty kilometres or so north of the city, which would place them in New Jersey, but if they continued westward they would soon be out of it. Frannie held Johann lightly on her lap. He was asleep again. Frannie had her eyes closed and her head back against the seat. She was really quite lovely.

There were only occasional lights now and few cars on the two lane secondary road. Altwasser studied the driver. He was a big man and judging by the size of his neck at least, he was well muscled. His large hands gripped the wheel lightly and he guided the heavy Packard sedan skilfully. His hair was blonde and short. Put a German army uniform on him, Altwasser thought, and he would fit into any regiment on the western front.

Altwasser leaned back and rested his head against the back of the seat. He would close his eyes and rest for a few minutes.

The lights flickering through the windows of the car awakened him. He sat up and looked out. They were in a small town with street lights, moving slowly past the closed stores, a hardware, a drug store, a couple of women's clothing stores. The car slowed and turned off the main street. Beside him Frannie stirred and opened her eyes.

"Where are we?" she asked, her voice thick with sleep.

"In a small town, from the look of it," Altwasser answered. "I would guess we are somewhere west of Philadelphia but I've been sleeping, too."

"I need a bathroom," Frannie said. "So does Johann, although I can change him here if we aren't going to stop soon."

As Altwasser leaned forward to speak to the driver, the car slowed and came to a halt in front of a large white house. The driver turned off the engine. "Wait here," he said without looking back at them. He opened the door and got out, closing it softly.

Altwasser watched him walk up a long gravel path to a large verandah, then knock on the door. It swung open immediately and he disappeared inside. The house was three stories high and set back from the street. The large lawn was spotted with tall trees. There would likely be flower beds, too, but the scene was only illuminated by a street light a couple of houses away and most of the yard was in shadows.

CHAPTER SEVENTEEN

Monday, November 18, 1940, Marsland Cove, Nova Scotia, Canada

Gilford watched the shore coming up, rocky and inhospitable, and wondered where they were landing. The two men in the boat had said nothing other than to tell them where to sit. They still had some distance to go and no doubt there was a good landing behind or around one of the rocks. Gilford took a perverse enjoyment from Klassen's obvious discomfort. As they had been boarding the boat, Klassen had rudely brushed aside the offer of a life jacket by one of the men in the boat. Gilford had slipped one on and tied it loosely.

"There they go," Katherine whispered, leaning toward him, her cheek brushing his to be heard over the noise of the motor. She was facing him, cradling Erich and rocking him gently.

Gilford turned to look over his shoulder and saw that the hull of the U 64 had already disappeared and the conning tower, tilted slightly forward, was sinking quickly. He felt a moment of anxiety as he realized that he and Katherine and Erich were now at the mercy of Klassen, without Captain Echart to act as a buffer. He thought of Bormann and his last instructions. Erich's life was critical. All others were expendable. He wondered what Klassen's orders were. He felt the small boat alter its heading and turned forward again. A small opening in the rocks was visible now and they headed toward it.

There was a fire in an old cast iron wood stove and it's heat was welcome at first after the bitter cold of the sea air. Now, however, after about ten minutes, it was becoming oppressive. The shack they were in was clearly a fisherman's shelter and was not intended as a permanent habitation. They would spend the night here and be moved in the morning. Klassen had objected pointing out that they should move under cover of darkness but one of the fishermen, a fat jolly man, pointed out that nothing moved hereabouts after dark. Klassen had difficulty understanding their heavily accented English. It reminded Gilford of a soft Irish brogue. It was a gentle, lilting English, sprinkled with a local vernacular.

There was a cot by the stove and an old double bed in a curtained off area in the back of the small shack. The two windows were covered with heavy drapes to prevent light from showing, although there wasn't likely to be a lot from the two coal oil lights, a rather pretty old glass lamp with a tall narrow chimney and a battered lantern.

"I apologize for the accommodations, my friends," the fat jolly one said. "But this old shack is only used by us when we're fishing in the bay here." He turned to Gilford. "I'd suggest you and the missus along with the wee one, take the bed in back." He turned toward Klassen. "You, sir, might take the cot."

"And where will you be sleeping?" Klassen asked sharply.

"Ah, now," the jolly one said, chuckling good naturedly. "I'll be spending the night with the wife in me own bed. That way she won't be wonderin' what I'm up to. Women have got suspicious minds, beggin' your pardon Mam." He glanced at Katherine with a wink.

"You are leaving us here alone?" Klassen asked.

"Well now, there's nought to be afeared of, is there? The ghosts of some dead cod fish won't be botherin' you, I should hope? Besides man," he added, dragging a large old watch out of a pocket in his overalls and consulting it for a moment. "It's after midnight, for heaven's sake."

Klassen glared at him.

"No one goes about at night around here and we'll be back early in the morning for you." With that, he nodded at them. "Good evenin' to you all. Sleep well," he said, and slipped quickly out the door, closing it firmly behind him.

"You take the first watch," Klassen ordered, staring angrily at Gilford. He glanced at his watch. "Wake me at two."

"There is nothing to watch, Klassen," Gilford said patiently. "You heard the fisherman. And even if someone did discover us here, what are you going to do? Shoot them? You watch whatever you wish. I am going to bed." He turned and walked the few steps toward the faded curtain that Katherine had drawn as she readied Erich for sleep.

"Very well, Doctor Shore," Klassen replied. "I will watch over you and your precious family, but your insubordination will go in my report."

"Thank you, Klassen," Gilford said softly. "I knew I could count on you."

"Of course you can," Klassen said, the sarcasm unnoticed.

Gilford pulled the curtain aside. He felt the confidence he had displayed with Klassen disappearing rapidly. In the dim light of the oil lamps behind him, he could see the outline of Katherine's body under the single cover. He looked around the small area and saw her boots beside the bed. She was lying on her back and had placed Erich between herself and the wall. She smiled up at him and lifted the cover, invitingly it seemed, on the empty half of the bed. Gilford pulled the curtains shut and sat down on the edge of the bed. He took off his boots, parked them beside Katherine's and then remembering his medical bag, he stood up and opened the curtain again. Klassen reclined in an old stuffed chair in one corner of the room, his Luger laid carefully on the arm, his head thrown back, sound asleep. Gilford walked over and looked at him, his blonde hair tousled, his handsome face no longer cruel in sleep, the cold eyes hidden. It was a strangely innocent face, he thought. Gilford silently picked up his medical bag, blew out the lamp and turned down the lantern to a soft glow. He listened carefully but could only hear the gentle lap of the ocean swells against the rocky beach. He smiled and made his way quietly back to the curtain. Slipping his bag under the bed, he stretched out beside Katherine and pulled the old quilt up.

Katherine moved over against him. "Thank you for looking after us so well, Gilford," she whispered.

"My pleasure," he whispered back. "Incidentally, Klassen is asleep."

"Good," Katherine whispered. "That way he won't hurt anyone."

Gilford lay quietly, waiting for Katherine to roll away from him but she slipped her arm over him and moments later her breathing deepened and she was asleep. He lay quietly, enjoying her closeness, her warmth, thinking of the events of the last few weeks, challenge, danger, even fun with Erich and Katherine. He put his hand tentatively on hers, resting on his chest, and stroked it softly. So much had changed. If they could survive the next few weeks then life would be a bit more certain.

Gilford came awake slowly. His back was cold. As he opened his eyes he was aware of a soft glow of light coming from behind him. He could feel Katherine's hair on his face and realized he was lying on his right side curled up close behind her, his left arm wrapped over her holding her close to him. He could feel the softness of her breasts against his forearm.

There was a different sound outside. Wind was moaning around the cottage now, gusting and rattling something on the roof. He gently moved his left arm, withdrawing it slowly. As he reached behind to pull the old quilt down over his back, Katherine snuggled back against him. He moved his arm back over her and she slipped her hand into his, intertwining her fingers. Gilford felt himself hardening and moved gently away but she pushed herself firmly back against him, wiggling slightly as she did so. He sighed and held her close to him. He thought about his wife back in Germany, an angry, dedicated, Jew-hating Nazi, and ironically, probably the reason he had been chosen for this job. He smiled contentedly.

CHAPTER EIGHTEEN

Monday, November 18, 1940 Graystown, Pennsylvania

Heinrich Stahl came awake slowly. He was in a small room in the attic on a rather hard cot. A high curtained dormer window occupied the wall at the foot of the bed and dull grey morning light seeped in around the edges of the flowered fabric. He slipped out from under the single coarse woolen blanket and moved to the window. Pulling the curtain aside he found himself staring into a soft morning mist. He could make out the shape of another house about a hundred metres away. It looked cold outside. The linoleum floor was certainly cold beneath his feet. His clothes were hung over the back of a chair in the corner of the room beside a wash stand and his small suitcase rested on the seat of the chair. He pulled on his socks and underwear and looked in the mirror. Other than being in need of a shave, he didn't look too much the worse for wear. He poured some cold water from the large pitcher into the porcelain wash basin, picked up a small bar of soap and began washing himself, quickly rinsing the soap off and drying himself before he got colder.

He had been spared military service because of his Gestapo status, but had heard a lot about washing in cold water, or not washing at all, and of the other assorted indignities of life in the army. His son had been conscripted into an infantry regiment a year ago and had been part of the force invading France. He had written sporadic letters, or in any event, they had arrived sporadically, and then two months ago, he received a visit from a fellow Gestapo officer to tell him his son had been killed by French Partisans.

He had not been close to him since his wife had left almost a decade ago, taking their ten year old son with her. Life with a dedicated police officer had not turned out the way she wanted it, and certainly not the way her rich parents had desired. But they had warned her before the marriage and had taken her and her son in when it had failed. Since Heinrich was living in Munich and her parents lived in Berlin, he had quickly lost touch with them both. Domestic life had taken such a small amount of his time when they were married that, by working a little more, he scarcely noticed they were gone, but he did miss his child and the chance to watch him grow and develop. He wrote periodic letters and dutifully sent his son gifts on his birthday and at Christmas. He had tried to make arrangements to see him but was routinely thwarted by his wife's father, who believed it best if the son simply grew up without him.

The last time he had seen him had been about six months ago. His son had been in Munich on a brief leave from the army before being sent to France. They had spent an evening together, dinner, schnapps, too much schnapps really, and had a good visit. Stahl had left that evening with some hope that perhaps as adults they might become friends.

Stahl was a good detective and it did not take him long to find out what had really happened to his son. In a small town on the outskirts of Paris, he had been on patrol with two other soldiers, enforcing the local curfew. They found an old man and his daughter out past curfew and were escorting them back to their house when they were accosted by an SS major, who had been out for dinner in a local restaurant and obviously had consumed a considerable amount of wine. The major explained to the young soldier that the old man and his daughter were Jews and ordered him to shoot them. He refused, whereupon the SS officer drew his luger and shot them both and then shot young Stahl, leaving his body in the care of his two companions to serve as an example.

He would find Major Johann Stickleman, SS Army Intelligence Group, Western Front. Stahl looked in the mirror, and with a small shaving brush began to lather his face. "Revenge," he whispered the old wisdom. "Is a dish best eaten cold." He picked up his razor and concentrated.

The kitchen was a large warm room, a wood burning cook stove in one corner, a slightly battered wooden table and six chairs in the middle of the room, with the walls covered in tall white cupboards. A counter with a solid wood cutting board and a sink lined one wall. A small electric refrigerator was located in one corner where a section of the cupboards and counter top and been removed to accommodate it. It reminded him of the large country kitchen in the summer home of his in-laws. It had been a hunting lodge at one time but most of the acreage had been sold off and the last he heard, it had been closed up as a wartime economy measure.

"Good morning, Herr Stahl," a woman said, looking up from the counter where she was rolling out some pastry.

"Call me 'Henry', please," Stahl replied and then recalling her name, added, "Good morning, Anna."

"You slept well?"

"Very well, thank you."

"I apologize for our attic room . . .", Anna began.

"Please." Stahl interrupted her gently, holding up his hand. "There is no need. I slept very well, the accommodations are excellent."

"Thank you," she said. "You are very generous. The nurse and the baby are in the parlour." She indicated a door on the opposite side of the kitchen. She held up her flour-covered hands and shrugged. "Please help yourself to coffee."

Stahl picked up a heavy china cup from the counter and seeing a pitcher of cream beside it, added a large dollop. A tall coffee pot sat on one end of the stove, the hinged lid open revealing a small wire handle that held a cloth bag with the coffee grounds.

"Danish coffee," Stahl observed. "How delightful."

"My mother worked in Denmark as a girl and brought the idea back with her."

Stahl filled his cup and took a sip. The coffee was rich and strong with no hint of bitterness. "This is fine coffee," he said, watching Anna smile self-consciously.

He walked into the parlour. "Good morning, Nancy," he said as he approached the rocking chair where she was holding baby Lienhard, bundled in a small blanket.

Nancy looked up at him and smiled. "Good morning, Herr Stahl."

"It would be better if you called me 'Henry'," he said. "How is our young fellow this morning?"

"I'm not sure," Nancy said, a worried frown stealing across her face. "I think he may have a slight fever. He was vomiting earlier but that may just have been a reaction to losing sleep on the flight, perhaps different food and water. He should settle down if that is all it was."

"Should I summon our doctor?"

"Perhaps he should check on the child this morning but I don't think there is a rush."

"Could I bring you some coffee, Nancy?" Stahl asked.

"If you don't mind, that would be lovely, thank you."

"Cream and sugar?" Stahl could see that Nancy was almost flustered by the attention. She was not the sort of girl that a lot of men would find attractive.

"Just cream, thank you."

Stahl returned to the kitchen as Anna was closing the oven door. "Biscuits," she said as she straightened up. She glanced up at a large wall clock. "In about fifteen minutes they will be ready."

Stahl added cream to a second cup and filled it from the pot on the stove. Returning to the parlour, he handed the cup to Nancy, who deftly shifted Lienhard to her left arm as she took the cup.

"May I?" said Stahl, holding out his hands toward her. "Let me hold him for a while so you can enjoy your coffee unencumbered."

"Are you sure?"

"Certainly," Stahl replied, with a smile. "I like children." And it was true. He did like children. He had quite enjoyed his own son as a child. He took the baby and expertly cradled him in the crook of one arm. Lienhard gurgled happily.

Nancy got to her feet and the two of them walked into the kitchen. Stahl picked his cup off the counter and drank some more of his coffee. Setting the cup down, he put the back of his hand lightly on Lienhard's forehead. He did feel hot.

"There is a telephone?" he asked Anna.

"Yes, but it is party line."

"Then others may listen in?"

"They may," Anna said with a quick laugh. "And they will. This is a small town without a lot of entertainment so we listen to each other's phone calls to amuse ourselves."

"It is very likely a town of good neighbours, then."

"It is."

The biscuits were delicious served with cheese, sausage and plum jam, made from plums that grew in the yard of the house. Throughout breakfast, Stahl held Lienhard lightly in the crook of his arm. He was a slight little lad without the usual baby fat that he associated with infants. He stood up and still holding Lienhard, added some more cream to his cup and filled it from the pot on the stove.

"You must come from a large family," Anna said, as he sat down again.

"Why do you say that?"

"The comfort with which you are holding the child. Most men have no idea how to do that."

Stahl smiled. "Actually, I am an only child, but I did have a son."

"And how old is your son now?"

"He would have been twenty next month, but unfortunately was a war casualty about two months ago." Stahl felt a lump rising in his throat. This was the first time he had spoken aloud of the fate that had befallen his son.

"I am so sorry," Anna said.

Stahl looked at Nancy and saw the trace of tears in her eyes. Wordlessly he handed her the child. "I think I will take a walk and see how our other group is doing. It is about a kilometre away, is it not?"

"Four blocks," Anna replied. "A kilometre would be about right. I am afraid I have been here so long that I think in blocks when I am in town and in miles when I am going somewhere else."

The early morning mist had dissipated but the air was crisp. Stahl turned up the collar on his coat and shoved his hands into the pockets. Anna had checked an outside thermometer and told him it was 35 above. He translated from Fahrenheit to Centigrade and concluded it was about 2 degrees above freezing, cold in any case. She had given him directions and as he walked down the wide streets, leafless trees dotting the broad lawns surrounding what looked like quite large houses, he was surprised at how generous Americans were with residential land. Several automobiles drove by as he walked along, all were large vehicles, clouds of steam coming from the exhaust pipes. He passed a woman bundled in a heavy coat, carrying a shopping bag. She smiled at him as they passed. "Good morning," she said merrily.

Stahl touched the brim of his tweed cap and smiled back at her. "Good morning."

He walked up to the front door of the other house and knocked lightly on the door. A moment later a woman opened it. "Yes," she said. "May I help you?"

"My name is Stahl. I am with the group who is staying with you."

"Of course, please come in, Herr Stahl." She stepped back and opened the door wide. "Forgive me for not recognizing you."

In the kitchen, much like the one in his own accommodation, he found Atlwasser, the nurse and the child, sitting around the large kitchen table. Altwasser stood and shook his hand. "You slept well?"

"Indeed I did," Stahl answered. "And you?"

"Very well."

"And how is your child adjusting to life in America?"

Atlwasser turned to Francine. She was holding the child who was asleep. "I think he likes it here very much."

"That is good to hear."

"And the other child?" Altwasser asked.

"I think he may be developing a bit of a fever. Perhaps you should have a look at him. Nancy thinks it may just be that he is tired, is eating and drinking different things, and that may well be the case. However, I would feel better if you could confirm that."

"Of course," Altwasser replied. "I'll get my bag and my coat."

"You have not been to America before?" Altwasser asked as they walked in the crisp morning air.

"No," Stahl replied. "Interesting country so far."

"What happens next?" Altwasser asked.

Stahl was silent for a moment. "If all goes as planned, the children will be picked up tomorrow and transferred to their permanent homes."

"Permanent homes? What are these places we are staying now?"

"For the moment, we are staying in temporary homes, people who are supportive of the German Reich, however, this is not where the children will remain when we are gone." Stahl smiled. "Part of our government's phobia about security, I suspect."

"So the children are transported tomorrow and we leave the next day:?"

"That is the plan unless young Lienhard holds us up."

"He shouldn't as long as it is nothing very serious," Altwasser said. "However, I have only my medical bag and that limits what I can do. I assume we can access the local pharmacy if we require additional medications?"

Stahl walked in silence for a few steps. "Let's see what the child requires."

Stahl introduced Altwasser to Anna, who took their coats before they went into the parlour. Nancy rocked gently back and forth holding Lienhard on her shoulder. Stahl immediately noticed the difference in Lienhard. His small face was red and his breathing was laboured. Altwasser watched the child for a minute and then took a thermometer from his medical bag. He rubbed it on the sleeve of his jacket to warm it slightly, gave it a shake to force the mercury to the bottom of the glass tube and then, while Nancy pulled the blanket down, he slipped it under his arm. He put his hand lightly on Lienhard's forehead.

"He certainly has a fever," Altwasser said. "In a moment we will know how high his temperature is."

"He looks worse than when I left," Stahl said, looking at his watch. "That was less than an hour ago."

"He vomited again just after you left," Nancy replied. "I have tried to feed him some milk but he spits it out. I have managed to get a little water into him."

Altwasser leaned forward and gently removed the thermometer. He held it up and read it. "40.8," he announced. "That is too high. He can sustain that temperature for a while but if it doesn't fall, I will have to give him something to break his fever."

"You have something with you?" Stahl asked.

"Yes," Altwasser said. "Simple aspirin will do it, but with his small body, only a tiny amount. The additional complication will be whether he can keep it down. It will irritate his stomach."

Half an hour later, Lienhard's temperature had risen another degree and Atlwasser ground up an aspirin, put a tiny amount on the end of a spoon mixed with a little plum jam. Lienhard reluctantly sucked at the end of the spoon and took the concoction into his mouth. A few minutes later, Nancy fed him a little water. He squirmed around and closed his eyes.

"We'll see if that helps," said Altwasser. "If it doesn't we may have to pay the local pharmacy a visit."

With considerable relief, they watched the redness in Lienhard's little face gradually fade. Altwasser took his temperature again and found it was almost back to normal. He checked his watch and discovered their vigil had only lasted about twenty minutes.

"I think the aspirin has done its work," he said. "Watch him closely, but he seems to have improved for the moment. Feed him a little more of the aspirin if his fever returns."

Stahl stood up with Altwasser. "What do you make of this fever?"

Altwasser picked up his medical bag. "If a small dose of aspirin has worked to relieve the symptoms, it is not likely anything serious."

Stahl nodded, clearly relieved. "I will walk you to the door."

CHAPTER NINETEEN

Monday, November 18, 1940 Graystown, Pennsylvania

Altwasser was relaxing in the parlour after lunch, reading a two day old copy of the New York Times. Lillian, the owner of the house, had announced earlier that she was going to the butcher shop and had asked if he wanted her to pick up anything. He had asked for a current Philadelphia Inquirer but they had been sold out. She had returned with the Times.

When he had lived in Philadelphia he had been amazed at the almost complete indifference Americans displayed about happenings in the rest of the world. They had a peculiar idea that what went on in America was relevant to them and what happened elsewhere was not. It projected a strange sense of isolation, of inward looking insularity. It didn't appear that this isolationist view had changed materially in the years he had been away.

He skimmed a number of articles trying to get a sense of what was important to America. He read an account of President Roosevelt's address at Hunter College stressing the need for better qualified teachers "so that youth would be better prepared for a complex civilization".

He recalled that in spite of the pride Americans took in their democratic institutions, they were still deeply suspicious and untrusting of their elected officials. He skimmed an article on federal grand juries investigating election irregularities. "The first investigations into alleged election frauds will start this week under direction of Maurice M. Milligan, special assistant to the Attorney General, the Department of Justice announced today in Washington."

And, of course, economic news was always at the forefront. An announcement noted that Westinghouse profits had increased and that they were offering for sale $45,000,000 in first-mortgage 3% bonds that would mature on November 1, 1960. He put his head back, set the paper on his knees and for a few moments tried to picture where he would be and what his life would be about on November 1, 1960. That was only 20 years away but given the turmoil of life in a country at war, it seemed a very distant reality.

Altwasser found these articles interesting because they illustrated the freedom found in America and the power of a free press to report on almost anything that went on in the country. Given the sorry state of the German press at the moment he had hoped to glean an objective view of what America thought of the events in Europe and the role German aggression played in them. However, if the New York Times was any gauge, in America there simply were not any thoughts about these events.

He noted a brief announcement, "Canada Gets Twenty More US Tanks". While the US was officially neutral, it was giving some support to the British war effort. The paper also reported that the Pope had decreed November 24 to be a day of World Prayer with the theme of "peace and comfort to the victims of war".

A couple of articles on the war in the Mediterranean caught his eye. One from Belgrade in Yugoslavia: "Neutral diplomats reported tonight that Germany is preparing to attack Turkey, through Rumania and Bulgaria, as soon as Italy's invading forces have established a stranglehold on Greece." A second article reported that Greek ships at sea were being advised to seek safe ports. "The British Broadcasting Corporation, acting 'on instructions of the Greek Government,' tonight advised all Greek ships at sea to put into United States, British or Netherlands Indies ports and not to enter any port in France or French possessions."

These accounts were written as factual reports, largely devoid of any political or ethical judgements. They were accounts of a war on the other side of the Atlantic that really had no bearing on life in America. Perhaps, he reflected, the United States would stay out of the war entirely. He shook his head. Somehow he doubted it.

He was about to set the paper aside when an article on the draft caught his attention. The headline, "Draft Opens Today for Nation's Youth; President Will Speak and Then Stimson Will Take First of Capsules From Bowl." He went on to read the ominous announcement that "The nation's first peace-time draft lottery will be opened at noon tomorrow by President Roosevelt."

Altwasser leaned back in his chair. So somewhere in the internal workings of the US government, somebody was seeing the need for a larger US armed forces. A strange country this was, with the constitutional promise of "life, liberty and the pursuit of happiness," where a military draft, which would override every basic individual democratic freedom, could be instituted in a time of peace.

He leaned back in the chair and closed his eyes. He had slept well but somehow was still tired, perhaps from the change in time zones, or the altitude in the aircraft, or perhaps it was just getting away from the horror of the trauma hospital and for once in months actually getting a full night's sleep.

A hand on his shoulder awakened him. He looked up at Frannie and smiled sleepily and then came upright in the chair as he saw the frown of concern on her face.

"Herr Stahl has just been here again," she said. "I'm sorry, I should say 'Henry'. He is concerned about Lienhard. He says the child has had a convulsion. When I told him you were asleep, he asked that I awaken you and tell you. He has gone back to see to Lienhard."

Altwasser nodded and stood up. "I'll go right over."

He pulled on his coat and put on the black fedora he had been supplied with. As he picked up his bag, he turned to Frannie. "How is our child?"

"Johann is fine. I'll watch him carefully just in case whatever Lienhard has is infectious."

Altwasser reached out and lightly touched her arm. "I'm glad you are here to care for him. I will see what I can do for Lienhard."

Lienhard was wrapped in a couple of blankets and Stahl was holding the child, rocking him gently and looking down at him with real concern. The small lad was crying softly and shaking. Altwasser took his temperature again and saw it was the same as the last reading. That was good but didn't explain the convulsion.

"What is your diagnosis, Emil?" Stahl asked, his brow furrowed. "He seems like a very sick little boy."

"I don't have one yet, but I think our first line of attack is to break his fever. Whatever it is, it is much more serious than lack of sleep, a change in altitude or a difference in food or water could account for." Altwasser opened his medical bag and found the aspirin. "Nancy, I will need a little more plum jam, a spoon and a small dish."

A few moments later, he tried to feed the small bit of plum jam with the ground up aspirin to Lienhard. With surprising dexterity, Lienhard managed to avoid the spoon by turning his head, by nodding up and down and by squirming about. Nancy held his head while Altwasser slipped the spoon between his reluctant little lips. He took the jam into his mouth and then promptly spit it out.

After the third time that he spit it out, Altwasser mixed up a new batch, but try as they might they could not get Lienhard to hold it in his mouth. Swallowing it was not going to happen.

Altwasser sat back and thought about his next move. "Let's try one more old fashioned trick. We have to bring his fever down and with his small body mass, if we bathe him in cool water it will draw some of the heat out of him."

"Whatever you think is best," Stahl said, handing the child to Nancy. "Where will we bathe him?"

"I think the kitchen sink," Altwasser replied. "We can control the water temperature better there. He is not going to like it very well, but among the three of us we should be able to manage him."

In the kitchen, Nancy found a stopper for the sink and filled it partially with lukewarm water. Altwasser stuck his hand into and nodded. It was slightly cool on his hand so it would be a good starting point.

"You have more blankets?" he asked Nancy.

She nodded.

"Good," Altwasser said. "Then just lower him slowly into the water with the blanket on."

Stahl leaned over the sink and very gently eased the little child into the water. For a moment there was no reaction, and then Lienhard screamed and began to kick. Stahl lifted him out of the water and looked at Altwasser.

"It will feel cold to him," Altwasser said. "But that is what we need to do for now. Get him cooled down."

Stahl nodded grimly and lowered the still screaming and kicking Lienhard back into the water. He held him there, partially submerged, his small arms and hands waving frantically, his screams continuing.

"How long do we leave him in here?" Stahl inquired.

"Let's try five minutes," Altwasser said. "But you had better brace your arms on something because you won't be able to hold him that way for long."

"Nancy, can you get a towel, a change of clothes and a dry blanket for Lienhard?"

"Of course," Nancy replied, and went out the door leading to the stairway up to the second floor.

"Henry," Altwasser said, leaning close to him. "You know what kind of physician I am. I am not a specialist in child diseases, I am primarily a surgeon. If this doesn't work we are going to have to get him some additional treatment here."

Stahl nodded. "If we have to do that to save his life we will, but let us first see how this remedy works."

"We can't wait very long, because if it fails, we will not have much time to act before the child is in serious trouble."

"What do you suggest?"

"As you know, I trained in Philadelphia. I had a colleague here who is an exceptionally fine child specialist. If I call him, I am sure he will help us."

Stahl shook his head. "I don't know, Emil." He looked down at Lienhard, his scream now reduced to a pitiful whimper, his strenuous thrashing about, now a feeble squirm. Either he was getting used to it or his energy was failing.

"I can't put his life at risk, Henry," Altwasser said.

"Is your friend politically opposed to us?"

Altwasser thought for a moment. "I am not sure," he said. "He and I corresponded after I left here but in the last couple of years, he has not answered my letters. There could be any number of explanations for that including our own censorship activities."

Stahl nodded and looked down at Lienhard. "If it becomes necessary, then talk to your friend and see how he feels. However, we cannot compromise our mission."

"He is a doctor, as I am," Altwasser said. "His first duty is to his patient and what is spoken between doctor and patient, in this case, me, is confidential. I am certain he would honour that."

Altwasser looked at his watch and saw that about five minutes had passed. "Lift him out of the water, Henry," he said. "And let's see how he is doing."

Stahl lifted the baby, water dripping from the saturated blanket, and laid him gently on the drain board beside the sink. Lienhard lay quietly, his eyes closed as if in resignation to what was being done to him.

"Let me change him," said Nancy, stepping forward with a dry towel and a fresh diaper. She opened the wet towel, deftly pulled the dripping night shirt over his head, slipped the wet diaper off and lifted him up. Stahl slid the wet towel out from under the child and laid a dry one in its place as Nancy carefully lowered Lienhard onto it.

Moments later he was swathed in dry clothes and wrapped in a dry towel. Altwasser took his temperature again and was relieved to see it was down slightly. As he was putting the thermometer back in his medical bag, Lienhard began to shake, a quiver at first, rapidly growing into an uncontrolled convulsion.

CHAPTER TWENTY

Tuesday, November 19, 1940 Marsland Cove, Nova Scotia, Canada

Katherine Shore heard voices as she drifted up out of a deep restful sleep. The first voice was soft and indistinct. She was lying on her back and as she opened her eyes and stared up at the ceiling she became aware of a strange sensation. She was lying perfectly still. There was no motion. A couple of metres above her, old weathered boards bore the faint evidence of a coat of pale grey paint. The dim light of a coal oil lamp seeped in around the curtain. She shivered and turned her head. Gilford lay beside her, breathing deeply, still sound asleep. Something bumped her shoulder on the other side and she looked to see Erich beside her, his small face creased by a smile.

Then she heard Klassen's strident voice. "As long as it is secure," he said.

The second voice murmured something reassuring.

With a rush she recalled where she was, in a small fisherman's shack somewhere on the east coast of Canada, Marsland Cove, one of the fishermen had told her. She reached over and gently touched Gilford's cheek.

He opened his eyes and turned toward her, a startled look on his face. Then he smiled. "Did you sleep well?"

She nodded. "I think our fisherman is back."

There was silence for a moment and then a light knock on the wall near the curtain.

"Thank you," Gilford said. "We're awake." He sat up on the edge of the bed and blew out his breath. It formed a faint cloud of mist in the chill morning air. He smiled over his shoulder at Katherine. "Time to face the day," he said softly.

They loaded their few belongings into the back of an old battered truck. It had been dark blue at one time but was now rusted in places, and a dull grey metallic colour in others. The truck smelled of fish, much of it obviously not fresh.

"Our first stop this morning will be to get you cleaned up and fed," the fisherman told her as she climbed into the small cab of the truck. She arranged Erich on her knee and tucked a small blanket around him.

"That would be wonderful," Katherine said, glancing over her shoulder to see Gilford and Klassen climbing into the box.

"I'll be taking you to my place," the fisherman said. "You'll meet the wife although she's not likely to say much. She doesn't like me helping out the Fatherland, although she certainly enjoys the extra dollars that it gets us."

After half an hour of jolting over a washboard road, the truck turned off the narrow road into a long driveway that ran through a wooded area. The trees had shed their leaves but were still dense enough that she couldn't see far through them.

A small old house, its wood weathered grey, emerged as they drove into a clearing.

"Home sweet home," the fisherman said as he drew up to a shed that had been built onto the back of the house. He got out of the truck and moved around to Katherine's door to open it for her and take Erich while she dismounted. He handed the child back to her and led her up to the door. He held it for her and ushered in.

Katherine looked around in the small shed. Garments, tools, some floats, a couple of heavy oil skin jackets and some things she couldn't identify, were hung at random on nails that had been hammered into the wall.

They moved quickly into the kitchen and the fisherman held Erich while she slipped off her jacket. It was a small room but warm and cozy. A few minutes later, Gilford and Klassen came in bringing their small duffle bags.

"Now Mam, there's hot water on the stove and just down the hall is the bathroom where you and the wee lad can freshen up."

The water in the small enamel wash basin had been warm when she had bathed Erich but had chilled by the time she had gotten him dressed and given him to Gilford. Now as she stood naked on a small towel in the bathroom and sponged off the soap and accumulated grime of two and a half weeks she was grateful. She had washed her hair with a bar of soap in the first basin of water and she shivered as she dried it with a thin blue towel and tried to fluff it into some semblance of order. Then she dressed, carefully removing each garment from the single wire hanger she had placed them on after she ironed them in the kitchen.

There had been a fire in the kitchen stove and a couple of flat irons were set on one end with a battered enamel coffee pot beside them. She and Gilford had sipped the coffee, strong and bitter from being boiled, while they had taken their few clothes from the sealed oilskin bag they had brought and she had ironed them. She offered to iron Klassen's clothes as well, but he had declined, quite politely, which surprised her, and said he would look after them himself. Perhaps he was capable of civil behaviour and was only unpleasant when he was cooped up in a submarine for a long time.

"I apologize for the facilities," the fisherman said, standing at the stove. Gilford was now in the bathroom taking his turn with some freshly heated water.

Katherine smiled at the fisherman. "Please don't be concerned," she said. She looked at him more carefully. In the boat and the light of the coal oil lamps of the previous evening, she had not really seen him well. Iron grey hair peeked out in fringes from under his knit cap. She guessed he would be somewhere in his fifties but still fit and energetic. He was not a large man, a few inches shorter than Gilford, but he looked solid and powerful, rooted to the floor by his heavy work boots. He was well-muscled by a lifetime of hard work. He had removed his heavy quilted jacket and was wearing a plaid flannel shirt under it.

"Where is Klassen?" she asked. She moved to an old wooden rocking chair in the corner of the kitchen, sat down and arranged Erich on her knee.

"Ah, him," the fisherman said with obvious distaste. "He's taken himself outside for a wee security check, or so he said. You'd best be watching him. He's wound tight, that one is."

Katherine nodded. "He is," she said.

"There's not much for breakfast," the fisherman said. "I hope some bread and smoked cod will take away your hunger pains." He smiled at her. "You've likely grown used to pretty good fare in that grand ship you arrived on."

Katherine laughed. "Food on a submarine is pretty basic," she said. "But bread and fish will be lovely. It sounds quite Christian, doesn't it?"

"Now so it does when you put it that way."

There had been no sign of the fisherman's wife when they arrived but as she took another sip of the coffee the back door opened and a tall slim woman came in, stamped her feet and closed the door behind her.

She looked at Katherine, smiling slightly. "Good mornin' to you," she said. She set a basket on the floor and slipped off a heavy jacket, likely one that belonged to the fisherman judging by the fit. "Just been gathering a few eggs and feeding the chickens."

"Good morning," Katherine replied, smiling at her. "It's very kind of you to let us use your home."

The woman nodded and glared at her husband. "You didn't tell me there was a woman and a child."

"I didn't know until last night and you were sleeping when I got home."

Holding Erich on her lap, Katherine rode again in the front of the truck with the fisherman, Gilford and Klassen in the back. A canvas tarpaulin covered the box of the truck, held aloft by a sturdy wooden frame. A couple of folded blankets provided some relief from the hard steel floor.

Katherine listened to the truck as it rattled and groaned over the gravel road. There were bumps and holes in the road and the fisherman slowed down for the worst of them and steered around the others.

"Where are all the other cars?" she asked.

"The other cars?" the fisherman replied, glancing at her. "Not many out on this road but we'll see a few more as we get nearer to Halifax. But gas rationing has taken a lot of them off the road."

Katherine nodded and looked out the window. They were driving through a wooded area, the trees like dark sticks against the grey sky. The narrow road was flanked by shallow ditches on either side and there were occasional culverts and driveways leading off through the trees. A couple of times she saw houses or buildings of some sort, in the trees, gray unpainted wooden structures like the small house they had washed up in this morning.

"You certainly charmed the wife," the fisherman said. "It's not often we get women guests, especially with a wee child."

"I enjoyed talking with her," Katherine replied. "I haven't spoken to a woman since we left Europe."

The promise of bread and fish had been replaced by scrambled eggs and fresh baked biscuits. It was evident that the fisherman's wife was not going to tolerate any second rate hospitality if there was a woman guest.

The fisherman had delivered them to a house on the outskirts of Halifax where a quiet middle aged couple provided them with new clothing and lunch before delivering them to the train station. Two hours later they found themselves waiting for a train on a long wooden platform, a brick station house behind them, three suitcases beside them and a small crowd of other passengers waiting with them. Gilford was wearing the uniform of a captain in the Royal Canadian Medical Corps, Klassen was dressed as a Lieutenant in the Royal Canadian Artillery and she was wearing a long dark brown dress, a pale brown overcoat that reached past her knees and a small hat that matched the coat. She had on a sturdy pair of shoes and heavy cotton stockings that did little to keep her feet warm.

Gilford looked handsome in his uniform, the fitted great coat accentuating his broad shoulders. She held Erich, bundled in a small suit the woman had called a snow suit, and wrapped in a woolen blanket. He was getting a little heavy and she knew that Gilford would be quite willing to take him for a while but she would miss the warmth of holding him against her.

Klassen had paced up and down the platform until Gilford took him aside and spoke to him. Since then he had remained beside her but continued to look up and down the platform. Katherine realized after watching him for a few minutes that he was nervous, perhaps frightened. He was in a strange country, an enemy country, impersonating a soldier. He spoke only the most rudimentary English with a heavy German accent and regarded himself as being responsible for them, or for their security, as he would likely think of it. She almost felt sorry for him.

CHAPTER TWENTY ONE

Tuesday, November 19, 1940 Graystown, Pennsylvania

During his years in America, Altwasser had not spent a lot of time in small towns although he had certainly driven through them. Unlike German towns of similar size, those in America seemed low and spread out, single houses on large residential lots, few buildings exceeding one story and the streets were wide. In early days this had accommodated wagon traffic on muddy roads and more recently, the automobile had confirmed the wisdom of this previous accident in design.

The centre of Graystown was dominated by a town square with a small gray stone memorial commemorating those lost in the Great War. It was set in a fenced area on a lawn, now brown, with flower beds mounded for the winter. A band shell, badly in need of a coat of paint, occupied one side of the park.

He looked around the square, enclosed on one side by a formal stone court house and what was likely a jail and police station combined. The other sides were commercial, a hardware store, a large grocery store, a cigar store, a pharmacy, some clothing stores, and on the side opposite the court house, the building he was looking for, the telephone exchange.

He walked across the square, following a graveled path past the war memorial and entered the telephone exchange. It had been a difficult task to convince Stahl that their only reasonable option was to contact Northrop Granger, but he had reluctantly agreed. Altwasser was grateful that their Gestapo companion cared seriously about the child. Any other agent he had encountered would have let the child die and then blamed the death on the incompetence of the doctor that had been sent to care for him.

A woman smiled at him from the other side of the counter. "How can I help you, sir?" she asked. She was short and heavy, and wore a telephone headset which covered one ear. Her dress, a rose colour with a large flowered print, was not slimming but her smile was good natured.

"I need to place a call to Philadelphia," Altwasser said. "This is the number," he added, handing her a small slip of paper on which he had written Northrop Granger's number. He looked around the small room. There were a few travel posters on the walls, one from California showing people on a beach, another from Colorado with an automobile on a steep road with spectacular mountain scenery in the background.

She glanced at the paper and then up again at Altwasser. "Are you visiting here?" she asked.

Altwasser nodded. "From Philadelphia," he said.

"I didn't think I recognized you," she said. "And in my job, I get to know pretty much everyone in town. You just have a seat at the table over there and I'll get the number for you. Anyone in particular you wanted to talk to?"

Altwasser hesitated a moment. "Northrop Granger," he said. "Dr. Northrop Granger."

He watched while she wrote the name on the slip of paper. "And who shall I tell Dr. Granger is calling."

"Dr. Altwasser," he replied.

"Dr. Altwasser," she said. "Could you write that down for me so I'll get the spelling right?" She pushed the slip of paper back to him and handed him a pencil.

Altwasser printed his name.

She turned away and sat down. She carefully transferred the names and number to a permanent record book by the switchboard and then plugged in a cord and began to dial.

Altwasser sat down at the table. The room felt close and smelled musty, like old cigarette smoke and some kind of cleaning compound. He was mildly concerned at leaving a record of the call, but shrugged his concerns aside when the phone on the table in front of him rang. He picked up the handset.

"Northrop Granger." Altwasser heard the deep, rich voice, as reassuring as a radio announcer's.

"Northrop, it's Emil Altwasser calling."

"So your operator said." Granger's voice sounded guarded. "How are things in Berlin?"

"Fine when I left," Altwasser replied. "But I am currently near Philadelphia, caring for a patient."

There was a pause. "Philadelphia? Are you kidding me?"

Altwasser laughed. This sounded more like the Granger he knew. "I am in Graystown, west and a bit north of Philly, I think."

"Yes, I know it," Granger said. "About an hour's drive as I recall. We pass through it occasionally on our way to the summer place. But what are you doing in Graystown? Are you going to get into Philly for a visit?"

Altwasser had been to the Grangers' summer cottage, a smaller mansion than the one they occupied in Philadelphia. "I am not sure, but I definitely want to see you before I leave."

"I should certainly hope so," Granger said.

Altwasser went on. "Northrop, I'm caring for a child at the moment and he has encountered some problems I'm not sure how to deal with."

"You are looking after a child?" Granger chuckled. "I thought you removed unnecessary organs from rich German women?"

Altwasser smiled in spite of himself. "I normally do that," he replied. "However, at the moment I'm here for a few days and I am caring for a one year old infant boy who is running a high fever, and he's had two convulsions. I'm not well prepared or equipped to diagnose this or to treat it."

There was silence for a moment. "You could be in Philadelphia and at my office in less than an hour and a half and I could have a look at him."

"Any chance that you could come out here?"

"Are you afraid to move him?"

"It could be awkward," Altwasser said carefully, unsure how much to say over a public phone.

"Awkward?"

"I'll have to check what our transportation options are," Altwasser said. "I may be able to arrange it."

"Call me if you can't," Granger said. "However, you know as well as I do, that I can treat him more effectively here than out of a medical bag."

"I know," Altwasser said. "I'm grateful for your help."

"Incidentally," Granger added. "It's wonderful to hear from you in person, Emil, but why haven't I heard from you in the last two years? I have written but get no replies."

Altwasser almost sighed with relief. "Censorship, I suspect, but I'll fill you in when I see you."

"Very well, Emil," Granger said. "It's now a little after four. I'll expect you by about six. Do you remember where our offices are?"

"Unless you have moved, or Philadelphia has changed a lot, I'll find you."

. . .

"Absolutely not! The child will remain here and you will treat him."

Altwasser looked at the tall imposing figure of the man who had driven them from the Philadelphia Municipal Airport to Graystown. He stood with his hands on his hips, the stance accentuating the breadth and power of his shoulders. He wore a brown leather jacket which reminded Altwasser of a pilot's flight jacket.

"And if the child dies?" Altwasser asked.

"Then he dies."

Altwasser looked at Nancy, cradling Lienhard gently in her arms, tears running silently down her cheeks. The child was quiet, breathing shallowly through his small mouth, his eyes closed. Their driver had arrived while Altwasser was calling Northrop Granger, and had been furious that one of the group had contacted an American doctor for assistance. He had told them to call him Helmut.

Stahl rose from his chair on the other side of the large kitchen table. "Come with me," he said curtly to Helmut.

The driver nodded his head but his expression did not suggest any sort of cooperation was likely to be forthcoming. His close cropped blonde hair and the jacket gave him a military bearing. He only needed a pair of high shiny boots so he could bang the heels together, raise his right hand and shout "Heil Hitler."

They walked into the living room and Stahl closed the door.

"They won't let him die, will they?" Nancy asked.

Altwasser looked at her and saw her anguish. "I won't let that happen, Nancy."

She answered with a small smile.

They could hear the murmur of voices from the next room but the words were indistinct. Then there was silence.

The door opened and Stahl and Helmut reentered the room. Stahl walked over to Nancy and looked down at the child, then over at Altwasser. "Do you think you could convince your child specialist to visit us here?"

Altwasser nodded. "Yes," he replied. "I think so."

CHAPTER TWENTY TWO

Tuesday, November 19, 1940 Toronto, Canada

Katherine looked up at the high vaulted ceiling of Union Station. It looked like it could be in Europe, with frescoes and cherubs, not what she had envisioned a Canadian railway station would look like. Throngs of people hurried through the terminal, a lot of them men in military uniforms, dark blue for the navy, lighter blue for the air force and the dull solemn khaki of the army. Erich was standing unsteadily beside her tugging at her finger. She saw Gilford coming back followed by a porter pulling a small trolley with their baggage. She thought Gilford looked quite handsome in his Royal Canadian Army Medical Corp uniform, the three brass "pips" glittering on the epaulets of his great coat. She watched Klassen, his arm in a sling, following the cart. Klassen looked handsome, too, but only from a distance, she reflected. As he got closer she could see he was tense, his eyes darting back and forth, searching for something amiss.

"We're back again, Darling," Gilford announced, kissing her lightly on the cheek. He looked down at Erich and then held out his arms. Erich jumped and Gilford swung him up. "There is a car for us," he said, motioning to the porter and to Klassen. "A driver, too." They headed toward an exit at the end of the terminal.

"Excuse me, sir," the porter said, doffing his red pillbox hat. "Military vehicles are picking up army personnel at the other end of the station."

"Mind your own business," Klassen snarled. "Just take our luggage where we tell you."

The porter recoiled at the force in Klassen's voice. Gilford spun around, fixing an icy glare on Klassen. Then he turned to the porter and smiled. "Thank you for telling us that, but we have private arrangements," he said quietly. "And please excuse the behaviour of my Lieutenant. As you can see he was wounded and he's still recovering."

"Yes, sir," the porter answered stiffly. He was middle aged, perhaps in his forties, but he looked frail and Katherine noticed he had a slight limp when he walked. A fringe of wispy grey-brown hair was visible below his red cap. He had a heavy black wool jacket on, done up to the top button and his black trousers were tucked into the tops of rubber galoshes, the metal buckles tightly cinched. He tugged at the trolley and moved along after Gilford. Klassen walked behind him, tense and alert.

Katherine looked up at a huge clock on the wall over the door. It was set in marble with Roman numerals and showed a couple of minutes before three. Gilford stood aside and ushered her into a revolving door and followed with Erich in the next section. As she stepped outside she was struck by the cold, a deep penetrating wet cold, not the crisp dry cold she was used to in winter. There was a wide sidewalk in front of her where a taxi was waiting. The street was covered with a dirty slush of snow and water. The cars that went by sprayed it out in fans from their tires. The clouds were a low dull grey in the gathering dusk. She often found herself looking up at the sky and around at the scenery since she had gotten off the U boat, a reaction, she supposed, to being locked in tube for most of three weeks. She pulled her scarf more tightly around her neck as she turned to see the porter lugging the trolley through a latched open door beside the revolving ones. She felt sorry for him. He seemed beaten and tired and much too frail for a job like that. Klassen came up beside Gilford.

"That idiot porter will give us away," he snapped.

It took Katherine a moment to realize he had spoken in German. She turned to see the porter was now behind them, a surprised look on his face. She glanced at Gilford who was staring ahead, his face grim. A young man in army uniform appeared before them.

He saluted. "Captain Shore?" he asked.

Gilford returned the salute. "Yes corporal, I'm Captain Shore."

"This way, sir," he said, and led them toward a large black car by the curb.

Katherine saw Gilford grasp Klassen's arm at the elbow and speak rapidly to him. She glanced back at the porter, who was following them with the trolley. He drew it up at the edge of the curb. The corporal opened the trunk and they began loading the duffel bags. Her two suitcases went in last.

"What are you doing at this entrance, Corporal?" The speaker was a tall, tough looking soldier with an armband that had the word "Provost" stenciled on it. A second soldier stood behind him. "Provost," she thought, and then remembered they were military police.

"Special pick up, Sergeant," the corporal said, coming to attention and saluting.

The Sergeant returned the salute. "Let me see your orders, Corporal."

Katherine watched the corporal go around to the driver's door. She saw Klassen, white faced and tense, the fingers of his right hand clenching and unclenching, and then moving toward the sling on his left arm. She stepped toward the Sergeant. "Excuse me, Sergeant, but can we get in the car while you straighten this out? We've had a long journey."

"Certainly, Mam," he said with a slight bow. He turned to Gilford and gave him a quick salute. "Captain, I apologize for the delay, just a routine check. Please get in the car if you wish."

"Thank you, Sergeant," Gilford replied, returning the salute. "Come along, Lieutenant." He opened the front door and motioned Klassen to get in. Klassen glared at him but did as he was told. "My dear," he said to Katherine, opening the back door. He handed Erich to her once she was seated and closed the door.

The Corporal closed the driver's door and Katherine watched him walk around the car and hand some papers to the Sergeant. Gilford stood beside him. The Sergeant checked the papers carefully and was about to hand them back, then checked something again and looked sharply at the Corporal. From the corner of her eye, she saw Klassen move and as she leaned forward saw him shrug off the sling and draw a pistol out of it. He reached for the door. Desperately, she tried to think of something to do.

"Stay where you are, Klassen," she said sharply. "If something is wrong, you are going to have to drive us out of here and you will be no damn use at all out there."

He froze and then began to slide across the seat toward the driver's side. "As you wish." He had spoken in German again. He looked at the gauges, the gear shift and down at the pedals.

"Call me Mrs. Shore," she snapped. "And no more German or you'll get us all killed." She returned her attention to the scene on the side walk. The Provost Sergeant handed the papers back to their driver and they exchanged salutes. Gilford turned and opened the door, sliding in beside her. She watched the two Provosts walk back toward the station entrance. The porter stood uncertainly with his trolley; he leaned forward and stared at Klassen in the front seat. As the driver slid into his seat, Klassen suddenly pushed open his door and stepped out. He grasped the porter firmly by the arm and shoved him into the front seat.

"Let's go," he snapped at the driver who turned to Gilford with a wide-eyed look.

"Stay where you are," Gilford ordered. He opened his door and stepped out, angrily yanking open the front door. He grabbed Klassen by the arm and hauled him out of the car, slamming the door shut.

Katherine watched them, Klassen's left arm clear of the sling, his left hand in the pocket of the great coat, holding his pistol she could only assume. Fear gripped her and then she was aware of the porter again. She leaned forward and put her hand gently on his shoulder. "Please excuse the Lieutenant," she said as reassuringly as she could. "He was shelled badly in France and we are taking him to a sanatorium for treatment. We thought he would be fine but he is reacting very badly."

Gilford pulled the front door open. "Please get out, sir," he said quietly to the porter. He held out his hand to help him from the car and pushed a bill into his hand. The porter stepped behind Gilford, keeping him between himself and Klassen. Gilford turned to Klassen. "Lieutenant," he said, motioning him into the car. "If you please."

Klassen was shaking with rage as he hurled himself into the front seat and slammed the door shut. Gilford turned to speak to the Porter again for a moment and then slipped into the back seat. "Let's go, Corporal," he said pulling the door closed.

The driver put the car in gear and glanced over his shoulder just as Klassen swung his door open again. The porter was a few steps ahead of him pulling his trolley back toward the station entrance. Katherine watched in horror as Klassen grasped him by the shoulder from behind. The porter's back seemed to arch for a moment and then Klassen was easing him down into a sitting position on the trolley. As he stepped aside, Katherine could see the Porter's head lolling to one side and as Klassen jumped into the front seat and slammed the door, she saw the porter gently topple off the trolley into the slush. As their car pulled away from the curb the two Provosts ran from the station entrance.

"We're safe now," Klassen announced. "That swine won't be telling anyone anything." He pulled a handkerchief out of his pocket, slipped a long vicious looking dagger out of the sling and wiped it off. "Here's your ten dollars back," he added, tossing the bill indifferently over his shoulder.

"Klassen," Gilford snapped. "You are an idiot. Your role is to protect us, not to get us killed."

The Corporal swung the car into the slow late afternoon traffic. Half a block ahead of them a stop sign blocked their way with two cars waiting. Katherine twisted to look out the back window. She saw the two Provosts standing beside the body of the porter. The larger one, the Sergeant, appeared to shout something at his companion and then began running down the street after them. The Corporal brought the large car to a smooth halt behind the two cars at the stop sign. A steady stream of traffic crossed the intersection in front of them. Finally the first car moved into a break in the traffic flow and the second car idled forward to the sign.

"Corporal," Klassen said tensely. "Drive around him. Get us out of here."

Katherine turned again to the back window. The Sergeant, pistol drawn, was only a couple of car lengths behind them. "Gilford," she said quietly. "Look." She pointed out the back window.

"Do as he says if you can, Corporal," Gilford said. "We are about to be visited by the Provost again."

"What?" Klassen snapped. He slipped his left arm back in the sling as the Provost Sergeant arrived at his door and wrenched it open. He stood clear and pointed the pistol at Klassen. "Get out of the car, Lieutenant. You too, Captain and you Corporal. Put your hands on the roof."

Gilford carefully opened his door and started to get out. The Corporal began opening his door as Katherine saw Klassen swing around in his seat and begin to awkwardly pull himself out with his right hand. He appeared to stumble forward as he stood up, his left hand flying out of the sling and slamming the Sergeant's right arm upward. She heard the roar of the Sergeant's pistol as it discharged harmlessly into the air and she caught a flash of Klassen's dagger as it arched upward into the Sergeant's chest, cutting effortlessly through the rough woolen material of his khaki battle dress jacket. Klassen eased him to the ground with surprising gentleness, wiped the dagger on the leg of the Sergeant's uniform and slipped back into the car. Gilford, still only half out of the back seat, swung back in and pulled the door closed. The Corporal slammed his door shut, put the car in gear and moved up to the stop sign. A moment later he swung the car into the evening traffic.

Katherine let her breath out in a sigh as she realized she had not been breathing. She gripped Gilford's hand in terror. What kind of psychopath was Klassen and would he turn on them as brutally as he had on the porter and the Provost Sergeant if it served his purpose?

CHAPTER TWENTY THREE

Tuesday, November 19, 1940 Graystown, Pennsylvania, USA

Altwasser sat uneasily in the kitchen. It seemed to be the gathering place in Anna's home although he wasn't certain why. She had made some cookies with oatmeal and raisins, not something he had encountered before. They were tasty enough but he couldn't really summon up any enthusiasm for them. She had also made fresh coffee, in the Danish manner, rich and dark and fragrant, but he wasn't really enjoying that either. The oak chairs which earlier had fitted him comfortably had become unbearably hard as the afternoon wore on.

He had trudged back to the telephone exchange and called Northrop Granger again, apologizing profusely for the inconvenience and explaining that he had no effective way of transporting the child into the city. Granger had sounded a bit perplexed but agreed to come to Graystown. He was finished with his patients for the day and was cleaning up some paperwork. He could leave shortly. In their discussion Granger had asked for more details of Lienhard's condition and then had suggested a chilling possibility. Diphtheria. Altwasser agreed that the symptoms fit but sitting in the confines of the telephone exchange with the operator a short distance away, he felt he couldn't respond in detail.

Following his return from the telephone exchange, Altwasser and Nancy managed to get Lienhard to swallow a bit of plum jam with part of a ground up aspirin in it and he was resting quietly for the moment although his fever was still high. Henry and Helmut were sitting silently in the living room. He looked at his watch again. It was about five-thirty and Northrop Granger wouldn't be here much before six. He wondered what he was getting his friend into. For that matter he was beginning to wonder what he and his colleagues were already into. What had started out as a child delivery mission was rapidly turning into something much more sinister.

He was increasingly grateful for the firmness that Stahl had displayed in the face of Helmut and his overriding demands. How bad could the situation get? He glanced over at Nancy who had Lienhard cradled in her arms, wrapped warmly in a small blanket. Her eyes were closed and she was resting deeply. He wished he could feel the same confidence but he had a sense of foreboding, nothing he could identify, but things were not unfolding as they should. He should be getting ready to return to Philadelphia, to board their plane back to Germany and the trauma hospital. Unpleasant a prospect as that was, it was still something he could deal with, a familiar environment made up of known problems, not emerging levels of uncertainty.

He stood up, gathered his medical bag and went into the small bathroom off the kitchen. It contained a white enamel toilet and sink, a small mirror above the sink and a pair of pale blue towels on a bar beside it. On a shelf below the mirror was a bottle of lotion labelled "Italian Balm". It was a glutinous grey fluid likely used by Anna for keeping her hands soft. Locking the door behind him, he opened his medical bag and stared down into the neatly arranged contents. He moved a couple of packages of sterile bandages aside and looked at the folded manila envelope lying in the bottom of the bag. He lifted it out and opened the unsealed flap, tipped the envelope slightly and allowed the Luger to slide out into his hand.

He had never been comfortable with guns and the Luger seemed out of place in a satchel filled with items designed to save lives, not take them. However, it felt solid and reassuring. He had fired one in the abbreviated basic training course he had taken as an army physician, and when in uniform he carried one although he had never taken it out of its holster. Unfortunately, knowing how to use a gun was quite a different matter from pointing it at someone and pulling the trigger. He looked in the small mirror above the sink and shook his head. Who was he going to shoot, anyway? He would let Henry worry about shooting. That was part of his Gestapo responsibility, but he felt some small confidence that, should the need arise, he would be equipped for an unanticipated emergency.

He slipped the Luger back into the envelope and set it in the bottom of his medical bag, placing the packages of sterile bandages over it. He flushed the toilet and waited a few moments before opening the door and returning to the kitchen.

Nancy opened her eyes and looked up at him, smiled, and then snuggled Lienhard against her. He seemed to have calmed down considerably since they had gotten the aspirin into him. Altwasser set his medical bag on the floor beside Nancy's chair. "I am going into the living room to have a chat with Henry," he said.

"We'll be fine," Nancy said.

Altwasser opened the door to the living room, stepped inside and closed the door. Henry was sitting in a carved wooden rocking chair, legs crossed. He was completely still. Helmut was seated on one end of a small navy blue sofa on the opposite side of the room. He stood up as Altwasser entered.

"Is something wrong?" Helmut asked.

"No," Altwasser replied. "The child is still asleep. The aspirin seems to have calmed him for the moment."

"Then we will not require the services of your Philadelphia specialist." Helmut said "specialist" as though it was a disease of its own.

"For the moment he is sleeping," Altwasser said. "That could change in an instant. But he may also be exhausted from his fever and we must guard against him falling into a coma."

Helmut snorted and sat down. "Childhood ailments are seldom serious," he said. "Bringing in an additional party is simply a waste of time and a threat to the security of this entire operation."

"I am charged with the responsibility of caring for this child and I will not put him at risk," Altwasser said. He felt his temper rising as he stared down at Helmut.

Helmut leaned back. "I am charged with the security of this operation, Doctor, and you are seriously endangering that."

"Listen carefully," Altwasser said, his voice a study in controlled fury. "I am a serving medical officer in the German Wermacht and my orders come directly from the office of the Fuehrer himself. If he deems the life of this child important then you have no authority to compromise his safety. Do you understand me?"

Helmut paled visibly and sat up straight. "As you wish, Herr Doctor."

"Excellent," Altwasser said. He turned to Stahl. "I need to talk to you for a moment."

"Of course," Stahl said, standing up.

Altwasser turned and opened the door to the kitchen, stepping aside to let Stahl pass.

"Where do you think you are going?" Helmut asked, rising to his feet. "You will not hold conversations about this operation without me."

Altwasser turned to face Helmut. "Herr Stahl and I are both members of the German Armed Forces. There are matters of security to the German Reich which we are not permitted to discuss with anyone else."

Helmut glared at him for a moment and sat down.

"These are not my rules," Altwasser said, trying to put a conciliatory tone in his voice. "These are rules set down by the Office of the Fuehrer."

Stahl nodded gravely and the two of them left the room.

"Clever of you to use the authority of the Fuehrer," Stahl said softly as the door closed behind them.

"Something has to convince that idiot," Altwasser said, guiding Stahl toward the far corner of the kitchen. "In any case, it is true. This operation really is being conducted by the Office of the Fuehrer."

"You are quite correct, of course," Stahl said with a smile. "I must remember that."

"I am concerned with how things are developing," Altwasser said. "I do not want any medical interference in the treatment of Lienhard, or of Johann either, for that matter. However, I am becoming worried about what will happen when we turn the children over to Helmut for delivery to their next destination."

"Helmut is merely the driver," Stahl replied. "Although he is taking his role a bit more seriously than I had expected. Anna will be in charge of the children when we leave here. She knows where they are going and Helmut will merely drive them to their new homes."

"I see," Altwasser said. "That is good to hear. But why has he decided that he is in charge of the security of our operation?"

"I am not sure," Stahl replied. "But someone has impressed upon him the importance of what we are doing and I suspect he is taking that quite seriously, which is good, so long as it doesn't get out of control."

"Anna will care well for the children from what I have seen of her," Altwasser said.

"I agree," Stahl said. "Her husband, Gustav, works in Philadelphia during the week and comes home on weekends. He will also be available to help should the situation require it."

"I wondered where Anna's husband was." Altwasser thought for a moment. "So you are comfortable with how things are going?"

"Except for Lienhard's illness and the necessity of bringing in your Philadelphia doctor friend, I am quite satisfied. We have moved the children from Berlin, through Portugal, across the Atlantic Ocean to Philadelphia and on to Graystown. We have only to deal with a child's fever and then return and our orders will have been carried out. This is going much more according to plan than most military operations."

Altwasser nodded. "You are right to put it into perspective like that."

They both heard the knock at the front door.

"I'll answer the door," Altwasser said, quickly walking down the hall. A coach light outside the front door outlined the familiar figure of Northrop Granger through the opaque glass. He grasped the door knob and pulled, then realizing it was locked, he released the dead bolt and swung the door open.

The two men stared at each other for moment. "Come in, come in," Altwasser said, smiling effusively and stepping aside. Granger set his medical bag down and they shook hands vigorously.

"So good to see you again, Emil," Granger said. "I was wondering if you were surviving over there."

"I'm fine," Altwasser answered. He took Granger's overcoat and picked up his medical bag. "Come this way." As he turned to lead Granger down the hall, Anna entered the hallway from the kitchen, Stahl behind her. Altwasser introduced them and then led Granger into the warmth of the kitchen.

"A lovely home you have, Anna," Granger said. "Now where is our patient?"

"This is Nancy, a nurse who is with us," Altwasser said.

"You have quite a contingent here," Granger said looking around the room. "Tell me about his symptoms, Nancy, and how long he has had them."

Nancy recounted Lienhard's recent history, as Granger checked him over. Using a thermometer he measured his temperature. He reached in his medical bag and pulled out a brown paper bag, a tongue depressor and a flashlight. He handed the bag to Altwasser. "I trust you haven't lost your taste for good scotch?"

He deftly slipped the small wooden depressor between the child's lips and shone his light into his mouth and throat. Lienhard tolerated this for a moment and then turned his head away. He set the wooden stick on the edge of the counter and retrieved a stethoscope from his bag, rubbing it lightly on the sleeve of his jacket to warm it before using it to check Lienhard.

Granger straightened up. "He has a fever, he is congested and judging by his throat I would say he has diphtheria."

Silence greeted this announcement.

"My God," Nancy said softly. "That is often fatal, isn't it? Especially in children?"

"It can be if not treated immediately," Granger said. "And in the past it was often fatal for anyone who contracted it."

"I wondered," Altwasser said. "But I haven't seen a case in years. It rarely ever shows up in my patients."

"You were right to call me," Granger said. "There is a very effective antitoxin for diphtheria and it is unlikely you have any with you." He looked at Altwasser and raised his eyebrows.

Altwasser shook his head in agreement.

Granger took a small syringe from his bag and filled it carefully from a glass vial. After wiping some alcohol on Lienhard's upper arm, he deftly slipped the needle into him. Lienhard squirmed for a moment and was still as he withdrew it.

"Now we will wait for a while and see how he reacts," Granger said. "There is a secondary problem, however. I assume the child has been coughing a lot in the last few hours and diphtheria is spread by the vapour released by a cough. I will have to give the antitoxin to all of you who have been in contact with the child."

"That would be an excellent precaution," Altwasser said.

A short time later Granger handed the last syringe to Altwasser and rolled up his sleeve. When Altwasser finished the injection Granger turned to Anna. "Perhaps you would have some glasses, Anna. I think it is time for some more adult medicine."

"It is indeed," Altwasser said. "However, we have two other members of our small group at another home nearby and if I can prevail on you for three more doses of the antitoxin I will administer it."

"Of course," Granger said.

Half an hour later, Altwasser returned and walked into the kitchen. "I asked Frannie if she would like to bring our other child over here and join us for a drink but Johann was sleepy and she decided to stay there."

"Likely a wise decision," Granger said. "Has the other child shown any symptoms?"

"None at all and neither has Frannie."

"Excellent," Granger said. "Now let's get back to the business at hand."

Stahl rose from his chair. "I will tell Helmut that everything is now under control and he can return tomorrow." He opened the door to the living room and went in.

Granger raised his eyebrows and looked at Altwasser.

"Helmut is another member of our group," Altwasser explained. "He is our driver."

Anna had set three glasses on the kitchen counter and taken the bottle of scotch out of the paper bag.

"So let's have a drink, a toast to old friends and new acquaintances, and you can tell me what you've been up to," Granger said, breaking the seal on the bottle and pouring a generous measure into each of the glasses. He looked at Anna and then at Nancy. "Ladies?" he asked. "Will you join us?"

Anna smiled. "Thank you, but alcohol doesn't agree with me."

"Nancy?" Granger asked.

"Just a little, please," Nancy replied. "I have never tasted scotch whisky before."

Anna got a fourth glass from the cupboard and Granger poured some of the rich amber liquid into it, not noticeably less than he had poured into the other three.

"Nancy, my dear," Granger said. "You're in for a treat." He held up the bottle. "Somewhere in Scotland twelve years ago, someone knew that we'd want to meet this evening and have a drink together. This whisky was made in 1928, the last year of happiness and prosperity in America. Emil, you and I were together in Philadelphia, beginning our medical careers, set to heal the sick and repair the injured of the world." He shook his head ruefully. "Those were truly good times. I miss them."

"I miss them, too," Altwasser said, reminded of how Granger could burst forth with an inspiring few words on almost any topic.

"Now, to truly savour good scotch I'm told that we need a very small splash of water in each glass. Anna, perhaps I could prevail on you for a small pitcher of water."

Stahl opened the door from the living room and came back into the kitchen. He caught Altwasser's eye and nodded slightly.

Anna handed Granger a small glass pitcher of water and he added a dollop of water to each glass. He picked up two of the glasses and handed them to Nancy and Altwasser, then a third to Stahl.

He raised his own glass. "To old friends and new. May the child we are caring for, outlive us all."

They raised their glasses and drank, Nancy taking a very tentative sip.

"And what do you think, Nancy?" Granger asked.

"I thought it would be harsh, but it isn't. It's very pleasant."

Granger laughed. "Indeed it is," he said. "With your permission, Anna, perhaps we could move to your living room and chat in there."

Anna remained in the kitchen while the others settled themselves on the sofa and chairs, Nancy holding Lienhard, carefully wrapped in a blanket.

"Now," Granger said, looking around at the other three. "Can you tell me what this is all about?"

Altwasser looked at Stahl and raised his eyebrows.

"I can tell you some of what this is about," Stahl began cautiously. "We are from Germany as I am sure you have figured out. We were charged with transporting two children here and will return to Germany in a couple of days. As you see, one child has unfortunately taken ill."

"How did you get here?"

"We flew."

"Across the Atlantic?"

"Yes."

"In what?"

"The aircraft is a Condor, a four engine passenger plane."

"And it can fly from Germany to America?"

"Yes it can. I believe its initial trans-Atlantic flights were from Berlin to New York, but we came via Portugal and stopped to refuel there."

"So if you put bombs in this Condor, it could be used to attack America?"

Stahl smiled. "I suppose that is possible, but it could return only if you permitted it to refuel after it dropped the bombs."

Granger chuckled. "These must be pretty important kids."

"Apparently," Stahl said.

"Emil is a doctor, and Nancy is a nurse," Granger said. "What is your role in this?"

"I am a police officer," Stahl replied. "I suppose I am really acting more as a bodyguard and looking after things other than medical matters."

Granger digested this information. "Thank you for your frankness, Henry. That sounds like all I need to know," he said, turning his attention to Altwasser. "Now, Emil, what have you been up to and how has being a partner in your father's practice worked out. As you may recall, my father was a banker which was one of the reasons I went to medical school. We quite enjoy each other but we could never work together."

"Excuse, me," Nancy interrupted. "But I will let you two old friends reminisce and I will put Lienhard down for a sleep."

"Call me immediately if there is any change," Granger said.

Nancy nodded as she stood up, Lienhard cradled in her left arm, her scotch held carefully in her right hand.

"If you don't mind," Stahl said. "I will follow Nancy's example and let you get on with your visit. Thank you again, Dr. Granger, for all you are doing for us."

"You're welcome, Henry. A drive in the country to see Emil is no inconvenience at all." He waited a moment until the door closed and then leaned forward. "Tell me if you can, Emil," Granger said. "Is Henry's account of what is going on here the truth of the matter?"

Altwasser nodded. "It is an honest account," he said slowly. "But the truth is, we don't know a great deal. We are charged with transporting the children from Germany to America but we don't know whose children they are or why we are doing this."

Granger sat back in his chair and sipped his scotch. "It would be safe to assume that there is some importance to this enterprise."

"Most certainly there is," Altwasser replied. "But I don't know what it is. If I had to speculate, I would guess the parents are high ranking Nazi's. I don't think anyone else could mobilize the resources required for this operation. But, of course, that is just a guess."

"It sounds like a good one. What else could it be?"

Altwasser shrugged. "I suppose they could be American children who by some accident or another were born in Germany and now are being returned." Altwasser took a sip of the scotch. "This is excellent, Northrop," he added. "Thank you for bringing it. In a country at war a lot of things are hard to come by."

Granger raised his glass. "To peace," he said.

Altwasser joined him in the toast.

"If these are American children, somcone over here must have great influence in Germany. Is that possible?"

"I don't know," Altwasser said. "But there is considerable concern that America will enter the war on the side of Great Britain."

Granger laughed. "Not much chance of that," he said, "although Roosevelt would certainly like to drag us into it."

"I hope you are right. I would not want us to be enemies."

"Our countries may go to war, Emil, but you and I will never be enemies."

An hour later, Anna brought a plate of food into each of them. "I have a room made up for you Dr. Granger. I trust you will spend the night with us?"

Granger looked toward the scotch bottle and the remaining few inches in the bottom. "I think that would be a good idea, Anna. Thank you for your hospitality."

CHAPTER TWENTY FOUR

Tuesday, November 19, 1940 Kitchener, Ontario, Canada

Katherine didn't know how long she had been sleeping when the car bumped to a halt. Gilford was holding her against him, her head on the shoulder of his great coat. Slowly she sat up straight, melted a small patch of frost off the window with her bare hand and looked out. It was still snowing. It had started before they got out of Toronto, big soft flakes splattering on the windshield with the wipers sweeping slowly back and forth, turning the snow into lines of dirty grey slush. The Corporal turned off the engine and it was quiet for a moment. She saw Klassen sit up with a start. He must have been sleeping too. Erich was cradled on Gilford's lap, wrapped securely in several small blankets. He was awake now, too, and stared up at her with his big serious brown eyes. She gave a short gasp as she suddenly remembered the porter, tipping slowly off his trolley and the Sergeant sliding into the freezing slush of the street. She turned in anguish to Gilford.

"It's all right, Darling," he said softly. "Everything will be all right now." He grasped her hand and squeezed it gently.

Katherine sighed as she returned the pressure. She felt reassured even though she knew that Gilford had only said what doctors and nurses always said to anyone who was upset.

The Corporal opened his door and got out. Klassen did the same and an icy blast of air and snow swept into the car. Gilford handed Erich to Katherine. "Stay here for a minute until we get the luggage organized and then we'll go and see our new home." He smiled warmly at her but anger burned in his eyes. Katherine looked out the window at the house. From the outline she could see in the darkness it looked like a wooden two story structure with a gabled roof which concealed either a substantial attic or some slope-ceilinged rooms on a third floor.

They had entered the house through a side door and found themselves in a coat room that led into the warm, cozy kitchen. Katherine was now seated in an ornate wooden rocking chair that squeaked softly as she rocked back and forth with Erich on her lap. Klassen and Gilford were sitting with steaming mugs of coffee at a large wooden table on the other side of the kitchen. They had all changed their clothes and the Corporal had taken the car and their uniforms and driven off.

Conrad and Edith, the owners of the house had not seemed pleased by their arrival but they were doing their best to be good hosts. Conrad was at the table with the others and Edith was busy at an ancient cast iron cook stove only a few feet from where Katherine sat. Edith looked tired and annoyed. Some fat in a large frying pan spattered onto her apron and she muttered a curse in German. She snatched up a spatula and turned over the offending piece of meat. A pot lid rattled as the water came to a boil and she propped the lid on the edge of the pot to let the steam escape. She wiped a greying strand of hair from her forehead, glanced at Katherine for a moment and tried to smile but it came out as a grimace.

"Can I help with anything?" Katherine asked.

"Thank you, no, Mrs. Shore," Edith answered. "You are our guests," she added firmly, but without much conviction.

Dinner had been a strained affair. Klassen had been bright and cheerful, animated like an active child looking for attention. Gilford was quiet and withdrawn, anger still seething within him. Edith served them schnitzel, boiled potatoes and some tinned vegetables, a mixture of peas and carrots. She apologized for not having a torte to serve with the dessert of canned peaches and explained that she had been expecting them the next day. Klassen waved her apology aside and was complimentary, even charming. Edith allowed herself a tiny smile.

Conrad said little over dinner. He was a large gruff looking man, somewhere in his fifties, the lower part of his square, rough-hewn face covered in a grey, late evening stubble. His eyes shifted warily around the table. He was clearly not charmed by Klassen at all and Katherine felt certain he just wanted them out of his home as soon as possible. She wondered what the next step was. Certainly they couldn't stay here for the duration of the war.

The upstairs rooms were chilly, and the small bedroom that Edith showed her into smelled musty from disuse. The walls were papered with a floral scene, little girls dressed in suspiciously French looking costumes flitted across fields of faded wild flowers with a few picked and placed carefully in the small wicker baskets they swung. The scene repeated endlessly as Katherine looked about the room. A matching border ran around the wall a couple of inches below the ceiling. One wall was taken up by a dresser, its antique brass pulls tarnished with age. There was a double bed "for you and the Doctor" as Edith put it, and a crib at the foot of the bed for Erich. Katherine looked at the double bed and in spite of an undefined nervousness, felt a gentle surge of pleasure at the prospect of sleeping in the same bed with Gilford. On the train from Nova Scotia to Toronto, she had slept in a lower bunk with Erich while Gilford had slept in the berth above them. Other than their fitful night in the cabin, the night they had disembarked from the U boat, they had slept apart. She smiled to herself as she recalled Gilford's arousal when she had snuggled back against him.

"Thank you, Edith," she said. "This will be fine. It has everything we need. And thank you for the delicious dinner."

"You are welcome," Edith said formally. "I will turn down the crib for your child and leave you. The bathroom is down the hall."

When she had gone, Katherine got Erich ready for bed and tucked him into the crib. She discovered the suitcase of clothes that she had been given in Halifax had been placed under the bed. Gilford's duffle bag stood in a corner beside his small leather medical bag. She lifted the suitcase onto the bed, opened it and dug out a long pale blue cotton nightie. She slipped quickly out of her clothes, and pulled it over her head. The cool cotton slid down over her and she shivered for a moment until it warmed with her body heat. She glanced over at Erich, who was watching her, a saucy smile on his face.

"What do you think, Erich?" she asked, pirouetting around. "Do you think he'll like it?"

Erich waved his small arms.

She put her clothes on a couple of wire clothes hangers on a hook on the wall, pushed off the light switch by the door, and pulling back the comforter on the bed, she slipped under it. She shivered again, wondering with a quick grin if Gilford would also find it chilly. Maybe he would curl up to her for warmth. She certainly planned on snuggling up to him. As she stretched out she realized she might have little choice as the mattress sagged in the middle.

It seemed like hours later when the bed moved and she felt Gilford climb under the covers. She lay quietly, facing away from him, breathing as steadily as she could and waited. The bed creaked slightly as he rolled up behind her and she felt him against her. She sighed as he slipped his arm over her and she snuggled back against him. She felt him stiffen against her but this time he didn't pull away.

"Katherine," he whispered.

"Mmmm."

He moved back from her and gently rolled her onto her back and leaned his face close to her ear. "Listen carefully, Katherine," he whispered.

"Mmmm," Katherine murmured. She turned to face him and kissed him fully on the mouth, her lips parted. She felt him recoil for a moment in surprise and then he responded, crushing her against him, running his hand over the back of her nightie and sliding it up. His hand was a soft caress against her skin and as she slipped her arms around him she realized he was naked. With her hand she traced the smooth muscles of his shoulder and his back and felt him tugging insistently at her gown. She lifted herself and felt it slide up over her waist. His mouth moved to her throat and she threw her head back. His hand crept up to her breasts and she shuddered as he gently touched her nipples in small circles. She ran her fingers into the soft fine hair of his chest and then moved down slowly dragging her finger nails over his skin to grasp his hard smooth erection. She moved her leg over him rubbed it into her wetness. With a groan he brushed her hand aside and drove himself into her.

They lay quietly together, their passion spent for the moment, the damp cotton gown crumpled around her breasts. Katherine felt content. Making love with Gilford had seemed so natural, so beautiful.

"Katherine," Gilford whispered. "I started to tell you something before..." His voice trailed off.

"Mmmm."

"We have to get out of here," he whispered, his voice authoritative again. "I don't trust Klassen and I don't trust his orders."

"What do you mean?"

"I think Klassen's orders are to get us here safely, likely stay a day or two to make sure that Erich is fine, and then kill us all and move Erich to a second family. Then Klassen disappears back to Germany."

"But why?

"Why else would we have Klassen with us at all? We could have brought Erich here and moved on to the next phase of our plan."

"What is the next phase?"

"There isn't one, and that's what bothers me. I was supposed to get additional instructions when we arrived here. I am not going to get anything from Conrad or Edith. They are just temporary hosts. The driver was only our transport. There is no one to tell us what to do next, so perhaps there isn't any 'next'."

Katherine was fully awake now. "Then what are we going to do?"

"We are going to leave."

"But where will we go?"

"I hoped that things would work out differently, but in case they didn't, I brought some things that might help us. But first we have to get safely away from Klassen."

"When do you think we should try to leave?"

"The sooner the better, I should think," Gilford answered.

"How do we do it?"

"I found out that Conrad has a car in the garage in the back yard. Apparently he has it all tuned up, full of fuel and ready to go in case we require it. I think he just wants us out of his house and this is a handy way to let us know that he's ready to help anytime we are ready to leave."

"So we just take the car and drive away?"

"That would be nice and simple but I doubt that Klassen would go along with that." Gilford kissed her gently on the cheek. "I would give a lot to know what Klassen's plans are."

"Have you asked him?"

"I asked him what his orders were and he told me they were to protect us and to make sure we got here safely. Nothing beyond that. But I doubt that Bormann or whoever gave him his orders would give him something like that. They don't leave loose ends like us around."

"Who's Bormann?"

"Martin Bormann. He is close to Hitler and the Nazi hierarchy."

Katherine thought for a moment. "What's he look like?"

"Short, somewhat fat, rather plain looking, powerful," Gilford replied, trying to think of some feature of Bormann that would stand out.

"He's a lecher," Katherine whispered.

"You met him?"

"He was the second man that interviewed me briefly and all he did was undress me with his beady little pig-eyes."

"Yes," Gilford reflected, smiling in spite of himself. "That's Bormann."

"He's a filthy disgusting man."

"Yes he is, but he is also one of the most powerful men in the Reich."

"So what will we do now?"

"If you can take care of Erich, I will try to look after the other details."

Katherine slipped her arm over Gilford and pulled him close to her. They embraced and held each other tightly. She kissed him on the mouth and then snuggled her head on his shoulder, kissing his throat, tasting a faint saltiness. She felt him becoming aroused again. She pushed against him playfully. "Can we save it until later?"

He hugged her tightly for a moment. "Of course we can, my Darling," he whispered.

"Darling," she echoed softly. "That has a nice sound to it."

"You'll get used to it."

"I hope so."

He released her and slipped out of bed. She heard him moving softly as he got dressed. The latches on his medical bag sounded loud in the confined space of their bedroom and then there was silence. She felt Gilford's weight on the edge of the bed and his face close to hers.

"Stay here and stay quiet," he whispered. "Someone else is up." She felt Gilford move away and his weight come off the bed.

Katherine listened intently and then she heard a faint creak from somewhere down the hallway. She lay quietly aware of her pulse quickening. It had to be Klassen. She caught a flash of light on the other side of the door. He must have a flash light. Then it was dark again. She heard a slight creak as the bedroom door opened. There was a soft light in the hallway and a faint silhouette of a man in the doorway. She waited, her eyes slits, wondering where Gilford was.

"Good evening, Klassen," Gilford said quietly. The flash light stabbed a beam across the room to the bed. Katherine lay frozen with fear. Then it swung across the small room. Gilford was leaning, almost nonchalantly, against the wall by Erich's crib, his arms folded. "A bit late for a social visit, isn't it? What seems to be the problem?"

"No problem, Herr Docktor," Klassen said in German. "No problem at all."

"Gilford," Katherine said, surprised by the calmness of her voice. "He has a gun."

The light swung to the bed for a moment and then back to Gilford. "Good evening, Mrs. Shore. How nice of you to join us. And you, Dr. Shore, I see you are dressed. Were you planning on going somewhere tonight? It is quite chilly out and still snowing a bit."

"Just to the bathroom down the hall."

"And for that you get fully dressed?"

"So it seems."

"Enough of this, Dr. Shore. Get undressed and back into bed. It will be more comfortable for you to die there than standing where you are."

"Why are you doing this, Klassen?" Gilford asked, still leaning against the wall.

"Quite simple, really," Klassen said. "You and the child are here safely. My job is to eliminate you, your wife and our hosts and move the child to another family nearby. Then I return to Germany."

"I see," said Gilford. "And do you really think that the Reich will leave a loose end like you wandering about? If I were you, Klassen, I would be wondering who was assigned to get rid of the last detail."

Klassen laughed. "The Gestapo looks after its own, Doctor. Now move back to the edge of your bed, take your clothes off and get back under the covers with your wife."

"And if I don't?"

"As your wife pointed out, I have a gun," Klassen said and raised it to point at Gilford's chest. "I will simply shoot you where you stand, undress you and put you back into bed with your dead wife."

"Cover your ears, darling," Gilford said quietly. "Guns are quite noisy in small rooms."

Klassen laughed. "Very well, Dr. Shore, have it your way."

Katherine watched as the gun steadied on Gilford and she screamed as she saw his finger tighten on the trigger, then nothing but the heavy click of the firing mechanism. Klassen slipped the flashlight under his arm and in one fluid motion snapped the slide back, ejected the bullet and jacked a new round into the chamber. It clicked a second time and Klassen angrily tossed it aside, snatching his dagger from a sheath on his left arm. Gilford stood unmoving for a moment and then slowly unfolded his arms, pointed a small pistol at Klassen and fired it. In spite of Gilford's warning, the sound was shattering. Klassen staggered back and Gilford fired twice more, the sound deadened as Katherine realized her ears still had not recovered from the first shot The flash light fell to the floor sending a beam of light spinning across the ceiling and then the room was plunged into darkness.

A moment later Gilford turned the ceiling light on. Klassen lay in the doorway, his right leg twitched for a moment and then was still. Gilford leaned over him, checked for a pulse and then came back to the bed. As her hearing gradually returned she became aware of Erich crying, standing in his crib and reaching toward her. She quickly slipped past Gilford and picked him up, holding him and comforting him. She realized that Gilford was saying something to her and then he stopped speaking, leaned over Erich to kiss her lightly on the cheek. He stepped over Klassen and disappeared down the hall. She heard him going carefully down the stairs and then she returned her attention to Erich.

She was buttoning up Erich's snow suit when Gilford returned. He looked at her grimly. "Klassen saved us for the last. Conrad and Edith are both dead, stabbed."

Katherine gasped in dismay. "How could he do that? Just kill innocent people?"

Gilford ignored her question. "Klassen has also dumped some gasoline down the basement stairs so I presume his plan was to burn the house when he left. I think we should do the same."

The car started easily and ran smoothly. Katherine sat in the front seat with Erich on her knees, wide awake, looking intently around from the small hood of his navy blue snow suit. Gilford backed the car out into the alley and drove it around to the front of the house. He left it running as he hurried up the walkway and around to the back door. Snow was still falling in large soft flakes, oddly hypnotic through the beams of the headlights. The windshield wipers flopped back and forth, clearing the slush from the windshield and a fan ran noisily, blowing slightly warm air around her feet.

Katherine looked out at the old house, now in total darkness. Judging by how the snow was falling, the night was calm. On the edge of the headlight beams she could see trees stretching off down the road.

She saw Gilford returning, walking fast, the collar of his overcoat pulled up and his face shielded by the brim of a hat. He opened the rear door of the sedan and fumbled in his medical bag for a moment, closed the door and slipped into the front seat beside her. He leaned over and kissed her quickly.

"The flames in the house will be visible soon," he said.

Katherine looked out at the house and saw a small flicker of orange through the kitchen window.

Gilford turned on the flashlight that Klassen had used. "Hold this," he said, handing it to her. He opened a brown envelop and slid the contents into his hand, two small dark blue booklets with gold embossed printing and a coat of arms on the front. He opened one of them and handed it to her.

She looked at a photograph and read the name. "Katherine O'Neill?" she asked. "Who is that?"

"That is your new identity," Gilford said. "Germany has the best forgers in the world. One of them was a patient of mine so I had him prepare these passports in case we needed them. It turns out we do."

"Ireland," she said softly. "I've never been there."

"Neither have I." He put the car in gear and she listened as the tires slipped in the snow for a moment and then gripped. The car moved off down the road.

CHAPTER TWENTY FIVE

Wednesday, November 20, 1940 Graystown, Pennsylvania

Stahl looked at the old wood framed clock on the wall as he walked into the warmth of the kitchen. It was four minutes after seven. He was assailed by a delicious mixture of smells, fresh coffee, pastry baking and bacon sizzling in a large cast iron pan on the stove top.

"Good morning, Henry," Anna said. She smiled at him warmly. "I trust you slept well?"

"Very well, thank you," Stahl replied, picking up a large cup from the counter and pouring it full of coffee from the pot set on the end of the wood stove. He had a trace of a headache this morning, perhaps from the generous glass of scotch whisky that Northrop Granger had poured for him the previous evening. He wasn't sure why but coffee often helped get rid of his occasional headaches. He returned to the counter and added a small amount of cream, watching it swirl about for a moment until he took a sip. He raised his cup in a mock toast. "Thank you, Anna," he said. "This is a lovely way to start a day."

Anna nodded, flustered by his comment. "You are most welcome." She pointed to the door to the living room. "Nancy is in there with the child."

Stahl entered the living room. It was dark save for the light of a small table lamp in one corner. Nancy sat in a rocking chair with Lienhard. "Good morning, Nancy," Stahl said. "And how is our patient this morning?"

"Much improved," Nancy replied, her voice barely above a whisper. "And he is sleeping for the moment. He seems almost back to normal so whatever Dr. Granger did has worked."

"Excellent news," Stahl said. "I am sure that your care and attention helped as well."

Nancy smiled up at him. "Thank you."

Stahl had learned early on in his life as a police officer that people being questioned responded much better to kindness and compliments than to harshness and intimidation. He had realized a few years later that he had unconsciously transferred this process to his dealings with everyone, and somewhat to his surprise, that his complimentary approach had become a genuine part of his personality. As a result, he had discovered that most of the time he was generally well liked, an unusual circumstance for a police officer and unheard of for a member of the Gestapo. Stahl returned to the kitchen.

"It seems that our child has recovered nicely," Stahl said. "We will have Dr. Granger confirm this, of course, but if he does then perhaps we can be on our way later today."

"Helmut will come after lunch," Anna said. "All the arrangements to transfer the children have been made and you will be able to leave for Philadelphia."

"I don't need to know the details, Anna, but are you the one who will be overseeing it?"

Anna nodded as she picked up a small towel and moved the cast iron pan with the bacon to the end of the stove where it would keep warm. "I am," she replied.

"I am glad to hear that."

They both turned as they heard footsteps on the stairs. A moment later Northrop Granger entered the kitchen.

"What wonderful aromas, Anna," he said, closing his eyes and breathing deeply. "I have not smelled a morning this good since I was a child."

Anna smiled self-consciously. "Thank you, Dr. Granger." She turned back to the stove.

"And how is the child this morning, Henry?"

"I think your magic has worked, Doctor," Stahl said. "The fever is gone and he is resting comfortably."

"Exactly as it should be," Granger said. "Is he in the living room?"

Stahl nodded and watched as Granger went through the door and closed it behind him. As he listened to the indistinct murmur of voices in the next room, he found he was beginning to relax. Things were working out. He would go to the telephone exchange and call the Biltmore Hotel, speak to the pilot, confirm their departure, they would leave for Philadelphia and the children would be delivered to their foster homes. He strolled over to the stove and looked at the bacon in the skillet and then stepped back as Anna picked up her small towel again and opened the oven to remove some biscuits. He watched as she deftly juggled the pan and set it on a mat on the counter.

The door to the living room opened and Granger reentered. "I'm pleased," he said. "Lienhard is doing well. He will likely sleep a bit more than usual today but otherwise he is fine." He picked a coffee cup from the counter and filled it from the pot on the stove, then took a sip. He looked carefully at the pot, noting the small cloth bag in the top that held the coffee. "This is a most interesting way to make coffee, Anna. I use a percolator and it doesn't produce coffee nearly as good as yours does."

Anna smiled. "An old Danish secret," she said. "Although I think that most of Scandinavia makes coffee this way."

"I must try it," Granger said. He turned to Stahl. "I think we have a fairly healthy child on our hands now. It was wise to call me since I have seen this sort of thing before and Emil likely has not encountered it in children."

"Thank you for all you've done," Stahl said.

"So will you be leaving soon, or do you have other duties to keep you here for a bit longer?"

"Unfortunately, we do not," Stahl replied.

"Well, Emil and I had an evening together and I guess in a time of war that is much to be grateful for."

"It is," Stahl said. "We will be leaving here later today and flying out of Philadelphia this evening."

Granger nodded and took a drink of his coffee. "Then I will return to the city after breakfast. It smells much too good to resist."

Altwasser came over about 8:30 am and he and Granger visited in the living room. Judging by the periodic bouts of laughter, they were reminiscing. Stahl found himself wondering when the last time was that he had heard people laugh. About 9:30 Granger entered the kitchen, thanked Anna profusely for her hospitality and said his farewells, wishing them all the best.

A few minutes before ten Helmut arrived. He came into the kitchen and greeted Stahl with a smile.

"Good morning, Helmut," Stahl said. "You're early."

"I had no other duties this morning so I decided to come over to see how the child is."

"The child is fine," Stahl said. "So it was wise that we brought Dr. Granger here to care for him."

"So it seems," Helmut said. "Then you will be leaving today?"

"Early afternoon, I think," Stahl said. "I will contact our pilot and tell him to expect us."

"I will go and make the necessary driving arrangements," Helmut said.

The wipers were clearing the rain off the windshield as they climbed into the car, Helmut holding the rear door for them. The rain was turning to sleet and it would make the paved roads dangerously slippery by evening if it continued. So there had been a small change in plans. They were leaving earlier. It was now about noon, and Lienhard and Anna would come with them. A second car would pick up Altwasser, Frannie and Johann from the other house. They would deliver the children first, then continue on to Philadelphia.

Stahl did not like changes in plans. About half an hour ago he had gone to the telephone exchange and called the Biltmore Hotel to confirm with the pilot that they would be arriving later that afternoon, but the pilot was out. He had left a message. He didn't like leaving messages either. He had wanted confirmation that they would be meeting at the airport. Helmut had assured him that he could call again on the way in, after they had delivered the children. At least he was pleased with the change in Helmut. Yesterday the driver had been surly and argumentative. Today he was polite and cooperative. Perhaps he was just relieved that the child had been cured and the operation was concluding. Whatever the case, the transformation had been a welcome one.

As the car reached the main street, it turned right, away from Philadelphia as far as Stahl could remember, and drove slowly down the street. This would add a bit more time to their trip back to the city if they travelled very far in this direction. A few people scurried along under black umbrellas, an occasional car was parked, diagonally against the sidewalk.

Anna turned and looked over the back of the front seat. "We are just a short drive from our transfer point. The children and I will remain there with Helmut and this car, and the four of you will return to Philadelphia in the other car."

"Thank you," Stahl said. "Perhaps you can satisfy my curiosity about something. How can a child show up in a family in a small community and not cause a lot of questions to be asked? How this is accomplished?"

"It's fairly simple," Anna said. "As you know, America has had a severe economic depression. Many families have had to move, most of them west, to look for work. Many farm families in the mid-west have been displaced by drought. So it's not unusual for family members to help each other out. Children come to live with relatives while their parents get reestablished, or their parents simply pass a child on for adoption to another member of the family, a sister, brother or even a grandparent, or sometimes a close friend, since they have no means to support and raise the child. So the arrival of two small children can be explained fairly easily. It will also explain the situation when they leave the community in the future to return to their real parents."

Stahl thought about this. It made sense and it would work both for the delivery of the children and for their eventual return.

"Do you have any idea when the children will be going back to Germany?" Anna asked.

"As I understand it, they will be returning when it is safe to do so," Stahl replied.

Anna looked at him with surprise. "Do you mean it is not safe in Germany now?"

"For the moment it is," Stahl said carefully. "However, a country at war can be full of uncertainties."

"But I thought that the war will soon be over?"

"When it started a year ago in September I thought so, too," Stahl said. "Now I am not so sure."

"Really?" Anna said. "Surely Germany will win."

"I am sure you are correct," Stahl said. "However, what started out as a small war to redress the unfairness of the Versailles Treaty of 1918 that ended the Great War, now seems to have expanded. Britain has also entered the war along with her empire and I don't think that was expected. So it may take a while longer than was originally anticipated."

"So the children could be here for some time?"

"I would think that is likely," Stahl said. "Perhaps a year, perhaps more."

"That will be fine," Anna said. "We will do whatever must be done to support the Fatherland."

Stahl looked out the small rear window of the car and saw the second car with Altwasser, Frannie and Johann, a shadowy outline in the sleet, some distance behind them. As he turned back, the car slowed, Helmut braking gently. Just ahead Stahl could see a small side road leading into a bluff of trees. Helmut turned the car into the driveway, stopped the car and got out to open a wooden gate that blocked the road. It was old and dilapidated and as Helmut swung it open he was almost carrying it. Long grass, withered and wet, separated the two tracks of the narrow road.

Helmut got back into the car and drove through the gate, the second car following, now close behind them. The road ran straight through a stand of tall leafless trees for a couple of hundred metres and ended in a small farm yard. Immediately ahead was a two story house, weathered grey with occasional patches of peeling white paint. As Stahl looked at it he saw that a window on the second story had two panes of glass broken, one of them covered roughly with boards. It looked abandoned.

"Times have been difficult around here, too," Anna said, as though reading his mind.

As Stahl was looking at the front door, it swung open and a man stepped out onto the small porch and waved at them. He smiled and started down the steps as the car drew to a halt in front of the house. Helmut got out of the car and opened the rear door for Stahl. Anna opened the other back door and reached inside to take Lienhard from Nancy.

"I bid you welcome," said the man from the house.

"Thank you," Stahl said, looking back at the second car. The driver was holding the door open for Frannie, Altwasser was already standing by the other door.

"Anna," Stahl said. "Surely we are not leaving the children here? This place is a derelict."

"You are quite correct, Henry," Anna replied. "This is the transfer point as I explained. Just as you are careful with your information, we must be with ours."

"I see," Stahl said. He slipped his hands into the pockets of his overcoat, feeling the comfort of the Luger in his right hand. Something was wrong here and he had been a policeman for far too long not to trust his instincts.

"What is happening, Henry?" Altwasser asked as he stopped beside Stahl.

"I'm not sure," Stahl replied. "But it appears we will leave the children here and carry on to Philadelphia. Is that correct, Anna?"

"That is correct."

Stahl turned toward Altwasser, shielding himself from Anna and the man from the house. He slipped the Luger out of his pocket and let the sleeve of his overcoat ride down to partially cover it. He held his hands behind his back in an at ease position.

"Very well, then," he said to Anna. "What is next?"

Anna looked at Helmut and nodded.

Helmut stepped forward. Stahl caught a movement from the corner of his eye and too late turned toward the man from the house. He was raising a gun, and as the tableau unfolded, Stahl noticed incongruously, that it was a 45 calibre automatic, a huge and ungainly weapon in his opinion. He dropped to one knee, as Altwasser lunged to one side, blocking his view. Stahl heard the blast of the big gun and Altwasser was hurled backward by the force of the bullet, his body barely missing him. He fired his Luger and the shot caught the man squarely in the chest, crumpling him backward onto the steps.

Stahl spun toward Helmut but he had disappeared. The driver of the second car shouted at him and he turned to see him holding Frannie with his gun pointed at her head. Another 45, he noted, with the odd detachment that had overtaken him.

It was a long shot with a hand gun but he raised his Luger and aimed carefully. They were all dead anyway, he thought, so if he hit Frannie, it would be unfortunate, but would not change the outcome. The man shouted at him again as Stahl squeezed the trigger, gently, and over the small gun site, saw the man's head explode as the nine millimetre bullet tore through the front of his skull.

"Get in the car," he shouted to Frannie. "On the floor."

As he threw himself to the ground behind the prostrate figure of Altwasser, he heard another shot from the other side of the car he had arrived in. He could see underneath the car and saw Nancy's body fall. There was blur of movement near her body and he fired at it but knew he had missed. The rear car door on the far side opened. Someone, Helmut, or Anna with the child had climbed inside.

"Give up, Stahl," Helmut shouted from the other side of the car. "Or I will kill the child."

"Go ahead, Helmut," Stahl shouted back. "He's not my child."

Stahl drew himself into a crouch. Judging by the sound of his voice, Helmut was still outside the car. If he could reach the steps perhaps he could see over the car and get a clear shot at him. Altwasser had not moved since he had fallen which likely meant the shot had been fatal, but he did not have the luxury of checking. He paused for a moment and then darted toward the steps. As he sprang onto the first step, it shattered under his weight and he fell heavily, dropping his Luger. He tried to roll clear as he saw Helmut stand up on the other side of the car and raise his gun. Helmut fired and he felt a sudden terrible searing pain in his right shoulder. He slumped in agony and through his half closed eyes he saw Helmut look at him for a moment and then walk back toward the second car.

He wondered where his Luger had fallen but it didn't seem terribly important, he just hated to lose things. He heard another shot and saw Helmut standing by the open rear door of the second car. Presumably he had shot Frannie. He emerged holding Johann in the crook of his arm, gently and carefully. He kicked the door closed and began walking back toward the first car. As he did so, Anna emerged from the rear door of the first car. Stahl noticed she was not holding Lienhard. Anna held out her hands to Helmut and he handed Johann to her. She turned back to the car, leaned inside, then emerged again and closed the door.

Stahl moved his good arm thinking he would sit up but his hand hit something rough. He looked down. It was the sleeve of the man from the house who had killed Atlwasser. His 45 calibre automatic lay a few centimetres away. Stahl closed his hand over it. It was cold, heavy and unfamiliar. It felt strange to hold a gun in his left hand. He stared at it for a moment and when he looked up, Helmut was walking toward him, his own gun held loosely beside him. Behind Helmut, Anna was walking toward him, too.

Helmut was about ten paces away when Stahl raised the gun. Helmut froze. Stahl glanced down at the gun and fired. The heavy recoil knocked it out of his hand. He looked for it but couldn't see it and when looked back at Helmut, he was still standing in front of him, the look of fear slowly fading. He smiled at Stahl, took a few steps toward him and raised the gun. Stahl closed his eyes and heard the shot. It sounded different, not as loud as the 45's had sounded earlier. He opened his eyes and saw Helmut stumble forward and fall to the ground. Anna stood behind him, a small revolver in her hand.

She walked to the foot of the steps and looked down at him. "I am sorry for this, Henry," she said. "Truly, I am. The children will be well cared for and will be returned to the Reich when they are needed. In the mean time they will be raised in America. Johann will become Jonathon and Lienhard will become Lincoln.

Stahl watched as she raised her gun, pointing it unwaveringly at his head. He closed his eyes again.

Philadelphia Inquirer, November 21, 1940
Police are still investigating the mysterious death of prominent Philadelphia physician, Dr. Northrop Granger. Dr. Granger's automobile was found in a ditch approximately thirty miles west of the city on the evening of November 20. Road conditions were treacherous at the time and it was initially assumed that Dr. Granger had lost control of the vehicle and crashed.

However, further examination of the accident scene and of the damage to Dr. Granger's car, a late model Lincoln, revealed that a second vehicle was almost certainly involved. No details have been released but the Coroner's Office has said that some of his injuries were not compatible with an automobile accident. Police are asking the cooperation of anyone who might have witnessed the accident.

Dr. Northrop Granger was a graduate of the University of Pennsylvania Medical School and had a large pediatric practice in the city. He is survived by his wife . . . "

PART TWO

April 1989 - January 1990

CHAPTER TWENTY SIX

Thursday, April 20, 1989 11:05 pm Winnipeg, Canada

"I suppose you enjoyed the Scriabin better than the Mahler?" Katherine O'Neill looked over at her husband as he touched the heater controls on the dash of the Mercedes.

"Umm," Gilford O'Neill murmured. They had only owned the car for a couple of weeks and he hadn't yet figured out where everything was. He glanced at her and smiled. "I usually prefer mad Russians to sane Germans," he said.

Katherine laughed, a clear sparkling sound. "The Winnipeg Symphony did well this evening, sanity and madness all in one concert."

Gilford turned on the windshield wipers to intermittent to clear the sleet and the occasional drop of rain that made it to the windshield without freezing. The road would probably turn slippery by the time they got to Portage la Prairie. Perhaps it might hold off for an hour, it was only about 80 kilometres. "There's a nice motel a few blocks ahead," he said. "Would you like to spend the night?"

"I plan to spend the night with you anyway, Darling, but I'd rather be in our own bed." She stared ahead intently for a moment at the six lanes of Portage Avenue glistening in the street lights. "Is the road slippery?"

"Not yet."

11:45 pm, Portage la Prairie, Canada

Marvin was really pissed. The bitch had turned him down. "Jesus Christ," he muttered. He fumbled in his pocket for the car keys, pulled them out and dropped them in the snow. "Fuck!" he swore, bending to retrieve them. As he straightened a wave of dizziness swept over him and the beer and the tequila shooters roiled up in his throat, harsh and acidic. He pushed the key at the lock but missed and dug a two inch scrape into the glistening black paint.

"Goddammit." He tried again and the key slid in smoothly. He turned it and pulled on the door handle. As the heavy door swung open he lost his balance and fell heavily to the ground. He lay back in the fresh snow and looked up, watching the large fluffy flakes of snow drift down, lit by the street light on the corner of the parking lot. The flakes settled softly on his glasses and melted, blurring and softening the light. It didn't seem cold lying in the snow, kind of refreshing actually. Then he thought of the bitch in the pub. Shit! She was a dog. She should've been grateful for the chance to go with him. She'd been hot for him for the last two hours and then when he finally made his move she'd told him to get lost. Get lost? For Chrissake, who the fuck did she think she was?

The anger seared through him again and he rolled over onto his hands and knees. He pulled himself up on the door and flopped inside into the deep bucket seat of the Camaro. Dragging his legs inside, he reached for the door, sounding the horn as he fell against the steering wheel. He jammed the key into the ignition, turned it and jabbed the accelerator viciously. He was rewarded with a roar of power, the engine torque rocking the car. He laughed. That bitch would never know what she was missing.

11:50 pm

Gilford gently eased his foot up on the accelerator as he approached the off ramp for Portage. It had been snowing for the last half hour, big soft flakes splashing across the windshield, falling hypnotically. It was like driving through space with cosmic particles flashing by. He glanced over at Katherine. She was still sleeping, her head turned slightly toward him, her hair like burnished silver on the dark blue leather head rest. Her lips were parted slightly. He had always marveled at how beautiful she looked when she was sleeping.

He glanced at the speedometer and saw the needle slipping slowly down toward 70 kilometres an hour. He steadied his foot on the accelerator as he left the divided section of the highway. Off to his right was a small museum, a yard light casting a white glow through the falling snow.

11:52 pm

Marvin pulled the gear shift into reverse and the car lurched backward. He spun the wheel and was suddenly slammed back into the seat. The noise of the crash seemed to come after. He looked over his shoulder. Some prick had parked right behind him. Serve the asshole right. He laughed again and pulled the gear shift into drive easing the car forward slightly. He tramped on the accelerator, letting up as he felt the car start to fishtail. He'd check the back of the Camaro in the morning.

As he headed east on Saskatchewan Avenue, six lanes wide, he poked at the tape deck and got the tape back in on the second try. "Lyin' Eyes" howled through the car. Good song for tonight he thought. He loved the Eagles, best fuckin' rock band ever. Those guys were poets. He pushed a button on the armrest. The driver's window hummed down and the frigid air poured through the car. Felt good. He watched the wipers flopping back and forth and wondered for a moment if he could get them hooked up to the stereo so they'd slap in time to the music. One of these days he'd come up with a million dollar idea. He glanced at the speedometer as he tore by the 30 kilometre zone sign at Victoria Elementary School, a hundred and twenty klicks, it said, the small numbers behind showed 75 miles an hour. He pushed the accelerator down, heard the pitch of the V8 winding up and felt himself being pressed back into the seat. Son of a bitch, this mother could move. He glanced down a moment later and watched the needle slide past 150 klicks, just coming up on 95 miles an hour. He laughed as he hurtled by the Portage Mutual Insurance building on the eastern edge of town. JoAnne worked there and he had just cancelled his life insurance that morning. There was one bitch that wasn't getting rich off him. The life insurance had been her idea but she'd walked out a week ago, when he'd come home and told her he'd been laid off. Who needed her? Still, ten years was a long time to be with one woman, but, of course, he'd spread it around a bit. No point saving it all for her, not that she would even have noticed in the last couple of years.

11:53 pm
Gilford slowed for the railway tracks, not that he was expecting a train, but they crossed the highway at an angle and he didn't want the front wheels pulling. Katherine murmured something as the Mercedes bumped slightly over the tracks. Gilford glanced over at her and saw her eyes were open. He smiled at her. They had been together now for forty nine years.

Katherine still teased him occasionally about making an honest woman of her but no ceremony could ever make him love her more. In any case, it would have been too difficult to go through anything formal, even dangerous perhaps, and after all this time it really didn't matter anymore.

The traffic had been light and the snow melting as it hit the road. That would likely change before morning and it would become treacherous. He wondered who was on call at the hospital tonight. It was a night waiting for accidents. Perhaps Laura . . .

11:54 pm
Ahead, Marvin saw the blur of lights at what had once been "Little Portage", a truck stop, now just a bunch of abandoned buildings. He slipped his glasses off, rubbed them across the front of his sweatshirt and slipped them back on. Now the blur was a smear but it was better. He felt the Camaro drifting a little, feeling light now. Squinting at the small numbers, he saw the needle hovering around 125 miles an hour, pushing past 200 klicks. He took one hand off the wheel and punched at the electric window button. He missed it, looked down at the arm rest and carefully put his finger on the button and pushed, watching his window rise against the shrieking wind. As he glanced up he saw the car had drifted a little to the left. He tugged at the wheel, gently now, and felt the tires break loose, the car drifting sideways, he spun the steering wheel back . . .

Friday, April 21, 1989 12:35 am Portage General Hospital
Laura Schaefer walked up to the coffee machine near the nurses' station. She put in a loonie and watched as an insulated paper cup fell down a chute and slowly filled with the brown sludge that passed for coffee. "It's Hard to Soar With Eagles When You Work With Turkeys" the faded photocopy on the

small cork board beside the machine informed her. She felt suddenly irritable. She wasn't a turkey and none of her colleagues were either. She ripped it off and crumpled it. A nurse looked up from her chart at the counter.

Laura smiled at her, embarrassed by her outburst. "I hate these signs," she said lamely. "I just don't think they're funny."

"Me either," the nurse replied. "How's it going, Dr. Schaefer?"

"Quiet so far," Laura said. "Just patched up a couple of guys who couldn't agree on something important."

"Couldn't agree?"

"Looked like it," Laura said with sheepish smile. "One of them pulled a knife on the other while the second one hacked the first one open with a broken beer glass. Lots of blood and stitches, no serious injury other than hurt pride." She sat down and took a sip of her coffee. It was vile.

"Dr. Schaefer to emergency," the paging system said softly. "Dr. Schaefer to emergency."

Laura got to her feet, walked over to a garbage container by the coffee machine, tossed in her cup headed down the hall. Moments later she walked into emergency. "What's up?"

"Ambulance coming in, three casualties, one dead, two close. ETA four minutes," the emergency room nurse said. "And you thought you were going to get a coffee break tonight."

"Doesn't look like it, Jeannie," Laura replied. "What happened?"

"Car accident," Jeannie replied. "Sounded like a head on but I didn't get a lot of detail."

Laura could hear the faint moan of the siren as she slipped the rubber gloves on and headed back to the emergency entrance. By the time she got there, the ambulance was outside the door, the strobes spinning slowly, throwing red and blue shafts of light across the parking lot and through the large glass entry doors. She watched the paramedics unload the first stretcher and wheel it toward them. The doors hissed open and she and Jeannie took over. Laura glanced at the pale grim face of the attendant and knew it was bad.

Wheeling the stretcher into a bay, Laura began the feverish ritual, checking for vital signs, passing orders to Jeannie, but she knew within moments she was going to lose this one. The styled white hair told her it was a woman, but her face was badly smashed, severe head injuries with an entire section of bone shattered on one side of her head exposing the brain tissue beneath. There was still a pulse, faint but regular and some movement of the rib cage suggested breathing although where the air was passing into her body was problematic. Two other nurses from Acute came in.

"What can we do, Dr. Schaefer?" one of them asked.

Laura glanced up, grateful for their presence. "Prep the other one," she said softly. "I'll be there in a moment." She seldom had to deal with this kind of emergency and was always surprised at her own reactions. There was an initial phase of anxiety which just faded away when she started to work, replaced by an icy calm. She worked fast and accurately.

In the next bay was a man, again with head injuries but mostly a lot of blood this time. One of the nurses told her the numbers, pulse, blood pressure, but Laura's heart fell as she saw that some of the blood was slowly frothing out of his mouth. Internal injury, lungs or nearby and bleeding into the lungs.

"My God, Laura," Jeannie said softly, wiping blood off the man's face. "It's Dr. O'Neill."

Laura froze for an instant and then carried on. She finished with the woman and almost elbowed Jeannie out of the way. It was Gilford O'Neill, her mentor, her friend, so many other things. She felt the tears burning down her cheeks, then took a deep breath.

Gilford O'Neill suddenly gripped her arm with surprising strength, his eyes open now, staring at her but she couldn't be sure he was seeing her. "Care for Eric," he murmured. "I should have told him. It's all written down. He can decide what to do." Then the grip went slack, his eyes closed and his ragged breathing began again.

At 7:00 am Laura walked out to her car. She had never felt this bad in her life, not even when she had lost her own parents. It was light out now, large snowflakes floating softly down over everything, unusual for this late in the season, winter's last gasp. She started the car and grabbed the scraper brush from the passenger side, stepped down and began brushing the snow off the windshield. The trouble with a 4 X 4 when you were short was that every time you brushed off the windshield you got covered in snow or mud or whatever was stuck to the side of the vehicle. She dabbed at her coat and then began to cry. She crawled back into the driver's seat and put her head down on the steering wheel, sobbing. She had tried so desperately to save them but she knew she never had a chance. Katherine was effectively brain dead when she arrived, probably within seconds of the crash. Gilford had simply bled to death but his internal injuries had been so massive that nothing short of a whole new set of organs would have helped.

She had loved them so much. And how could she ever tell Eric? She thought of Gilford's last words and wondered what he had meant by them. She sat up and rummaged in her purse for a moment, pulling out a prescription pad. She started to write down what Gilford had said and suddenly stopped, stunned by the realization that he had spoken to her in German.

CHAPTER TWENTY SEVEN

Thursday, April 20, 1989 35 Foot Sail Boat, Pegasus, West of Tahiti

Eric O'Neill watched the sun come flying up out of the eastern horizon into a cloudless sky, bleaching the pale pinks and burnished golds to a clear intense blue, driving the darkness into the western sea. During the night, the wind had been steady from the southwest at around ten to twelve knots, pushing the boat along at a steady four and half knots. He made coffee and watched the spectacle, and as the warmth of the morning sun crept into the cockpit, he slipped out of the nylon shell and the woolen sweater that had kept the night chill away.

Setting the mug in a holder in the corner of the cockpit he stood up, and stretching his arms above his head, he slowly twisted his body from side to side. He was stiff from sitting, muscles tensing and relaxing with no conscious thought, balancing him against the swells that had rolled under the boat all night long, drifting four thousand miles across the Pacific from Australia.

He knew there would not be a lot more mornings like this. He had been sailing for eighteen months, losing himself in the vastness of the ocean, finding himself in the solitude of single handing his boat. He hadn't been sailing the whole time, of course, but when he had been in a port, or anchored in a bay on some tropical island, he had managed to remain largely apart from fellow sailors, had transacted the business he needed to, buying food and other supplies, having a few repairs done, taking on fuel and fresh water, but not becoming involved in the lives of others. He had found it profoundly satisfying. He knew that his friends and colleagues in Toronto and his family in Manitoba thought his behaviour quite bizarre, a mid-life crisis, or like some social throwback to the 1960's, a search for the meaning of life. He thought of the wise words of Peer Gynt. "To search for the meaning of life, is like peeling an onion, looking for the core. All you are left with is tears." He might not have the quote exactly word for word but it was close enough to make him laugh.

He had been asked how long he was going to keep sailing. He had always answered that he would know when it was time to stop. On this leg from Rarotonga in the Cook Islands, to Tahiti in French Polynesia, he had decided it was time. He was at peace with himself, as healed as he was likely to get, and if not entirely ready to reenter the real world, at least content to leave his world of solitude.

He released a line and furled in the head sail. Then he stepped lightly up to the cabin top and made his way forward to the bow. He attached a halyard, sheet and guy to his small cruising spinnaker and moved back over the cabin top, casting his eye up the mast as a fast check on the rigging. In the cockpit he hauled on the halyard, winching it to the top of the mast, and watched as the parachute-like sail exploded softly out over the port bow, the wedges of deep emerald and royal blue material at the top of the sail lit by the rising sun. He saw the knot metre slide up to five. Half a knot didn't seem like much but it was eleven percent faster. He looked forward again and adjusted the sheet, tightening it in to take a flutter out of the edge of the sail. He smiled and waved at the large white-winged horse, Pegasus, floating majestically in the middle of the spinnaker.

At 8:00 am he tuned into the morning single side-band radio net and registered his position, heard the scoop from the other sailboats in that region of the south Pacific and picked up the met report. The weather folks were predicting deteriorating conditions as the day wore on, a small Pacific low, they had said. "Intensifying as the day wears on." He was reminded of an old joke. "Do you know why God created weather forecasters?" The answer: "To make economic forecasters look good."

By noon, the western sky became hazy and any remaining traces of blue were driven off by early afternoon. He downed the spinnaker and replaced it with a partially furled jib. By late afternoon the sky was covered in clouds from heavy gray to ominous black. He lowered the main sail to the second reef point as the wind gradually shifted from the southwest across his stern to the northwest and picked up.

It seemed that today the weather forecasters had gotten it right. By half an hour before sunset, the wind was up to thirty knots, gusting to forty at times. The ocean had changed from a benign deep blue to black and when Pegasus was in a trough between the waves, the wave tops looked about the same as the height of the mast, about fifty feet. The only good news was that now with a storm jib and double reefed main sail, he was pushing along at just over seven knots. The bad news was that the sea was building, the wind was rising and the night ahead would be long and dark.

He was carrying too much sail to head into the night and with the seas still building he decided to strip off the remaining sails and hoist the small storm tri-sail.

When he was finished, he poked his head around the bulkhead and glanced at the barometer. It had fallen again since his last check about an hour ago. He sat in the cockpit for a few minutes to get sense of how Pegasus was handling with the single tiny sail. It would do little but give the boat a bit of stability. Then he unclipped his safety harness and swung down the companionway into the cabin.

Earlier he had stowed and secured everything, putting the safety latches on the storage lockers and cupboards to keep cans and boxes from turning into missiles if they got loose in heavy seas. He stood beside the chart table, bracing himself against the stairs. According to his chart and the last satellite navigation fix he had taken about an hour ago, he was approximately a hundred nautical miles west of Tahiti and around sixty south of Bora Bora, the island James Michener had described as the most beautiful tropical island in the world. It was certainly one of them. There was nowhere to run to but he knew that he was far safer out here, clear of islands, shoals and reefs, and with a hundred miles of open ocean ahead of him, he wouldn't hit anything before the storm abated.

From the locker next to the chart table he got out his survival suit, a bright orange jumpsuit with built in floatation. He slipped out of his safety harness, put on the jump suit and replaced the harness. He went up into the cockpit, clipped the safety line onto his harness and closed up the companionway to keep water out of the cabin. When he was finished he sat down, bracing himself into a corner in the cockpit. He watched the wheel turning, stopping and turning again, mysteriously keeping the boat on course as the self- steering mechanism compensated for the waves rising under the stern, trying to push the boat off course. The knot metre had picked up a bit and was again bobbing around seven knots.

He looked past the stern. A band of bright gold was trapped between black clouds, their ragged undersides streaked with orange, and the dark hazy line of the western horizon that disappeared and reappeared as the boat rose and fell in the swells. He wondered what an old time mariner would have made of it, what prediction he would have drawn from it.

Just before midnight he crawled forward, waves and spray washing over him, and stripped off the storm tri-sail. Back in the cockpit, he lashed the wheel and waited to see how the boat adjusted. The first large wave broke over the stern washing through the cockpit and floating him toward the life lines before slamming him down on the gunwale. The water foamed out the transom as the wave passed under the boat and the bow rose, heaving a sheet of water into the wind. Although he couldn't see them, Eric knew by the motion of the boat that the waves were towering over the stern. The wind moaned and whistled through the rigging, a sound that told him it was pushing up near 40 to 45 knots. Spray was continuous, rattling off the rubberized nylon hood of his suit. In the faint red glow of the knot metre, he could see the needle swinging between seven and eight knots, rising as the boat surfed down the front of a wave, and then falling to two or three knots as the wave passed under him and boat rested for a moment in the trough.

Eric unclipped his harness and crawled carefully down the companionway closing the hatch tightly behind him. Pegasus was now running before the storm with bare poles, rocketing down the faces of the waves, plunging into the troughs and rising again.

Months ago, in a marine supply store in Auckland, Eric had chatted one day with an elderly couple who had been caught in a hurricane years before. He was beginning to appreciate what they had been through, but, at the moment, he was mostly grateful that he had taken their advice and equipped Pegasus with safety straps to belt himself into a berth to keep from slamming around inside the cabin.

Pegasus was heaving ominously, rolling almost flat in the water and rising upright only to be slammed over once more, plunging the bow completely under the water, standing nearly on end before bursting through the surface again. Eric had never been in anything like this before. He knew the boat was solid, but did any boat builder come out in a storm like this and then go back to the drawing board? He doubted it. Over the howl of the wind screaming through the rigging he heard a new and terrifying sound, like the roar of a freight train bearing down on him. Then Pegasus shuddered with the awful impact of a breaking wave and rolled. Eric hung upside down for what seemed like minutes and then the boat slowly came upright. He heard the sound of smashing glass in one of the lockers. Scotch or gin?

The sudden thud of something slamming down on the cabin top startled him. Something was loose on deck or he had drifted into something. He listened intently straining to hear what it was over the shriek of the wind and the roar of the water. A strange noise, like the crack of a whip, sounded against the side of the hull.

"Jesus," he murmured as he realized what it was, a shroud, an eery name for a heavy stainless steel guy wire that supported the mast. Then Pegasus shook as though she had been hit in the side with a battering ram. She had been dismasted, Eric realized. The danger was not that he couldn't survive without a mast, the problem was that the mast was still connected to the boat by the wires that held it aloft and in these waves it would batter the boat into kindling.

He reached above his head and pulled the radio microphone from its clip. "Pan. Pan. Pan." He was surprised at the calmness of his voice as he uttered the international distress call. "This is the sailing vessel Pegasus." He gave his approximate position. "I have been rolled, dismasted and am trailing a spar. I estimate winds of 60 to 70 knots, high and breaking waves. Over."

As he held the mic, he felt his first flash of real fear. If he had to go on deck with a pair of bolt cutters to cut the mast loose, could he do it without being swept away? Or dragged and drowned? Or tangled in the rigging as it went down and dragged him with it. As if in answer to his speculation, the boat heaved up and the mast slammed into the starboard cabin top with a sickening thud.

The radio crackled. "Pegasus. Pegasus. Pegasus. This is Tahiti Rescue station. We are monitoring."

"Tahiti Rescue," Eric began. Suddenly Pegasus was lifted, almost tossed upward, and the roar of a breaking wave was right under him. "Oh shit!" Eric said. In the split second before she fell, he knew what was happening. He grabbed the sides of the bunk and hung on desperately. Pegasus dropped over the crest of the wave in a free fall, bow down, the roar of the breaking wave deafening, as she plunged her bow into the trough and thousands of tons of water foamed over her driving her down, end over end.

Slowly, agonizingly, he felt the boat rising, her rigging and mast smashing against the cabin top and then the hull as Pegasus broke the surface. He snapped on his flashlight, swept it around the cabin. Everything was holding for the moment although water was sloshing on the floor, forced in from somewhere. He heard the bilge pump running, trying its best to pump the water out. This told him that at least some electrical systems were still working.

He squeezed the mic again. "Tahiti Rescue. This is Pegasus. I have pitch poled and am taking water. Will assess damage."

This time the answer was immediate. "Pegasus. Tahiti Rescue. Standing by."

Eric undid the strap across his waist as the boat heaved again. He hung on as it settled and then stood up, gripping a hand hold beside the bunk. A wave rolled Pegasus flat in the water. Eric grabbed for the side of the bunk as the companionway hatch cover exploded, splintering and smashing apart as the end of the boom drove into the cabin like a battering ram. Water gushed in over him and then subsided for a moment. He snapped on his flashlight, clipped it to the pocket of his survival suit and swung himself across the cabin to the companionway stairs. He heaved on the jagged aluminum spar but it was jammed firmly through the opening. A wave surged in over the cockpit and water gushed in over him again.

He stuffed a life jacket between the aluminum boom and the splintered cover. The spar moved slightly and the wind sucked the jacket out into the storm. The sea poured in over him like a low pressure fire hose, the salt burning his eyes.

Choking and coughing, Eric looked down, he was almost knee deep in water. He watched as it sloshed up the bulkheads. The pump could never handle this much. As he fumbled for another life jacket to close the hole he was deluged again. Hundreds of gallons of water were surging around inside the cabin. Pegasus was now completely unstable. He knew if she rolled over again or pitch polled once more, it would be her last. He waded across the cabin, grasping the hand hold by the bunk. He hit the EPIRB button on his emergency locator transmitter, clipped to his survival suit and plucked the radio mic out of its clip.

"Tahiti Rescue. This is Pegasus. May Day. May Day. May Day. I am holed and sinking. Out."

CHAPTER TWENTY EIGHT

Thursday, April 20, 1989 Harrisburg, Pennsylvania

Jon Falken stood outside the front door in the darkness, listening intently, trying to hear sounds above the gentle rain that was falling on the lawn behind him. The door was ajar and a light from inside cast a faint shadow on the broad front step. He was crouched slightly, ready to move instantly in any direction. Old reflexes die hard, he thought, as he held the gun pointing upwards, his index finger outside the trigger guard. He gently pushed the door open and moved smoothly into a firing position. The entry foyer was tiled, big square creamy white tiles embossed to look like marble. They were shiny and the light glistened from a single set of wet footprints going through a partially open door on the other side of the foyer. A suitcase stood outside the second door and he could hear someone in the room crying softly.

He was aware of Marianne behind him as she touched his sleeve. "Why have you got your gun, Jon?" she whispered.

She pulled her hand away as he glanced back at her and shook his head slightly. "Because we don't know what's going on."

He stepped into the foyer and crossed the tiled floor in a few fast steps. Crouching by the second door, he pushed it open fully, sweeping his eyes across the scene. Irene Delgado was huddled like a small child in the corner, whimpering, a cordless telephone receiver clasped against her shoulder, a look of sheer terror on her face. Marianne was behind him again. He had told her to wait in the car but she had refused as he knew she would. He needed his wife with him, as a witness if for no other reason.

Frank Delgado's study was an elegant room. Old oak book cases lined two of the walls, filled with leather bound editions of classics in literature, art, philosophy and a range of other subjects. Jon was always amazed to find that Frank had an interest in these esoteric topics and in most cases, had considerable knowledge of them. A huge gilt-framed painting of a cavalry charge dominated a third wall, the beautiful chargers fierce and terrifying with nostrils flared and iron shod hooves thundering into a line of infantry.

The floor was covered with a Persian carpet, its intricate pattern representing the tree of life, as Frank had once explained to him. He had acquired the carpet during a brief posting to Tehran and it had graced his study ever since. His ancient oak desk, inherited from his father, sat squarely, heavily in the centre of the room, its scarred and darkened top worn to a dull sheen.

Frank Delgado was sprawled back in the large dark leather chair behind his desk, his head thrown back. His face was pale, his eyes open, staring sightlessly at the ceiling. Fragments of bone and brain tissue were splattered on the back of the brown leather chair and in an arc across the books on the shelf behind.

Jon straightened and turned to Marianne. "Don't come in here," he said gently, blocking her way. "Frank has shot himself."

She glanced at him and then slipped past him into the room gasping as she took in the scene. She turned to Jon her eyes huge, her mouth open in a silent scream. Taking a single deep breath she turned back, crossed the room and dropping gracefully to the floor, curled Irene into her arms, slowly rocking her back and forth.

Jon slipped the gun into the pocket of his windbreaker, went over to them and took the phone from Irene. Slowly and deliberately he punched in the numbers. 911

When he ended the call a few minutes later he set the cordless receiver carefully on the corner of the desk. "Let's move to the living room, Honey," he said, crouching beside them. "I'll make us a drink."

Marianne nodded dumbly. She tried to pull Irene to her feet and after a moment Jon slipped in behind her and gathered her up in his arms, carrying her like a child, her head limply on his shoulder.

In the living room he set her down in the corner of the chesterfield. Slowly she looked around, as if coming out of a trance. She stared at Jon, then at Marianne and then buried her face in her hands as though to shut out the world.

"I'll be back in a moment," Jon said and walked across the entry foyer. He stepped out into the cold air, leaving the door ajar and stood for a moment on the front step and took several deep breaths. This would soon be over. He felt himself calming, becoming centred again. He slipped his hand back into the pocket of his windbreaker and felt the cold steel of his service pistol, the same model that had killed Frank and that was lying on the floor beside him.

Head down, he jogged across the short distance to his Ford Explorer, pulled open the passenger door and slipped in. He carefully locked the pistol in the glove box, just as Pennsylvania law required, then stepped back out into the rain and locked the door.

Returning to the house, he closed the front door behind him, slipped off his shoes, and padded across the tiled entry to an old oak sideboard behind the chesterfield. In the second cupboard that he tried, he found the scotch decanter and poured a generous amount into each of three heavy crystal highball glasses.

Irene seemed calmer now, her head resting on Marianne's shoulder. He handed each of them a glass. Irene took hers and swallowed a large gulp. She leaned back and sighed.

"How could he do that?" she whispered. "How?"

Jon said nothing and took a small sip of his drink. It wasn't a question that had an answer. He swirled the scotch around on his tongue, savouring the rich mellow flavour. He would likely have to give it up for bourbon when he was a congressman.

As he watched the two women, he thought back over the years that he and Frank had been together, from junior officers in Vietnam, to positions in the Pentagon. It had been a long road. He thought of his last meeting with Frank, yesterday, when he had asked him to work on his congressional campaign, although he knew that it would never happen. Frank had become unreliable, perhaps the booze, perhaps too many other things. Who knew the mind of another man? Frank had agreed to help him, of course, and they had left the officers' mess together and come to Frank's house for a drink.

The door chimes jarred him out of his reverie. He strode across the room and opened the front door. A uniformed policeman stood there, his cruiser parked behind Jon's Explorer.

"Come in, please. I'm Jon Falken."

"Officer Rainier," the policeman replied, stepping into the foyer and closing the door behind him. "You called 911?"

"I did," Jon said. "Thank you for your quick response."

The policeman nodded. "The dispatcher said you called in a suicide."

"Yes," Jon said.

"May I see the body?"

The policeman removed his hat as he walked across the living room. He was tall, slim and looked about sixteen. Take the uniform off and he could pass for a high school basketball player.

Jon led him to the door of the study and stood aside as he peered in to examine the scene.

"You've been in the room?" he asked Jon.

"Yes, to get his wife."

"I'll have to ask you not to enter the room again. We have a couple of detectives on the way who will take your statements and initiate the investigation."

"I understand," Jon said.

The policeman walked back to the front hallway with Jon following. "I have a few questions now," he said, taking out a small hard covered notebook. "Were you the one who called 911?"

"I was."

For the next few minutes Jon continued to answer a series of basic factual questions. He knew the procedure. The cop would secure the crime scene, although in this case there wasn't much to secure and he wasn't certain whether the police would consider a suicide to be a crime scene. He would gather basic information and then turn the investigative part over to detectives.

Jon heard a car door slam and a few moments later the door chimes rang again. He opened the door. Two men in rumpled business suits stood on the step, their dark sedan parked beside the Explorer.

The taller of the two detectives was black, solid and muscular. Jon guessed he would have been a lineman in college. He offered a small leather ID folder for Jon's inspection. "Good evening, Mr. Falken," he said, his voice surprisingly high and lilting. "I'm Lieutenant Gardner, this is Sargent Odaka.." He motioned to a short Asian looking man behind him, also holding out a leather ID wallet. Jon shook hands with both of them. Since he'd decided to run for Congress shaking hands had become almost a reflex.

He ushered them into the foyer closing the door behind them. "Where would you like to start, gentlemen?"

"We'll chat with our colleague for a moment and then we'd like to talk with you," Gardener replied.

"Of course," Jon said. He walked back into the living room leaving the two detectives and the uniformed police officer by the front door.

A few minutes later, Lieutenant Gardner entered the living room and motioned for Jon to join them in the foyer. "Perhaps we could talk here for a moment, "Gardner said. "What happened?

"This is the home of Frank and Irene Delgado, close friends of ours." Jon glanced at his watch. It was a few minutes after ten. "About half an hour ago, perhaps a bit more, we got a call from Irene. She was hysterical and said that Frank was dead. We came right over."

"And you are the one that called 911, Mr. Falken?" Gardner asked.

"Please call me Jon. Yes, I was."

"Did you make the call from home or from here?"

"From here," Jon replied.

"Why not immediately from home, Jon?" Gardner's eyes narrowed as he stared at Jon. "Why did you think it necessary to come here in person before calling 911? Was something wrong?"

CHAPTER TWENTY NINE

Thursday, April 20, 1989 The Poconos

Lincoln Carswell heard them before he saw them, a faint rustling of last fall's leaves, then a twig snapped. A chipmunk chattered quickly for a moment, scolding something, and then silence. He felt the warmth of the sun seeping slowly through his Ghillie suit, but he was only peripherally aware of these things. He breathed slowly and relaxed, his eyes staring unfocused into the bare trees across the clearing, beech and birch soaring like empty talons reaching upward, a light breeze swaying them against the clear blue sky. Bracken and low shrubs grew close to the ground broken by an occasional small animal trail that wound through them.

One of his pursuers moved into sight on the far side of the clearing, the spotted camouflage blending him into the background, the smoky black rifle a dark scar across the front of his uniform. A second man appeared behind him. They scanned the clearing and then moved quickly across the open area and crouched behind a fallen log a few yards to his right.

Lincoln slowly shifted his gaze to the left. Two more soldiers moved out of the bush and slipped quickly into position behind separate trees. Basic fire and movement tactics, he thought, standard stuff but well executed. The first pair moved again, out of his line of sight, shuffling softly through the leaves and loam. The next moment would tell. They would look back over him to signal their partners and if they saw him he would have a second or two to respond before they caught him in their cross fire. He watched an ant crawl slowly across his gloved hand and onto the dull steel of his weapon, then veer back to the comforting warmth of his leather glove.

The two soldiers on his left were moving again, slipping quietly past his left flank about twenty feet away. He listened and heard the first two men move again and a few moments later the second two. He stared ahead, listening intently. Slowly he raised his head and then turned as he sat up, emerging like some leafy monster from a cocoon. He peered through the branches of the bush behind him, easily picking out the first pair. They were in position facing a rocky outcrop looking for a way to flank it. It was a perfect ambush site and judging from their approach, they would expect him there. For a moment he couldn't find the second pair and then they moved, farther away from the first pair than he had expected. A crow, glossy and black, came drifting down and settled on the branch of a tree above him. It looked down at Lincoln and squawked a couple of times. Frozen in his half sitting position, he waited to be spotted but none of the soldiers looked back.

He swung his rifle carefully toward the two men on his left, lined one of them up and squeezed the trigger. The rifle bounced lightly on his shoulder and he saw a red stain blossom on the back of the soldier's jacket. He caught the second man as he turned, a solid upper body shot.

The other two were scrambling for cover. He snapped a shot off at one of them as he ducked behind a gnarled old beech tree and caught a glimpse of red on his upper arm or shoulder. The second one fired back but the shot was well to the left. He hadn't been sighted yet.

Lincoln crouched, utterly still, and watched as the last soldier scanned the clearing looking for him. Lincoln waited until his head was turned away, then raised his rifle, aiming carefully, a bit high, and squeezed the trigger. The soldier looked back toward Lincoln as a red blotch exploded on the plastic face cover of his helmet.

Lincoln slowly stood up and watched as the others got to their feet. He walked forward toward the first two he had hit.

"Jeez, Linc," one of them said. "You did that really well."

"Yeah," the other one said. "You make a great fox."

Lincoln smiled. "You guys were very good hounds. You just didn't expect me to be hidden in the open." They had been executing a stalking game, they called it Fox and Hounds, where one of them was given a ten minute head start and the other four came after the first one.

He heard the sound of a motor and moments later an ATV towing a small trailer pulled into the clearing. The driver waved at them. "Ready to go?" he asked.

The stalkers got into the trailer. Lincoln mounted the seat behind the driver and they set off.

The Free America Militia was a form of therapy for Lincoln Carswell. It was a physical outlet for his pent up energies, but more importantly, it built his self-esteem in a way that his other talents had failed to do. He had wanted to go to Vietnam but asthma and allergies kept him out of the armed forces. The recruiting sergeant told him he had a great attitude but a random sneeze could get him killed, his buddies too. So he had become a fitness buff, working out, building muscle and endurance.

After years of tests and medical consultations he had started researching on his own. He read everything he could find on asthma and allergies. There were suggestions it was stress related. He took up Transcendental Meditation, a simple process, easy to learn, that involved the repetition of a mantra, essentially a nonsense word, and have the mind become aware of nothing but itself. At first that made no sense to him at all but as he had become more adept at it, he had accomplished it. He had done a couple of twenty minute sessions almost every day since. It worked amazingly well to alleviate stress. He changed his diet, organic food, no night shade vegetables, no red meat. Gradually, with these and other changes, the asthma receded. He rarely used his medical puffer anymore.

The allergies were more difficult to deal with since they seemed to be seasonal, pollen and other things in the air. He had found a naturopathic physician and undergone a series of homeopathic treatments which helped to some degree. Living in the city avoided a lot of the natural irritants. He had an excellent air filtration system in his home but he still took an antihistamine this morning before the militia exercise.

The ATV pulled into a clearing occupied by a single low building, nothing more than a large metal machine shed, painted an olive drab colour. They dismounted and went inside, chatting a bit more about the exercise. Carswell said little. He was finished with the morning. He had won again as he usually did when he was the fox. Very few in this group trained rigorously. Most were here for the political rhetoric, the talk of America in decline, the greatest enemy being the enemy within. Their job was to protect themselves and their families and perhaps all of America eventually against the threat of the Federal Government. No other force in the world could destroy the liberties and freedoms that the founding fathers had fought for and that were enshrined in the American Constitution. They believed Government was involved in an insidious process that day by day, year by year, slowly eroded these fundamental rights as surely as the Colorado River had eroded the Grand Canyon.

Carswell spun the combination on his locker, pulled it open and got out of his camouflage suit, hanging it carefully so it would be ready for his next exercise. He cleaned his paint ball rifle, and snapped it into a clip inside his locker. He grabbed a bar of soap and wrapped a towel around his waist. As he walked past the picnic table where his four companions were drinking beer, one of them waved a can at him but he shook his head.

"C'mon, Linc, ya gotta loosen up," the guy with the can said.

"Thanks, Johnny," Carswell said. "But I've got to work this afternoon."

The shower area was a small room with a drain in the concrete floor and four shower heads coming out of the wall. He hung his towel on a hook and turned on the one of the shower heads, waiting for a couple of minutes until the water turned from icy cold to lukewarm. He only stayed in the shower long enough to get the sweat off since he knew he'd be showering again as soon as he got home. He dried himself, wrapped the towel around his waist again and returned to his locker. On his way back, he noticed his buddies were opening a second six pack. This would lubricate the developing political rant.

As he pulled his clothes on he wondered, not for the first time, why he enjoyed doing this so much but had so little interest in the political agenda. He was politically on the far right but he didn't view the Federal Government as the enemy. He doubted that they could get well enough organized to present a serious threat to America.

In his view the "enemy" was the legion of citizens with a sense of entitlement. They thought that by virtue of being American they were entitled to the full American Dream, and that they only had to find out who was going to give it to them. A few of them worked hard, most of them did nothing, but they all believed in the American way of life, a house in the suburbs, a couple of cars in the driveway, an RV in the back yard or a summer cottage or a ski chalet somewhere else, good schools for the kids. This, or something close to it, was their birthright. The responsibility of government was to make it happen. This citizen view of the country was common to every society in history as it entered the final stages of decline and fall. America deserved better.

He closed his locker, snapped on the padlock and went out the door. The sun seemed brighter now. He pulled a pair of sunglasses from the pocket of his jacket and slipped them on as he got into his Ford half ton truck. Back to the real world, he thought, as he drove out of the compound.

CHAPTER THIRTY

Friday, April 21, 1989 West of Tahiti

Eric O'Neill came awake suddenly and tried to roll to a sitting position inside the small fully enclosed inflatable life raft. He managed to pull himself half upright with one of the small handles inside. He gagged and coughed, his throat burning with the taste of his own vomit. The raft heaved gently and settled back. As he reached up to the zipper on the sealed canopy over his head, he felt a twinge of pain in his shoulder. Pulling the zipper up, he peered out at the ocean as the small survival raft rose on the crest of a swell. The morning light was a gray tinge in the blackness ahead of him.

For a few moments he breathed in the fresh air, barely a sniff at first and then in great gulping lungfulls. He dropped back onto the floor of the raft. It had taken in a little seawater during the night and judging by the smell, a lot of the contents of his own stomach as well. Not much wonder considering the storm had tossed it about like a beach ball, throwing him around inside it, until he had managed to hook himself into the straps. Then the beating had lessened somewhat. He reached up and pushed the zipper open a little farther and looked out again. Light was creeping across the eastern horizon.

The wind had dropped back to a few knots and with it the waves had moderated, leaving long swells rolling gently under him. He checked himself carefully, moving his fingers, wiggling his toes, slowly stretching his arms, legs and neck. Every movement caused a little discomfort but when he was finished examining himself he was confident that nothing was broken or seriously damaged. The aching and stiffness would disappear in a day or so. In the faint light he began a methodical check of the raft, first bailing out what looked like a couple of gallons of vile bilge from the floor. His emergency supplies had survived intact, zipped into their pockets around the perimeter. He took a small drink of what was dubiously labelled "Fresh Water". It tasted stale but at least it wasn't salty. The small light glowed on his emergency radio beacon which should mean that a signal was going out to Tahiti Rescue or anyone else who monitored the signals. By the time he was finished checking the raft it was fully light, the dull grey sky and dark pewter sea stretching endlessly off to the horizon. He zipped up the enclosure and sank back against the edge of the raft. It rocked gently, mocking the fury of the night. He laughed out loud and was seized with a fit of coughing. His ribs ached. It was good to be alive. Faintly at first and then louder, he heard the distant thwacking sound of a helicopter.

Friday, April 21, 1989 Papeete, Tahiti

As he waited at the counter in the Port Captain's office, he was glad he had taken the time to shower, shave and put on clean clothes before he came ashore this morning. The French navy had outfitted him with white shorts, a military cut shirt, soft-soled canvas shoes, a razor and personal kit and a bag to put his old and new possessions in. The air conditioner was on high and the bureaucrats were starchy formal in their white uniforms. He had finished filling out his customs and immigration forms and had been passed on to another official.

"You are Canadian, Monsieur," the clerk behind the counter said in French. "But your boat was Australian?"

"I bought the boat in Australia and kept the registry," Eric replied in French.

The clerk smiled. "Oui, Monsieur O'Neill, I understand. Please accept my sincere condolences on the loss of your boat."

"I am grateful for the rescue by your navy," Eric said formally.

The clerk leaned over the counter and offered his hand. "Enjoy your stay in French Polynesia, Monsieur."

Eric stepped into the street and as the mid-day heat settled around him, his forehead beaded with perspiration. Funny how the world seemed hotter when he was on land, the loss of the sea breeze perhaps. He walked slowly down the seawall, glancing up at the majestic row of palm trees that skirted it. A large open parking lot lay between him and a cruise ship wharf, a small one by most standards. A navy lieutenant had told him it was transformed each evening at dusk into a food market, small stalls and trailers appearing magically and dispensing all sorts of food, even a few crafts if you looked carefully.

To his left, traffic hummed by on the main thoroughfare, two lanes in each direction for the most part but adventurous souls sometimes extended this to three. The French seemed to have exported their style of driving to Tahiti. North Americans tended to use the accelerator and the brake as the two main instruments in driving, other than the steering wheel. The French favoured the accelerator and the horn.

He waited at a street light and crossed after the third car had gone through the red light. A block down he turned into the American Express office, offered his American Express Gold

Card, and left a few minutes later with some French Pacific francs and information on where to make long distance calls. There had been no mail for him but he had expected that.

At the telephone exchange, another block away, he gave the number to the operator behind the counter, handed her several French Pacific bank notes and went to a booth to wait. The phone rang after a couple of minutes and the operator explained in French that she was getting a recorded message in English that she could play through for him but as she didn't speak English, she didn't know what it was saying. Eric hung up and waited again. The phone rang and he picked it up. "The number you are calling is no longer in service. Please check the number you have dialed and try again."

Eric stepped out of the small phone booth and heard the hiss of the traffic punctuated by the muted sounds of horns coming through the closed door of the telephone exchange.

An old man and a little girl were sitting on a bench near the operator's counter. They stared at him as he walked across the small room. The little girl tugged at the worn sleeve of the man's old grey jacket, then covering her mouth with her hand, she said something to him. The old man wore a black beret, pulled rakishly to one side, with a small pipe protruding from the other side of his mouth. He pulled the pipe from his mouth and leaned to whisper something back to her. She stood up and faced the old man, smoothing her dress. He smiled down at her as she peeked over her shoulder at Eric.

Back at the counter, he checked the number with the operator but she confirmed that she had dialed the correct number. He thanked her and stepped outside, enveloped by the heat again, the soft tropical air smelling faintly of gasoline and diesel fumes from the traffic on the boulevard. He stood for a moment breathing deeply and then strolled down the street. A couple of blocks from the telephone exchange he found a small restaurant with a raised outdoor patio area, climbed the two steps, pulled a chair around into the shade of the table's umbrella. As he sat down, he realized he was tired, emotionally drained from his last night on the ocean.

Looking out over the street and the traffic, he watched the afternoon breeze ruffle the waters of the harbour. In the distant haze he could make out the mountains of Moorea, twelve miles away, if he remembered his charts. A waiter strolled over and he ordered a cafe au lait and a couple of pastries, surprised by his sudden hunger.

He had been fortunate to have his wallet and passport in his survival suit. Had he really expected to lose Pegasus or was he just being a prudent sailor? But now without the boat he realized he had a new set of choices to make, or at least to think about. He could buy another boat and continue on his journey, wherever it was that he was going. He could end his sailing adventure and return to Canada. He could sit here and enjoy his coffee and think about it. He chuckled. There was a time when the third option would not have even occurred to him. Maybe that was progress.

"Monsieur," the waiter interrupted his reverie as he set a tray down on the table, picked up two small ceramic pots and poured streams of rich dark coffee and steaming milk into a cup. He set the pots down and put a plate of pastries in front of Eric.

"Merci," Eric said, smiling up at him.

The waiter nodded and turned away

Eric took a sip of his coffee and stared off toward Moorea again. He took a bite of the pastry, something flaky with a tart lemon filling and thought about his phone call. If no one answered, he normally got a message recorded by his father, but phone systems weren't always reliable. Still, the recorded message had been from Canada, or some other English speaking country, not from Tahiti. He would try again later. He called his parents every month or so to let them know where he was, that he was alive and well and to get caught up on any news he needed to hear. It was funny how he needed that contact with his origins. He wondered if Laura was still there. Perhaps he would phone her to check on his parents. Something else to think about. Calling home had worked well for the last two years.

Two years? Had it really been that long? He knew it had but some days it seemed like he had been out a few weeks. At other times he felt like he had spent all his life at sea. He sipped his coffee again, strong and rich, smoothed with the hot milk. Had this sojourn really helped him sort things out? Perhaps, but more importantly it had given him a sense of peace. Maybe running away hadn't been such a bad idea after all, although most people who did it didn't wait until they were his age. He smiled at the thought of turning fifty this fall and wondered what he would do to celebrate. Dierdre would have known what to do, at least at the socially correct level, but his wife was gone. Was that part of the peace he felt? No point in getting too introspective about it.

A couple with three small children came up the steps and into the patio area. They looked around and selected a table with a large umbrella in the corner opposite to where Eric sat. He listened to the children chatter as they squirmed in their seats, the parents telling them, with little success, to sit still and wait. The father's voice carried clearly and Eric suddenly recognized the accent and the patterns of speech. Quebec. They were Canadians but many from Quebec regarded that as an accusation. He hadn't encountered many Canadians recently and none from La Belle Province in the last eighteen months.

He had left behind everything he had, which wasn't much more than a lot of money and a successful career. He smiled at that. He knew people who would kill for what he'd walked away from. He'd also had a marriage that people envied. Not just the perfect couple, it went far beyond that, the perfect couple in the perfect lifestyle, the perfect home, the blindingly successful career, the beautiful child. He shook his head, saddened by the memory that such success could result in so much unhappiness and also by the vision that others had of their perfection. It had felt fraudulent at the time. It was socially fraudulent in a way to be part of that image, to set up something that others might strive for and if they got it, find it a hollow and meaningless shell as he had. But maybe others would have made a success of it where he and Deirdre had failed.

Sweet Deirdre, so beautiful, so elegant, so tragic. He had loved her too much in some ways, not enough in others. He exceeded all her expectations and those of her family, too. He knew what her family thought of him when he married into it, some Manitoba peasant from some hick town west of Winnipeg, which was, after all, just a bigger hick town. It was called "Portage-something-or-other." He wondered why they let their precious daughter marry him at all. He wasn't from the right class, and that name, O'Neill. It was Irish, wasn't it? He wouldn't be blowing things up, would he? He wasn't Anglican! My God, he wasn't Catholic, was he? At least he wasn't a Jew. Apparently there were a lot of them in Winnipeg. There was something quite wrong in Winnipeg when they could elect a man like Jacob Penner to their City Council, the only duly elected communist in North America. But somehow Eric had passed their scrutiny, had taken the humiliation and set it aside.

In time he discovered his mother-in-law was a lush, his father-in-law a businessman who was in way over his head and who would have foundered without his intervention. This made them hate him, where before they merely looked down on him. But all this, too, had been hidden under the public image. The joyful family circle, expanded to include young Eric O'Neill, "Keep your eye on him, he'll do great things". And he had. But here he was, alone with his cafe au lait, in a small bistro on the waterfront of Papeete, trying to phone home to Portage la Prairie, the hick town fifty miles west of Winnipeg that his in-laws had never been to and listening to a telephone voice thousands of miles away telling him no one was there, or perhaps that there was no phone any more.

Here he was, too, a survivor again, this time from the fury of the sea. He shuddered as he thought of his last minutes aboard Pegasus. Every offshore sailor wondered how he would react if he ever faced a serious storm. As near as he could tell, he had done everything right but he had still lost his boat. Launching the survival raft had been terrifying with waves smashing over him, wind howling by him and the awful fear it would tear the raft away before he could get in it, or that it would snag in the flailing rigging and go down with Pegasus. Would this bring a lifetime of nightmares? He was rather surprised that as he was trying to phone his parents, he really hadn't figured out what he was going to tell them other than that he was well. He was definitely not going to tell them about last night's adventure.

He leaned back and closed his eyes, felt the heat of the afternoon sun though his eyelids. Home. Funny thing to call the small prairie city where he had grown up but that was where he was going to go next. Go home . . . for a visit . . . not to live . . . not to see Laura, she was married . . . or not *just* to see Laura.

He left a handful of francs on the table and walked into the street again. On the large concrete apron in front of the harbour, vendors were setting up small stalls, some of them out of the backs of cars, others in small trailers towed from somewhere, a few canvas shelters. He crossed the street and stopped by one of them selling pareaus, large rectangles of colourful gauze-like cotton that could be wrapped like a skirt, tied like a dress, used as a table cloth. He laughed at the enthusiasm of the old woman as she slipped it around her ample body in a variety of styles. He picked a blue one with pale waves of creamy white running through it. Perhaps he would give it to Laura. On an impulse, he walked back toward the telephone exchange. He could at least phone her.

Would he give up his vagabond life and return to reality? Not today, he decided.

CHAPTER THIRTY ONE

Thursday, April 20, 1989 Harrisburg, Pennsylvania

Jon stared back at Lieutenant Gardner, shaken as much by the question as the tone. Why would Gardner ask if something was wrong? He paused for a moment. "I don't know . . . I guess we were just overcome . . . we only live a five minute drive away. I suppose I wasn't thinking clearly."

Gardner's voice softened. "Please don't be concerned, Jon. These are traumatic circumstances."

Odaka spoke for the first time. "Could we see the body, please?"

Jon led them to the door of the study and motioned them inside. They both peered in through the door. "Did you enter the room?" Odaka asked. He pulled on a pair of surgical gloves.

"Yes," Jon replied. "My wife and I found Irene in the corner of the room. I called you from here."

"Did you touch anything?"

Jon thought for a moment. "I don't know. I might have touched the desk but nothing else."

"Except the phone?" Odaka asked.

"Yes, of course," Jon said.

"That's the phone on the corner of the desk?"

"Yes."

Odaka stepped into the room and looked carefully at Frank's body sprawled back in the leather chair. Then he turned and left the room, slipping off the gloves as he went out the front door.

Jon looked at Gardiner and raised his eyebrows.

"Sergeant Odaka will call in the details from the car."

Gardner led Jon back to the foyer. As they passed through the living room Jon saw that Marianne and Irene were still huddled together in the corner of the chesterfield. Marianne was comforting Irene but from the expression of anguish on her face, he knew she was also badly shaken. He felt strangely nervous.

"When Mrs. Delgado called you, did she say that her husband was dead? Or that he had committed suicide?" Gardner asked. He took a small notebook from an inside pocket of his suit and wrote something in it.

Jon thought for a moment. "She said Frank was dead."

Gardner looked at him carefully. "It likely isn't important, but are you certain that is what she said?"

"Yes. She said that Frank was dead."

Gardner nodded. "Okay," he went on. "When you were in the study did you see a note or anything resembling one?"

"I'm sorry, Lieutenant, I just saw Frank and Irene and I didn't think of much else but to call 911."

"Of course." He paused while he noted something in the small book. "I take it you were a good friend of Frank Delgado's?"

"We served together in Vietnam and in a number of other military postings. He was my adjutant for a while."

"So you knew him well?

"I guess as well as anyone, except Irene, of course."

"Any reason you can think of that would make Mr. Delgado take his own life?"

Jon shook his head. "Not really," he said slowly. "But he retired a year ago and seemed kind of rootless after that. He was always a social drinker, nothing more than that, but in the last year he was drinking rather heavily."

Gardner nodded his head sympathetically. "I wonder if you could expand on that a bit. What do you mean by 'heavily'?"

Jon thought for a moment. It seemed like as good a time as any to tell him. "The last time I saw Frank was yesterday. We met at the mess around two for a drink. Frank had already had a few drinks when I arrived. We talked for a while and around 4:30 or so came back here. He had borrowed a book of mine some time ago and I needed it back. I wanted to get a quote out of it for a speech I'm preparing. While we were at the mess he was having doubles, I was having singles and he was still ahead of me when we left."

"How many drinks did you have, Jon?"

"Three, as I recall."

Gardner looked up from his notebook. "So Mr. Delgado would have had perhaps four doubles in about two and a half hours?"

"I'd say that was about right."

"Was he showing any obvious signs of intoxication?"

"Like slurring his words or something like that?"

Gardner nodded.

"Perhaps a little but nothing too obvious. He was talkative but that was normal."

"Did you drink anything when you came back here?"

"Frank poured us each a drink in his study. We chatted a bit more, I got the book and then left."

"The drinks that he poured here, would they have been doubles, too?"

"At least."

"Do you know if this was his daily pattern of drinking?"

"I think Irene could answer that better than I could."

"What was Mr. Delgado doing when you left him?"

"He followed me out to the front door and made some comment about another TV dinner night. Irene was away visiting some relatives for a few days and just got home tonight."

"So he was alive and well when you left?"

"Yes, he was a little drunk, but fine otherwise. He seemed in good spirits."

"About what time would that have been?"

"I would guess close to 5:30."

Odaka joined them. "Forensics will be along shortly," he said.

"Could we chat to your wife for a few minutes? Perhaps in another room?"

"The kitchen," Jon said. "Follow me."

Entering the living room, Jon introduced the detectives to Marianne and Irene and showed Marianne and the detectives into the kitchen in the rear of the house. He returned to Irene and sat down on the chesterfield. She seemed calmer now, staring vacantly across the room. He took her glass and got up, pouring them each another scotch. He could hear the murmur of voices from the kitchen but couldn't make out the words.

He handed the glass back to Irene, walked over to the gas fireplace on the opposite wall, and switched it on. It burst into flame, the tendrils of fire weaving a flickering pattern around the ceramic logs. It was peaceful and reassuring. He walked back and forth in front of it for a moment, then sat down close to Irene. She snuggled against him and he slipped his arm around her, drawing her comfortingly close. She still felt good.

He took a sip of his scotch and thought back on his last conversation with Frank. He had confronted Frank, had tested him in a sense, and Frank had failed. Frank had never been a very convincing liar. He was too much of a straight arrow to be truly valuable to him in his emerging political career.

Marianne walked back into the living room. "Lieutenant Gardner wants to talk to you." She looked at the scotch he was holding and took it from him. He reluctantly disengaged himself from Irene, got up and went into the kitchen.

"Please sit down, Jon. This will only take a moment," Gardner said. "We just need to tie up a couple of things."

Jon nodded and sat down opposite Gardener.

"By the way, are you the retired Colonel Jon Falken that's going after the congressional nomination?"

Jon nodded again. "That's me," he said, smiling.

"I read about you in the paper the other day, "Gardner said. "You had quite a military career, didn't you?"

Jon smiled again, wondering where this was going. "A lot of Americans serve their country."

"You certainly did that, Colonel, and a lot of your time was in Special Forces, wasn't it?"

"Yes," Jon replied. "A lot of it was."

"So you can't talk much about it in your campaign?" Gardner said. "That's a real shame, sir."

"You sound like you were in the services, too."

"I was, sir. Two tours in Vietnam. I was in the marines." Gardner leaned back in his chair. "Now that brings me to a couple of things we need to clear up." He leaned forward again, staring intently across the table at Jon. "Your wife said that when you entered the house this evening you were carrying a gun. Why was that, sir?"

"I wasn't sure what was happening and I guess I wanted to be prepared."

"Colonel, you have had a lot of experience with this kind of thing and I just don't understand why you did that."

Jon stared back silently. There was a sudden hum behind him as the refrigerator came on.

"You see, sir, if you knew Frank Delgado committed suicide, you'd have known there was no danger and you wouldn't have needed the gun. Am I correct, sir?"

"Yes, but I didn't know that he had committed suicide. I only knew he was dead." Jon stopped as he realized he was answering questions that hadn't been asked.

"Yes, sir. That's what you said." Gardner wrote something in his notebook. "So what did you think was happening over here when you got the phone call from Mrs. Delgado?"

"I wasn't sure. I just knew that something was terribly wrong."

"Like maybe a robbery?"

"I suppose so," Jon replied.

"What about a heart attack or some other natural cause?"

"I didn't really think about it, I just came over. He was my close friend."

"Exactly, sir. That is just how a normal person would react. But you are not a normal person, Colonel. You are an experienced soldier, a Special Forces combat officer with years of experience in situations of this type. I find it hard to understand why you entered a danger zone when you knew one of your officers was dead, that you did this alone, a handgun drawn, with no backup and without notifying anyone of your course of action. I find it particularly difficult to understand why you chose this course of action with your wife right behind you, fully exposed to whatever danger there might have been. That is not what I would have expected someone like you to have done."

Jon was silent. Then he shook his head ruefully. "You're right, of course, Lieutenant. It was stupid of me. I just wasn't thinking straight."

Odaka spoke. "Either that, Colonel," he said softly. "Either that, or you knew there was no danger."

"What the hell is that supposed to mean," Jon snapped.

Odaka sat back in his chair and regarded Jon coldly.

Gardner spoke quickly. "I think the Sargent is just covering all the bases, Colonel. Of course, you were upset and we don't always act as rationally as we would wish when that kind of personal stress hits us."

Jon backed the Explorer out of the Delgado driveway.

"Didn't you have any idea at all, Jon?" Marianne asked. "Surely there must have been some clue."

Jon put the vehicle in drive. "I only wish there had been some sign, something he had said to me, some hint that I might have reacted to, but there was nothing." He glanced at her. "There was nothing unless you count having a few more drinks than usual as a sign, and we both know that Frank was drinking more than usual in the last few months."

He slowed at an unsigned intersection and then drove on. "It's no consolation, Marianne, but thousands of other Vietnam vets have also committed suicide."

Marianne was silent.

"Frank chose his time to die," Jon said quietly. "A lot of soldiers don't get that choice."

"All that macho bullshit might be comforting to you, but when a man kills himself at forty eight after he's gotten through all the wars he's ever going to fight and has the rest of his life to live, I think it's a tragedy, not a choice."

It was Jon's turn to be silent.

"I'm sorry, Jon," she said softly and reached over to squeeze his hand. "I shouldn't be angry when you say things like that. It's just that they don't comfort women a whole lot."

"They don't comfort men a whole lot either."

CHAPTER THIRTY TWO

Friday, April 21, 1989 Portage la Prairie, Canada

Dr. Laura Schaefer sat at her desk staring into the pool of light spilling across the scarred surface of her old oak desk. She was reading a file but as she got to the bottom of the first page she realized she had no idea what she had just read. She took her reading glasses off and set them on the paper. The old brass clock on her desk ticked softly and seemed to stare accusingly at her with its white enamel face. Its hands told her it was 7:30 pm. The round brass bell on the top with the little knocker beside it was silent, thank God. Once in a while when she wound it, she pushed something she shouldn't and it went off a few hours later and almost stopped her heart. She reached back and massaged her neck. Time to go home. She shook her head. Time to go to where she lived, at any rate. Darrin would be into his third rye and coke by now wondering where the hell dinner was. She looked at the calendar on the opposite wall to see what night it was. Tuesday. Not his poker night so he'd be waiting, watching a hockey game, eating another of the endless bags of junk food he kept around for snacks when dinner didn't "happen".

As she stood up and turned off the desk lamp the phone rang in the outer office. She picked up her glasses and put them in the case. She was taking her coat off the hanger on the back of her office door when the night answering machine came on. She listened to her receptionist's voice, so formal for a small town doctor. "Thank you for calling the office of Dr. Laura Schaefer. Office hours are . . ." She slipped her coat on, closed her office door as she stepped into the reception area and then she froze.

"Hello Laura," the familiar voice said, still quiet with that faint huskiness that made her think of leaves rustling in the fall. "I'm sorry to bother you but . . ."

She snatched up the receiver. "Eric."

The line was silent for a moment. "Laura?" The voice sounded faint and far away, hollow and electronic but it was still Eric.

"Yes," she replied and swallowed as she realized her throat had gone dry. "It's Laura. Where are you?"

"I'm in Tahiti," Eric said. There was a noise in the background, like the rush of traffic or maybe waves on a beach. "I tried calling home but all I get is a recorded message telling me that the number is no longer in service."

"Funny," Laura thought. "He still calls it 'home', his childhood home that he hasn't lived in since he was seventeen. "Eric," she said quietly. "There's some bad news." She listened to the silence on phone. "Oh God," Laura whispered to herself as she realized the enormity of what she was about to tell him.

"I'm sorry, I didn't hear what you said."

"Eric," Laura said. She had gone through this conversation a thousand times and it was a painfully new experience every time she did it, especially painful now. She took a deep breath. "Your parents were killed in a car accident last night. There was no way to get in touch with you. I knew you called them every month or so. Katherine told me. She always let me know after one of your calls. Oh, Eric, I am so sorry to have to tell you this."

There was a long sigh and then silence for a moment. "I'll be home soon. Has anyone been to the house or done anything?"

"I have a key," Laura said. "Katherine gave me one a few years ago because I volunteered to look after Mergetroid when they went travelling."

"Mergatroid," Eric repeated softly. "Is that old cat still alive?"

"Still alive but I picked her up today. I thought she could live with me for a while." Laura wondered why she hadn't said 'live with us'. "I've been to the house, Eric, but just to make sure the heat is on and to water Katherine's plants. I haven't done anything else. I cleaned out the fridge." And I went to your room and laid on your bed, she thought, and remembered the nights a long time ago when we lay there together and talked about our dreams and listened to the crickets call in the long twilight evenings of the last summer we were in love. Oh shit, why did this have to happen.

"Thank you, Laura," Eric said. "And thank you for telling me. I know that couldn't have been easy."

Nothing with you has ever been easy, she thought. Not loving you, not leaving you, not losing you, not even seeing you now and then, and most of all not thinking of you married to that rich moron.

Laura was looking at the mirror on the back of the door to her reception area. She watched herself come into a blurry focus through the tears, her dark blonde hair tousled, no make-up left, her baggy coat open. Haggard, that's what she saw.

Her face was drawn, her eyes especially gave her away. They were just dull, dead. There was no sparkle at all. It was easy to blame it on a lack of sleep last night but she knew it went a lot deeper than that. She sighed. Underneath she was still pretty good but you'd never know it by looking at her.

Why was she even thinking about this? She knew why. Every time Eric showed up in her life she got a weak feeling in the pit of her stomach. It was there now, she realized, deep and pervasive underneath the overwhelming sadness of losing Gil and Katherine.

"Are you still there, Laura?"

"Yes," she whispered. "When are you coming home? I guess you have to put your boat in storage or whatever you do to it and get a ticket out of there."

She listened to the silence for a moment. "My boat sank in a storm last night. I was rescued by the French Navy so at least I don't have to worry about that."

"My God, Eric! Are you all right? That must have been terrifying."

"Yes, it was, but I'm fine, Laura, really I am." He paused again. "I'll try to get a flight out of here tonight or tomorrow. It'll depend on when flights are available."

"Call me when you know?"

"I will."

She tried to think of something to say. "I am so sorry, Eric."

"Me too."

"I'll hear from you in a few days?"

"Is it still easier to get you at the office?"

"Yes, just call here." Laura was pleased in a small way that he had remembered their last conversation and her comment that it was better not to call her at home as she was seldom there. They both knew that wasn't the real reason. "Leave a message if I'm not here."

"Okay. Thanks again for all you've done."

"It wasn't much," she said. "Goodnight, Eric."

"Good night, Laura." There was still the sound of waves rushing in the background. "I'll be in touch."

She put the phone back in its cradle, scarcely aware of when she started to cry but she put her head down on the desk and sobbed. Her body shook. She was so tired of it all, of all the things that might have been. After a few minutes she stood and went back into her office. There was a small bathroom off to one side. She turned the light on, slipped her coat off and tossed it at her office chair. After washing her face she felt a little better.

She replayed her conversation with Eric. He must be in shock. She hadn't handled it well, not like she should have. She should have been professionally sympathetic and understanding and she had just blurted it out. She knew Eric would understand but it didn't help a lot. She thought back to the last time she had seen him in 1980 at the high school reunion and then again, briefly in 1983 at his sister Lisa's funeral. God what a tragic life he'd had. She felt almost guilty worrying about her own small cares and woes. But they weren't small, Godammit. They were her life. The life she could have had. The life she chose not to have or maybe she and Eric both chose not to have. Not choosing was still a choice. She felt tears, hot and angry, welling into her eyes again.

Her whole face felt puffy but she doubted that Darrin would notice. He rarely noticed much. How had she ever gotten herself into this life. She had wanted kids but none ever came. She had wanted a marriage that was full of a rich and enduring love. Whatever she was enduring, it wasn't rich and it wasn't love. It had started well, full of fun and promise. Where had it gone? A long story and not one she felt like thinking about right now.

She did a final check in the mirror, patted down her hair, switched the light off and went back into her office. Retrieving her coat, she glanced at the old brass clock and saw it was now a little after eight. Snow was falling softly as she let herself out, hopefully the last snow of a long winter.

CHAPTER THIRTY THREE

Friday, April 21, 1989 Harrisburg, Pennsylvania

Jon Falken stared across his desk and out the window into the late afternoon rain, angling across the lawns, soaking the carefully tended flower beds with their few green shoots breaking through, drifting down through the skeletal trees, their buds invisible through the mist. He stood up and stretched, feeling as he always did, the brief twinge of pain in his right thigh where a few small pieces of shrapnel still resided. The new chair helped the stiffness a bit if he had to sit for long periods. The chair had been designed by some Pentagon physiotherapist for survivors with leg wounds or some types of back wounds. Jesus, with the stuff they did there these days you would hardly know the Pentagon was the heart and soul of the American military, but then he seriously doubted that the American military had a soul anymore. It had fled the military body, dissipating into the ether somewhere during Vietnam and gone wherever institutional souls go. Maybe that was something he could restore. He would have to work on a heart transplant as well. He thought about the analogy for a moment and wondered if he could use it in a speech. It would depend on the audience.

He walked over to the French doors that led outside. They were old, their maple frames checked and scarred under generations of varnish. He had resisted all attempts to have them double-glazed or to replace them with aluminum or vinyl or whatever the hell they made doors out of these days. He knew they were drafty and inefficient. He swayed rhythmically back and forth, unconsciously standing at ease, his hands clasped loosely behind him, the scene outside distorting gently as his gaze shifted from the centres to the corners of the small panes. The days were getting longer; already spring weather was common, but this afternoon looked like a fall day, a day when the world was dying a little.

Jon turned from the window. The small fire crackling on the grate in the corner fireplace warmed the room. The sparkling light it threw took the edge off the dull dreariness of the rain. He picked a book off his desk that he had been reading, Fascism: A Reader's Guide. It contained part of a speech by Leon Degrelle. Jon had met him once about ten years ago in Spain, a fiery old Belgian, an ex SS general for whom World War II had been the highlight of his life. The SS had aged well in Leon's mind. It had become like a mystical order entrusted with a sacred mission, rather than a branch of the German armed forces. Jon stared down at the page and then read aloud in his deep baritone voice. "True elites are formed at the front, a chivalry is created there, young leaders are born. When we see a revolutionary, from Germany or elsewhere, we feel that he is one of ours, for we are one with revolution and youth. We are political soldiers, we prepare the political cadres of the postwar world. Tomorrow, Europe will have elites such as it has never known. An army of young apostles, of young mystics, carried by a faith that nothing can resist."

He laughed aloud and tossed the book on his desk. Old Nazis never die, they just miss the point. Power in the modern world is primarily economic, not political, and there are many roads to economic power. The only real example of political power he could think of was the presidency of the United States. Now that's power.

Too much looking at the pyramids. He smiled. So many people, movements, countries and cultures, too, for that matter, spent too much time looking back at their own pyramids, the things they had done in the last decade, the last century or the last millennium or two. He had been in Cairo a few years ago and had been taken through the squalor of the city to see the pyramids at Giza. A couple of months later, he and Marianne had gone on a brief holiday, one of the few they had taken, to Mexico. They had been stuck in Mexico City for a couple of extra days because someone had screwed up their airline reservations. They had taken a tour to Teotihuacan, out through the sordid poverty of Mexico City to the great pyramid site to the north. Jon had marveled at the irony of their guide, likely a Spanish descendent, taking such pride in a thousand year old achievement of an Indian culture that his ancestors had entirely destroyed. But the real questions that pyramid-gazers missed was what have you done last week? What are you planning for the next year, the next decade, the next century or the next millennium?

"Jon?" Marianne's voice interrupted his reverie. She peered around the open door of the study. "Are you on the phone?" She walked into the room, attired in an afternoon dress, as she liked to call them, something a little dressier than what she would wear in the morning but less so than what she'd wear in the evening. He sometimes wondered if she spent her entire day choosing what to wear and changing into it. "I thought I heard you chatting to someone."

"Just reading aloud."

"Keep practicing," Marianne said. "You're going to need it." She walked over to his desk, reached up and kissed him on the cheek. "It's 4:30 and we should be getting ready to go over to the O'Donnells'."

"O'Donnells'?"

"The people who moved into the old Sutton place a couple of years ago and..."

"I know who they are, Marianne," he interrupted. "I'd just forgotten we were going over there."

"Well," Marianne said, slowly as though she was explaining something simple to someone even more simple. "They do have a lot of money and we do need to build the war chest. They asked us over for drinks and then we're going on to the Club for the Foundation Ball."

The Club, Jon thought, and flinched. No one who had spent time in an officer's mess should ever have to go to golf and country clubs. But he did need the war chest and his campaign committee had identified a list of contacts he had to deal with and some important ones would be at the Foundation Ball. Planning a congressional campaign was worse than planning a military one. He shook his head and walked out of his study. Time to get cleaned up and into his new "dress uniform", or at least that was how he regarded his tuxedo.

Half an hour later, as he pushed the studs through the cuffs on his shirt, he watched Marianne toweling herself off in the ensuite bathroom. At forty five, she still had a beautiful body, slim shapely legs, a rounded butt and full breasts that hadn't yielded to either age or gravity. She had smooth white skin and that rich auburn-red hair, both, she claimed, part of her Irish heritage. She could easily pass for a woman in her mid-thirties. A pity she wasn't much interested in using her body for what the Celtic gods had intended when they had given it to her. However, she was certainly decorative, charming, and in her own way, intelligent and shrewd, tough, too, as he had found out on more than one occasion over the years. She would make a fine political wife even as she had been an asset all through his military career, although the colonel's rank he had retired with a year ago was something he had earned himself.

And her family's money didn't hurt either. Marianne was the last daughter of the O'Briens. She was an only child which ensured her parents' money had ended up with her when they died in a plane crash ten years ago. She had also been an only niece for her two maiden aunts, both gone of natural causes in the last couple of years, so the entire O'Brien fortune was now reunited. About 80 million dollars the last time he had checked, a small fortune to be sure, but one that would sustain them through the coming years.

Marianne strode naked across the plushly carpeted room toward him, seemingly unaware of her sexuality. Jon felt a stirring in his groin and reached out for her as she went by. She pirouetted out of his grasp letting his hand linger on her breast for just a moment. Then she moved back and hugged him, kissing him quickly, letting her soft wet tongue slip into his mouth and out again. She laughed as he flushed and she strolled insolently away.

He smiled ruefully as she winked over her shoulder at him and stepped into the large walk-in closet. Sex with Marianne had been pretty rare in the last couple of years but she could still do it to him. She rarely drove him wild like Lee did, but Marianne could be fabulous in bed when she put her mind to it.

He watched as she slipped the long dark blue gown over her head and wiggled it down her body. It clung suggestively to her. "Are you wearing anything under that?" he asked.

"I don't think so," she answered moving toward her make-up table. "This way you'll pant after me all evening."

"I thought I was supposed to be raising money tonight." He picked up his tuxedo jacket and slipped it on, turning to check his image in the full length mirror. He was tall, the few traces of grey in his temples adding maturity and distinction to his slim but well- muscled body. The carefully tailored tuxedo fitted him perfectly.

"You are, Sweetheart, this will just keep you motivated."

He sighed. "And I'll get my reward at the end of the evening?"

"Did you mean me?" She turned and smiled and then moved into her dressing room to put on her makeup. Jon watched her as she stared at herself in the mirror. She still retained a youthful face, smooth-skinned, a few pale freckles dusting her high cheekbones, giving her a wholesome, innocent quality when she went without makeup. When she was made up, she became sophisticated and elegant. She could certainly be seductive if she chose to but she rarely did. She seemed to prefer to be the beautiful and cool but elegant wife of a rising star, a decorated soldier and a soon-to-be distinguished congressman.

He watched the concentration as she moved the liner across her eyelid. "You've been sleeping with Lee again." It wasn't a question.

Jon was stunned. "What did you say?"

"You heard what I said. You were with that Vietnamese slut on Tuesday night."

"What are you talking about?" Jon felt his pulse rising. He forced himself into an icy calm. "I was at a regimental meeting on Tuesday night."

She switched to the other eye. "Bullshit," she said quietly.

"Marianne, I don't know what you're talking about. What was the name again?"

"Lee Marcoux." She leaned forward as she applied a pale shadow above her right eye. Her voice was conversational but there was steel under the softness. "How can you risk our future over some Asian swamp rat?"

Denial, denial, denial, the three key words in any disinformation operation. He walked up behind her and put his hand on her shoulder. "Marianne," he said softly and sincerely. "What's this all about?"

"Don't touch me." She struck his hand away. "You got used to fucking them while you were in Vietnam." She switched to the other eyelid, finished it in silence and then picked up her mascara and began to brush a light coating on the lashes of her right eye.

Jon stepped back. "I don't know what to say." He affected a stammer. "I just don't know what you're talking about."

She didn't answer him for a moment, finishing her mascara. She picked up a tube of lipstick and spread the deep red colouring over her lips. "You were fucking that Vietnamese slut you see in Philly. I know it and you know it. It's a weakness Jon and it is going to wipe out everything we've worked for." She glanced at him and then back at the mirror. "If I catch you fucking her again, I'll destroy you." She glanced at him again and then back at the mirror. "Don't worry, I won't cut your balls off." She blotted her lipstick. "Worse than that, Honey, I will cut your money off." She tilted her head for a final check in the mirror and then stood up and turned to face him. "How do I look?" she asked cheerfully.

He stared at her and nodded silently.

"Good," she said and walked up to him. She brushed her body against his as she picked a piece of lint off the satin lapel of his tuxedo. "Shall we go?" She moved beside him and slipped her arm through his.

CHAPTER THIRTY FOUR

Monday, April 24, 1989 Philadelphia, Pennsylvania

The coffee and pastry shop across the intersection from Eastwood Towers was not busy at 11:15 am although there were a few people coming and going. The barista had addressed Marianne Falken with a French accent and slipped smoothly into the language when Marianne answered him in French. One of the few useful things an expensive finishing school did, she reflected, was to equip one with essential skills that were never required. She had taken the early morning flight into Philly for a late afternoon hair appointment and a visit to an art show opening at the Liberty Gallery. Another, and not incidental reason was to sit in this small coffee shop across from Lee Marcoux's condo. Why she sat here she wasn't really sure. She certainly wasn't going to ring the bell and ask for admittance. Or maybe she should. She didn't expect to see the slut, but she had to admit that she did wonder about the woman that Jon had been screwing. The operative word was "had". All she knew for sure was that her name was Lee Marcoux, she was Vietnamese and she lived in Eastwood Towers. She had no idea what she looked like but small and Asian was a good guess.

Marianne saw a slim woman come out of the condo, her hair in a scarf, wearing jeans and a baggy sweatshirt with Philadelphia Eagles on it. She chatted to the doorman for a moment, then slipped on a pair of sunglasses moved to the crosswalk to wait for the light to change. Marianne went back to reading her magazine.

When the door to the coffee shop opened a couple of minutes later, she glanced up to see the slim woman in the Eagles sweatshirt come in the door.

"Bonjour Gerard," she said. Her voice was low and husky.

"Mademoiselle." Gerard beamed at her. "Espresso as usual?"

"Oui, merci. And you have a croissant left for me?"

"Of course, Mademoiselle."

The woman glanced around the small shop and caught Marianne looking at her. The woman nodded. "Good morning," she said brightly.

"Ah, Mademoiselle," Gerard said from behind the counter before Marianne could answer. "You are in luck today. Another Francophone."

"C'est vrai?" she said to Marianne.

"Oui," Marianne replied. "But I haven't spoken much French in quite some time."

"But Madame does it so beautifully," Gerard said.

"Please," Marianne said, indicating the other chair at the table. "Join me."

"Avec plaisir," the woman said, taking the chair.

Lee Marcoux was in the door of the café chatting to Gerard when she saw Marianne Falken. She knew immediately who she was. She had seen pictures of her and the hair gave her away instantly. There couldn't be more than a handful of women on the east coast with hair that colour. And now that goddamned Gerard was introducing her and Marianne was inviting her to sit down. The question was, did Marianne know who she was? Impossible, she decided, but she definitely knew something or she wouldn't be here, sitting across the street from her condo. She smiled and offered her hand. "I'm Liselle," she said, using her full name.

"Hi, I'm Marianne."

"Do you live around here, Marianne? I don't think I've seen you before and with that gorgeous hair, I'm sure I would have remembered."

"Thank you," Marianne said. "Harrisburg. I'm just in town for the day. I have a hair appointment and when I come into Philly I like to pick a different part of town and wander around a bit."

"What an interesting way to learn the city," Lee said. "Anything in particular you're interested in?"

"Galleries, primarily," Marianne replied. "The large ones are all listed but there a lot of small studios around that you never hear of unless you stumble across them. I'm going to the Liberty Gallery opening tonight. But what do you do in Philly? You are French?"

Liselle waited while Gerard put the small china cup of espresso in front of her and set the croissant on a plate beside it. "I am half French," she said. "The other half is Algerian. I work on contract to the French government, sometimes for the embassy in Washington, sometimes for the UN delegation in New York, so Philadelphia is a good halfway location." She took a sip of the espresso. "And you, Marianne?"

"I'm just a housewife." She nodded as Gerard hovered by her with a carafe of fresh coffee. He poured some more in her cup. "My husband was in the army and we got transferred around a lot so I never really had time for a career. I guess I actually had the time but we were never in one spot long enough to really get started on anything."

"I know what that can be like," Liselle replied sympathetically. "My father was in the French armed forces and we moved around a lot when I was a child." She found herself liking Marianne Falken. There was a warmth to her that was quite surprising in light of what she had heard from Jon. She took a sip of her espresso and looked over at the counter. "Gerard," she said. "Be a dear and wrap up my croissant for me. I'll take it with me." She took a sip of her espresso and looked at her watch.

"I'm keeping you, Liselle," Marianne said.

"No, not at all," Lee replied. "I have an appointment with a decorator at noon and I just couldn't face him without one of Gerard's espressos."

"Mademoiselle is too kind," Gerard said smiling broadly as he picked up the plate with the untouched croissant. She took a final sip of her espresso and stood up. "A pleasure to meet you, Marianne. A bientot."

"Yes," Marianne said. "That would be nice."

Marianne watched as Liselle took the small package from Gerard and with a final smile at her and a small wave, went out the door. She had thought about asking her for a card. Perhaps she could call her for lunch sometime when she was in Philly. She wondered if she should have asked her about her fellow resident, Lee Marcoux. She stood up, put a five dollar bill on the table and turned to the counter. "Gerard?"

"Oui, Madame."

"Do you know Mademoiselle Liselle's last name?"

"Alas, Madame, I do not." He shrugged. "There are so many clients that come to my humble shop, it is all I can do to remember their first names, and many of them I forget from time to time. But you, Madame, with your magnificent hair, your name is engraved in my mind."

Marianne smiled. "Merci, Gerard. A bientot."

"Merci, Madame Marianne. I, too, hope to see you again soon."

As she walked out the door she suddenly wondered about the name "Liselle". Could its short form be "Lee"? But Vietnamese were short Asians, not elegant and French.

Monday, April 24, 1989, Philadelphia The Liberty Gallery

Lincoln Carswell watched the woman staring intently at the painting. He strolled up behind her and stopped, aware of her scent, something light and fresh. She'd be somewhere in her late thirties, he guessed, a decade younger than he was, but he knew he wasn't much good at guessing women's ages.

Suddenly, she stepped back and bumped gently into him. "Excuse me," she murmured glancing over her bare shoulder, a look of mild dismay on her face. She put her hand on the sleeve of his blazer and then looked at him more closely. "Do I know you?" She smiled and pulled her hand back.

Lincoln returned her smile. "I certainly hope so," he said, offering his hand but not his name. He leaned gently on the cane. She glanced down at it and then back at his face. The cane was a great prop. It made people uncomfortable and then they didn't look as closely at the rest of the disguise.

She shifted her champagne flute to her left hand, adorned by a plain gold wedding band. "Marianne Falken."

"A pleasure to meet you, Marianne," Lincoln replied, taking her right hand in a firm grip. Her hand was small, soft and delicate and he held it for just a few seconds longer than he needed to. "I'm Ross Albright." She was expensively dressed, the simple long black gown clung to her, accentuating a slimness that was relieved by full breasts and the curve of her hips. Had he chosen to look further, he was certain that the slit in the side of the dress would reveal a shapely leg. But it was the crown of rich auburn hair that held his attention. It was the colour of burnished copper.

She took a sip of champagne. Her mouth looked soft with just a trace of a pout.

"Do you like the painting?" he asked.

"I like a lot of the paintings in the exhibition but especially this one. The precision of the brush strokes, the blades of grass in the foreground, the details of the harness on the horses, the rosebushes around the verandah in the background. The detail and the precision are just stunning."

He looked closely at her but she was quite sincere. "You're very descriptive," he said. "A pity it's sold."

She laughed. "Not really." She put her hand on the sleeve of his blazer again. "I bought it."

"That's great," he said, laughing with her.

"But what do you think of the exhibition?" Marianne asked.

"American Heritage," Lincoln said reflectively. "A Celebration of Values." He glanced at the cover of the art gallery brochure that Marianne was holding, the print embossed in gold lettering, an American eagle frowning ferociously at the top. "Very impressive."

"I love Lincoln's work," she said.

He glanced at the brochure again. "Lincoln Carswell," he murmured. "Yes, I do, too."

She looked at the painting again. "It captures something about a peaceful America that we just don't seem to have anymore. The horses and the carriage, and the couple in the carriage just seem to embody a simpler life, a purer kind of existence than we have now."

Lincoln looked at the painting and nodded his agreement. Of course, he didn't agree with her assessment at all. American Heritage: A Celebration of Values was just nonsense. It was a brilliant sales gimmick and he was a great marketer. He knew he was a technically fine artist, but the concept was just plain stupid. The entire show had been sanitized, sterilized. The man holding the bridle of the team of horses to steady the carriage while the elegantly attired couple prepared to descend was white. In reality, he would have been black, of course, and appropriately subservient. Maybe he should do a series called American Reality: A Celebration of Contemporary Values and show pickers' shacks, Watts burning, Detroit on fire, a couple of Jews screaming at each other in one more mindless New York sitcom.

Marianne touched his arm. "You just left for a minute, didn't you?"

Lincoln was jolted from his reverie. He smiled warmly. "Just thinking."

"Want to talk about it?" she asked with an impish smile.

He laughed. "Sure. I was thinking of how we remember only the good in the past. How those folks in the carriage had a life expectancy of about forty-two. How the pain in their heads from the sherry and bourbon they are going to drink would not be relieved by the aspirin that hadn't been invented yet."

She laughed. "You're very descriptive. But do you like the painting?"

"It's beautiful."

A man in a tuxedo moved slowly by them. Marianne placed her empty champagne flute on the tray he was carrying and picked up a full one. She arched her eyebrows at Lincoln.

"No, thank you," he said.

"You don't like champagne?"

"Something like that."

She looked around the gallery. People were still strolling in, some in tuxedos and long gowns, some in business attire and some, from the practising arts community, had slipped on a clean sweater or blazer with their jeans. She turned back to Ross. "I was told he'd be here. He's always at his openings, isn't he?"

"Always," Lincoln replied. "He wouldn't miss one. Have you met him?"

"No, I only saw him once at a New York opening a couple of years ago."

"The New World Exhibition."

"Yes," she said thoughtfully. "I think that's what it was called. A lot of works that focused on frontier themes."

"What did you think of it?" Lincoln asked, suddenly aware that her opinion mattered to him.

"I liked the work but not the theme," she said. "I guess the theme was fine but nothing in the show would have fitted into my home. They would have been wonderful in a home with a Santa Fe decor."

Lincoln nodded. "Nice to meet you, Marianne. I have to wander along. I can't stand in one place too long or my leg seizes up." He held out his hand. She took it again. "It's been a pleasure talking to you."

"I've enjoyed it, too," she said. They smiled at each other. "Do you have a card?"

"Yes," he replied, reaching into an inside pocket in his blazer. He handed her one.

"Ross Albright," she read softly. "AlphaCon Consultants. What do you do when you're consulting, Ross?"

"I'm afraid I'm an economist," he said with a smile. "Mostly business consulting, that sort of thing. Pretty boring stuff."

⁂

In the change room in the rear of the gallery Lincoln quickly stripped off his clothes. He tugged the slightly greying wig from his head and wiped off the light makeup. His short cropped dark brown hair hadn't suffered much under the slightly shaggy wig and without the glasses, the wig and the make-up, his face was ten years younger. He slipped into his formal clothes, the white slimly tailored dinner jacket replacing the padded blazer that had added a dozen pounds to his girth.

CHAPTER THIRTY FIVE

Monday, April 24, 1989 Philadelphia, The Liberty Gallery

Years ago Lincoln Carswell had wondered whether his undergraduate minor in theatre arts would ever be of any use, other than as some undefined broadening of his knowledge of graphic arts. However, he found it quite useful in wandering around art shows, especially his own, and finding out what people really thought. The moment they knew who he was all honest criticism and comment dried up. He snapped on the gold Rolex and looked at his image in the full length mirror. Ross Albright, the ageing but affable consultant was gone and Lincoln Carswell, the dynamic young artist had emerged. Forty-nine years young, he reminded himself, and in the mirror he could see he carried the years well. So he should, he worked hard at it.

As he slipped into the gallery a few minutes later and lifted a glass of champagne from the tray of a passing waiter, he was engulfed in the babble of voices. He saw the curator and his entourage sweeping down on him as his eyes searched the room for Marianne Falken.

"There you are, Lincoln," the curator said as he stepped up beside him. Allan Jensen called himself a "curator" but in reality, he was the owner of the Liberty Gallery and essentially a salesman. His knowledge of art was fairly skimpy but quite effective. He knew what sold. Jensen affected a kind of breathless exuberance and had a set of mannerisms that placed him somewhere between heterosexual and gay. "Picture time," he said. A photographer fired off a couple of informal shots as they stood together.

"Let's move down into the exhibition and get a few shots with the paintings in the background," Lincoln said. He spotted Marianne Falken. She had moved to the centre of the room.

Lincoln smiled, shook hands, chatted easily with the patrons, graciously accepting their compliments. He stopped a few times to answer questions that were more serious but kept moving inexorably toward Marianne Falken. He stopped with Allan Jensen at a couple of paintings and posed for the photographer.

From the corner of his eye he saw Marianne was moving through the crowd toward him. A moment later he turned to her and smiled, offering his hand.

"Lincoln Carswell," he said. "And what do you think of the exhibition?"

There was a flash as the photographer captured the moment.

"It's quite impressive," she replied. "I'm Marianne Falken."

"Have you found a favourite piece?"

"As a matter of fact, I have," she said.

"Where is it?

Marianne pointed across the room. "I liked it so well I bought it."

"Really?" Lincoln said, feigning surprise. "My patron."

He turned to Allan Jensen. "Allan, let's get a photograph with the painting Marianne just bought."

Looking back at Marianne he asked. "Will you lead the way?"

She nodded and led him slowly across the room to the painting. A small crowd gathered around them as they posed by the painting and photographer snapped a series of pictures. Lincoln waved a waiter over, set his half empty champagne glass on the tray and took two fresh ones. Handing one to Marianne, he touched the brim of his glass against hers. "Thank you," he said.

"It's my pleasure," Marianne replied. "I should be thanking you."

Lincoln smiled at her. "Don't go away," he said. He took her hand, squeezed it gently and released it.

"Okay."

Lincoln moved to another painting and chatted with a few people who had been watching him and Marianne in front of the painting she had purchased. As the group dispersed and moved on he walked back to Marianne.

"Do you mind a personal question, Marianne?" Lincoln asked.

She laughed. "I don't mind the question at all," she replied. "But no guarantees on the answer."

"Fair enough," Lincoln said, joining in her laughter. "I wondered if you had ever had your portrait painted."

"No," she said shaking her head. "I've never thought about it."

"You should," Lincoln said. "Your hair is simply stunning. May I?" He reached out and touched her hair, just above her left ear.

"It's real and it's natural." She watched him carefully.

He nodded and pulled his hand back. "You're beautiful as well, of course, but there is much more to you than that." He put his hand lightly on her bare shoulder. "You have skin like satin."

"Thank you," Marianne said. "You're very kind."

"I'm not trying to be kind," Lincoln said. "I'd like to paint your portrait."

"I'm not sure I could afford that," she said with a quick laugh.

"Good heavens," Lincoln said, joining in her laughter. "I'm not trying to hustle your business, I am trying to create a work of art. I wouldn't dream of charging you for the privilege of painting you."

Marianne was silent.

Lincoln reached into the pocket of his white dinner jacket and pulled out a card and a pen. He wrote a number on the back of the card. "Here is my card with my unlisted personal number. Will you think about it and give me a call."

Marianne took the card. "I will," she said.

"Please call me whatever you decide." He smiled. "And now I do have get back to hustling my art."

Monday, April 24, 1989, Philadelphia Eastwood Towers

Jon Falken leaned back on the cool silk pillows, stretching his long muscular body for a moment before relaxing. He tugged the black silk kimono down to his knees and then smiled at himself. It would soon be removed. He reached over to the small bedside table, picked up a highball glass and took a small sip of scotch. He let it burn slowly across his tongue, the rich smoky flavour seeping out as it reached his throat. Lee walked slowly into the bedroom, the deep red silk clinging to her body. She smiled, pirouetted and bowed slightly as she moved toward the bed. She sat and let her hand drift lightly and slowly up his right leg, pushing his kimono aside.

"Welcome home, lover," she murmured, the faint hint of a French accent adding a sexual dimension to everything she said. "Thank you for the gift." She stood up and slipped the peignoir off her shoulders, titling her head to one side, running the tip of her tongue over her bottom lip as she watched him. He followed the red silk as she controlled its fall, letting it slip gently down her arms and then guiding it with her hands, down over her slim hips to the floor. It gathered around her feet in a sensual red pool.

He stared at her in the dusky light, her perfect skin so pale and smooth, the aureolas around her nipples tinged brown not pink, a small triangle of black at the top of her slim shapely legs.

She sat down again on the edge of the bed and traced her fingers over the scars on his right leg. "Does it still hurt?" she whispered. She lay back against him and ran her hand into his thick dark hair.

"Not if you touch it that way," he murmured. And it was true. The few bits of shrapnel he still carried with him caused some discomfort at times, but often even a slight distraction would make the pain disappear. He put his hand over hers. She had such flawless skin, such delicacy. He reached for her breast and ran his fingers over her nipple. She squirmed and snuggled against him closing her eyes. He saw the shadow of a smile spread across her lips. He was going to have such an evening of pleasure. He always did and he knew he was going to miss it so desperately when it was gone.

She kissed him softly and put her head on his shoulder. "I met your wife this morning," she whispered. "She's very beautiful"

"You what?" Jon sat up abruptly. She held on to him and moved back.

"Easy, lover," she said. "She didn't know who I was but she certainly knew where I lived."

"What happened?"

"I walked into Gerard's and there she was."

"Just sitting there?"

"Umhm." She tilted her head to one side. "Do you want to tell me what's going on?"

Jon leaned back on the pillows. "Last Friday, Marianne told me she knew about us. Apparently a friend of ours, Frank Delgado, had told her. Frank had been drinking a lot lately and I guess he let it slip."

"Go on," she said, running her fingers through the light hair on his chest.

"Frank committed suicide," Jon said. "Actually the day before Marianne told me."

"And he was your close friend?"

"Yes."

"It is so sad to lose a good friend," she whispered. "Are you okay?"

"I'm fine."

"And now you are going to lose me, too?"

"I'm afraid so, my love."

"Will we be able to see each other at all?"

"I don't think that would be wise."

"Perhaps not," she said softly. "But I will miss you terribly."

Liselle closed the door behind Jon, waited a moment and then turned the two dead bolts and slipped on the security chain. She walked across the foyer of the penthouse, stopped at the small Buddhist shrine and watched the water gurgle over the rocks and splash softly into the small pool. She put her hands together and bowed slightly. The water flowed in an endless stream, hour after hour. Of course, she knew that it was same water cycling back to the top of the shrine and running down but she liked the illusion. She smiled. She liked a lot of illusions.

She went down the two steps into the living room, kicked off her shoes and carried them into the bedroom. She stripped the black silk sheets off the bed and tossed them on the floor. She quickly remade the bed, white cotton sheets this time, and changed the pillow cases. She didn't like sleeping with the smell of stale sex around her and she didn't like silk sheets much either, too cool and they slipped off in the middle of the night. She gathered them up and tossed them into a laundry hamper in the closet.

In the marble bathroom she turned on the shower, as hot as she could stand it, and stepped in. She thought about her meeting with Marianne Falken this morning. She had found herself liking Marianne and if circumstances were different she would have met her again. Perhaps she would anyway, now that Jon was out of her life.

The water poured over her and she turned slowly between the two shower heads. Breathing the steam seemed to cleanse her inner soul and gradually she relaxed. Perhaps she should suggest that Marianne replace Jon? Marianne would eventually be privy to Jon's secrets.

Liselle squeezed a jasmine scented lotion from a tube and stepped out of the streams of water as she spread it onto her skin, over her breasts, down across her flat, smooth stomach, into her pubic hair. She stroked herself softly and shuddered before she stepped back into the jets of water. So Marianne was going to the Lincoln Carswell exhibition tonight. She hadn't seen Lincoln in a while, a couple of months anyway. She would have to call him and catch up. He was such a gorgeous man. She wondered what Lincoln would think of Marianne and smiled. She'd find out.

Back in the bedroom, she sat naked at the small white French provincial desk and wrote a short note on embossed stationary. She wrote quickly in French, the letters small and round, almost like calligraphy. She slipped the note into an envelope, wrote an address on it and sealed it.

Finally, she went into her large walk-in closet and retrieved a small stool. She set it under a light fixture mounted on the wall above and to the right of the bed. Pressing a tiny catch on the base of the fixture, she hinged it up and removed a small surveillance camera with a built in sound recorder.

CHAPTER THIRTY SIX

Wednesday, April 26, 1989 Winnipeg and Portage la Prairie, Canada

Snow was piled like a dirty curb in front of the rental cars at the Winnipeg International Airport. Eric was freezing as he slid behind the wheel of the new full-sized Chevrolet Caprice he had rented. He hadn't chosen it, he had been "upgraded", which likely meant they had already rented the car he had reserved. The heater blew frigid air around his feet and into his face. He shut it off to wait for the engine to warm up. He would have to buy a sweater and a winter jacket. Perhaps there was still a men's clothing store in Portage. One consolation was the sunshine, bright and beautiful, and it was warming up the world. As he backed the car out of its stall, he could see the dirty snow was yielding a trickle of water. Long distance travel always amazed him. A few hours ago he had been on the other side of the world in a tropical paradise and now he was watching snow melt and thinking of sweaters and insulated jackets.

He felt a tension coming back into his life, pervasive and a bit unfamiliar. He was planning and organizing again and dealing with a lot of external detail. He would have to decide what to do with the house, the summer cottage at Delta, the cars, the furnishings, his parents' other possessions. He supposed there would be a will that would require probating, decisions about a memorial service, disposing of all the accumulations of two lifetimes. He knew that some of this was his way of avoiding thinking about the terrible emotional impact of losing both his parents. For the moment, he was suffering an emotional numbness but that would fade. It would be a difficult time.

He always had the same feeling when he drove into Portage, a sense of coming home, an odd sensation since he hadn't lived here since he finished high school in 1957. He remembered spring days like this as a child, sitting on the front steps of the big old house, facing into the sun, letting it warm his face, opening his winter jacket and letting it inside. As long as he could find a spot out of the breeze, days like that had been tolerably warm. He remembered watching the ice break up on Crescent Lake. He smiled at the thought of being grateful for the warmth of a day like this, kind of like dropping a brick on your foot because it felt good when the pain went away. Prairie winters were like that.

As he drove into the east end of the city it looked seedy. It had been a long time since Portage la Prairie had been a prosperous town. It was too close to Winnipeg, only an hour's drive away, to fully develop commercially, although it had been an important railway town, a division point in the days when steam engines had to stop every fifty miles or so for coal and water, and it was an agricultural supply centre, as well as having two military airports nearby, both now closed. It even attracted some light manufacturing but those companies seemed to fail or move away with disconcerting regularity.

He drove past the Portage Mutual Insurance Company building, one of the local success stories, and a few blocks further on, Victoria school, a classic old brick school onto which some architect had stuck a hideous stuccoed addition. He glanced involuntarily down Fourth Street where Laura's parents had lived. They had both died a few years ago but he hadn't learned of their passings until months later. He had written Laura a letter of condolence each time and had received formal thank you notes.

Eric knew that Laura and Darrin lived out in a new subdivision, Koko Platz, on the southeast side of Crescent Lake, built a few years after he had left Portage. It was the kind of place Darrin would like to live, nice homes, good life style although it was a bit of a drive to the golf course, but then in a town the size of Portage with its 14,000 or so residents, nothing was very far from anything else.

At the street light on the corner of Saskatchewan Avenue and Royal Road, he turned right. There was a vacant parking spot across the street from the small building where Laura's office was located. He pulled into it and got out of the car. He was suddenly cold again and realized he had forgotten to stop to buy a sweater and a jacket. He also realized he was a little nervous at the prospect of seeing Laura again although he had spoken with her from Tahiti to let her know he would be arriving this afternoon. He had even called again from Vancouver last night to leave a message on her answering machine confirming his arrival. Maybe it was natural to be nervous around old girlfriends, especially if you still carried a flame, such an old fashioned way of describing his feelings but he didn't really want to look too closely at those feelings right now.

Glancing at his watch, he saw it was a little after four. He wondered what time Laura closed her office. Maybe five. She told him to come to her office whenever he arrived. Maybe she would be free for dinner or free to come to the house with him. Maybe Mergatroid had learned how to fly. Quit dreaming, he told himself, she's happily married to your former best friend. Well maybe not completely happily married, he had felt some tension between them the last time he had seen them and sensed that everything wasn't well in spite of Darrin's comments about life being great.

It was surprising how sensitive he was to them but perhaps not entirely so, since the two of them had been his best friends in his last years in high school. He shrugged, plugged a couple of dimes into the parking meter and walked across the street. Royal Road, he thought, named for the fact that when King George VI and Queen Elizabeth visited the town on a Sunday morning in 1939 they had been driven from the train station up what was formerly First Street North East, to the United Church to attend the service there. The town council had promptly renamed the street. The King had read the scripture. The church still had cushions on the seats they had occupied and had installed a commemorative brass plaque screwed onto the back of the pew. Long memories in this town, he thought as he opened the glass-paneled door, "Dr. Laura Schaefer" embossed in gold across the glass.

It seemed strange to be serving a take-out pizza in the kitchen of his family home. Ordering fast food was something his parents rarely did, had done, Eric corrected himself. He left it in the box on the kitchen counter and set plates and utensils on the round oak table in the corner. He went to the old cherry wood French provincial china cabinet in the dining room to get wine glasses. He chose heavy crystal goblets. They would hold the Chianti nicely. He had been pleasantly surprised by the wine selection in the local government liquor store.

He was nervous again, looked at his watch and wondered if he had time for a quick shower. He decided he did and went up the broad staircase in the entry. He had tossed his single bag in his old room, largely unchanged from his teenage years. He slipped out of his clothes and went down the hall to the large bathroom he used as a kid. He opened the closet and pulled out a towel, it was full of them. He shook his head. His mother had been prepared for everything. A circular curtain rod and a shower head had been retro-fitted on the huge old claw-footed tub. As the hot water coursed over him he thought of his meeting with Laura.

There had been three young mothers with their children in the waiting room, only one child was crying and that was more a snuffle than a howl. Laura's receptionist, Gloria, looked at him with more than common interest when he told her his name. He had waited among the moms and the children for about ten minutes before Laura ushered out the patient she'd been seeing in her inner office, another mom with a child. He stood up as she'd walked over to him, formal in her white coat, and shaken his hand. They chatted for only a couple of minutes and he scarcely recalled what they had said, except that it was Wednesday, and Laura had told him it was the night Darrin played poker, normally going straight from work. So he must have asked her if she was free for dinner. She'd said she'd come over after work, likely around 6:30 or so.

He stepped out of the shower and quickly toweled himself dry. He had turned up the thermostat when he had come in but the house still seemed cold. He shivered as he walked down the hall, clad only in the towel, tied lightly around his waist.

In his room, he zipped open his bag pulled out a polo shirt and slipped it on. It was wrinkled but he didn't feel like tracking down an iron. He'd hang up the rest of his stuff later but hanging things up made him think of moving in, of staying a while. Maybe he would be. He opened one of the drawers in his old dresser. It was full of sweaters, a sprinkling of cedar shavings mixed in to keep the moths away. His mother never threw out any of his things. The cedar chips were her addition. He lifted the corners of the sweaters and came to a deep brown mohair crew neck. He slipped it out of the drawer, shook it out and pulled it over his head. It was a sweater with memories.

He heard a noise downstairs and glanced at his watch. It was 6:20. She was early. He quickly finished dressing. As he came down the staircase into the entry hall, he saw a black wool winter coat tossed over the bottom post of the stair railing and a small pair of snow boots parked by his running shoes. He smiled at the contrast, but running shoes or sandals had been his choice and he'd figured sandals wouldn't keep out as much snow.

He paused in the archway leading into the kitchen. Laura had her back to him and was lifting the corner of the pizza box, peering intently inside. In her other hand she held one of the crystal goblets half full of the deep red wine. She turned as she heard him behind her.

"Hi again," he said, trying not to stare. Her hair was brushed loosely, still dark blonde with scarcely a trace of grey. She was wearing black slacks and a pale blue sweater, the collar of a white blouse peeking out the top. She had a little makeup on but she still had a natural and wholesome scrubbed look about her.

"Hi yourself."

"I hope you like ham and pineapple on pizzas."

"Sounds tropical."

"Hawaiian."

He walked to the table, wanting desperately to hug or kiss her but resisted the urge. He picked up the other goblet and poured some wine into it. He held out his glass and she clinked hers against it in a silent toast.

"I thought we'd eat in the kitchen."

"It's not a formal dinner, is it? I'm not really dressed for it."

"Me either," Eric said. "Like my sweater?"

Laura nodded. "August 1957," she said. "It was a good summer for mohair sweaters."

"It kept me warm in Toronto."

"It was supposed to." Laura laughed, set her glass down and stepped toward him. She took the goblet from his hand, set it on the table beside hers and slipped her arms around him, pressing her face against his chest. He enfolded her and felt her against him, soft and yielding. He nuzzled his face into her hair, smelling something faintly of a flower he couldn't identify. They stood holding each other for a long time and gradually she released him.

"The pizza is going to get cold," she whispered into his chest.

"I think there's an oven about somewhere."

Laura laughed. "Always prepared, aren't you?"

"Not always, but I try." He released her and they picked up their wine glasses. "Let's have dinner. And thank you for coming. It's good to have you here. You should be here. You meant so much to my parents."

"I loved your parents, Eric," Laura said. "After mine died, I guess I kind of adopted them. Your father was especially helpful to me. As he gradually retired from his practice he passed many patients on to me, a lot of them men who thought that all women in the medical field were nurses. That took a lot of courage."

"He had a lot of courage." Eric pulled a chair back for her and pushed it in as she sat down. He set the box in the middle of the table, lifted the lid and picked up a slice, all stringy with melted mozzarella and put it on her plate.

"I wondered if you would stop at Dick's Cafe and get Saratoga chips with gravy," Laura said, cutting off the end of the pizza slice. "But I'm not sure they even make them anymore."

"I thought of it but I never really liked them all that well." He set a slice of pizza on his plate remembering that Darrin had loved Saratoga chips with gravy.

"How are you doing with this, Eric? I feel badly that I blundered into telling you the way I did. I'm supposed to be good at that sort of thing."

"You are good at it, Laura. If anyone was going to tell me that news I'm glad it was you." He thought for a moment. "I'm as okay as I can be at the moment. I feel lonely, kind of numb. I feel like my source of wisdom is gone. I guess as long as you have parents there is always somewhere to go, someone who will love you totally, unconditionally, no matter what you've done or where you've been. I guess I'm missing that a lot even though it's not something I need at the moment. Hard to explain. But please don't worry about how you told me. I'm just grateful it was you."

She ate in silence for a moment. "Thank you," she said. "I'm glad it was me, too."

CHAPTER THIRTY SEVEN

Wednesday, April 26, 1989 Harrisburg, Pennsylvania

A secretary ushered Jon Falken wordlessly into the law firm's small board room. It was a gloomy place that got little relief from the north-facing floor-to-ceiling windows. Deep brown drapes were hung at both sides of the glass as though ready to swoop across the panes at the first sign of serious light. The other three walls were lined with dark wood shelving filled with books, bound tomes of statutes from the look of it. The centre of the room was occupied by a large rectangular walnut table with a dozen leather armchairs pulled up around it. The black suits worn by the two men standing by the window fit perfectly into the decor. They turned as Jon was shown into the room. As they watched him cross the room toward them, neither one smiled.

"Jon Falken," he said, extending his hand with a broad grin.

"Clark Einfeld," the taller of the two replied, taking Jon's hand in a short firm grip. He was slim and doleful, an odd contrast to his quiet but powerful voice. He sounded like a radio announcer about to deliver the evening news. "My associate, Steven Clayton."

Jon shook hands with Clayton and nodded. Clayton was shorter, solid and muscular, the result of well spent time in a gym pumping iron judging by his build. His hair was sandy brown and he looked as though he had to work hard to keep from appearing happy but was apparently prepared to do so. Jon decided he didn't like either of them much.

"Please sit down, Mr. Falken." Einfeld said.

"Call me Jon."

"As you wish," Einfeld replied, indicating a chair at the end of the table. Einfeld sat down to his left, Clayton to his right. "Thank you for agreeing to meet with us on such short notice, Jon. We do appreciate it."

"My pleasure," Jon replied. "I know your names, but who am I meeting with? Who do you represent?" There had been a message on his answering machine when he had returned last night from Frank Delgado's funeral reception. It had merely said that Clarke Einfeld would like to meet with him to discuss financially supporting his candidacy for the United States Congress and asked him to confirm a meeting time the next morning at a small downtown law firm.

Einfeld leaned forward on his elbows. "We'll get to that shortly, Jon, but first we would like to know how serious you are about running for Congress."

Jon leaned back in his chair, annoyed by the superior tone of voice as much as by the question. He didn't have time to waste. "How much do you know about me?" he asked indifferently.

"Quite a lot of your background, Jon," Clayton said, speaking for the first time. His voice was high pitched, almost feminine, ingratiating. It irritated Jon. "What we don't know is the depth of your commitment." He almost lisped. Faggot, Jon thought, and unconsciously moved his chair back.

Jon looked from onc to the other. "What would you like to know that you don't already know? My military career speaks for itself. Anything I have ever undertaken I have done successfully and well. I've developed and maintained good connections with the party, especially since I retired. There is no other serious candidate at the moment to replace Congressman Fry when he retires at the end of his current term and I've worked quietly within the party organization to let it be known that I will be a candidate."

"So you are really serious?" Einfeld asked.

"I am totally committed."

"Have you thought beyond the House of Representatives?" Clayton asked.

Jon turned at the sound of Clayton's voice. He nodded silently, looking carefully at Clayton. You couldn't always tell, but he would have done something about that voice if he wasn't gay.

"And what have you decided?"

"That after two terms in Congress, I hope to be in a position to go after the presidential nomination."

Clayton and Einfeld looked at each other and nodded. Then Einfeld spoke, his radio announcer's voice deep and foreboding. "That should be entirely possible. However, we do not at present think you are serious about your political career."

Jon sat forward, suddenly angry. "What the Hell do you mean, not serious?"

"No need to raise your voice, Jon," Clayton said in his annoying whine. "Every political candidate has three lives; a public life, a private life and a secret life. You have an exemplary public life and an enviable private life but your secret life will destroy your political hopes."

"If you are going for the presidency you've got to be clean," Einfeld added.

"Squeaky clean," Clayton said. "And squeaky clean does not include being married and having a French girlfriend."

Jon thought of denying it but if they knew that Lee was French, they were not guessing. "How did you find out?"

"That doesn't matter, Jon," Einfeld said. "What matters is that if we can find out, so can others."

"Are you intending to stay married, now that your wife knows about your mistress?" Clayton asked.

"Jesus Christ," Jon muttered.

"Calling on a deity isn't likely to provide much help in these circumstances," Clayton added primly.

"So what is going on here?" Jon asked. "Blackmail?"

Einfeld and Clayton looked at each other and Clayton smiled. "Quite the opposite, Jon," Einfeld said. "We want you to win in congress and we want you to win the presidency in 2000. That's only eleven years away but youthful adventures have a way of coming back to haunt one."

Jon sat in silence, shaken by their revelations. How could they have found out about Lee? How could they have known that Marianne knew about Lee? He had been more than discreet. He had been secretive.

Einfeld leaned forward. "Jon," he said quietly. "You have to start getting clean. Step one is to get rid of Lee Marcoux."

"Gentlemen, I am no longer involved with Miss Marcoux," Jon said.

Einfeld and Clayton looked at each other again, then Einfeld spoke. "And when did this development occur?"

"Two nights ago."

"Please accept our apologies and our sincere congratulations, Jon," Einfeld said. "That was a very wise decision."

"Step two," Clayton said, his voice subdued but still whiny, "is to rebuild your relationship with your wife. We are not going to support a divorced candidate."

Jon looked at each of them in turn. "I appreciate your candour, gentlemen," he said. "But what makes you believe that I either want or need your support?"

Einfeld and Clayton looked back at Jon. This time there were no smiles. Then Clayton spoke. "We are the nucleus of your support team, Jon. We want your political career to unfold exactly as you do. We will provide logistical support, a national network, extensive financial support..."

"You are not answering my question," Jon interrupted sharply.

Einfeld spoke next. Jon recognized the basic interrogation technique, sit the prisoner between two interrogators so that he has to look back and forth, like watching a ping pong match, and can never see the two of them simultaneously. "As you know, Jon, to be president of the United States, you must be born an American citizen."

"I was born in Philadelphia."

"No you were not, Jon," Einfeld continued relentlessly. "Regardless of what your birth certificate says, you were born in Germany in October 1939."

Jon leaned back in his chair and was silent. This was not new information to him but it was buried so deep that no one, other than his parents, could have known. Together, they had told him when he had joined the armed forces and he had never told anyone. His birth parents must have been powerful and important, and in 1940 in Germany, that meant that they were Nazis as well, but he had no idea who they might have been. His adoptive parents were both dead now and he was confident that they had never revealed his secret to anyone.

From the corner of his eye he saw Clayton lean forward. The whiny voice was soft but that made it even more irritating.

"You see, Jon, you do not have a choice in the matter. We are your campaign support."

Einfeld took over. "No one will ever know we are behind you unless you choose to tell someone and we wouldn't advise that. We will approve everyone who works on your campaign and who works for you when you are elected. We will provide you with staff and all the support you need."

"You only have to stay clean, Jon," Clayton added.

CHAPTER THIRTY EIGHT

Wednesday, April 26, 1989 Philadelphia

Lincoln watched as the white BMW coupe rounded the circular driveway and came to a halt in front of the entrance to his home. He opened the front door as Marianne Falken swung her legs out of the car, stood and closed the door. She seemed unaware of what a sensual image she projected by just getting out of her car. She walked towards him and he watched the afternoon light glisten in her hair as it bounced slightly. She had called two days earlier and they had chatted for a while, easily, like a couple of old friends. Lincoln had learned a long time ago that being open and personal with women worked well, whether he was trying to put them at ease when they were posing, or whether he was trying to get them into bed. One often preceded the other. He wondered how it would unfold this time.

She mounted the broad front steps and came to a stop in front of him. "Hi," she said.

He gave her a quick hug. "Thank you for coming. I'm so glad you decided to sit for the portrait."

They walked through the front door into the large open foyer. "I could hardly turn down an offer like that from one of America's finest artists."

"You flatter me."

Marianne looked at him. "I don't think so," she said. "But I didn't know you painted portraits."

"I only do them occasionally and only when I choose to. I don't accept commissions."

As she turned her back to him, he slipped her black leather hip-length jacket off her shoulders and hung it in a small coat room.

"This room is striking," Marianne said. "Are you also an interior designer?"

"Not really," Lincoln replied. "I had a bit of help from some colleagues who are interior designers and architects." He had designed the entry area to be exactly what Marianne had called it. Striking. It was open, high-ceilinged, with angular walls entirely in white, a couple of abstract sculptures, one on a pedestal, a larger one rising from the floor about twenty feet toward the ceiling. He took her hand. "Come on, I'll show you around."

They walked down a short hallway which led into a large open room, entirely glass on two sides. Half of the room was focused around a huge fireplace with white leather chesterfields and white marble, glass-topped coffee and end tables. The other half of the room was a dining area with a large glass-topped table and white leather chairs. Beyond the dining area was a kitchen, again in white with black marble counter tops, and four high white leather stools pulled up to the counter facing into the kitchen.

Marianne looked around the room. "You designed this, too?"

Lincoln nodded. "I did the design and layout of the room, the entire house, actually, but I did have some help with the furnishings." He released her hand. "The windows open completely so in the summer the wall can just disappear and the patio becomes part of the living and dining area."

"Are you a Buddhist?" Marianne asked, pointing at a statue set on the edge of a patio area with a small fountain and a couple of covered outdoor lounge chairs nearby.

"No," Lincoln replied. "But I have read a fair bit about it. The fountain and the statue are peaceful and I like tranquility. "

He watched her reaction to the room. She was correct in her assessment. It was a stunning room, especially with the view of the flagstone patio flanked by a low stone wall and the landscaped shrubbery and trees in the background. It was an enclosed area but managed to appear open and spacious.

"There's more," Lincoln said. He led the way down another short hallway and opened a door on the right and ushered her into the room. He switched on the lights to reveal a small but well equipped fitness centre with a treadmill, fitness machines and free weights. One wall was windows, again looking out into a landscaped area, two other walls were entirely covered in mirrors, giving the room a feel of spaciousness and reflecting the outdoor area. The remaining wall was equipped with pulleys and other fitness devices.

"Do you actually use all this stuff?" Marianne asked.

"Every day," Lincoln replied. "I guess to be honest, I use some of it every day."

Marianne looked at him carefully. "You must be very fit."

"I was told once that your twenties is your last maintenance-free decade. After that you have to work to keep fit." He switched off the light and they returned to the hallway.

"Next on the tour is the music studio, then we'll move on to the art studio and get at your portrait."

"You're a musician, too?"

"Just a hobby," Lincoln replied, opening another door. They stepped into a closet-like space. A second door led into the studio. Lincoln switched on the lights.

"Was that some kind of air lock?" Marianne asked.

Lincoln laughed. "No," he replied. "It's a sound lock, I guess. This is a music studio but it's also a recording studio."

She looked around the room. "You play all these?"

"It looks like a lot, but there are really only two kinds of instruments in here, guitars and keyboards." He gestured toward a grand piano. "This side of the room is for acoustic instruments, the other side is for electric ones."

"What's behind the glass?" Marianne asked, gesturing at a wall to her right.

"That's where the recording goes on," Lincoln replied. "It's a twelve channel recording system with the technical stuff to make it all work. I'll take you in there if you like."

Marianne laughed. "I'm a technical idiot I'm afraid. I wouldn't know what anything was." She strolled over to the piano and hit a couple of keys. "Nice," she said.

"Do you play?"

"I did as a child, the usual classical piano lessons. I didn't enjoy it much." She walked over to a guitar hanging on the wall and looked at it carefully. "This is beautiful. Another of your works of art?"

"No," Lincoln said. "It's just a beautiful guitar. My father was a luthier and made it. I was raised in Nazareth."

"Nazareth in the Holy Land or Nazareth, Pennsylvania?"

Lincoln laughed. "Pennsylvania, I'm afraid. My father worked for the Martin Guitar Company, mostly building the high end models."

"That explains the music but how did you get interested in art?"

"My mother," Lincoln replied. "She was a painter, mostly water colours. She was actually quite good at it. She taught me to sketch things from the time I could hold a pencil, and then showed me how to compose a picture, how to use colour and texture and all the other stuff. I was very fortunate."

"So you were born into a creative family. Did you go to art school?"

"I got a degree in graphic and performing arts," Lincoln replied.

"You're an actor, too?"

"Not at all," Lincoln said. "I enjoyed the program but it was a minor and I didn't follow it up."

"So you inherited your love of music from your father and the art from your mother. How wonderful to have creative genes like that."

Lincoln laughed again. "Actually, I am an example of environment triumphing over heredity."

"How so?"

"I was adopted."

"Really?"

"Yes," Lincoln replied. "I don't have much detail about my birth parents, but I was born in Germany in October, 1939 and deported to America in 1940."

"Deported?" Marianne said. "You must be joking."

"I am," Lincoln said. "I was moved here in a program to relocate German children who had been orphaned. Or that's what my parents were told at the time they adopted me. So I expect my birth parents were casualties of the war."

"I'm sorry," Marianne said.

"Don't be," Lincoln answered. "I had a wonderful childhood here, unscarred by war. My parents loved and nurtured me. I had an older brother, the biological son of my adoptive parents, who didn't have a musical or artistic gene in his body. I really don't know where mine came from."

"You had a brother?"

"He was killed in Vietnam."

"That whole debacle was such a tragedy," Marianne said. "An entire generation scarred by it in one way or another."

Lincoln nodded. "He was two years older than me and he was my hero."

Marianne looked back at the guitar. "Would you play me something?"

Lincoln reached past her and lifted the guitar off its rack. He slipped the strap over his shoulder. "Do you know the Riddle Song?"

Marianne shook her head.

Lincoln strummed a chord and began to pick a simple melody. Then he sang the words.

"I gave my love a cherry that had no stone
I gave my love a chicken that had no bone
I told my love a story that had no end
I gave my love a baby that's no cryin'."

He stopped. "There you are. Your private concert."

"You play beautifully," Marianne said. "I think I've heard the song before but it was a long time ago. Would you sing me the last verse?"

Lincoln began again.

"A cherry when it's bloomin' it has no stone
A chicken when it's pippin' it has no bone
The story that I love you, it has no end
A baby when it's sleepin' is no cryin'."

"Thank you," she said softly. "I don't think anyone has ever sung me a song before." As the sound of the guitar faded she looked at it more closely. "Such a beautiful instrument."

"Yes, it is," Lincoln said. "It was made the same year I was born. 1939. It's a real classic. Eric Clapton uses the same guitar."

"1939," she echoed. "That's the same year my husband was born."

"It must have been a good year," Lincoln said. He slipped the guitar strap off, hung the guitar back in its frame on the wall.

"You play and sing so beautifully," Marianne said. "Did you ever do it professionally?"

"Sort of," Lincoln replied. "When I was in university I tried singing in coffee houses. I even wrote some songs but no one liked them very much."

"What were they about?"

"Kind of anti-protest songs. Songs supporting our efforts to preserve freedom in South East Asia. Not exactly pro war songs, but sometimes they got interpreted that way."

"That's too bad."

"It seems that the folk-singer composers of the 60's were all in favour of freedom, justice, equality and tolerance but not for songs or ideas they disagreed with. They only tolerated one popular song that glorified war."

"What song was that?"

"The national anthem."

Marianne laughed. "I guess it does but I never thought about it before."

Lincoln took her hand again and led her back into the hallway. "Now let's get at your portrait."

His studio was on the north side of the house, large windows providing natural light, but equipped with curtains to shut it out if he chose. It was a spacious room but also a messy and littered workspace. Several large canvases in varying stages of completion were scattered on easels around the room.

Marianne looked around. "Is this your next show?"

"I don't know," Lincoln replied. "I don't really think in terms of shows. I'm a fairly prolific painter so I do pretty much what I want. When I have a number of canvases finished, I can usually find a theme in them somewhere, or a unifying idea that gives at least some of them something in common."

Marianne strolled around the room, looking at partially finished works. "How do you choose what to paint?"

Lincoln thought about the question. "I get ideas from all over. I travel and take photographs, I see ideas in magazines and books, friends suggest things. Sometimes I start a sketch and I know it isn't going to work, so in part, it's also a process of rejection, of what not to paint."

"So what's next?" Marianne asked.

"Come over here," Lincoln said, leading her to a high stool near the windows. "I'm going to take some photographs first."

Marianne climbed onto the stool and looked at Lincoln, raising her eyebrows as the shutter clicked for the first photo.

He circled around her taking photographs from a variety of angles. He told her to smile, to frown, to look angry, sultry, lustful, sad. He then turned on some lights mounted on stands and took more. He shut off the lights and stood in front of her. "Okay," he said. "I have the head and shoulder shots. Now we have to decide how to pose you. Where do you think you would like to be in this painting?"

Marianne looked at him quizzically. "I'm not sure I understand the question."

"Background," Lincoln said. "Would you like to be posed in front of the Eiffel Tower, a woodland meadow, on a boat, reclining on a couch?"

Marianne nodded. "I see." She was silent for a moment. "I think I would rather be outdoors than indoors, more casual than formal. Does that help?"

"A lot," Lincoln replied. "What mood would you like to be in?"

"More happy than sad but I don't want to look like an air-head."

Lincoln laughed. "I don't think I know how to paint an air-head. Come with me to the costume house."

Marianne slipped down off the stool and followed Lincoln over to a corner of the studio. There was a rack hung with clothes and a couple of boxes on the floor.

Lincoln rummaged on the rack for a moment and handed her a man's white dress shirt. Then he opened one of the boxes and after a moment's search, handed her a pair of short white shorts. "I think these will fit."

Marianne looked at the shorts. "Am I going to be a beach bunny?"

"No," Lincoln replied. "I was thinking of posing you on a boat. It's casual and whenever advertisers want to show class and opulence, they use boats. It's an image that would suit you well." He pointed to a door. "There is a change room in there. See if they fit."

"The shirt is miles too big."

"I know," Lincoln said. "Roll up the sleeves, leave it untucked and tie the tails together at the front. The look you are going for is sensual and casual."

Marianne smiled. "We'll see." She opened the door and went in.

CHAPTER THIRTY NINE

Wednesday, April 26, 1989 Portage la Prairie, Manitoba

Laura Schaefer pushed the button on the garage door opener as she swung her car into the driveway. As the door slowly rose it revealed a second car. "Oh shit," she murmured softly. Darrin's car was there so either he was home early or the poker game had been canceled. She glanced at the dashboard clock as she drove into the garage. 10:15. Not late but hard to explain. Dammit, why should she have to explain? Eric was an old friend to both of them and had suffered a terrible personal loss, on top of some other losses in the last few years. All she had done was to be his friend again for a few hours. She knew that was all true but that Darrin wouldn't buy it. She also knew that Darrin was right. There was a lot more to her feelings for Eric than being an old high school buddy. She sighed and opened the door. Might as well get it over with.

"Hi Honey," she called cheerily from the entry way. There was no response, just the sound of a hockey game coming from the TV set in the family room. A funny name for a room in a house where there were no children. She walked down the short hall to the kitchen, saw the nearly empty bottle of rye on the counter, and peered into the family room. Darrin was glowering at the TV and after a moment glanced up at her.

"Where the hell have you been?" he snapped. He took a large drink from the highball glass in his hand.

Laura took a deep breath. "I stopped by the O'Neill house. Eric got in today and he wanted to talk about the details of his parents' death."

"So lover boy's back, eh?"

"Eric is back for a few days dealing with his parents' estate."

"Well, you just let him deal with it all by himself," he said quietly. "Is that clear enough for you?"

"What is this about, Darrin?" she asked. "He used to be your best friend."

"Yeah, well, that was before he knocked up my wife."

"He didn't knock up your wife," she said.

"Well you're my wife, aren't you? Or you were the last time I checked."

"I wasn't your wife when I got pregnant," she said patiently. How many times had they been through this, always when Darrin was drunk.

"Goddammit, Laura," Darrin shouted. "You got pregnant with that son-of-a-bitch but you sure as hell didn't with me."

"You know we tried."

"Well not bloody hard enough." He took another drink.

"I'm going to bed, Darrin."

"You fucking well don't walk out in the middle of this conversation," he shouted. "You spent all evening sitting around talking with that prick, you can Godamn well sit down and talk with your husband. Did you have a drink over there with Lover-boy?"

"A glass of wine."

"A glass of wine," he mimicked. "Well, well, isn't that classy. Rye not good enough for you anymore?"

"Darrin, you're drunk and your language is abusive."

"I'll tell you when I'm drunk, Godammit." Darrin got out of the chair and stood, swaying unsteadily. "And I'll tell you when this fucking conversation is finished."

"This isn't a conversation."

"Not a conversation?" he shouted. "What do you call it then? You got time to talk to your old lovers, you can fucking well take time to talk to me."

"So talk to me, Darrin," she said with a sigh, knowing what was coming next before he spoke.

"That bastard knocked you up, right?"

Laura stood silently looking at him, wondering why she stayed. Some rye slopped over the edge of his glass and ran down his hand before dripping onto the carpet. His shirt had come untucked, the sweater he wore had crumbs on it from the bag of pretzels he'd eaten, the empty bag lay crumpled beside the chair. His thinning grey hair was mussed. He looked like the middle-aged lush he was.

"Right?" Darrin shouted. "Answer me, Godamn you,"

"Right, Darrin, he knocked me up."

"And you had an abortion in Vancouver. Right?

"Right, Darrin."

"And then you couldn't get pregnant anymore? Right?"

"If you say so."

"I don't need to say so. There's nothing wrong with me or my Godamn sperm. You screwed yourself up with that fucking abortion because that son-of-a-bitch knocked you up."

"Whatever."

Darrin suddenly hurled the glass at the brick wall behind the television set. The tumbler shattered noisily and the remaining rye trickled down the wall, leaving a faint brown stain on the white bricks. "Don't you talk to me that way. I'm your husband you frigid bitch."

Laura looked at the wall and then back at Darrin. "Goodnight, Darrin." She turned away and walked back through the kitchen.

"You stay away from that prick, you hear me?"

Laura hung her coat in the small mud room by the garage entrance.

"You hear me? Godammit I'm talking to you."

Laura walked back into the kitchen. Darrin still stood in the same place, a caricature of his own belligerence. "I hear you, Darrin."

"Well you just stay away from him."

Laura turned and walked down the hall toward her bedroom. She heard Darrin stumble into the kitchen, likely in search of another highball glass and another bottle of rye.

Eric lay in the darkness. He knew he wasn't going to sleep for a while but it didn't really matter. His body was still confused by the jet lag, eight and a half hours from Tahiti to LA, another three hours north to Vancouver, a night of broken sleep in an airport hotel and two and a half more hours in the air to Winnipeg. The evening with Laura had been marvelous, restful and peaceful. He had wondered what they would talk about, old times maybe, or his marriage or hers, but they hadn't. Their conversation had been about the present and about what they had grown into. It was as though they had been trying to tell each other the kind of persons they had become, not boasting or complaining, just talking about things that mattered.

He felt alive and awake. He decided sleep wasn't coming for a while so he slipped out of bed and dressed quickly. He could think about the evening and get a start on the affairs of his family at the same time.

His father's study on the main floor hadn't changed much since he was a child. It was lined with books. The room was dominated by a huge oak desk, a deep lustrous brown, it's surface clear except for a pen set and a reading lamp. In the corner behind the desk were a couple of old wooden file cabinets. The swivel chair sat still and empty behind the desk and his father's favourite reading chair, a large brown leather arm chair with a matching stool, sat in another corner with an old fashioned tri-light behind it.

Eric moved slowly across the room and finally sat in the swivel chair. Where on earth should he start? How could he deal with his father's life, the life of a small town doctor who had been loved and respected by everyone who knew him.

He pulled open the centre drawer of the desk and started. He found a ring with several keys on it, a couple he recognized as being for the summer place at Delta, a couple he didn't recognize, one was a safety deposit box key and there was one small one. He held it up and looked at it carefully. It was old and brass and was for a small lock of some sort. He set the key ring aside and continued working his way through the drawers. An hour later he discovered the bottom left hand drawer was locked and the small brass key fit. He turned it and pulled open the drawer.

A dusty folder lay at the bottom underneath a single envelope and a small metal box. He took the items out and set them on the desk top. The folder contained a single letter, written, as far as he could tell, in German. The stationery was heavy and embossed with an eagle clutching a globe, emblazoned with a swastika. What on earth could this be about? How could it be connected to his father? He shook his head and set it aside.

He lifted the lid on the box and peered inside. An object was wrapped in a layer of cloth, lightly infused with oil. He unwrapped it carefully to reveal a small metal cylinder, about nine inches long, a miniature submarine, painted grey and in a fine square script on the conning tower were the letters 'U64'. It was a detailed rendering, small propellers on the ends of two fine shafts protruding from the stern, a tiny square door marked in the metal above them. He wondered what it was for, perhaps the aft torpedo tube door. A tiny cannon was mounted on the fore deck, its barrel pointed straight forward. Such detail. No wonder his parents hadn't given it to him as a toy to play with. It would have been broken in the first few minutes.

The metal box also contained another small box, a little bigger than a ring box. He opened it to reveal a shiny badge with the word "Kriegsmarine" engraved on it, yet another mystery.

The envelope was addressed to him. It was old and stiff and he carefully slit it open with his father's brass letter opener. He took out the single sheet of paper, read it and sat stunned by what it said. He read it again and again but the words stayed the same. He felt like the foundations of his world had been shaken. He folded it up and slowly slipped it back into the envelope.

CHAPTER FORTY

Wednesday, April 26 1989 Harrisburg, Pennsylvania

"Could we have coffee?" Jon asked. He was seated again at the boardroom table with Einfeld and Clayton. It was early afternoon and the north facing windows were letting in a bit more light from a sunny spring day.

Clayton rose to his feet. "Of course," he said and went to a telephone on a side table at the other end of the room. He returned and sat down. "It will be here momentarily. But first of all, Jon, we would both like to thank you for agreeing to meet with us again today. I feel like we may have gotten off on the wrong foot this morning and I want to assure you that we are your allies and your supporters, not your enemies."

"Thank you, Clark," Jon said warily. "Let's see how the afternoon unfolds, shall we? Just to establish a time frame, I have only an hour to meet with you today. I have another appointment."

Einfeld frowned. "Fair enough. This afternoon we need to cover some background, Jon. We were not informed as to how much you know about your origins, other than the fact that we know you are aware of your birth place as Germany."

"I know that, yes," Jon said cautiously. "But why don't you assume that I know little else and tell me the rest."

"Good move, Jon," Clayton said, with a short chuckle. It was the first sound of humour Jon had heard from either of them. "In case we don't have accurate information or you think we are trying to bluff, you'll find out."

Einfeld ignored Clayton's comment. "All right, Jon," he began. "Here is a brief history of what we know of your origins."

There was gentle knock on the door behind them and the secretary who had shown Jon in entered with a tray. She set it down in front of Clayton. "Thank you," he said and the woman nodded, turned without a word and left the room.

"You take your coffee black, I believe," Clayton said, pouring a steaming mug full and setting it in front of Jon.

Jon nodded, wondering what else they knew of his personal habits. He took a sip. It was strong and rich as he liked it. "Thank you."

Einfeld shook his head as Clayton raised his eyebrows and pointed at a cup. "You were born in a small town in southern Germany. The date on your birth certificate is accurate, but it claims you were born in Philadelphia and that is not true. In the fall of 1940 you and another child, also about a year old, were flown from Berlin to Lisbon in Portugal, and after refuelling there, you continued across the Atlantic to Philadelphia. You were accompanied by a doctor, two nurses and a security officer. After your arrival, you were placed with a German family in a suburb of Philadelphia. The rest of your growing up you know."

"I didn't know how I was transported here," Jon said. "I hadn't really given a lot of thought to how I got here and I didn't know there was another child. What happened?"

"We can't tell you that, Jon."

"Why not?"

"Because you don't need to know anything about him."

"Does the other child know anything about me?" Jon asked. "Because if he does he can compromise my political future."

"He doesn't know of your existence, Jon, and will never be a threat to you in any way."

Jon looked searchingly from one to the other as he pondered this information. They had better have it right. "Fair enough," he said. "So now I know how I got here."

"There was a third child that was sent to Canada but he and the people with him died in a fire a few days after they arrived there. This is of no concern to you other than giving you a fuller picture of what was going on."

"A third child," Jon murmured. "Also born in the small town in Southern Germany?"

"That is correct," Einfeld said.

"Is there more?"

"Much more," Einfeld went on. "How you got here is the simple part. Why you were sent here is the interesting question. Can you imagine the kind of power it took in 1940 when the Fatherland was fighting a war, to free up a Condor aircraft and crew plus the medical personnel involved, to take a child to North America?"

"I can imagine," Jon said quietly, remembering the difficulty that junior officers had in Vietnam in moving personal things about, but also recalling that high ranking officers seemed to have little trouble in commandeering planes, trucks or other military resources to solve personal problems. However, in 1940, an aircraft capable of transatlantic flight would have taxed their ingenuity.

"You are likely the son of a very high ranking German officer who was also in a position of considerable power within the Nazi party. We don't know the precise identity of your parents, but we do know that people close to Adolf Hitler himself were involved."

"How do you know that?"

"Because the man who became Hitler's principal secretary made the arrangements. Martin Bormann."

Jon was silent for a moment as he thought of the implications of this. "But why would Bormann bother with a child?"

"Bormann got a bad press after the war. He was a bureaucrat but he also had a good head for numbers and knew what Germany's production capacity was. He did some simple arithmetic and calculated that Germany could not sustain the war that Hitler had in mind. He was likely the first senior minister in Hitler's government who knew that Germany was going to lose the war. By 1940 he knew the Third Reich would not last a thousand years; it would be lucky to last five. He was pretty accurate."

"I still don't understand why he would send a one year old child abroad," Jon interjected.

"The Fourth Reich," Einfeld said quietly.

"The Fourth Reich?" Jon echoed incredulously. "You mean those old Nazis wandering around South America living on fifty year old dreams of glory?"

Clayton laughed, cutting it short as Einfeld glared at him. "I do not," Einfeld said sternly. "The Third Reich was a political entity attempting to spread National Socialism across Europe and eventually across the world by means of political negotiation, and where that failed, by military conquest."

Jon smiled in spite of himself. Surely he wasn't going to be treated to a tirade about the revival of the Nazi movement. The skin heads and the militia nut cases weren't going anywhere.

"Humour me, Colonel Falken," Einfeld said. "And I will bring you up to date on the last fifty years of the Nazi movement in the world. What I am about to tell you is not fantasy or invention, it is not some stupid James-Bond-like plot or some silly world conspiracy dreamed up by an obsessive American novelist."

Jon took a sip of his coffee and held the cup out to Clayton who refilled it. He leaned back in his chair.

"Do you know who Walter Schellenberg was?" Einfeld asked.

"A Nazi general in World War Two."

"Correct," Einfeld said. "After the Battle of Stalingrad in January 1943 the realists in the German army knew that the war was lost and they began to shift their attention from the Fuhrer's concept of 'lebensraum', 'living space for the master race' would be a very loose translation, to defending western civilization against communism, and for those of them who still believed in the master race nonsense, from the 'Asiatic mongrel peril'.

"The communist east and the capitalist west were developing a tenuous kind of cooperation to ensure the defeat and the restructuring of post-war Germany. So in December of 1942 Schellenberg initiated contact with the Americans through Allen Dulles in Switzerland. You will recall that Dulles controlled the Office of Strategic Services operations in Europe, the OSS being the forerunner of the CIA. Schellenberg pointed out that Germany and the US had far more in common than the US and the Soviet Union and he suggested a rapprochement with the US to allow Germany to defeat the Soviet Union. This in turn would allow the US to focus on defeating Japan in the Pacific. Apparently, Dulles thought it wasn't an entirely foolish idea."

Jon set his coffee cup on the table and stood up. "Have you forgotten that I was a high ranking military officer and I know military history rather well?" He stepped back from the table and looked at them. "Either tell me something I don't know or quit wasting my time."

Einfled nodded. "Please be patient with us, Jon. There is a point to telling you this."

Jon turned to look out the window. "Very well, but can you make soon?"

Einfeld continued. "Just a little more background, Jon. Schellenberg also contacted the Soviets to fuel Stalin's well known paranoia, and let them know that their trusted ally, the USA, was making secret deals behind their back with the German high command.

"This in turn promoted Allen Dulles' fear that the Germans would make a deal with the Soviets and then turn their full attention on Western Europe which at the very least would prolong the war and consume US military resources required to defeat Japan. Dulles loathed communism and believed that in the post war world, an alliance with Germany would be much preferable to one with the Soviets and so the seeds of the cold war were planted."

Jon returned to the table and sat down. "I am familiar with history of World War Two," Jon said. "Does this have some relevance to my being sent abroad in 1940?"

"It does, Jon," Einfeld replied. "Please indulge me."

Jon looked at his watch. "Very well."

Einfeld continued. "At the end of World War II Germany and much of Europe was in ruins. You may be aware that a lot of senior people in the Nazi party and the German Wehrmacht got out of Germany, many thousands of them, in fact. There were no end of fanciful plots developed by the invading forces as to how this happened but the truth of it was that in the chaos of the last days of the War it was relatively simple. Tens of millions of dollars, most of it in gold, had been moved out of Germany beginning as early as 1940."

"To South America?" Jon asked.

"About 25,000 kilograms of gold was moved to Argentina alone, as an example of what went there, but a lot also went to Switzerland, to Spain, Portugal, the Scandinavian countries, the US, Canada and other countries as well. In those days bankers tended to accept gold without asking a lot about its origins." Einfeld paused. "Does that answer your question?"

Jon nodded. "Thank you."

"By the end of the War an economic base had been established abroad but the Nazi movement was entirely discredited."

"To put it mildly," Jon interjected.

"Yes," Einfeld said. "To put it mildly."

Jon looked at his watch again and saw that they had been chatting for about forty-five minutes. This whole lecture was getting tedious. There were a few bits of personal information that he hadn't known but most of the rest he knew or at least knew something about. He rose to his feet. "Gentlemen," he said. "I apologize for running out on you but I have to be getting on to my next meeting. Thank you for your time."

"The thanks is all ours, Jon," Einfeld said. "We aren't quite finished our briefing. In fact most of the really relevant material has still to be covered. Do you have any time tomorrow?"

"Would tomorrow afternoon at the same time work?" Jon asked.

"That would be fine," Einfeld replied. "We'll look forward to seeing you then."

As he walked out of the board room, Jon rolled his eyes. Surely this couldn't go on for too much longer.

CHAPTER FORTY ONE

Wednesday, April 26, 1989 Philadelphia

When Marianne stepped out of the change room, Lincoln knew he had been right. She would be a great subject. She was barefoot and had tousled her hair a bit, either purposely or by accident when she had slipped off her sweater. The shorts fit well, tight enough to be sexy but not so tight as to be lewd, but the white shirt was the best part of the costume. She had tied the tails around her waist, done up three buttons and to his surprise had removed her bra. The way the shirt rounded over her breasts was full of promise.

"What do you think?" she asked, turning slowly in a circle.

"I think you're very beautiful," Carswell replied softly. "And I think I am a genius for choosing those clothes."

Marianne laughed, a bright sparkling sound. "That good?"

"That good," Carswell confirmed. "If it's summer and you're on a boat you'd be wearing sunglasses. Do you have a pair with you?"

"I do," Marianne said, walking over to the purse she had set by the stool. She picked it up and withdrew a pair of plain dark-lensed glasses. "Do you want them in my hair or on my face?

"On your face," Lincoln said. "That way I can show reflections. It can be quite an interesting technique for adding intrigue to a painting."

"Intrigue?"

"Who is the mysterious stranger watching her?"

"I'm going to be on a boat with a mysterious stranger?"

Lincoln laughed. "It won't be a mystery to you but it should be to the viewer, although I just used that as a example. There could be the reflection of several people, or of another boat nearby, or of someone about to dive into the water. Really anything we decide to put on the lenses."

"Sounds interesting."

"Now I want to pose you on a boat. It will be a sailboat, and you will be holding the wheel. That puts you in control and will add a sense of power to your image. Stand over by the stool and put on your sunglasses."

Marianne did as she was told. "How do you want me to be standing?"

"I want you to feel the deck of the boat under your feet. It's a moving platform so your feet will be slightly apart, bracing yourself against the motion of the boat. The wheel will give you stability against falling forward or backward. Hold your hands up as though they were on the wheel. It will be about four feet in diameter and your hands will be at about 11:00 o'clock and 1:00 o'clock."

Marianne stood by the stool as Lincoln had described. "Where am I looking?" she asked.

"Into the distance," Lincoln replied. "There are other people on the boat but you're ignoring them because you're guiding the boat. You're in charge."

She smiled. "I like that."

"Good," Lincoln said. "Then it'll feel natural." He picked up his camera again and walked around her taking a number of photographs. "Don't lock your knees," he said. "You will be on a slight angle, ready to respond to changes in the wind or waves."

She adjusted her pose.

"Now I need a small smile," Lincoln said. "It will express pleasure because you love what you're doing. It will convey self-confidence because you know how to sail a boat and you're doing it well. Others on the boat are watching you, some of the women with envy, the men with something close to lust. You look fabulous and you know it."

Marianne shifted her body slightly and a faint smile appeared on her face.

"Perfect," Lincoln said, his amazement showing in his voice. "Just perfect." He snapped another series of pictures, switched to a portrait lense and snapped a few more from different angles. "Can you hold this a little longer?"

Marianne nodded.

Lincoln picked up a sketch pad, and worked rapidly, sketching her pose, her face, the outline of her hair. He tore off the page and did a second and then a third sketch. Then he stopped, stood up and walked around her. "I am really grateful you've agreed to do this. If I can capture what you look like and put it into context, we will have a really fine painting."

"Can I relax now?"

"Of course."

Marianne shrugged her shoulders, turned her head and stretched her arms out in front of her. "That feels better," she said. "I just thought of it while you were sketching me. What happens to this portrait when it's finished?"

Lincoln smiled at her. "What would you like?"

"If it is as good as you say, I would like to have it myself."

"You wouldn't mind if I put it into a show first?"

"I don't think so, but I'm not sure what it will reveal about me."

"Almost anything you want."

Marianne laughed. "That's a clever answer, but I don't want it to be too suggestive."

"It will certainly suggest things but I hope nothing that will dismay you."

A few minutes later, Marianne emerged from the small changing room, her costume gone and her formality restored.

Lincoln looked up from his sketch pad. He had been roughing out some background, working out a composition. "Hello, again," he said.

Marianne came up behind him, rested her hands lightly on his shoulders and watched him draw. Lincoln finished an outline sketch of a woman, no facial features, or body characteristics, with a circle in front of her, a sloping line under her feet, some lines in the background. The outline of a man took shape, leaning back against a railing or a line, his hand braced on something, his featureless head facing toward the woman.

"Who's the guy?" Marianne asked.

"Who would you like him to be?" Lincoln asked. "It could be your husband if I had a photograph of him or if he'd like to pose for one. Or anyone else you think you'd like to go sailing with."

Marianne was silent for a moment. "I don't think my husband would go sailing."

"Anyone else then?"

"Could it be you?"

"Certainly."

"Then let's do that," she said. "Do you do much sailing?"

Lincoln laughed, tore off the sketch and closed the pad. "I've never been on a sailboat. I don't really like water much unless it's mixed with good bourbon."

"I've never been on one either so this painting will be a new experience for both of us." Marianne withdrew her hands as Lincoln stood up.

He looked at his watch. "It's almost five," he said. "Can I offer you a glass of wine?"

"Sure," Marianne said. "I'd enjoy that."

"I'm not keeping you from your next appointment?"

"Not at all. My next appointment is with rush hour traffic and I'd be happy to put that off for a while."

Lincoln gathered up his sketches and put them on a desk in the centre of the room. He picked up his camera, pushed the rewind button and popped a roll of film out of the back. He did the same with a second camera.

"I didn't realize you were using two cameras," Marianne said.

"One is colour, one is black and white," Lincoln said. "Your hair is so dominant that in a colour photo it just takes over. The black and whites give me a better sense of composition and better shadows and highlights."

He turned off the lights as they left the studio. They walked back down the hall, returning to the living room area. Lincoln passed through it and into the kitchen. Marianne followed him and climbed onto a stool by the counter facing into the kitchen work area.

"Red or white, or something else?" Lincoln asked.

"White, please."

"Chardonnay, Sauvignon Blanc or something else?"

"Where's the Chardonnay from?"

"California or France."

"France," Marianne said.

Lincoln moved to a small refrigerator with a glass door and removed a bottle. He set it on the counter in front of her with the label facing her. "Are you familiar with this one?"

She glanced at it and shook her head.

He peeled the foil cover off the top of the bottle and removed the cork. Turning back to the counter on the other side of the kitchen, he slipped two glasses out of a rack and placed them in front of her, carefully pouring each of them half full. He pushed one toward her and picked up his own. "Cheers," he said and they clinked the glasses together.

"This is lovely wine," Marianne said as she set her glass back on the counter. She looked at it appreciatively.

"Thank you," he said. "I'm glad you like it. Let's go sit in the living room. It'll be a bit more comfortable than that stool." He picked up his glass and led her to a love seat facing the fireplace. They sat down.

"How long will it take you to do the portrait?" Marianne asked. She pulled her knees up and sat facing Lincoln.

"A week to a month, depending on how it goes."

"That's interesting," she said. "Why the uncertainty?"

Lincoln thought for a moment. "Sometimes it flows really fast and smoothly, other times I have to work much harder. I expect your portrait will be fairly fast."

She raised her eyebrows.

"I'm inspired." Lincoln laughed. "Tell me more about yourself, Marianne." He leaned back against the soft leather cushions of the love seat. "When you arrived this afternoon you had a lot of questions for me and I answered them but you didn't tell me much about yourself."

Marianne took a sip of her wine. "What would you like to know?"

"I know you're married, or at least wearing a wedding ring." Lincoln rose from the love seat and strolled over to the kitchen counter. He picked up the bottle of Chardonnay and returned, setting it on the coffee table in front of them and sat down again.

"I'm married to Jon Falken, a retired army officer, who is thinking of running for congress."

"I've heard of him," Lincoln said. "But I didn't make the connection. Any children?"

"No," she replied. "Neither of us really wanted children. I saw too many Army brats running around the bases where we were stationed and I didn't think that was much of a life for a kid."

"Where are you from?"

"Originally, from California," she said. "My father was a real estate developer at the right time after World War II and made a lot of money. I'm not sure why he worked so hard at it because he inherited a lot, too. He told me once that some people like to spend money and some like to make it. He liked to make it."

"What about you?" Lincoln asked.

Marianne sipped her wine again and tipped her head to one side. "I haven't really thought about it. I grew up with wealth so money has never been very important to me. My husband grew up in a poor family so money is a huge deal to him." She paused. "I don't care so much about spending it but I like good things, and money gets good things. I like nice clothes, good cars, fine art, which I guess brought me here."

Lincoln picked up the bottle and added some wine to both their glasses. "Brothers or sisters?"

"I'm an only child," Marianne replied. "I like it that way. I can be independent, not worry about family squabbles or anything like that. I guess I'm missing the closeness of a sister or a brother but I've never had it so what's to miss?"

Lincoln glanced at his watch. "Could I convince you to stay and have dinner with me?"

Marianne met his eyes, held them for a moment and nodded. "That would be nice," she said. "You're a very peaceful person to be around."

Lincoln smiled at her. "I've never been told that before. Thank you." He stood up and held out his hand to Marianne. She took it and as she rose to her feet she was close to him. He stood there for a moment and then stepped back, releasing her hand and picking up his glass and the wine bottle, now almost empty. He turned and walked back to the kitchen.

Marianne followed him and climbed on a stool at the kitchen counter as Lincoln went around to the other side. He took two fresh wine glasses from a cupboard and set them on the counter. "I think we'll switch to a Sauvignon Blanc for dinner if that's okay?"

"Don't feed me too much wine," Marianne said. "I still have to drive."

"No worries," Lincoln said. "I'll feed you exactly the right amount." He opened the refrigerator and removed a chilled bottle of wine, deftly removed the cork, and poured a generous amount into each of the glasses. He picked up his and raised it in a toast. "To art." They touched their glasses together.

Turning back to the refrigerator, he lifted out a bowl covered in plastic wrap. He set it on the counter near her and removed the plastic. "I hope you like prawns."

"I love them."

"They've been marinating in some herbs and Cointreau."

"Are you always this prepared for dinner?" Marianne asked.

"No," Lincoln said. "I was being presumptuous. I was hoping if our sitting went well that you would stay and have dinner with me."

Marianne was silent. She took a sip of her wine.

"And was I?" he asked.

"Being presumptuous?"

Lincoln nodded as he removed a wok from a cupboard under the counter and set it on the stove.

"Yes, you were," she said. "But I love prawns."

As Lincoln prepared a salad, they chatted about art and galleries they had been to. Lincoln found himself enjoying Marianne a lot. Most people were too aware of his stature as a professional artist to talk to him about art but Marianne was not intimidated in the slightest.

"Can I help?" Marianne asked.

"Sure," Lincoln replied. "You can set the table." He added a splash of peanut oil, some butter and two cloves of crushed garlic to the wok, waited a moment until the butter began to bubble and dumped in the prawns.

Marianne came around the counter into the kitchen and stood beside Lincoln, her arm brushing against his, as she peeked into the wok. The prawns were sizzling as he tossed them with a large metal spoon and the kitchen was rich with smells of butter, garlic and Cointreau.

"Cutlery is in that drawer," he said, pointing to one in the counter.

Marianne opened the drawer, gathered the utensils and set them on the counter. "Place mats?" she asked.

Lincoln pointed to another drawer. She pulled it open, removed three and walked to the table, setting one in the middle, and then two together on one side facing the window that looked out into the small garden. She retrieved the cutlery and set it on the place mats, then stood back and looked over the table. She took the wine bottle and placed it on the centre placemat.

"Ready?" Lincoln asked. He approached the table with two plates, steam rising from them, and set them down.

Marianne retrieved their wine glasses from the counter, set them beside the plates and sat down.

"Do you say grace?" Lincoln asked.

Marianne laughed. "Not since I was a child." She picked up her wine glass. "But I do like toasts." She turned to Lincoln and raised her glass. "To good food and new friends."

Lincoln raised his glass and joined her, repeating the toast.

After dessert, Lincoln made coffee in a French press and they sat on the love seat again and drank it, laced with Kaluha and cream. He picked up a remote control from the end table beside him and clicked it. The gas fireplace burst into flame casting a soft yellow glow over the room.

"That was a beautiful dinner, Lincoln," Marianne said. "I've never had a man prepare dinner for me before."

"Really?"

"Really," Marianne said. "Thank you."

They sat in silence for a few moments.

"Will you give me your recipe for chocolate mousse?" she asked.

"Of course," Lincoln said. "It's a recipe I got from a friend who grew up in Algeria. It's fiddly, full of egg yolks, whipping cream and the like and takes about an hour to put together, but I find it's worth the time."

"I've never tasted chocolate that good."

"Thank you."

"When can I see my portrait?" Marianne asked.

"When will you be back in Philadelphia?"

"I'm not sure but it's a short flight."

"Where are you staying?"

"With a girlfriend," Marianne said. She glanced at her watch. "Speaking of whom, I should call her and let her know where I am."

"Does she know you're at a portrait sitting?"

"Yes, but that was the afternoon."

"Does she know who you're sitting for?"

"No," Marianne replied. "I left it vague."

Lincoln smiled. "Is she likely to worry about you?"

"Maybe, but if I could use your phone, I'll let her know I'm still alive."

"How much wine have you had?"

Marianne laughed. "More than usual."

Lincoln looked at her seriously. "Me too," Lincoln said. "Are you comfortable driving to her place from here?"

"I have her car so I'll have to be careful with it."

"I have a guest suite that you're more than welcome to use."

Marianne looked at him silently. "Now you're being presumptuous again."

Lincoln laughed. "Not at all," he said. "I feel responsible for you. I fed you dinner and a bunch of wine and I don't want you getting into an accident on the way home. I don't have any ulterior motives."

Marianne continued staring at him, a slow smile stealing across her lips. "All men have ulterior motives."

Lincoln was silent for a moment. "You're probably right, Marianne," he said. "But there's a lock on the door if you're really worried about my motives."

Marianne laughed. "Let me call my girlfriend."

Lincoln handed her a cordless telephone receiver from the end table beside him.

She dialled the number and then stood up, walking toward the fireplace. Lincoln rose and went into the kitchen to give Marianne more privacy and load some dishes into the dishwasher. He finished and wiped off the counter. Marianne was still on the phone. He could catch the occasional word but not the conversation. To occupy himself, he opened the refrigerator, though nothing in it needed his attention.

"Okay."

Lincoln turned. Marianne was standing on the other side of the counter.

"Okay?" he said.

"Okay, I'll take you up on your guest suite invitation."

Lincoln nodded. "I'm glad."

"My girlfriend was too, once I convinced her that I might bash up her BMW if I drove it to her place."

"The guest suite has a tooth brush and all the other things you're likely to need."

"I'm fine," Marianne said. "I have my overnight bag in the car."

Lincoln laughed. "Is it your turn to be presumptuous?"

"Celeste picked me up at the airport. I haven't been to her place yet."

CHAPTER FORTY TWO

Thursday, April 27, 1989 Portage la Prairie, Canada

Laura Schaefer sat at her desk and stared at the neat stack of files that Gloria had set on one corner before she had gone home yesterday, patient files that she should look through quickly to familiarize herself with who she was seeing today. She would do that and then head up to the hospital for her morning rounds. Glancing at the old brass clock she saw it was a few minutes before seven.

She thought about last night, about the beautifully peaceful time she had spent with Eric and the vicious verbal attack from Darrin when she had arrived home. When she was leaving Eric's house, he held her coat as she slipped into it. She'd wondered if he would kiss her goodnight. She smiled. She'd wondered that the first time he'd walked her home and now, thirty-two years later, she was wondering the same thing again. Maybe she was a slow learner. Maybe she and Eric were starting over again. Yesterday she'd felt again the same nervousness, a combination of wishing he'd do it and fear that he would. As she had turned to him, doing up the buttons on her coat, he'd stepped back and watched her hands. She'd stood by the front door for a moment before she opened it. She had thanked him for dinner and a pleasant evening. He'd stepped up to the door, leaned forward and given her a quick hug, kissing her softly on the cheek. Well, she thought, there's thirty-two years of progress.

On her way to work this morning, she had peeked quickly into Darrin's bedroom. He was lying on the bed, fully clothed, snoring gently. Another night of drinking until he passed out. Those had become all too common lately. The separate bedrooms was his idea, years ago, when he had grown tired of phone calls in the middle of the night; a mother about to have a baby, a patient in the hospital emergency ward, a car accident and she was on call. For years she had been grateful for the arrangement.

The phone rang in the outer office. She listened to the clicks on the answering machine and then picked up the receiver at the sound of Eric's voice. "Good morning, Eric," she said, realizing her voice sounded a little breathless.

There was silence on the line for a moment. "You're in early this morning."

"Not really, this is about my normal time. I was about to go up to the hospital to do my rounds. My first patient appointment isn't until 10:00."

"I won't hold you up then," Eric said. "Do you still read and speak German?"

"A bit," Laura replied. "I don't use it much anymore since my parents died except on the occasional German speaking patient. Why?"

"Did you ever speak German with my parents?"

Laura was silent, wondering how she could tell him of the last words his father had spoken. "Eric," she said. "The night your father died, just before he lost consciousness, he grabbed my arm and said something to me. I was so busy, I didn't realize until later when I went to write it down that he had spoken to me in German. I was going to tell you." She paused. "I never heard your mother use it."

"What did my father say, Laura?"

"Just a moment, I wrote it on a prescription pad in my purse." She reached into a small compartment on the outside of her purse and retrieved the pad. "He said, 'Care for Eric. There is so much I should have told him. It's all written down. He can decide what to do.'" Laura paused. "But what's this about?" she asked.

"Last night after you left I started going through some papers in my father's study and I came across a file that contained a single sheet of paper, a letter of some sort, that's written in German."

"That's odd, but they might have been medical records or patient information from someone who was German."

"I don't think so but there are some notations on the papers. I'm no handwriting expert but I'm pretty sure it's my father's handwriting and it's in German."

"How strange."

"I wondered if you could tell me what it says?"

"Probably, if it isn't too complicated."

For a moment the phone was silent again. "I guess I'd be pressing my luck to ask if you were free again for dinner tonight?"

Laura laughed at the tentative tone. "No, it would be pressing my luck, not yours, but I could stop over for a few minutes on my way home. I think I should be done about five today unless something happens, which it often does in this job."

"That would be wonderful," Eric said. "I don't want to cause any difficulty between you and Darrin, Laura. I know he's a bit sensitive about you and me."

"Just a bit," Laura said, wondering if Eric would pick up on the sarcasm. This morning she didn't care.

"Anything I can do?"

"Nothing," Laura said. "Nothing you can do and nothing you should be concerned about." She thought she should feel disloyal talking to Eric about Darrin but she felt nothing. She really had no feelings left for Darrin and not much else but some fond memories of their early years together. More recent memories she just didn't think about.

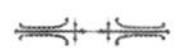

Eric glanced at his watch and saw it was a few minutes after five. He stood up and stretched. His father's desk chair was comfortable but sitting anywhere for very long made him want to stretch. He walked out to the kitchen, opened the refrigerator and took out a beer, one of the six pack he had bought on his way home. There seemed to be lots of liquor in the house and he had even found a store of wine in a cool room in the basement. He hadn't remembered that his parents had kept wine there but perhaps it was a more recent habit. He'd decided to round out the collection and picked up some beer. He snapped the cap off the bottle and took a long drink. It was cold and refreshing. He walked back to the study and sat down again. His mind felt numb, overloaded with information. What to make of it, or perhaps even, so what?

He heard a light knock on the front door and listened as it opened. "Eric?"

"In the study, Laura." He stood up and came around to the front of the desk.

She walked into the study and slipped her arms around him. "You look tired, Eric. Is there something wrong?"

"I don't think so," he whispered into her hair. He released her and gently placed the miniature U boat in her hand. "I found this little toy in my father's desk and there was a note explaining its origins at the bank, in the family safety deposit box,. It was made for me by a German sailor who was on a U boat that brought me across the Atlantic Ocean in 1940."

"A U boat?" Laura asked. "All the way across the Atlantic. There must be quite a story there!" She reached behind him and picked up his beer bottle and took a long drink from it. "Can I have one of these, too?" she asked.

"Of course," Eric said. "I'm forgetting my manners. Sit down." He guided her toward the leather chair. "I'll get you one."

Eric returned a minute later. "Do you still drink beer from the bottle or would you like a glass?"

Laura laughed. "A bottle is fine." She tipped it up and drank. "So what did you do today?" she asked.

"Some odds and ends of shopping but for the main event I went to the bank and checked the safety deposit box. There were a few surprises. I found my parents' Canadian passports and also two very old passports, dating from 1938 and issued in Ireland. They always told me they were born in England. However, the really exciting finds happened during the night when I couldn't sleep. I found a letter from Mom and Dad that really threw me. I just don't know what to do about it. In one sense it simply doesn't matter but in another it tells me things about my origins that are intriguing. Upsetting, I guess if I'm honest about it. I'd really value your take on the letter. And another letter in German, dated 1940, October, I think. I can't read it but I am hoping you can." He paused. "Otherwise, just a day of sifting through things. Putting my parents estate in order. However, deciding what to do about this information is going to take a bit longer than I thought it would."

"I'm glad."

"You sure?"

"Not at all sure, but it's nice to see you again." She looked up at him. "To hang out with you for a while."

Eric was silent for a moment. "Maybe you'll change your mind. Have a look at the first mystery letter." Eric handed her an envelope. She removed the single sheet of paper and began to read aloud.

September 1957

Dearest Eric,

If you are reading this letter, it is likely that we are both gone. As you can see from the date on the letter, you have now finished high school and moved to Toronto to begin the next phase of your life. As your parents, we will always be a part of you, but our role in shaping you and your life is now over. Henceforth, you will find your own way.

Over the years that you have been our son, we have debated whether to tell you the following information or to simply let it pass with us. We finally concluded that you had a right to know and that you would have to decide what to pursue, what to ignore and what to do, if anything, about the knowledge you will now have regarding your origins.

You are our adopted son, not our birth son. However, you must never question our love for you, Eric, it is total. We adopted you, in a manner of speaking, when you were one year old. You were born, not as your birth certificate says, in London, England, but in Germany. We brought you from Germany to Canada in the fall of 1940 to ensure you would have a safe childhood. It was a rather arduous trip by train across occupied France and then via U boat across the Atlantic. Others were to return you to Germany, but after World War II ended there wasn't much of a Germany to go back to so we stayed here. Incidentally, we were both born in Germany as well.

We do not know who your parents were but they went to considerable effort to get you out of Germany, and in 1940 that probably meant that your father was an important man in the armed forces or the government or both and almost certainly a figure of prominence and power in the National Socialist Party.

Should you decide to explore your origins more fully, you must do so with great care as we do not know what you may find at the end of your journey. We have provided some additional information with this letter that might help. Of course, your origins need not concern you at all if you choose to ignore them and this may well be the wisest course for you to follow.

We are immensely proud of you, Eric, and love you deeply. You have been a source of great pride and satisfaction for both of us.

With all our love,
Your Mother and Father.

Laura read it through a second time in silence. "So what do you think?"

"I honestly don't know. I think I'm still in shock. They are my mother and father, I've never known any other. But why all the mystery? Why not just tell me when I turned fifteen or something?"

"I've known patients who were adopted children and who desperately wanted to know about their real parents and can't find out much. Others just don't care and are quite happy to go through life with their adoptive parents. It's a very personal choice, Eric, but you're fortunate to have the choice. Not many do."

Eric tipped his beer bottle and took a drink. "Maybe so, but there's more. In the safety deposit box there was an envelope with some banking information. It gave me account numbers and codes for an account in Switzerland, mysterious and numbered, of course." He paused and smiled. "That sort of thing I understand. I've had lots of clients looking to hide their money from the Canadian tax authorities and the secrecy of Swiss banking laws are well known to anyone in the financial business. These days most of the money goes to other tax havens like the Bahamas or Grand Cayman. Anyway, I called my old firm in Toronto today and started the process of tracking down what's there. They will get back to me shortly, I expect. There may well be nothing there, the account may have been closed after all these years. However, I need help with something else." He handed Laura a small box.

She opened the box carefully and examined a shiny metal badge set on a blue velvet liner. "Kriegsmarine," she said softly. "This is a German navy insignia of some sort, a badge for a cap, perhaps." She handed it back.

Eric opened a file folder and passed a single sheet of stationary to Laura. "What's this?" she asked.

"I don't know," Eric replied. "But read on."

It was a letter in German, typed and dated October 12, 1940. The single sheet was a heavy bond paper, embossed with an eagle clutching a globe adorned with a swastika. He watched her read through it slowly. She looked up at Eric when she was finished. "You're quite right, it is in German. The embossed stationary with the eagle, the globe and the swastika likely means it originated somewhere in the Nazi hierarchy. It's an itinerary of sorts, written like a military order for a group of three, a man, woman and a child, who are traveling from Berlin to L'Orient, wherever that is. It instructs anyone who is asked, to furnish whatever assistance may be required to the bearer of this letter. The bearer is identified as a Captain Schiller, a doctor in some medical corps, but I don't understand enough military organization to grasp it."

"What about the notations?"

"They seem to be changes in the orders, made by Captain Schiller. Apparently they changed from railway to motor car at some point."

"You knew my father's handwriting, Laura. Are those notations in the margin in his writing?"

"It sure looks the same."

"That's what I thought, too. So was Captain Schiller later to become Gilford O'Neill?"

"I don't know," Laura said. "But did you look at the signature, Eric."

Eric shook his head. "I just saw it was in German, looked at a couple of the notations that looked like they were written by my Dad and left the rest for you."

Laura read aloud. "By Order of the Fuhrer, and it's signed, 'Martin Bormann'."

"The man who became Adolf Hitler's principal secretary," Eric whispered.

CHAPTER FORTY THREE

Thursday, April 27, 1989 Surrey, England

Martin Bormann stood at the window of his study staring out at the rain. He was used to it now, this incessant rain, or drizzle, or fog, the air seemed always to be full of water. No wonder the English were such a sallow race, every shred of colour was constantly washed out of them. He looked out over the green lawn to the trees, shadowed in the mist, a hundred metres away. Perhaps it would clear a bit later so he could go for a walk. He heard a noise behind him as the door to the study opened. He turned.

"Good morning, sir," his aide said, entering with a tray bearing a silver coffee pot and a china mug. He walked carefully across the thickly carpeted floor and set the tray down on the large oak desk. Heinz had been with him a long time, had come with him to England in fact, although they'd been separated for a couple of years while the English learned Bormann's secrets. Bormann smiled. The English were such an interesting combination of sophistication and naivete. He wondered if it came from sending the elite to private schools and teaching them the rules of fair play. Maybe they just trained the deviousness out of them. At any rate, Bormann had made a deal and kept it. The English brought him out of the conflagration that was Berlin in 1945 and gave him a new life. In return, he gave them more information than they had dreamed of but all they wanted, it seemed, was history, who did what, when had it happened, what about the camps, and so on. They never asked him much about the future, although to be sure, they did want to know where the money went, the Reichbank gold, the plunder. He gave them some of that, too. But they never asked about the future of the National Socialist movement. Strange.

Heinz poured coffee into the china mug. "Will there be anything else, sir?"

"Not for the moment, Heinz. Thank you." Bormann walked over to the desk and picked up the coffee. He took a tentative sip, strong and rich. He rather liked it black, now that he was used to it. His wretched doctor had taken the cream and sugar out of his coffee a few years ago and changed his entire diet, no alcohol, lots of fresh fruit and vegetables. Where the hell did you get fresh fruit in England? And they boiled their vegetables to mush. He made some small changes to appease the physician. He expected he would have to make a few more. He sat down, the large leather chair groaning slightly as it always did. He swiveled the chair to the right and took in the large portrait of Adolf Hitler, draped in two Nazi flags, a golden eagle clutching a globe at the top of the picture frame. Two or three generations had spent vast amounts of time and energy trying to explain Hitler, to understand him. Bormann often wondered why. Hitler had been at heart a fairly simple man, a psychopath who needed to impose his will on the world.

A few years ago, Bormann learned that one of his grandchildren had been diagnosed as autistic. It was a recently discovered form of autism called

Asperger's syndrome, named after the Austrian doctor who had identified it. He had never seen any of his grandchildren except in pictures, nor any of his nine children, his wife or any other relative since 1945. He had officially died in the railway switching yards near the Lehrter Station in Berlin in the early hours of May 2, 1945 and he preferred to keep it that way. However, he did get occasional reports on his family.

He asked his secretary, Joachim, to find out about Asperger's Syndrome and the moment he began to read about it a picture of Adolf Hitler emerged. Bright, full of ideas with no ability to prioritize any of them, a restless energy, a need to be the centre of attention and to dominate any conversation he was part of, a need to lecture, to explain and to impose his point of view. In children it was referred to as "the little professor" syndrome. Bormann laughed when he read about the complete lack of sensitivity and social skills that was a common feature of the disorder. The parallels went on and on. Which was why he, Martin Bormann, the "plodding bureaucrat", as Hitler had once called him, ended up choosing the priorities, making the decisions and directing much of the operations of the Third Reich.

He shook himself out of his reverie and rolled his chair up to his desk. Simple man or not, even in death Adolf Hitler could still exert an immense influence on his thoughts. He shrugged and opened a file that Joachim had placed there. Joachim had been with him only twenty years. The file contained the estate accounts. Bormann had discovered years ago that he enjoyed the process of running his estate. He puttered in the gardens and had come to like roses, they grew well in England. The land holding of a few hundred acres was covered in trees, had a bit of wild life in it but, other than the flower and vegetable gardens, it produced nothing. Except for his personal staff and the security staff, it hired no one. Income came from bank accounts in the Channel Islands. So it was all quite simple. Still, he enjoyed the weekly review of the accounts. In his youth he originally was trained to run agricultural estates. The training had been thorough and transferable too, he mused, since it had taken him through the ranks of the Nazi party to the post of Adolf Hitler's principal secretary, a position of power in the Third Reich exceeded only by Hitler himself. Now, at 88 years of age, he still liked numbers, production figures and income figures. They gave him a picture. He still liked the game too, political intrigue and manipulation, although that was largely limited now to his last project, but it was still running after all these years. He sipped his coffee and ran his eyes down the page.

There was a soft knock on the door. "Come in, Joachim," Bormann said quietly.

The door opened and Joachim entered. He was tall and slim, dressed in a dark suit, white shirt and dark tie, always the same uniform, winter and summer, every day of the year. Bormann had learned the English word "cadaverous" some years ago and it fitted Joachim well. Bormann wondered if he ever took the suit off but it was always meticulously pressed. "Good morning, sir."

"Good morning, Joachim." Bormann watched as he strode confidently across the room and sat in a chair on the other side of the desk. He recalled in the old days, that while the important things were done by men, secretaries under his direction were always young and attractive women, usually willing, too, if they planned to work for long in the Reich Chancellery.

"We may have a problem with the Project, sir."

Bormann stared at him intently. Joachim was a bit tense this morning. "What sort of problem? Has something happened to Falken?"

"No, sir, at least not directly." Joachim set a thin folder on the edge of Bormann's desk. "The Schiller account has been activated."

"What?" Bormann was incredulous. "That's impossible."

"Yes sir," Joachim replied. " Nonetheless it has happened."

"But Dr. Schiller, the nurse and the child were burned to death in a fire in the fall of 1940, November, I believe, within a few days of reaching Canada."

"That is correct, sir,"Joachim said patiently. "But the account was activated late yesterday. I have put together what I could find out."

"And . . ."

"And it appears that the child is alive, although almost fifty, now. I have prepared a report for your consideration." Joachim pushed the file folder toward Bormann. Joachim always prepared reports for "consideration", never for "information" or "implementation" or any of the other things a report could be prepared for.

"Thank you, Joachim," Bormann said, suppressing a rising excitement. "I'll read it later. Tell me the facts now."

"The man who activated the account calls himself Eric O'Neill. He did so through the offices of a brokerage house in Toronto, in Canada. He contacted the National Commercial Bank in Geneva yesterday and he had the information on the account and the codes. Everything was in order. Of course, they immediately contacted us as the arrangements we have with them dictated."

"But is it him?"

"I am still checking on that but so far it looks like it could be."

"But how did he get this information?"

"I don't know the answer to that yet, sir. However, he had been abroad and returned to attend to his parents' estate. Apparently, they were killed in an auto accident about a week ago."

"What were the names of his parents?"

"Gilford and Katherine O'Neill."

"Schiller to O'Neill?" Bormann nodded slowly. "Captain Schiller seemed very resourceful at the time. Perhaps he survived and raised the child himself."

"Do you have any instructions, sir?"

"I will read your report, Joachim," Bormann said. "Then we will decide what has to be done. In the meantime, continue to find out everything you can."

"Very well, sir," Joachim replied.

"Anything else this morning?"

"Only routine matters, sir, and they can wait," Joachim replied. "The 24 hour security report is positive, no intrusions."

"Thank you, Joachim." Bormann stood to indicate the meeting was over.

Joachim nodded, rose and left the room.

Bormann walked slowly around the study, past the dark oak book shelves, the ornate old fireplace that produced more smoke than heat and which hadn't been lit in years, and ended up back at the window behind his desk, staring out through the morning mist. Could it be possible? Could Eva's child still be alive? All three children had been fathered by Hitler but he had always felt there was somehow a greater legitimacy to the child Hitler had had with Eva Braun. My God! What a development.

What kind of a man had this one developed into? He turned to his desk and sat down abruptly pulling a sheaf of papers from the file Joachim had left, suddenly anxious to know more.

As he went through the material, he was amazed again at the amount of information that was available on any individual. The files of the Gestapo had nothing compared to the detailed records that modern democracies kept on their citizens. It was only necessary to have the right contacts, to know where to look and to know what to make of it when you found it. Joachim was good at this.

The written report provided more detail than Joachim had delivered verbally. Gilford O'Neill had been a physician, so had Gustav Schiller. There was no employment record for his wife, so perhaps the nurse hadn't made it, or perhaps she had decided not to work. They had two children, a son, Eric and a younger daughter who had died in a drowning accident in 1983. Bormann breathed in sharply and softly slapped his hand on the desk. A copy of the birth certificate. Eric O'Neill. The same birth date, October 30, 1939.

"Ha!" Bormann exclaimed. Eric O'Neill had to be authentic or else someone was going to an immense amount of trouble to fabricate this. He continued on through the material, photocopies of his passport, bank statements, income tax returns. Bormann slowed and examined these carefully. Passport photos were notoriously bad but O'Neill's showed a good looking man, wavy light coloured hair although it was difficult to tell from the black and white picture. He went on to the financial information. Apparently Eric O'Neill had made a great deal of money, a good sign. Bormann admired wealth, not for its own sake, but rather for the effort it revealed, the commitment to succeeding, the drive that it took, and obviously O'Neill had a lot of these characteristics.

Bormann finished the material and sat back in his chair. What could he surmise from the facts that Joachim had so far assembled? He knew that Eric O'Neill was well educated, financially astute and hard working. After spending a number of years learning his trade by working in other brokerage houses, he had created his own financial firm, quite successful from the look of it. This would suggest that he must be willing to assume risk and must have both organizational and leadership skills as well as the financial knowledge and business acumen he needed. It would be interesting to know what his employees and peers thought of him. He took a long black pen from a holder on his desk and jotted a note at the bottom of the page.

A troubling item of information though, was the fact that about a year and a half ago he had simply disappeared. This had occurred in the wake of his son's death and that of his wife, a few months later. But what did this signify? Was it a time of healing? Was it a mental breakdown of some sort? No doubt Joachim would track down where he had gone and what he had been up to, but at this point it appeared that he had withdrawn from his business and vanished, only to reappear following the deaths of his parents. Nonetheless, an interesting man and certainly one worthy of a lot more study.

Assuming that Eric O'Neill was authentic how should he proceed? There were now, suddenly, three heirs apparent, and while Bormann was not a serious student of history, he knew enough of human nature to know that when there is only one throne, there can not be three princes with no clearly defined order of ascension. Jon Falken had been the clear choice until now. Lincoln Carswell was bright, organized and focussed. His high profile could do a lot for the movement but he had never demonstrated any interest in being a leader. Perhaps he had merely lacked the opportunity. But now, with Eric O'Neill in the picture things might be different. Falken had flaws, not the least of which was his over-riding ambition. No doubt O'Neill had flaws, too, and time and Joachim would reveal what they were.

He would need to know more about Eric O'Neill, but he now knew his next course of action. He would let the contenders themselves determine who would win the throne. He pushed the intercom button on his phone. "Joachim, could you come to the study, please."

"Certainly, sir." The reply was immediate and moments later Joachim sat across from Bormann, a pen poised over an old fashioned steno pad.

"Thank you for all the information you have assembled, Joachim," Bormann said softly. "Please continue and when we have a clearer picture of what Eric O'Neill is about, and in particular, that he is authentic, then I think we will bring them together, let them get to know each other."

CHAPTER FORTY FOUR

Thursday, April 27, 1989 Harrisburg, Pennsylvania

"Do you know who Reinhardt Gehlen was?" Einfeld asked.

"Wasn't he the head of West German intelligence after the War?" Jon was sitting at the board room table again. He stifled a sigh, wondering where Einfeld was going today.

"He was until 1968. But during World War II he was the head of Hitler's intelligence network in Eastern Europe and the Soviet Union. At the end of the war he simply walked over to the Americans and offered his services to the OSS."

"Excuse me," Jon said. "But are we going to go over post war history? I have a reasonable working knowledge of it so perhaps we can save some time if you just give me the short version."

Einfeld stared at Jon for a moment. "I can understand your frustration, Colonel, but please bear with me. I am trying to establish for you the power of the organization that is behind you."

Jon sighed. "Very well."

"I will try to keep it as brief as I can," Einfeld said. "The Americans accepted Gehlen with open arms since neither they nor the British nor anyone else had a functioning espionage network in the east. So he became the west's primary source of intelligence on what the Soviets were up to and he was able to pass on enough misinformation to push the Americans and the British into the cold war with their former ally, the Soviet Union. Details of Russian troop movements were falsified, strengths were augmented, and a host of other indicators were either exaggerated or completely fabricated and passed on. Once the Cold War started, it survived on its own momentum."

Jon shook his head. "Why would Gehlen do something so stupid. Surely he knew he would be caught?"

"But he wasn't," Einfeld said triumphantly. "He wasn't! But you have asked why? I am surprised it isn't obvious to you. If two dogs both want the same bone, they will snarl at each other, bark, bite and fight each other until one of them drives off the other. The bone remains intact during this process. Think of Germany and National Socialism as the bone. Two huge political forces engaged in a struggle for world domination themselves, had little time to spend on what you have so eloquently described as a bunch of 'old Nazis wandering around South America living on fifty year old dreams of glory?' That is exactly the image we intended people should have. The reality is far different."

"You mean there are not old Nazis wandering around South America?" Jon asked, doing little to hide his sarcasm.

Einfeld looked at him sharply. "The fact that you ask that question is a testament to how successful we have been." He turned to Clayton. "Please be good enough to get me some water."

"Of course," Clayton replied, getting up quickly and going to the phone again.

"There are old Nazis all over the world," Einfeld continued. "While many of them slipped off to South America, they certainly didn't have to. They were welcomed in many countries. Franco, in Spain, for example, embraced them, their money, their expertise and their business acumen. By the late 1940's there was a German 'colony' in Madrid of more than 16,000 of what you have termed 'old Nazis'. But there are also a lot of young Nazis."

"I see a few of them around," Jon said. "You can generally tell by the haircuts and the costumes."

"Ah yes," Einfeld said. "The skin heads. And what do you make of them, Colonel?"

"They are disaffected punks wearing clothes that offend people, posturing and sometimes acting out their aggressions, like burning Turkish hostels in Germany, for example, or establishing paramilitary organizations here like the militia movement."

"Have you ever noticed how much attention they get from police, from your FBI in this country, and from law enforcement agencies wherever they show up?"

The door opened and a woman walked in with a large pitcher of ice water and three glasses on a tray. Jon hadn't seen this one before. She was wearing a short tight black skirt and a top that revealed a generous cleavage as she leaned over to set the pitcher and the tray down in front of Clayton.

"Instability," Einfeld continued. He picked up a glass and filled it.

"What kind of instability are you talking about?" Jon watched the provocative swing of her hips as she left the conference room.

"All kinds." Einfeld took a long drink and went on. "Once economically established outside of Germany and with the commencement of the Cold War, the two major powers in the world were occupied. But wherever there is political instability, disillusionment, unemployment, injustice, any of those things, then a doctrine which promises salvation can take hold. For most of the last two thousand years, in Western Europe, that has been Christianity but in an age of rationalism such has prevailed in the last century, it has failed. But look at Nazi movements. In one form or another, they arose in Japan, in Germany, in Italy, Spain, Portugal and after the War in most of the middle east and South America."

"So you create instability?" Jon reached for a glass and filled it. He took a sip. "How has that worked here in America. I don't see much instability around here."

"Instability is half of the equation. The other half is infiltration. We take over and control companies, political parties, movements, governments." Einfeld paused and drank some water. "And this is the important and relevant part for you, Jon. If things work as we have planned, then you will 'infiltrate' the presidency of the United States."

Jon sat utterly still. Suddenly it made sense.

Einfeld went on. "Jon, let me give you some examples to illustrate. It is crucial that you understand and believe what we are capable of."

Jon nodded.

"I am only going to give you a few examples that you can check. There are numerous operations that have and will remain secret." Einfeld took a sip of water. "You are familiar with the details of the Iran-Contra scandal a few years ago and the efforts of Colonel North to supply the Contras in Nicaragua with weapons?"

"I am," Jon replied.

"Have you heard of the Kintex Corporation?"

"No."

"It is an import-export enterprise based in Sophia, Bulgaria and is a significant player in the international trade in arms and drugs. It is full of Soviet spies as well as Bulgarian secret service folks. It imports drugs through connections in Turkey, and exports arms to the middle east among other places.. We are not talking here about a few rifles and mortars, Colonel. The Kintex Corporation has quite a variety of NATO armaments available, Leopard tanks and your very effective Cobra assault helicopters, for example. The CIA used the Kintex Corporation to ship arms to the Contras." He paused and leaned forward, placing his elbows on the table. "We control the Kintex Corporation."

Einfeld paused for a moment and took a sip of his water. "By the 1960's more than 200 West German military officers occupied important posts in NATO, among them, eighteen former World War Two German Generals, including Hans Speidel who served as the commander of all NATO forces in Western Europe.

"You can't be serious," Jon said incredulously. He had been aware of a few Wehrmacht veterans holding positions in NATO but nothing on this scale.

Einfeld smiled grimly. "Jon, these are just a few simple examples to convince you of the seriousness of our power. In time you will come to learn more fully the scope of the movement. It is immense."

"Are you aware of the full scope of the movement?"

Einfeld shook his head. "As I am sure you are aware, Jon, in all organizations that are vulnerable to infiltration, members are informed on a 'need-to-know' basis. So there is a great deal that I don't know, especially in the finance areas."

"Why is that?"

"Mostly because my field is political action, not economic action or military action. The specific military examples I am giving you are in deference to your own distinguished military career and are all ones that you can easily check."

Jon nodded. "Is there more?"

"Does the name 'Otto Skorzeny' mean anything to you?"

"He led the commando team that rescued Mussolini in 1943."

"Correct," Einfeld replied. "Skorzeny was another one of ours. Ever hear of the 'Paladin Group'?"

"No."

"That was a brainchild of Skorzney's that he established in Spain in the early 1950's. It was headquartered near Alicante on the Mediterranean coast. It was basically a commando training school and it has a fairly illustrious alumni. The South African secret service trained there. The Spanish Interior Ministry sent staff there so they could continue their clandestine warfare on the Basque separatists. The Greek Colonels who seized power in 1967 sent troops there as did Muarmmar Qaddafi of Libya. The Egyptians sent people, among that group a little known Arab of the time named Yassar Arafat. They provided logistical support for some Palestinian terrorist groups. Even some US Green Berets on their way to Vietnam trained there." Einfeld smiled. "In the best traditions of American education, it was a non-segregated equal opportunity school."

"Have you ever heard of Hans Rudel?" Einfeld asked.

"The name doesn't ring a bell."

"Rudel was the Third Reich's most decorated Luftwaffe pilot. After the war he made his way to Argentina, with the help of the Vatican, incidentally, became an advisor to the Argentine government and close personal friends with Juan and Eva Peron. Through his efforts he was able to secure positions in the Argentine Airforce for more than a hundred former Luftwaffe members. For many years he represented Siemens, the giant German electronics firm. He died seven years ago, in

1982, and was buried in Germany. Over 2000 people attended his funeral and two Luftwaffe jets swooped down over the site dipping their wings in salute. There were howls of protest from leftists all over Germany at what they regarded as an outrageous recognition of an unrepentant Nazi, but to illustrate our political influence, the West German minister of Defence refused to investigate the unauthorized flight." Einfeld looked down at the folder in front of him and read a quote. "I do not know Rudel's political opinion, but even if I had to reject it, I have high respect for the man for his achievements as a soldier." Einfeld looked up at Jon. "That is a quote from Manfred Worner, who later became the Secretary General of NATO."

Jon sat very still and absorbed what Einfeld had told him. If these few examples were typical of what these people could achieve then the presidency was within his grasp. "Thank you," he said softly. "What is the next step?"

Einfeld smiled. "You have just made the wisest political decision of your life, Jon." He reached across the table and offered his hand. Jon shook it firmly. "You will fly to London for further briefing a week from today." He nodded at Clayton who pulled an envelope from the inner pocket of his suit jacket and handed it silently to Jon. "These are your airline tickets and reservations in London. You will need to rearrange your appointments so this can happen and, of course, you must keep this information entirely to yourself. You may not tell your wife. Ostensibly, you are being invited to London to speak to a group of retired British military officers about the Vietnam War and what you and the US armed forces have learned from it."

"The second part of the talk would be very short," Jon said. "Neither the armed forces nor the political establishment learned much."

Clayton nodded. "You will be contacted and given further instructions when you arrive in London."

CHAPTER FORTY FIVE

Thursday, April 27, 1989 Philadelphia

Marianne Falken rolled onto her back and stretched. She stifled a yawn as she opened her eyes and stared up at a strange ceiling, disoriented for a moment until she remembered she was in the guest suite in Lincoln Carswell's home. She sat up and looked around the room. A bedside clock told her it was 8:12am. She had slept longer than she intended. There were four back-lit buttons built into the table beside the clock and she recalled one of them was for the lights. She didn't remember which one but she pushed the nearest one. She heard a soft whirring sound and light began to flood the room as the drapes covering the windows opened. A small table and two chairs sat in a window alcove. She pushed the next button but nothing happened. The third button turned on the ceiling lights and those in the ensuite bathroom she could see adjoining the bedroom. She didn't bother with the fourth button.

She pushed back the duvet, slipped out of bed and walked, naked, into the bathroom. She turned on the shower, a spacious, partially enclosed glass stall, adjusted the water temperature and stepped into the steaming hot spray. As she soaped herself, she wondered why she didn't have a hangover, not a headache, not even the dull feeling she often got after drinking a glass or two of wine. She slowly turned, letting the hot water play over her shoulders and upper body. She breathed in the steam and felt refreshed.

Stepping out of the shower, she toweled herself off before slipping into a soft white terry cloth robe hanging on a hook near the shower. As she walked back into the bedroom, she could smell coffee. Looking around, she spotted a large mug on the table in the alcove. She walked over to it, picked it up and took a sip. It was a latte, or likely a double latte judging from the taste. A note beside the mug read, "I'm in the studio. L."

She turned and looked back toward the shower in the en-suite, clearly visible from the table. She smiled at the thought of Lincoln watching her.

The sun was shining into the garden outside the windows. A rock wall flanked by low shrubs enclosed the area. Several rose bushes, none in bloom yet, surrounded a grey stone fountain in the centre, water rising in a steady column about a foot high and then falling back into a basin before running over the edge into a pool at the base of the fountain.

Marianne sat down at the table and thought about last night. It was one of the most pleasant evenings she had spent in a long time, relaxed and interesting, excellent food, fine wine and enjoyable company. A small brown bird landed on the edge of the fountain, splashed itself with water and shook the drops off before flying away. She didn't recognize it but she knew nothing about birds other than that some birds had webbed feet and some didn't. That seemed to be enough.

She drank some more of the coffee. And what would today bring, she wondered? She was meeting Celeste for lunch, returning her car and had to catch her five o'clock flight back to Harrisburg. Celeste would pester her about what she had been doing all night and would not likely believe the truth when she heard it. Celeste was her only really close friend and had been since they were room mates in college in California. There wasn't much that mattered that they didn't know about each other.

She picked up the coffee and returned to the bathroom. Before going to bed she had set out her personal kit. It was silly how military terms like "kit" had invaded her vocabulary. She ran a pick through her wavy hair and it fluffed into place.

Marianne put the pick down and drank some more of her coffee. She wondered what Lincoln's plans for the day were. There was only one way to find out. As she walked to the door she thought of getting dressed but decided the robe was quite comfortable and demure enough for morning wear. She wondered about makeup but knew she looked fresh and innocent without it. I might as well let Lincoln see the unsophisticated woman.

She found him in the studio sitting at a large drafting table, a latte resting near his right hand. He was using a T square. She only knew what it was from dating an architecture student in college. He looked up as she crossed the room.

"Sleep well?" he asked. He picked up his coffee.

"Yes, thank you. Very well and too long."

"You look rested and refreshed," Lincoln said.

She came around the table and stood behind him, looking at the large sheet on the drafting table. A series of lines and curves led her eyes across the paper. "What's this for?"

"Composition," Lincoln replied. "I know what I'm going to paint but not entirely how I'm going to paint it, so I'm drafting out where all the bits and pieces will go so when you look at it you'll be drawn into the painting and it'll feel balanced and complete." He stood up.

"Which am I?" Marianne asked.

Lincoln looked confused for a minute and then laughed. "A bit or a piece?"

"Yes."

"Neither," Lincoln said. "You're the central focus of the painting. Everything will lead to you, enhance your image, cause the viewer to focus on you."

Marianne looked at the series of lines and curves again. She didn't see a painting there yet but at least had a sense of what he was doing.

Lincoln stood up and put his hand lightly on her back, guiding her away from the table. "Your coffee is likely getting cool. Let's go to the kitchen and I'll make us each a fresh cup."

"Thanks for this one," Marianne said. "How did you know I was awake?"

"You pushed the 'call' button."

"The one between the drapes and the lights?"

"That's the one."

"What's the fourth button for?" Marianne asked as they reached the studio door.

"The gas fireplace."

"I didn't notice a fireplace."

Lincoln smiled down at her. "That's because there isn't one yet."

As they walked into the kitchen, Marianne saw the table was set, bowls, small plates and cutlery, this time with champagne flutes in front of the place mats.

"I hope you like fruit," Lincoln said. He pushed a button on an ornate cappuccino machine in the corner of the counter and set two small stainless steel pitchers to catch the espresso as it came out.

As he worked in the kitchen, Marianne noticed how efficiently he moved, everything set out where it was needed. She watched his hands, long fingered and delicate, almost feminine except they looked strong and powerful. She wondered how they would feel on her. "Do you mind a personal question, Lincoln?"

"Not at all."

"You're single. How come?"

He turned to look at her. "I get that question a lot, especially from the wives of friends who think a single man is an affront to the feminine world." He set two lattes on the counter. "I got married shortly after I graduated from art school. My wife waited patiently for about a year for me to start earning a living with my art and then decided she wanted me to get a real job. She worked in a bank and came to resent the fact that I didn't have to go anywhere when I got up in the morning. The house we rented always smelled of paint and turpentine and my art stuff was all over the place. We moved to a slightly larger place that had a garage and I did my painting out there. After about five years of this she picked up and left. She said she was tired of being married to a deadbeat who wasn't going anywhere. After that experience I decided that marriage and art didn't make a good combination."

"What's she doing now?"

"The last I heard, which is about ten years ago, she was remarried, to an accountant, had a couple of children and had moved to the mid-west somewhere, and become a deadbeat."

"A deadbeat?"

"She gave up her day job."

"Marianne laughed. "Funny how that works for a woman but not for a man."

"She didn't think it was funny when I was staying at home painting."

"And you haven't met anyone who thinks that marriage and art would go well together?" Marianne asked.

"Not yet," Lincoln replied. "But at my age all the eligible women are married or divorced. If they're married they aren't available and if they're divorced they're predatory."

"Predatory?"

"They married the first time for love, the second time they want money and security. That sounds a bit cynical, I know, but it fits well with my experience."

Marianne sipped her coffee and thought about what he had said. She had divorced women friends who fit that description perfectly.

Lincoln opened a built in oven and put a pan in it, closed the door and set a timer. "I hope you like croissants."

"I like them a lot, thank you." She looked down and saw that the robe had come open revealing her legs. She was about to pull it closed and then decided to leave it since her legs were under the counter at the moment. Besides, if he had seen her in the shower there wasn't much to hide. "Do you miss female company?" she asked.

"Sometimes," Lincoln replied. "But I have a lot to fill my days and like a lot of single folks, I have a wide circle of friends. If I want female company I can always find a married woman to paint." He looked at her straight-faced and then laughed.

She laughed with him. "I suppose that's the safe thing to do. Single women might want something lasting."

The timer on the stove behind him rang, a soft bell sound, not the sharp irritating ping of her own oven. He turned, slipped on oven mitts and took the pan out. The aroma of fresh baked croissants filled the kitchen.

"What are your plans for today?" Lincoln asked. They were standing side by side at the kitchen counter, cleaning up a few things after breakfast.

"I have a plane to catch at five," Marianne replied. She held a champagne flute up to the light, wiping a smudge off the rim. "And I told Celeste I'd meet her for lunch."

He picked up a champagne flute from the counter and took the other one from her, his fingers brushing her hand. He turned and hung them in a rack under a cabinet behind them. "When will you be back in Philly?"

"It's not a long flight," Marianne replied. "When will you have something for me to look at?"

Lincoln smiled. "In about a week. You can look at how the portrait is developing and we can make any changes you'd like to see."

In the studio, he picked up the two rolls of film he had taken yesterday of Marianne posing for the portrait. He stuck them into his pocket, retrieved his car keys from a drawer in the kitchen and drove six blocks to the Landsend Mall.

A few minutes later he walked into the Android Camera Shop, assailed by the smell of chemicals, and wondered how people could work in a place that smelled this vile.

"Lincoln," the owner said coming out from behind the counter and shaking his hand. "How are you?"

"Fine, Jake," he replied. "I'm doing a portrait and I need your best work on these."

"Hey," Jake said. "You always get my best work."

Lincoln laughed. "I know I do. Can you do them now?"

"You got it," Jake said. "Come back in half an hour."

Lincoln wandered over to a nearby Starbucks, went inside and bought a small latte. He sat at a table and picked up a newspaper that was lying there. He looked at it but couldn't concentrate. Visions of Marianne kept floating into his mind, vivid, beautiful, intense, her laugh, her hair, her luscious body.

"Just a couple of minutes," Jake said as Lincoln walked back into the camera shop.

"No problem," Lincoln answered. He walked over to a shelf filled with compact cameras. He selected one and peered through the view finder. It was small and would fit into a pocket. It would be a good travel camera although the picture quality wouldn't be as good as his studio cameras. On an impulse he turned and set it on the counter. "I want one of these, too," he said.

"I'll get you an unopened one," Jake said, reaching under the counter and retrieving a small box. "That's a great little camera. I think you'll be impressed with the quality and you can take it anywhere." He set two rolls of film and a package of batteries by the camera.

"Thanks, Jake."

"And remember if you don't like it, bring it back."

"That's another reason I keep coming here," Lincoln said.

"Here are your pictures," Jake said, placing two envelopes on the counter beside the camera box. "That is one gorgeous woman in those pictures, Lincoln. Where did you find her?"

Lincoln picked up the envelopes. "At an art gallery, actually," he replied.

"I need to come to your next show," Jake said.

Lincoln sorted through the photographs and set about a dozen of them out on the counter. "I need eight by tens of these."

"In an hour?" Jake asked.

"Tomorrow will be fine. I can work from the small prints for a day or two. I'll need the enlargements when I get to the detail."

"They'll be ready when you need them."

CHAPTER FORTY SIX

Monday, May 1, 1989 Portage la Prairie, Canada

Eric O'Neill sat quietly in the pew. He felt numb, lifeless, as dead as the two small urns of ashes sitting among the flowers on the ornate table a few feet in front of him. Miles Crawford, the family lawyer, had made the arrangements. Eric was grateful that he and his parents had had friends like these.

He was aware of Miles sitting on his left, his head bowed in grief. Laura sat on his right side. He had asked her about Darrin but she had merely said, "He sends his regrets." She had looked away too quickly so he knew there was more to it than that. Likely some sort of disagreement or perhaps even an ultimatum. He was grateful for the courage she had shown in coming with him and sitting in the section reserved for family. It couldn't have been an easy decision for her, to be there publicly with him in the absence of her husband, although why Darrin hadn't just come along too was a bit of a mystery. Surely for one day he could have set aside his animosity. After all, as a teenager, Darrin had spent innumerable hours in the O'Neill home.

As they had filed into the church he saw that all the pews were filled and people were standing in the back. It was a small town and his parents had been among its preeminent citizens. He was aware, too, of some curious looks, family friends and acquaintances who hadn't seen him in years, wondering what Katherine and Gilford's son had been up to. No doubt some of them remembered that he and Laura had been high school sweethearts too, and that would spark its own kind of reflection.

The Anglican priest entered and the congregation hushed. Canon Clarke began the service, his voice as rich and resonant as Eric had remembered. The words were soothing but it was more the voice than the content. Eric stared up at the huge stained glass windows that dominated the nave of the church, pious looking saints in long colourful gowns, their halos lighted by the afternoon sun streaming in, low angled, from the south. One of them, presumably Mary, held a small child in her arms and looked lovingly into his face. Adjoining windows featured bearded shepherds, bearing crooks and loving stares. He pulled his thoughts away from the mythology.

Eric felt a movement beside him as Miles stood. He walked to the pulpit, stooped, aged and tired. He looked over the congregation and then pulled a paper from the inside pocket of his jacket and began to read the eulogy.

Eric thought of his mother, beautiful, elegant and charming, so sophisticated in an old world sense in such a small prairie town, but loved and respected by so many. Summers at their cottage, "the summer place", as his mother had referred to it, taxed her patience at times. The memory of a small incident came to him. She was standing in the kitchen of the cottage, hands on her hips, staring down at him. He was about ten and on his hands and knees gathering up the pieces of a broken china plate. Mrs. Owens from the cottage next door had been over to borrow something. She was standing behind his mother.

"I don't know why you have china and crystal at a cottage anyway, Katherine," she had said.

As Eric looked up at his mother she had winked. "We may have to spend our summers out here, Evelyn, but we don't have to live like peasants."

Eric found himself smiling at the memory. He had asked her later what a "peasant" was.

Monday, May 1, 1989 Arlington, Virginia

Jon Falken had always thought that the National Memorial Cemetery at Arlington was one of the most beautiful spots in the world, its peaceful lawns rolling off into the distance, the orderly white markers in rows at attention, a final parade for the fallen. It was a sunny day, a light breeze wafting through the tree tops that weren't quite in leaf yet, a gorgeous spring day full of the promise of life.

He felt Marianne's hand on his arm. He glanced down at her as she wiped the tears from her cheeks. He couldn't see her eyes for the large dark sunglasses she wore. He felt a twinge of sadness too. The moment of silence to honour fallen comrades that he had always started his staff meetings with would now include one more name.

There were familiar faces around the grave side but it wasn't a large crowd, a couple of dozen, perhaps. He felt Marianne squeeze his arm reassuringly. He watched as the honour guard raised their shiny rifles and fired a salute over the coffin. The lonely sound of a bugle playing the Last Post always brought tears to his eyes. He pulled a tissue from his pocket and wiped them away. He didn't like signs of emotion but there were times when compassionate tear ducts conveyed an appropriate message. Moments later a sergeant snapped the final folds into the American flag and presented it to the grieving widow.

She stood quietly, almost catatonic, supported by her two children who had come home from California. Jon looked at them. The son was tall, about six one, the daughter, too, although it was harder to guess her height with heels on. Nice looking kids, kids any parent could be proud of. He hoped they would stick around for a few days and give their mother some support.

As the service concluded, he and Marianne walked around the grave to the family. He shook hands with the son, Jason, as he recalled, and the daughter, Janet. He hugged Irene gently. "When things settle down in few days," Jon said. "Please call me if there is anything at all that I can do."

Monday, May 1, 1989 Portage la Prairie

"We are not here to mourn the passing of Katherine and Gilford O'Neill, but to celebrate the joy they both took in living, to rejoice in the good fortune that a loving God has bestowed on us to have had two such wonderful people in our lives." Miles paused and looked up. Eric could see the tears in his eyes but Miles continued.

"It was my honour to know them for almost forty years, to call them my friends..."

As Miles went on, telling a funny story, relating a compassionate incident, detailing an unknown contribution, Eric was aware of tears running down his face. He felt Laura's hand slip into his and squeeze it reassuringly. He pulled a tissue from the pocket of the suit jacket and wiped his eyes, then using both hands, blew his nose. He returned his hand to Laura's.

He stared at his father's urn, the small Grecian vase holding a handful of ashes that was all that was left of his father's body. Unbidden, an image slipped into his mind. He was about eight years old, it was summer and he and his father had walked over the bridge to Island Park and along the trail by the shore of the lake to where an old man rented a few row boats and a couple of canoes. His father had chatted with the boatman, Mike? He thought that was the name. They had rented a small green row boat, his father taking the oars and with Eric on the seat in the back, they had skimmed across Crescent Lake as flat as a sheet of glass, the late afternoon sun glinting off its surface like a mirror, his father's powerful arms and shoulders straining at the oars. Near the other side there were some reeds and he had stopped rowing and let the boat drift silently. They watched a pair of mallards and a couple of grebes paddling about, turning their tails to the sky and disappearing under the water, popping to the surface again a few yards away.

Monday, May 1, 1989 Arlington, Virginia
Jon and Marianne drove slowly through the cemetery, towards the exit. "Irene seems to be holding up better than I thought she would," Jon said.

"How did you think she would act, for God's sake," Marianne snapped.

Jon sighed. Marianne was so tense and angry lately. "I only meant to pay her a compliment," Jon said softly. "I wasn't trying to analyse her behaviour."

"The reception is at four?" Marianne asked.

"Yes."

"Let's try not to stay too long, shall we?"

"Only long enough to pay our respects, talk to the children and so on," Jon said.

"Try to act like you care."

Jon sighed again and concentrated on driving.

Monday, May 1, 1989 Portage la Prairie

At the reception people gathered around Eric in clusters, shaking his hand and talking to him about his parents. A lot of them he knew but there were also many younger people and others he had never seen before. He was surprised by the personal warmth so many of them displayed, hugging him fondly, taking his hand in both of theirs, kissing his cheek. Although he enjoyed it, he wasn't used to this kind of physical contact, but slowly he felt comforted, enveloped in their care.

"Saved my life, your Dad did." An old man stood in front of him, ramrod straight. He transferred his cane to his left hand and shook Eric's hand. His rich silver hair gleamed in the fluorescent lights of the church hall. "Went to a specialist in Winnipeg who was no help at all, but your Dad knew what was wrong."

"Thank you," Eric said, resisting the impulse to ask what the ailment was.

"You need anything, young man," the old gentleman said solemnly. "Anything at all, you call me." He handed Eric a card.

Eric glanced down at it, a simple white business card with the crest of a small cannon on it and the words "Lt. Colonel Jason R. Stuart, Retired" followed by some regimental numbers and information.

"Thank you, Sir. I will."

Monday, May 1, 1989 Arlington, Virginia

The military reception room was hushed, old furniture and older paintings, large gloomy scenes, almost pastoral but for the soldiers running and the field guns belching fire and the skies with roiling clouds of smoke. In a couple of them cavalry horses charged, nostrils dilated and steaming, sweat pouring from their flanks, their riders with raised curved swords ready to decapitate the hapless foot soldiers that survived the horses hooves.

Jon enjoyed the old paintings. The scenes of glory, courage and sacrifice set an appropriate tone to remember a fallen comrade. He knew Marianne was appalled by the carnage in them, viewing them as glorifying nothing but male brutality. He became aware of her at his side, returned from the rest room.

"Shall we pay our respects?" she asked quietly. "And then we can get the hell out of here. This place is just too depressing."

Jon smiled. "Dignified, my dear."

Marianne looked up at the paintings with undisguised contempt. "Whatever," she murmured, and tugged his arm to draw him toward the small group of people around Irene and the children.

Monday, May 1, 1989 Portage la Prairie

Eric looked around the church hall. Two women were carrying plates of small sandwiches out to the kitchen, a third was busy unplugging a coffee pot. Laura picked up the urn and moved toward the kitchen with it. He felt a tug on his arm.

"Eric, it's good to see you."

He didn't recognize them for a moment. "Mr. and Mrs. MacGregor," he said as their names came to him. They were both frail and much older than he remembered.

"Edwin and Aldeth, please," Mr. MacGregor said. "We haven't seen you since you went off to Toronto. That was a long time ago."

"It was," Eric said. They had lived two doors down from his parents. "Thirty one years ago the first time, but I was back in the summers for a few years."

"We miss Katherine and Gil," Aldeth said. "They were the best friends and neighbours anyone could ever ask for."

"Thank you," Eric said. They shuffled slowly toward the door, Aldeth with her arm linked through her husband's, his cane appearing to support them both.

"How are you doing?" Laura asked, slipping her arm through his.

"Fine," Eric said. "So far at any rate."

"I have to go up to the hospital to check on a couple of patients," she said. "Then if you'd like some company, I'll stop by your place."

Eric looked at her for a moment, wondering about Darrin. "I'd like that."

The last funeral Eric had attended had been his wife's and he had felt numb, disconnected from what was happening. He had talked to Laura about it last night. She asked him if he wanted anything, a tranquillizer, a sleeping pill. He thanked her for the offer but declined, he just wanted to talk. He probably kept her out late enough to provide Darrin with a reason for not coming today.

Laura had asked about Dierdre's passing. "By the time Dierdre died, there wasn't a lot left between us. We started out like a lot of newly-weds but after Geoffrey was born something died between us. I wondered if she was suffering from some sort of post-partum depression but that wasn't it. She just lost interest in me. I took it personally, of course, but I shouldn't have." He smiled at his comment. "She lost interest in all her friends. I think she loved me in her own way, but all the intimacy just evaporated."

"Did you lose interest too?"

"Eventually," Eric said. "But the death of my feelings was a slow process. There was no single event. I would come home at the end of the day and Geoffrey would hug me, Dierdre would smile. The kisses stopped. She would turn her cheek instead of offering her mouth. We used to shower together. I loved soaping her body. But then she began to complain that I got her hair wet. So I stopped. I used to come up behind her and fondle her, you know what I mean?"

Laura nodded.

"In the first couple of years that could lead to a kiss, a cuddle or even to bed. At first she seemed to enjoy the attention, then she began to push me away after a moment and eventually she didn't seem to notice at all. So I stopped. I could give you a thousand examples and not one of them would matter in itself." Eric paused and picked up his scotch off the coffee table, staring into the fire for a moment.

"I spent most of my days working with numbers." He smiled and shook his head. "I don't think you can ever quantify something like this but one day I tried. We were married for almost 20 years. This cumulative rejection started about the third year and I gave up about two years before she died, about a year before Geoffrey's death. So if you take fifteen years, times 365 days, times this sort of rejection about three times a day, it comes to 16,425. That sounds so stupid when I say it, but after fifteen or twenty thousand times, people learn to change their behaviour."

"You were a slow learner," Laura said softly.

Eric looked at her sharply, wondering if she was being mocking, but he saw tears in her eyes. Perhaps she was talking about the two of them.

"Did you ever find someone else?"

"Another woman? An affair?" Eric asked.

Laura nodded.

"No," Eric said shaking his head slowly. "I guess I just took it out at work. There never was another woman, although I suppose there were the usual opportunities."

"I know," Laura said. "I could have been one of them."

Eric looked at her and smiled. "Yes," he said slowly. "You could have been." He thought about adding "You are," but he resisted.

"Could you tell me about Geoffrey's death, or is that too painful?" she asked, wiping her eyes with a tissue. "I know he was killed in a car accident but I never really heard what happened."

"Such a terrible thing," Eric said. "He borrowed his mother's car, got drunk with a couple of his friends and drove into a concrete abutment on the Don Valley Parkway." Eric took another sip of his scotch. "His two friends had some cuts and bruises, Geoffrey was killed. It was the evening of his seventeenth birthday."

Laura slipped her arm around him and pulled him against her. Eric continued. "He wasn't killed outright, he died a day later from internal injuries. He had an odd type of blood and they used all they had. I volunteered my blood but it didn't match. A strange thing, I thought, because I knew that Deirdre and I had the same blood type. About a month after Geoffrey died, I asked my doctor about the blood match. He didn't want to talk to me about it but I said I would just ask another doctor. He told me that Geoffrey could not have been my biological son."

Laura went rigid. "Not your son?" she asked. "How did you feel?"

"Hurt and angry, of course," Eric said quietly. "But the fact that another man was Geoffrey's biological father didn't change the fact that he was my son. That issue was between his mother and me, not between Geoffrey and me."

"Did you ever find out who the biological father was?"

"No," Eric said. "I never tried to find out."

"Didn't you talk to Diedre about it?"

"I thought about it, but she was such a wreck after his death that I just didn't have the heart to add one more thing."

"And Dierdre died the same year?" Laura asked.

"About six months later."

They sat in silence staring at the fire. "What happened, Eric?"

"Dierdre had a drinking problem even before we were married although I didn't notice it for a few years. Both her parents were practicing alcoholics and it seemed to come naturally to her. After Geoffrey's death, she just gave up any attempt at hiding it. I tried to get her help, to talk about it, but I guess I didn't approach it very well. She ended up screaming at me and drinking more. In our last days together she became particularly vicious. She accused me of killing Geoffrey, because if I had been around more when he was growing up, he wouldn't have started drinking, hanging out with bad kids, and so on. There was no response to this because I did spend time with him. He didn't drink much and the kids he was with the night he was killed were perfectly fine young people."

"I wonder why she would say those things to you?"

"Alcohol to some degree, but she also was carrying a terrible guilt. The night Geoffrey was killed was the first time she had ever let him drive her car, but she had also bought him a bottle of vodka for a birthday present and the remains of the empty bottle were in the wreck."

"My God, Eric," Laura whispered.

Eric was silent, staring at the fire.

"How did Dierdre die?"

Eric took a drink from his glass. "About six months after Geoffrey's death, on Christmas eve, we went out to visit some friends, a happy cheerful evening for a change. When we came home, it was quite early, around 9:30. Deirdre said she had a headache and was going to bed. I went into my study to wrap a small gift I had bought for her. When I had finished I checked on her and she was sleeping. I went back to my study and read for a while. A couple of hours later I went back in the bedroom and she was dead. There was an empty prescription bottle on her night side table. Sleeping pills," Eric said quietly. "Suicide."

With a crumpled tissue, Laura gently wiped the tears from Eric's cheeks, softly blotting his eyes, and then held him tightly against her.

Monday, May 1, 1989 Arlington, Virginia
Jon Falken manoeuvred the rental car through the late afternoon traffic. He kept his attention firmly on his driving, well aware that the three drinks he had consumed at the funeral reception had slowed his reflexes.

"Now that Frank is gone I suppose you'll have to get someone else to cover for you?" Marianne said.

Jon ignored the comment and concentrated. An agitated commuter in a silver BMW hurtled by, swerved in front of him and shot down an off ramp.

"Did you hear what I said?"

"I heard you," Jon replied. "Can we talk about whatever is bothering you when we get to the motel?"

"Of course, Dear, but what makes you think something is bothering me?"

Jon glanced over at her. "Your bitchy tone of voice."

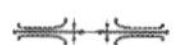

Half an hour later Jon opened his travel bag, pulled out a bottle of scotch and poured a stiff measure into a plastic glass supplied by the motel. He walked to the phone, punched "one" and asked for ice and for a couple of real glasses.

Marianne came out of the bathroom and glanced at his drink. "Where's mine?" she asked. "Or are you going to drink alone? That's a bad sign." She sat on the edge of the bed and kicked off her shoes.

"I called down for ice and some real glasses. I'll make yours when they arrive."

Marianne patted the bed beside her. "Now what is this business about me being bitchy?"

Jon sipped his scotch but didn't sit. "You seem tense and irritable lately, Marianne. I'm not sure why."

Marianne looked at him with raised eyebrows. "Really?" She stood up, walked across the room and turned to face him. "I discover my husband has been having an affair with some Asian swamp rat, putting at risk the political future we've both worked so hard for. I discover that he has been lying about it, which is understandable. I wouldn't tell you either, if I was having an affair. But what else are you lying to me about or just not telling me?"

Jon sighed. "Marianne, I am profoundly sorry. You are quite correct. I let my hormones take over my brain. But somehow we have got to put this behind us and get on with our lives."

There was a discreet knock on the door. Jon rose from the bed and handed Marianne his drink. He opened the door and pushed a five dollar bill into the young man's hand, then took the tray with the ice bucket and two glasses.

He set the tray on the dresser, poured his own drink into one of the glasses, added scotch to the second and added ice to both. He handed a glass to Marianne. "To a better future," he said, raising his glass and touching the brim of hers.

"It had better be," Marianne responded grimly. "And I meant what I said about Frank. You had better not need someone to cover for you in the future."

Jon smiled. "I trusted Frank a great deal. We both did and we have to continue trusting Irene."

Marianne looked at him sharply. "Are you talking about the times we got intimate with them?"

Jon nodded.

"That was years ago, Jon, and it only happened a few times when we'd had too much to drink."

"But it still happened and there are a lot of people who would judge us harshly, whether we were drunk or not."

"A lot of couples swap partners, Jon. There are books about it, even magazines about the lifestyle. It's open and honest compared to sneaking off on your own and having an affair." She took a sip of her scotch. "Besides, it was a lot of fun." She smiled knowingly at him. "At least I had a lot of fun."

CHAPTER FORTY SEVEN

Wednesday, May 3, 1989 Zurich, Switzerland

Eric O'Neill hadn't been to Zurich in a decade and except for a few details, he couldn't remember much about the last time. He couldn't see a lot from the car but he remembered the blue trams when one rumbled by. The back seat of the taxi felt like a capsule enclosing him in a world of grey. Outside, the rain dulled everything but the small flashes of light spinning by. The heater of the Mercedes was turned up to sauna levels. The taxi slowed and pulled up in front of a building with a large grey awning reaching out to the curb. The driver stopped and turned expectantly. Eric handed him some bills as the door opened and a liveried doorman welcomed him.

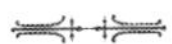

The hotel room was large, high ceilinged and spacious with an ancient-looking four poster bed, although its size looked suspiciously like a modern queen sized bed. The porter put his suitcase on a stand in one corner by a large closet with some upholstered hangers and showed him the room's amenities, a bathroom with a claw footed bath tub, a shower retro-fitted to it, a televison set with a remote control, windows that didn't open covered by drapes that did. Eric tipped the porter and thanked him. He opened his carry-on bag and took out the duty free scotch he had purchased in Toronto. It had been an impulse thing as he wandered in the airport waiting for his Lufthansa flight to Frankfurt.

Two heavy crystal glasses sat on a silver tray on top of an antique dresser. They were reflected in a small framed mirror behind them that was checked with age. He poured scotch into one of the glasses and set the bottle on the tray. Adding a little water from a sealed plastic bottle beside the tray, he took a tentative sip and nodded to himself. Nice.

He sprawled in a comfortable old armchair in one corner of the room, leaned back and crossed his feet. The flight from Toronto through Frankfurt to Switzerland had left him jet lagged, tired but not sleepy, that strange state of exhaustion that besets travellers and that only a few days of staying in the same place seems to cure. What next, he wondered. He had an appointment with the bank tomorrow but in the back of his mind he was questioning what he was really doing here. He didn't need the money, whatever the account contained. He was worth several million dollars, eighteen or so the last time he had checked and that was not counting the value of his partnership in the firm. More money was generally preferable to less money but he knew that was not what was driving him.

He had grown up with parents he loved and regarded as his only mother and father. So why was he in Switzerland trying to track down roots that he didn't care about? If he had Nazis in his closet from fifty years ago, it was an interesting mystery, to be sure, but did he really care to find out more? Perhaps he did, but then what?

On his way from Vancouver to Switzerland, he had spent a couple of days in Toronto in the high rise condo that he and Deirdre had shared during most of the twenty years they were married. When he had left Toronto two and a half years ago he'd arranged for the condo to be checked and cleaned once a month and when he walked in a week ago it was cool, sterile and empty. It was evening, an oddly clear one for Toronto, and when he pulled open the drapes in the living room, the view over the city lights was as magical as ever, but it had seemed like someone else's view, as though he were in a rented apartment. He had no sense of belonging, or of coming home. He had stood in the doorway of the master bedroom; the furniture was still there, the closets were closed and a small battery clock on the bedside table still kept the correct time.

He'd spent his last days in Toronto in the guest bedroom but when he wandered in there it seemed even less familiar. His clothes were still hanging in the closet, neatly encased in plastic storage bags. Other clothes would be in the master bedroom closets. He had only brought some working clothes into the guest room.

He wandered back to the living room There were strangely few memories or associations even though there were photographs on the wall, framed ones on a couple of end tables and assorted souvenirs about the place. This was quite unlike his experience of going home to Portage and walking into his parents' home. There was a sense of roots there, of a presence that held him. Here in Toronto there was nothing, just some possessions, some mementoes of a life he didn't feel connected to anymore.

He picked up a grade twelve graduation picture of his son, handsome in his cap and gown, smiling, head tilted slightly. It showed a handsome young man full of promise. It had been taken about a month before he died. Eric sighed and put it down. Geoffrey had always been Deirdre's son far more than his, and not just in the way that mothers have a bond with their sons. It was as if she had never wanted Eric to be part of raising him and perhaps in their last days he had discovered why.

He thought of Laura. Was he running from her? Maybe. But she was married, happily or otherwise, and was established in her life. He wondered about the old wisdom "you can never go back". But he didn't think he was trying to go back. Still, there wasn't much point in reflecting on Laura, or on what it would be like to have her back in his life even if she were free to make that choice. He chuckled. When they were high school sweethearts she had often affectionately called him "arrogant" and here he was assuming that if she were free of Darrin she would run to him. He took a sip of the scotch.

Maybe he should just buy another boat and go sailing again. However, he had done that originally to heal himself, to think about what he wanted to do with the rest of his life, and, of course, because he had always wanted to go off shore sailing. As he thought about it, he realized that his two year sojourn in the South Pacific on Pegasus had worked better than he had realized. There were still some unanswered questions in his life but his time in Toronto told him he was as healed as he was going to get, at least from the wounds that he had received there.

"Coffee, Herr O'Neill?" The secretary stood in front of him with his hands clasped.

"Yes, thank you," Eric replied. "Black, please." He looked around the waiting room in the International Commercial

Bank building as the secretary walked with slow dignity to a door in the opposite wall. It was quite different from the kind of office he was used to. It was as still as a funeral home and with a similar decor, designed to make one think of peace and eternity, dull muted colours, still life paintings devoid of anything suggesting motion. The furniture was so heavy it looked as though it would take a small crane to move it. No image of a dynamic investment house here, just solidity, endurance and old luxury. There were no magazines on the small table by his large uncomfortable chair. Perhaps the clients who came here couldn't read. He smiled at the thought. More likely, they didn't stay here long enough.

The door on the opposite wall opened and the secretary returned. "If you will follow me, Herr O'Neill." He indicated a second door and opened it, ushering Eric into an inner office, clearly done by the same decorator but with a desk planted firmly in the middle of the room.

"Good morning, Herr O'Neill." A small balding man in a black suit rose from behind the desk. "I am Alfred Koenig, vice president of the International Commercial Bank."

"Good morning, Herr Koenig," Eric said. "Thank you for seeing me."

"Please sit down," Koenig said, indicating a chair in front of his desk. He waited until Eric was seated before sinking into his own chair, one that looked considerably more comfortable than those reserved for visitors. He looked up at the secretary. "I believe you were about to bring us coffee?"

The secretary nodded and left the room.

"I trust you had a pleasant flight from Canada?"

"It was fine," Eric replied leaning back in the chair as far as it would allow. "But long distance travel is always a bit tiring."

"Indeed," Koenig said. "Now Herr O'Neill, how can we be of service."

"I believe you have my correspondence on the matter I wish to discuss. Apparently, I have fallen heir to one of your accounts. I would like to learn the balance and the history of the account."

"Of course," Koenig said. "As I am sure you know, we are very conscious of the security of our clients' accounts and for that reason require identification."

Eric silently slid his passport across the desk. Koenig picked it up, read the opening page carefully, looked at the picture and then at Eric. He closed it, nodded and set it down. Eric heard the door behind him open and a moment later the secretary set a large silver tray on the desk. Koenig handed the passport to the secretary who nodded and left.

Koenig stood and picked up an ornate silver coffee pot and poured two small china cups full. "I think the Swiss like coffee even better than Americans," he said.

"You make it better, too," Eric replied. He picked up the delicate china cup and sipped. It was strong and rich but not harsh or bitter. "Very nice."

Koenig's desktop was empty, clear of everything save a single leather folder placed squarely in front of him. He opened it. "Your account presents us with some interesting problems, Herr O'Neill. It was created decades ago, during World War II, actually, and as you know, in recent years we have become more sensitive to the issue of wartime accounts."

"I understand the issues, Herr Koenig. You are concerned about Nazi gold and currency transactions. Do you have any reason to believe that my account falls into this category?"

Koenig picked up his china cup, took a drink of the coffee and stared at the folder on his desk. "We really don't know, Herr O'Neill. We were hoping perhaps you could tell us."

"All I can tell you is that my parents were killed in an automobile accident recently and among their personal effects was information on this bank account, all of which I communicated to you. My parents were Irish and I was born there as my passport shows so I assumed the account was originated from there."

"A natural assumption, Herr O'Neill."

Eric heard the door behind him open again. The secretary walked silently to the desk and handed the passport to Koenig with a curt nod.

Eric smiled at Koenig. "And am I who I appear to be?"

"Of course, Herr O'Neill," Koenig said, smiling for the first time. He leaned back in his chair. "Your account was opened in September 1940, not quite a year after you were born. Incidentally, your account is US dollar denominated and all deposits to it have been in US dollars. Each September another deposit was made until the last one in September 1944. After that, the account had no activity at all until a few days ago. Then another large deposit was made." Koenig paused and took another sip of his coffee. "In spite of your Irish birth, Herr O'Neill, and the Irish citizenship of your parents, all deposits, including the one that occurred a few days ago, were received as transfers from the Rutgers Bank of Berlin, a rather small institution that managed to survive the war."

"A few days ago?" Eric was incredulous. "Who would put money in my account now?"

"Apparently it was someone who has considerable resources, Herr O'Neill."

"Why do you say that?"

"The deposit was for five million dollars US," Koenig said quietly.

CHAPTER FORTY EIGHT

Thursday, May 4, 1989 West Berlin

Eric remembered Berlin, or at least West Berlin, as a vibrant, exciting city, almost manic in its energy, always on the edge of extinction, living every day as though it were its last. But that had been August 1979 and he had spent a week meeting with some German financial managers to set up investment arrangements for some of his high value clients. After day time hours in a boardroom working out the details, they had shown him the city, its cafes, its entertainment and even its brothels although he had declined those. His hosts had not.

That week in August the sun had shone every day and the place had sparkled, but today it was raining, a dull grey drizzle with a cold mist hanging low, resolutely obscuring the city. And, of course, he was alone. He had dredged his memory for the name of the small hotel he had stayed at but couldn't come up with it. He had flown from Zurich to Frankfurt and then had taken a train to Berlin. The train had been a kind of whimsical decision. He liked train travel and as a child had often taken the train for an hour from Portage to Winnipeg for a day of shopping with his parents.

As the train had rolled across the countryside outside Frankfurt, everything was lush, green and gently rolling, squared by little fields of what looked like grain and fodder crops. Every two or three kilometres he passed by or could see in the distance, a small village, the houses tall, two or three stories under steeply pitched red slate roofs. The border stop was short, to allow East German armed guards to board the train before it moved on again. They made their slow, methodical and unsmiling way through the compartments checking tickets, passports and other official papers. To Eric, the checks seemed cursory, as though the guards were going through the motions rather than hunting out potential spies and traitors. He had smiled at his silly cold war imagery.

Once into East Germany the towns had looked seedy, worn and shabby. At one point the train slowed and passed another train in a siding, full of Russian troops, tanks and armoured personnel carriers on flat cars. As they travelled farther east, the landscape flattened until it looked almost like the Canadian prairies, huge fields with the occasional large tractor in the distance. Periodically he saw along the tracks, on what was likely the railway right-of-way, small gardens, a few metres square with tiny cottages like children's play houses tucked neatly in a corner, rows of vegetables and flowers waiting for the summer sun. These were the summer cottages belonging to apartment dwellers from nearby towns, cared for with great pride.

The phone purred softly beside the small chesterfield in his hotel suite. He had called Karl Krause, one of his hosts from ten years ago, and had left a message with his secretary. "Good afternoon," he said cheerfully.

"Eric O'Neill, please."

"Hello, Karl."

"So it is really you?"

"Indeed it is."

"And you're in Berlin?"

"I am. Thanks for calling back. I need some information."

"You will need to eat dinner as well. Shall I pick you up at seven?"

"That would be fine, Karl."

Eric put the phone back and stood up. His suite was larger than he needed but it had been the only one available when he had shown up to register. He had decided on the Ravensburg Hotel, caught a cab at the Zoo train station, and had been taken directly to the hotel. There was a small kitchen, a spacious living room, bathroom and a separate bedroom. Since he expected to stay a couple of days he had hung up his few clothes in the generous closet, set out his toiletries in the bathroom and settled in.

A small store nearby had provided some fresh fruit, half a kilogram of coffee, a bottle of Alsatian white wine and some buns and butter. He wasn't sure why he had purchased the food but he had organized all the items neatly in the small refrigerator and it seemed to normalize his surroundings a bit to have some things in the kitchen.

Now it seemed he would be eating dinner with Karl. They had sent occasional notes back and forth over the intervening years and Karl had been in Toronto at a meeting in the early '80's and they had spent an evening together. They enjoyed each other's company but distance and the demands of their careers had just gotten in the way of a closer friendship. He found himself looking forward to the evening.

He had decided to make his appointment with Rutgers Bank after he had chatted with Karl and found out something about it, assuming Karl knew anything. If not, perhaps he could direct him to some useful sources. Eric didn't know what he was going to talk to the Rutgers Bank people about. He was fairly certain they wouldn't provide him much information on the early transfers of money, even assuming their records had survived. They were even more unlikely to tell him about the recent five million dollar transfer.

He had been stunned by the balance in the portfolio. The deposits in September 1940 and 1941 had each been for $500,000 US. But for the following three years they had been for one million each, huge sums for those days. So by September 1944 the account had held $4,000,000 US. Prior to the five million dollar deposit made a few days ago, the account balance had stood at just over $46,000,000, a sum which made him extremely nervous. Quite aside from the origins of the money, it was a staggering amount. A police detective had told him a few years ago that the going rate in Toronto to have someone murdered was between $500 and $10,000, depending on who you hired, who the target was and the difficulty of the task. If people would kill for $10,000, what would they do for $51,000,000? However, so long as the money remained in the National Investment Bank in Switzerland, no one else could get at it whether he was dead or alive.

He had been surprised at the amount but a rough calculation told him that the original four million had been compounding for the last forty five years at about five percent per year on average. Still, a pile of money in excess of $50 million dollars could be a real problem, especially when he had no idea who was behind it all. He wondered what would happen if he simply withdrew it all and transferred it to the off-shore bank where he kept his own "international" money.

A few minutes before seven, he took the stairs down to the lobby. When he was travelling he avoided elevators and took the stairs whenever possible, building in a small bit of exercise whenever the opportunity presented itself.

Karl pulled up a few minutes later in a large black BMW. He parked in the small loading zone in front of the hotel and jumped from the car, running around to the entrance to embrace Eric. "It's been too long, my friend," he said, releasing Eric. "Much too long."

"It has," Eric replied, laughing at Karl's exuberance and shaking his head slightly as he had forgotten just how big Karl was. He was easily six foot four and had to weigh 250 pounds but was so well proportioned that you didn't realize how big he was until he was standing near you or crushing you in an embrace.

The restaurant was small, hidden away in a side street and judging by the welcome that Karl received when they entered, he was a regular. They had barely been seated when a waiter delivered a chilled bottle of white wine. "Each fall Heinrich, the owner of this place, spends a week wandering around the Rhine Valley buying up his year's supply of wine, so most of the wine here is not what you would encounter in other stores or restaurants but it is usually pretty good."

Eric picked up his wine glass and held it by the stem, looked through it for a moment and then tasted it. It was rich and fruity, smooth as butter and surprisingly dry and crisp. He smiled with pleasure. He wasn't a wine connoisseur by any stretch of the imagination but he did enjoy good wine and this was perhaps the best tasting white wine he had ever encountered.

Karl leaned forward, his handsome face creased in a frown. "What do you think?"

"Marvellous, Karl," Eric replied. "Just marvellous."

Karl picked up his own glass and they touched their goblets together in a toast. "Welcome to Berlin, Eric."

Karl had ordered dinner for them both, a schnitzel so delicate it literally melted in his mouth. They had chatted about their last time together, about the current state of markets in Europe and when the conversation had shifted to North American markets, Eric had explained to Karl about his two year sojourn away from the world of finance and his lack of current information on the state of them.

"But what a wonderful adventure," Karl said when he had finished. "Why would you ever go back to an office?"

"Good question," Eric said thoughtfully. "I may not. I'm still not certain what I'm going to do."

"Well, you are lucky to have that choice."

"Surely you could do the same if you wished."

"Ah, my friend," Karl said, leaning back in his chair and pushing it away from the table. "Until a year ago I would have agreed with you. Then my wife left and took half of everything I owned. Now I am a poor man again."

Eric laughed. He didn't know Karl's precise worth but it was in the millions. "You? Poor?"

Karl laughed too. "Well, poverty is a relative thing," he said. "Besides, now that I have no one to spend my time with, why would I retire?" He paused. "But then that is precisely what you did, isn't it?"

Eric nodded and smiled. "If you are lonely when you are alone, then you are in bad company. Its an old Canadian proverb, Karl, but I'm sorry to hear about your wife leaving." He recalled meeting her on his trip to Berlin in 1979 and remembered her as blonde and blue eyed, tall, slim and striking.

"It's quite a story," Karl said. A waiter appeared by their table and he and Karl had a short conversation in German. "I've ordered us coffee and liqueurs. You are not in a hurry?"

"Not at all, Karl."

"Well, Angela, you will remember she adopted this silly American name, complained a bit about the hours I worked but not a lot since her own job with the broadcasting company often took her out of town and I complained, too, just to keep things even. Well, she found someone else about four years ago and then a year ago, she moved out."

"I'm sorry to hear that," Eric said. "I only met her once but I liked her."

"So did I, and she looked like a Nordic goddess as you will recall. But she went through a difficult time in a number of ways, none of which she ever discussed with me and then she left. She claimed she had fallen in love. She told me I was the only man she could ever love, but that she had fallen for another woman."

Eric was silent.

Karl shook his head with a good natured grin. "But I am over it and we are now good friends again. Not so good that she wants to give back the money, but good enough that she trusts me to manage it for her."

"You seem to be surviving well in spite of the trauma," Eric said.

"Well, you should see the other woman," Karl said, laughing again. "If I wasn't still in love with Angela I would fall in love with her." Karl leaned forward. "But you didn't come here to learn of my love life. So what can I do for you?"

Eric had wondered how to raise the subject but decided that he would just go at it directly and trust that Karl wouldn't pry too hard into his reasons. "What do you know of the Rutgers Bank?"

Karl raised his eyebrows and sat up. He stared thoughtfully at Eric for a moment. "Not a lot," he said seriously. "It is small, old, exclusive. It seems to cater to low profile, high value clients as far as I know." He paused. "What sort of information are you looking for?"

"Any kind really," Eric replied.

"Are you a client of theirs?"

"No."

"Thinking of doing business with them?"

"No."

Karl leaned forward again. "There are always rumours in our business, as you know. Rutgers is rumoured to have been one of the banks the Nazis used during and immediately after the war to move money out, to Zurich, to Spain, South America and all the other spots that welcomed their investments. However, they were never convicted of anything."

"But the rumours persist?"

"Yes they do, and so we don't deal with them."

"Anything else I should know?"

Karl looked at him thoughtfully. Eric noticed for the first time that a tinge of grey was creeping into his temples, making his thick pale blonde hair almost white in the candle light of their table. "Have you heard of the Reichbank robbery?"

"The one that occurred near the end of World War II?"

"The very same."

"I've only heard that it was large, confused and involved a lot of people."

"Correct," Karl said. "Millions of deutschmarks, pounds sterling, Swiss francs, American dollars, gold bullion and all the other sorts of things that central banks hold, were taken from Berlin in March 1945, supposedly to be safeguarded from the invading Allied forces and to be returned to the new German central bank when hostilities ceased and peace and order were restored."

"It was moved south, wasn't it?"

"Some of it was, some of it was placed in depositories in other banks, some was buried, some sunk in lakes, a lot was recovered and returned just as it was supposed to have been, but a huge amount of it simply disappeared."

"Where did it go?"

"No one knows," Karl said and then smiled. "Of course, someone knows but no one is telling. The part that went missing was never found, no one was ever charged and the money, mostly US dollars and gold, never showed up, or no one spotted it when it did."

"And the Rutgers Bank?"

"One of the chief suspects in moving it and laundering it."

"But never charged?"

"Never even investigated."

"Why not?"

"Too well connected, I suspect."

"How so?"

"You North Americans like to think that you made the world safe from the Nazis in 1945. You didn't. Lots of them survived. Some of the more prominent ones moved to South America or Spain, or Egypt or wherever they could sell their talents. But most of them stayed right here in Germany and either retained their positions of prominence or quickly regained them, unless they had been involved in the death camps or other war crimes."

"Can this be true?"

"Most certainly," Karl said. "Let me give you a couple of examples of what I mean. The Allies tried, with virtually no success at all, to break up German industrial and manufacturing conglomerates to prevent another arms build up. But no one seriously considered breaking up the German banking system. They looked at the financial collapse that occurred following World War One and realized they just couldn't risk that again."

The waiter arrived with a silver coffee service and a decanter of cognac and poured for each of them.

When he left, Karl continued. "Once the Cold War began, Allied policy shifted immediately from punishing Germany for World War II to rebuilding it as a bulwark against communism, and who better to rebuild it than those who had rebuilt it the last time?"

Eric sipped the brandy and felt it softly warming his stomach. "So they let old Nazis back into power?"

"Much better than that," Karl said. "The Marshall Plan, as you will recall, poured tens of millions of dollars into rebuilding Western Europe. West Germany got the largest share. In fact, Hermann Abs, a Deutsche Bank director, who had been marked for prosecution as a war criminal until the second round of the Nuremberg trials was cancelled, was involved in distributing Marshall Plan dollars and graciously sent much of it to West Germany. Conrad Adenauer and his Christian Democratic Union party won the 1953 election. His government was full of ex-Nazis."

"But surely this is past now," Eric said quietly.

"I wish it were," Karl replied earnestly. "But this kind of infiltration is not merely political or within our financial institutions.

By the mid 1970's the German Bundeswehr, our armed forces, had 217 generals commanding the largest standing army in Europe. All but three were Third Reich veterans. There are thirty-seven military bases in West Germany named after soldiers who made their reputations during the Hitler years.

"One last example, Eric, and then I'll stop. In the spring of 1985, just four years ago, the remains of forty-seven SS men were buried at Bitberg Cemetery with 2000 Wehrmacht soldiers. Ronald Reagan came by to lay a wreath to commemorate the end of World War II. He offered some comments on human rights abuses during the war but limited them to those committed by communist countries. He depicted the Third Reich as the work of one maniac and even suggested that the SS men were victims of Hitler just as surely as the victims in the concentration camps were. He conveniently overlooked the fact that the SS was heavily involved in running the death camps."

"That is just astonishing," Eric said.

"This is just the tip of an iceberg and my simple examples cover the entire post-war period. These people simply scare the shit out of me. And to come back to your Rutgers Bank, Eric, I would not be surprised to learn that they are an integral part of this whole process."

CHAPTER FORTY NINE

Thursday, May 4, 1989 West Berlin

Eric O'Neill walked slowly up the stairs to his hotel room. His head was spinning from the information Karl had given him regarding the Rutgers Bank. In reality, he knew that some of the spin was due to the wine and the schnapps that he and Karl had consumed with dinner.

He took the key from his pocket, inserted it in the lock, turned it and tried to open the door. The door remained locked. Puzzled, he turned the key the other way and the latch opened. Odd, he thought. Could he have left the door unlocked when he went out earlier? He stepped into the room, switched on the light and hung his coat in the small closet in the entry way. He straightened his navy blazer on the hanger. A pair of slacks were coming loose on their pant hanger and he rearranged them as well. He must have knocked things out of kilter when he had taken his trench coat from the closet on his way out. He slipped off his loafers and set them together on the floor of the closet before he closed the door.

He saw his bed was turned down and two chocolate wafers were carefully placed on the small end table beside it. He smiled. Hotels always seemed to leave chocolate by the bedside, never jelly beans or gum drops, which was fine by him.

In the bathroom, he noticed the towels had been changed, the damp ones he had left from his shower had been replaced with fresh ones. His shaving kit had been moved from the right to the left side of the wash basin. It was an odd thing for a hotel housekeeper to do. Then he noticed a faint smell, familiar in a way but he knew it wasn't one he could name, perfume, perhaps, or a man's cologne.

He left the bathroom and pulled open the closet door again. Picking up his old briefcase, he carried it to the small dining table in the alcove by the kitchenette. He looked at the numbers on the combination lock. Deirdre had given him the briefcase for his thirty-fifth birthday and he had set the combination at 035. He had not locked it so the open combination was still showing. The numbers still read 035 but they were in perfect alignment, something that occurred only when he fiddled with them to get them even, a task he rarely bothered to undertake. Someone had opened the case, then taken the time to align the numbers, probably assuming he kept them that way. Someone had been through his room, his papers, his clothes.

Rapidly he flipped through the few files in the case. Nothing appeared to be missing but the files were not in the same order in which he had arranged them. His daily planner was there, but had been turned upside down, so whoever had looked knew his schedule although there was nothing in it for the next few days. Perhaps that would be confusing. He walked quickly to the door and locked it, throwing the deadbolt and putting on the safety chain.

Suddenly he felt nervous, even a bit frightened. Somcone now knew the balance in his Swiss account as well as the number of the account. All they lacked was the identification code.

He sat down in the comfortable arm chair. Should he call the front desk or the police to report a robbery in which nothing was stolen? For which the main clues were a faint scent he couldn't place and the alignment of numbers on a combination lock? Relax, he told himself. But someone was watching him, following him. Why? A Swiss account with a $51 million balance was why, but who knew about that? The folks who had added $5 million a week ago knew. Herr Koenig of the National Investment Bank of Switzerland knew. Laura knew the account existed but not the balance. Laura.

He picked up the phone, then looked at his watch. It was after midnight. He did a quick subtraction and concluded it would be 5:20 in the afternoon in Portage. He had promised to phone Laura when he knew something. Well, now he knew something. And it would be comforting to talk with her. He dialled the hotel switchboard, asked them to place the call and set the receiver back on the cradle. The thought of a scotch was appealing but his head was already fuzzy enough.

The phone rang and he picked it up. "Hello."

Laura's voice sounded faint and far away. "Eric?"

"Yes," he answered. "How are you?

"Fine. Where are you?"

"Berlin. I was in Switzerland for a couple of days and now here." He had been about to say he was leaving as soon as he had been in touch with the Rutgers Bank but suddenly wondered if the phone line was secure, or whether he ought to be using the hotel phone at all. Paranoia was a strange thing. "Can you talk for a minute or am I interrupting the health care system?"

Laura laughed, a rich warm sound. "I'm glad you called, Eric. I was wondering when I would hear from you." She paused.

"I was at your house last night checking on things. I think someone else had been there. Does anyone else have a key that you know of?"

"No," Eric said, suddenly feeling cold. "Was it a break-in?"

"I'm not sure," Laura replied. "I went into your Dad's study and things just didn't look right. The papers and files we had looked at before you left had been moved around." There was silence for a moment. "I have been to the house a couple of times since you left, both times in the evening, and just sat in your father's big leather chair in the study and read through those letters again. I wanted to make sure I had the German right so the second time I took a dictionary with me. That is a such a quiet, serene room." There was silence again. "Before I left the second night, I tidied up the desk top, put the files in a neat pile, chronologically and when I was there last night, they were not as neat and were in a different order."

"Did you check the rest of the house?"

"No. I was afraid to," she said, her voice suddenly quiet. "I was afraid I might find someone there so I just left."

"Did you report anything to the police?" Eric asked.

"No, I didn't call them. I had been in the kitchen before I went in the study and everything there seemed fine. All the crystal was still there. I poured myself a glass of wine before I went into the study but after I found the files out of order I just grabbed my coat and left. It was a strange feeling. Do you want me to call the police?"

"No," Eric said. "Unless you think it would be wise?"

"There isn't much to report other than the suspicions of a middle aged woman and they might want to know what I was doing in your house anyway."

Eric smiled at the comment. "We middle aged folks are entitled to a little paranoia, I think."

They were both quiet for a moment. "Eric," Laura said softly. "Do you know when you are coming home?"

"I don't know," Eric replied, realizing oddly that he was comfortable with the idea of 'home'. "In a few days I should think. I have pretty much run out of leads. There isn't much to do here."

"Good," she said. "I miss you."

"I miss you too."

Silence again.

"I should let you go," Eric said. "I'm sure there are patients waiting to see you."

"Just a couple."

"I'll call you again in a few days."

"Okay. Is there anything you'd like me to do about the house?"

"No," Eric said. "Maybe you should just stay away in case there is some danger there."

"Okay. Please be careful, Eric."

"I will."

"Bye."

"Bye."

Eric sat quietly and thought about his conversation. He had not told Laura about someone being in his room here. He had intended to but decided not to worry her any further, and then there was the phone. He had not told her of the $51 million either. There would be time for that later.

The Rutgers Bank was small and old and treated people who phoned them very graciously. In the morning, he called for an appointment and was given one for two o'clock. They sent a car to his hotel to pick him up, a large black Mercedes with a driver who looked like a bodyguard, big, tough looking and silent. He smiled and nodded at Eric but other than asking his name and wishing him a good day, or at least that is what Eric had assumed he said, he had not spoken. He wore a black suit that was perfectly tailored to cover his large muscular frame but there was no trace of a swagger or of any awareness of the physical power that emanated from him.

They drove for ten minutes down the Kudamm, the busy traffic of mid-afternoon Berlin flowing smoothly, and then turned up in a narrow street stopping in front of a small, old, gothic looking building. The driver ushered him in and handed him on to an elderly, white haired gentleman who greeted him in flawless English, touched by traces of a British accent, but Eric couldn't place it much closer than that.

None of the trappings of a normal bank were evident, no tellers' cages, no flow of customers in and out, no evident place to make deposits or withdrawals, only a large foyer with a telephone switchboard operated by a man, and another desk, empty for the moment but likely belonging to his white haired greeter.

A small modern elevator took them up to the fourth floor. As the door opened, two men stepped forward. "Good afternoon, Herr O'Neill," the taller one said. "Welcome to Rutgers Bank. My name is Heinrich Hoffner and this is our financial vice president, Wolfgang Schwartz."

"Thank you," Eric said, and shook hands with both of them. In other circumstances he would have wondered if they were a comedy team. Hoffner was tall with a shock of silver hair, slim and dressed elegantly in a black suit. Scchwartz was short, balding and portly, and his navy blue suit hung over him rather than on him.

"It is an honour to meet you, Herr O'Neill," Hoffner said. "We've been expecting you."

"Really?" Eric said with genuine surprise.

Hoffner smiled at him warmly. "Come this way, please," he said and led them into a large room furnished more like a residential living room than a bank board room. It contained sofas and chairs, coffee and end tables, all large heavy and comfortable. The paintings on the walls were gilt-framed still lifes. A delicate crystal chandelier hung from the centre of the high ceiling, looking oddly out of place, as though the room had been converted from a dining room and someone had forgotten to change the light fixture.

"Coffee?" Hoffner asked.

"That would nice, thank you."

Schwartz rose and left the room.

"I expect you have come to inquire about your Swiss account, Herr O'Neill."

Eric nodded, surprised. "I would like to learn what I can."

"Of course," Hoffner said. "Before we begin would you mind showing me your passport?"

Eric reached inside his blazer. "Not at all." He handed the small navy blue folder over to Hoffner.

Hoffner opened the passport, glanced at it in a cursory manner and handed it back. "It must have been rather disconcerting to discover that you had an account at all, and even more so to learn that it had a substantial balance."

"To say the least," Eric said.

"I understand your own background is in financial markets."

"That's true. I worked for a brokerage firm in Toronto for a number of years and then started my own firm, primarily portfolio management for high value clients."

"That is not unlike our own operation here."

The door opened and Schwartz entered balancing a coffee pot on a tray with three white china mugs bearing the bank's logo, an ornate coat of arms. He set the tray down on a sideboard and poured, handing out the mugs and sitting down with his own.

Hoffner continued. "Your account was established in the fall of 1940 with our bank. Due to the unstable nature of things during wartime, we arranged with a correspondent bank in Switzerland, the National Investment Bank, to move your account there where it has remained since. I trust you are satisfied with their management of it?"

"I haven't really had time go over a lot of the details but it seems that they have done a credible and conservative job of it."

"What else would you like to know, Herr O'Neill?"

Eric smiled at the question. "I'm sure you can guess, Herr Hoffner. I would like to know who put $5 million into it a week ago, who was responsible for setting it up and making the original deposits from 1940 to 1944."

Hoffner smiled at the question. "The first deposits came from the office of the Reich Chancellery. That would be like your prime minister's office, although it was done by staff in the office. So the short answer to your question is that we don't know who, precisely, is responsible. As to the recent deposit, it came in the form of a bank transfer from a correspondent bank in England with instructions to deposit it to your Swiss account. Again, we do not know specifically who originated the transaction."

Eric drank his coffee in silence. The Reich Chancery, run by Martin Bormann if he recalled his history correctly and an English correspondent bank. What was the connection?

"We do have some further information for you," Hoffner said, interrupting Eric's reverie. He picked up a small folder from the side table by his chair. "An airline ticket, a flight to

London, scheduled three days hence. These arrived by courier this morning from the same correspondent bank in London so I assume you will get some further answers when you get there." He handed the slim Lufthansa folder to Eric.

Eric nodded and took the folder, opened it to check the departure dates. It was a one way ticket from Berlin to London. The folder contained no other information.

"I take it you have friends here in Berlin, Herr O'Neill?"

Eric nodded. "A couple of acquaintances that I know through business."

Hoffner took a sip of his coffee. "I believe you had dinner with one of them last night," he said with a smile. "Karl Krause? I believe he works for one of our competitors."

Eric was somehow not surprised. "You are well informed."

"We are, Herr O'Neill, and very careful with the interests of our clients. During your stay here, we would be pleased to arrange anything you would wish. Opera? Theatre? The Berlin Philharmonic is playing this week. There are some fine art galleries."

"Thank you," Eric replied. "That's very kind."

"Wolfgang has prepared a list of some of West Berlin's better attractions," Hoffner said.

Schwartz pulled a folded sheet of paper from his inner suit pocket and handed it to Eric. "I've taken the liberty of inviting you to a reception the bank is hosting tomorrow evening. It is for some of our more prominent clients and their wives. Otherwise, please feel free to choose anything on the list or anything else you would like to attend and we will arrange tickets for you. We have also put a car and one of our drivers at your disposal while you are here."

"That's very gracious of you," Eric replied.

The silent driver dropped him back at the Ravensburg Hotel half an hour later. Eric thanked him and dismissed him, telling him he would not require his services for the rest of the day. The driver had seemed relieved.

But what was waiting in London in three days? The only information that Hoffner and Schwartz had provided was that he would be met there and his questions answered. So he was in Berlin, being followed or shadowed or whatever was happening. The folks at Rutgers Bank had offered to keep him busy and engaged with the cultural life of Berlin for the next three days and he had a plane ticket from someone to go to London. There was just too much control here. He was losing the initiative. He had come here to find out about his origins and he felt like his life was being directed by forces he didn't understand.

There might not be a lot he could do about changing that but he did not have to take part in it either. In his room, he didn't bother to take his coat off. He put his briefcase on the dining table, got his personal kit from the bathroom and moved the essentials to his briefcase. He closed it and left the room, locking the door behind him.

He walked down the three flights of stairs and waited at the front desk for a couple of minutes as a young couple checked in. The lobby was empty except for a middle aged man sitting in an armchair reading a newspaper. Eric had seen him earlier when he left for the Rutgers Bank. Perhaps he was some sort of hotel security type. The young couple picked up their luggage and headed for the elevator. Eric spoke to the clerk at the front desk, extending his stay to Sunday, three days from now, and walked out the front door.

A couple of blocks down the street he found another large hotel. He entered and approached the concierge. Tipping him generously, he asked for a taxi.

"Tegel Airport, please," he told the driver.

CHAPTER FIFTY

Thursday, May 4, 1989 British Airways Flight 479, New York, JFK to London, Heathrow

Liselle Marcoux stared out the window, deep in thought, only peripherally aware of the constant white noise of the 747. Far below, the Atlantic was a deep flat blue and the early afternoon sun sparkled with almost painful brightness on a few light clouds. She turned away as the first class flight attendant asked her something, and then shook her head at the champagne bottle. She had enjoyed one glass, more would make her sleepy and she still had work to do.

She turned her attention to the black zippered binder on the small table in front of her and squirmed in the soft leather seat. It was the size of a small armchair. She opened the binder and stared at the first picture. It was a colour 8 X 10, a head and shoulder shot of a man taken on what looked like a street corner. The back of a second man covered some of the foreground. The subject was smiling, almost laughing, tanned, healthy, good-looking rather than classically handsome. It had been a bright day and his hair appeared sun bleached, dark blonde roots with bleached ends. It was thick and wavy and looked like it would tousle easily.

"Nice looking guy," the man beside her said, brushing against her arm as he leaned over for a better look. "Your boyfriend?" He had introduced himself earlier, Ralph Walters, an account executive for a Wall Street firm, mid-forties, perhaps, darkly handsome with a wedding ring on his left hand and definitely interested in her. There were times when a casual liaison of the sort he was likely offering might have some appeal but she was working on this trip so she had decided on her quiet and friendly but cool and unattainable personality and it had done its job. She had asked questions, made him feel important and listened with some genuine interest as he had chatted about life on Wall Street. Inside information on anything was useful. After lunch, served with two glasses of red wine, he had ordered a Courvosier and drunk it rather more quickly than the lovely old cognac deserved. Then he had fallen asleep.

"Yes, he is a good looking man," Liselle replied, ignoring the boyfriend question. She smiled at him. "Feeling rested?"

Ralph sat back in his seat. "These flights are always too long and tedious."

Liselle nodded and looked away, amused by the comment. What did that make her?

"So you never really told me what you do in New York," Ralph asked.

"I'm a head hunter," Liselle replied. "I specialize in finding people to fill difficult jobs."

"What sort of jobs?"

"Look-alikes for movies, adventure guides, a variety of people."

"And this guy in the folder?"

Liselle laughed. "I'm sorry, Ralph, but I can't disclose personal information of that sort."

"You remembered my name. I'm impressed," Ralph said good-naturedly. "But I understand. Same thing in my business. When I go to the movies I'll keep my eyes open for this guy."

"Good idea," Liselle said and then pointedly turned her attention back to the binder and turned to a second photograph. This one was taken in a bar or a restaurant booth. There were two other people there but he seemed to dominate the table even though he was the one listening. His face was in repose, serious and concentrated, slightly in profile revealing a full, straight nose. His lips were a little thin but the mouth was still strong, sensual in a way. But it was his eyes that were the dominant feature. His head was tilted slightly and he was focussing on the man across from him in the booth. The eyes were a deep dark brown, compelling and powerful. She wondered if they would be revealing eyes. The photograph had been taken without a flash and the natural shadows accentuated his features. He was wearing a navy blazer with a lighter blue turtle neck under it.

As she turned through the next few pages, other pictures confirmed the initial impression without adding much to it. She went on to the printed pages and read the tomb stone details: Eric Gilford O'Neill: Height: 6'; Weight: 175 lbs; Hair: light brown; Eyes: brown. This stuff must have come from his passport, she thought, not very accurate. Birth Date: October 30, 1939, London, England.

So he will turn fifty this year she mused. I wonder how he'll handle that? The next page was headed "Biographical Information". Liselle glanced at Ralph but he was deep into Fortune Magazine. She turned her attention back to the page.

> Subject was born in Dublin, parents emigrated to Canada when he was a child. No records to confirm this have yet been located. Raised in a small prairie town, Portage la Prairie, Manitoba, just west of the city of Winnipeg. Played high school sports, did well academically and moved to Toronto in the fall of 1957 to attend university. Graduated in 1961 with specialties in finance and economics. Was employed by the Bank of Canada, Securities Division for two years, and spent the second year in London, England.
>
> Subject left the Bank of Canada in fall 1963, returned to Toronto, joined a brokerage firm and left in 1966 to start his own firm. Married in August, 1967 to Deirdre Allison Hudson, daughter of an old and wealthy Toronto family. They had one son, Geoffrey Forsyth, born May 1969, who died in an automobile accident, June 21, 1986. Wife committed suicide December 24, 1986.
>
> Subject left Toronto, early March 1987, destination unknown, and resurfaced in Portage la Prairie, MB in April 1989, following the deaths of his parents in an automobile accident, April 20, 1989.
>
> More detail to follow.

Liselle shut the binder and leaned back in her seat. She closed her eyes and thought about Eric O'Neill. The cold facts told so little in some ways but so much in others. How had he handled the double agony of losing his only son and his wife within six months of each other? Where had he been for the last two years and what had he been up to? She knew they would find out, perhaps by the time she reached London and her second briefing. Success, tragedy, adventure, wealth, power and now a search for his roots. An interesting man.

She had been contacted by her control late yesterday and told she was going to London the next afternoon. She would be given a file at JFK and would be met at Heathrow and more fully briefed. She wondered about a coincidence. Jon Falken and Eric O'Neill had identical birth dates, although Jon had been born in Philadelphia. She wondered about her assignment to Jon Falken being followed by her assignment with Eric O'Neill.

CHAPTER FIFTY ONE

Thursday, May 4, 1989 Frankfurt, West Germany

Eric had managed to get a flight from Berlin to Frankfurt within an hour of arriving at the airport. Now in Frankfurt, with only his brief case, he passed quickly through the entry points. A few minutes later, as he stood in the concourse looking about for directional signs he caught sight of a familiar figure. For a moment he couldn't place the man and his eyes swept on looking for directions to the international ticket and departures area. There was an overcoat and a hat now but he had gotten a clear look at the face. He swung his eyes back quickly but the man had disappeared in the crowds. He was fairly certain It was the man from the hotel lobby in Berlin, the man who had sat there reading. Was it a coincidence that he should now be in Frankfurt, or was it that a lot of German men looked equally nondescript and that he was merely being paranoid? He felt shaken, suddenly fearful.

He started walking and spotted the sign he was looking for. A few minutes later he was standing in front of a Lufthansa ticket counter with a short line of people in front of him. He scanned the departures board behind the counter, then glanced at his watch. It was 6:30pm.

"Paris," he said. "Do you have a seat available on your 9:10 flight?"

"One moment, sir," the clerk replied. She was short and dark and spoke English with an odd accent that was not German. Karl had told him a lot of Turkish citizens worked in Germany.

"We only have seats available in business class on that flight, sir."

"That will be fine," Eric said and slid his credit card and passport across the counter.

He looked around as he strolled slowly away from the ticket counter but he saw no familiar figures. Perhaps his imagination was becoming overactive. He realized he was hungry. The flight from Berlin had been short and he had turned down the offer of tea, coffee or a drink. A few minutes later he found a small restaurant and bar and ordered a beer and a sandwich. The beer was dark and smooth, almost thick tasting. The sandwich was made from something that tasted like corned beef and came on thick rye bread. Delicious.

He was finishing his beer and beginning to relax when the man walked into the restaurant and without glancing at him, went directly to the bar and sat down on a stool. This time Eric was more certain. The man took his hat off and set it on the counter. In the hotel he had only seen him from the front but there was a mirror behind the bar and in it Eric could see the man's face. When he turned to look about and Eric was sure it was the man from the hotel.

Should he walk over and confront him? Or perhaps greet him like an old friend and offer to buy him a drink? Or maybe just get the hell out of the restaurant.

He finished his beer and waited until the man from the hotel had been served. He gathered his briefcase and his overcoat and walked to the cash register at the entrance to the restaurant. He was only a few feet from the man at the bar. He glanced over at him while he waited for someone to take his money. Their eyes met for an instant and the man looked away.

"How was everything, sir?" the manager asked.

"Just fine, thank you," Eric replied, handing him the bill and some marks.

"Thank you, sir," the manager said, handing Eric his receipt and some change.

"I wonder if you could direct me to a currency exchange," Eric said. "I need to get some French francs."

"Certainly," the manager said, and proceeded to give him directions to the nearest currency exchange kiosk. "Enjoy your flight."

Eric glanced at his watch. "I will," he said and walked out of the restaurant heading quickly down the concourse towards the money exchange kiosk. He turned a corner and saw it in the distance just where the restaurant manager had said it would be. There were two people in line at the kiosk when Eric arrived. He stood behind an elderly woman and scanned the route he had just covered but there was no familiar figure.

He turned and walked away. His shadow now believed he was going to France. Eric crossed to an escalator and took it down a couple of levels following the directions to the train station in the lower airport concourse. He located the ticket counter and scanned the departure board. He bought a ticket for the next train to Hamburg leaving at 8:15 pm, in about 45 minutes. All he had to do was stay out of sight until then. He looked around for a men's washroom.

The 8:15 train to Hamburg left at 8:15, a refreshing change from his experience with Canadian trains. He had reserved a seat in a non-smoking compartment and shared it with a young couple. They chattered in a language that Eric didn't understand, perhaps Norwegian or Swedish. Two large green back packs were stuffed in the overhead racks above their seats. Eric was grateful to be ignored.

He tried to lean back in the seat but the cushions were hard and back didn't recline. He watched the lights of Frankfurt flash by and then they were into the countryside and his reflection in the window was broken only occasionally by the lights of a village or a station they passed.

He thought about what he was doing. Running. Perhaps not running so much as taking control again. By the time he had left the Rutgers Bank, he had the feeling that forces he didn't understand, or even necessarily want to understand, were controlling his agenda, a distinctly uncomfortable feeling although he was not certain why he felt this way. After all, he had come to Europe to find out something of the mystery that his parents had left him with, so what had he expected? He had hoped to find out about the bank account, perhaps a little of its history, an intriguing detail or two of his own history and origins, and then fly away home, wherever he eventually decided that might be, but likely back to the security of his childhood home in Portage for a least a short while. He realized that he had not expected a large bank account balance, nor to discover a movement, or whatever it was, of the sort that Karl had outlined.

There was the added complication of the watcher from the hotel. Was he a guardian angel, a hostile element or a figment of his own paranoia? He had wasted some money on a flight to Paris to try and get rid of him whatever his affiliation or his reality.

So was he going to London or not? He guessed that he was but on his own ticket. He set his briefcase on his lap and opened it. From one of the compartments in the lid he removed a manila envelope. He took out his mother's and father's Irish passports.

He glanced at the young couple opposite him. The woman had fallen asleep, her head leaning against the young man's shoulder. The young man was reading a paperback book. He returned to his parents' passports, looking carefully at the long-ago photos, both staring straight ahead at the camera, his father looking a bit stern, his mother with a trace of a smile. They made a handsome couple. He wondered if the intruders in his Berlin hotel room had discovered them. If so, what would they have made of a couple of identity documents from 1938?

Who were thc intruders? Thieves who had taken nothing? If it had been a simple case of thievery then he had nothing to be concerned about.

The organization that was responsible for the Swiss account seemed like a good possibility and they might simply have wanted to learn more about him. If that were the case he didn't have much to be concerned about either, since a five million dollar deposit would indicate they were well disposed toward him. He wondered for a moment what they might be expecting from him for five million.

In the meantime, he would find a hotel in Hamburg for tonight. Tomorrow he would fly to Dublin. That would give him what remained of Friday and all day Saturday to sort out the passport mystery, and perhaps even to track down a little family history if there were anything there to track down.

For the moment he felt free.

CHAPTER FIFTY TWO

Thursday, May 4, 1989 Heathrow Airport, London

Liselle Marcoux knew it was coming, it was just a matter of when, and it happened rather later than she had expected, just as the giant 747 was touching down at Heathrow. She was looking out the window at the rain flashing by in the runway lights. What else in London? She glanced at her watch. It was a little after 8:30 in the evening. Transatlantic travel was always a drag, she thought. She had left New York about seven hours ago and, with the addition of five time zones, had arrived twelve hours later

"How long will you be in London?" Ralph asked.

"I'm not sure," Liselle replied. "It'll depend on my assignment. How about you?"

"I'm here for a week," Ralph said and then gave her a boyish grin. "Would you join me for dinner this evening? Or do you have other plans?"

Liselle put on a reluctant smile. "That would be lovely," she said. "But I have a meeting this evening as soon as I get off the plane."

Ralph nodded. "They work you pretty hard, do they?"

Liselle laughed. "Not at all. I'm freelance, so I work myself this hard."

"How about tomorrow evening?" Ralph asked. "Or Saturday?"

"That sounds tempting but my plans at this point are really uncertain. Why don't you give me your card," Liselle said. "Tell me where you're staying and if I'm free I'll give you a call."

Ralph gave her a look that said he didn't really expect the call. He pulled a business card out of the breast pocket of his suit jacket and quickly wrote an address on the back of it. "I'd also be happy to talk to you about investment opportunities when you're back in New York."

"Thank you," Liselle said, taking the card. "That's very kind of you."

They cleared British customs quickly and Liselle began walking toward the baggage claim area, Ralph close beside her. A man in a navy blue suit wearing a British Airways customer service badge fell into step beside her. "Miss Liselle Marcoux?" he asked.

"Yes," Liselle said, stopping. Ralph stopped, too.

"Would you come with me, please."

"Is there a problem?"

"None at all, Ma'am."

Liselle turned to Ralph with a dazzling smile and held out her hand. "I enjoyed the chat, Ralph."

"So did I," Ralph said, holding onto her hand. "I hope we'll meet again."

"You never know," Liselle said. She retrieved her hand and turned to leave with the BA attendant.

"Where are you staying?" Ralph asked.

"Not sure yet," Liselle answered over her shoulder.

⸻

The British Airways First Class lounge was opulent. Liselle followed the BA attendant across the rich blue plush carpeting to a corner chesterfield. A lone man was seated there. He looked up from his London Times as she approached. When he stood he was the same height as she was, about five seven. He was chubby, bald and when he smiled his face crinkled, a Santa Claus look-alike minus the beard and hair. He stuck out his hand.

"Welcome to London," he said, his voice soft and husky, a smoker's voice.

"Thank you," she said and sat down, sinking into the pale brown leather. She crossed her legs and glanced out at the panoramic view over the runways, lights sparkling through her reflection in the glass.

"Would you like anything before we start? A drink? Coffee?"

"Water would be nice."

He waved at a steward and sat down. "Bring us a pitcher of water and a couple of glasses, please."

Liselle was trying to place his voice. It sounded like Brooklyn with some education and a few years in California, definitely American melting pot.

"I hope you don't mind meeting here," he said. "We can't safely use the embassy."

Liselle looked around at the richly furnished and appointed lounge. “This is just fine.”

He was silent until the steward had brought the water and departed. “How was the flight?”

“Good but long.”

“You met someone.”

Liselle laughed. “Just someone looking for company.”

He smiled. “Guys do that sometimes.” Then he became serious. “Call me Harry.”

She nodded.

“You got a briefing file at JFK?”

“I’ve read it.”

“Good,” Harry said. “We have a few things to add. The pictures in the file were taken in the last couple of days so they are current.”

That would explain the bleached hair, Liselle thought.

“You also need to know a little more background,” Harry went on. “You know Jon Falken?”

Liselle nodded.

“Eric O’Neill and Jon Falken were born on the same day, same year,” Harry said.

“Coincidence?”

“No relation or connection as far as we can determine but we don’t believe in coincidences so we’re following it up.” Harry took a drink of his water. “We found out what Eric O’Neill was doing from early 1987 until a few weeks ago. He was sailing in the South Pacific, all by himself. His boat was caught in a storm near Tahiti and sank. He was rescued by the French navy.”

“He was sailing for two years?” Liselle asked, surprised by the idea. “Just floating around out there?”

“Sounds like it,” Harry said. “But we still have a lot to learn and hopefully you will learn some of that for us.” Harry picked up his water glass, took a sip and glanced over toward the steward. "Eric O'Neill came back to his home town the last week of April, a few days after the death of his parents. This guy is full of coincidences. His parents get killed in a car accident the same day that his boat sinks. Anyway, he comes back to Portage la Prairie, this little hick town, hooks up with his old high school girlfriend, gets his parents affairs in order and then flies to Toronto for a week. Last Sunday he flies to Zurich. Can you imagine why?"

Liselle shook her head.

"He has a bank account with the National Investment Bank of Switzerland, or rather his parents did, or someone else did, and he has the numbers and access codes. It contains a lot of money. And every time someone shows up at a Swiss bank with an account containing a lot of money, especially money originating in World War II, that triggers our interest. We only learned about the bank account on Monday, two days ago, when he showed up at the bank."

Harry waved at the steward again. "Sure you wouldn't like something stronger than water?"

"No, thank you."

"Can you bring me a scotch?" Harry asked the steward.

"Certainly, sir. Do you have a preference in brand?

"Naw," Harry said. "Just bring me a nice single malt. You decide."

"Very good, sir." The steward turned and walked away.

"So Eric O'Neill meets with the Swiss bank people on Monday and then on Tuesday, flies to Frankfurt and takes a train to Berlin. He has dinner with an investment analyst Tuesday evening, we think this guy is a friend, and Wednesday he goes to the Rutgers Bank for another meeting. Know anything about the Rutgers Bank?"

Liselle shook her head again.

"Old bank, owned and run by a bunch of Nazis." He paused as the steward set his scotch on the large coffee table in front of them.

"Laphroig, Sir," the steward said, naming the scotch.

"Thanks," Harry said to the steward. He went on. "It seems his parents have left him some peculiar stuff including some papers and information from the early years of World War II, the details of which you don't need to know, and which he left in Portage la Prairie. This old girlfriend seems to be keeping an eye on his parents' house. He spent a bit of time with her in the few days he was there. She's married and she reads and speaks German, which he apparently does not."

"What's the old girlfriend like?" Liselle asked, strangely curious about her.

"Her name is Laura Schaefer, she's the same age as O'Neill and she's a doctor," Harry said. "What else can I tell you?"

"Harry," she said with some exasperation. "If I'm supposed to meet Eric O'Neill and get to know him, then I need to know the kind of women he's attracted to."

"Oh," Harry said. "Yeah, I see. We got a couple of pictures of her." He reached down to a briefcase on the floor beside the chesterfield and pulled out a file. "She's small, pretty," Harry said. "Here's one." He handed her a picture, another eight by ten colour print.

Liselle looked at the picture. It showed a woman in a white coat or jacket, she couldn't tell since only her head and shoulders were visible above a counter. It had been taken in a hospital judging from the background. Her eyes were looking down. She was reading something. Her hair was like Eric's, dark blonde and tousled although not sun bleached. She was frowning and looked puzzled, but she was at least pretty. .

"You said she was married," Liselle said.

"Yeah," Harry said, still flipping through some papers in a file. "We didn't follow it up. We could if you need to know."

"Not for now."

"Here's the other one," Harry said, and handed her another picture.

This one was taken outdoors. She was standing beside a man in a parking lot. In the background was a building with an ambulance in front of some sliding doors, likely the emergency entrance to the hospital. She was laughing. She looked beautiful.

"Is this her husband?" Liselle pointed at the man.

"Don't think so," Harry said. "Want me to find out?"

"No."

Harry picked up his scotch and took a sip. He nodded appreciatively. "Anything else you want to know about the old girlfriend?"

"Not for now."

"Okay," Harry said. "Then we'll get back to Eric O'Neill. The only things he seems to have brought with him, other than personal effects, are the bank information and a couple of old Irish passports issued in 1940 in the name of his parents."

Liselle nodded thoughtfully. "You're very thorough considering you've only had a couple of days."

"Yeah," Harry said. "We had someone slip into the Portage house and we tossed his room in Berlin. Not much there." Harry took another drink. "But Eric O'Neill is a man of many parts. After he went to Rutgers Bank, he was driven back to his hotel. He extended his reservation at the hotel through to Sunday. After he did this, he took a walk and didn't come back. We traced him to Frankfurt, a Lufthansa flight late this afternoon from Berlin. Then he vanished. He was supposed to be on a flight from Frankfurt to Paris this evening. He bought the ticket in Frankfurt, but just before you walked in, I got a call that he hadn't shown up for the flight. He's disappeared."

"Is he running?"

"Don't know," Harry said. "But it's a good bet."

"Why?"

"Maybe he's finding out things that are scaring him. Someone else is tailing him, too, although we don't know who."

"So where has he gone?"

"Don't know," Harry said again. "As I said, he has a hotel reservation in Berlin until Sunday. He also has a ticket for a flight from Berlin to London Sunday afternoon, but I'd bet he doesn't take it."

"Is he in any danger from the other people who are shadowing him?"

"Don't think so," Harry said. "They seem like they're watchers, just keeping an eye on him, but that was before he disappeared. Maybe that'll change now."

Liselle leaned back on the chesterfield. Why was Eric O'Neill in Europe at all? His parents had died, he had come into some information and had gone on a search to track it down. She thought about it for a moment. "Ireland," she said suddenly. "He's going to Ireland."

CHAPTER FIFTY THREE

Thursday, May 4, 1989, Philadelphia

Marianne walked into the studio, Lincoln close behind her. The morning light from the north facing windows lit the room softly. Lincoln turned on some overhead lights as they entered. An easel with a large mounted sheet of what looked like some kind of drawing paper sat on an easel in one corner of the room. The walls on both sides of the easel were covered in eight by ten prints, some in colour, some black and white, all of her.

"I feel like a movie star," she said, looking at them. "These are the photos you took of me last week?"

"The very ones."

Marianne walked up to the easel. "I thought you painted on canvas?"

"This is the first stage, laying everything out, consulting with you and making any changes we need."

Marianne saw the sailboat, with her at the wheel, and other figures in front of her. Lincoln had been right about her figure being the central focus of the painting.

"This is the layout," Lincoln said. "I've added a bit of colour using oil pastels so you can get a better sense of what is developing."

"What are oil pastels?"

"Like high class crayons."

She stepped back and looked everything over. She liked it. "I thought it would be bigger."

"It will be," Lincoln said. "Much bigger. This is like a model."

"Then I'll just wait for the finished portrait." She looked carefully at her figure but it was only sketched in. "You will give me some facial features and a better shape, I hope?"

"You will be magnificent."

Lincoln Carswell lay on his back in the master suite of his home. He was looking up at the ceiling, a silly smile on his face, or so he thought. He felt like he was floating around in a post orgasmic paradise. Marianne lay curled up beside him, a leg and an arm thrown over him, her head on his shoulder. His arm enfolded her, pulling her against him, her breasts pushing into his side. He nuzzled his face into her hair, soft and fresh smelling. He moved his hand on her back caressing her satin skin.

She snuggled more tightly against him for a moment, then rolled away and sat up, smiling down at him.

He looked into her eyes. "Wow," he whispered.

She leaned over him and kissed him softly, dragging her breasts across his chest. Then she sat up again. "You are a beautiful man, Lincoln Carswell."

Her cheeks were still flushed, her mouth pouty from kissing, her hair tousled like a burnished copper halo. She was as beautiful in passion as she was in repose.

"I have to go," she said. "Come and shower with me."

Lincoln glanced at the bedside clock. 2:10pm. "Do you really have to go?"

"I'm meeting Celeste for a drink before she takes me to the airport."

⁂

"When will you be back in Philly?" Lincoln asked. They were standing by the front door. He held her coat as she slipped it on.

"I'll be gone about a week but I'll be in touch when I get back."

"Where are you going?"

"My husband has some boring military conference in London and I'm going with him. We're leaving Saturday."

"In two days?" Lincoln laughed. "Then you don't have to be home until tomorrow."

Marianne smiled up at him and slipped her arms around him, holding him tightly. "I wish," she said. She stepped back and looked up at him. "It's likely a good thing that I'll be away for a while. I don't know what to do with you."

"What would you like to do with me?"

"Don't ask," she replied.

"Where are you staying in London?"

"At the Raphael," she said. "Why?"

Lincoln nodded. "I'll have something for you to look at when you get back."

"I bet you will," Marianne said.

Lincoln drew her close and held her. "Be careful in the big city."

He watched her drive away, her fingers fluttering in a farewell wave out the driver's window. He walked back into the house. "Now what?" he thought. When this sort of thing happened, as it did occasionally, his first thought was usually how he was going to get out of it or at least how he was going to avoid an entanglement. But not this time. This time he wanted more of Marianne, more of her time, more of her company, more intimacy. "Wow," he whispered again.

He strolled back into his bedroom and picked up a pillow. It had the scent of her hair. He tossed it back on the bed. "Shape up, Carswell," he said aloud.

CHAPTER FIFTY FOUR

Friday, May 5, 1989 Dublin, Ireland

Eric O'Neill stood on the corner waiting for the traffic light to change. He was scarcely aware of the rush hour traffic swishing by on the rain slicked pavement, or the wind whipping his trench coat around his knees, or the occasional spits of rain gusting down on him. He glanced at his watch and saw it was nearly four. He had been in that damned office for nearly four hours.

A car stopped in front of him and he realized that the traffic light had changed. He crossed the street with a crush of people, a few of them with umbrellas open but most of them just taking the gusts of rain as they came. On the opposite corner he stopped again to get his bearings. The Dublin Dreams Hotel was only a few blocks away. He stepped back under a narrow awning and pulled a Dublin street map from the inside of his overcoat. He partially unfolded it, careful not to lose it to the wind. If he turned left at the next corner he would only have about five blocks to walk. The fresh air would clear his head.

As he folded the map and shoved it back into his trench coat pocket he became aware of someone else under the awning. She was looking at her watch too, and then out at the traffic as though waiting for a car. She was wearing a black raincoat with a dark red scarf tied lightly around her hair partially obscuring her face. She had a small black leather purse slung over one shoulder and carried a closed umbrella in her other hand.

Eric seemed to take in the details in slow motion as a young man in shabby clothes pushed past him and then stumbled into the woman. He shoved her roughly back against the shopfront window, looped his hand through the strap on the purse and deftly slipped it off her shoulder. As he sprinted away the woman screamed.

With a sudden burst of inexplicable rage, Eric raced after him, pushing through the swath of people in the crowded street. The assailant was slim and fast but couldn't get through the crowd quickly enough. Eric was rapidly gaining on him. The young man came to the entrance of a narrow alley and raced around the corner. Eric tore after him, the frustration and anger of his day pouring into his running.

Garbage cans and dumpsters were piled along the right side of the alley, debris spilling out of them. The assailant veered to the left to avoid a puddle and slipped. He fell hard and rolled over twice, then stumbled to his feet. Eric was almost on him when he turned, dropped into a crouch and pulled a long vicious looking knife from under his jacket.

Eric stopped and stood facing him from about ten feet away. He was older than Eric's first impression of him, likely in his thirties anyway, not the teenaged punk he had taken him for. He was breathing hard and had a streak of mud on the side of his face from his fall. His wool seaman's cap was still pulled down to his eyebrows as he stared ferociously at Eric.

Suddenly he threw the purse at Eric, turned and sprinted away. Eric picked up the purse, shook the water off it as best he could and started slowly back up the alley to the street, his breathing returning to normal. He felt oddly exhilarated, the anger of his day quickly melting away.

She was waiting for him at the entrance to the alley, her umbrella open now, her eyes wide, lips parted, looks of shock and relief vying for dominance. Wordlessly, he handed her the leather purse.

"Are you all right?" she asked.

No trace of an Irish brogue here, he thought. "I'm fine," Eric answered. "But I usually warm up a bit before my afternoon jogging routine." He smiled and tried to put her at ease. "Really, I'm fine."

"How can I thank you," she asked. "You saved my purse, my passport, everything . . ."

"You make it sound more heroic than it was," Eric replied. "I guess I just reacted on impulse."

She moved closer to him and held her umbrella to shield them both from the rain which was now coming down lightly but steadily. "Can I at least buy you a drink?"

Eric nodded. "Yes," he said. "That you could."

The pub was all old dark wood with small heavily framed pictures, mostly landscapes, hung in clumps around the walls. It was noisy and crowded as they threaded their way toward a small empty table in the corner, still littered with the debris of the last occupants, two empty glasses and a greasy plate. A television set was mounted high in one corner, a soccer game on with no sound. Like real pubs everywhere, the faint scent of old beer floated on the air.

Eric pulled a chair out for her. She slid her raincoat off and gave it a quick shake before laying it over the back of a vacant chair. Then she sat and slipped the scarf off her hair. Eric pulled his trench coat off and sat down opposite her.

"I don't even know your name," she said, leaning back in the chair.

He looked at her carefully for the first time. Without the scarf, the coat and the umbrella obscuring various parts of her, she was really quite lovely. "Eric O'Neill," he said. "And yours?"

"Liselle Marcoux," she said. "I live in Philadelphia." Her voice was soft and husky but still carried easily over the conversational noise at the adjoining tables.

"Jameson, water on the side, please," Eric said to the waiter who arrived to clear their table.

"And what would you be havin' dear?" he asked Liselle.

"The same, please." She smiled at Eric and shrugged. The waiter left with their orders. "I've never had a Jameson. What is it?"

Eric laughed. "You're a brave woman, "he said. "Jameson is Irish whiskey."

It was her turn to laugh and it was a light sparkling sound. "I'll see if it's bravery or foolishness, I guess."

"I'm sure you'll enjoy it," Eric said. "But what brings you to a Dublin street corner?"

"My husband had family here. I was in London on business and slipped over to spend a few days with them. I got back to Dublin this morning and I was actually trying to do some shopping when you came along."

Eric noted the past tense and wondered if she were widowed or divorced. "I was also hoping to do a little sightseeing today but I got tied up in a meeting a bit longer than I expected."

"That's too bad," Liselle said. "There seems to be a lot to do and see in Dublin, although I haven't really been able to do much yet. Perhaps tomorrow."

The waiter arrived with their drinks and set them on the small scarred table. "Enjoy," he said and winked at them.

Eric added a little water to his whiskey, picked up the glass and swirled it lightly, setting it back on the table. He watched as Liselle did the same and saw a single gold band on the fourth finger of her left hand. He lifted his glass in a toast. "May the road rise up to meet you, may the wind be always at your back, may the Lord hold you forever in the hollow of his hand, and may you be a day in heaven before the Devil knows you're gone."

Liselle stared deeply into his eyes, her own suddenly wet. "That's so beautiful," she said softly. "Irish, of course?"

"Of course," Eric said, surprised by her reaction. "But it's not a blessing to be sad for."

Liselle reached for her purse and pulling out a tissue, she dabbed her eyes lightly. "I'm just being silly," she said. "But I don't think anyone has ever blessed me so eloquently."

"My pleasure," Eric said. "Where are you staying in Dublin?"

"At the Dublin Dreams."

"What a coincidence," Eric said. "So am I."

"Really?" Liselle said. "Then please have dinner with me this evening. My treat. I am just so grateful for what you did." She paused. "I'm sorry," she said. "I shouldn't just assume that you're free or that you would even be interested, but if you are I would really like to buy you dinner."

Eric nodded. "I am free," he said. "And I'd enjoy that but it's my turn to buy."

In his hotel room, or suite as they called it, Eric slipped out of his trench coat and hung it in one end of the closet away from his other clothes, leaving the closet door open to dissipate the moisture, although he wondered how effective that would be given the nature of Irish weather. He looked carefully at the other things he had hung in the closet, a couple of shirts, a tie, a sweater, a pair of slacks, all of them new, the result of a short shopping expedition late yesterday afternoon, to replace the items he had left behind in his Berlin hotel. All of them looked exactly as they had when he left. Next he checked his briefcase and the personal items in the bathroom. Nothing seemed to have been moved or disturbed, so either no one had searched his room or they were getting better at it. He shook his head. The last couple of days he had thought so much about what was going on that he wondered if he was effectively distinguishing between reality and fantasy.

However, he had a dinner date in a couple of hours and that was real. He smiled at the thought. Tough way to get a date. But she was lovely, cultured and exotic. The exotic part he had noticed in the pub, a trace of something oriental about her eyes, her cheek bones, a slight olive cast to her skin. And she had a beautiful laugh. It would be a pleasant evening. When had he last had a date with an attractive woman? If he didn't count Laura, it had been years, and he wasn't quite sure how to count Laura. His feelings for her were still strong, still deep but he didn't want to examine them too closely. That was how you got hurt, striving for things you could never have. She was married. He had to keep saying it to himself. Just get on with life.

He undressed and entered the marble tiled bathroom. An old fashioned tub had been retro fitted with a shower, not unlike what his parents had done with the Portage house. He turned it on full, adjusted the temperature and stepped in, letting the hot, heavy streams of water cascade over him. Gradually he felt his muscles relaxing. He had not been particularly aware of being tense but he was certainly aware of the tension flowing out of his body.

He toweled himself dry and put on a heavy white terry towel bath robe, tightening the sash around his waist. In the living room of the suite, he picked up the phone by the chesterfield and punched zero. Giving the operator Laura's office number in Portage, he asked her to place a person to person call for him and then hung up the phone. He looked around the suite. It was furnished with antiques from a variety of periods he guessed, the only consistency was that everything looked old and all the wood was dark. The walls were a rich gold colour with white wainscoting and a white ceiling with textured designs in the plaster. A heavy gilt framed painting on the wall above an old roll topped desk showed some shaggy brown cattle grazing under a dark and dismal sky, black clouds rolling across the horizon. He shuddered as he realized it reminded him of the sky on his last night on Pegasus. A barn, decayed and crumbling with age, graced the background and a slow flowing creek meandered across the foreground in front of the cattle. The artist might have been trying to achieve a sense of pastoral serenity but to Eric it looked like a scene of rural desolation and loneliness. However, with the exception of the painting, the room was quite elegant.

While not normally much of a hard liquor drinker, he had enjoyed the Jameson he had consumed earlier with Liselle. He rummaged in the small refrigerator fitted into an ancient sideboard. There was no Jameson but he found a miniature bottle of Bushmills Irish Whiskey, proclaiming itself to be twelve years old. He poured it into glass and was adding a splash of water to it when the phone rang.

"Eric?" Laura asked.

"The same."

"Where are you?"

"Dublin, at the moment."

"Oh," Laura said. "Checking out your parents' passports? What did you find out?"

Eric laughed. "I found out that the Irish take a very dim view of people forging Irish passports."

"Forging?" Laura's voice was full of surprise. "I wouldn't have expected that of your parents."

"There are lots of surprises from my parents but it appears that they were not the ones doing the forging. However, someone did, and I spent four hours waiting, detained and rather vigorously questioned really, while they brought in an expert to confirm the forgeries. Apparently they were produced in Germany by a Jewish forger. The expert had encountered his work before, even knew his name, although I don't recall it now, and declared that these were among the best he had seen. He was so pleased that they were in such excellent condition that he kept them. The passport folks were very firm and very insistent on knowing where I got them."

"What did you tell them?"

"The truth," Eric said. "That I found them in a safety deposit box after my parents died. Also that I understood that if I had a parent or a grandparent born in Ireland, I was eligible for Irish citizenship and an Irish passport of my own and that was why I was there."

"Is that true?"

"Well, it's not why I'm here but the rest is true," Eric said. "Lots of North Americans are checking it out since they will be able to travel throughout the European Union countries on one passport if it's from a member country. There are other reason's too, but they're complicated. Banking and tax stuff."

There was silence for a moment. "Are you all right, Eric? Have you learned anything else?"

"No, I haven't, but I'm fine," Eric replied. He was about to relate the purse snatching incident and then realized that it wouldn't make Laura feel any more secure about his adventure. "I'm okay, really I am."

"Will you be there long?"

"I'll likely go to London on Monday."

"And then home?"

"Then some meetings with banking people first."

"Take care, Eric."

"I will."

Silence.

"I miss you, Eric."

"I miss you, too."

He sat and sipped the whiskey, smooth and rich, closer to Canadian rye than to Scotch, but still distinctively different. He thought about Laura. He did miss her but to what end? She was still married to Darren, she showed no signs of leaving, and even if she were willing, was this a relationship he wanted to embark on? He thought about that for a moment. Likely it was, but it was also likely to be one of those things which just wasn't fated to happen.

However, his dinner engagement was. He stood and walked over to the closet to see which of his two new shirts he would wear this evening.

They had arranged to meet in the dining room and Liselle was already seated when he arrived. She was looking at a menu as he strolled across the room behind the tuxedoed waiter. Her head was tilted slightly and her white even teeth were just visible, resting on her lower lip. She looked up as he approached and her face burst into a dazzling smile.

"I seem to have developed a taste for Jameson," she said as he sat down. There was a glass in front of her partially filled with the amber liquor and a small carafe of water beside it. "I ordered you one as well," she added. "I hope that was all right?"

Eric sat down. He nodded. "Thank you," he said. "That was thoughtful of you."

She looked at him quizzically, almost as though she was looking for sarcasm. "The menu looks wonderful and the wine list is pretty impressive, too."

She was dressed in black, a high necked design, her bare shoulders and arms covered by a black lace shawl. She looked more exotic, more oriental tonight, perhaps it was the subdued light, maybe the black outfit or her makeup. Eric knew he wasn't much good at these subtleties. He picked up the heavy crystal glass of Jameson, and sipped it. Setting it down he added a small splash of water and swirled it gently. When he looked up, Liselle was watching him. He smiled self-consciously. "What do you see?"

She tilted her head slightly. "An interesting man," she replied in her husky voice.

Eric nodded. The words sounded like a pass but the way in which she had said them did not. "Thank you."

"So tell me a little more about yourself," Liselle said. "I know you're a Canadian from Toronto and you're in Europe on a holiday with some business mixed in."

Eric took another sip of the Jameson. "What would you like you to know?"

Liselle stared at him for a moment. "You choose."

"I grew up in a small prairie town, went to university in Toronto, and after working a year in London, lived and worked in Toronto for a number of years as a stockbroker. I took some time off a couple of years ago and I'm still trying to decide whether I want to go back to work again or do something else. Any suggestions?"

"It's nice to have that choice," Liselle said thoughtfully. "I guess if I have a suggestion it's a simple one. Do what you want, not what someone else wants."

It was Eric's turn to be thoughtful. "I guess I'm trying to do that. I just have to figure out what I want."

"Most men want money and power."

"I suppose so. But I have enough money," he said. "And power, or at least power over other people, doesn't really interest me much."

"So what have you been doing for the last couple of years?"

A waiter approached and hovered by their table. "Would you like a few minutes more to decide or are you ready to order?"

Liselle looked at Eric and arched her eyebrows. "Would you like a few more minutes?"

"Have you decided?"

Liselle nodded. "The breast of duck."

Eric looked up at the waiter. "That sounds good. Make it two."

"Very good, sir."

Eric turned his attention back to Liselle. "Sailing," he said.

"Sailing?"

He nodded. "I left Toronto in early 1987, flew to Australia, bought a sailboat and lived on it and sailed it around the South Pacific until a few weeks ago."

"That sounds wonderful," Liselle said. "So romantic."

Eric laughed. "I wouldn't describe it quite that way, but most of the time it was a lot of fun and I enjoyed it."

"What parts did you not enjoy?"

Eric thought for a moment. "Bad weather and storms are obvious ones. Occasionally I was lonely."

"You did this all alone?"

Eric nodded. "I wanted time to myself and you don't get that kind of time if you don't choose to be alone."

"I suppose not," Liselle said quietly. "What a luxury that would be. Time to yourself." She picked up her drink and had a sip. "But what brought you back if you still didn't know what you wanted to do?"

"Two things," Eric said. "My parents were killed in an automobile accident. I'm an only child so I had to come home to sort out their affairs."

"That's always such a difficult thing to deal with."

"Yes, it is," Eric said. "Have you lost your parents, too?"

She nodded. "A few years ago, and it upset me far more than I expected it would." She took a sip of her drink. "Somehow I knew that as long as I had a parent alive there was a place I could go where I would be loved and nurtured and accepted, no matter what I'd done." Liselle paused. "It's not that I even needed it or used it, but it was always there and it was hard to believe that my last sanctuary was gone." She was silent for a moment, then looked up at him and smiled. "Sorry to be so heavy. What was the other reason you came back?"

"My boat sank."

"Sank?"

"I got caught in a storm about a hundred miles west of Tahiti and it sank."

Liselle put her hand to her mouth. "How terrifying," she whispered. "How did you survive?"

"In a life raft," Eric said, smiling at her reaction. "I was rescued by the French navy the following day."

"That sounds dreadful," she said.

"The life raft? Or the French navy?" he asked.

She laughed, the delightful sparkling sound again.

The waiter arrived with a small wicker basket, a linen serviette carefully folded around several small slices of dense white bread. He placed a silver butter dish beside it.

"Your turn," Eric said. He lifted the serviette and moved the basket toward Liselle.

She took a piece of bread from it and set it on a plate beside her cutlery. "I was born in France, and I discovered at an early age that I liked languages so I studied them, learned English and some others. But what I really wanted to do was to become a motion picture star. So I went to drama school for a couple of years, but I just didn't have the talent for it and I wasn't willing to meet the expectations of film directors and casting agents."

Eric took a bite of the bread. It was soft and smooth. He frowned at her last comment.

Liselle pushed the silver butter dish toward him. "Expectations?" she asked. "I mean I wasn't willing to sleep with people to get a role in a movie."

"I thought that was a thing of the past."

Liselle laughed. "Perhaps in Canada, although I doubt it. Certainly not in France. However," she continued, "My father was posted as a military attache to the French UN delegation in New York. My mother had died four years previously and so I went with him and lived there for a couple of years. I didn't go back to France with him and I've been in America now for about ten years."

"You mentioned your husband has relatives here."

Liselle nodded. "My husband passed away three years ago," she said. "He was American."

"I'm sorry," Eric said. "I didn't mean to pry."

"That's quite all right," Liselle said. "I was about to ask you the same question."

Eric nodded. "Unfortunately," he said quietly. "I have the same answer. My wife died about two and half years ago."

Liselle reached across the table and put her hand on his arm. "I am so sorry," she said.

Eric glanced at his watch and saw it was a little after midnight. They were waiting in front of the elevator. He realized he was feeling very mellow, the Bushmills, the Jameson, the bottle of French chardonnay with the superb breast of duck and the final Irish cream liqueur they had enjoyed in the bar after dinner had all worked their magic.

"Thank you for a lovely evening, Eric," Liselle said, slipping her hand through his arm.

The elevator door opened and they stepped in. "It was my pleasure. I really enjoyed myself." The door closed softly behind them and Eric pushed their floor numbers, five for him, three for Liselle.

She giggled and squeezed his arm, resting her head on his shoulder for just a moment, her breast pressed against his arm, warm and intimate. The elevator stopped with a quiet ping and the door opened. Liselle turned and stood on her tip toes and hugged him briefly, brushing her lips on his cheek. "Call me in the morning?"

Eric nodded and looked down at her. He wanted to kiss her, to hold her for a moment more. Instead, he smiled. "I will."

She stepped out of the elevator and waved her fingers at him as the door closed.

CHAPTER FIFTY FIVE

Saturday, May 6, 1989 Surrey, England

"We've found him," Joachim announced triumphantly as he strode across the heavily carpeted study, his black suit and white shirt impeccable as always. "Eric O'Neill is in Dublin." He sat down in the chair opposite Bormann.

Martin Bormann leaned back in his large leather chair and nodded. "I was confident you would. And how did you accomplish this?"

"He called the Schaefer woman in Canada, in Portage la Prairie, the doctor who was his high school sweetheart."

"Yes, yes, Joachim," Bormann interrupted. "I know who she is. How did you find this out?"

"We took the liberty of tapping her phones, at her office and her home, and O'Neill called her office late yesterday from Dublin."

Bormann absorbed this. "Well done, Joachim," he said.

Joachim nodded and smiled at the rare compliment. "And since he made the call last night we have located him. He is staying in the Dublin Dreams Hotel, a five star establishment. He is renting a suite there."

"And we have someone there keeping an eye on him?"

Joachim frowned. "Not yet, Sir," he replied. "But we will have someone in place this morning, by noon at the latest."

"Do we know why he is in Dublin?"

"Not yet, sir."

"That's an odd place for him to go," Bormann reflected. "There is no money there, no relatives or ancestors or anything else for him to find out about, is there?"

"Not that we know of."

"Very well," Bormann said. "Anything else?"

"Nothing of importance," Joachim said. "However, in the course of our phone taps on the Schaefer woman's home, we discovered that her husband has a relationship with another woman."

"A mistress, you mean?"

"It would appear so."

"It's hard to know whether that is significant to us at this point or not, I suppose," Bormann said. "Keep me informed."

"Very well, Sir," Joachim said. "The arrangements for Falken are proceeding as planned. He will arrive this afternoon at Heathrow and we will transport him here late this evening. We'll get him settled in and he will have lunch with you tomorrow."

"Excellent," Bormann said. "And what about Carswell?"

"There may be some difficulties there. As you are aware, he is an artist. We know that his beliefs are well right of centre but he is politically indifferent and has not shown any interest or involvement in the US political process. He may be reluctant to travel here since he seems to accept how he got to the US from Germany as part of an orphan's program. He doesn't need money. He is involved in a right wing militia group that does military training but he seems to treat that like belonging to a recreational baseball team."

"His lack of interest is something we have known for some time, isn't it?"

"That's true, but there is now a slight additional complication. Carswell may be having an affair with Jon Falken's wife."

"May be?" Bormann asked. "How has this happened?"

"She bought one of his paintings at an art show recently and is now having Carswell do a portrait of her."

"Interesting," Bormann said. "And what makes you think that an affair is in progress?"

"She spent a night at his place."

"I see," Bormann said. "Does Falken know anything about this?"

"No," Joachim replied. "Not as far as we know but it may change the dynamic of things a bit when the three of them meet."

"So Carswell may not want to come to England," Bormann said.

"We will take the necessary steps to bring Carswell here, if necessary, so perhaps we will learn more then."

"Good," Bormann said. "And what about O'Neill?"

"His arrangements, conveyed to him by Herr Hoffner of Rutgers Bank, were to have him arrive at Gatwick Airport tomorrow, overnight in London and then be transported here on Monday morning."

"And what alternative arrangements do we now have in place?"

"We are hoping that O'Neill will still arrive at Gatwick tomorrow afternoon from Dublin but we should know later today if he has made any arrangements to do so. Failing that, we can pick him up and bring him here."

Bormann stood up and turned to look out the window. He would have to meet Eric O'Neill, one way or another, preferably voluntarily on O'Neill's part, but if not, he would simply have to be brought here. "Good. I do need to meet him and assess his potential."

"Very good, Sir," Joachim said, standing up. "I will see to it."

Bormann remained standing long after Joachim had left, staring out the window of his study. The weather had turned and the sun was shining. The rose bushes along the perimeter of the house were coming out in leaf late this year. He smiled as he recalled the arguments he had had with his security people over planting rose bushes close to the house. "Cover and concealment," they had said. "It would make it too easy for infiltrators to reach the walls."

Bormann had told them it was nonsense. The bushes were covered with thorns and it was only necessary to plant lots of them to ensure that infiltrators couldn't get near the place without being permanently scarred.

He shook off the reverie. Carswell likely didn't want to come here, didn't really give a damn about his origins. Perhaps he wouldn't care about the future of National Socialism either, but maybe when he knew what the potential was, he would change his mind. Somehow Bormann doubted that.

And what to do about Eric O'Neill. He was again displaying an independence, a freedom of spirit and action that made him unpredictable. There was a time in his younger years when Bormann would have regarded that as a weakness, a fatal flaw, but not now. Now was a time that required boldness, a willingness to seize the moment, a pragmatic approach above all else. A fragment of a decades-old conversation drifted into his mind. Erwin Rommel was speaking to Hitler, defending his actions in North Africa. "More opportunities are lost to indecision than through bad decisions."

CHAPTER FIFTY SIX

Saturday, May 6, 1989 London, England

"What the hell is this?" Jon Falken snapped.

"It is exactly what it appears to be, Jon," the slim man in the black suit said quietly. He had introduced himself as Lyle Copeland. "It's a blindfold. Now please put it on." Copeland was in the jump seat of a Bentley limousine facing Jon and he was holding a wide black band of cloth.

"A blindfold?" Jon said, incredulously. "Do you know the kind of security clearances I have? You people are supporting my candidacy for the Presidency of the United States of America and you want me to wear a fucking blindfold? Are you insane?"

A tired smile flickered across Copeland's face. "I hope not, Jon." He continued holding the blindfold out to Jon.

Jon sighed and leaned back into the soft enveloping leather of the back seat of the Bentley. He glanced out the tinted glass of the windows but the darkness was only broken by the lights of other vehicles. They appeared to be on a divided highway but that was about all he could tell..

"You do know that I used to earn my living doing this kind of clandestine shit?" he asked, his anger barely under control. He glanced at his watch and saw it was almost midnight. "You have pulled me out of my hotel, driven me around London for an hour and now we're headed out of the city. I have no bloody idea where I am or where I am going and you want to blindfold me?"

It was Copeland's turn to sigh. "It's nothing personal, Jon, but yes, I must insist you wear the blindfold if we are to proceed any further. This is just how we operate. You will be required to wear it on your return to London as well."

"And when will that be?"

"Probably Monday evening if all goes as planned."

Jon reached out and took the blindfold. He was tired and angry and he didn't need any more irritation from these bloody amateurs. The day had started with excitement and anticipation. He was going to meet some people who would give him a shot at the presidency. Even getting up at 4:00am to get to JFK in New York by 6:00am so they could board their flight at 8:00 had not dampened his enthusiasm. He had survived the seven hour flight to London, the loss of another five hours in time zone changes, and had been impressed by the elegant suite in the Raphael Hotel where they had been taken by stretch limo from Heathrow. He and Marianne had stayed there on previous visits to London although not in the "royal suite" as their accommodation was called. He had pleasant memories of former visits there.

He was relaxing over a scotch with Marianne, moving into the subtle ritual of flirtation that preceded their rare bouts of lovemaking, or at least they seemed rare these days. She was tired and unresponsive but he hoped he could change that when they got to bed. Then the damn phone had rung.

Someone called Copeland was in the lobby and wanted Jon to join him. They were going to their first meeting and would not be back until late tomorrow. Marianne was understandably suspicious but his assurances had seemed to allay her fears. He knew that getting caught in an affair with Liselle Marcoux had destroyed whatever trust she had and now a mysterious phone call that he could not entirely explain but that would take him away overnight stretched his credibility, to put it mildly. He would not have believed it either.

He had met Copeland at the front desk and embarked on this stupid motorized adventure. Anticipation turned to anger and disillusionment. This was not what he had envisioned at all. He had been looking forward to a night of passion followed by sleeping in Sunday morning, perhaps with a repeat performance, followed by a truly splendid brunch somewhere, perhaps at the Belvedere in Holland Park with its Fin de Siecle decor and surrounding flower gardens, then a stroll around some small galleries and museums. Monday would be the day for sedate and civilized meetings in some elegant city board room.

"Thank you, Jon," Copeland said, relief evident in the tone of his voice.

Jon glanced to his right where a second man sat silently slouched in the corner apparently indifferent to the discussion that had just transpired. Copeland had introduced him as Dunhill, Alfred or Albert or something like that. He had been so angry he hadn't really paid attention. Dunhill was overweight and looked soft. He might have been handsome but for the jowls. Jon looked at the blindfold, basically a panel of black cloth with an elasticized band to fit around the back of his head. He held it up to his face, covered his eyes with it and slipped the band over the back of his head. He adjusted it slightly for comfort.

Dunhill spoke for the first time. "Excuse me, Jon," he said, his voice barely more than a whisper. "Could you just lean forward for a moment and I'll fix the band on the back."

Jon obediently leaned forward and turned his back slightly toward Dunhill. He tried to turn back as he felt the hypodermic needle sink expertly into his neck but Copeland had gripped his arm with surprising strength. His last moment of awareness was a euphoric drifting upwards.

Marianne Falken couldn't get to sleep. The bedside clock read 1:34 AM. The wine over dinner had relaxed her. She expected with the additional scotch she had drunk with Jon before he was called away, she'd have no trouble getting to sleep. She had even taken a couple of melatonin pills to help with the jet lag but she was still wide awake.

Whatever Jon was up to, she found she didn't really care. She thought she might if it compromised his political future, but at the moment she was indifferent even to that. She was simply tired of the lies and evasions. Before he left, she had recognized the signs of Jon's rising sexual expectations. They would have been easy enough to fend off, fatigue from the long day, a headache from the long flight, but the truth was, she just didn't feel like having sex with Jon, not tonight anyway.

She couldn't get Lincoln Carswell out of her mind. How the hell had that happened? One minute they were in his kitchen, the next they were in bed having the most spectacular sex she could remember. And it wasn't just the sex. He was kind, thoughtful, gracious, funny . . . simply delightful to be with. She had laughed more with Lincoln in the few hours they had been together than she had with Jon in the last year. That was a dangerous reaction and she knew it. She also knew she was in a vulnerable state of mind after discovering that Jon was having an affair. She was constantly managing Jon's political aspirations, fundraising events, social meetings, coffee encounters, and keeping Jon's attention focussed on his brain not his dick. She didn't like the man that Jon had become. He had been a caring, compassionate, understanding man when she first met him but in recent years she had rarely seen those qualities. Now he was calculating, cold and exploitive, although these qualities were still covered, in public at least, by a veneer of charm.

Maybe Vietnam had changed him as it had millions of other Americans. Maybe the care and compassion had been burned out of him. Whatever the reason, life with Jon was not a lot of fun and hadn't been for many years.

So what was she going to do about Lincoln Carswell? Wisdom would suggest that she not see him again. But she knew that she was going to. She had just condemned Jon for risking their political future. Now she was doing the same. Maybe she had been concerned with their political future because she didn't see much personal future. Could there be a personal future with Lincoln? Not likely. Lincoln had tried marriage once and it had failed. He now seemed quite content to live as a bachelor.

She wondered what Lincoln was doing. She looked at the bedside clock again and saw it was 2:04 AM. That would make it 9:04 PM in Philadelphia. He would be having a drink, a glass of white wine. He would be looking at the pictures he had taken of her. He would be thinking about making love with her, correction, having sex with her. Or maybe it was making love. "Don't go there," she whispered.

CHAPTER FIFTY SEVEN

Saturday, May 6, 1989 Philadelphia

Lincoln Carswell stood back and looked at the evolving portrait of Marianne Falken. The balance and composition were perfect. No matter where they looked, the viewers' eyes would be led to Marianne. They would not be able to stay focussed on any other part of the painting. The next phase was to start the detail, the part that would make the portrait stunning. He found he had to keep holding back on painting Marianne to make sure the structure of the painting was what he wanted. It had taken him two days of concentrated work but it was done. Tomorrow was Sunday. Maybe he would pretend he was a Christian and take the day off. He'd see how he felt in the morning. In the meantime, he was finished for the day. He'd relax with a glass of Chardonnay and think a bit more about the portrait.

He was taking a bottle of California chardonnay out of his wine refrigerator when the phone rang. Would Marianne be calling? He couldn't get her out of his mind. Not from

London, surely, but not many people had his unlisted number. He picked it up.

"Lincoln Carswell?" The male voice was deep.

Lincoln paused for a moment. "Who is this?"

"My name is Clark Einfeld and I would like to meet with you."

"This number is unlisted, Mr. Einfeld. How did you get it?"

"I have a lot of resources at my disposal Mr. Carswell and I have a proposition to make to you that I believe you will find interesting."

"So tell me about it."

"I would prefer to do that in person."

"I don't take commissions," Lincoln said.

"This is not about your art."

"What is it about, then?"

"May I talk with you in person?"

Lincoln thought about it. He didn't have a lot on in the next hour or so. "I take it you are in Philadelphia?"

"That's correct, Mr. Carswell. We could be at your home within half an hour."

"No," Lincoln replied immediately. "And you said 'we'."

"I have a colleague with me, Steven Clayton."

"Why would I want to meet with you and your colleague?"

"We have some information on your origins and an interesting opportunity for you to consider."

Lincoln thought about it for a moment. "Do you know where the Landsend Mall is?"

"We'll find it," Einfeld replied.

"I'll be there in half an hour. There's a Starbucks there."

"Thank you, Mr. Carswell," Einfeld said. "I really do appreciate your taking the time to meet with us."

When he walked into Starbucks a few minutes later, two men stood up. He walked over to them.

The taller one held out his hand and smiled. "I'm Clark Einfeld," he said. "Thank you for meeting with us. This is my colleague, Steven Clayton."

Lincoln shook hands with both of them and sat down. "So what's this all about?" he asked.

"We would like to give you some information and then tell you about an opportunity."

"Are you buying coffee or should I go get some?" Lincoln asked.

Einfeld looked at Clayton. "Steven?"

Clayton rose and walked to the counter.

"You told me your names, but who are you and who do you represent?" Lincoln asked.

"We are from an organization that was, in a sense, responsible for moving you from Germany to the US," Clayton replied. "But I think this will become clear as we talk."

"Okay," Lincoln said.

"I believe you know that you were born in Germany in 1939 and came to the US about a year later."

Lincoln nodded.

"You were told you were an orphaned child and that your parents were casualties of war. Is that correct?"

"Yes."

"That is not entirely accurate. You were not an orphan, and your parents were not war casualties. Your father was a high ranking military or political official in the Third Reich and you were moved here for your own protection. The plan was to return you to Germany at the end of the war but Germany lost the war so there wasn't much to return you to."

"So what has all this got to do with me, other than curiosity about my origins which I don't really care much about?"

"We'd like you to suspend judgement about that for the moment and to come to London with us and find out more."

Lincoln leaned back in the chair and laughed. "You guys really get right to the point, don't you?" He paused for a moment. "Let me get this straight. You two call me, out of the blue, tell me some nonsense about my biological parents being Nazis or soldiers or whatever the Hell they were, which I don't really give a damn about, and you want me to fly off with you to England to find out even more?" He paused. "Does that about cover it?"

Clayton arrived back with two large coffees and set them on the table, one in front of Lincoln, the other by Einfeld.

Einfeld stared at him. A trace of a smile crossed his face and then vanished.. "That is the essence, Mr. Carswell, but we would like you to take our proposition seriously."

"Why?"

"I think you will find your origins interesting and worth exploring a bit further."

"So let's hear the proposition."

"We would like to you to come to London for three days, meet some members of our organization, get some further information and then decide if you would like to work with us. We will pay you $100,000 for your time, regardless of your decision."

Lincoln looked from one the other. "What makes you think I need money?"

"I'm not suggesting you do. We are merely offering to compensate you for your time."

"And if I don't want to go at all?"

"We wouldn't advise that course of action," Clayton said, speaking for the first time.

"I'm not looking for advice from you. I don't really want anything from you. So if there is nothing else you have to say, please excuse me." Lincoln stood up. "Thank you for the coffee."

"I believe you know Marianne Falken," Einfeld said, standing up to face Lincoln.

Lincoln was surprised. "Yes."

"This involves her to some degree and her husband to a much greater degree."

"I've never met her husband."

"Please sit down for a few minutes more, Mr. Carswell. We do have a couple of further items to discuss."

Lincoln sat down. He took a drink of the coffee.

"Marianne Falken purchased one of your works at your recent show at the Liberty Gallery. Correct?"

Lincoln nodded.

"The photographer that evening took a number of pictures of you, several of which were with Marianne Falken. We think your attraction to her was obvious in the photographs."

Einfeld paused but Lincoln remained silent.

"We have also discovered that she was at your home a week ago and spent the night with you." Einfeld leaned back in his chair.

Lincoln was shaken by this revelation but he kept his face a mask and picked up his coffee mug. "And your point is . . . ?"

"Her husband is going to run for a congressional seat and may at some future point run for the presidency of the United States."

"And what has this got to do with me?" Lincoln said. His mind was racing. Where did these guys get their information?

"We do not want your relationship with Marianne Falken becoming public knowledge."

"I don't have a relationship with her. She bought a painting of mine and came to look at some others. We had a couple of drinks and she stayed over in my guest suite. End of story."

Einfeld nodded thoughtfully. "You are a dynamic, good looking man with a bit of a reputation as one who doesn't turn down a sexual opportunity. Mrs. Falken is a very attractive woman who just spent the night with you. If this ever became public, who do you think the tabloids would believe."

Lincoln laughed. "Your version, of course, but I don't really care. Scandal sells art."

"Scandal defeats politicians, destroys reputations and breaks families apart," Einfeld said. "We are intent on Jon Falken securing the congressional nomination and winning the seat. This would be much more difficult if he or his wife were the subject of a scandal."

"All you have to do is to be discreet about your faulty information," Lincoln said. "I have absolutely no intention of talking to anyone about Marianne Falken."

Einfeld smiled. "You just have."

"So what are you guys about? Who do you represent? The committee to elect the next congressman? Or what?"

"We represent a large and powerful international organization. We are asking for your cooperation, for a small favour, if you wish to call it that, and for the courtesy of learning the answers to the questions you just asked."

"So that's it?" Lincoln asked. "Why don't you just tell me and then we can all get on with our day."

"To understand what is going on there are some other people you will have to meet."

Lincoln shook his head. "This is really not my problem." He stood up, nodded to them both. "Good afternoon, gentlemen. Thank you for the coffee."

Lincoln drove, thinking through the meeting he had just been subjected to. What was the point of it all? These nut cases must have something to do with getting Marianne's husband elected. Were they part of his election machine? Were they from some security agency whose job it was to protect political wannabees. Who cares? He certainly wouldn't knowingly hurt Marianne. Perhaps there was some way to warn her but warn her about what?

He turned his truck into the residential area where he lived. As he turned he glanced in his rear view mirror. Was that Clayton driving the car two vehicles behind his? He couldn't be sure but he was when he turned into his own long driveway and the car turned in behind him. He drove up to the front door and stopped. Clayton parked behind him. Einfeld got out of the passenger's side and walked toward him.

"There is one more thing we didn't mention to you," he said. He pulled a pistol, a Glock nine millimetre, from the waist band of his slacks and pointed it at Lincoln. "You are coming with us to London, willingly or otherwise."

CHAPTER FIFTY EIGHT

Saturday, May 6, 1989 Dublin, Ireland

Somewhere a phone was purring, a soft insistent irritation, not quite a ring. Liselle Marcoux was warm, almost hot, as a series of images fluttered like a kaleidoscope through her mind, shimmered away and disappeared. She opened her eyes and fumbled for the phone.

"Hello."

His voice was soft and husky, a morning-after voice. "Good morning. Did I wake you?"

"Just a little." Liselle stretched and sat up, pulling her knees up and wrapping her arm around them.

"How about breakfast?" Eric asked. "Or do you have other plans?"

Liselle smiled to herself. "I'd like that," she replied. "What time is it?"

"About nine."

She looked at the bedside clock. The green numbers read 9:07. "I slept in."

"Good sleep?"

"Delicious," she answered. "What time and where?"

"How about room service in my suite and you pick the time?"

Liselle smiled again. She had wondered how and when she'd get into his room. "Ten."

"Coffee will be here. Why don't you decide from the menu in your room what you want and have it sent to mine."

"I could do that," Liselle said. "But perhaps I should preserve your reputation. Why don't you just decide."

He chuckled. "Okay, see you at ten."

Liselle set the phone down. Breakfast and then what? Maybe some sightseeing. She slipped out of bed and walked naked across the room to the bathroom. Turning on the shower, she glanced in the mirror. Her hair was tousled a bit. She'd wash it and blow-dry it. That would make it fluffy and innocent looking. Eric had already seen her sophisticated side last night. She turned back to the shower and realized that her head hurt. Not a lot but enough to remind her that she had drunk a lot more the evening before than she usually did.

Eric O'Neill was an interesting man. She stepped into the shower and put her head under the stream of hot water, massaging her temples lightly. He was friendly and gracious, almost old-fashioned in the way he treated women, or perhaps he was just out of practice. She squirted shampoo into her hand and rubbed it into her hair. She liked her hair, thick and black and so easily managed if she got a decent cut. He had shown bravery yesterday with the purse snatcher and she hadn't needed to go to plan B, which was simply to play the helpless woman and ask for his assistance. When he had returned her purse he was breathing deeply but not hard so he must be a jogger or a runner or do something to stay in reasonable physical shape.

She turned her back to the stream of hot water and let it flow over her shoulders. She stepped forward and soaped her breasts and then ran her hands down over her flat stomach into her pubic hair. Eric had been an entertaining dinner companion, too. He had talked openly about his life and his travels although not with a lot of personal detail and he had listened with a disconcerting interest in what she had to say. Most men she associated with were easily led into talking about themselves and their accomplishments. Eric seemed to want to know about her and when he fixed his large brown eyes on her, his beautiful large brown eyes, she reminded herself, she felt like she was the most important woman in his universe, and it didn't seem phony, quite the opposite, there was a genuine warmth and interest there.

She turned to face the shower, raised her arms above her head in a luxurious stretch and then put her head under the stream. Eric had another remarkable quality, too. He was fun to be with, just plain fun. He had a self-deprecating humour. He wasn't critical of himself but it showed he didn't take himself or his achievements all that seriously. Fun was something she seldom had with men. "Stop this," she whispered sternly to herself. It was fine to play the role and enjoy it but she was working, whatever she thought or felt about Eric O'Neill.

She turned off the shower and stepped out of the stall. She dried herself, and then turned on her small travel hair dryer and ran her fingers through her hair as she fluffed it. A quick check in the mirror confirmed the look of tousled innocence she was striving for. Still naked, she opened her makeup kit, a light facial lotion, a little eyeliner, a touch of eyeshadow so subtle he wouldn't know it was there, a swipe of lip gloss. In the bedroom she slipped into a bra and panties, pulled on a pair of erotically tight jeans and slipped a large powder blue bulky knit sweater over her head. She winked at herself in the mirror. Ready for breakfast.

Eric swept open the door and ushered her in. This was definitely upscale compared to her room. As he closed the door behind her she was aware he was looking at her, appraising her really, and she turned to face him. "So what do you think?" she asked, doing a small pirouette.

Eric nodded and smiled. "You look very lovely," he said, his voice still husky.

The sincerity in his voice caught her off guard and she looked intently at him for a moment. "Thank you."

"Over here," he said, slipping his hand under her elbow and guiding her toward a small round table set in one corner of the living room. "Coffee, or Irish breakfast tea, if you prefer it, and Irish soda bread with butter and preserves."

Liselle sat down in the chair that Eric had pulled out for her and saw that he had taken the items off the tray and arranged them on the table. "This is much nicer than a restaurant," she said.

The sun sparkled over the Irish Sea, or at least that was what she thought it was, unless the beautiful bay below them went by another name. They were standing beside a low stone wall, their rental car, a small French Renault, parked tightly against it. This was supposed to be a lookout but there was precious little room to park. They were about an hour out of Dublin driving north along a coast road. Traffic wasn't so much heavy as crowded and busy feeling, slow as they passed through small towns and villages. And, of course, they drove on the left side of the road, too, which somehow made it feel more crowded. Eric seemed to adapt to the right-hand drive car easily even though he said he hadn't driven much in recent years.

"Gorgeous," he said quietly looking off into the distance.

"Are you seeing yourself out there in a sailboat?" Liselle asked.

He turned and laughed. His face transformed when he laughed, his eyes sparkling, his cheeks slightly dimpled. "How did you know?"

"Just the far off look, I guess."

He turned back to the vista and slipped his arm around her. "If you look out beyond the headland...out there just to the left..." He leaned closer to her and pointed.

He smelled nice. She snuggled up against him. "A boat with sails," she laughed. "How clever of you to find one."

"I guess looking for a sailboat is almost an instinct," he said, removing his arm and turning back to the car. He opened the door and held it for her while she got in and then closed it.

She had a couple of feminist friends who would have been insulted by this but she thought it was just gracious. She watched him climb in the other side. "Thank you," she said.

He gave her a questioning look.

"For holding the door for me."

He nodded and started the car. "Sounds like you haven't been hanging out with the right kind of men," he said with a quick chuckle. Then he turned and faced her. "I'm sorry," he said. "That was a thoughtless comment."

"What do you mean?"

"I didn't mean to imply that your departed husband wasn't thoughtful."

Liselle nodded. She was forgetting her widowed image in the enjoyment of being with Eric. "He was thoughtful, but I'm just not used to being treated this way. It's very nice."

She reached over and squeezed his arm lightly. "Please don't worry about it."

She looked over her shoulder as they pulled back into the traffic. For a few miles before they'd stopped at the lookout, there had been a small dark green delivery van behind them. She couldn't be certain but she thought she'd seen it in Dublin just after they had left the hotel, but she hadn't really been paying much attention at the time. Sloppy field craft. She resolved to watch more carefully. A couple of cars had usually been between them and the van but it had still seemed to be pacing them. Now it was gone. If someone was following them, who would it be? Her own people would have told her if they were doing it, so if there really was anyone back there it must be someone connected to Eric. Harry had told her at Heathrow that there were others watching him. A large Swiss bank account could do that.

A couple of miles down the coast road they passed through a small village. The little dark green van was parked in front of a pub, the rear door open. She could see boxes piled inside it. It must be just a normal delivery van. She read the printing on the side as they drove by. "O'Connor Brothers Delivery Service". There was smaller print below it but she couldn't make it out.

Why was she looking for trouble? She realized she was enjoying herself, enjoying herself a lot, and she ought to get herself back to reality. She was working and the job was to find out as much as she could about Eric O'Neill, not get fond of him.

They drove into the yard of a small stone manor house that had seen better days. There had been a small hand lettered sign by the driveway. It simply read "TEA". They got out of the car and stood in the heat of the mid afternoon sun. Liselle turned her face to the sky and felt the warmth. She looked at the huge old trees that must have been there forever. The back part of the yard was overgrown with bushes and wildflowers just coming into bloom. She touched Eric's arm and pointed to the wildflowers. "Isn't that beautiful?"

"The flowers?" Eric asked.

She nodded.

"Ah," he said softly, his husky voice taking on a slight brogue. "And that's where the Leprechauns would be living."

She laughed and slipped her hand through his arm. "You're a good mimic."

A door opened in the old house and a little girl of about six or seven came skipping over toward them, her frilly dress flouncing and the ruffles on her small hat bouncing up and down. Liselle knelt and looked at her.

"Have you come for tea?" she asked.

Liselle nodded. "What's your name, Honey?"

"Meagan," the child said, a large smile revealing a missing front tooth. "But you can call me Meg. Everyone else does."

She took Liselle's hand as she stood up and led her toward the door. Looking over her shoulder, Liselle shrugged and smiled at Eric. He was pointing a small camera at her and it flashed.

"Come on," Liselle said. "You'll be late for Meg's tea."

"Oh," said Meagan with great seriousness. "My mother makes the tea."

The tea room was low ceilinged but bright and warm. A row of windows faced out onto the yard where they had parked the car. Meagan's mother was a small slim woman with an infectious laugh and an accent that was almost incomprehensible. She fussed around them making sure they could see well, pointing out a dozen varieties of wild roses that were climbing up a series of latticed frames, offering to get a more comfortable chair for Eric.

"And would this be a special occasion for you two?" she asked as she set a plate of scones on the table in front of them and then quickly refilled their almost full cups of tea.

Liselle looked at Eric and nodded. "Yes it is," she said.

"A celebration?"

"Yes," Eric said. "A celebration. Our first day together."

The woman straightened up, hands on her hips, eyebrows raised, eyes wide in surprise. "Well now," she said. "That I would never have guessed. But from the look o' you, it's a grand thing you're doing."

They all laughed. "Thank you," Eric said. He reached across the table and touched Liselle's hand.

As Liselle looked at him and squeezed his hand, she knew she was in trouble. This kind of affection could only compromise her mission. She felt a quick tear in her eye and turned to look out the window just as the small dark green delivery van drove slowly into the yard.

CHAPTER FIFTY NINE

Saturday, May 6, 1989 Surrey, England

Martin Bormann was kneeling beside an ailing rose bush, one called French Lace, which produced a particularly delicate and fragrant white rose. "Aphids," he murmured. "The little bastards are out early this year." He examined the shoots of garlic, now a few inches high, which were growing near the roots of the rose bushes. A horticultural magazine he had read a couple of years ago suggested that planting garlic around the bases of rose bushes kept aphids away.

He pushed himself carefully to his feet and leaned on his cane. "Must be a new garlic-resistant strain of aphids," he muttered, smiling at the idea. He saw Joachim walking across the grounds toward him. He was holding some papers in one hand and was walking quickly, almost breaking into a jog, quite uncharacteristic.

"Bad news, sir," Joachim said as he arrived breathing heavily. "It's about Eric O'Neill in Dublin." He held one of the sheets of paper out to Bormann.

Bormann took it and examined it. It was a fax, a grainy black and white picture of Eric O'Neill and a woman coming out of a building. "Who is the woman?"

"That's the bad news, sir," Joachim said, regaining some of his formality. "We have confirmed from the photograph and from the hotel registry that the woman is Liselle Marcoux."

Bormann recognized the name and searched his memory for the connection. "Yes," he said quietly, still looking at the picture.

"She is the Vietnamese woman who was having an affair with Jon Falken," Joachim added.

Bormann looked more carefully at the photocopy. It certainly looked like her although he had only seen one other picture of her. He looked up at Joachim.

"She is registered in the same hotel as O'Neill under her own name. This photograph was taken this morning outside the hotel. O'Neill rented a car late this morning and they have gone touring out of Dublin."

Bormann looked at the photocopy again. They were laughing, looking carefree and happy.

"Apparently, they had dinner together last night," Joachim said.

"She doesn't look Vietnamese," Bormann said, wishing he could push off the inevitable identification.

"Her father was French," Joachim offered.

"Why would she use her own name?" Bormann wondered aloud as he looked across the peaceful yard. The ancient oak trees that marked the limits of the open space around the manor cast long shadows across the lawn in the late afternoon sun. A couple of birds chased each other out of the trees and then swooped around the corner of the house. They looked like small hawks and some years ago he would have known for sure.

His eyesight just wasn't that acute anymore. He turned his attention back to Joachim.

"Perhaps she doesn't know about us," Joachim said.

"There are no coincidences, Joachim," Bormann said softly.

"Correct, sir."

"If this woman has been with Falken and is now with O'Neill, she knows far more than she should. She works for someone who is providing her with a lot of support because no one person would have the resources to make the connection between them." He watched as the birds soared over the roof of the manor and dived toward the lawn. They certainly looked like hawks. "But we need to know who she is working with or working for and I am still puzzled about why she would use her own identity."

"Perhaps there wasn't time to fashion a new identity for her."

Bormann nodded. "Perhaps," he said, his tone of voice suggesting he was clearly not convinced.

"Shall we pick her up, sir?"

"What do we know about her?"

"Quite a lot, actually," Joachim said. "I have put the file on your desk for your consideration but I wanted to tell you immediately of the problem."

"Very good, Joachim," Bormann said. "What is the other piece of paper you have?"

Joachim handed it to him. "Another faxed photograph, sir, taken early this afternoon as our men drove by their vehicle. They were stopped at a lookout."

Bormann looked at the picture. It was slightly blurred but showed the same two people, this time in profile, leaning together, the man with one arm around the woman, his other arm extended, pointing at something. He nodded and handed the photos back to Joachim, then turned and started slowly back toward the house, limping slightly, his right knee a little stiff from his bout with the ailing rose bush. "Tell me what we know," he said.

"We know something of her origins, mother Vietnamese, father French military. She has French citizenship and works for their embassy in Washington and their UN delegation in New York, both arrangements on some type of contract as she is not listed on the rosters of either organization."

"Could she be working for the SDECE?"

"The French Secret Service?" Joachim asked. He was silent for a moment. "I will check it out but there is no evidence of that, so far at least."

"Good," Bormann replied. He didn't need the French on his trail. The SDECE made the Gestapo look like a benevolent children's daycare centre. They were a shadowy, notorious organization that stopped at nothing to get results and Bormann knew that few intelligence organizations in existence were as ruthlessly efficient at producing results. He felt chilled at the thought that they might be closing in after all these years. "We have observers in Dublin?" he asked.

"Yes, Sir."

"They are well experienced?"

"Yes, Sir."

"Good," Bormann said. He thought about this woman that had shown up in Jon Falken's life in Philadelphia, an inconvenient but essentially harmless affair that had been successfully concluded, and then days later across the Atlantic Ocean in Dublin she shows up again with Eric O'Neill. He shook his head sadly. The two small hawks came soaring out of the trees, rocketing over the rooftop. Their grace and beauty reminded him of the old Messerschmitt ME 109's. He hated euphemisms, words like eliminate or terminate. "Kill her," he said softly.

CHAPTER SIXTY

Saturday, May 6, 1989 North of Dublin, Ireland

Eric was looking at Liselle as she suddenly pulled her hand away. She was staring out the window of the tea room where a small green delivery van had pulled into the yard. It stopped and then drove slowly forward. The driver was casting his eyes around the yard looking for something. He came to the corner of the old house where their car was parked and then stopped again. Eric watched it for a moment more as it backed around toward the house and stopped and then he turned his attention back to Liselle. "Is something wrong?"

She looked at him, her eyes wide, and silently shook her head. She picked up her cup and took a sip of tea, then a tiny bite of a scone before looking back to the yard.

The small green van drove forward, out of the yard, stopped for a moment at the junction and then turned right back onto the road and disappeared. Eric leaned back in his chair and watched as Liselle visibly relaxed. "Someone step on your grave?"

She turned to him. "Step on my grave?" she asked.

"Did something upset you?" Eric said. "Did you see a ghost? It's just an old saying." He looked at her carefully and saw a vulnerability in her, almost fear. With little makeup and her hair blown about a bit she looked younger today, more innocent, perhaps even a little frightened. Maybe she was still carrying the images of yesterday's purse snatching incident.

She smiled and shook her head. "Nothing like that," she said. "I'm fine."

"You sure?" Her voice didn't match the look in her eyes.

She leaned forward and covered his hand with hers. "My husband was killed in a car accident. His car was hit by a green delivery van. Every time I see one it just makes me uncomfortable."

"And how is everything?" Meagan's mother asked as she came up to their table.

"Lovely," Eric said. "This is a beautiful spot you have here."

"Why, thank you," she said. "It's been in the family a long time."

"There was a delivery van that just drove into your yard and then out again," Liselle said.

Meagan's mother looked out the window. "Was there now?" she said. "I was in the kitchen."

"It was dark green," Liselle said.

"Oh there are a few green ones around here, you know. It's a popular colour in Ireland." She laughed.

"O'Connor Brother's Delivery," Liselle said.

"Never heard o' them," Meagan's mother said. "But you're a very observant young woman to be readin' the sign."

The small pub a couple of blocks from the Dublin Dreams Hotel was warm and cozy. They were standing at the bar enjoying a Jameson waiting for one of the small round tables to become available. Eric had turned the car in while Liselle had gone to her room to freshen up. She had brushed her hair and wore a little more makeup now but her jeans were as tight as ever. Nice body, he thought as the Irish whiskey warmed him, but he knew it wasn't just the whiskey, nor even her body. It was the day, the time together, the small intimacies that had unfolded between them. It had been so long since he had really enjoyed time with a woman, other than Laura, his now married former high school girlfriend, he reminded himself

"Do you mind a personal question?" Liselle asked. They were looking at each other in the mirror behind the bar.

"Not at all," Eric said, turning to face her and smiling. "But no promises about the answer."

Liselle smiled, too. "Fair enough," she said. "I was wondering about your wife. You told me she had died but you didn't tell me anything about her. What was she like?"

Eric took a drink from his glass and thought about the question for a moment. Laura had asked the same kind of questions. Why did women want to know about a man's former wife? "Deirdre's family was very wealthy so she grew up rich, maybe spoiled, but she was a very beautiful woman, full of fun and energy. She was also given to bouts of sadness, perhaps depression."

Liselle touched his arm. "Our table is free," she said. "Shall we grab it before someone else does?"

Eric nodded and they made their way to the corner of the room and sat down. The sky had clouded over on the drive back and it had been spitting rain as they came into the pub. A couple of patrons came in the door, one of them folding and shaking an umbrella.

"What happened to Deirdre?"

Eric looked at her for a moment. "It's a very sad story. The short version is that Deirdre was an alcoholic. Our son was killed in an automobile accident in June 1986. He was seventeen. About six months later, she committed suicide. It was Christmas Eve."

Liselle put her hand on his forearm. "How awful. I didn't mean to bring back painful memories."

"I haven't really talked much about it, but as the old saying goes," he said. "Shit happens." He watched a tear roll over the edge of her eyelid and down her cheek. "But I am coping with it fairly well and getting on with my life. A couple of months after her suicide, I stepped out of my business and went sailing for two years as I told you the other evening." He paused. "I hope I haven't shocked you with being so blunt about it. There isn't another way to tell the story."

"Thank you for telling me, Eric. I am enjoying getting to know you, even the sad parts."

"And I don't mind talking to you about it." He smiled. "You must be a good therapist."

Liselle looked at him seriously, then a trace of a smile stole across her face. "I've been called a lot of things but never a therapist."

"What can I tell you to make you happy?" he asked.

"I don't trust happiness," Liselle said, pulling a tissue from her purse and wiping her eyes. "Maybe you can teach me how."

"Maybe I can," Eric said.

"You can tell me that I can buy you dinner," she said. "That would make me happy. I think it's my turn."

Dinner had been fun. Liselle had talked to him about growing up in France, going to convent schools and how she and her friends had developed more and more elaborate and devious ways to get around the teaching sisters and their rules. He had chatted about his youth in Portage la Prairie, the summers at Delta.

After dinner, as they waited for the elevator, Liselle slipped her hand into Eric's. "Thank you for spending the day with me," she said. "I'm still a bit shaken about that purse snatcher and I needed to be with someone. And thank you for letting me get to know you better."

Eric squeezed her hand. It was soft and small, delicate but surprisingly strong. "I enjoyed it, too."

The elevator door opened and they stepped in. Liselle leaned against him and rested her head on his shoulder for a moment, then turned to face him and slipped her arms around him. He held her lightly against him, smelling the freshness of her hair. As the door opened on the third floor, she tilted her face up and kissed him lightly on the mouth, her lips soft and cool, and then she stepped back out of the elevator. "See you in the morning?" she asked.

Eric stepped forward to block the door from closing. "I'm flying to London tomorrow, early afternoon."

Liselle frowned. "Breakfast then?"

"Same place only an hour earlier?"

"Sounds good." She blew him a kiss. "Good night, Eric."

Eric came instantly awake and listened as the phone rang again. Was this Laura calling and had she gotten the time zones wrong? He reached over and picked up the receiver, glancing at the bedside clock. 12:23am. "Good morning," he said.

"I'm sorry, Eric," Liselle said, her voice a whisper. "But I'm having a nightmare. Can I sleep on your sofa?"

"Of course," Eric replied.

"I'll be there in a minute," she said. "Thank you." The line went dead.

Eric slipped naked out of bed, turned on a light and hunted in the bedroom closet for a white terry towel robe he had seen earlier. Slipping into it, he wondered if this was some elaborate ploy to sleep with him. He smiled at the idea. If Liselle had wanted to do that, she would only have had to persist a little more in the elevator. He walked into the living room and turned on another light. There was a light tap on the door.

Liselle stood there, her hair tousled from sleep, her eyes wide. She was wearing the same robe as he was, but clutched a pillow in front of her. He stepped aside and ushered her in.

"I feel so stupid," she said. "I just had a terrible nightmare about that purse snatcher and I woke up so frightened."

Eric slipped his arm around her and led her to the sofa. "Everyone has bad dreams, Liselle," he said. "Don't worry about it."

"I woke up scared and called you."

She got up and went to the closet in the living room. She opened the door and on the top shelf there was a pillow and two blankets. "I'm so sorry about this," she said, returning with the bedding. She spread the blankets on the sofa and put a pillow at one end.

"Would you like me to stay up with you for a while?" Eric asked.

"No, please," she said. "Just go back to bed. I'll be fine. I feel silly, but I feel better here."

Eric slipped the bath robe off and crawled back into bed. He lay awake thinking about Liselle. Why hadn't he just suggested she sleep in here with him? Because that would be taking advantage of her fear. He wondered about his scruples. He wondered if he would keep in contact with her when he left. He knew he wanted to. Nothing serious yet, but there was little point in mooning around about Laura, she was married, and whatever his feelings there, and whatever future they might have had, she was simply not available. Maybe Liselle wasn't either. He hadn't really asked.

Eric came awake slowly. He was lying curled up on his left side, the pale morning light seeping in around the drapes. As he stretched slightly he became aware of someone curled tightly behind him. Peering cautiously over his shoulder, he saw Liselle's glossy black hair on the pillow next to his. Her arm was thrown over him. He lay quietly, enjoying the intimacy, aware of a growing arousal. Had she awakened again in the night, frightened by another dream? As he slipped out from under her arm, she murmured softly in her sleep.

Eric retrieved the terry towel robe from the floor and glancing at the clock saw it was a few minutes before eight. He moved quietly to the ensuite bathroom and closing the door, turned on the shower. He let the hot water stream over him but he could still feel the imprints of Liselle's breasts in his back, the feel of her arm over his. So soft. He hadn't been in bed with a woman since Deirdre.

He dried himself thoroughly and put the robe back on before he entered the bedroom. The bed was neatly made and the door to the living room was open. "Liselle," he called softly. There was no answer. He strolled into the living room but it was empty. On the coffee table there was single folded sheet of paper. He picked it up.

"Thank you for everything, Eric. I've enjoyed our time together more than I can tell you. Sorry, but I can't make breakfast. I'll be in touch. Fondly. Liselle."

Eric picked up the phone and dialed her room number. He listened to it ring and hung up after ten rings. He dialed zero.

"Good morning, Mister O'Neill, how may we help you."

"Good morning, could you connect me to room 307 please.

"One moment, sir." Silence. "I'm sorry, Mister O'Neill, but Miss Marcoux checked out a few minutes ago."

CHAPTER SIXTY ONE

Sunday, May 7, 1989 England

Lincoln Carswell felt like shit. His head hurt, he was nauseated and he had a raging thirst. He had just awakened in an aircraft, a private jet from the look of it. He was in a partially reclined seat, the seat belt buckled loosely around his waist. Through half-open eyes, he saw Clark Einfeld sitting in the seat opposite him. There was no sign of Clayton but he was likely somewhere about.

"Can I have something to drink?" he asked, his voice barely a whisper.

"Of course, Mr. Carswell," Einfeld replied. He looked past Lincoln and raised his hand.

A moment later Clayton appeared with a large glass of orange juice and handed it to Lincoln.

He took a long drink. It was sweet, cold and refreshing. He looked around the interior of the aircraft. He had been in private jets before but none this opulent. Everything seemed to be covered in a pale cream leather, the seats a little darker. It was also quieter than others he had been in.

"Take these," Clayton said, holding out a couple of small white capsules.

Lincoln looked at them, popped them into his mouth and downed them with a swallow of orange juice. If they wanted to do him harm, they didn't need to give him pills.

He handed the empty glass to Clayton and closed his eyes. He thought back to yesterday, or maybe it was the day before. Einfeld had pulled a gun on him in front of his home and told him he was going to London. He wasn't going to argue with a man who was pointing a gun at him. So they had gone into his house while Clayton had driven his truck into the garage. They waited and watched as he packed. They told him he'd only need clothing for three days.

He chose a carry-on suitcase, stuck in underwear, socks, a couple of shirts and sweaters, a wind breaker and a blazer. He packed his personal things and managed to put in a small makeup kit. He asked if he could take a sketch pad and some pencils and packed them in an artist's case. He put in his new camera and a couple of rolls of film although he didn't really expect to be taking a lot of pictures. He always took these things with him when he travelled.

Then he locked up the house, put on the alarm system and Clayton drove them to the airport. They had gone to a small terminal and boarded an opulent private jet which had taken off immediately. When they reached cruising altitude, Clayton had served them wine. That was the last thing Lincoln remembered.

Lincoln wondered how to approach his current situation. Aside from kidnapping him and drugging him, they seemed well disposed toward him. He smiled at that in spite of his aching head. He would rest awhile, gather his strength for whatever lay ahead.

A slight bump awakened him. He heard the engine thrusters slowing the aircraft and realized they had landed. He opened his eyes. His headache was gone as well as the nausea but he was still thirsty.

Einfeld sat opposite him reading a magazine. He looked up. "Welcome to England, Mr. Carswell."

Lincoln looked out the window. The sun was shining. He consulted his watch and saw it was 2:35. He added five hours. 7:35, early morning in England. The aircraft slowed and turned off the runway, coming to a stop in front of a small building. He listened as the engines spooled down and stopped.

Clayton appeared beside him and held out a glass of orange juice. "Good morning, Mr. Carswell."

"Thank you," Lincoln said, taking the glass and drinking about half of it. "Would you have coffee as well?

"When we're off the aircraft," Clayton said.

Lincoln finished the orange juice and looked at Einfeld. "So what now?"

"We are at a small airport in rural England. We will proceed to an estate nearby and get you settled in."

"And then I'll meet these folks that are so bloody important?"

"That's correct," Einfeld replied. He unfastened his seat belt and stood up.

Lincoln undid his belt and leaned forward. He felt a bit light-headed, almost dizzy, and as he started to rise, he felt Clayton's hand on his elbow steadying him. After a few moments the dizziness passed.

They went down the stairs, Lincoln holding on to the railing for balance. At the foot of the stairs was a liveried driver holding open the back door of a black limousine. The three of them entered and sat down. Clayton opened a small compartment and removed a plastic insulated cup with a lid and handed it to Lincoln.

"Coffee?" Lincoln asked.

Clayton nodded. "A latte."

Lincoln leaned back and drank the coffee. He watched the countryside roll by, rich green fields with clumps of trees. They passed through a village on a narrow winding street, old stone and wood houses, a small church and then they were back in the country again.

Lincoln handed the cup to Clayton, leaned back in the soft leather seat and closed his eyes. His next awareness was the car coming to a halt and a rumbling sound as a garage door closed behind it. A moment later the chauffeur opened the door and they got out.

Lincoln looked around. There were four cars in the large garage, the limousine he had travelled in which he saw was a Bentley, a silver Jaguar sedan, a green Austin Mini and another small car he didn't recognize.

"This way," Einfeld said, leading them to a door in front of the Bentley. It opened into a storage area, with boxes and large plastic containers neatly arranged on shelves. A second door led into a large kitchen. At the end of the kitchen, a table was set for three. Clayton hung the car keys on a small rack by the kitchen door and they sat down.

A plump elderly woman walked over to the table and set a plate of food in front of each of them, scrambled eggs, a large sausage and two buttered English muffins.

Lincoln stared at the food. "Is this safe to eat?" he asked. "Every time I drink something I fall asleep."

Einfeld smiled. "There was nothing in your coffee, you were just tired."

Lincoln started to eat, realized he was quite hungry in spite of his overnight ordeal, and finished his plate quickly.

"Would you like anything else, Mr. Carswell?" Einfeld asked.

Lincoln shook his head.

"Very well, we'll take you to your suite. You can shower and freshen up, rest if you wish, and then you will meet our host."

"Who is he?"

"He prefers to introduce himself," Einfeld said. "I'm sure you'll find it interesting to meet him."

Lincoln shrugged. "Whatever."

An hour later Einfeld led him to a small outdoor patio area, furnished with white wrought iron furniture, consisting of a couple of chairs and a bench with upholstered cushions and a round table. Sunshine filtered through an overhead lattice framework covered in climbing roses, mostly pink, their fragrance floating in the still air. An elderly man sat in one of the chairs, a cane leaning against the arm. He slowly stood up as Carswell approached him.

"Good morning, Lincoln," he said, his voice betraying the remnants of a German accent. "I apologize for the circumstances under which you were brought here." He held out his hand.

Lincoln stood silently before him, ignoring the outstretched hand. He nodded and looked around. Nice grounds, pleasant surroundings. He wondered what this old geezer wanted.

"Please sit down, Lincoln. We have some things to discuss." The old man lowered himself carefully into the chair.

Lincoln took the next chair, slightly facing him. "So let's discuss," Lincoln said. He looked pointedly at his watch. "Then you can fly me back to Philadelphia."

The old man watched him for a moment. "I am Martin Bormann," he said.

Lincoln smiled. "Right," he said. "I'm the Lone Ranger."

Bormann chuckled. "I am not surprised by your skepticism, but I really am Martin Bormann."

"Tell me why I should care, even if you are?"

"Because I may have a lot to offer you."

Lincoln was silent. This old guy was as vague as Einfeld. Why couldn't they just get to the point?

Bormann continued. "There is a large and powerful international organization, well established, well financed and effective at influencing international affairs. I would like you to learn a bit more about us and if you still are disinterested, then we will return you to your home."

"Is this a Nazi organization?"

"Its origins are, but it is now much more."

Lincoln leaned forward in his chair. "Listen carefully, Mr. Bormann, or whoever you are. I am a successful American artist. I paint pictures and sell them. I have no interest in international affairs, or events, no interest in politics and no interest in your money. I am financially independent and happy doing what I do." He paused. "So let's not waste your time or mine."

Bormann stood up slowly and retrieved his cane. "Come for a short walk with me, Lincoln. I would like to show you something."

Together they walked back into the house, entering a glassed-in room, furnished similarly to the patio area they had just left. Bormann turned to the left and walked slowly down a hallway. He opened the second door they came to and ushered Lincoln in. There was a sofa against one wall, a coffee table in front of it and three of his paintings on the opposite wall. Two were from his American Heartland Series, one an agricultural landscape with a man following a plow pulled by a team of horses. The rich black soil was turned in furrows, a clump of trees decorated the background and through the foliage were the outlines of a white farmhouse. The second one was a street scene from a small American town, likely set around the year 1910. He smiled. The inspiration for that one had been the small town America exhibit in Disneyland. Nobody did fantasy better than Disney.

"We have been following your career for some time, Lincoln," Bormann said.

Lincoln examined the third painting. It was smaller and had come from a show he had done in LA. "American Patriots", he had called it. There had only been about twenty pieces in the show, all military scenes. This one was from World War Two and depicted a single American soldier, battered and bleeding, standing in a wasteland of smoke, mud and fire, wrenching his bayonet from the body of a German soldier, whose face was a mask of agony.

"Thank you for supporting my art," Lincoln said. He tried to recall who had purchased these pieces but couldn't. But many were purchased by agents for collectors or galleries, so it was unlikely that he would have connected Bormann to any of these.

"It has been our pleasure," Bormann replied. He sat down on the sofa. "Please let our support continue."

"So what do you want?" Lincoln asked. He sat down beside Bormann.

"You know your origins lie in Germany. You know you were moved to the US when you were one year old. Others were moved in the same way and tonight you will meet two of these men. You share the same background and you have much in common, although you have all developed into quite different and unique individuals."

"So who are these other two?"

"One is a Canadian, a stockbroker by trade. The other is, like you, an American, and has had a distinguished military career. He may have a political future as well."

"Do these men have names?"

Bormann smiled. "That is the first interest you have shown. Yes, they do. The Canadian's name is Eric O'Neill. The American you may have heard of. His name is Jon Falken."

Lincoln felt as though he had been punched in the stomach. He knew his surprise must be showing.

Bormann tipped his head to one side, and then as though he was reading Lincoln's mind, said, "Please relax, Lincoln, Colonel Falken is here alone."

CHAPTER SIXTY TWO

Sunday, May 7, 1989 England

Eric O'Neill stood patiently with the small carry-on bag at his feet. The line at customs wasn't long but it was slow. Gatwick was a smaller airport than Heathrow but still huge by Canadian standards. He felt sad and withdrawn. Since he had read the note that Liselle had left this morning there had been a hollowness in the pit of his stomach. He wondered if he had done something to make her run. Relax, he told himself. People make choices, all life is a choice, and she chose to leave in a hurry this morning. It could have been as simple as embarrassment at having spent the night with him. He smiled. Maybe she didn't respect him in the morning, as the old saying went.

"Sir?"

He came out of his reverie, moved forward to the customs and immigration counter and handed his passport to the agent.

"Welcome to the United Kingdom, sir," the agent said, looking carefully at him. "Is your visit here for business or for pleasure?"

"Pleasure," Eric replied. "Just a short holiday."

The agent stamped his passport. "Enjoy your stay, sir."

Eric glanced at his watch and saw he was still two hours ahead of the arrival time that had been on the original ticket he had been given in Berlin. He was sitting in a booth in a food court, sipping a cup of bad coffee. As he pushed the mug away having decided he didn't want coffee badly enough to drink this, two men walked up to the booth and sat down, one across from him, the other sliding in beside him.

"Eric O'Neill?" the one across from him asked, his voice quiet, but deep and resonant. "My name is Clark Einfeld," he said without waiting for Eric to answer. "My colleague, Steven Clayton," he added, indicating the man seated beside Eric.

Eric nodded. "Gentlemen."

"We've come to take you to a meeting," Einfeld said. "I presume your presence here confirms that you wish to attend?"

Eric nodded again. "What it confirms is that I am curious, Mr. Einfeld. I am interested in learning more, one step at a time."

"Please call me Clark," Einfeld said. "Very well, Eric. I can provide you with a little information. What would you like to know?"

"There is some large, well-financed organization at work here. What is it and who is involved?"

Einfeld stared at him for a moment. "What do you know of your origins?"

Eric smiled. "I thought you wanted me to ask the questions?"

It was Einfeld's turn to smile. "Good point. Here is the short answer. Following the collapse of Germany at the end of World War II, a group of businessmen set up international corporate ties, foreign subsidiaries and the like, which over time developed into a large and powerful network. As you may know, you were born in Germany, moved to Canada as a child and until recently, a matter of a few days ago actually, we had assumed that you and your guardians had died in a fire in the fall of 1940. We would now like to get to know you better and provide you with more information on this network. As well, we would like to provide you with the opportunity to get to know us better."

"Why would I want to do that?"

"You're here," Einfeld said.

"So I am," Eric replied. "And there is a meeting?"

A black Bentley was waiting in front of the airport. The driver took Eric's bag and Einfeld and Clayton ushered him into the car. There was a rear bench seat with a rear facing jump seat. Clayton took the jump seat.

"There are elements of secrecy to our organization as I am sure you know by now," Einfeld said. "We are taking you to meet one of the principle leaders who will be better able to answer your questions. However, his whereabouts is one of our security concerns and shortly we will be asking you to don a blindfold for the remainder of the journey. Is this a problem for you?"

Eric looked from one to the other. "Not really," Eric said. "But I'm not sure I'm much interested in finding out about an organization that operates this way. I understand concerns regarding industrial espionage but secret leaders just sounds paranoid."

Einfeld smiled again, a relaxing, engaging smile that made him look quite likeable. "I realize it must appear that way to you but you will understand why when we arrive."

Eric awakened slowly. He opened his eyes and stared at the ceiling, high and ornate, white, and as he turned his head he saw that the rest of the room was white as well. He was in what appeared to be a small hospital room with a single bed. He sat up slowly and dangled his legs over the edge. Someone had taken off his shoes and he noticed his jacket was gone as well. His tie had been loosened. He felt a little sleepy but otherwise fine. The last thing he remembered was Clayton fitting a blindfold on him as they had turned on to a freeway.

The door opened and Einfeld entered. "How are you feeling, Eric?"

"Fine," Eric replied. "But was the drug really necessary?"

Einfeld nodded sympathetically. "Just our standard operating procedure, Eric. My apologies." He handed Eric his jacket and pointed to a chair in the corner of the room. "Your shoes."

Eric stood up gingerly but there was no nausea or dizziness. He slipped the jacket on, walked over to the chair and put on his shoes.

"Ready for tea?"

Eric glanced at his watch. A little after four. "Coffee?" he asked hopefully.

"In England the term 'tea' covers a multitude of sins."

They left the dispensary and walked down a wide hallway. They were clearly in an old house, large, luxurious and beautifully maintained. Ornately framed paintings, most dismal landscapes, were hung at intervals, and an occasional small table, chair or sideboard was placed under the paintings. "Nice place," Eric observed.

"It is," Einfeld said. "Like a lot of old English country estates it was built and added to over several centuries."

They turned a corner and went through a doorway. Eric saw two heavy brass striker plates in the door frame as they passed through it so the locks were definitely modern. A moment later they entered a large parlour filled with ornate furnishings but still retaining a light, airy feeling about it. There was nothing gloomy about the place despite its age. They passed through a set of French doors that led into a glassed in sun room, obviously one of the more recent additions. The perimeter was filled with large leafy plants, and a white cast iron table with a glass top was set in the centre of the room with two comfortable looking upholstered chairs drawn up to it. An old man sat in one of the chairs and watched as they entered and crossed the room. With the aid of a cane, he rose slowly to his feet. He was short and a bit portly, with wispy white hair.

Einfeld and Eric stopped in front of him. The old man looked Eric over carefully and then nodded, seemingly satisfied. His eyes twinkled. "So you made it?" he said. His voice was strong and firm, the words slightly accented. "Welcome to England, young Eric, and thank you for indulging an old man." He held out his hand and Eric shook it, surprised at the strength of the grip. "I am Martin Bormann. Please join me for tea."

Eric stood holding Bormann's hand for a moment. "Thank you," Eric said quietly and let his hand drop. How could this be, he wondered. He knew little about the details of the Third Reich but he was confident that Martin Bormann had been killed in the dying days of World War II.

"You are surprised to find me alive, Eric," Bormann said, easing himself back into his chair. "Reports of my death have been greatly exaggerated.'" Bormann motioned for Eric to be seated. "So have reports of my life in South America." He glanced past Eric. "Thank you," he said to Einfeld who nodded and left the room.

"I am surprised," Eric said. "Stunned, really."

"Well so am I, Eric. We had no idea that you and your guardians had survived but I must say I am pleased that you have."

A tall man in an impeccable black suit entered the sun room bearing a tray with a silver coffee pot and other accoutrements. "Thank you, Joachim," Bormann said as Joachim set the tray on the table and poured coffee for each of them. He set a plate of biscuits, small bowls of jam and clotted cream and another plate of small sandwiches on the table. "Will there be anything else, sir?"

"Not for now, thank you," Bormann replied.

Eric took a sip of his coffee, dark and rich, and noticed a slight metallic taste in his mouth, a leftover reaction from the drug, perhaps.

"Over the next day or two, I will fill you in on the last few decades of history but for the moment I would like you to tell me something. While you were in Ireland you met a woman, Liselle Marcoux. Correct?"

"You are well informed."

Bormann smiled. "I haven't survived this long on bad information. However, what do you know about Miss Marcoux?"

Eric looked at Bormann and wondered where the questioning was going. "I met her in Dublin, by accident really. A young man snatched her purse and I retrieved it for her. She bought me a drink and it turned out we were staying at the same hotel."

"Did this strike you as an odd coincidence, this adventure with the purse and then the discovery that you were staying at the same hotel?"

"No," Eric replied, recalling the situation. "Not really."

"And then you had dinner together. Yesterday you rented a car and the two of you drove about to see a few sights. Correct so far?"

Eric nodded. He picked up one of the small sandwiches and took a bite. Ham and mustard but still with a faint metallic taste.

"And dinner again last night?"

"Correct."

"And then this morning Miss Marcoux vanished," Bormann said, leaning back in his chair. "Do you know why?"

Eric shook his head.

"Let me tell you a couple things about her that you probably do not know." Bormann picked up his coffee cup and took a sip. "I'm not supposed to drink much coffee. My wretched doctor tells me it's bad for my heart." He took another drink and set the cup down. "I was having you watched while you were in Dublin. I was not trying to pry into your private life, Eric, please believe me. I was trying to make sure you came to no harm. So last night I sent two of my agents, well trained men, to meet her, to ask her some questions. They were waiting in her room when she returned from having dinner with you. Can you guess what happened?"

Eric thought of the middle-of-the-night phone call, of Liselle at his door, tousled and wearing a white terry robe, of the nightmare that had broken her sleep. He remembered awakening to the feel of her nakedness on his back. He shook his head.

Bormann leaned forward, the twinkling eyes now cold and hard, his voice soft. "She killed them both."

CHAPTER SIXTY THREE

Sunday, May 7, 1989 Surrey, England

Jon Falken was tired of being cooped up. The security people would not let him go for a run or even a walk around the grounds. He was to stay in the old house, elegant as it was, and look out at the sunshine. He was assured it would be worth his while, but he was not impressed. He had discovered a fitness centre installed in one wing which the security people used to keep in some semblance of physical conditioning but the three of them he had seen so far looked more like fat rent-a-cops than serious threats. However, he had spent a couple of hours working out a few of his own frustrations. He had been blindfolded, drugged, brought here, and then nothing. He had met with Einfeld and that faggot, Clayton, last night and again early this morning over breakfast and had learned a little more about the dreams of the old Nazis. After that he had been turned over to one of the security people who had a room temperature IQ and all the social skills that went with it. Einfeld and Clayton had gone somewhere immediately after breakfast and had returned after lunch. They had briefed him a bit more and had promised that at dinner this evening things would become clear. They had better, he thought darkly, or he wouldn't be around for the morning briefing.

He stripped off the shorts and tee shirt that the security guy had given him and turned on the shower. At least the suite he had been given was nice. Marianne would have loved the elegance and the old art, too. It was all pale colours and white frilly furniture with gold leaf trim and tapestry seats. Not his style, but definitely upscale.

The knock on his door came exactly at 7:00pm. It was Einfeld.

"Good evening, Jon," he said. "I hear you had a workout this afternoon."

"Right," Jon said irritably. "There wasn't much else to do."

"I apologize for that but I think you will find this evening to be more productive."

They entered the main body of the manor house and strolled into a parlour. Heavier furniture here, more of a masculine touch, Jon noted. Einfeld led him to a grouping of heavy upholstered chairs in one corner of the room. As they approached, an old man rose to his feet with the aid of a cane. Jon wondered if this was the token "old Nazi".

"Good evening, Jon," the old man said quietly. "A pleasure to meet you." He held out his hand.

"Good evening," Jon said respectfully, shaking his hand. Strong grip for an old guy, he thought.

"Please sit down," the old man said. "We will go in to dinner shortly. I am Martin Bormann."

Jon stared at the old man, transfixed. Adolf Hitler's private secretary in the flesh, the most sought after war criminal in history. He was supposed to have died in May 1945, or escaped to live in South America, or defected to the Soviet Union, but here he was in England, still alive. Jon sat down. "An honour to meet you, sir." He stared at Bormann, taking in every detail, all thoughts of dreaming old Nazis gone.

"Thank you for coming here, Jon," Bormann said. "I apologize for the inconvenience I've caused you."

"Not at all, sir," Jon said. As he looked at Bormann, he could see there was still a sense of power and confidence about the man, an energy but also a stillness in him.

"You are going to meet two other men this evening. They have come here under similar circumstances to your own. You all have quite different backgrounds, skills and interests to contribute, should any or all of you choose to become involved in our enterprise."

A tall man in a black suit entered the room. "Dinner is ready, sir. Mr. Carswell and Mr. O'Neill are there."

"Thank you, Joachim," Bormann said, rising slowly with the aid of his cane. "We will join them now."

A set of French doors led to a large formal dining room. It was the first room Jon had seen that was furnished in dark wood. The table and chairs were heavily constructed, likely walnut from the look of it and a long sideboard against one wall matched them. Einfeld stood in the far corner of the room, a drink in his hand, talking to two other men, O'Neill and Carswell, whoever they were. Carswell was a familiar name but he couldn't place it.

Jon walked in slowly keeping pace with Bormann. The three men turned as they entered. The taller of the two strangers was a nice looking man, the dark blonde hair was a bit on the long and unruly side, but his features were regular and he looked slim and fit, likely around six feet tall, about the same age as he was. He smiled at something Einfeld said. He looked comfortable and relaxed. No military in his background, Jon decided. It was just something about how civilians stood, too casual.

The other man was shorter, dark haired, more intense looking, perhaps annoyed at something. He clutched his wine glass as though afraid he might drop it.

"Jon Falken, meet Eric O'Neill and Lincoln Carswell," Bormann said. The three of you have a lot in common."

Jon shook hands with O'Neill and Carswell. "I believe you know my wife," he said to Carswell, the shorter one with dark hair. "You're an American painter, aren't you?"

Carswell nodded. "I am," he replied. "What is your wife's name?"

"Marianne Falken."

"I met her at a show I was having and she very kindly bought one of my paintings."

Over dinner, Bormann explained how they had been smuggled out of Germany to the US and Canada. He merely nodded and smiled when Jon asked if he knew who their parents were but declined any further comment.

"What I would like to do this evening is to give you a general sense of what our movement is about," Bormann said. "Jon, I understand that you expressed the concern that we were a bunch of old Nazis running about South America living on fifty year old dreams, or words to that effect. I want to assure you that there is a far more serious enterprise underway than that." He paused and smiled. "However, you are partially correct. There are, in fact, some old Nazis doing exactly what you so eloquently described, but they have nothing to do with our organization. I also understand that you have been briefed by

Clark Einfeld on some of the military accomplishments in our recent history?"

Jon nodded. "Yes, sir."

Joachim entered the room set a bottle of Courvosier and three large brandy snifters on the table beside Bormann. He gathered dishes off the table and left.

Bormann poured a tot of cognac into each of the three snifters and passed them out. "Here is a brief outline of what we have accomplished," Bormann began. "At the end of the War Germany was in shambles, physically, economically, militarily, even spiritually. Our losses were staggering, conditions unimaginable, but today Germany stands rebuilt and is the strongest, most prosperous nation in Europe. At the end of the War some of the Allied countries, notably the Soviet Union, wanted to break up the German industrial conglomerates but no one, including them, seriously considered breaking up the German banking corporations. After all, look what had happened at the end of World War I? Hyper-inflation and the collapse of the German economy, precisely the conditions ripe for the rise of National Socialism."

"Excuse me," Eric interjected. "Surely no one could have been concerned about the resurgence of the Nazi party in the late 1940's regardless of the developing economic conditions."

Bormann looked at Eric for a moment. "You are quite correct," he replied. "But to be certain that the German banking community survived intact, the United States went so far as to cancel the second round of the Nuremberg trials to prevent members of the German banking community from even testifying. This also served to cover the close prewar ties they had enjoyed with the US. Some of that was our doing, much of it was not." Bormann raised his eyebrows. "Does that answer your question?"

"Thank you," Eric said.

Bormann continued. "Now our movement is world-wide and for the last forty-four years we have attempted to rebuild National Socialism from a political movement confined to Germany and briefly to the territories it conquered, to an international economic force. We have learned something the Jews have always known. Real power is economic, not political.

"By the end of the War we had moved vast sums of money out of Germany and these were used to invest in enterprises all over the world. We have managed to keep the United States and the Soviet Union in a state of war; we have seen right wing political movements that support our political and economic aims develop in a variety of countries around the world."

Jon listened to Bormann drone on, his voice becoming more animated, powerful and even strident at times, his hand gestures more pronounced, slapping one partially clenched fist into the other hand for emphasis. He had watched old films of Hitler doing the same thing. He was leaning forward on the edge of the table, his head nodding with his hand gestures, his features almost fierce. He was deeply involved in his own fantasy, Jon decided, but there were certainly resources here to be used so long as the Nazi connection could be disguised or even better, eliminated.

"We have prospered and grown on instability, political, economic, social, even cultural instability, and we have fostered these in a variety of ways."

Jon had heard all this from Einfeld. He glanced over at O'Neill, sitting there listening, quite focussed judging by the look on his face, his head tilted slightly to one side. So O'Neill was another one of Bormann's orphans sent abroad to be recalled when needed, an interesting man but not someone that Jon would ever get close to. Carswell looked bored, as though he could hardly wait for this diatribe to be over.

Jon had been stunned to meet Bormann alive but once he had gotten over the initial shock of it he had wondered if Bormann was just another old Nazi, in this instance sitting around England, living on fifty year old dreams. So far it sounded that way. And surely Eric O'Neill could not be considered any kind of heir apparent to all this? He was a bloody stockbroker. Carswell was an artist, for Christ's sake. What could a painter know of international issues?

"Over the next short while I will give you details of what this organization consists of and what some of its achievements have been," Bormann said. He looked tired and spent as he leaned back in his chair. His hand quivered slightly as he picked up the bottle of Courvoisier and passed it around the table. "But I would be interested in any initial reactions that you might have."

Jon waited a moment to see if O'Neill or Carswell were going to say anything. Carswell shook his head. O'Neill nodded at Jon and said, "You go first, Jon."

"Thank you for the information, sir, and for trusting us with it," Jon began.

"Excuse me for just a moment," Bormann interjected. "But trust to this point is not important. If you left here with what you now know and went about telling people that Martin Bormann was alive in England, living in retirement in Surrey and that the Fourth Reich was on the move, you would be treated like mad men. I have not trusted you yet and I have not decided whether I will."

Jon took a sip of his cognac. Tough old bastard, he thought. "Very well, sir," he said. "Then I will work to gain that trust. But for the moment I don't have a lot of comments other than the fact that you and the organization seem to have done an amazing job of survival and rebuilding."

"What are your thoughts, Lincoln?" Bormann asked.

"I don't really have any comments," Lincoln replied. "Fascinating as this is, I'm still not the slightest bit interested in joining you and your organization."

Bormann turned to Eric and nodded. "Any comments you'd like to make, Eric?"

Eric picked up the cognac and sipped it, shaking his head, a faint trace of a smile creeping across his features. "I am afraid I do have a couple," he said, setting down the snifter. "To start with, I think you are all mad."

Jon watched Bormann stiffen at the comment.

"The world is far too politically fragmented to ever become an empire again. I agree with you that if there were any hope at all, it would be economic, but there is no hope there either. The aggregations of power required to exert that kind of control are just too massive. Only the Arabs have even the beginnings of that kind of money and even they don't have nearly enough, never mind the peculiarities of their governments. They're like the Nazis of your generation, blinded by their own racial and religious lenses, driven by an ideology that is essentially destructive and anarchic. The kind of economic power and control that you're talking about is a function of long term order, of economic activity relatively free and unfettered by government interference, shareholder demands or the niceties of social or environmental consciousness. Nowhere in the world do these conditions exist together. Perhaps the mafia or the Chinese triads or other organized crime syndicates come somewhere near your ideal but they're also too small and are not driven by Nazi ideology or anything close to it."

Eric paused and took a sip of the cognac. "It's fashionable these days to talk about economic colonialism of the sort practiced by large international corporations who set up businesses, commonly in developing countries, where they influence or even direct governments and their policies, fly their own corporate flags and in some cases become the driving force in national economies."

He leaned forward and spoke softly, gently to Bormann. "I'm sure that when we get to the details, we will learn that your organization is involved with some of these multinationals as well as having various other international influences, but if your idea of the Fourth Reich is controlling a multinational oil company or an international soft drink company or something of the sort, then I will stay with my original contention. The entire idea of an economic empire on the scale you are suggesting is utter nonsense. You are mad."

Jon had to hand it to O'Neill. He certainly had balls telling this old Nazi he was crazy. He watched Bormann, his face flushed, push himself to his feet. He stood there, grasping the edge of the table, a study in fury.

"How dare you?" Bormann snarled. "How dare you dismiss four and a half decades of commitment by innumerable people? People who have dedicated their lives to this organization. We have been the most powerful force in the twentieth century."

Eric spoke again, his voice still soft and gentle. "I'm not suggesting that World War Two was not the major event of this century . . ."

"I am not speaking of the War," Bormann roared. "I am talking of the post war achievements of our movement. Achievements that you know nothing about, but that you are dismissing as trivial, as madness."

Jon was startled by the power in his voice. Bormann's complexion was a deep red now. Jon wondered if the old man had heart condition. Maybe he should say something to slow him down.

"We were the architects of the Cold War between the United States and the Soviet Union. Reinhard Gehlen, our eastern intelligence director, was taken to the US, to Fort Hunt, Virginia in September 1945, to be specific, and he stayed there for ten months. When he returned to Germany in July 1946, he became the major source of Soviet intelligence for the US and England for the next twenty-two years until he retired in 1968 and we were able to feed on Stalin's paranoia and that of the American CIA, whose paranoia was at least as great as Stalin's.

"We were able, for example, to convince the US that a small post war incursion into a country no one had ever heard of was a dress rehearsal by the Soviets for the invasion of Western Europe. You will remember the Korean War."

Bormann was speaking rapidly and forcefully, his complexion had paled again. Jon took a sip of his cognac and stole a glance at Eric. Eric was staring back at Bormann, the expression on his face was neutral but to Jon's eye, he still looked unconvinced.

Suddenly Bormann relaxed. With a long sigh, he eased himself back into his chair and turned to Eric again. "How can I convince you of our power and importance, Eric?"

"I am not certain that I can be convinced," Eric replied. "All sorts of organizations take credit for things. Why should yours be any different?"

Bormann waved at Joachim. "Bring me a snifter, if you please."

Joachim set one in front of Bormann and reached for the Courvoisier. Bormann brushed his hand away and poured himself a generous splash. He raised his eyebrows to the others. Eric pushed his glass toward Bormann. Jon shook his head. He wanted a clear mind for this. Carswell was holding on to his snifter as though he thought it might fly out of his hands.

"I am 88 years old, Eric, and I don't have much time left. I would not go to the trouble to prepare some complicated fabric of lies to convince you of something that wasn't true." He took a sip of his cognac. "Let me offer you a few more examples of how we have directed the events of the twentieth century." He leaned back in his chair and picked up the brandy snifter.

"We are an entirely pragmatic organization. We will do whatever it takes, whatever works; we will form alliances with any government or group or individual to forward our cause." A trace of a smile crossed his grim features and he seemed to relax a little more. "In other words," he went on. "We operate in essentially the same way that the US government operates, the end justifies the means. So we have supported everything from the Aryan Nations movement in the US to the World Muslim Congress. We have supported the growth and development of extremist groups of all political persuasions in every country where we have found them because they all have one consistent dynamic. They are driven by ideologies that are intolerant and that permit no deviations. As a result, they argue and fight among themselves, they split up and they reform. They seldom achieve anything more than a protest rally, an assassination or a hijacking. Because they keep reforming themselves, they absorb immense US and Soviet resources trying to track and infiltrate them because each country imagines the other is using and directing these organizations to achieve their own ends. Occasionally they are correct.

"The United States has more secret police than the Third Reich ever dreamed of. This is an odd commentary on the world's bastion of individual freedom and open democracy. The FBI, the CIA, the NSA, US military intelligence organizations, the US Secret Service and virtually all the others are driven by the fear of communism and communist infiltration so anyone with a right wing bias is welcomed. We have numerous deep penetration agents in all these organizations. Similarly, we have infiltrated the Soviet KGB and their other state security agencies using their fear of anyone with right-wing leanings."

Jon nodded in agreement. He hadn't really thought about the US intelligence establishment in comparison with that of World War II Germany, but there were certainly too goddam many spooks in the US these days, none of them talking to any of the others.

Bormann went on. "The CIA and US military intelligence organizations along with considerable assistance from Reinhard Gehlen were able to convince the US government that the Soviets and the Chinese were on a course to extend the veil of communism over the entire region of South East Asia. As a result the US decided to intervene in the democratic elections in South Vietnam when it became apparent that the communists would win. As you know, they soon escalated their involvement in Vietnam to the status of a full scale war, again with the result that American interests were diverted from Western Europe allowing the further resurgence of our organization and the development of a united Europe."

Bormann took a sip of his cognac and smiled ruefully. "We even tried to fund Alfred Kinsey's sex research with the idea that this would help to undermine American sexual morality but it seems that this was scarcely necessary." He became serious again. "We also were strong supporters of the American civil rights movement, the anti- Vietnam War movement and anything else that the US government considered subversive.

"You will recall the assassination of Robert Kennedy by an Arab? Did you wonder who trained him? In 1981 Pope John Paul II was shot by Mehmet Ali Agca, a member of a Turkish Grey Wolf organization that we supported. The same year John Hinckley shot Ronald Reagan. John Hinckley was a follower of Frank Collins and the National Socialist Party of America. Also in 1981, Anwar Sadat, the president of Egypt was murdered after he made peace with the Israelis. This was ironic as our ties with Sadat went back to Rommel's time in North Africa during World War II. Among our agents in Egypt working against the British at the time were a couple of young Lieutenants by the names of Gamal Abdel Nasser and Anwar Sadat. Nasser became the president of Egypt and Sadat succeeded him. Incidentally, Sadat's connection to the Third Reich was well established and following the War he spent three years in a British prison for his trouble. However, sometimes people outlive their usefulness."

Jon nodded in agreement, fascinated. He had known about Anwar Sadat's support of the Nazis against the British and had heard or read rumours of some of the other incidents, but Bormann's summary was chilling, exciting, too, if he were honest.

Bormann gave a long sigh and shook his head slightly. He stared into his cognac for a moment as though looking for inspiration in the rich amber liquid. He looked up at Eric. "There is such power here to influence the world."

Eric stared back, pale and unsmiling now. "Such destructive power it seems," he said softly. "Why kill people, destroy the dreams of a generation like the Vietnam War did, cause such grief and anguish in the world? You believe the end justifies the means, but what is the end?"

CHAPTER SIXTY FOUR

Sunday, May 7, 1989 London, England

"What the hell was I supposed to do?" Liselle Marcoux stood with her hands on her hips, utterly exasperated. "You sent me in with a day's notice, with no warning that there were enemies about and you're angry that I survived." She threw herself into an armchair. She was tense and tired. "Thanks a lot."

Three men sat across from her, two on a sofa and one on another armchair. They had just gathered in the living room of a hotel suite in central London. The two on the sofa were young, likely in their early thirties, one wore glasses and had a day's growth of dark beard, or maybe he always looked like that, the other was pale and smooth skinned. The third man was older, perhaps in his early fifties. She hadn't worked with any of them before although she had met the older man once.

"Liselle," the older man said comfortingly. "We are delighted that you survived. We did not know or expect that there would be enemies around. If we had, we would certainly have warned you and sent a support team with you." His voice was gentle and carried the trace of an east European accent that she couldn't place. He paused and picked up a glass of wine from the coffee table in front of him. He stared into the large tulip glass for a moment as he swirled the deep red wine around. He wore half glasses and closed his eyes as he brought the wine glass close to his nose to smell the aroma. He took a sip and set the glass down. "Marvelous," he commented. He looked over the top of his glasses at Liselle again. "But was it really necessary for you to kill them both?"

Liselle stared at him in disbelief. "No, Aaron," she said softly. "I didn't have to kill them. I could have let them rape me and interrogate me and then kill me. But given the circumstances, I thought I made a pretty good choice."

Aaron raised his eyebrows in surprise. "They were going to rape you?" he asked.

"Jesus Christ, Aaron," she snapped. "A woman can tell about these things."

Aaron nodded. "So let's move on?" he said, glancing at the younger men seated on the sofa. "What did you two find out?"

"Eric O'Neill was met by two men at Gatwick Airport late this morning and taken by car to an estate in Surrey," said the smooth skinned one. "Local pub talk tells us that an old man lives there, has some retainers, or security people on site. He is apparently a complete recluse. There is some suspicion that he may be a holocaust survivor but I doubt that. We would be aware of who he is if that were the case."

"An old man," Aaron said quietly. "Aren't they curious?"

"Likely, but the English accept eccentricity and privacy better than most of us and they seem content with it."

Aaron leaned forward and picked up his wine again. "Tell me, Nathan," he said to the smooth skinned one. "Why do you think they took Eric O'Neill there?"

Nathan looked at Aaron thoughtfully. "I'd assume that these people are connected somehow to the money that was put into O'Neill's Swiss account a few days ago so that makes them Nazis in one form or another. But O'Neill seemed to know nothing about it until he was told, indeed, really nothing about the contents of the account until he arrived there. So I would guess they are meeting with him to brief him."

"Why not just do it in London?" Liselle asked.

"I don't know, but I'd guess that either they want him isolated or the people he is meeting with can't or won't come to London."

Aaron nodded. "Thank you, gentlemen." He stood up and the others rose to their feet. "Liselle, I need to talk to you a little more." The two men left the room and Aaron sat down again.

"I"ll have some wine now, please," Liselle said.

Aaron poured some and handed her the glass. "I need to know more about Eric O'Neill," he said. "What he is like, what he thinks. Anything you can give me."

Liselle took a sip of the wine. Aaron was right, it was marvelous. She leaned back in the chair and stretched her legs out in front of her. She switched the wine glass to her left hand, still feeling a slight throbbing in edge of her right hand where she had struck one of her assailants. "Eric O'Neill is a gentleman. He is kind, caring, courteous, listens well and can be quite charming. He is very bright, shrewd and analytical, but I'm certain you know that from what he's done. He's brave, or at least foolish enough to go after your purse snatcher."

"You sound as though you like him," Aaron interjected.

Liselle felt a slight blush creeping up her throat. "I do like him," she said quickly. "He would appeal to a lot of women. But don't worry, Aaron, I'm not losing my perspective."

"I never thought you would, Liselle," Aaron said. "Your professional reputation precedes you."

Liselle nodded. "What else would you like to know?"

Aaron ran his hand through his thinning grey hair and looked at her again over the top of his glasses. "Did you sleep with him?"

This time Liselle did blush. "You mean have sex with him?"

"That's the usual connotation."

"Of course not," Liselle said. "I was only with him for a day and a half."

"But you could have?"

Liselle thought about the question. She nodded. "Yes, I think so."

"So why didn't you?"

"My task was to learn about him, assess him personally, not screw him," she said. "And I didn't think that doing that would tell me anything I couldn't find out by other means." She paused. "Besides, I was trying to come across as a widowed professional woman on a holiday who meets a widowed attractive man, not as some harlot in heat." She was amazed sometimes how men just didn't get it. How could they run intelligence organizations when they had such a flawed understanding of how women thought?

Aaron nodded. "Thank you," he said. "Now let me tell you how things are going to unfold over the next few hours. When I am finished, you will need to tell me, with complete honesty, if you can continue to work on this project."

"Okay," Liselle replied. She sat up straighter in the chair. She was getting sleepy and the wine wasn't helping.

"There is another person at the Surrey estate that you know," Aaron began. "His name is Jon Falken."

"Jon Falken?" Liselle said. "What the hell is he doing there?"

"We are not entirely certain, but likely the same thing as Eric O'Neill. He arrived in London on Friday and was taken to Surrey yesterday," Aaron replied. "But just hear me out and then you have a decision to make. Okay?"

"Okay."

"We think the Surrey estate is a Nazi safe house of some sort. We are interested in O'Neill and Falken. I will spare you the details but we think they are very likely the children of high ranking Nazis, perhaps members of Hitler's inner circle. Since the old man is meeting with the children of these high ranking Nazis, it follows that he is very likely a high ranking Nazi himself, although at this point we don't know who it could be. We have accounted for most of them. "

"Why would you think Falken and O'Neill were children of high ranking Nazis?"

"Because they were born in Germany in the fall of 1939 and moved from there to the US and Canada in the fall of 1940. Only a few at the very top of the Nazi hierarchy could command the resources necessary to accomplish that. Because Eric O'Neill has a large Swiss bank account with World War II connections, which is to say, with Nazi connections. Jon Falken had a similar account but we were able to intervene and confiscate it. We only discovered O'Neill's account a few days ago."

"Do you know who the parents actually are?"

"No we don't. But we have speculated that one of them might be the son of Eva Braun, the mistress and for the last few hours of her life, the wife of Adolf Hitler." Aaron leaned back in his chair.

"My God," Liselle said softly. "How could that be?"

"Interesting question, since our research has always claimed Hitler was impotent or sterile at the very least. But then what else would it say? An impotent monster was better than the other kind. However, at this point we don't really know."

"Jon Falken," Liselle said quickly.

Aaron looked at her carefully. "Explain."

"Jon is unprincipled, ambitious, deceitful if it suits him. He wants power and control and he will use people to get it. He can be a vicious son-of-a-bitch." She stopped as she realized her voice was rising. She thought of Eric. It just couldn't be Eric.

Aaron nodded. "I see," he said thoughtfully. "That certainly accords with our profile of Colonel Falken."

Liselle set her wine glass on the coffee table. "I just cannot imagine Eric O'Neill as Hitler's son. He is honourable, gracious, kind . . ."

"And perhaps very good at revealing only a part of himself?"

Liselle shook her head in denial. "I don't know," she said. "Of course, I don't know."

"In any case, Liselle," Aaron said. "We are going to meet again in an hour with an assault team. We are going into the estate to extract Falken, O'Neill and the old man and find out what is going on. We will also take what papers and documents we can find."

"I want to be part of the team," Liselle said in a whisper. "I have to be."

CHAPTER SIXTY FIVE

Monday, May 8, 1989 Surrey, England

Eric O'Neill couldn't sleep. The revelations that Bormann had poured on him, Lincoln Carswell and Jon Falken after dinner kept streaming through his mind. And Jon, the man-who-would-be-king. What was he all about? A retired soldier becoming a US congressman. But Eric sensed there was more to it than that. Jon wanted the kind power Bormann was talking about, whether he got it through the US political system or through Bormann's organization, and Eric still didn't have a very clear idea of what that organization was. Perhaps just as well, he thought. The more he learned the less likely it seemed that he would walk away from this place, although, to be fair, there had not been a trace of threat or intimidation. Probably Bormann just could not believe that anyone would turn down an opportunity like this. Lincoln certainly was turning it down. He just didn't give a damn about any of it, as far as he could tell.

Perhaps his father had been right. He should have left the whole business of his origins alone. He didn't seem to be much closer to finding out who his biological parents were than when he had started. Maybe he should quit now and leave. Life in Portage la Prairie, simple as it might be, was developing an appeal. What was Laura up to? It had only been a few days since he had phoned her but it seemed a long time ago. Surreal happenings made it seem longer.

And what was Liselle up to? He had met her, enjoyed his time with her, found her really quite attractive, and then she had vanished, apparently after killing two men in their hotel and spending the rest of the night with him. That seemed nonsensical. Surely there must have been a mix-up of some sort. She didn't seem at all capable of that.

He sat up in bed and stretched forward. He felt stiff. No exercise for most of the last week. Maybe tomorrow there would be time. He stood up. He was thirsty and his stomach grumbled. Turning on the bedroom light, he slipped on a pair of slacks and pulled a polo shirt over his head and did up his shoes. He put a windbreaker around his shoulders. He had felt cold ever since he arrived here. As he turned the handle on his bedroom door he half expected it to be locked but it wasn't. The hallway was dimly lit and as he came to the first corner a security guard stood up and literally snapped to attention.

"Good evening, Mr. O'Neill," he said. "How can I help you."

Eric was startled. The guard stood to one side of the hall and was not blocking his way but it seemed clear that if he didn't answer the question he would not pass. He smiled at the guard. "Good evening," he said. "I'm just having trouble sleeping and I was thinking a glass of milk and a snack would help. Could you direct me to the kitchen?"

"Certainly, sir," the guard said, still standing at attention. "However, I can also have it brought to your room if you wish."

"I think I'd rather just see what there is, if that's okay."

"Of course, sir," the guard replied, and gave Eric directions.

Eric started off and a couple of minutes later was back in the living room area with the glass sun room where he had first met Bormann in the afternoon. He noticed several doors leading off from here and thought back to the guard's directions but he couldn't remember which one to take. Shrugging, he crossed to the nearest one and opened it. He found himself in a short hallway, dimly lit like the others, but with a stronger light coming from a doorway at the end of the hall. He moved forward slowly, confident now that he had taken the wrong door but curious where it led.

As he stepped into the doorway, Martin Bormann looked up at him from behind a large dark wooden desk. He leaned back in the leather chair and it groaned slightly. He stared at Eric for a moment. "Please come in, Eric," he said, smiling. He slipped off his small frameless glasses and set them on the desk. "Spend a few minutes with an old man and his memories."

Eric stepped inside the room and looked around, astonished. He felt as though he had stepped back in time. The only light in the room came from a lamp on Bormann's desk. Heavy drapes covered the wall behind. The shadowy light revealed heavy, dark book shelving lining the other walls, but to his left two large flags hung from short staffs, some brass or gold ornament on the top of each staff. A pair of small floodlights came on suddenly. Bormann must have done it from his desk. The flags were a deep rich red, and although he could not see all the detail in the folds, Eric knew that the black circles and lines in the centres were swastikas. However, it was the huge, gilt-framed portrait between them that drew his attention, a colour portrait of Adolf Hitler taken in his prime, a powerful visionary depiction. He stepped closer.

"Quite a photograph, isn't it?" Bormann said softly.

Eric nodded, mesmerized by the strength and power of it. He pulled his eyes away and turned to Bormann. "I didn't mean to disturb you," he said. "I was on my way to the kitchen and took a wrong turn."

Bormann nodded. "Good," he said. "I couldn't sleep either, but as they say, I will soon have all eternity to sleep." He motioned to a chair on the other side of his desk. "Please sit with me for a little while."

Eric sat down.

"We didn't get off to a good start this evening, Eric," Bormann said. "You seemed horrified at what we've accomplished. I gave you examples that I thought would illustrate the power we have to effect change, to direct the course of events. I sense that you simply did not understand what we are about."

Eric nodded. "I don't doubt the power. I am mystified by the goal, and quite frankly, I am horrified by what you and your organization have done."

"Lest you blame us for all the ills of the world, let me assure you that we are not as destructive as you might think. Let me give you an example. Martin Luther King."

"You were responsible for his assassination, too?"

"No," Bormann said. "We were not. We had nothing to do with it. King was causing the US government no end of grief. They had to deploy all sorts of resources to deal with him. He was a great help to our cause, albeit, unwittingly and certainly unwillingly.

"One last example and I will stop. When the Cold War began to thaw a little in the early sixties we had to prevent that. You will recall the assassination of John F. Kennedy?"

Eric shook his head in disbelief at the enormity of where this was leading.

Bormann continued. "The assassin, Lee Harvey Oswald, was widely regarded as a communist since he had visited the

Soviet Union. He was not. He was just a simple man, easily manipulated. In one of Oswald's notebooks were the names and addresses of Dan Burros and George Lincoln Rockwell. Do you recognize either of those names?"

"Wasn't Rockwell the head of the American Nazi Party in the 1960's?" Eric asked.

"Correct," Bormann said. "Although he had nothing to do with our organization. We used him and later eliminated him. He was what you would call a 'nut case'. Burros as well. He was the editor of their magazine, 'Stormtrooper', a silly, trivial publication."

Bormann sighed. "There has long been a conspiracy theory around the assassination of John Kennedy. Who was responsible is part of it, but a more ephemeral part of the theory deals with the existence of the second assassin. Forensic investigators have been puzzled by the angle of the entry wound and so on, but no one has ever conclusively proven that there was one, nor identified who it might have been. This is surprising because in the art of assassination, if I may call it that, especially if the target is an important one, there is almost always a backup, a second shooter, sometimes known to the primary assassin, sometimes not. The details of the Kennedy assassination are of no consequence, but I can assure you that there was, in fact, a second assassin." Bormann paused and leaned back in his chair. It squeaked slightly as his weight shifted. "I do want to impress on you that we can and have changed history."

Eric sat still, stunned by the revelation, horrified that this pleasant old man could sit and regale him with stories of such horror.

Bormann looked at Eric and shook his head sadly. "You have spent most of your life in the economic sphere. so perhaps I should use other examples, examples that we are not responsible for, incidentally, and ones that may make our ultimate goals a bit clearer for you. Have you ever visited a sweatshop in India or South East Asia?"

Eric shook his head.

"Neither have I," Bormann said quietly. "But members of my staff have and they tell me that they make the slave camps of the Third Reich look like benevolent employers. Women and young children are jammed into fetid holes to sew endless piles of designer clothes for Europeans and North Americans, items like the golf shirt you are wearing, for example.

"Every major government in the underdeveloped world is part of the international trade in heroin, cocaine and other illegal drugs. Have you ever seen a ten year old girl addicted to heroin, selling her body to support her habit, while her pimp looks on?"

Eric shook his head again.

"I have seen film of this. Our agent who took it put himself at some risk when he abducted the girl and turned her over to a convent. Incidentally, he killed the pimp." Bormann stared at Eric intently. "There are tens of thousands of young girls and boys who live like this, not for long, unfortunately."

He paused. "Are you aware that international pharmaceutical companies routinely test drugs in Africa and Asia on diseased populations so that they can work out their worst side effects before they are released in Europe and North America? And these same companies then deny the use of their drugs to the same populations they have tested them on by pricing them beyond the reach of any but the rich."

Eric nodded, wondering where this next line of horror stories was leading. "I have heard of examples of that."

"These are not isolated examples, Eric. These are the normal practices of such companies, whether they are assembling electronic equipment, producing garments, developing drugs or exploiting human weakness. These examples illustrate the standard operating procedures of most of the world. People look back today on what they call the horrors of the Third Reich because it makes them feel righteous. They were not part of what they regard as the murder of six millions Jews. Modern economic exploitation kills more people than that annually."

"Excuse me," Eric interrupted. "I understand that the world has many horrible examples of economic exploitation. The industrial revolution was based on it as was the economic colonization of the underdeveloped world, a prominent example being what historians call the British Empire. However, I'm losing the connection to your organization. What has this got to do with a resurgent Nazi movement?"

Bormann looked at Eric thoughtfully. "Please be patient for a few more moments. I hope I can make it clear." He paused and then continued. "The US collects and destroys surplus food while the children of the world starve. The UN dithers while one tribe of Africans butchers another using weapons sold to them through the government agencies of the industrialized world, and in a truly astonishing leap of logic, your government, the government of Canada, sends your armed forces to these places as UN Peace Keepers, to prevent these people from killing each other. The world is a schizophrenic kind of place."

Eric was getting tired now. Was Bormann trying to justify old slaughters with new ones? "Yes, but where does your organization fit into all this?"

"Order," Bormann said quietly. "These atrocities can only happen in a world of chaos, a world lacking in any form of moral discipline, a world with no goals, no vision, no leadership and no heros."

"And you are going to provide this?"

"No, Eric," Bormann said, his voice barely a whisper. "You are." He looked past Eric at the door behind him. "What is it, Joachim?"

"My apologies, sir," Joachim said, walking quickly across the room. "Our surveillance system is reporting intruders."

CHAPTER SIXTY SIX

Monday, May 8, 1989 Surrey, England

Liselle felt the van slowing and turning to the right. It bumped over something, not a real off-road feeling but they had definitely left the paved secondary road they had been on for the last while. She looked at her watch, and pushed the small button to illuminate it. The red glow showed 3:07am.

There were four others with her and five more in the first van somewhere ahead of them. She knew none of the men but they had apparently all worked together before. At the briefing it had become clear to her that they didn't have enough information, not about the estate, nor the building, nor the location of the people within the building. They were relying on the estate being lightly guarded and not well secured.

She shook her head wondering why they were doing this. They were certainly well equipped but too many things could go wrong. Her job was a simple one. She was to stay back and identify, make sure that they had snatched the right people. It wasn't out of any deference to her gender, the Mossad was surprisingly free of those biases, although she suspected that the assault team was made up of Israeli commandos borrowed from some branch of the military, rather than regular Mossad agents. Still, they had accepted her presence without question.

The van came to a halt and the section leader gave a quick thumbs up as the rear doors opened. They were on the edge of a heavily wooded area. The ten of them gathered quickly in a tight circle.

"As I said in our earlier briefing, I'm not happy about this project," the team leader said softly. "We are going in blind. What little intelligence we have suggests that we will encounter very little resistance. There are a few security guards or maybe they're servants of some kind, and three targets, two men about fifty plus an old man that we're going to snatch. Just because we don't know about their defenses doesn't mean there aren't any. So let's move in expecting strong resistance and let's be careful." He looked around the group. "Any questions?"

There were none. He shone a dim red light on a sketch map of the area and split them into three teams of three. Liselle would stay by a small outbuilding in the woods that would be their rendezvous point after the attack.

They made a final time check and weapons check, then fitted and switched on their night vision goggles and moved off through the woods. Liselle stayed with the team leader and the two commandos who were with him. She had a 9mm Browning automatic strapped to her thigh and carried a standard Uzi submachine gun. She didn't like the Uzi much. Its high rate of fire was devastating but it just lacked any finesse. Her real preference was a sniper's rifle but it wouldn't likely be of much use in tonight's exercise. If she had to carry an assault weapon she preferred a Scorpion. However, this assault was conceived of as close encounter fighting, if indeed there were any fighting at all.

The pale green world revealed by the heavy night vision goggles was sharp and clear and a few minutes after entering the woods they came to the small outbuilding. It had a large overhead door in one end and a small window in one side. The team leader nodded at her and the other three moved forward.

She crept up to the building and peered through the small window. She could see the dim outline of a vehicle, an older Land Rover from the look of it, or a small van, perhaps. She moved back to the door and sure enough, there was a faint set of ruts leading off through the woods, a clear path back to the road, although they hadn't known it was there and likely wouldn't have taken it even if they had. If there was a surveillance system operating, a clear trail like this one would be a certain place to put sensors.

She moved away from the building, and squatted at the base of a large tree, leaning against it for support. It was a somewhat uncomfortable position but she knew if she got really comfortable she would fall asleep.

Eric and Jon, she thought. What would they think of each other? Jon would probably think Eric was some kind of money grubbing stockbroker and would be entirely unable to fathom a two year sojourn on a sailboat, particularly alone. Jon was not personally reflective. He had somehow arrived at answers to life's questions that satisfied him, or more likely had never asked them. Maybe he didn't know there were any questions. She smiled silently at the thought. Eric wouldn't judge Jon so much as be curious about him but he would certainly pick up on Jon's ambition. Everyone who met him did that.

Suddenly there was a burst of light off through the woods toward the manor house. She shoved her night vision goggles up and squinted toward it. It must be from flood lights, not flares, it was too steady and not high enough for flares and it was most certainly not something the assault team was doing.

Moments later she heard bursts of gunfire, at first the light staccato bursts from the Uzis, probably trying to extinguish the flood lights, and then the heavy solid pounding of thirty calibre machine guns, several from the sound of it.

"Jesus," she whispered softly.

CHAPTER SIXTY SEVEN

Monday, May 8, 1989 Surrey, England

Jon Falken was dreaming, an intensely erotic dream. Liselle lay naked on a huge satin-draped bed in front of him. He stood over her as she beckoned to him. Then she changed. She was on a cot in a small thatched hut and she became a child, a Vietnamese child, perhaps ten or eleven, wearing a short yellow cotton dress with small blue flowers on it. He was alone with her although he knew there were others nearby. He could hear gunfire in the distance. He had only moments before the others came. He yanked the short dress up, ripped the small cotton panties down, forced her legs apart and jammed his hand between them. Someone was knocking on the door, he felt a hand on his shoulder and was suddenly awake.

"Colonel Falken." It was one of the security guards, shaking his shoulder. "Come with me, sir. There is nothing to worry about but we are under attack."Jon sat up abruptly and heard the short bursts of gunfire in the distance, small calibre, nine millimetre, probably Uzis, judging by the rate of fire. He slipped out of bed and pulled on a dark jogging suit he had set out for his morning workout. He stuck his feet in the running shoes and as he bent to tie the laces he heard heavier calibre machine guns open up. The sound came from somewhere above him.

He looked up at the guard. "Browning 30 calibre machine guns?"

"Yes sir," the guard replied. "We have four of them mounted in the third story of the manor. They cover all the approaches to the building.""Sensors, too?"

"There are motion sensors in the woods and on the verge of the lawns that alert our security centre to anything entering the grounds."

"Wouldn't the deer or other wildlife trigger the sensors?" Jon asked as he finished tying his shoe laces and stood up.

"There are also infrared cameras."

Jon listened to the 30 cal's for a moment, old, reliable and deadly.

The guard opened the door and they moved down the hallway at a jog. Jon was surprised at how quickly the guard moved even though he was a good thirty pounds overweight. They came around a corner and another guard waved them on. They paused at a closed door and the guard motioned him back, drawing his handgun and cautiously opening the door. Not good field craft, Jon thought. They were looking into the darkened living room area which adjoined the glassed-in sun room. The guard stepped into the room and motioned Jon to follow him just as the glass wall exploded in a thousand fragments hurling the guard back into Jon and knocking him to the floor.

Lincoln Carswell awakened to the muffled sound of gunfire. He lay quietly for a moment. What the Hell was this about? There was a knock on the door and it was pushed open. His darkened room was suddenly illuminated by light from the hallway.

One of the guards stood in the doorway, then stepped inside, closed the door and switched the light on. "Excuse me for bothering you, sir," he said. "Our security system is reporting intruders. We should have the situation contained momentarily. Please get dressed and I will come back for you in a few minutes if it becomes necessary to move to safer quarters."

"Safer quarters?"

"Yes, sir. You are quite safe here for the moment." With that the guard stepped out of the room and closed the door.

Lincoln sat up and looked around the room. Heavy drapes covered the only window in the room but as he recalled it faced into an interior courtyard, so he would be safe enough until the intruders got into there, if they did.

Maybe it was time to get out of Dodge, as the old expression went. He walked to the closet opened his suitcase that was sitting on a small foldable stand. He took out his make-up kit, a wig and set to work.

Eric stared at Martin Bormann in disbelief. "You believe that I will be the leader of this new order?"

Bormann nodded calmly. "Could you close the door, please," Bormann said." Joachim is rarely wrong. This place is not impregnable but it is well protected."

Eric rose and walked to the door. He heard a distant popping noise. It came in small bursts. Gunfire, he wondered? He pushed the heavy door closed. It swung smoothly on well lubricated hinges and clicked solidly into place. He turned back to Bormann. "What's going on?"

"I don't know, Eric," he said. "Perhaps someone has followed you or Jon or Lincoln here, although we tried to make that difficult. Perhaps someone has found out who the mysterious old Jew who lives here really is."

"Old Jew?"

Bormann smiled. "Local rumour has it that I am an elderly Jew, a death camp survivor, who lives as a recluse and who is frightened enough of the real world to keep guards about the place."

Eric nodded. It was a workable ruse. A sudden banging sound came from somewhere above them and Eric involuntarily looked up.

"Those are our weapons," Bormann said. "Courtesy of the British Army surplus. We have machine guns mounted on the third floor which cover all the approaches to the manor." He reached down and retrieved a leather briefcase. Setting it on the desk, he pushed it across to Eric. "Take this, please."

"What is it?"

"The material in the briefcase will tell you about our organization. It will tell you about your mother, too. She is alive and well and living in Portugal."

"Who was my mother? My father?"

Bormann smiled and shook his head. "If I tell you that, young Eric, you might not read the material."

An explosion shook the room. It came from nearby and was followed by short bursts of gunfire. Then silence. Bormann opened a desk drawer, pulled out an envelope and slid it across the table to Eric. "Take this, too, Eric. It is a map and a set of instructions that will lead you out of here and to safety in London. You might require them. If the Israelis overrun the manor, I don't want them to find you here."

"Israelis?" Eric asked. "How the Hell do you know that?"

"Who else?" Bormann said, his voice still calm. "They have been hunting me for forty-four years. No one else really gives a damn anymore. It certainly isn't the British. They only have to pick up the phone."

He stood up and slowly walked across the room to the portrait of Adolf Hitler. He slipped his hand in behind the Nazi flag on the right of the picture. A moment later the huge portrait and the section of wall that it was hanging on swung open to reveal a dark narrow passage. "This is your escape route if you should need it, Eric. Just follow this passage and read the instructions if you have to."

"Why would the Israelis harm me?"

Bormann laughed, the sound was almost merry. "Because if you are here they will believe you are a Nazi and will kill you. Now go into the tunnel and if no one comes to get you in fifteen minutes or so, then follow it out of the estate." Bormann held out his hand. Eric shook it firmly. "Thank you, Eric. It is an honour to have met you."

Eric nodded and released Bormann's hand. As he stepped through the entrance to the passage, two gunshots rang out, close by from the sound of them. He lifted a small flashlight from a clip just inside the entrance. As the door swung shut behind him he heard another shot.

Jon lay quietly in the hallway for a moment, quickly checking himself for wounds. Everything seemed fine except that he noted the unusual quiet and realized the explosion had deafened him, temporarily, at least. He pushed the guard's body off him and touched his hand lightly to the throat searching for a pulse. There was none. He picked up the pistol and peered carefully around the doorframe into the room. In the shadowy light he saw a figure slip silently into the solarium and crouch beside a large urn with some spiky tropical plant growing out of it. He waited. A moment later a second figure scurried past the first, through the shattered glass wall between the living area and the solarium and dropped into a crouch behind one of the heavy old chairs. Still Jon waited. The first figure came through the same opening and moved off to the right, crouching behind another chair. They looked like aliens, the heavy battery operated night goggles pushed up on their foreheads. They certainly hadn't needed them crossing the floodlit grounds and now they could see with the dim light coming from an open door on Jon's right.

The one on the right stood up slowly and moved toward the door where the light was coming from. The second one got into position to cover the first one. Jon stepped quietly into the doorway and aimed the pistol carefully at the second one. A head shot, he thought, they would almost certainly be wearing body armour. He squeezed the trigger gently. The pistol jumped in his hand, its muffled crack confirming that his hearing was coming back. Hollow point rounds, Jon thought, as he saw the commando's head explode with the impact. The other commando spun around and dropped to a crouch by the door as Jon fired again, the impact of the bullet throwing the commando against the door frame. As he fell to the floor, Jon sprinted across the room, crouched beside him. He looked down into his eyes. The commando stared back. Jon saw no fear there, only defiance and fury. Blood was oozing from a wound in his upper arm. He smiled at the man and fired a second shot directly into his forehead.

CHAPTER SIXTY EIGHT

Monday, May 8, 1989 Surrey, England

Martin Bormann stared at the picture of Adolf Hitler, stood and brought his heels together. Slowly he raised his arm, pushing it forward, fingers together, the Nazi salute. "Sieg Heil," he whispered. "Hail Victory." It sounded so hollow in translation. He dropped his arm and shuffled back to his desk. When he touched the small switch on the underside of the top, just by the right hand drawer, the portrait dropped back into darkness. Bormann sat heavily in his chair. "We shall see," he murmured.

It was quiet now. He switched off his desk lamp and swiveled his chair toward the heavily draped window behind his desk. In the darkness he peered out through a small gap in the drapes onto the grounds of the estate. The floodlights illuminated the lawns, the shrubs and everything out to the tree line. About halfway between the manor and the trees there appeared to be a couple of crumpled bodies. He couldn't be sure. Why would they bother after all these years? Did they never give up? The Jews were more paranoid than Hitler. For decades they had invented tales of him roaming about South America and he had never set foot on the continent, nor anywhere in the tropics, full of heat, hurricanes and health hazards he had read somewhere. If they found him it would only take a couple of questions for them to decide he was not a Jew. But that didn't seem likely tonight.

And what would they do with Eric if they found out about him? Or Jon? Or Lincoln? Eric, Jon and Lincoln. An interesting problem. Eric had the characteristics he needed to assume the leadership of the organization, but he didn't have the interest. Jon had the interest but his drive for personal power was just not compatible with what the organization needed. Lincoln just didn't care. It would sort itself out or not as the case might be. He stifled a yawn and let the drapes fall closed. He had done what he could.

Eric shone the flashlight down the tunnel. A couple of metres further on it turned into a narrow stone staircase leading downwards. If this was an escape route perhaps now was a good time to take it. Bormann had given him the means to leave and if there were Israelis running about the manor, they were hunting Nazis and probably wouldn't bother with the niceties of checking his political affiliations. He moved to the staircase and shone the light down. He could see the bottom but it was about twenty feet down. He felt his heart beating harder, his breathing speeding up.

He had never been claustrophobic but by the time he got down the stairs he was beginning to wonder. The staircase was old, narrow and not equipped with any kind of hand rail. At the bottom it turned into an equally narrow stone-lined tunnel with a few inches clearance on either side and a couple above his head. The air was cool and musty and as he shone the light forward he was surprised to note there were no cobwebs. Someone must sweep the tunnel regularly, he thought. Or perhaps it was just too toxic down here for insects. He smiled grimly and moved carefully forward about twenty metres by his best estimate, and then the tunnel turned sharply left and was blocked by a heavy steel door. He tried the handle and it swung open easily.

The stone tunnel changed into what looked like a large galvanized steel culvert about eight feet in diameter. As he stepped forward the heavy door swung closed behind him and clicked solidly into place. He turned and shone the light on it. There was no handle on this side, no way back. He closed his eyes for a moment and forced himself to breathe deeply and slowly. He opened his eyes and shone the light down the tunnel. It disappeared into the distance. A culvert, Eric thought. Did that mean that it carried water?

Jon Falken removed the Uzi from the dead attacker's shoulder and stood up. He stepped into the corridor and as he touched the light switch, everything went dark. He listened to the silence, still uncertain how much of his hearing had returned, but the 30 cals above him had stopped and the small arms fire from outside had ceased. He moved over to the shattered glass wall and stared out across the floodlit grounds of the estate. He shook his head. They must have been insane to have tried crossing a killing ground like that, but the lights would not have come on until they were part way across.

There was a slight movement at the edge of the tree line. He stared intently at it. It looked like one man dragging another so at least a couple of them had survived. The floodlights went out, plunging the estate into darkness. Jon hesitated a moment and then sprinted out through the shattered wall, running fast, directly toward the movements he had just seen. If they saw him coming at all he would be a dark running figure and they would assume he was one of them, coming back out of the manor house. About halfway across Jon swore. He was getting sloppy. He remembered the night vision goggles that the two intruders he had shot had been wearing.

Lincoln Carswell had waited for the security guard to return and then thought, Screw it! I'm getting out of here. He left his room and made his way slowly down the dimly lit hallway. He was heading toward the central area of the house. Once there, he could find the kitchen, the keys to the cars and the garage.

The earlier gunfire had ceased and it was now eerily quiet. As he rounded a corner he saw a body ahead of him lying in the doorway that led into the glassed-in area where he had first met Martin Bormann. He paused for a moment but there was no sound or movement. He reached the body, one of the guards, judging by the uniform, and knelt beside it. He saw his holster was empty. He rolled the guard onto his side, extracted his wallet and opened it. He quickly counted 70 pounds. Not a lot but it would have to do until he could change some American dollars to pounds.

He stood up, stuffed the bills in his pocket and glanced around the corner into the glassed-in area. Two more bodies lay crumpled on the floor, both in camouflage dress, night vision goggles lying on the floor beside the first one. He watched them for a moment but neither moved. He walked quickly across the room, crouched beside the first body and removed a pistol from a belt holster, a Glock nine mil, a weapon he was familiar with. He stood up, clicked off the safety, and moved through the dining room toward the kitchen.

CHAPTER SIXTY NINE

Monday, May 8, 1989 Surrey, England

Eric had come to the end of the long galvanized pipe. A set of wooden stairs led upward. He sat down on the bottom step. He was sweating and breathing hard in spite of the cool air and only the gentle exertion of walking slowly. He was scared. He was in a long tunnel somewhere under the grounds of the old manor, likely under the wooded area by now if his sense of distance and direction was accurate at all. He couldn't go back the way he had come and he had seen no other way out until now. The temptation to run up the wooden staircase and out the door at the top was almost overwhelming. But what if there wasn't a door at the top, or perhaps only a door like the one at the other end of the tunnel, one that only opened from the other side.

But surely Martin Bormann would not go to the trouble of bringing him here, briefing him and then burying him in a tunnel. Still, Bormann's instructions had been to wait in the tunnel for fifteen minutes and then to follow it out as an escape route if no one came to get him. He had not followed those instructions.

He tore the end off the large manilla envelope that Bormann had given him and pulled out the contents, shining his flashlight on them. There was a road map of southern England and a city of London street map with a small slip of paper containing a phone number, stapled to one corner of the London map. Some set of instructions, Eric thought. He put the London map with the phone number back in the envelope and spread the road map open on his knee. After a few moments he found a small "X" on the map and a highlighted route into London. He refolded the map carefully with the "X" on top.

Let's find out what's next, he thought as he stood and started carefully up the stairs.

Liselle had left her position by the small outbuilding moments after the floodlights had come on and had moved carefully from tree to tree toward the edge of the woods staying well back in the cover of the trees. What she had seen was appalling. The three teams had spread out along the edge of the tree line and had approached the manor from three different points, racing across the open ground toward the cover of the house, a tactic that had been a dismal failure.

She counted six bodies strewn across the lawn. Where were the other three? As she swept her eyes over the scene there was an explosion on a wall of the manor directly across from her vantage point. As the debris settled she could see it must have been some kind of solarium or glassed in sunroom so maybe the other three were inside. They must have smashed the glass and tossed in a hand grenade. They wouldn't have used their C2 on glass. The machine guns from the manor had ceased firing and it was silent. Then some muffled shots from inside the manor and silence again. The floodlights went out plunging the scene into darkness.

⸻

Jon Falken kept running. Without the night vision goggles they would see him coming as clearly as if he were running in daylight and as soon as he got close they would know he was not one of them. He veered to his right, away from the spot where he had seen the movement. He strained his eyes against the darkness, trying to sort out the detail of the woods in front of him, waiting for the burst of gunfire, praying that their moment of indecision would last long enough for him to get to the cover of the woods.

Then suddenly he was there, a tree looming in front of him. He grabbed it and spun around it to stop, then crouched low in the underbrush and listened. His breathing sounded loud and harsh but he knew it would subside in moments. He looked back across the lawn to the manor house, faintly silhouetted against the night sky and tried to estimate how far he had diverged from the point where he had seen the movement. He crawled back onto the grass and began worming his way along the verge of the trees, too many twigs to snap the other way. He stopped every few feet and listened. It had been a long time since he had been in combat. He felt alive again, in a way he hadn't felt in years, felt the adrenaline surging through his body. God dammit, it was good to be back.

⸻

Liselle slipped her night vision goggles back down and saw a body nearby that she had missed before. It moved and then started to crawl slowly toward the edge of the woods. She watched for a moment and sprinted out the few metres to the wounded commando and dragged him back to the edge of the woods. It was the team leader. He had been hit in the right shoulder and lower right leg. He was conscious but bleeding badly. She pushed her night vision goggles up and quickly checked the wounds. He would not make it and she couldn't take him with her. He moaned.

Liselle glanced up toward the manor as she felt for a morphine ampoule on the commando leader's body. Someone was running out of the house toward her. Maybe one more survivor. She jabbed the syringe into the commando's shoulder and pressed the plunger. She pulled it out and moved her night vision goggles down again, glancing toward the running figure. He had changed course. She could see him clearly now, a pale green running man in a jogging suit, carrying an Uzi. Jesus Christ, she thought, he's not one of ours. She snatched up her own Uzi and brought it up just as the figure disappeared into the trees.

She pulled out her own morphine ampoule, pushed it into the commando's shoulder and pressed the plunger. Combined with the two wounds and heavy bleeding, it should be enough to kill him. It was the best she could do.

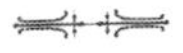

Somewhere ahead Jon heard the trace of a sound, a movement in the grass or the brushing of cloth against a tree, a night animal scurrying home perhaps. No, it wasn't an animal. There had been a moan this time, closer than he had thought. They would know by now that whoever had run into the woods was not one of them. Had they left a wounded man? Not likely in this sort of attack. They would take their wounded with them or kill them if they couldn't. They would carry out their dead, too, if they could. So what was the moan about?

He lay still and listened. He had only sound and the faintest of light to guide him. They had night vision goggles to spot him. So he would just have to be better. He relaxed and looked ahead, keeping his eyes as unfocused as he could. His peripheral vision caught a slight movement in the edge of the woods about fifty feet in front of him. He willed himself not to look directly at it since he would spot it better with his peripheral vision. There it was again. He froze completely and then with infinite care he slowly brought the Uzi to bear on the spot. He held it firmly and closing his eyes against the burst of light from the muzzle blast gently squeezed the trigger. The blast of gunfire ended abruptly as he released the trigger and rolled into the undergrowth. He lay there, utterly still, his face pressed into the grass waiting for a response. There was nothing but silence.

Eric paused on the landing at the top of the stairs and examined the door. It was another solid metal door but with a handle and a dead bolt. He turned the dead bolt, held his breath as he tried the handle. The door swung open smoothly and easily and he stepped forward into a small garage. His flashlight revealed an older model Land Rover. He heard the door click shut and turned but there was only a wooden wall behind him now, no evidence of a door at all.

The Land Rover was the classic pale blue, clean but not shiny. He opened the right-hand door, dropped his briefcase in the back and slid into the driver's seat. The key was in the ignition and on the dash board in front of him was a small black garage door opener. Pulling the door shut behind him, he switched off the flashlight and sat quietly for a moment. He could wait here and walk back to the estate when it got light. He looked at his watch and saw it was a bit after 4:00am. First light would be along shortly.

He really just wanted out of here, out of the whole mess. He wasn't a Nazi, he didn't want the power or whatever Bormann was offering, assuming, of course, that he wasn't just a senile old man with delusions of some past grandeur. He just wanted out. For the moment, he had a vehicle, a map and an escape route. He did not have his passport but he did have his wallet with his driver's license, cash and a couple of credit cards. He also had a contact number in London. However, that would put him right back where he didn't want to be. There was the Canadian High Commission in London if he could get there, which might be difficult if someone were intent on stopping him. He shook his head. One step at a time. He pushed the button on the garage door opener.

Lincoln Carswell opened the door into the kitchen, scanning it quickly, the Glock held steadily in front of him. The kitchen was empty. He crossed it quickly, pausing by the doorway leading to the four car garage. He found a small rack with keys where he had remembered it when he arrived. He felt for a light switch and flicked it on. The kitchen lit up, he pulled all four sets of keys from their hooks and turned off the light.

He pushed open the door that led into the garage. It was dark. He waited a moment to let his eyes adjust and felt his way to the first car. It was the Mini. As he opened the driver's door the interior light came on. He slid in, pushing the key into the ignition and setting the pistol on the passenger seat. He tossed the other three sets of keys into the back seat and closed the car door. No sense in leaving the keys to a chase vehicle. He hoped the English put garage door openers on the sun visors like Americans did. He found it and pushed the button. An overhead light came on and the garage door began to rise. He started the engine and backed out, spinning the steering wheel hard, braking, shifting and then accelerating down the long driveway.

CHAPTER SEVENTY

Monday, May 8, 1989 Surrey, England

Martin Bormann leaned back in his leather chair. It creaked comfortingly. He was tired, exhausted but exhilarated, too. He had watched as the small red light appeared on his desk console telling him that Eric had gone through the first security door in the tunnel. So he had decided to run. Well, he had the information he needed to make a decision, if he read it, of course, but if he didn't, then that was his decision. In a peculiar way he trusted Eric, an uncommon reaction, he thought. After a lifetime of manipulation and subterfuge, he rarely trusted anyone, and it surprised him that he trusted Eric with the information he had given him, whether he chose to use it or not.

He opened a bottom drawer in his desk and pulled out a bottle of schnapps and a small glass. He carefully filled it and set the bottle on the desk. Raising his glass in a silent toast, he tipped the liquid into his mouth and swallowed it. He smiled and set the glass down. What his doctor couldn't see surely wouldn't hurt him.

What to do now? Eric was on his way somewhere or nowhere as the case might be. Lincoln was still here, probably wondering how to get safely back to Philadelphia and on with his painting, or, if the rumour were true, perhaps thinking of getting in touch with Marianne Falken. She was in London but he wasn't sure whether Lincoln knew that or not.

Jon was still here, too, dangerous and power hungry. He frowned. For years he had watched Jon and had been well pleased with how he had developed. Now that he had met the man, gotten a sense of him, he just wanted him gone, out of the movement. Bormann had spent years of his life managing one psychopath and was not about to deal with another if he could help it. But what could he do about Jon?

As he picked up the bottle of schnapps again and poured himself another glass, he saw a second small red light blink on the console. Eric had left the tunnel.

Liselle propped the dying commando leader up against the base of a tree. He was unconscious now from the morphine. She tried to set him so he would have a silhouette against the trees and then she crawled quietly back into the woods, working her way toward the small outbuilding. She knew there would be no other commandos returning so her job now was to get out. She would take one of the vans, disable the other.

She froze as she heard a slight movement behind her on the edge of the woods. Surely whoever had run from the house couldn't have reached the commando yet. As she peered over her shoulder toward the edge of the trees there was no longer any silhouette of a man. The noise must have been the commando leader falling over. She was turning her head back when a blast from an Uzi ripped through the night.

⁂

Jon Lifted his head slowly and peered through the underbrush, then carefully crawled back out onto the grass. This time he moved forward quickly, the Uzi held in front of him at the ready. He wasn't sure how many rounds it had left, likely not many so he wouldn't be able to rely on it for more than a short burst or two.

He paused. Off to his left, somewhere in the woods, he heard a movement, he listened and heard it again. Someone was moving, fast by the sound of it, but there was no point in shooting into the trees. The movement was away from him. At least one of them was escaping.

He started crawling again. Achieve one objective at a time. A couple of yards in front of him there was a break in the geometry of the trees, an unnatural outline, a body slumped against the base of a tree. He paused, then moved into a crouch and sprinted forward. There had been time to see him and kill him if someone had been there to do it. He knelt beside the body running his hands quickly over the equipment, two more magazines for the Uzi and a Glock nine millimetre pistol. The body took a ragged breath. One still alive. He might make it for interrogation. Jon continued his search of the body. He touched something around the attacker's neck, his night goggles. Jon smiled exultantly as he pulled them off.

Then somewhere in the woods he heard a different sound. A hum followed by an oddly familiar clattering sound.

⁂

Liselle crouched beside the small outbuilding where she had waited before the attack. She was startled by the noise of the large garage door opening. Someone had gotten into the garage and was about to drive the Land Rover away. She pushed the "how" and "who" questions aside as she stepped to the edge of the door. The starter growled and the engine turned over and caught. She was on the passenger side and as the vehicle moved out she grasped the handle and yanked the door open, swinging herself into the passenger seat in one easy motion. She levelled her Uzi at the driver as she pulled the door shut behind her. "Drive," she ordered and jammed the barrel of the machine pistol viciously into the driver's ribs.

⁂

Jon pulled the night vision goggles over his head, touched the small switch to turn them on, and smiled as the darkness of the night vanished and a pale green world appeared. He scanned the woods ahead of him and began moving swiftly, silently from one tree to the next. He heard a car start and moments later heard it begin to move. A small building loomed ahead of him, about the size of a large suburban single car garage. He moved to one side as the vehicle emerged and raised the Uzi taking rough aim at the driver's door. He squeezed the trigger.

⁂

Liselle gasped in surprise as she found herself staring into Eric's face, contorted with fear and surprise, frozen in an adrenaline rush. The only emotion missing was recognition.

"Drive, God dammit," she shouted at him.

He pushed the accelerator down, snapped on the headlights and the Land Rover shot forward, bouncing unevenly over the narrow, rutted path, turning sharply and then heading off through the trees.

Jon felt the Uzi jump in his hand, a short burp, as it spewed out its last two rounds. He swore softly as he ripped the empty magazine off and jammed a new one into place. As he raised it the world turned white, washed out by the Landrover's headlights. He knocked the goggles up and raised the Uzi again loosing a long burst of fire at it as it turned sharply away from him. He raced after it and as he came to the turn in the trail, emptied the magazine down the narrow defile in the trees.

"Son of a bitch." He threw the Uzi to the ground, knowing his last burst of fire was pure frustration. He caught a red glow from the tail Lights as the vehicle got to the road and then it disappeared. "Shit." He knelt and picked up the Uzi, pulling the goggles back down.

Eric jammed on the brakes as the Land Rover broke out of the woods and he saw a small embankment in front of him. He pressed the accelerator again and it easily mounted it.

"Turn left," came the terse command from the passenger seat.

He did as he was told and wheeled the Land Rover left onto a narrow paved road. Trees lined both sides of the road heightening the sense of speed. From the corner of his eye he could see his new companion still holding the gun steadily on him. His heart was pounding and his hands were shaking slightly on the wheel but it seemed for the moment, at least, he was going to survive.

"You don't recognize me, do you, Eric?"

The voice was feminine and familiar. He glanced at her. Black clothes, tight fitting black hood, camouflage paint on her face. He looked back at the road. Still, the voice was familiar. "Liselle," he said, recognition flashing into his mind. He heaved a sigh of relief and then was hit by fear again. Another glance told him the gun was still as steady as ever. "What the hell is going on?"

CHAPTER SEVENTY ONE

Monday May 8, 1989 Surrey, England

Jon stopped at the edge of the woods beside the body of the commando he had taken the Uzi and the night vision goggles from. The commando was dead. Interrogation might have revealed something but was no longer an option. He stood up and moved out of the woods and onto the lawn, his hands empty and raised, the 9mm pistol stuck into the waist band of his jogging pants, the Uzi on a sling around to his neck. He had dropped the night vision goggles beside the dead commando he had taken them from. He didn't need them anymore in the first light of dawn, but he also didn't want to be mistaken for a surviving attacker and get shot. Some of the security people didn't seem all that bright and he was dressed in a black jogging suit.

However, as he walked across the lawn no one accosted him. He knelt by the crumpled bodies of two of the dead attackers. Same equipment as the one on the edge of the woods.

That body had been a decoy propped up to slow him down. He wondered why the retreating commando hadn't used it to ambush him. Maybe he was the last one and didn't want to risk getting pinned down in a fire fight with first light coming. He wondered who the hell these people were. No doubt Bormann would know, or Joachim.

He stood up and walked toward the shattered glass of the solarium where he had run out of the house only minutes ago, it seemed, but a glance at his watch told him he had been gone almost forty minutes. After the Land Rover had driven off he had followed it out to the road and discovered two mini vans, rental units from the look of them, both abandoned. He hadn't touched either one in case they were wired with explosives.

He had made a sweep back through the woods, checked out the small garage where the Land Rover had been parked but it hadn't yielded anything either. That was a real puzzle. Why the hell would there be a Land Rover stowed in a garage in the middle of a forest? And why would the attackers have a key to it? More questions to ask. Bloody slack security arrangements around here, it seemed.

He listened to the sounds of the early morning, birds chirping, a breeze rustling the leaves of the trees behind him. Glancing up he saw a small early-morning hawk drifting in a slow circle watching. Maybe it was a late-night owl. He didn't know much about birds. He breathed deeply. The morning air was fresh and cool. He smiled. It was good to be alive.

He stepped carefully over the slabs of broken glass that littered the floor of the solarium. The bodies of the two attackers he had shot earlier had been removed. He checked the hallway where he and the security guard had entered the living room area and the guard's body was gone, too. They must have a morgue in here somewhere, Jon thought grimly. He glanced out onto the lawn again and saw three of the security people near the two bodies he had encountered on his way back in. One of them was armed and remained standing while the other two rolled one of the bodies on to a stretcher.

"Colonel Falken," Joachim said, entering the room from one of the hallways. He closed the door behind him. "We were worried about you. We couldn't find you for a while."

Jon nodded. "I'm fine," he said. He saw that Joachim was wearing black slacks, likely the pants to his suit, and a black turtle neck sweater. He carried a pistol in his left hand. "Who the hell were these people?" Jon asked.

"Israeli commandos, I think, or perhaps Mossad agents," Joachim replied. "Hard to tell, really. But you survived, uninjured from the look of it."

"Yes," Jon said. "One of your security guards was taking me somewhere and they blew out the solarium wall and came through it just as we entered this room."

"Ah," said Joachim. "And you shot the intruders?"

"Yes."

"I wondered," Joachim said. He seemed relieved. "The premises are secure again. We have to clean things up as I expect the local constable will be along in an hour or so to see what the ruckus was all about. He called a few minutes ago and said someone had phoned in a complaint about noise." Joachim smiled slightly and shook his head. "The English love understatement."

Jon let the heat of the shower pour over his shoulders and down his back. He stretched the tension away. He was still exhilarated but he felt content, like he had done a good day's work, and as a soldier, he told himself, he had. He turned and let the water course down the front of his body. He turned up the heat a little and breathed the steam. He felt cleansed, purified.

As he was drying himself off, he thought he heard running footsteps in the hallway, and voices. He wrapped the towel around himself and walked quickly to the door and pulled it open, but the hallway was quiet and empty now. He closed the door and locked it while he got dressed. He put the pistol into his pocket and a few minutes later left his room and made his way back to the central part of the house. It seemed quiet and deserted.

In the dining room he discovered a pot of coffee and a tray of pastries. He suddenly realized he was quite hungry. He poured the steaming coffee into a large china mug and picked up one of the pastries and bit into it, some kind of jam or preserves inside dribbled out onto his fingers. He licked it off and quickly ate the rest. He picked up a second one and ate it, too.

He added some cream to his coffee, took a sip and strolled out of the dining room back into the living room area adjacent to the shattered solarium. The broken glass had been swept up, the shards removed from the frames and except for a gentle breeze wafting into the room it was hard to tell the glass was missing. The early morning sun lit up the grounds, streaking it with long shadows from the tree line on the eastern side. A doorway on his right opened and one of the security guards stepped into the room.

"Good morning, sir," he said and stood aside as a second guard came through with a dolly containing three large cardboard file boxes. He pushed it across the room and into one of the hallways. The other guard dutifully closed the door behind them.

Jon walked toward the door where the guards had come from and pulled it open. Strolling down a short hallway he came to an open door on his right and peered in. It was a large room, a study or an office, the walls lined with dark wooden bookcases. Joachim was seated in a leather chair behind a desk and was pulling a few things out of a drawer. Jon noticed a liqueur bottle and a small glass on the desk.

"A bit early for a drink, isn't it?" he asked, taking another sip of his coffee.

Joachim looked up, his face a mask of tension. "I beg your pardon, Colonel? A drink?"

"The bottle and the glass," Jon said, smiling and walking into the room.

Joachim continued staring at him blankly.

At the edge of the desk, Jon pointed to the bottle and Joachim looked down.

"Oh," he said. "Yes, I see what you mean. Sorry, I didn't understand."

"Is something wrong?" Jon asked.

With a long sigh, Joachim leaned back in the chair. It groaned slightly with the shift in his weight. He looked up at Jon and shook his head slowly. "We knew it was coming," he said softly. "But still, one is never quite prepared."

"I thought your defenses were very well prepared," Jon said. "You were alerted in time and repelled them."

Joachim shook his head. "Not the attack, Colonel," he whispered. "Reichsleiter Bormann is dead."

CHAPTER SEVENTY TWO

Monday, May 8, 1989 West of London, England

Lincoln drove the Mini hard for the first few miles, wanting to get some distance from the Surrey estate. What a madhouse, he thought some old geezer claiming to be Martin Bormann, alive forty odd years after he was supposed to have died. Maybe he was Bormann, maybe he wasn't. Tell someone who cares. And dreaming, or maybe hallucinating was a better word, about some Fourth Reich rising from its ashes to become a world force again. What insanity. And Eric O'Neill, a nice guy, but how the hell did he get involved? Jon Falken was weird. He took all that shit seriously. At least O'Neill had listened and called it nonsense.

He slowed as he drove through a village, down shifting smoothly. He braked hard and swerved slightly as a dog ran across the road in front of him. He drove on, more slowly now. Nice sleepy little town, he thought, as he passed a few more old stone buildings. He accelerated and shifted up as he left the town. The sun peeked over the horizon, and then burst across the landscape in front of him, lighting a low stone wall on his right, casting long shadows from bushes on his left. He pulled the small sun visor down and glanced again in the rear view mirror. There was no sign of pursuit. He would drive the car for a while longer but keep his eyes open for a train station. There were supposed to be commuter trains all over the place heading into London and it might not be long before the car and its license number were in the hands of the local constabulary.

The next question was what to do when he did reach London. Catch a flight to Philadelphia. Would that present any problems since there would be no record of him having entered England? Perhaps he would have to do as the English were reputed to do, muddle through.

Marianne Falken was in London, staying at the Raphael Hotel, if he remembered correctly. Could he safely contact her there? Would Jon Falken be leaving Surrey as well and returning to his hotel? He didn't want to encounter Jon again, especially not in the company of his wife.

⁂

The glare of the rising sun was streaming in under the visor of the Land Rover. Liselle had been silent for the last while, glancing back down the road behind them every few minutes. At least she had quit pointing the gun at him and that was an improvement. Eric watched the small steps she had taken to subtly reassert her feminine side. She had pulled the black hood off and fluffed her hair up with her fingers. Then she had tried to wipe the camouflage paint off her face with some tissues from a package in the glove box but there were still smudges and streaks that had resisted her efforts.

She held the Uzi on her lap and began to strip it. Then she rolled down the window and threw one of the pieces out into the shallow ditch that ran beside the road. She continued doing this every few minutes until she had thrown all the pieces away.

The secondary highway was still narrow as they passed through small villages and hamlets, the stone pubs and churches looking like they were built to last forever. He slowed as they rounded a corner and entered another village, a small sign announcing it was Lower Beeding. At least the sun would be out of his eyes for a little while. Glancing at his watch, he saw it was a few minutes before six. "When this is all over, Liselle," he said, trying to keep his voice conversational. "It would be interesting to drive around this area. . . like we did in Ireland." He glanced at her.

She looked at him, her eyes expressionless. "Yes," she said softly. "In a simpler life, it would be."

"Are you going to tell me what's going on? Where we're going? What's happening?"

"We're going to London," she said. "If you have any hope at all of surviving this, Eric, I am it. Just trust me."

Eric glanced back at her and smiled grimly. "What's my second choice?"

She smiled for the first time. "You don't have one." She slumped back against the seat. "Neither do I at the moment."

Eric began to accelerate as they left the village. On the outskirts there was a service station, its large green and white BP sign lit up.

"Pull in there," Liselle said. "Don't stop at the pumps, pull around to the side and turn off the engine."

Eric slowed and swung the Land Rover into the parking area. A couple of small trucks were at the gas pumps. He braked the vehicle to a stop and turned off the ignition.

"Eric," Liselle said, turning to face him. "This is where the trust part comes in. I can't tell you what is going on but I want to impress on you that you have wandered into a situation that has put your life in danger."

"I was just looking . . ."

"Eric," Liselle said sharply. "Listen to me. There are people who want to know a lot more about you and what you are up to."

"But I'm not up to anything," Eric said. "I'm just looking for information on my background."

"There are people who will kill you for that information."

"Who would do that? Who are they?" Eric felt fear like a knot in his stomach.

"It doesn't matter who they are," Liselle said. "I can only tell you that I am your single hope of staying alive. I am going into the ladies room and get cleaned up. You can walk away and be gone by the time I get out but that wouldn't be a wise decision."

Eric stared at her wordlessly.

"Do you believe me?"

Eric nodded. "Yes, I believe you, Liselle." He stared at her intently, trying to assess what she was telling him. "We were becoming friends and now I don't know what we are." He shrugged. "I guess you're my saviour or my guardian or something like that. I'm trying to work out our new relationship."

Liselle shook her head. "Don't try, Eric," she said. "Just trust me." She reached over and pulled the keys out of the ignition, swung the passenger door open and was gone.

Lincoln down-shifted the Mini as he entered a town, a bit bigger than most he had come through. He was enjoying driving the little car, powerful, responsive and it handled like a dream. He saw a red sign with black lettering, Train Station, and a couple of blocks further on, an arrow and a directional sign. He turned off the main road and drove slowly into a large parking lot. On the far side of the lot there was a low red brick building, the train station, he assumed. A sign read, London Road, Guildford.

He gathered his small suitcase from the rear of the car, locked the doors and walked toward the station. About half way there he stopped and returned to the car. Opening the driver's door, he put the key back in the ignition and left the door unlocked. He wasn't sure about the habits of English car thieves but in Philadelphia an unlocked car with the keys in it would last about five minutes.

At the station he found the men's room and went in. He checked his disguise. His grey wig gave him an unkempt look, reinforced by the wrinkles in his blazer. He looked a bit tired and seedy. He used the facilities and walked out onto the platform to check the London timetable. Glancing at his watch, he saw a train was due in fifteen minutes. He walked back into the station to the ticket counter and purchased a ticket for London, Waterloo Station. Then he sat down on a bench and picked up a discarded newspaper. He opened it and watched as a number of people came on to the platform, likely locals who knew the schedule.

Eric opened the glove box and checked the contents, just papers which he didn't bother to examine. He pulled open the ashtray. It was full of coins. He sat quietly for a moment, then scooped the coins out of the ashtray and pushed the driver's door open. The morning air was fresh and cool. He walked into the petrol station. The attendant was chatting to one of the truck drivers, the other driver was smoking a cigarette and reading a paper. Eric walked to a cooler in the corner of the small room. He removed two soft drinks and looked at the green bottles. "Lilt", mango and mandarin. He had never heard of it. As he approached the counter, the attendant glanced at him as Eric handed him some coins.

"Sorry, Yank," the attendant said with a good natured grin. "We haven't got your coffee habit here yet."

Eric returned the smile. "No problem." He wondered how the attendant knew he wasn't British. Likely his clothes, but did he really stand out that much as "foreign"?

He climbed back into the Land Rover and opened one of the soft drink bottles. He took a drink. It was cold, refreshing and sparkling in his mouth, the mango and orange flavours making a nice combination. One of the drivers came out of the station and climbed into his truck just as Liselle opened the passenger door. Eric looked at her and took in the tousled black hair, the fresh scrubbed look of her face without a trace of makeup, a complete study in innocence. She pulled off a vest and tossed it in the back. It landed with a thump.

"Protective vest," she said. "Some people call them bullet proof."

"Oh," Eric said, feeling strangely shaken .

She leaned over and touched his arm. "They are kind of like your waterproof watch, which is really only water resistant. They are bullet resistant, not bullet proof." She smiled at him, some warmth back in her expression as she pushed the key back into the ignition.

Eric nodded. "Bullet resistant," he said quietly, handing her a soft drink. "That's an interesting idea." He started the engine, backed up and drove out onto the road.

"I know you must be confused by all this," Liselle said. The bottle made a small hiss as she opened it. "Thank you for not running away back there."

They drove in silence for a while, sipping the cold drinks, watching the small fields go by, the trees and low stone fences by the road producing a welcome sense of order.

"So was Ireland all just a set up?" Eric asked. "The purse snatching? The drink in the bar? Dinner?"

Liselle was silent for a moment. "It started out that way."

"And?"

"Don't go there, Eric," she said softly. "There is just no point in it. You are a kind, caring, honourable man caught up in some wretched circumstances you know nothing about and over which you have no control."

"That isn't what I was asking, Liselle."

"I know what you were asking," she replied. She was silent for a moment and then let out a long sigh. "Ireland was a set up. However, I met you, I liked you and I had a lot of fun being with you. Is that what you want to know?"

"Thank you," he said. "I had a lot of fun, too."

"Just let it go for now, Eric."

He slowed for the next town. As they entered the outskirts it looked a bit bigger than ones they had recently passed through.

Liselle was watching the streets intently and then suddenly said. "Turn right at the next corner."

Eric did as he was told and about two blocks along the street a parking area with a couple of dozen vehicles in it and room for several times that many.

"We'll leave the Land Rover here," Liselle said. "And take a commuter train into London."

She pulled a small black plastic bag out of a pocket in the leg of her slim fitting dark green jumpsuit. The line of the legs was broken by two zippered cargo pockets, one on each leg. She drew a small pistol from a holster strapped to her right leg and put the handgun into the plastic bag. Then she popped open the glove box and pulled out a slim booklet for the Land

Rover and dropped it into the bag as well. She saw Eric's curious look. "I need to break up the silhouette of the gun in the bag." She unstrapped the holster from her leg and handed it to Eric. "Toss this in the first trash barrel we come to."

"Are we going to need a gun?"

Liselle shook her head. "I doubt it, but I don't want to leave it here." She turned and pulled the vest back into the front seat. Turning away from Eric, she took a few things out of small pockets on the vest and put them into the cargo pocket on her left leg. "How much money do you have?" She put the bag with the gun in the right cargo pocket.

"I'm not sure," he said. "About two hundred pounds, I think, plus some Euros."

"That'll do for the moment but we'll have to get more in London." She opened the door of the Land Rover. "Don't lock it and leave the keys in the ignition. With any luck, someone will steal it."

Eric got out of the Land Rover and retrieved the briefcase from behind the driver's seat. Liselle handed him the vest. "Toss this with the holster."

As they walked toward the station to get their tickets, Liselle put her arm through Eric's and gave it a squeeze. "Look happy, Honey," she said softly. "We're supposed to be together." She slid her hand down his arm and slipped her hand into his.

Eric paused by a large trash barrel near the steps leading up to the platform and dropped the vest and the holster into it. He felt the softness of her small delicate hand in his and squeezed back.

CHAPTER SEVENTY THREE

Monday, May 8, 1989 Surrey, England

"Dead?" Jon asked. "How could that be? The attackers never got into the building except for the two by the solarium."

Joachim sighed. "A heart attack, Colonel."

Jon shook his head incredulously. The most hunted Nazi war criminal in the world had evaded capture for forty four years and had just escaped an Israeli assault only to die of a heart attack.

"He had been ailing for some time," Joachim said. "He knew he didn't have long. However, these things, expected or not, still come upon us as a surprise."

"Where did it happen?"

"Right here," Joachim replied. "Right in this chair. I came in about an hour ago and found him. Since then we have just been carrying out his instructions." His eyes were wet as he looked up at Jon and shook his head sadly. "Reichsleiter

Bormann was the quintessential bureaucrat right to the end. Beyond his death, really."

"So what now?"

Joachim sighed and stood up slowly. "Some housekeeping things first, as he called them. We have long had an arrangement with a sympathetic local undertaker to dispose of the Reichsleiter's remains when that became necessary. He has no idea of the identity of the body. We also have an incinerator on the estate to dispose of records and other materials."

"I see," Jon said, wondering how to switch the conversation around to what Bormann's plans might have been for his own future.

Joachim went on. "He also wanted certain artifacts and emblems removed from this room and incinerated. A large photograph of the Fuhrer, some Nazi battle flags and accompanying paraphernalia, for example, and some smaller personal items."

"They would be worth a fortune to collectors," Jon observed.

Joachim looked at him sharply. "Yes, Colonel, they would, which is precisely why the Reichsleiter's instructions have been carried out so expeditiously. He was always appalled by the trade in Nazi artifacts. He did not wish to have his personal belongings traded like so many baseball cards."

"Quite understandable," Jon said. "On my way in here I passed a couple of your security people with some file boxes on a dolly. I suppose those were the articles you were speaking of?"

Joachim shook his head and turned his attention back to the desk. He picked up the empty glass and the bottle of schnapps and placed them carefully in a box. He looked up at Jon. "The file boxes you saw were his personal files. They were being taken to the incinerator."

"His personal files?" Jon said. He realized his alarm was evident in his voice.

Joachim stared at him for a moment. "Colonel," he said softly. "Reichsleiter Bormann kept extensive personal files on a variety of things. They outlined the background, the hopes, the expectations, the possibilities that he foresaw for the re-establishment of the Nazi movement in the world. They were very personal in many respects. They could be highly damaging both to individuals and to the movement that he sought to perpetuate.

"They also contained the particulars of what he termed 'The Last Option'. These were the files on you and the others who were smuggled to North America in 1940. They contained details of how it was accomplished. There was information on financial arrangements, contact information, etc. In your case, for example, there was a detailed dossier on your years at school, your distinguished military career, your marriage, your family finances, your political ambitions so far as we could determine them, and your parentage."

"My parentage?" Jon asked. "So you know who my parents were?"

"I'm sorry, Jon, there were sealed portions of the file that I never read. The identity of your parents was in one of those and I was not permitted to read it."

"Not permitted?" Jon's voice was rising. "You could have opened it now or better yet, have given me that file."

Joachim's face registered shock. "I never could have done that, Colonel. The Reichsleiter's instructions were quite clear. They were to be burned upon his death."

"Jesus Christ," Jon fumed.

"And by now all the files have been incinerated."

Jon paced across the office and back. "God dammit," he muttered. He turned away from Joachim and breathed deeply several times, quieting himself and regaining his focus. He turned back. "What of the future of the movement?"

Joachim looked at him for a moment. "You deserve an answer to that, Colonel. Sit down, please."

Jon sat down in a chair on the other side of the desk. It was a low leather chair and he sat forward on the edge of the seat.

"Reichsleiter Bormann had a dream that one of the children he was able to get out of Germany would emerge to lead the movement."

"Excuse me," Jon said. "You keep referring to children. Were there others than Lincoln Carswell, Eric O'Neill and me?"

"No," Joachim replied. He paused. "What you need to know is that the Reichsleiter made a decision on who he wished to lead the movement. His decision was that it be Eric O'Neill."

CHAPTER SEVENTY FOUR

Monday, May 8, 1989 London Road, Guildford,
Railway Station

Lincoln Carswell was looking over the top of his paper, slowly scanning the flow of people arriving to catch the next train. He gasped in surprise as he saw Eric O'Neill walk onto the far end of the train platform. He was holding hands with a woman who looked vaguely familiar. As they got closer his surprise turned to astonishment when he recognized the woman he was holding hands with. He hadn't seen her in a year or more, but it had to be Liselle Marcoux, nattily dressed in a close fitting dark green jumpsuit. He knew Liselle from the art scene in Philadelphia, not well, but they had met a few times, and then he hadn't seen her again until now.

His first instinct was to stand up and greet them, but he stayed seated. O'Neill had obviously "escaped" from Bormann's lair, too. Whether this made him a friend or someone he should be suspicious of wasn't clear. He could reveal his identity at his leisure if it seemed wise. For the moment he would wait and watch.

Lincoln looked at Liselle more closely. Her figure was as trim as ever but he realized she was wearing no makeup. He had never seen her heavily made up, but she always did her eyes and used lipstick. He smiled at the thought that perhaps she and O'Neill had spent the night together and this was her just-out-of-bed look. But that couldn't be. O'Neill had been at the Surrey estate last night and Liselle had not been there.

As he watched her, he suddenly realized that the jumpsuit she was wearing had an uncanny similarity to the one worn by the dead attacker he had taken the pistol from in the solarium. The attacker's had been partially covered by a bulletproof vest and there was a holster and other items on it, but the colour was similar. An odd coincidence. Or was it a coincidence?

They disappeared into the station, presumably to purchase their tickets as he had, and emerged a couple of minutes later. They turned and walked away, back toward the end of the platform where they had entered. Lincoln watched them sit down on a bench and lean toward each other. Liselle was talking, then O'Neill said something and she shook her head emphatically.

The whistle of the arriving train drew his attention away from them. He folded the paper, stood and picked up his suitcase. He moved down the platform toward O'Neill and Liselle. Were they going to London, too?

He looked at his ticket and checked the coach and seat numbers as the train ground to a halt beside the platform. He entered the coach, found his seat and stowed his suitcase in the overhead rack. As he sat down, he saw Liselle and O'Neill enter the coach and move down the aisle toward him.

CHAPTER SEVENTY FIVE

Monday, May 8, 1989 London, England

The coffee house was dark and cozy, with a low ceiling, crossed with heavy black beams. It was furnished with small round table and chair sets. Eric sipped his coffee and looked around at the other inhabitants, about a dozen, mostly in business suits reading papers. The coffee was vile. No wonder the habit had never really caught on in England. He glanced at his watch. He had been here about ten minutes but it seemed a lot longer. Liselle had parked him here and said she would be back as soon as she could, likely half an hour or so, but not to worry if it was longer. What if she just didn't come back? Was he supposed to sit here all day, all week? But she would hardly have gone to the trouble of bringing him to London in the first place if she had intended to dump him. However, he reminded himself, he had been on the way to London on his own when she had joined him, or maybe "hi-jacked" him, was more accurate.

The door was pushed open and a stream of sunlight briefly lit up the room as an older man shuffled through the door. He paused for moment and looked around and then moved off toward the other side of the room, almost dragging a small suitcase with one hand while supporting himself with a cane in the other. He was wearing a navy blazer and grey slacks with a typically English tweed cap perched on his head, likely an old soldier from another time and place.

Eric pushed his chair back and set the briefcase on his lap. It was a heavy case, metal reinforced under the dark brown leather, and had a six digit combination lock. As Bormann had instructed him, he entered the digits of his birth date, 39-10-30. He tried the latch and it popped. Lifting the lid he scanned the neatly organized contents, files in the compartments of the lid along with several computer disks, and some maps, a bound package and two envelopes in the main compartment.

He picked up the envelopes, opened a small manilla one and pulled out his passport. He checked it and it seemed fine. He slipped it back into the manilla envelope and picked up the smaller white envelope. It wasn't sealed and he pulled out a folded letter. He scanned it quickly, instructions from Bormann on finding his way in London, a phone number to contact, a second number and a third one if the first two failed. He was not to use any number more than once. A couple of days ago he would have laughed at all the secrecy, now he wasn't even smiling. He skimmed some more. Portugal. He stopped reading and went back a paragraph. A contact in Portugal would provide information on his parents. A single phone number this time. He sat back in the chair. Was he going to go there? Maybe. He wondered if he really cared anymore. Still, he had gone through a lot to just walk away. He would go and find out maybe, then get out.

He lifted the package, it was heavy, like a book but it flexed, not solid. He loosened the tape holding the end of the package closed. I was bundled currency. He would check it later in private. He replaced the tape and put the package back in the briefcase.

He pulled a thick file out of the lid, closed the case and set it on the floor beside him. He opened the file and began to read. Financial information. At last something that he could understand. He began to read it slowly and then more quickly, scanning through the pages, focussing on some key numbers, a fact, a name, a company, in the US, in Europe, Japan, South East Asia, even a few in Canada. He was familiar with many of them and the information was easily verifiable.

He glanced up, startled by the waiter. "Will there be anything further, sir?"

Eric stared at him for a moment, looked at his almost untouched coffee. "Tea, please," he said.

"Thank you, sir," the waiter said. He smiled as he picked up the cup. "Coffee not to your liking, sir?"

Eric looked at him for a moment, still distracted. "Fine, just cold. But I would like tea now, thank you."

The waiter nodded and left.

Eric plunged back into the folder. After a few minutes he closed it. He was surprised by what he had just gone through. He picked up the briefcase and pulled out another file, replacing the first one. It was not as thick and contained information on German companies. He skimmed it quickly, finding the same patterns as he had in the other file. He didn't bother with a lot of the detail, there would be time for that when he could analyze it in depth. He replaced the file and closed the briefcase, leaning back in his chair. He saw a cup and a small tea pot on the table. He hadn't been aware of the waiter setting them down.

He poured some tea and took a sip. It was good, hot and refreshing. What an interesting set of information Bormann had provided. He wondered if Bormann had any idea of the limitations this financial information contained. Likely not. Although the portfolio was quite large, he would certainly never control the world with it. Not even close. Perhaps there was more somewhere else. He took another drink of tea and set the cup on the table. He lifted the briefcase onto his knee and turned the combination to lock it.

He put some money on the table and stood up. He would stroll around outside for a few minutes and keep an eye on the place so that when Liselle came back he would see her. He was approaching the door when Liselle opened it and stepped inside. He scarcely recognized her. She was transformed into a fashionable cover girl. Gone was the jumpsuit and the tousled image of innocence. She now wore a navy blue suit, the skirt clinging at her hips, slightly flared at the bottom, a white blouse with a simple red scarf at her neck.

"I was going out for some fresh air," he said. "I can't drink the coffee."

Liselle smiled. "Fine," she said. "Let's carry on, but first we have to get you cleaned up."

"Cleaned up?"

"I think a shower and shave are in order and then we'll find you a tailor."

Lincoln Carswell watched Liselle Marcoux come in the door of the coffee house just as a waiter arrived with his coffee. Now this was the Liselle he was familiar with. He watched as they chatted for a moment and then went out the door. He put some money on the table and stood up. He gathered his suitcase and his cane and headed for the door, resuming his shuffle as he stepped outside. A short distance down the street at the corner of the block, there were two of London's unmistakable taxi cabs. As he moved down the street, he watched Liselle and O'Neill get into the first one.

He was in luck, as he had been at Waterloo Station earlier, when he had been able to take the next cab and follow them to the coffee house. While in the cab he had retrieved an old tweed cap and his collapsible cane from his suitcase. Then he had paid the cabbie and watched them go in. He had been shuffling toward the door when Liselle came out, turned away from him and strode off down the street. He watched the provocative swing of her hips in the tight fitting skirt and wondered again what she and O'Neill were up to.

The cab with O'Neill and Liselle waited for a break in the traffic, moved smoothly forward and turned the corner. Lincoln picked up his pace as he hurried toward the second cab. He was about a hundred feet away when two women rounded the corner and got into it. He watched in dismay as it pulled out into the traffic and drove away.

He smiled grimly. He had been lucky this morning but he knew it couldn't hold forever. First he had ended up at the same commuter station as O'Neill and Liselle, gotten seats in the same coach and escaped their detection. O'Neill had mostly sat still on the train ride into London but Liselle had fidgeted, glancing around, looking at other passengers and leaning toward Eric to talk. She looked nervous, O'Neill looked resigned. At Waterloo Station, Liselle had walked out to the taxi line, glancing around as though looking for someone, and almost pushed O'Neill into a cab.

But now he had lost them. Perhaps it didn't matter. Another cab pulled up to the corner and parked. He walked up to it and got in. Time to move to Plan B. "The Raphael

Hotel, please," he said to the driver. He leaned back in the seat, opened his small suitcase and began to transform himself back into Lincoln Carswell.

Liselle was right, a shower was in order. The water poured over him in a heavy stream from a large, solid chrome shower head. Liselle had checked them into a hotel, requesting a deluxe suite. Eric had wondered if this was so they would have separate beds if they stayed here long enough to sleep. He was really too tired to care at this point. They were posing as husband and wife now with a gold wedding band adorning her left hand.

She had taken his sizes, told him to enjoy his shower and said she would return within an hour. He stepped out of the shower, toweled himself dry, combed his hair and looked in the slightly fogged mirror. He was clean shaven, his dark blonde hair damp. There was a tension and a tiredness around his eyes. He recognized it from years ago but in those days it had been caused by long hours of work. He sighed, tossed the towel over the shower stall and slipped into a white terry towel robe hanging on the back of the bathroom door.

He wandered back into the sitting room. Seeing the briefcase on a desk in the corner of the room he sat down, and was about to dial the combination when he saw it was already set to his birth date, 39-10-30. He thought for a moment and was certain he had spun the dials to lock it when he had closed it in the coffee house. He smiled. Liselle was a woman of many talents.

Opening the case he retrieved the white envelope and extracted Bormann's letter of instructions. He read it through carefully again and wondered what to do, who to trust. Really, what he wanted to do was just to get the hell out of this entire situation. But what was the best route? Trust Liselle who was apparently an Israeli agent who likely didn't know about who his parents were supposed to be. Truth to tell, he didn't know either. Trust Bormann's contacts in London? Trust his own judgement and initiative? Maybe just walk out of here? The last course was tempting but he wondered how far he would get.

He looked at the London phone numbers for a moment and then glanced at his watch. It was a few minutes before noon. He picked up the phone and dialled the first number.

"Garrick," a voice answered abruptly before the first ring was completed.

⟿⟾

The large bed invited him to lie down. He pulled back the covers, dropped the bathrobe and slipped into the bed. He wondered about the phone call, sorry in a way he had made it. All Garrick, whoever he was, wanted was for Eric to come to his place or failing that, to tell him where he was. He had chatted to Garrick but had not agreed to meet him nor to tell him where he was staying. Enough for now, he thought. He was tired. The pillow softly enveloped his head as he closed his eyes.

CHAPTER SEVENTY SIX

Monday, May 8, 1989 Surrey, England

"A fucking stockbroker?" Jon shouted incredulously, leaping to his feet. "He picked a fucking stockbroker? That's insane." He paced across the room and then turned back to face Joachim who was still sitting behind Bormann's desk, transfixed by his outburst. He walked slowly back to the chair. "What did Eric O'Neill have to say about that?"

"I have no idea, Colonel. The Reichsleiter spoke to him privately."

"Well, where the hell is he now?"

"He's gone."

"Gone?"

Joachim nodded.

"Gone where?"

"London, I believe."

"When?"

Joachim looked at his watch. "About five hours ago."

"Jesus Christ," Jon fumed. "This whole organization is falling apart and O'Neill has gone to London."

Joachim nodded.

"All right, Joachim," Jon said, leaning over the desk. "Enough of this bullshit. Where is he in London?"

"I don't know, Colonel."

Who is he with?"

"He's alone."

"How did he get there."

"He drove."

Jon straightened up and looked past Joachim, out the window onto the lawn. He slipped his hands into the pockets of his slacks. His right hand encountered the pistol. He gripped it tightly, comfortingly, and thought about what to do next. Eric O'Neill was not going to inherit the empire if he could help it. He looked down at Joachim and smiled ruefully. "Please excuse my outburst, Joachim," he said softly. "I was just disappointed. I have been a team player all my life, a soldier who takes orders from superiors, who obeys them without question." He paused. "How can I get to London?" he asked, his voice still quiet but insistent. "If Eric O'Neill is to be the new leader, then I need to meet with him to determine where my place in the organization will be, to receive whatever orders he chooses to give me."

Joachim looked at him carefully. "Thank you for that reassurance, Colonel Falken, but I don't know where he is. I do have some contact numbers for London but I don't know whether Eric was given them or not. However, nothing is going to happen for a few days or more likely, for a few weeks, so I think your best course of action would be to return to America. We will be in touch and I am certain that there will be a prominent role for you in the movement. What could be more prominent than a congressional seat, or ultimately the American presidency?"

"Thank you, Joachim," Jon said. "But I believe there is a greater urgency than you apparently do. I want the phone numbers and I want a car."

"I don't think I can do that, Colonel."

Jon sighed. "I think you can, Joachim," he said as he pulled the pistol out of his pocket.

"You are going to shoot me for some phone numbers?"

"No, Joachim, for the phone numbers and a car."

Joachim stared at him coldly. "Very well, Colonel," he said. "They are in the desk and I have to open the drawer. Come around here if you wish to reassure yourself."

Jon moved around behind Joachim and watched as he took a Rolodex from the upper right hand drawer and set it on the desk. He picked up a pen and wrote a number on a note card, turned the Rolodex to a second card and then a third, writing each number on the card. When he was finished he handed the card wordlessly to Jon.

"Thank you, Joachim," Jon said. "And now a car."

Jon moved to the side as Joachim pushed the chair back, stood up and slowly reached into his pocket. He pulled out a ring of keys and removed one. "There is a Mercedes sedan in the garage." He handed the key to Jon.

"That's better," Jon said. "Sit down please. I need one last piece of information. O'Neill has gone to London. Why London?"

"I believe he will leave the country and he is likely to do that through London."

"And these numbers are his London contacts?"

"Yes."

"Good," Jon said. He stepped behind the chair and pushed the pistol back in his pocket. He slipped his hands around the back of the chair, and for just a second, positioned his hands on Joachim's head in a feather-light touch before grasping it firmly and giving it a sharp twist. Jon smiled at the faint snap of Joachim's neck breaking.

CHAPTER SEVENTY SEVEN

Monday, May 8, 1989 London, England

Liselle watched as the cab pulled up to the hotel entry. She tipped the doorman as he opened the door and ushered her into the taxi. She glanced down at the business card to confirm the address that she gave to the taxi driver. She turned the card over and read it. "Ralph Walters" was followed by some letters, financial designations she assumed, and the name of the investment firm where he worked. It had been four days since she had met Ralph on the BA flight from New York to London when he had asked her out for dinner. She felt confident he would remember her.

Ten minutes later she alighted from the vehicle, waited until it disappeared into the traffic and walked back a block and up a side street. She looked up at the facade of a modest sized but quite luxurious commercial hotel and read the marquee, Georgian Place Hotel.

In the lobby she sat at a small table and picked up the house phone. She looked at her watch and saw it was near noon. He would likely be out but no harm in calling anyway. "Could you connect me with Ralph Walter's room, please." Her sophisticated English accent was impeccable.

"Thank you, M'am," the operator replied.

Liselle listened to the phone ring twice and then surprisingly it was picked up on the third ring. "Ralph Walters."

"Hello, Ralph," Liselle said, slipping easily into the east coast accent she had used when she had met him on the plane. "It's Liselle Marcoux. You may not remember me, but we sat beside each other on the flight from New York to London last Wednesday."

"Of course, Liselle," Ralph said. "How nice to hear from you."

"Thank you," Liselle said. "I was surprised to find you in your room."

"I'm just finishing up some work here before I head out for my afternoon appointments. It seems the English don't do a lot of my kind of business in the mornings. But what are you up to?"

"I finished my business yesterday and I'm just in town for the day doing a bit of shopping. I'm free this evening and I wondered if your dinner invitation was still open?"

"It certainly is,"Ralph said. "Where are you staying?"

"With friends in the country," Liselle said.

"That's wonderful," Ralph replied. "Would you like to come here for a drink and then we could go for dinner."

"That sounds marvellous, Ralph," Liselle said. "Around seven?"

"That would be fine," Ralph said. "I'm going out shortly to a couple of appointments, and I will likely have to endure a drink or two at one of their dreary clubs when I'm finished. But seven would be just fine. That will give me time to get back here and freshened up."

"I'll look forward to seeing you later, Ralph."

"That'll be great," Ralph said.

"Oh," Liselle said. "Could I ask a small favour?"

"Of course."

"I'm shopping, as I mentioned, and I wondered if I could drop off a couple of my parcels in your room this afternoon. My arms will simply fall off if I have to carry them around much longer."

"No problem," Ralph said. "I'll tell the front desk and you can leave them with the concierge."

"Would it be too much to ask you to leave a key for me at the front desk?" Liselle said, putting just a trace of huskiness into her voice. "Then I could freshen up, too, if I got there a bit early."

"Consider it done," Ralph said eagerly. "I'll arrange it when I leave for my appointments."

"You're a darling, Ralph," Liselle said.

He laughed. "Anything to oblige."

"See you later," Liselle said softly and set the phone down. She arose and strolled across the lobby into the bar. It was almost empty at this time of day and she took a seat in the far corner, shielded from the lobby by a large artificial palm plant, although she could still observe the hotel registration desk.

A server approached her table. "Good morning, Ma'm," he said. "Can I bring you something?"

"Coffee would be lovely," Liselle said, her impeccable English accent back again. "And a copy of the Times if you have one."

"Certainly, Ma'm."

If things worked out, she and Eric could be on the Dover ferry to France tonight. If not, they would make it in the early morning. There were risks either way.

She had met with Aaron while Eric was trying to drink his vile coffee and had reported the appalling results of the assault on the Surrey estate. Aaron had been stunned. Whoever lived there must have been vastly more important than they had realized to merit that kind of security and defence system. She had resisted saying "I told you so". He had grilled her on the details and she had told him what she could. Then she had showered and Aaron had gone out, saying he would be back in the afternoon to talk some more. He had a lot of things to do. She had told him she just needed to sleep and that was true enough. She had not told him that she had Eric O'Neill waiting in a coffee house a couple of blocks away.

And what was she doing with Eric O'Neill? The mission had been clear. Get Eric, Jon Falken and the mysterious old man and deliver them to the tender mercies of Aaron and his colleagues. But here she was, hiding Eric. He just did not seem to deserve the interrogation that Aaron certainly had in mind for him. She would find out from Eric what was going on in Surrey, who the old man was and then decide what to do. For the moment she was going to protect him.

Liselle relaxed in the upholstered chair in the bar and set her large purse on the floor beside her. She had another couple of hours, she guessed, before Aaron returned and discovered she was gone, perhaps a couple more after that before he did anything about it. She thought of Ralph Walters again, and smiled as she recalled the lust in his voice. So many men were ruled by their hormones, not their brains. Jon Falken certainly was but she was fairly sure that Eric O'Neill was not.

She nodded at the server as her coffee arrived. He laid the folded paper on the table beside the coffee. "Will there be anything else, Ma'm?"

"Not for the moment, thank you."

It was almost an hour before Ralph arrived at the registration desk, a coat over his arm and carrying a briefcase. Liselle watched as he spoke with the clerk behind the counter and then headed out the door. She glanced at her watch. It was nearly one o'clock. She waited ten minutes and then approached the bar. She paid for her coffee and walked into the hotel registration area.

"Good afternoon," she said to the clerk behind the counter. "I'm Liselle Marcoux. I believe Ralph Walters left a key for me?"

"One moment, Ma'm," the clerk replied. She turned to a set of pigeon holes behind her and retrieved a large brass key. Turning back to Liselle she placed it on the counter. "Our security procedures require that I ask you for identification." She kept her hand on the key.

"Of course," Liselle said. She pulled out a wallet and removed a driver's licence. The picture was a reasonable likeness. She held it out to the clerk, carefully keeping her fingers over the jurisdiction information. It was obviously not a British licence but there was no point in revealing where it did come from.

The clerk nodded and pushed the key toward her. "Thank you, Ms. Marcoux," she said. "Is there anything else we can do to assist you?"

"That's all for now," Liselle replied. "Thank you."

The key turned smoothly and she stepped into Ralph Walter's room. Five minutes later she was back on the elevator heading down to the lobby. Ralph had left only his clothes in the room so she would have to see him for dinner. Damn.

Two hours later, Liselle entered her own hotel room and set her parcels down inside the door. She walked quickly along the short hallway and into the bedroom area. Eric lay sound asleep, his lips parted, breathing deeply, one muscular shoulder and arm uncovered. She looked at him for a moment, his tousled dark blonde hair on the pillow. It was tempting to crawl into bed with him again, bring him gently awake and see what would happen from there. She smiled. She knew pretty clearly what would happen if she were directing things, and, she told herself, she would be.

Retrieving the packages from the hall she quietly unpacked them and hung Eric's new clothes in the closet, a black top coat, a dark grey suit, a couple of ties, two white shirts, black socks, underwear. The shirts and accessories had been simple and she hoped his suit size hadn't changed. He had told her he took a size 42 regular in North American measurements but added that he hadn't bought a suit in a couple of years.

She looked in on Eric and saw he was still sleeping, then quietly slipped out of the room. She glanced around the hotel lobby and walked out the entrance, down to the corner and across the street to a pharmacy. A few minutes later she was back in the room.

She sat down on the edge of the bed and ran her fingers into his hair, ruffling it lightly. He opened his eyes slowly and looked up at her with a sleepy smile. "Time to wake up, Prince Charming," she said, still moving her hand through his hair.

He put his hand on hers and squeezed it lightly. "This is a nice way to wake up."

Liselle withdrew her hand and stood up. She retrieved the bathrobe from the floor and tossed it on the bed. "You have to get decent now, we have some things to do."

Eric sat up lazily and pulled the bathrobe around his shoulders. "Have you had any sleep?" he asked.

"Just on the train this morning," she replied. "But you must get up now, I have to work on changing your appearance."

Eric swung his legs off the bed and stood up, pulling the bathrobe around him and tying the sash at his waist. "What's wrong with my appearance?"

"Nothing, except that you look too much like Eric O'Neill."

"Is that a problem?"

"It is if we're trying to get out of England."

"And why are we trying to get out of England?"

"To keep you safe."

"I feel safe here."

"You are safe here, but we can't live here."

"Liselle," Eric said. "Sooner or later you are going to have to tell me what is going on."

"I know," she said, taking some things out of a bag and placing them on the bathroom vanity. "Bring a chair in here," she said. "The small one from the desk will do."

Eric picked up the chair and carried it into the bathroom.

"Sit," she ordered, draping a towel around his neck. "I'm going to cut your hair."

Ten minutes later she was finished, the bleached ends were gone, and Eric's hair was short. The waves were still visible but not dominant as they were when his hair was longer.

"Stay here," Liselle said. "I'll be back in a moment." She returned to the bedroom, unbuttoned her blouse and took it off, then her skirt, half-slip and panty hose. She returned to the bathroom clad only in a bra and panties with a bottle in her hand. She watched Eric's eyes widen appreciatively. She smiled and ruffled his hair teasingly.

"Just relax," she said. "I'm not going to attack you, just your hair."

"Help yourself," Eric said.

Liselle turned the water on in the sink. She laughed and pushed his head toward it.

CHAPTER SEVENTY EIGHT

Monday, May 8, 1989 London, England

Lincoln Carswell paid the taxi driver and stepped out of the cab as the liveried doorman at the Raphael held it open for him.

"Good morning, Sir," the doorman said, touching the brim of his top hat, his dark blue uniform matching the gold trimmed navy awning that sheltered the entry. "May I help you with your bag?"

"I'm just meeting someone for breakfast, thank you," Lincoln replied.

"Very well, sir. Enjoy your time with us."

Lincoln walked into the spacious lobby and located a house phone, picked it up and asked for Marianne Falken. He listened to the phone ringing and wondered what he would say when she answered. However, a moment later, the system switched to voice mail. He set the receiver back on its cradle. He wouldn't leave a message that Jon Falken might inadvertently retrieve. He sat for a moment and pondered his next move. Was Marianne a morning person? He didn't know since he had only spent part of one morning with her.

He stood up with his small travel bag and strolled across the lobby. A few moments later he was in a restaurant. A man in a morning coat directed him to a small table on one side of the room. The furnishings were beautiful, chairs upholstered in deep red velour, white table clothes, real silver ware. The English certainly knew how to do elegance. He scanned the large eating area but there was no sign of Marianne. He sat down and picked up the breakfast menu, glanced down the extensive list of fare and set it aside as a hostess arrived with a pot of coffee.

When she walked away he looked up and saw Marianne standing in the entrance. He stood and watched her as she looked about the room, saw her gasp of surprise and the smile that followed when she spotted him. She walked across the room toward him and he felt his pulse rising. She was beautiful in a slim fitting dark brown pant suit, the jacket open, the pale teal blouse revealing the lush fullness of her breasts.

"What are you doing here?" she whispered as she slipped into his arms.

He kissed her cheek. "Looking for you, of course."

"I'm flattered," Marianne said, releasing him and stepping back. "All the way to London to see me?"

Lincoln nodded and smiled. "Yep."

They sat down and the hostess appeared again with the coffee pot.

"You came here with your husband, as I recall?"

"I did," Marianne replied. "But he left on Saturday evening for some meetings and hasn't come back yet. I expect him later today. He phoned this morning and said there was a change in plans. We were going to leave Thursday morning to go home. Now it seems as if we'll be traipsing off somewhere else." She shrugged. "But what are you really doing in London? Surely you didn't come all this way just to have breakfast with me?"

Lincoln laughed. "It's a bit more complicated than that but I did remember your hotel and when I discovered I had the morning free, I decided to find you." He picked up his coffee and tasted it. It was quite good by English standards. He thought about what Marianne had just told him. He already knew that Eric and Liselle were in London. So was Jon, or he soon would be if he was meeting Marianne. Were they all going somewhere? Did he care?

"You're thinking about something and I don't think it's me," Marianne said. "Wanna tell me about it?"

Lincoln set his cup down. "I was wondering how I could spend some time with you."

Marianne looked at him, a slow smile creeping across her face. "I was wondering the same thing," she said softly. "Where are you staying?"

"Nowhere at the moment, I just got into London this morning."

"The Raphael is nice."

"It is," Lincoln said. "But is it safe to stay here?"

"Jon is not a spontaneous man," Marianne said. "He will phone ahead and get things organized. I doubt that he will just show up."

CHAPTER SEVENTY NINE

Monday, May 8, 1989 Surrey, England

Jon Falken eased Joachim's body out of Bormann's chair and dragged it over to the doorway of the study. There was a small closet there and he manipulated the limp corpse into a crumpled position on the floor, covering it with a large brown shawl he found on the top shelf. That would do for a few hours. Then he went back to Bormann's chair and sat down. The rich old leather was still warm. He smiled at the thought that the last two people who had sat in this chair were now dead.

On the broad surface of the desk, he laid out the contents of the cardboard box that Joachim had been filling. There were a few mementoes, a letter opener, a couple of brass paper weights, all engraved with swastikas, the bottle of schnapps and the empty glass, and four file folders. He opened the first folder. It appeared to be the accounts of the estate. The second file contained a couple of seed catalogues and some folders on new hybrid roses. The third and fourth folders similarly dealt with mundane matters, charitable donations to the local orphanage, contract information on the power and phone utilities. There was nothing.

Jon leaned back in the chair. He could get out of here but with little information on where Eric O'Neill had gone he was stymied. He knew O'Neill had gone to London but where in London? It was an enormous city. He got up, walked back to the closet, opened the door and pulling the shawl off Joachim's body, he dragged it out onto the floor. He quickly searched Joachim's clothes, retrieving a ring of keys from a pants pocket. He reached his hand inside the breast pocket of the black suit and pulled out a thick white envelope. Tossing it on the floor he completed his search but found nothing else. He maneuvered the body back into the closet, covered it again and closed the door. He noticed that it had a lock and he searched Joachim's key ring, found one that fit and locked it.

Picking up the envelope, he ripped it open and sat down at the desk. It was a copy of a letter from Bormann to Eric O'Neill. He leaned back in the chair and began to read. When he came to the phone number contacts in London, he compared them to those on the card that Joachim had given to him. "You sly son of a bitch," he murmured, as he saw that each phone number had one incorrect digit.

He suddenly straightened. Portugal, the Algarve. His mother might be alive in Portugal, or O'Neill's or Carswell's mother. He relaxed. If Eric O'Neill had traipsed around Europe looking for his roots he wasn't about to give up now. He was headed to Portugal. So if he couldn't intercept him in London, he would do it there. Besides, the Algarve was beautiful this time of year. Jon smiled. He could do with a little sunshine and relaxation. He would call Marianne.

He was folding the letter to put it back in the envelope when there was a knock on the door. He was startled for a moment but finished inserting the letter and stood up, putting the envelope in his pocket. "Come in," he said loudly.

The door swung open and Clark Einfeld appeared. "Colonel Falken," he said, clearly surprised by Jon's presence in the room. "I just heard about Reichsleiter Bormann." He looked around the study. "What are you doing here?"

"Come in, Clark," Jon said, stepping around the desk and moving across the room. He grasped Einfeld's hand firmly and shook it. "Devastating news."

Monday, May 8, 1989 London, England

Jon Falken stood with his hands on his hips staring out the window. There was little to see other than a short narrow street with four parked cars and a few passing pedestrians but he was too agitated to sit. He was about to close in on Eric O'Neill and with him a source of power and wealth that would assure his future. The solution was a simple one. Find Eric O'Neill and kill him. Take whatever documents and information that Bormann had given him and move into position. In order to achieve his political ambitions he would have to fill the sort of role Bormann had. He could not be a public power figure in this organization since a US congressman, or perhaps a US president, could not be associated with the modern Nazi movement, but he could certainly wield the power and direct the resources, especially the financial ones and military ones if there were any.

Clark Einfeld and Steven Clayton were seated on a chesterfield, relaxed and apparently quite comfortable. At the moment, Jon needed all the manpower he could get but at the first opportunity he would get rid of Clayton, the simpering little faggot. Both Einfeld and Clayton had accepted his story that Eric O'Neill had stolen a case full of documents, financial and organizational information and had fled to London.

They had taken his direction easily when he had told them that Joachim had instructed him to organize the three of them to track down O'Neill, eliminate him and recover the documents. Sometimes life was simple. He had called the first London number on Bormann's list, had gotten a man named Garrick, and here they were, waiting for him.

He heard a movement behind him and turned as Helen Garrick entered the room. She was carrying a tea service. "I thought you'd like some tea, Mr. Falken," she said and set the tray down on a small end table next to the chesterfield. "Mr. Garrick should be along shortly."

"Thank you, Helen," Jon said and turned away from the window. "That's very kind of you."

"No trouble at all, I'm sure," she replied. She picked up the china tea pot, a large ornate one decorated in pink flowers, wild roses perhaps, and poured tea into three delicate white china cups. She set the pot down. "Now Mr. Falken, you come and sit down and have your tea. Do you take anything in it?"

"Nothing, thank you," Jon replied and obediently sat down on a hard embroidered chair. Helen handed him the cup and saucer and then served Einfeld and Clayton. "I hope you'll join us, Helen," Jon said graciously.

"And that's kind of you," Helen replied. "But I'm certain you gentlemen have things to talk about and I have some chores in the kitchen." She was somewhere in indeterminate middle age, her sandy greying hair pulled back in a bun, her gait somewhere between a walk and a shuffle, her glasses old fashioned, wire-framed and sliding down her nose.

Jon took a sip of the tea. It was hot and soothing.

"And here's Mr. Garrick," Helen said as a door slammed shut somewhere in the back of the small house. "We're in the parlour, dear," she called.

Jon set the cup and saucer down on a small side table and stood up as Garrick entered the room. Einfeld and Clayton rose as well. Garrick was a small man wearing thick glasses and dressed in a black suit, his hair slicked back like a 1920's movie star. He stood ramrod straight as he saw Jon. He stared at him for a moment.

"I'm Jason Garrick," he said as he walked quickly across the room. He stopped in front of Jon, a little too close, and looked up myopically, holding out his hand.

Jon smiled and grasped his hand in a firm shake. "Jon Falken," he said. "We just got in from Surrey."

Garrick looked around at the other two. "Americans?"

"Yes," Jon replied. He quickly introduced Einfeld and Clayton.

"I've just poured your tea, dear," Helen said, handing a cup and saucer to Garrick.

He took it, retreated a few steps to a small upholstered chair opposite the chesterfield and sat down. Balancing the cup and saucer on his knee, he reached up and tugged at the knot in his tie, loosening it, and then undid the top button on his shirt. "And you've come from Surrey," he said.

"That's right," Jon said. "I've been there the last several days meeting people and being briefed. As I explained to you on the phone, a man named Eric O'Neill, who was also being briefed has turned out to be a traitor and has escaped with a case of quite valuable documents. We must recover them and deal with O'Neill."

"I see," Garrick said. "I've never been to Surrey. Pleasant place, I'm told."

"Yes," Jon said. "Lovely spot." And then steered Garrick back. "What have you been able to find out?"

"He called, as you suggested he might, and we traced his call to a small luxury residential hotel. We have a couple of watchers in place. He appears to have a companion."

"A companion?"

"A woman, dark short hair, quite attractive, five foot five or so."

"Who the Hell would that be?" Einfeld asked.

"An accomplice of some sort, I guess," Jon said, as puzzled as Einfeld was. "Are they still at the hotel?"

Garrick pulled an old fashioned watch on a gold chain out of his vest pocket. "O'Neill called about noon. We had watchers in place by 1:00pm. It is now about 4:30. The watchers reported that the woman came back about an hour ago."

"Where had she been?"

"We don't know," Garrick said. "She had already gone out when the watchers arrived, but after she returned she came out again a few minutes later and visited the pharmacy across the street."

"A pharmacy?" Jon asked.

"Yes," Garrick repLied. "She bought some dark brown hair colouring."

"Of course." Clayton spoke for the first time. "To colour O'Neill's hair."

"How far away from here is this hotel?"

"Half an hour, a bit more now that rush hour is on."

"Shall we go over there now?" Jon asked.

Garrick looked taken aback. "What is it you intend? The watchers are very good and they'll do whatever is required."

"Have they identified O'Neill?" Jon asked.

"They haven't seen him, if that's what you mean, but they didn't have to," Garrick replied. "He and the lady are registered as husband and wife, Mr. and Mrs. Eric O'Neill."

"I see," Jon said, and took a sip of his tea. It was getting cool. He set the cup and saucer down. "Then tell the watchers to revise O'Neill's description. His dark blonde hair is now dark brown." A phone rang somewhere in the back of the house.

Garrick stood, set his tea down, and nodded at the three of them as he left the room. He was back a few moments later. "The woman has left the hotel again, by cab. A watcher is after her."

CHAPTER EIGHTY

Monday, May 8, 1989 London, England

Liselle Marcoux had no intention of having dinner with Ralph Walters but she didn't see an easy way out of having a drink with him. Besides, he deserved that, considering what he was going to do for her. When she heard a key turn in the lock, she was sitting in the single large armchair in his room, her feet propped up on a stool, a weak bourbon and water on the end table beside the chair. A moment later, Ralph Walters walked into the room. His face lit up in a smile of pleasure, a little too much anticipation there, Liselle thought.

"Hi, what a lovely sight to come home to," he said, stopping to stare at her for a moment. "I'm glad I left you a key." He set his briefcase down, took off his top coat and tossed it onto the bed. "Been here long?"

"Just a few minutes," Liselle said. "I hope you don't mind my making myself at home. I found your bourbon on the dresser, fixed myself a drink and took the most comfortable chair." There was another chair, an office chair with wheels, in front of a small walnut desk that nestled against one wall, but it was not designed to lounge in.

"Not at all," Ralph replied. He kicked off a pair of shiny dark brown loafers and walked across to the dresser.

"Did you have a good day of shopping?"

"Pretty good, a couple of outfits, but I was able to send them home with a friend."

"The one you're staying with?"

"Yes," Liselle said. "She's a relative really, a cousin of my husband's." She paused to let that sink in for a moment. Ralph had his back to her pouring himself a bourbon.

"I didn't realize you were married," he said without turning around. He tasted the bourbon and added a little more.

"Widowed."

Ralph turned to face her, a look of genuine concern on his face. "I'm sorry," he said. "I didn't mean to pry. I just noticed that you weren't wearing a ring."

"That's okay," Liselle said. "It happened five years ago, a car accident, and I'm pretty well over it now."

Ralph sat down on the edge of the bed and raised his glass in a toast. "To London," he said.

"To fun in London," Liselle replied and raised her glass. They both drank.

Ralph poured his third bourbon and sat down on the stool in front of Liselle's chair. She moved her feet over and he patted her calf lightly. "That's fine," he said. "There's lots of room."

She smiled at him. "We were going to have dinner," she said. "But I'm so comfortable here that I really don't want to move."

"We could order room service," Ralph said.

"Nice idea," Liselle said. "Let's do that."

Ralph stood up with his drink and walked over to a desk against the far wall. He returned a moment later with a slim, leather bound folder containing the room service menu. He perched on the arm of the chair and handed it to Liselle.

She set her drink down and sat up, opening the folder. Ralph leaned forward to see it, draping his arm across the back of the chair. Liselle could feel his breath on her hair and turned her face up to him. "What do you feel like?" she asked, her mouth only inches from his.

He looked at her mischievously. "Interesting question."

She touched his leg and laughed. "I walked into that one, didn't I?"

He lowered his face to hers and kissed her. Liselle relaxed and responded. She parted her lips slightly as his tongue pushed gently into her mouth.

Liselle glanced at her watch as she entered her own hotel room. It was a few minutes after nine. She could see a flicker of light from the television in the bedroom. Eric waved as she entered. He was reclining on the bed, wearing the gray slacks from the suit she had purchased for him and one of the new white shirts. He was watching a golf match. "How's the golf."

He pushed a button on the remote and the television went silent. "Only interesting if you play golf." he said, sitting up.

"I'm going to have a shower and freshen up and then we'll order in some dinner. Want to check the room service menu?" She draped her coat over the back of a chair and began to take off her clothes. "Any excitement while I was gone?"

"Not really," Eric replied.

"Good," Liselle said, pulling her dress over her head. "The more anonymous we are here the better."

"Do you think someone will try to find us?"

"Perhaps your friends from Surrey will."

Eric was silent for a moment. "They know I was coming to London," he said. "In fact they sent me to London, gave me a briefcase full of information, which I gather you've had a peek at, so why would they be trying to find me?"

Liselle turned to face him, now down to her bra and panties. She gauged the look on Eric's face more as one of appreciation than lust. "I needed to know in a general way what they had given you, Eric. I didn't read any of the detail."

"There were some phone numbers in a letter. I was supposed to call one of them when I got to London."

Liselle's eyes widened. "Tell me you didn't phone."

"Just the first one."

"Jesus Christ," she said. "When did you do that?"

"I was in the shower when you went out this morning. I phoned when I got out of the shower, so I suppose it was around noon."

"God dammit, Eric, that was stupid." She turned her back to him, pulled off her bra and panties and hurried into the bathroom. "Start packing," she called as she turned on the shower. "We have to get out of here."

"I didn't tell them where we were."

"Doesn't matter," Liselle said. "They'll find us." She stepped into the shower. She should have thought of it. Of course they would have given him contacts and why wouldn't he call them? He was confused enough. But he just didn't get it. She scrubbed herself vigorously, turning her body in the scalding hot water. She had wanted a long cleansing shower, maybe a bubble bath but she wasn't going to get it now. She wasn't especially worried about the people in Surrey but if Jon Falken was involved, and he had been out there, then they definitely had a problem. She turned off the taps and stepped out, rubbing herself briskly with the towel. She wrapped it around herself and went back into the bedroom. In other circumstances she wouldn't be in a rush to leave.

"I'm sorry, Liselle," Eric said. It was just a statement, he wasn't contrite or worried, just apologizing because he had done something which upset her. "I don't understand what's going on."

"What's done is done," she said. She turned her back to him, dropped the towel and slipped on a clean bra and panties. She turned back. Eric had the small suitcase on the bed and had placed his few items in it. He was wearing the suit jacket now and had chosen the dark blue tie with the faint dark red pattern on it. He looked smashing, she thought. The newly cut hair, now a rich dark brown, suited him well. He still had enough of a tan to carry it off. "Listen carefully, Eric," she said. "How long were you on the phone and who were you talking to?"

Eric thought for a moment. "Ten minutes, perhaps," he said. "Likely less but I wasn't counting. A man answered, he identified himself as 'Garrick' and seemed to think the name would mean something to me but it didn't."

She put on a blouse and quickly did up the buttons, then slipped into the slacks and jacket of her business suit. "Did you tell him you were with anyone?"

"No," Eric said. "And he didn't ask. He seemed mostly interested in how I got here, and where I was. I didn't tell him but I did get the address of his place. He also gave me the address of a pub near where he lives and said we could meet there. He wanted to give me directions but to do that he would have needed to know where I was."

"Did you give him the phone number?" Liselle went into the bathroom and rapidly applied some makeup. Eyes and lips would have to do.

"No," Eric said. "I told him I would call him back. He seemed annoyed, maybe that's too strong, but he definitely wanted to meet with me."

"Let's go," Liselle said. She snatched up her coat but as she was about to put it on, Eric took it from her and held it. "Thank you."

He nodded, slipped into his own coat and picked up the suitcase and the briefcase.

"I'm going to check us out," she said, handing him a wallet and a passport. "Look these over and have the doorman get us a taxi."

"Well," Liselle asked him a few minutes later as she joined him at the front door. "Do you think you can pull it off?"

Eric nodded. "Who is Ralph Walters?"

"You don't need to know," she replied. "You just have be him for the next few hours."

He looked at her intently. "How did you get this stuff?"

She slipped her arm through his and touched her head to his shoulder. "You don't want to know," she said softly.

CHAPTER EIGHTY ONE

Monday, May 8, 1989 London, England

Lincoln Carswell lay quietly on his back, staring up at the ceiling. It was a peach colour with antique gold mouldings around the edges and a small chandelier in the centre, softly lighting the room. He felt exhausted and exhilarated at the same time. He rolled onto his side and snuggled up behind Marianne. She squirmed against him as he slid his arm over her and cupped her firm full breast in his hand. He felt her nipple harden as he stroked it gently.

"Are you trying to get my attention?" she asked.

"Mmmm . . ." Lincoln replied, nuzzling his face into her hair and kissing the back of her neck.

She rolled over and pulled his face toward hers, kissing him deeply, running her fingers into his hair, lightly scratching the back of his head.

Lincoln moved his hand slowly down her stomach and between her legs. He felt her legs move apart and she pushed up against his hand. She was wet and slippery from their earlier lovemaking. She moaned softly as he stroked her.

She grasped him. "I want you inside me," she whispered, rolling on top of him and sitting up. She guided him and then sat down forcing him deeply into her. She moved rhythmically back and forth. Her eyes were closed and her lips were parted. "You feel so good," she murmured.

Lincoln thrust upward as she rocked back. She leaned forward and dragged her lush breasts across his chest, then sat up again. She opened her eyes and smiled down at Lincoln as she moved her hand down and began to slowly stroke herself. Her breathing increased and she gasped, going into spasms as she reached an orgasm. Lincoln grabbed her hips and slammed himself deeply into her as he reached his own.

Marianne collapsed forward on him and they held each other tightly.

"Can I ask you a personal question?" Marianne said, brushing her fingers lightly across his chest. They were lying facing each other, the afterglow of their lovemaking intensifying everything.

"Of course," Lincoln replied. They were still naked, a sheet pulled over them. The Raphael had the softest sheets he had ever felt.

"Why are you here?"

Lincoln was silent for a moment, looking into her eyes. "Do you want all the reasons?"

Marianne laughed. "Sure."

"You are beautiful, charming, sensitive, caring and fabulous to make love to. I should say 'make love with'." He paused. "And I'm really fond of you."

"And you are quite eloquent."

"Why I'm here is simple," Lincoln said. "Most of the men you know would love to go to bed with you, me included. I'm single but you're married to a successful, dynamic man, with considerable political aspirations. Why are you here?"

"I keep asking myself the same question." She sighed. "When I married Jon, I was thinking more with my brain than with my heart. Oh, he was handsome and dashing in his uniform, and dynamic is a good word to describe him, and he was and is very ambitious, even charismatic. I saw a good future with Jon. But as I got to know him, I realized that something was missing. I'm not sure I can explain it. It's like he doesn't have a soul. I don't mean he can't tell the difference between right and wrong. He can, but he doesn't care. He does what's good for him, for his career and for his personal life."

"Sounds like a psychopath," Lincoln said. "I think the term is sociopath now."

"Maybe, but I don't understand that stuff well enough to know. You said 'making love to me' and then corrected it to 'making love with me'. I don't think Jon has ever made love 'with me'. Sex is something he does 'to me'. And a lot of other things are like that."

"Maybe Vietnam changed him," Lincoln said.

"I'm certain it did," Marianne said. "But I think it mostly made him more like he already was."

"Are you still in love with him?"

Marianne shook her head. "No, I'm not," she said. "I haven't been for a long time."

"So why are you still married?"

"Are you being naive?"

Lincoln laughed. "Maybe I am, but not deliberately."

"Love is only part of a marriage and maybe not even a really important part. Jon and I get along well most of the time. I enjoyed being a colonel's wife. I may enjoy being a congressman's wife or even the first lady." She paused and then rolled onto her back. She stared at the ceiling. "At least that's what I've been telling myself. Now I don't know. I've never really considered any other alternative. I don't love Jon. I don't even like him very much." She turned her head to look at Lincoln. "When you were married, were you in love?"

Lincoln nodded. "Yes, I was, although the nagging about getting a real job was getting to me by the time she left. Eventually it just wore me down." He stared into Marianne's eyes. "So when she left I mostly felt relief, not pain or sorrow. Maybe I wasn't in love by the end." He thought for a moment. "And I didn't like her very much by then, either."

Marianne stroked his cheek. "If I tell you something will you promise not to be scared and run away?"

Lincoln laughed. "I'm not running anywhere."

"I've been thinking of leaving Jon."

"Really? How long have you been thinking about this?"

"For the last few months."

"Anything special happen in the last few months?"

"A few things," Marianne replied. "You, of course, but Jon's political ambitions are really becoming a nuisance. Our social life is driven by who can support his run for a congressional seat politically or financially. A lot of our friends are from his military days and most of them are not rich or politically connected so we just don't see them anymore. I don't much like the new political friends." She turned her head and stared up at the ceiling. "I also found out he was having an affair."

"Surely not." Lincoln said. "Married to you and he is with another woman?"

Marianne smiled. "Afraid so, loyal fan."

Lincoln shook his head. "Hard to believe."

"Did you ever cheat on your wife?"

"No, although near the end of our marriage I was feeling a bit vulnerable and I guess if there had been someone I was really attracted to, I might have fallen from grace."

"What a quaint way of putting it."

"Is Jon's affair over now?"

"I think so," Marianne replied. "It better be."

Lincoln kissed her cheek and ruffled her hair. "So what now?"

"When we get home I will break the news."

"Get a lawyer first and develop an exit strategy."

Marianne stared at him. "An 'exit strategy'? That sounds weird."

"If you're going to leave, do it cleanly, do it soon and do it right."

Marianne laughed again. "This feels strange, lying here with you, discussing my pending separation and divorce."

"Will Jon fight it?"

"Vehemently."

"Then think about not going home."

"Really?" Marianne said. "Where would I go?"

CHAPTER EIGHTY TWO

Monday, May 8, 1989 London, England

That damned Eric O'Neill was proving to be more clever than he had anticipated, not dangerously so, just deviously so. However, Jon Falken had learned decades ago to never underestimate an adversary. He looked around Garrick's living room, neat and tidy again after Helen had served them some dreadful casserole that they had all complimented her on. No wonder Jason Garrick was such a scrawny little shit, eating that kind of crap.

He hated waiting. He especially hated it when he had no control, when the purpose of waiting was to learn how events had unfolded. As he had moved up through the ranks of the military he had learned that the higher up you got the more you waited. And now he was doing it again. The attractive woman with Eric O'Neill had left the hotel a couple of hours ago and gone to another hotel, the Georgian Place, a commercial hotel some distance away.

The watchers had called in to confirm her arrival. About an hour later a man had shown up at the Georgian Place, a man that matched O'Neill's new description, right height and build, dark brown hair. But the watchers at the other hotel had not reported O'Neill's departure. In fact, they had not seen Eric O'Neill at the other hotel at all. Usually, the simple explanation was the correct one and the simple explanation here was that O'Neill and this woman had checked into the first hotel under O'Neill's name, then moved on to the Georgian Place and gone to ground there.

So Jon waited. He decided to wait for a couple of hours, to give them time to get to bed, preferably to go to sleep, and then to take them. Some questions would be in order first, and the retrieval of the briefcase as well, but neither O'Neill nor his mysterious companion would likely leave the room alive.

The phone rang in the kitchen. Jon jumped to his feet but before he reached the kitchen he heard Garrick speaking. As he entered the room, Garrick put his hand over the mouthpiece of the phone.

"The woman has just left the Georgian Place Hotel," he said.

"Is she alone?"

Garrick nodded.

"And O'Neill is still in the room?"

"Yes."

Jon thought for a moment. "How many watchers do you have at the Georgian?"

"Three," Garrick replied. "One of them is following the woman, although she's waiting for a cab in front of the hotel at the moment."

"Good," Jon said. This new development called for a change in plans. "Wait until she leaves and then send the other two into the room. We'll meet them there as soon as possible."

Garrick nodded and spoke quickly into the phone.

Jon and Garrick went up in the elevator alone. They had parked Garrick's car and he had told Einfeld and Clayton to wait in the bar. Garrick tapped on the hotel room door and a moment later it swung open. They stepped in to the room. Jon pushed past the watcher who had opened the door and walked in. He spun around.

"What the fuck is going on here?" Jon asked.

"We had an accident, sir," one of the watchers said. He was about five foot nine, sandy hair, plain features, a small mustache, wearing a dark brown suit.

Jon sat down on the edge of the bed. A man was lying on the floor wearing a white terry towel robe with "The Georgian Place" embroidered on the breast pocket.

"What happened?" Garrick asked.

"Well, sir, we knocked on the door, and when the gentleman opened it, we asked if he was Mr. O'Neill, you know, sir, official sounding."

Jon stared at the man on the floor for a moment, wondering who the poor bugger was. He stood up. "And what did he say?"

"He asked us to repeat the name, which I did, but he said he'd never heard of anyone by that name and tried to close the door." The watcher looked at Garrick as though unsure who was in charge, then back to Jon. "So we forced the door, calmed him down and . . ."

"Calmed him down?" Jon interrupted. "What the hell did you do to calm him down?"

"My colleague just applied a little persuasion, sir. He took his arm and led him away from the door."

Jon looked at the other watcher, reclining in a large lounge chair. He was wearing a navy blazer and flannels, white shirt and club tie. He looked tough and solid but still wouldn't stand out in a crowd.

"Sorry, sir," the man in the blazer said.

"Did you question him?" Jon asked the first watcher.

"Yes sir," he replied. "We sat him down at the desk over there, told him we were hotel security and did he know he wasn't allowed to have professional ladies in his room? He said he didn't give a damn but he was going to call the front desk. Now, we couldn't have that, of course, but he was quite insistent, stood up, shoved us out of the way, quite a forceful gentleman, really. We grabbed him but he got away, tripped he did, and smacked his head on the corner of the desk. We checked him carefully, sir, but he was gone."

"You mean he's dead?"

"Yes, Sir," said the watcher with the blazer. "Frightfully sorry."

Jon let out a long sigh. "This man is not Eric O'Neill."

The watchers looked at Garrick. There was silence for a moment.

"Then who was he?" Garrick asked.

"I have no idea," Jon said. He knelt on the floor beside the body and checked the throat for a pulse. There was nothing. He moved the head slightly and saw a small pool of blood seeping into the carpet from the back of the skull.

"There was a woman in here tonight and this accident could easily have happened with her," Jon said. He stood up and turned to the watchers. "So wipe the place down and perhaps the police will come to the logical conclusion that he was mugged by a hooker. But first let's find out who this guy really was."

"We checked his briefcase, sir," said the watcher in the brown suit. "Here's his business card." He held it out to Jon.

Jon looked at the card. "Ralph Walters," he murmured. "Sorry about this, Ralph.

Where's the briefcase?" he asked, hoping beyond any reason that it might be the one he wanted.

"In the closet, sir." The watcher retrieved the briefcase and handed it to Jon..

He opened it and rifled the folders and papers quickly. Just financial stuff, nothing he wanted. He closed it and handed it to Garrick. "We'll take it with us. You and I will leave first." He turned to the watchers. "You two wipe this place down, not totally, but everywhere you've been. I want finger prints left for the police to find, just not ours."

"I'll get Einfeld and Clayton from the bar," Jon said a few minutes later as they strolled into the lobby. "There's a pay phone near the entrance. Call home and see if there is any word from your other watcher."

Jon walked into the bar, spotted Einfeld and Clayton at a table in one corner and nodded at them before turning back to the lobby. As he approached the entrance of the hotel, Garrick hung up the phone and turned to him.

"The woman and a man matching O'Neill's description are checking out of the other hotel."

CHAPTER EIGHTY THREE

Monday, May 8, 1989 London, England

Eric O'Neill felt Liselle suddenly stiffen against him. She squeezed his arm tightly for a moment. He glanced down at her as the cab drew up in front of the hotel entrance. She was looking back into the hotel foyer.

"Shit," she murmured. "Get in the cab and I'll join you in a moment." She turned and walked quickly back into the hotel.

The doorman ushered Eric into the back of the cab and handed in the briefcase and the small suitcase. He left the door open and as Eric looked past him he saw Liselle approaching, her coat draped over one arm, the other looped through the arm of an older man dressed in a dark business suit. She smiled at the doorman.

"Mr. Smith is joining us, dear," she said to Eric, her impeccable English accent back in place, as she guided the older man into the back seat. She slid in herself and nodded at the doorman.

"Leicester Square," Eric said to the cabbie as he pulled away from the entrance.

Liselle was sitting in the jump seat facing Mr. Smith. She moved her coat slightly to reveal a small handgun pointing unwaveringly at their new companion. "You are following us," she said. "Why?"

"Miss," he stammered, clearly frightened. "I've no idea what you're talking about."

"You were in the lobby when I returned this afternoon. You were in the pharmacy with me a short while later. You were on the phone when I left again a couple of hours ago and you're here now."

Smith stared at her. "M'am, I just work part time for the hotel. I'm security."

"And why did you follow me to the pharmacy?"

"Just a touch of a headache, M'am," he said. "I was picking up something for it. That's all, really."

"Bullshit," Liselle snapped. "You are following us and reporting our movements to someone and if you don't talk to me about it, you will be doing your job out of a wheel chair." She moved the muzzle of the gun against his right knee cap.

"Liselle," Eric protested. "What the hell is going on?"

"You heard what I just told him," Liselle replied, her eyes unwaveringly on Smith. "He is watching us. He wasn't there when we arrived but he's been there every time since. As we were leaving he was on the phone reporting that, too. I heard him."

Eric turned to look more closely at Smith. He was likely in his late fifties, thinning grey hair, slim but somehow not quite fitting into the business suit image he was striving for.

"Who are you reporting to?" Liselle asked.

"This is not likely worth losing a leg over, is it?" Eric asked.

Smith looked at him for the first time. "You wouldn't shoot me in a taxi."

"Do you want to take that chancc?" Liselle said.

"You wouldn't."

"Cover your ears, dear," Liselle said. "Even a small gun can be quite noisy in a confined place." She arranged her coat loosely over the gun. "My coat will absorb most of the sound." She pointed the pistol again at Smith's knee.

"Garrick," he said.

"Is that the name of the gentleman you were chatting on the phone with earlier?" Liselle asked Eric.

"The same."

"Now, you see," Liselle said. "That wasn't so difficult, was it? And you can still walk, for the moment at least. What are you to report?"

"Just when you and Mr. O'Neill come and go from the hotel."

"How many of you are there?"

"Three."

"Where are the other two?"

"They followed you when you left a while ago and they haven't come back yet."

Liselle sighed and leaned back in the seat. She looked at Eric. "We will have to find you another identity, I'm afraid."

"What's happening?"

"We'll talk later." She turned to the partition and spoke to the driver. "There must be a pub along here somewhere. Can you pull over at the next one we come to?"

"Certainly, M'am," the driver replied.

A couple of blocks further along, the cab pulled into the curb and stopped. "Here we are, M'am," the driver said. "The Shire Arms, a nice spot. Will you be getting out here?"

"Thank you," Liselle said. "We will." She reached for the door handle and pushed it open. "Out you get," she said to their companion. "Slowly and carefully." She glanced at Eric. "Pay the fare," she said, as Smith moved to the door and stepped gingerly onto the sidewalk. She held the gun steadily on him as she got out of the cab.

Eric handed the cabbie some bank notes and thanked him, gathered the briefcase and the small suitcase and then joined them on the sidewalk. He watched the taxi drive away.

There was an alley beside the pub. "Let's take a stroll down here," Liselle said.

A short distance in there were some trash cans against the wall.

Smith turned to face Liselle. He moved very quickly for a man his age. He threw himself forward on her, grasping her wrist and wrenching it to one side and shoving her against the wall. Eric dropped the briefcase and the suitcase, grabbed at his arm to pull him off Liselle, then grasped a handful of his thinning hair and yanked. Smith's head snapped back and Liselle's left arm uncoiled in a blur as the heel of her hand smashed into his face. He slammed back against Eric and slumped to the ground. His body twitched a couple of times and he was still.

Liselle stared at Smith for a moment. "Thank you," she said to Eric. "That was well done."

Eric was breathing heavily, more from the burst of adrenaline than from the exertion.

"Give me the wallet and the passport that I gave you," Liselle said.

Eric handed them to her and knelt beside Smith. He had a trickle of blood running from each nostril, his eyes were staring and his mouth gaped open. "Jesus Christ, Liselle," he whispered. "This guy's dead."

"Yes," Liselle said. She was busily wiping at the wallet and the passport. "He is. Did you take anything out of the wallet?"

Eric shook his head as he stood up. "I just looked at the name and the picture on the passport."

Liselle dropped the wallet and passport into her purse. "Help me move him," she said. They dragged him over to the wall and propped against it behind some trash cans.

Eric suddenly started to shake. He had just helped to kill a man.

CHAPTER EIGHTY FOUR

Monday, May 8, 1989 London, England

Marianne Falken was reclining in the large bathtub in her room at the Raphael, the hot water up to her chin. The bubbles from the foaming bath crystals she had added tickled her nose. They smelled like roses. She put her arms over her head and stretched. She felt like she had come from a workout at the gym although much more relaxed and content. "Contentment" was the word. She recognized it as almost a new emotion. Amazing what sex could do. More than sex, she thought. Lincoln had said "making love" and that was what it had been. Dangerous thinking, but the contentment was real.

She lay there mulling over Lincoln's advice. An "exit strategy" he had said. It was an Interesting idea, a plan to withdraw from her marriage. She laughed. Jon would be impressed with her. Her money was safe enough from him, buried in a family trust that no one could get at but her. He could have the house and the other stuff. She would need a lawyer, one of her own, not one of Jon's old cronies.

She sat up, raised her knees to her chest and wrapped her arms around them. She felt so deliciously relaxed, a bit tender between her legs, but so good. She slowly stood up and stepped out of the tub, taking a large white towel from a pile on a small wooden stand at the foot of the tub. She dried herself, tossed the towel into a large wicker basket in the corner, took a second towel and drew it around her.

In the bedroom, she pulled the duvet back on the king size bed, dropped the towel in a heap and slipped between the sheets. She reached over to a master switch on the bedside table, snapped it off and reveled in the darkness. She rolled onto her side, grabbed a pillow and put it between her legs. She smiled and closed her eyes.

A shaft of light from the half open bathroom door awakened her. Or maybe it had been something else, a noise, perhaps. She was confused for a moment. Then she saw Jon's silhouette in the doorway before he turned off the light. She closed her eyes and lay still, breathing deeply. The mattress shifted slightly as Jon got into bed. She felt him curl up behind her, felt his erection against her. His hand crept over her and grasped her breast. It was rough compared with Lincoln's gentle caress. She didn't move, didn't respond, feigned sleep.

He removed his hand from her breast. Then she felt him manoeuvring his erection between her legs. She squirmed slightly, sighed and rolled onto her stomach. She had awakened once, early in their marriage to discover Jon screwing her from behind. She had asked him why he did this while she was sleeping. She recalled his simple, crude answer. "Because your cunt feels better than my hand." Not tonight, Jon, she thought, and rolled over further, thankful the room had come with a king sized bed.

CHAPTER EIGHTY FIVE

Tuesday, May 9, 1989 Paris, France

The escape from England, if that was what it had been, was an anticlimax. Eric and Liselle took the train to Dover and the ferry to Calais. Eric used his own passport. They reasoned that the only people who wanted to stop him were those from Surrey and they would not want to involve police or border security. There had been no questions and no problems. Then they took the train to Paris.

Outside the station, they picked up a taxi. Liselle turned to Eric. "So far, so good."

"Where are we going?" Eric asked.

"First we are going to a small hotel where we will change taxis. Then we are going to a private apartment."

"A private apartment?"

"It belonged to my parents. Now it belongs to me. I stay there when I'm in Paris."

"That must be convenient," Eric said.

Liselle nodded. "It gets us around the strange habit the French have of taking the passports of every visitor who registers in a hotel and reporting their presence to the authorities." She tilted her head to one side and looked at him for a moment. "I will trust you, Eric. No one knows about this place and I have never taken anyone there."

Eric smiled. "I'm honoured," he said. "But if it belonged to your parents how is it that no one knows about it?"

"After my father's death, it was sold." She paused. "I bought it under another name."

Eric nodded. "I see," he said. "So we can just disappear?"

"Sort of," Liselle replied. "But we will still have to get new identities, yours a permanent one."

Eric nodded, leaned back and closed his eyes, oblivious to the passing traffic, the lights of Paris, the noise of the city. His mind filled with images of the man they had killed in London. He thought of the murder as something "they" had done, not something Liselle had done. True enough, she had struck the fatal blow, but he had positioned the poor soul for the strike. It had happened so fast. Surely, there must have been another way to deal with that situation other than killing the watcher.

Liselle leaned over and covered his hand with hers. "Don't think about it, Eric," she said. "It's over."

Eric nodded. "I know," he said. "But surely we didn't have to kill him."

Liselle squeezed his hand. "No we didn't, but he would have called Garrick, and his colleagues would have been on our trail immediately. In any event, he struck first. There is greater danger here than you think."

"There seems to be," Eric said. "But I don't understand why."

"I know you don't." Liselle sighed. "It's not about you, it's about your parents."

Eric sat up and looked at her. "You mean the mysterious high ranking Nazi's or whoever they were?"

"Exactly."

"Do you know who they were?"

"No," Liselle replied.

He slumped back against the seat. "My God," he said. "Will this ever go away?"

"No, it won't."

A small lift rattled slowly up to the third floor and opened onto a landing with four doors. Liselle retrieved a key from her purse and opened one of them, switching on a light to reveal a short hallway with a small wooden bench and an old fashioned coat tree, both in dark wood. She motioned Eric through the door ahead of her and locked the door behind them. Then she moved down the hallway, turning on lights as she went.

"When I was a little girl, this was my bedroom," Liselle said, as she opened a door and ushered Eric into a small room. The only evidence of it having been a child's room was a small dark wooden rocking chair in one corner with a bedraggled blonde coloured teddy bear leaning over one arm.

"This is Chou," Liselle said. "She will keep you company and protect you."

"Chou?"

Liselle laughed. "Yes, it means cabbage."

Eric joined in her laughter. "I know what it means but it's such an odd name for a teddy bear."

"At first I called her Chou Chou, a term of endearment, like Honey or Darling would be in English, and then I just shortened it to Chou."

Eric set his small suitcase on the bed and Liselle opened a closet. It was full of clothes but she pushed them to one side. "There should be room for your wardrobe in here," she said. "I normally hang my clothes in here as well as in the master bedroom closet."

Eric suddenly felt tired, exhausted. He sat down on the bed and took a deep breath.

"Are you all right?" Liselle asked, sitting beside him.

"I think so," Eric replied. "I'm just tired. I've been through a lot today and none of it was normal or not normal for me at any rate."

Liselle stood up. "Hang your clothes up and I'll be right back."

Eric was closing the suitcase when Liselle returned. She had a glass of water in one hand and a pill in the other. "Take this," she said, sitting on the bed beside him. "It'll help you sleep."

Eric stared at her. "Am I going to need it?"

"Trust me. You will."

"I've been trusting you all day," Eric said with a rueful grin. "I guess one more time won't hurt." He took the glass from her and swallowed the pill.

CHAPTER EIGHTY SIX

Wednesday, May 10, 1989 London, England

"Portugal?" Marianne asked. "Why Portugal?"

Jon was spreading marmalade on a piece of toast. They were sitting at a small table by the window of their suite, looking out at a dismal day, drizzle and fog.

"I'm finished here and we have a few days free. I have one more bit of business in Portugal and then we can fly home from there. I'm told the Algarve on the south coast is quite lovely this time of year."

"So am I going to sit in a hotel room in Portugal like I have been in London?"

Jon smiled at her. "You haven't exactly been wasting away in the hotel room, have you?"

Marianne looked sharply at Jon. "Well I did go shopping and found a few things. And London shops are a nice change from Philadelphia and New York."

"Exactly," Jon said. "A change. And this will be another change. We can walk on a beach, have a romantic dinner and enjoy the Mediterranean."'

"And how long will this idyllic interlude last?"

"Three or four days."

"And how long will your one bit of business take?"

"An afternoon, maybe a day, but no more," Jon replied. He picked up his toast and took a bite.

"Why don't I just stay here?" Marianne asked.

"You could, I suppose, but I'd like you with me. We haven't had much time together lately and may not again any time soon."

Marianne poured more coffee into her cup. She would rather stay in London with Lincoln than go to Portugal with Jon. She would rather be with Lincoln than Jon, not just in London, either. This came as a surprise to her. She looked up at Jon. He had said something.

"I missed that, Jon."

"I said we'll have to get packed and leave this afternoon. I've made reservations for a two o'clock flight to Faro."

Marianne nodded. All arranged with no reference whatsoever to what she might want. SOP as Jon would say, "Standard Operating Procedure".

"We're flying to Portugal this afternoon, two o'clock, but I don't know what airline." Marianne spoke softly into the phone although there was no need to be quiet. Jon had gone out shortly after breakfast, saying he would return around eleven. Marianne had waited twenty minutes to make sure he wasn't coming back for something he had forgotten, and then phoned Lincoln.

"So that gives us the rest of the morning," Lincoln said. He sounded relaxed, lazy.

"No," Marianne said. "That gives you the rest of the morning. I have to pack and be ready to leave by the time Jon gets back."

"How about staying in London with me?"

"I suggested staying in London but Jon wanted me to come with him and I didn't have any excuse, or none that I could explain to him."

"So how long will you be in Portugal?"

"Jon said three or four days, so that would be until the weekend."

"So I can go to Portugal or fly back to Philadelphia and wait for you."

Marianne was silent, as she thought of the implications. Wait for her. Did this make her uncomfortable? She decided it didn't. "What would you like to do?"

"Three or four days seems like a long time."

A smile crept over her face. "It does now, doesn't it?"

"You go ahead and pack. I'll figure something out, but don't be too surprised if you see me there."

"I'll watch for you."

"Watch for me in the cathedral square," Lincoln said. "Every city in Europe seems to have one."

"I'll find it."

They were both silent for a moment, then Lincoln spoke. "A bientot."

"I didn't know you spoke French."

"I have many talents but speaking French isn't one of them. I only know a few tourist phrases."

"I'm glad you know that one. I'll see you soon, too."

Silence again for a moment and then he started to sing softly.

"I'll see you in the morning light
You're everywhere it seems,
I'll see you in the stars at night
And love you in my dreams."

Marianne felt tears gathering in her eyes. "Whcre did that come from?"

"I wrote if for you this morning."

"It's beautiful. Thank you."

"Be safe, Sweetheart."

"I will," Marianne replied and gently set the receiver down. She thought of the last line in the song as she set her suitcase on the bed and gathered her clothes from the closet and the dresser drawers. Neither of them had used the word 'love' before. Where was this going?

CHAPTER EIGHTY SEVEN

Wednesday, May 10, 1989 Paris, France

Eric came awake slowly, blinking up at the pale pink ceiling. He looked to his left and saw Chou, the teddy bear protector, still slumped in the child-sized rocking chair. He could hear muffled street sounds, cars honking, the hum of tires on pavement. Slowly, he sat up and swung his feet off the edge of the bed. He remembered the pill that Liselle had given him. It had certainly worked. He felt as though he was coming out of a coma, but refreshed and rested.

There was a bath towel on the end table by the bed. He stood and wrapped it around his waist, opened the bedroom door and strolled down the short hallway to the kitchen.

Liselle glanced over her shoulder at Eric as he entered. "Sleep well?"

"Wonderfully well," Eric replied. He looked carefully at Liselle as she turned back to the kitchen counter. She was clad in a short red satin kimono, her dark hair just a little tousled. She took a kettle off the stove and poured boiling water into a

French press coffee maker, picked up a spoon and stirred the contents briefly. This was yet another image of her, Liselle in a kitchen.

She turned back to face him and smiled. He was struck again with her beauty, so natural and uncontrived. "Coffee will be served shortly," she said. "If you hurry you can have a shower before it's ready."

Eric nodded and turned back down the hall.

A few minutes later, he returned to the kitchen, clad now in slacks and a shirt. Liselle handed him a mug of coffee and led him through the small living room to a set of French doors, which led out to a recessed balcony. "I love this feature of the apartment," she said. "I can sit here and watch the world go by and no one can really see me." She sat down on a wicker love seat and patted the cushion beside her.

Eric sat down and took a sip of the coffee. "So what's the plan for today?"

"First, I am going to leave you for a while and get us new identities, then we are going shopping for a few things. Later in the day, we'll pick up our documents."

"How can you do this so easily?"

"Paris is my home town."

"Sounds like a nice, relaxing day," Eric said.

"Don't get too relaxed," Liselle said. "This evening we're flying to Portugal, if you still want to go there."

Eric thought about this. Did he really want to go? Did he really give a damn anymore? A simple trip to learn about a bank account in Switzerland and check on the identity of his parents had turned into a nightmare. He had met a woman in Ireland, had a gently romantic sightseeing drive and dinner, only to find out that she was some kind of agent who killed people. At the moment she seemed well disposed towards him and that was fine since others seemed less so.

In Surrey, he'd met a man who claimed to be Martin Bormann, the most hunted war criminal in history, escaped an attack on Bormann's manor house and fled to London. He had been given a briefcase full of documents on some neo-Nazi movement. Jesus Christ, why would anyone think that he cared about that shit? And now he was on the run from someone, either Bormann's people or someone else, who wanted to do him harm. How real and how severe was the danger he faced? Liselle obviously thought it was very real.

It all seemed surreal, an Alice-in-wonderland accident, and he had fallen down the rabbit hole. He looked at the date on his watch. "Wed, May 10". This fantasy had started in Dublin only five days ago. He just wanted to wake up and find it was gone. Jesus, what a mess.

"If I don't go to Portugal," he said. "What are my alternatives?"

Liselle looked at him for a moment. "You can go anywhere you want, but in your case the old saying, 'you can never go back', is your new reality. You can't go back to Portage la Prairie and resume your old life."

Eric looked sharply at her. "Do you know everything about me?"

Liselle laughed. "Not everything, but quite a lot." She put her hand on his arm. "I know about Laura, your high school sweetheart. I don't know how you feel about her but I know you've been staying in touch with her."

Eric nodded. "So no life in Portage? Not likely in Toronto either, at least not in my former life there?"

Liselle shook her head. "Sorry, Eric," she said. "That life is gone. Eric O'Neill is gone, too, or will be when we get your new identity later today. So if there is anything in your current life you want to take with you, you had best get on with arranging it."

Eric was stunned. Now he was going to vanish or his identity was. This whole thing was getting worse and worse. "You've got to be kidding? Is this going to be permanent?"

"For the foreseeable future."

"Shit," Eric whispered. He looked at her intently. "Why?"

"They will hunt you."

"Who the hell are they?"

Liselle sighed. "They are Nazis who want you to lead them. They are Israelis who want you dead. There may well be others, but those two will do for a start."

"Whatever for? I'm just a bloody stockbroker."

"It's not what you do it's who you are, and far more importantly, who your parents were."

"All right, then, who the hell were they?"

"I don't know. But they were very important in the Third Reich. And if I understand correctly, you are going to Portugal to meet your mother? Perhaps you can learn something from her."

"Maybe," Eric said.

"Maybe you are going? Or maybe she is your mother?"

"Maybe both." Eric leaned back on the love seat. "The sins of the father . . . "

"I'm afraid so."

Eric sighed and stared, unseeing, at the street scene below him. "So I have to disappear?"

"You do."

Eric thought about this. What did he want to take with him? Money, he supposed. There was the condo in Toronto and the house in Portage but he couldn't take them. In time he could arrange for their sale but making money, bank accounts, securities and so on, disappear and reappear was something he could do.

"What about Laura?" he asked.

"What do you want to do about her? Take her with you into the new nether world? Or walk away and not see her again?"

"I don't know whether she would come with me even if I asked her. She's married with a medical practice and a lot of roots in Portage."

Liselle shrugged. "You'll have to decide that, Eric."

"What about you, Liselle?" Eric asked. "When this is over will you disappear? Or will you be coming into the nether world, too?"

"I'll likely disappear," Liselle replied. She tilted her head to one side, smiled at him and raised her eyebrows. "But is that an invitation?"

Eric was silent for a moment and smiled back. "I don't know."

CHAPTER EIGHTY EIGHT

Thursday, May 11, 1989 Faro, Portugal

Jon Falken was about to sit down on the small balcony and join Marianne for what passed as breakfast in Portugal when the phone rang, a short shrill sound. Even the goddamned phones couldn't ring properly here. He turned back into the bedroom and snatched up the receiver.

"Falken," he said sharply.

Einfeld's deep voice always sounded like he was announcing something. "Lincoln Carswell just got off the ten o'clock flight from London."

"Really?" Jon was astonished. "What the hell is he doing here?"

Einfeld was silent for a moment. "I don't know," he said cautiously. "But he's here."

"You're sure it's Carswell?"

"He rented a car. I got a real good look at him."

Jon was puzzled. Why would Lincoln Carswell come to Portugal? It could be coincidence. Perhaps since he was in England, he had decided to come here. But Jon didn't believe in coincidences. Carswell was following him, or more likely, was following Eric O'Neill. Perhaps Carswell had changed his mind about Bormann's operation and had decided that he might as well lead it as anyone else. But he had been so indifferent in Surrey. Maybe that was just an act. Who the hell knew? But more to the point, how had Carswell known to come to Portugal? Maybe Bormann had talked with him privately as he had with O'Neill.

"What's he doing?"

"At the moment he has gone to the men's room. I expect he'll pick up his rental car and drive into town."

"Follow him," he said to Einfeld.

"I will."

Jon set the phone down and realized that Marianne was standing at the table behind him. She was buttering some kind of bun.

"Who was that?" she asked, looking up at Jon.

"Einfeld," Jon replied.

"And what did Einfeld want?"

"Nothing," Jon said. "He was just checking in with me. I asked him to phone this morning." Jon looked at her carefully. She was wearing a pair of tight white slacks and a bright turquoise blouse with the top buttons undone to reveal a deep cleavage. Marianne turned away with her buttered bun and walked back to the balcony. She pulled her sunglasses down out of her hair, put them on and sat.

Jon watched her walk away, took a deep breath and realized he was aroused. Marianne could be so sensual, so sexual, and at the same time so completely indifferent to his needs. He walked out and sat down at the small table with her.

"So what's happening today?" she asked.

"I have a short meeting in a couple of hours and then I should be free for the rest of the day."

"So I can wander around Faro and amuse myself?"

"If that's what you'd like to do," Jon said. "I can have Clayton go with you."

Marianne wrinkled her nose. "When you told me we were going to Portugal, you didn't tell me about the entourage."

"Einfeld and Clayton are here at my request. They need to be at the meetings, too."

"I didn't realize that congressional campaigns attracted European donors as well as American ones."

Jon had told Marianne that the meetings in Portugal were with some possible campaign donors but he realized that might have been a mistake. Too late now. He would have to keep fabricating the story. "European donors like American politicians because they may be able to influence trade deals and things like that. I don't expect much to come of it." He took a small bite of the crusty roll. "Mainly, I wanted to come here so we could spend some time together."

Jon thought about Einfeld's call. He had posted him at the airport yesterday to check flights from London to spot O'Neill when he arrived. However, O'Neill and his mysterious lady friend might have come in Tuesday night. Or he might not be coming at all. It had never occurred to him that Carswell might come here, too. The question now was what to do about him. Keeping him in sight would be a good tactic, at least until he could find out more. He thought back to his short time in Surrey and his introduction to Carswell. He suddenly remembered the reference to Marianne. She had bought one of his paintings and knew him or at least had met him. He wondered if he could use her to find out what Carswell was up to. It might be worth a try.

"You know Lincoln Carswell, don't you?" he asked.

Marianne appeared startled by the question. Her coffee cup stopped half way between the table and her mouth. "I know of him and I've met him."

"Einfeld knows him by sight and apparently he's just landed at the airport."

Marianne took a drink of her coffee and set the cup down. "And . . .?"

"I haven't told you much about the meetings I was at in England."

"You haven't told me anything about them."

Jon smiled. "And at this point I can't really tell you much."

"Back with all this clandestine crap again, are you?" Marianne stood up. "Just don't try using it to cover up another affair."

"Please sit down," Jon said. "I haven't told you anything because there really wasn't much to tell. I met with a wealthy English landowner and investor and some others. The discussion centred around whether I, or one of the others, would like to join the organization and play some leadership role in it. There is a lot of money and power involved but I didn't learn much of the detail. That's another reason why we're here."

Marianne sat down. "So you're here to learn more. And then what?"

Jon ignored the question. "There were two other men at the meetings in England. One was a stockbroker and the second was Lincoln Carswell."

Marianne was silent.

"We each met individually with the investor and it's beginning to look like he told each of us different things." Jon paused. "It would be helpful to know what he told the others."

Marianne poured more coffee into her cup and looked up at Jon.

"Since you know Carswell, I'd like you to meet him and find out what he knows."

"Really?" Marianne said. "And how do you propose that I do this? I scarcely know the man."

"Einfeld will follow Carswell into town, find out which hotel he is staying at, and from there it shouldn't be too difficult for you to meet him."

The phone rang again. Jon got up and walked back into the room. He picked up the receiver. "Falken," he said.

"I've lost him," Einfeld said. "As I told you, he went into the men's room but he didn't come out. I waited around and eventually went in to check but he wasn't there."

"Is there only one way in and out?"

"Exactly," Einfeld replied. "I have no idea how he got out. He's disappeared. I gave the rental clerk a twenty to tell me what car Carswell had rented. I went out to the parking lot to check and it's gone."

"Goddamn it," Jon whispered. He closed his eyes for a moment. "Well if he's here to follow us or O'Neill, we'll encounter him sooner or later. No sign of O'Neill and his lady friend yet?"

"Not yet," Einfeld replied. "But if they came in Tuesday night or from somewhere other than London we would have missed them."

"My fault," Jon said.

"I'll stay around the airport for a while," Einfeld said.

Jon set the receiver down, walked back out to the balcony and sat down.

"Who was that?" Marianne asked.

"Einfeld again," Jon said. "Apparently, he's lost Carswell or missed him leaving the airport in any case."

CHAPTER EIGHTY NINE

Thursday, May 11, 1989 Albufeira, Portugal

Eva Braun sat in a comfortably padded chaise lounge on the terrace in the sun, sipping coffee with just a hint of cream. Early morning was her favourite time of day, the sun was bright but not yet hot and the terrace was her favourite place to be. It was tiled with creamy white limestone. Part of the terrace, the section near the house, was covered with grape vines climbing up trellises on the sides and across a framework forming a roof and a shaded sitting area. The rest of the terrace was open with a low stone wall around the edge that was a long planter. She liked the annual flowers that were in bloom this time of year. They spilled from the planter and caressed the sides of the wall.

She looked down over the hillside below at the shrubs and grasses that were turning brown. There hadn't been any rain this spring. She had read that the Sahara was spreading, slowly desiccating the northern fringes of Africa. Perhaps it was spreading into southern Portugal as well.

Traffic on the highway above the villa hummed faintly. When she had first moved here in 1949 and settled into the villa, it had been just a local road and traffic noise hadn't been much more than an occasional horn blast aimed by one angry local at another, or just as often, by one friendly local acknowledging another.

She set her coffee cup down on the small table beside her. Below the hillside the ocean sparkled. A couple of fishing boats were specks in the distant haze. As she heard the door open behind her, she picked up her cup and held it out for Anna to refill. She had been with her for twenty years.

"Thank you," she said, speaking Portuguese.

Anna filled her cup and set the coffee pot down on the glass table beside Eva's chair, placing a bowl of chilled fruit next to it.

Eva stared out over the ocean again. She had received a phone call from Jurgen yesterday. He lived in a cottage west of Faro. Jurgen was the only one from the old days who knew how to contact her and even Jurgen did not know her real identity nor her location. Jurgen had called to say that a gentleman wanted to meet with her and had been sent by Herr Bormann. That was not likely since Martin was even less prone than she was to let the world know of his existence but the man with Jurgen had been quite insistent. He had taken the phone and had spoken to her. His German had been learned in America from the sound of it. He obviously did not know who she was either, but was quite determined to meet with her. What nonsense.

She had told him she did not receive visitors. He said he would call back. She smiled. He could wait in Faro the rest of his life and she wouldn't see him. Still, it was a troubling development. She picked up a small apple from the bowl beside her. It was crisp and sweet as she bit into it. She put her head back on the chair and looked up at the sky. She closed her eyes and savoured the taste of the apple.

Anna was touching her shoulder and saying something. She sat up, realizing that she had fallen asleep.

"Jurgen," Anna whispered and handed her the telephone receiver.

Eva sighed. "Good morning, Jurgen," she said. She looked at her watch, slim and black faced with no numbers on it, adorned only by five small diamonds set in a diagonal across the lower face. It was about 9:30.

"Good morning," Jurgen said, speaking German as he always did. "I have another man who wishes to see you. He is with a woman."

"Tell them I don't see people," Eva said. She heard Jurgen say something, then the other man came on the line.

"Good morning, M'am," he said in English. "I understand why you might not wish to see me, but I think you might be my mother and I was hoping that I could meet you."

Eva sat with the phone against her ear. She felt as though her heart had stopped. "You must be mistaken," she replied in English. "I don't have any children."

"Perhaps I am mistaken, then," the man said. "I was born on October 30, 1939 in Germany, in a small town in Bavaria, and I was sent from there to Canada on a U boat, in November 1940. The trip was arranged by Martin Bormann." He paused.

"I don't know anyone by that name," she said, her response automatic, but she sat still, staring out across the hillside to the ocean, seeing nothing, hearing herself in an argument with Bormann about the fate of her child.

The voice went on. "Shortly after I arrived in Canada with my guardians, the house we were staying in burned down and we were all supposed to have perished in the fire."

Eva Braun gasped. How could he have known this? Bormann had only told her after the war. It had been the summer of 1947 and she had been depressed for a year and a half. Then she had come here and slowly started to heal. Was this some terrible joke? Had Bormann gone senile?

She shook her head. "What do you look like?" she asked.

"I am about six feet tall, my hair is wavy, dark blonde, I have blue eyes, regular features."

She sighed. "And you want to meet with me?"

"I do because I thought you might be my mother," the man said. "I was raised in a small town in Canada by the man and woman who accompanied me on the U boat, a doctor and a nurse. They were killed recently in an auto accident and left me some information about my origins which led me to Germany, then to England and now I'm here."

Eva Braun closed her eyes. The description could fit. But then it could also be that of thousands of others. What if he were her son? What if he were not? Was this an issue she wanted to reopen after all these years of peaceful acceptance. "You are in Faro?" she asked.

"Yes, I am," he replied.

"There is a woman with you."

"My wife."

"Do you have children?"

"I had a son who was killed three years ago in an auto accident."

Eva Braun sighed again. "I'm sorry," she said. Her grandson, perhaps. She thought for a moment and realized she would have to meet him. "Find the Algarve Terrace. It is a restaurant. Jurgen knows where it is. If I can meet you, I will be there for dinner at nine this evening."

CHAPTER NINETY

Thursday, May 11, 1989 Faro, Portugal

Lincoln Carswell walked into the Faro airport and went directly to the Hertz rental counter. As he was signing the papers he caught sight of a familiar figure. It took him a moment to recall the face, but it was Clark Einfeld, one of the minders from Surrey and one of the men who had taken him from Philadelphia to Surrey. Einfeld glanced toward him and then walked away. Strange, Lincoln thought, why would Einfeld be here? He felt a twinge of fear. The estate in Surrey had been attacked. He had taken a car and driven off to London. He had just wanted to get the hell out of there. And now Einfeld was here. Perhaps Einfeld hadn't recognized him. Maybe Einfeld was here with Jon. But maybe it wasn't so strange in the context of his experience in Surrey where everything had been positively weird.

"Enjoy your time in Faro, Mr. Carswell," the rental clerk said.

"Thank you, I will," Lincoln replied. "Do you have a map of the city?"

The clerk reached under the counter. "Here you are, sir."

"Thank you."

He picked up the map and the rental contract and walked toward the men's rest room. He had no intention of spending his time in Portugal with Einfeld so he might as well get rid of him now, if he could manage it. He entered one of the stalls, closed the door, set his suitcase on the toilet and opened it. He took off his blazer, folded it and placed it in the suitcase, unfolded his cane, put on his cap and a pair of sunglasses, and closed the suitcase. He didn't really have time for make up so this would have to do. But people looked for what they expected.

He bent over slightly and shuffled back out into the airport concourse. He spotted Einfeld near the Hertz counter, watching the entrance to the rest room. Einfeld seemed to take no notice of him as he walked slowly over to a currency exchange counter and traded some US dollars for Portuguese escudos. Then he strolled out of the terminal exit.

He drove the small Fiat into the centre of Faro and found the Santa Maria Hotel

that the London travel agent had booked for him. He parked the car, leaned back in the seat and took a deep breath and relaxed.

"Good morning," the hotel clerk said as Lincoln walked up to the counter. "Welcome to the Santa Maria."

He checked in and was shown to his room. It was an old hotel, but his room on the fourth floor had what felt like a comfortable bed when he sat on it, a clean bathroom and a small balcony with a couple of white plastic chairs. He unpacked his few belongings and checked the map. Marianne hadn't known where she and Jon were staying in Faro when he'd talked to her in London. But all European cities had a cathedral, usually with a square in front of it, and they had chosen that as a meeting place, ideally around the noon hour. They would try to check there each day.

Lincoln looked at the bedside clock. It was 11:26. He put on his cap, gathered his cane and his sunglasses, took a sketch pad and a couple of pencils from his suitcase, and returned to the lobby.

"Do you have a business card?" he asked the clerk. "In case I get lost and need the address?"

"Of course," the clerk replied, indicating a small pile of them on the right side of the counter.

Lincoln picked up a couple of cards and walked out of the hotel, spotting the doorman off to one side having a cigarette. "Can you get me a taxi and tell him to take me to the cathedral?"

A few minutes later he got out of the taxi and strolled across a large open square. He chose a small outdoor café and sat down at a table. A waiter walked over and handed him a menu.

Across the square, he had a good view of the stone entrance of the church. It was different from a lot of cathedrals he had seen, the front entry structure was stone, a beige colour that could be limestone, but the main body of the building was white, perhaps whitewashed brick or stone. The tower at the front was low and blocky, not the soaring structure that was more common in European cathedrals. Judging from the steady stream of people going in and out, it appeared to be well patronized by the faithful.

The waiter returned to take his order. Eric glanced down the short menu and ordered a croissant. The waiter said, "Coffee?"

"Espresso."

Just as the waiter arrived with his order, a bell in the cathedral tolled announcing the noon hour. It was a warm sunny day, a pleasant spot to be watching pigeons foraging for scraps or gathering around people who were feeding them.

He leaned back in his chair and opened his sketch pad. First he drew an outline of the cathedral, roughing in the doors and windows and a bit of the detail of the low tower at the front. On the second page he began a series of panoramic sketches of the shops, cafes, benches and the like around the periphery of the square. As he was adding a couple of figures entering the square from the opposite side, he was surprised to see another familiar figure, another of the minders from Surrey. He searched for a name and it came to him. Clayton. Steven Clayton.

Clayton was looking intently around the square, clearly trying to spot someone or something. Lincoln went back to his sketch, deftly adding Clayton as a small figure, standing in front of a restaurant a few doors down from the café. When he glanced up Clayton was gone.

Lincoln scanned the square again and saw Marianne Falken, her head covered in a white scarf, strolling slowly across the square toward the cathedral entrance. She was wearing a shawl around her shoulders which covered most of a bright turquoise blouse complemented by a pair of tight white slacks.

He started a new sketch of the tower as he watched her enter the cathedral. He thought of following her but decided to wait a few minutes. The stream of people going in and out continued. He had never understood people with a deep and abiding faith in something as ephemeral as religion, but in a way, he did envy the comfort they derived from it. It would be a fine thing to have all the answers to all of the questions, crises and problems of life and to be forgiven for everything one did wrong, or failed to do right. He had thought about it but it seemed more like a handy way to avoid responsibility for his own actions. He was shaken out of his reverie by the sight of Clayton walking into the church. What kind of forgiveness was he seeking?

He picked up his croissant and took a bite, light and flaky, suspiciously like a French croissant, and followed it with a swallow of coffee. Two more bites and the croissant was finished. He looked around and the waiter appeared at his side. The waiter retrieved a bill from a pocket of his apron and put it on the table, clearing away the dishes.

Lincoln set some escudos on the table, closed his sketch pad and stood up. He opened his city map and began to stroll toward the cathedral entrance. He stood outside for a moment, looking up at the bell tower. Then he held the map carefully in front of him and kept an eye on the entrance.

Marianne walked out, pulled a pair of sunglasses from her purse and put them on. She looked around as Lincoln approached her.

"Excuse me," he said. "Are you American?"

She looked at him, recognition slowly dawning. "Yes," she replied. "But I'm in a hurry."

Lincoln set a hotel business card on the map as he held it in front of her. "Do you know where this is?"

Marianne picked up the card. "Sorry, I don't," she said, and walked away.

Clayton came out a minute later. Lincoln continued looking at his map and glancing around, the picture of a confused tourist. Clayton strolled across the square after Marianne.

CHAPTER NINETY ONE

Thursday, May 11, 1989 West of Faro, Portugal

"Nine o'clock this evening then," Eric O'Neill said quietly, handing the phone back to Jurgen. Maybe the search would be over then, or maybe just beginning. Jurgen was a small old man, bent over and white haired. He seemed to be a gentle soul. "Thank you for your help."

Jurgen nodded and said something in German. Liselle smiled and answered him in German. They chatted for a moment and then Liselle frowned and spoke quickly. While Eric couldn't understand what they were talking about, Liselle was clearly distraught. Then she reached out and touched the old man's hand, nodded and smiled at him. Jurgen held out his hand and in turn, both Liselle and Eric shook it slowly and formally, as though concluding an important agreement.

"They're here," Liselle said as they made their way down the narrow gravel driveway to the small green Renault they had rented at the airport.

"Who?"

"Whoever is chasing you," Liselle said. "Jurgen said we were much nicer than the other man. I asked him what he meant and he said that yesterday a man showed up looking for the old woman. It sounded like Jon Falken."

"Jon Falken?" Eric asked. "How do you know him?"

"It's a long story that doesn't matter," Liselle replied. "But he was with you in Surrey, wasn't he? What did you think of him?"

Eric thought about the question as he held the car door for Liselle. He got behind the wheel, backed the car around and started up the narrow road to the highway. "Bright guy, very ambitious, kind of scary in a way."

"Scary is a good description," Liselle said. "He is also ruthless and dangerous."

"How do you know all this?"

Liselle stared ahead. "I knew him in Philadelphia," she said quietly. "You just need to know that he will kill you without a moment's hesitation if it serves his purpose."

"Kill me? You can't be serious."

"Eric, what can I do to make you understand?"

"Tell me what's going on."

"I have told you," she said. "But did Jon tell you about the plans for his future?"

"No."

"He plans to run for a seat in congress, then in another four or eight years, to run for the presidency of the US."

"Ambitious man," Eric said.

"You are aware that the US president must be born in the US?"

Eric nodded. "I see," he said. "And Jon was born in Germany like I was."

"But Jon claims he was born in Philadelphia."

"So he can't be president.

"He can if no one finds out," Liselle said. "But you know and that makes you a threat to his future."

"So you think he would kill me to silence me?"

"In a heartbeat."

Eric drove on in silence.

"What was she like?" Liselle asked.

"The old woman on the phone? Surprised, reserved I guess," Eric said. "I suspect she's meeting us to satisfy her curiosity. She seemed quite firm when she said she had no children, but who knows, maybe it's just a natural reaction."

"How are you feeling, Eric?"

"About the possibility of meeting my mother?"

"That too, but just in general."

Eric was silent for a minute. "I wish I had taken my father's advice and left the whole damn thing alone. Nothing I've learned means a lot to me and now I have to change my life and I don't want to." He paused. "If Jon Falken is a serious danger to us do we have a plan to avoid him or deal with him?"

"I hope so," Liselle said. "But leave that to me."

"Gladly."

Liselle touched his arm. "I'm really sorry about the changes in your life but I don't see any other way."

As they entered the outskirts of Faro, Liselle spoke again. "Drive along the waterfront and let me out."

Eric turned the little car down a narrow street and turned toward the waterfront.

A couple of minutes later, Liselle said, "This will do."

He pulled over to the curb and stopped. Liselle leaned over to him, kissed him lightly on the cheek, and opened the door.

"I'll be gone for a while," she said.

"Would you like me to come with you?"

"No," she replied. "We have to stay separated as much as possible."

Eric looked at her and smiled. "Sometime when this is all over, are you going to tell me who you really are? Or all of the people you really are?"

Liselle laughed brightly. "Maybe I will," she said. "Or some of them at least." She squeezed his hand. "I'll be in touch. Stay in your room." She smiled.

"What are you smiling at?"

"My own last comment," she said. "I sounded like a mother talking to a little boy."

Eric chuckled. "I'll do as I'm told."

He watched the swing of her hips in the tight blue jeans as she strolled off down the street. She glanced over her shoulder, saw him watching her and waved her fingers at him. He knew she was staying near here somewhere but she had insisted that they register in separate hotels this time. He had to appear to be alone to anyone who found him, and she would not tell him where she was staying.

A few minutes later he parked the Renault in the yard behind the small hotel where he was registered. He had rented a suite on the top floor, which was only the third floor, but the suite was quite spacious. It had a bedroom, a bathroom, a kitchenette, a living room and a balcony. Eric lay down on the bed and thought through the last few days. He wondered again what the hell was he doing here chasing a background he didn't really care about. But he must care, or he wouldn't be doing it. Maybe it was like a poker game. He had too much on the table to fold. He had to see it through.

Whatever the logic or lack of it, now they were in Faro. Tonight he might meet the woman who was his mother. He might even find out who she was, other than an older

German woman who had some connection to a high ranking Nazi fifty years ago.

He got off the bed and sat down at the desk. He set the briefcase in front of him and opened it. He looked through the financial materials, list of money transfers, some with notations, most without any indication of what they were for. And then he came to a series of codes that meant nothing except for the word "Portugal". He removed the page and studied it, then folded it, stood up and put it in his jacket pocket, a slim bit of evidence that might be handy to have if he really was meeting a woman who might be his mother.

He thought about Laura and looked at his watch. It was 10:30. That would make it early evening in Portage. He picked up the phone and asked the hotel operator to place the call. A couple of minutes later the phone rang and he heard Laura's voice.

"You're working late tonight," he said.

"Eric?" she answered. "Where are you?"

"I'm in Portugal, on the south coast, a city called Faro."

"It's wonderful to hear your voice."

"Yours too."

"And how is your search working out?"

"I wish I had never bothered with it," Eric said. "It isn't leading me anywhere I want to go and what I'm finding out, more than anything else, is that I really don't care about a fifty year old personal history."

"Don't rush it, Eric," Laura said. "You're still forty nine!"

Eric smiled. "I guess I am for another few months. How are things in Portage?"

The line was silent for a moment. "In Portage things are okay. But I've made a change in my life that I'll tell you more about when I see you. The short story is that I've left Darrin."

"Really?" Eric said. He found himself smiling at the idea she was free and at a complete loss for words.

"Really," she said. "I have a favour to ask."

"Of course."

"I didn't have anywhere to go so I'm staying in your parents' house for the time being. Is that okay?"

"Certainly. I'm sure they would have wanted you to and so do I."

"You're sure?"

"Absolutely."

"Do you know when you're coming home?"

Eric was silent for a moment. How much could he explain? "I should be finished here within a day or two and then I'll be in touch."

"That sounds good."

"I may not be coming home for a while. Some complications have come up about my origins but I'll tell you more when I know more."

"That sounds very mysterious," Laura said.

"Yes, it does," Eric said. "We'll figure things out."

"I hope so."

"Me, too.

CHAPTER NINETY TWO

Thursday, May 11, 1989 Faro, Portugal

Marianne Falken sat in her hotel room and looked at the business card Lincoln had passed to her. The "Santa Maria Hotel", it read, with an address on Rua du Portugal. She had no idea where that was but there was also a phone number. She wondered about calling him.

Steven Clayton had followed her wherever she had gone this morning. Jon had said he would have Clayton accompany her if she was going shopping. When she protested Jon merely said he wanted her to be safe and Clayton could carry her shopping bag. She refused this arrangement but discovered Clayton not very discreetly following her anyway.

After she left the Cathedral and put Lincoln's hotel card safely in her purse, she confronted Clayton and told him if he insisted on coming with her, he might as well be useful. She went into a shop that sold scarves, shoes and purses. She loved the rich copper colour of her hair but it was a mixed blessing.

She had to be quite careful with the colours she wore. As she was holding several scarves up to see how they looked, she idly asked Clayton what he thought. She was surprised when he picked up another scarf, a pale teal colour, and suggested it might be a better choice. It was and she thanked him. For the rest of her short shopping expedition she consulted him several times and found he was helpful. He also smiled and even laughed a couple of times, something she hadn't seen before. She decided she enjoyed his company and quite liked him.

When she got back to the hotel, Einfeld was there and Jon was waiting to leave, ostensibly to go a meeting. Clayton joined them and they left. Jon said he would be gone a couple of hours and suggested she stay in the hotel while he was away. What nonsense.

So now she knew where Lincoln was. She picked up the phone and then set it down. Maybe the hotel logged calls. She went to the bathroom to freshen her makeup, grabbed her purse and went down to the lobby. She thought of catching a taxi but wondered if Jon would check with the front desk when he returned. She smiled. There was more to having an affair than just going to bed.

She walked down the street, looking in the windows of several shops until she came to another hotel. She approached the doorman and asked him to get her a taxi. He waved his hand imperiously and small blue car emerged from a side street and stopped in front of her. Marianne tipped the doorman, got into the rear seat of the car and handed the driver Lincoln's card. He nodded and handed it back.

She looked around as she entered the lobby of the Santa Maria Hotel. It was older and more modest than where she was staying. She approached the front desk. "Would you call Lincoln Carswell's room, please?" she asked.

The clerk smiled at her. "I'm sorry, but Mr. Carswell went out a while ago and I don't believe he's returned. I'll call his room to make certain." After a few moments the clerk shook his head and hung up the desk phone. "Would you like to leave a message?"

"Yes, please," she replied.

The clerk handed her a slip of paper and a pen, then looked past her and smiled again. "Here is Mr. Carswell, now," he said.

She turned and saw Lincoln, still with his cane and his cap, walking into the hotel lobby. "There you are," she said, moving toward him and extending her hand.

"Indeed," Lincoln said, shaking her hand and holding on to it.

They got into a small elevator, still holding hands. It rattled slowly up to the fourth floor.

"Thank you for the card, Mr. Carswell," Marianne said, as they got out of the elevator.

"My pleasure, Ms. Falken."

They both laughed as they walked down the hall. Lincoln took a large old fashioned key from his pocket, unlocked the door and ushered her into his room. She turned, slipped into his arms and held him tightly.

"I missed you," she whispered.

Lincoln kissed her, his cane falling to the floor. He backed her toward the bed and pushed her down.

Later they sat on the balcony, the two small chairs pulled close together.

"You didn't tell me you met my husband," Marianne said.

Lincoln looked at her for a moment. "No," he said. "There didn't seem much point and besides we seemed to find other things to do."

"We did, didn't we?" Marianne said. "So you and Jon and some other guy met with an English investor who runs some large concern?"

"Actually, he was German, not English," Lincoln replied. "And the other guy was a Canadian stockbroker. Nice guy."

Marianne smiled. "Here is something ironic for you. Jon recalled that I had met you in Philadelphia and wants me to meet you here and find out if this investor told you anything that he didn't tell him."

Lincoln laughed. "I think the investor, as Jon calls him, is a bit of a nut case. The only time he spoke to me was when he talked to the three of us over dinner so he didn't tell me anything that Jon didn't hear."

"A nut case?"

"He is an old guy in his 80's with a bunch of money and he wants someone to run his organization." Lincoln paused. "I'd rather have a root canal."

Marianne laughed. "Well Jon thinks that this old guy talked separately to each of you and told you different things. He wants me to find out what he told you."

"Well now you know."

Marianne looked at him thoughtfully. "So why didn't you tell me in London what was going on?"

"I'm not sure I know what's going on," Lincoln replied. "Do you remember my telling you that I was born in Germany and brought to the US as part of some plan to rescue and resettle orphaned German children?"

Marianne nodded. "And you were adopted by a family in Nazareth, Pennsylvania."

"Right," Lincoln said. "And this old guy brought the three of us together because we were all born in Germany and brought to North America in 1940, I assume under the same program."

"That can't be right," Marianne said. "Jon was born in Philadelphia,"

"Not according to this old guy."

"But I've seen Jon's birth certificate and his passport. They both say Philadelphia."

Lincoln shrugged. "I wouldn't know. However, as I said, I'm not quite sure what's going on."

Marianne was stunned. "If this is true, and Jon was born in Germany, he can't run for the presidency."

"I guess not," Lincoln said. "Where does Jon say he was born?"

"He's always claimed it was Philly."

"If Jon is seriously thinking of running, then whoever knows this can stop him," Lincoln said. "Unfortunately, I'm one of the people who knows this and Jon knows that I know. I don't care about politics and have no intention of talking about this but Jon doesn't know that."

Marianne looked carefully at Lincoln and thought about Jon. What would he do with people who knew? Would he ignore them or perhaps bribe them? She didn't see Jon doing either. The thought crept unwillingly into her mind. Would he have them killed?

Lincoln ran his fingers into the back of her hair. "You're deep in thought," he whispered.

Marianne nodded. "Jon is deadly serious about getting a congressional seat and then running for the presidency. If he really was born in Germany he'll do anything to keep this information secret." She paused. "Surely he would have told me," she whispered. But even as she said it, she knew it wasn't true.

CHAPTER NINETY THREE

Thursday, May 11, 1989 Faro, Portugal

Yesterday, Jon Falken had sent Clayton out into the country to watch Jurgen's cottage to see if O'Neill and his lady friend showed up and early this morning they had. Now Jurgen was reluctant to tell him what he and O'Neill had talked about. Well that was just too Goddamned bad for Jurgen.

Jon was developing a grudging respect for Clayton. He had reported O'Neill's visit and then followed Marianne on her morning excursion. Marianne seemed to like him so he had gained her confidence. But then women often seemed to like faggots. Still, Clayton did what he was told, did it well, was observant and even resourceful.

Jon turned his attention back to Jurgen. He and the old man were facing each other sitting on two battered wooden chairs in the small kitchen of the cottage. He had asked Jurgen if a man and woman had come to see him this morning. Jurgen had nodded but had declined to tell him much else. Jon sighed. He looked up at Clayton. Take his right hand and break one of his fingers," Jon said quietly to Clayton in English. "Any finger will do."

He looked back at the old man. "Hold up your right hand," he said in German.

The old man looked at him inquiringly and raised his right hand.

Clayton stepped forward and grasped his hand, deftly bending back the index finger. The snap was audible.

The old man howled, wrenching his hand free and doubled over in pain.

Jon reached forward and lifted Jurgen's chin. Tears were running down his wrinkled old cheeks. "You must answer my questions," he said, his voice soft and comforting. "Or this man will hurt you again."

The old man nodded. "No more, please," he whimpered.

"A man and a woman came to see you?"

The old man nodded.

"Did they tell you their names?"

No."

"What did they want?"

"They wanted to talk to the old woman, like you did."

"So they used your telephone to do that?"

"Yes."

Did she agree to meet with them?"

"I think so."

"When?"

"Tonight."

"Where?"

"In Faro, at the Algarve Terrace."

"What is that?"

"It's a fancy restaurant."

"Who is this old woman?"

"I don't know."

Jon sighed and leaned back in his chair. Perhaps the old man didn't know. Perhaps he did. He looked up at Clayton. "Break another finger," he said quietly. "The other hand this time."

Clayton moved behind the old man and grasped his other arm.

"Stop," the old man shouted. "I know nothing. She is some old Jewess who hides from the world. I have never seen her. I don't know where she lives."

Jon held up his hand, signaling for Clayton to stop. Clayton kept his grip on the old man's arm.

"You have her phone number."

"It is the one I used when you were here. It is a number for Albufeira."

"Where is that?"

"Down the coast, a fishing village."

Einfeld spoke for the first time. "I saw it on the map we got with the car. The guide book says there's not much there but a fishing village and some tourist condominiums."

Jon looked back at the old man, whimpering softly, clutching his hand, rocking on his chair with the pain. Jon stood up and looked around. "There are some stairs down to the cellar," he said, speaking to Clayton.

Clayton nodded. He came around to the old man's left side and very gently helped him to his feet. Jurgen cringed in fear, pulling away from him. Clayton patted him reassuringly on his back and led him across the kitchen. He stopped near the old black stove and stepped behind him. Slipping one arm around the old man's neck, he braced the other one and with a quick hard motion broke his neck. Jurgen slumped toward the floor but Clayton held him. He dragged him to the top of the stairs, balanced him there for a moment and let him topple forward, head first down the narrow stairway. Then Clayton went down the first few steps and returned a moment later.

"I undid one shoe lace," he said. "In case anyone wonders what he tripped on."

Jon nodded at him. "Nice touch."

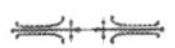

Jon Falken sat on the small balcony of their hotel room. He glanced at his watch. It was a few minutes before five. He didn't normally have a drink before five but he decided this was close enough. He stood up and walked back into the room. He had arrived home to discover that Marianne had disobeyed him and left the hotel room. Christ, he thought, he should be used to it by now. He picked up a bottle of Johnnie Walker Black, not his favourite Scotch, but very nice, nonetheless. It was the only decent Scotch they had in the small liquor store on the corner across from the hotel. He poured some in a glass, added ice, and walked back out to the balcony. He thought better with a Scotch in his hand, and he had some things to think about.

First, who was this old woman whose contact information he had found in the papers he had taken from Bormann's office? It sounded as though she was the mother of one of them, Carswell, O'Neill or him. If she were a Jew, as Jurgen had said, then a Jew might end up leading Bormann's organization. He smiled at the irony. But that couldn't be. Bormann hated Jews far too much. It must be a cover identity. So if she wasn't a Jew, she could be the wife or, more likely, the widow of some important Nazi. Who cares, he decided. She no longer had any obvious influence in the world, if she ever did have.

"Who was the father?" was the more interesting question. Perhaps she could tell him, but as he thought about it, he realized that at this point in his life he didn't really give a shit. He was his own man, personally successful in every endeavour he had ever undertaken. His origins wouldn't change that. He was a self-made man. He smiled wryly as he thought of the old saying. "A self-made man is a horrible example of unskilled labour." Bullshit! But she might lead him to O'Neill.

O'Neill was the second problem. He had the information on Bormann's organization and he would have to give it up. Since a lot of it would be financial information and since O'Neill was a stockbroker and would understand that stuff, it would be useful to get his take on it. But accountants were a dime a dozen and once he had the information, Einfeld could no doubt find a discreet and sympathetic one.

An additional problem, but one with a simple solution, was that the secret of his birth in Germany was now known by both O'Neill and Carswell. He heard the door to the hotel room open. He looked over his shoulder and saw Marianne closing the door.

"I'm on the balcony," he called. "Pour yourself a Scotch and join me."

Marianne walked over to the bedroom dresser and poured herself a drink, added some ice and water and strolled out onto the balcony.

"I asked you not to leave the hotel room," Jon said as she sat down.

"You did," she said, taking a sip of her drink. "But you also said I should find out what your English investor told Lincoln Carswell and I can't find that out sitting here."

Jon looked at her in surprise. "And did you manage that?"

"I think so," she replied. "I took a taxi to the old town, wandered around the square in front of the cathedral, went into a few shops and then I saw him, taking pictures of the square."

"He was just being a tourist?"

"So far as I could tell," Marianne said. "Anyway, I walked up to him, introduced myself. He remembered me from one of his shows, or at least was gracious enough to say he did, and he bought me a drink."

"Of course he would remember you," Jon said. "You bought one of his paintings."

Marianne nodded. "So we got chatting and I said, 'I hear you met my husband recently at a meeting.' He said he had and I asked him about it. He told me your English investor was actually German and that you all had dinner together."

"Who had dinner?" Jon asked.

"The old German guy, you, him and another guy, a stockbroker. Incidentally, he thinks the old guy is crazy. He called him a 'nut case' and said he really didn't understand what it was all about and left as soon as he could."

"Did he have a private meeting with the investor?"

"It didn't sound like it," Marianne replied. "He said you all had dinner together and the old guy told you about his organization. That was the only meeting he had from the sound of it."

"You're sure?"

"I'm not positive, but it sounded like it was."

"Where is he staying?"

"I didn't ask."

"Why not?"

"Think about it, Jon," she said. "I meet a man I scarcely know, he buys me a drink, and I ask him where he's staying. I'd sound like I was coming on to him."

"I see what you mean."

"Besides, you didn't tell me to find that out."

Jon looked at Marianne. She was staring off down the street. Then she leaned forward to pick up her Scotch. The cleavage was still there. God, she had nice tits.

She turned to look at him. "So what's next?"

"Tonight we are going out for dinner," Jon replied. "I heard about a good restaurant, overlooks the ocean. We have a reservation for 8:30."

"That sounds pleasant," Marianne said. "What's it called?"

"The Algarve Terrace," Jon said. "Just the two of us."

"I think I'd like to lie down for a little while," Marianne said. "I have a slight headache and this Scotch isn't helping it." She leaned over and poured the remainder of her drink into Jon's glass. Her breast brushed against his arm as she did so but she didn't seem to notice.

When Marianne was gone, Jon thought about the evening ahead. When he showed up at the restaurant, O'Neill would certainly recognize him. He wondered how he should handle it. Go over and chat with O'Neill? Buy him a drink? Invite him to join them?

If O'Neill were meeting the old woman there for dinner he would certainly want to be alone with her and find out what she was all about, Nazi, or mother, or whatever. So perhaps the wisest course would be to leave them alone and then later question O'Neill. Clayton and Einfeld would not be in the restaurant but when they had checked it out on their way back from dealing with Jurgen, they had seen there was a bar area separate from the dining area. He would put them in there. It would be an interesting evening.

CHAPTER NINETY FOUR

Thursday, May 11, 1989 Faro, Portugal

Lincoln Carswell tried on a dark brown sports jacket in the small menswear shop down the street from Marianne's hotel. The fit wasn't perfect but good enough. He had on a new pale blue tie and a beige shirt. He had left his cap in the hotel room but had put on a dark brown hairpiece with grey at the temples, and had picked up a pair of black framed reading glasses with a point five diopter correction, the weakest ones he could find. He often wore reading glasses when he was painting fine detail. He had left the cane in his hotel room. In the dressing room he looked in the mirror at his new image. It should work.

Lincoln paid for his new wardrobe and was just getting into his car, parked around the corner but still with a view of the front of the hotel, when he saw Marianne and Jon come out of the hotel entrance. Jon spoke to the doorman and a taxi pulled up. They got in and it drove off. Lincoln followed the taxi as it headed toward the ocean, then turned west briefly before pulling into a drop off area in front of a restaurant. He drove by, turned down a side street, made a U turn and headed back to the restaurant. He found a parking spot in the lot and turned off the engine, deciding to wait a few minutes before going in.

The parking lot had been paved a long time ago and was showing bulges where roots of the large trees around the perimeter of the lot were pushing it up. The lines delineating parking spots had long since worn off.

He rolled down the windows and let the fresh evening air drift through the car. Rustling leaves combined with the gentle sound of the waves breaking on the beach below the restaurant were almost hypnotic. He leaned back in the seat and relaxed careful to keep his eyes open.

Where was this romance leading? He had been married, had a few semi-permanent women in his life for varying periods of time but, except for his wife, had never had any interest in a permanent relationship, if that wasn't an oxymoron. And now there was Marianne. She was beautiful and he was enormously attracted to her. But there was more than that. She was intelligent, thoughtful, insightful and fabulously good in bed. He realized he was trying to rationalize falling in love. He smiled. "Rationalization is the aspirin of mental health," as Charlie Brown once said.

A car drove past him and parked a few spots away. Two men got out and walked toward the entrance to the restaurant. Einfeld and Clayton again, the minders from Surrey. Were they following Jon? Or were they with him? He decided to wait a while longer and a few minutes later he was rewarded.

Eric O'Neill drove in and parked two spaces over from his car. O'Neill got out and walked across the rippling pavement, up the broad set of stairs and through a large set of double doors into the restaurant. Moments later he walked out and returned to his car. He sat there and waited. Lincoln looked at his watch. It was a few minutes before nine. This whole thing was getting more and more bizarre.

A large black Mercedes drove up to the entrance of the restaurant and stopped. The driver got out and opened a rear door. He offered his hand to a woman who stepped out of the car and stood there for a moment. In the lights from the entrance, he could see that she was slim and dressed elegantly in a tailored black suit. She looked around in a leisurely way, taking in the entrance, the parked cars, the palm trees around the building, without really pausing on anything. It wasn't an arrogant look, just a survey of the surroundings, perhaps a trace of boredom or even amusement in how she stood.

Lincoln heard a car door close nearby and watched as O'Neill walked rapidly toward the Mercedes. He stopped and spoke to the woman. Her wavy dark blonde hair bobbed as she nodded in response to something that O'Neill said. They shook hands, continued chatting briefly and then they both got into the Mercedes. The driver who had been standing behind the woman closed the rear door, then climbed into the front and drove off.

CHAPTER NINETY FIVE

Thursday, May 11, 1989 Faro, Portugal

"Take us to the Citadel," she said, naming another restaurant on the waterfront. The driver pulled onto the street and drove slowly eastward.

Eva Braun glanced at the young man sitting beside her. She realized that he would be almost fifty, but at seventy seven, she thought of him as young. It was dim in the back seat of the car so she couldn't see him clearly. In the uneven light of the restaurant entry she had seen his handsome regular features. He appeared slim and fit, overall a very nice looking man.

"I thought your wife was with you?"

"She's not feeling well this evening," Eric said.

She looked at him closely. "You said your hair was dark blonde. It looks dark brown."

Eric smiled. "I colour it. It's naturally dark blonde. The same colour as your hair."

He had an engaging smile but already there was the hair colour and no wife. Perhaps she had made a mistake.

The car pulled into a parking lot and stopped. The driver got out and opened the door for her. Eric got out the other side.

"Come back for us in an hour," she said to the driver. An hour should answer her questions but she also knew that her driver would not be far away if she needed him.

Eric offered her his arm as they went up the broad stone steps and into the lobby. The large foyer looked like the entrance to a small castle, stone walls, some old looking coats of arms, and on the counter, two small but detailed model wooden sailing ships.

She spoke briefly in Portuguese to a young man at the reception counter and he led them to a table for two set against a large window overlooking the ocean. He held her chair as she sat and then lit a candle in a glass lamp near the edge of the table. She ordered a glass of white wine for each of them, a crisp vinho verde, with just a touch of sweetness. If this young man was her son, she could choose for him, if he weren't, then it didn't matter.

Finally, she turned her attention to Eric. His head was tilted slightly, a trace of a smile on his lips, his blue eyes wide, looking expectantly at her. She was stunned. She gasped and put her hand over her mouth.

His expression changed, replaced with one of concern as he leaned toward her.

She shook her head silently, staring at him. Then she whispered. "You have your father's eyes."

Eric sat back like she had struck him. "You knew my father?"

Eva nodded.

"Then will you please end this dreadful mystery and tell me?"

She was getting over her initial shock. "Perhaps I am mistaken," she said, forcing a smile. "Your eyes remind me of someone I knew a long time ago."

The waiter arrived and set a crystal glass of white wine in front of each of them. He spoke to Eva in Portuguese. She shook her head.

"Will you tell me his name?" Eric asked.

"Not yet," she said. "Let's talk a bit more. I don't want to give you information that may not be true."

Eric nodded. "Very well," he said. "What would you like to know?"

"Tell me again about your background. You said you went to Canada in a U-boat during the fall of 1940. Is that correct?"

"Yes," Eric replied. He recounted the details of the information he had found.

Eva listened intently. "And tell me again how you learned this."

"My adoptive parents were killed in an auto accident a few weeks ago. The safety deposit box in their bank contained an account of my move from Germany to Canada and some banking information. They didn't know who my birth parents were but speculated that they must have been important in the hierarchy of the Third Reich, either politically, militarily or both, to have accomplished this."

"And what was the point of sending you to Canada?" Eva asked.

"To keep me safe until Germany won the war and then to return me to Germany."

"Yes," Eva said softly, nodding her head. "There was such a program."

"Apparently there were at least two other children who were also sent abroad, although they were sent to the United States, not Canada."

"Really?" Eva said. This was a surprise. Who were these others? Could one of them be her son? She picked up her glass and sipped the cool crisp wine. Perhaps none of them were.

"You said you had a son," she said.

"I did," Eric replied. "He was killed in a car accident almost three years ago. He was seventeen and about to graduate from high school. Geoffrey was a very fine young man."

"Do you have a picture of him?"

"Not with me," Eric said. "But I could send you one. He looked a lot like his mother."

"His mother is with you?" She watched Eric frown.

"It's a bit complicated," he said. "His mother died about six months after he did." He paused. "She committed suicide."

"I'm sorry," Eva said. "I didn't mean to ask painful questions but who is the woman with you now? The one you referred to as your wife?"

"We've been living together," Eric said. "But we aren't married."

"I see," Eva said. What could she tell this earnest young man? If he really were her son, perhaps the truth. If she was wrong she would pass on a burden he might not wish to carry. Of course, that could be true even if he were her son. She would also expose her own identity and that could be a lethal decision. Still, if he were her son, perhaps he deserved to know who his parents were.

The waiter arrived again. She ordered halibut for both of them. He refilled their glasses, although Eric had scarcely touched his wine. She was surprised to see her own glass was nearly empty. She had no recollection of anything but the first sip.

"Can you tell me now who my father and mother were?"

Eva thought for a moment. "Come with me," she said, standing up. "This will seem strange but please indulge me." She led him to the entrance of the women's rest room. "Wait here," she said and went in the door. A moment later she was back. "Come in here with me," she said.

She saw the look of surprise on Eric's face and smiled. "Come on. There's no one inside. We'll only be a moment."

She took his hand and led him into the small room and over to one of the sinks where the overhead lights shone down.

"Lean forward," she said. "I want to look at your hair."

"I told you that it's coloured brown," Eric said.

"It's not the colour I want to see."

He obediently leaned forward and she pushed her fingers into his hair just where it was parted on the left side. She probed and pushed the hair back and then she saw it, a small scar about an inch above his hairline. Her hands shook for a moment and she felt tears welling into her eyes. The accidental scar from his birth, put there by the wretched doctor who had delivered him. She touched the scar gently, leaned forward and brushed her lips over it.

Eric stood up, a puzzled look on his face. "Are you okay?" he asked.

Eva nodded and turned away, pulling a tissue from a dispenser on the counter and wiping the tears from her eyes. She looked in the mirror but her eye makeup was still intact. "Come," she said, taking his hand again. She led him back to their table.

Eric held her chair, then pushed it in as she sat down. "Can you tell me what that was all about?"

"I can tell you some of it," she said. "You were born in a small town in Bavaria in a private clinic. I can give you the name of it if you wish to check their records but you won't learn much more. Your birth name was Erich, spelled with an 'h'. Your parents in Canada anglicized it." She looked carefully at him and wondered again how much trust she could put in a man she had just met, even if he were her son.

"When you were born, the attending doctor took over from a midwife and his clumsiness left a small scar just above your hairline. That is what I was checking in the rest room."

"How did you know this?" Eric asked.

Eva glanced past Eric and sat back in her chair as the waiter arrived with their halibut. He set the plates in front of them and ground some pepper over each of the filets. Eva nodded and waved him away.

Eric was looking at her expectantly.

"Because I was there," she said. She took a deep breath and let it out slowly. "Because I am your mother."

"But you said . . ."

"I know what I said," she replied. "And when we are finished with this conversation I will say the same thing again. I don't have any children."

Eva watched Eric's reaction. His eyes were wide, almost startled looking. She saw the blood drain from his face. He stared at her and nodded slowly. "Found and lost again, all in one evening."

"You said you were raised by parents who loved you and nurtured you. You are very fortunate. You don't need any other parents. Certainly not me."

"You haven't told me your name."

"No," she said. "Is it important to you?"

"I don't know," Eric said. "I guess I have a natural curiosity."

"You are correct to assume that one of your parents was a powerful figure in the Third Reich. Do you know much about the Third Reich?"

"Only what I learned in high school history and from watching TV accounts."

"And what are your thoughts?"

Eric was quiet for a moment. "It seems like the entire country went mad. I can understand how one inspiring madman could become a leader but I don't understand the kind of mass hysteria that must have prevailed to have led to the horrors of the Third Reich. I have read that if Adolf Hitler had died in the early 1930's he would have been regarded as one of the great leaders of Germany because of his economic recovery program. But the holocaust, the death camps, the horrors of World War II made him the most reviled leader in history." He paused. "You must have lived through that."

Eva nodded. "I did." She looked down at her plate. "Shall we eat our dinner before it gets cold?"

CHAPTER NINETY SIX

Thursday, May 11, 1989 Faro, Portugal

Marianne Falken saw Jon look at his watch and glance around the restaurant again. He had been doing this continually for at least the last fifteen minutes. The restaurant had few customers when they arrived but more were coming in fairly steadily. She took a sip of the dark red wine that the waiter had recommended. It wasn't anything she was familiar with. It had a trace more acidity than she preferred but it was pleasant.

The Algarve Terrace was on the ocean front, and the outdoor terrace itself was sheltered on the west from the prevailing wind by a high stone wall. A fire burned in an outdoor fireplace against the wall. Still, it was almost on the verge of being cool. Jon had chosen the terrace because he said it was more intimate, the tables were farther apart and they would be able to talk more freely. The inside area was full of larger tables seating six to ten people and they were crowded together in a warm noisy atmosphere.

She glanced at her own watch and saw it was a little after 9:30. "Are you expecting someone?" she asked.

Jon looked at her distractedly. "Expecting someone?" he said. "Yes . . . perhaps."

"And are you going to tell me?

"One of the people who was at the meetings in Surrey."

"So would that be the stockbroker, the old German nut case or Lincoln Carswell?"

Jon looked angry. "Don't make fun of this. It's serious."

"I'm not making fun of anything, Jon. You told me that we were going out for a romantic dinner in an ocean side restaurant. So far all you've done is drink wine, pick at your dinner and look at your watch. You haven't said a dozen words to me all evening."

Jon's look of anger softened. "I'm sorry," he said. "I was told that the stockbroker, whose name is Eric O'Neill by the way, might also be here. He seemed like a pleasant guy and he's in Faro with a lady friend, perhaps his wife, I'm not sure. I thought it would be an opportunity for you to meet them."

"And I would want to meet them because . . .?"

"There really isn't a pressing reason, I just thought . . ."

"So our romantic dinner alone was going to include another couple? And that's not counting your two friends, Einfeld and Clayton, who are sitting in the bar?"

"Marianne, I can only say I'm sorry."

"No Jon, you can do better than that," she said. "You can take me home and then carry on with whatever adventure you have planned for the rest of the night. I just don't care anymore."

Jon looked at her sharply, then reached across the table and squeezed her hand. "I am truly sorry. Tomorrow will be different."

"Yes it will be. I'm flying home tomorrow."

Jon withdrew his hand. "We still have the weekend ahead of us."

"We do indeed and I hope you'll enjoy your time in Faro but you'll be doing it without me."

"We'll talk about this in the morning," Jon said.

Marianne picked up her wine glass, surprised at how calm she felt, and drained the last mouthful. She set the glass down and stood up.

Jon stood as well, setting his napkin carefully across the food on his plate. "I'll have Clayton take you home."

"No you won't," she said. "I'll take a taxi."

CHAPTER NINETY SEVEN

Thursday, May 11, 1989 Faro, Portugal

Eric watched as the woman across the table from him, his mother, picked up a piece of halibut on her fork and placed it in her mouth. His mother. He looked at her carefully. He had her hair, the colour as well as the waves. Perhaps something of the shape of her face, it was hard to tell, but except for a brief smile at the washroom door, he had only seen her looking serious. He was searching for details but there weren't a lot of similarities.

She looked up at him, a trace of a smile flitting across her face. "Eat your dinner, Eric," she said.

Eric couldn't help himself. He shook his head and smiled, suppressing a laugh. "Yes, Mother," he replied.

She watched him for a moment. "Thank you for calling me that. I don't deserve it but it's nice to hear."

Eric took a bite of the halibut, flaky, delicious, a trace of garlic and lemon. He picked up his wine and took a generous drink of it. Lovely. It seemed strange but he felt comfortable with this woman who claimed to be his biological mother, whoever she was but he felt a sense of rising frustration. When was she going to tell him who she was, who his father was. He felt like she was playing with him.

"In your phone call you mentioned a man who had told you about me."

"Yes, I did," Eric replied. "He didn't tell me about you. He only gave me a contact, Jurgen, as it turned out, and said he could provide information about my parents. Jurgen put me in touch with you."

"This man in England claimed he was Martin Bormann?"

Eric nodded as he took another bite of halibut.

"And what did you think of him?" Eva asked.

"The experience was completely surreal. I was supposedly in the presence of a man who had died in the spring of 1945 and he was alive and well. I have no way of knowing whether he really was Martin Bormann or merely a deluded old man. He certainly had enough paraphernalia around to be convincing. He had some bizarre idea that I would take over the leadership of some phantom organization that he had either preserved or constructed from the ashes of the Third Reich. Or perhaps he was just having a long hallucination. It was the weirdest thing I've ever encountered."

Eva nodded. "He really is Martin Bormann."

Eric looked at her. "Do you know about this neo Nazi organization of his?"

"I know a bit about it," she replied. "It's primarily about money, investing it, moving it around, distributing it and so on. There is not really a physical component to it. There are few people who work for it."

"Who deals with the money?"

"Bankers as I understand it," she replied. "Martin issues instructions and they do the rest. It isn't a very active organization any more. I think the original idea was to fund the development of some kind of Fourth Reich, or prominent international Nazi organization, but nothing like that ever happened. Quite understandably, the world was too disillusioned to trust Nazis with anything. So they funded bits and pieces all over the place hoping that somewhere something lasting would happen. No one trusted the old Nazis and no new ones of sufficient stature emerged. So the Fourth Reich didn't develop and I don't think it ever will."

"So it's a financial organization," Eric said. "That may explain why he picked me. I'm a stockbroker."

"That would make sense," Eva said. "But what other choices did he have?"

"The other two children that were sent abroad in 1940 were also at the meeting I attended. One is a retired US military officer, Jon Falken, the second is an American artist, Lincoln Carswell."

Eva frowned. "The fact that there were three of you was likely just Martin making sure that if something happened to one of you there would be a back-up plan." She paused. "So what are you going to do about Martin's offer?"

"I don't know," Eric said. "I have absolutely no interest in it. He gave me a briefcase full of information. I've looked through it and have a sense of what it contains. Do you have any advice?"

"Close it down."

"Really?"

"Yes," Eva said. "Just get rid of it. It no longer serves any purpose. There is quite enough chaos in the world without trying to foment more."

Eric nodded. He had thought of this but it was good to have the idea confirmed. But he wasn't here to get financial advice.

"Will you tell me now who you are?"

Eva sighed. It was time to make a decision. Martin had trusted him. Perhaps she could, too. "I will tell you, Eric, but it could be a burden. The information I give you could be fatal if you ever told anyone, fatal for you and fatal for me. So be sure you want to know."

Eric thought for a moment. He had come a long way for this, apparently giving up his current life to find out. "I would like to know."

She reached her hands across the table and took Eric's hands in hers. "Very well, my son, my name is Eva Braun."

CHAPTER NINETY EIGHT

Thursday, May 11, 1989 Faro, Portugal

Lincoln Carswell got back into his car after a short walk around the parking lot to get rid of the stiffness of sitting there for the last hour.

Moments later, Jon and Marianne walked out of the restaurant and stood at the top of the steps. A taxi pulled up, they descended the steps and Marianne climbed into the back seat. Jon held the door for her but didn't get in. As the taxi drove away, he walked back up the steps and joined Einfeld and Clayton who had appeared from inside the restaurant.

He thought of following Marianne, but he was certain she was going back to the hotel. Perhaps he would see what Jon and his friends were up to before leaving. He slouched down in the seat as they strolled across the parking lot. Jon was talking animatedly, moving his hands. His gestures looked angry. Perhaps he had been hoping to meet Eric O'Neill? Who knew in this bizarre world?

The three of them walked over to the car that Einfeld and Clayton had arrived in. They got in but didn't drive away. What could they be waiting for? Lincoln could see their outlines but nothing else.

Eric stared at Eva Braun, stunned at the revelation. Surely this couldn't be the Eva Braun who had been Adolf Hitler's mistress and for the last few hours of his life, his wife. She had died with him in the bunker in Berlin.

As though reading his thoughts she said, "Yes, Eric, your father was Adolf Hitler."

Eric shook his head slowly. "But you died in 1945."

"I was flown out of Berlin in a Storch, a very small plane. A double died in my place."

"But how could that be?

"There was great interest in identifying Adolf, but very little concern about me. I was, in the modern parlance, the 'dumb blonde' mistress. No one cared."

Eric was silent. He felt numb. He had wanted an answer and now he had it. "Jesus Christ," he said softly.

Eva squeezed his hands gently. "Not quite, my dear," she whispered, a trace of a smile crossing her face.

"Adolf Hitler was really my father?"

Eva nodded. "He was." She stared intently at Eric. "Tell me how you are feeling."

"Numb," Eric replied. "Just numb. I don't feel anything."

"That's good," Eva said. "There is nothing for you to feel. You did not know either of your biological parents."

Eric was quiet as he thought about what she had said. "But you knew that I had been sent abroad."

"I knew that you had been killed in a fire shortly after you arrived in Canada. So I no longer had a child. I saw you for a few hours, perhaps five or six times during the first year of your life and not again until this evening."

"Why?"

Eva sighed. "Your birth was a secret. If it's any consolation, your father never knew you existed and since you had died, there was no point in telling him."

"But the birth record in the clinic?"

"You were born to Eva Schmidt."

Eric shook his head. He wondered if something would soak in, if he was in shock, or what? He simply felt nothing. He thought of Katherine and Gilford O'Neill. They had loved him and sent him on this journey, or at least provided the impetus for it. Eva Braun had said that after they were finished with their conversation that she would again say that she didn't have any children. Perhaps that was the wisest course. When he was finished with this conversation his only parents would be Katherine and Gilford O'Neill.

But still . . . he was the son of the most reviled man in history, a madman responsible for the deaths of millions, for the destruction of Europe. Perhaps feeling numb was a blessing. And now Martin Bormann, who surely knew who he was, wanted him to carry on with some neo-Nazi organization. He set down his fork, overcome by a feeling of nausea. He would end the madness, one way or another.

Lincoln Carswell watched as a lone figure strolled across the drop off area in front of the restaurant, hands in his pockets, head down. He appeared to be deep in thought. It was Eric

O'Neill. Lincoln watched as Jon and his two companions got out of their car. They moved toward Eric and were about half way across the parking lot when he spotted them. He stopped and for a moment it looked like he was about to run but he didn't. The three of them walked up to him and Eric and Jon began talking.

"So how did the meeting go with the woman who might be your mother?" Jon asked sarcastically. "She might just as easily be my mother, you know."

"She said she didn't have any children."

"So why was she meeting with you?

"She wanted money."

"Money?"

"She said if I paid her $10,000 US she would give me more information."

"So what did you do?"

"I talked with her," Eric said. "But I decided not to pay her. The odds are very high that both my parents are dead, if not in the war, as a result of old age. Besides, I'm getting tired of all this."

"Sounds like a good decision, Eric," Jon said. "Now we are leaving together. We can do it quietly, if you wish." He pulled back his jacket to reveal a pistol in the waistband of his slacks. "Or we can do it with fireworks. It's your choice. But either way, you are coming with me."

"Very well," Eric said.

"The car is over there," Jon said, pointing across the parking lot.

"Wait here a moment," Clayton said. "I want to check something out."

"What is it?" Jon snapped.

"There's a guy sitting in a car who's been watching us ever since we came out of the restaurant."

"Watching us?" Jon asked.

"Maybe, maybe not," Clayton replied. "But he's slouching down like he doesn't want anyone to see him."

"Make it quick."

Clayton nodded and walked off toward their car. He would come up to the other car from behind. There was a chance the occupant would see him but the way he was slouching meant he likely couldn't see much in the rear view mirrors and in any case it was dark behind the car.

He pulled his gun from a shoulder holster as he walked up to the open window on the driver's side. "Just relax my friend," he said, pointing the gun at the driver's head. "Tell me what you are doing watching us."

The driver snapped upright in his seat staring in sudden fear at the face and the gun in the window. "Nothing. I'm not watching anything."

"Then what are you doing here?"

"Waiting for my wife," he stammered. "She works here."

"So why are you slouching down trying to hide?"

"I was relaxing, trying to rest."

"Please get out of the car." Clayton stepped away from the door and as the occupant got out, Clayton had a flash of recognition. He reached forward, grasped the man's hair and pulled hard.

The man grabbed at the hairpiece but was too late.

Clayton smiled. "Good evening, Mr. Carswell. Please join us."

Eric watched as Clayton walked across the parking lot toward them, slightly behind a second man, presumably the occupant of the car he had checked out.

"Carswell," Jon said as they got closer. "How kind of you to join us."

Carswell was silent. He nodded at Eric.

"Shall we be on our way?" Jon said.

As they walked toward the car, Eric recalled Liselle's chilling words, that Jon would kill him without a moment's hesitation if it served his purpose. He knew he was certainly no match for three men, all probably trained in violence, so he would just have to make certain that killing him didn't serve Jon's purpose. And now Lincoln Carswell was part of the scene as well, whatever that meant. He felt a rising sense of fear but somehow he couldn't quite grasp the idea that Jon would hurt him. After all, in Surrey they had dined together, a small group that met with Martin Bormann, all so civilized.

Jon opened the rear door and ushered Eric and Lincoln into the back seat and climbed in beside Eric. The other two got into the front, with Clayton driving. Jon leaned back in the rear seat of the car and turned to Eric. "First we'll go back to your motel and retrieve the briefcase."

"What is it you want, Jon?"

"Bormann made a big mistake choosing you as the heir to the movement," Jon said. "And I intend to fix that."

"I agree with you," Eric said. "I didn't seek it and I don't want it. Take the briefcase and carry on."

"I will," Jon said. "But I need to know what Bormann told you about the movement and its future." He glanced past Eric to Lincoln. "You, too, Carswell."

"I have no bloody idea what you two are up to but I want no part of it," Carswell said.

"You aren't married," Jon said. "So who were you waiting for? Certainly not your wife."

"You're right, of course," Carswell said. "But when someone shoved a gun in my face, I just said the first thing that came into my mind. Actually, I was waiting for a girl I met in the bar a couple of nights ago. She works there."

"Ah," Jon said. "That explains the hairpiece."

Carswell was silent for a moment. "I'm just vain, that's all, and I was wearing it when I met her."

"No matter," Jon said. "I want to know precisely what Bormann told each of you about the movement and its future.

He looked back at Eric. "What the hell are you smiling at?"

Eric shook his head slowly. "There is no movement, Jon."

CHAPTER NINETY NINE

Thursday, May 11, 1989 Faro, Portugal

"All right, smart guy," Jon Falken said. "Show me."

Jon, Lincoln and Eric were seated at a small table in Eric's hotel room. Einfeld lounged against the wall behind Eric, and Clayton was sitting on a sofa in the living room area.

Eric opened the briefcase slowly and pulled out some folders. "Where do you want to start?"

"Let's start with the money," Jon said.

"It's just a portfolio," Eric said. "A large one, around a hundred million US, I would estimate, although I'd have to do a bit more work to be accurate."

Lincoln stood up. "I don't want to hear any of this shit. I was taken to Surrey against my will, as Einfeld and Clayton can confirm, and I took no part in any discussions that you weren't at. So why don't you two sort this out without me. It has nothing to do with me. I paint pictures for a living."

Jon stood up slowly. "Sit the fuck down, Carswell. You are part of this because you were there, willingly or otherwise. You will cease to be part of this when I tell you."

The two men glared at each other, then Clayton moved behind Carswell and drove his fist into Carswell's kidney. He staggered forward against the table but before he could fall, Clayton grabbed the back of his jacket and slammed him down in the chair.

Jon sat down and turned to Eric, speaking quietly. "Please continue."

Eric stared at Carswell, shaken by the violence, and then turned to Jon. "Was that necessary? He knows nothing about this and won't unless you force him to stay and hear it."

"I will decide what is necessary and what is not. Is that clear?"

Eric shrugged. "Bormann basically took the money that he managed to get out of Germany at the end of World War II and had it invested by Swiss bankers. Some of it's in bonds, some in short term money market stuff, a lot in stocks, mostly US and European and the European money is about two thirds in German companies. As near as I can tell, none of the stock positions represents anything even close to a controlling interest, not even a seat on a board of directors."

"So all there is, is a lot of money?" Jon asked. "It could be worse."

"There is a bit more than that," Eric said. "With that kind of money, you can certainly influence things but I don't see any evidence of the kind of impact that Bormann implied there was."

Jon was silent for a moment. "So how do you get at the money?"

"Not easily," Eric said. "There is a system of holding companies registered in a number of jurisdictions that would take a forensic accountant some time to figure out. It's set up very well from that point of view. However, I haven't looked for a way to get at the money. I assume you mean to transfer control to yourself?"

"You are a quick learner, Eric."

"Take all this stuff and maybe you or your accountants can figure it out," Eric said. "But be careful who you show it to since most of what is going on here would contravene your IRS rules and I'm sure, lots of other US federal laws."

"I intend to take it, Eric," Jon said. "Now what about this organization or movement that Bormann was going on about?"

"There is nothing about it here," Eric said. "As near as I can tell, Bormann's explanation to us was quite accurate. He and some other survivors of the War were able to divert the Allies' attention from hunting down Nazi war criminals and shackling German industry by creating a fear of the Soviet Union and their supposed expansionist ambitions in Western Europe. To do this they funded a variety of organizations both within Germany and in the rest of Europe, primarily."

"So there is an organization that does the funding."

"There is a list of employees in the briefcase. Most look like the security people we met in Surrey. There are a few others but their roles are not clear. Einfeld and Clayton are on the list and identified as being in the US. There are a few others in different countries."

Jon glared at Eric, then banged his fist on the table and stood up. He paced across the room and turned to face the table.

Eric spoke again. "If this movement existed as some pervasive world-wide conspiracy, it seems to have faded with the years, perhaps because it just isn't necessary or very relevant any more. Immediately after the War and perhaps as late as the 1970's, former Gestapo types were still training security forces in the Middle East, parts of Africa and South America. So if you want to be the head of some kind of Secret Police Academy that trains thugs in how to torture people, be my guest. I think this whole thing is just a dream. It simply doesn't exist any-more, if it ever did."

"What about the assassinations?"

"As Bormann told us, they were carried out by others, dis-affected souls, who could be manipulated. There is nothing in this information that tells whether he, or other Nazis, were actually involved or even paid. And that happened twenty years ago." Eric paused. "If it's that kind of power you want, Jon, then take over the CIA or some other outfit that actually exists."

"This is bullshit," Einfeld exploded. "Just bullshit. The movement does exist. Look at Clayton and I? We're part of it. There are teams like us all over the world."

Eric turned to look at Einfeld. "Like a good World War II German, Bormann and his colleagues kept records. You are the only two employees in North America. There are half a dozen others in England and we've likely met most of them. You are all paid out of bank accounts in the Channel Islands."

"You mean there are no others at all?" Jon said incredulously.

"There are coded payments recorded here," Eric replied. "But I can't tell whether they are paid to people, for contracts or for other goods and services. They are just payments and the codes required to figure it out aren't here. In any event, they might total a few million dollars a year, hardly a large organization."

Jon leaned forward, elbow on the table. "So how did Bor-mann come to pick you?"

"I haven't the faintest idea," Eric said. "I would certainly have chosen you, with your military background, leadership background and so on. He doesn't need someone to manage the money, it is already being done adequately, and that's all I can offer. So why don't you just assume command and take it over. I certainly don't want any part of either the movement or the money."

"Thank you, Eric," Jon said. "That is exactly what I intend to do. Now tell me what happened at Surrey? How did you get to London?"

"I was in Bormann's office when the manor was attacked. I had gotten up to find something to eat and wandered in there by mistake. He was sitting at his desk and had just packed a bunch of information in a briefcase. When the attack got underway, he opened a panel on the wall of his office, the one with the portrait of Adolf Hitler and the battle flags on it, and . . ."

"What portrait?" Jon interrupted. "I was in that office and I didn't see a portrait?"

"Really?" Eric said. "It was on the left hand wall as you came in the door. Quite imposing really. At any rate, he opened the panel and directed me into a passage on the other side. Told me to wait a few minutes and if no one came for me, to follow the passage and I would get out of the estate."

"So where did the passage lead?"

"It ended up in a wooded area in a small garage with a Land Rover," Eric said. "I escaped in it but not before someone shot at it."

Jon leaned back with a chuckle. "That was me," he said. "Too bad we couldn't have ended the whole damn thing right there." He went on. "So how did you get to London?"

"Drove part way, left the Land Rover in a parking lot and took a commuter train."

Einfeld spoke again. "You are reported to be travelling with a woman."

Eric had been expecting the question. "My wife," he said.

"Your wife died three years ago."

"My second wife,"Eric said. "I was married in Toronto shortly before I came over here."

"Really?" Jon said. "So where is your wife now? Women have a way of leaving their mark in a hotel room."

"Gone back to Toronto," Eric said. "She flew out earlier today."

"What does your wife look like?" Einfeld asked.

"About five foot six, dark hair, slim, pretty . . ."

Einfeld nodded at Jon. "Sounds like the one."

"So who is Ralph Walters?" Jon asked. "Your new wife visited him in his hotel room in London the night you left."

"Ralph is a colleague of hers," Eric said smoothly, surprised at how easily he was learning to Lie. "He works in the New York office of the same company she works for."

"All right, Carswell," Jon said. "What's your story? How did you get out of Surrey?"

Lincoln straightened in his chair. "After the attack I took a car from the garage and drove part way to London, then took a commuter train. Basically the same as Eric did."

"And what did Bormann tell you?"

"Nothing," Lincoln replied. "I arrived and had tea. He apologized for having his goons kidnap me and told me he admired my art. He showed me three of my paintings that he had arranged to purchase. Later we all had dinner together and I heard what you heard."

"That's all?"

"That's all," Lincoln said. "In my opinion, he's just a rich old man who's locked himself away in a country house to hallucinate about a bunch of dead Nazis. There are a lot of kinds of senility."

Jon stood up. "Thank you both," he said. "I think you've given us about all the information we need." He picked up the files and put them back in the briefcase, closed it and handed it to Einfeld. "Shall we go?"

Clayton moved beside Carswell. "On your feet, my friend." He gripped Carswell's arm and nearly lifted him out of the chair.

"I thought you said you were finished with me?" Eric said, slowly getting to his feet. His discussion with Jon had been firm and his fears had gradually faded as Jon's focus on money and power became apparent. He now had all he wanted, but Eric went cold. He recalled again Liselle's warnings about Jon and suddenly the realization struck him. Jon was going to kill him, and Carswell, too.

"And so we are, Eric," Jon said. "But we have one more stop to make this evening. You've been there before, I believe, an old man named Jurgen, the one who helped you contact your mother or whoever she is."

"What's the purpose of that?" Eric asked, although he sensed all too well what it might be.

"If I understand your history accurately," Jon said. "I believe you were supposed to have been burned to death in a fire in 1940, is that correct?"

"Apparently there was a fire but we escaped."

"I don't think you are going to escape this time."

CHAPTER ONE HUNDRED

Thursday, May 11, 1989 Faro, Portugal

Eric looked out the window of the Mercedes as they drove by the last lights of Faro and passed into the country side. He was frightened. He had been frightened before, frightened for his life the night that his boat had sunk. Was that only a few weeks ago? But out of the fear had come a calm resolution that he was not going to die. It was entirely irrational but it had sustained him and when he achieved that state he could act. He could feel that same calmness settling over him now and he began to consider his options.

They were heading west out of Faro, travelling about a dozen kilometres to the small side road that led down to the old man's cottage. Was he in on this, too? It seemed probable since Jon had tracked him to the restaurant. Perhaps they had forced the information out of the old man and were going to kill him too.

A truck passed them heading into Faro. Eric looked over at Jon as the headlights lit his face. He was frowning, perhaps confused by the information he had received. A moment later a car overtook them and passed. Then the road was empty.

Eric stared out into the darkness. If he weren't stuck between Jon and Lincoln, he might jump from the car but that would likely kill him assuming he even got the door open. He would have to wait until they got to the old man's cottage, perhaps run off in the darkness, the sky had clouded over and the country side certainly looked black. He would have to wait for an opportune moment. Certainly overpowering three men was not on. He had never been a fighter, had never been trained in any kind of physical combat unless you counted sports. He didn't doubt his own courage, just his abilities. He was physically as fit as his captors, likely more so, but that wasn't going to count for much when they had guns.

He felt the car slowing and saw the narrow turn off in the headlights. The heavy car lurched slightly as it left the pavement and then bumped along the road heading down the gentle hill to the cottage. Eric stretched slightly and then tensed his muscles as the car pulled to the side of the narrow track and stopped.

"Don't even think of running, Eric," Jon said quietly.

Eric looked over to see Jon's gun pointing at him.

"Just wait until my colleagues get out of the car and then get out slowly."

Eric closed his eyes and leaned back on the seat. Clayton opened the driver's door and the overhead light came on.

"Turn that damned light off," Jon snapped.

Clayton turned it off. Jon opened the rear door and slid out as Clayton and Einfeld got out of the front of the car. Jon stood there, looking relaxed, his gun pointing almost nonchalantly at Eric. Jon motioned with the gun for Eric to get out of the car, stepping back as Eric slid across the seat and got out. Clayton opened the other door and waved Lincoln out. There was no room to run and little chance of success with three guns pointing at the two of them.

"Shall we go, gentlemen?" Jon said and began walking toward the cottage.

Eric took a deep breath. The air was cool and fresh, it smelled of something like heather, or sage. He wondered if they grew here. He looked toward the ocean and saw a few lights sparkling along the shore. Summer homes perhaps, he couldn't tell.

"Let's move along, shall we?" Clayton said from behind him.

Eric nodded and started walking slowly toward the cottage, Lincoln beside him. Jon was waiting for them at the door and as they approached, Jon stepped inside and turned to face the doorway, gun still levelled at Eric. He snapped on a light switch and a single bulb hanging in the centre of the ceiling on an old frayed cord lit up the room behind him.

"Son of a bitch." Einfeld's deep voice was a whisper, almost a gasp. He was staring past Jon into the room.

Jon spun to see what he was looking at. All Eric glimpsed was the old man sitting in a chair at the table, but he didn't care. He slammed back into Einfeld knocking him into Clayton and as they stumbled backwards and fell, he was running. Running as hard as he could, as fast as he ever had, hoping that the old man, Jurgen, his name popped incongruously into his head, had kept the small yard free of holes. He was almost to the road when he heard the first shot and feet pounding behind him and then he hit something, doubled over it and was thrown backwards to the ground. He felt sharp pains in his stomach and for a moment he thought one of the shots had hit him. Then Clayton and Jon were dragging him to his feet.

Jon pointed a small flashlight at the area in front of them. "Didn't see the fence?" he asked. The light revealed a single strand of wire, waist high, rusted and worn with age. "But I admire your courage. Running from three men with guns was a gutsy thing to do, even if you didn't stand a chance."

Eric stood, slightly bent over catching his breath, mostly knocked out of him from hitting the wire. Jon was a few paces away on one side, Clayton, the same on the other. He had no chance to run again.

"One more time, my friend," Jon said, stepping behind him and giving him a heavy shove back toward the cottage.

Eric was just getting his breath back by the time they got to the door of the cottage. Lincoln was standing on one side of the door, Einfeld, with his gun pointing at Lincoln, on the other side.

"Now, Clayton," Jon said. "Check out your handiwork. I thought the old man was dead."

In the dim light of the cottage, Clayton moved across the room to the old man in the chair. He leaned over and looked carefully without touching him. "He's dead, all right," Clayton said. "But who the hell set him up like this?"

Eric was aware of a slight movement to his right and then a flash and a deafening crack. Einfeld's head exploded. Jon hurled himself backward through the door as a second shot seemed to come straight at Eric. He felt a faint rush of air passing his right ear. He threw himself to the floor. Einfeld crumpled on top of him. A third shot took out the light bulb and the cottage was plunged into darkness.

Eric felt a hand shaking his shoulder. Someone was talking to him but he was still deafened by the noise of the gunshots. He touched the hand that was shaking him, a small hand, Liselle's hand. He looked up at her but she was only a shadow. Outside a car started and then Liselle was gone, jumping lightly over him.

As he rolled to one side and pushed Einfeld's body off, a beam of light came from a flashlight that Einfeld had apparently fallen on. In the faint light he saw Lincoln getting to his feet and Clayton on the floor, holding his left shoulder. Lincoln stepped toward Clayton, picked up his gun, glanced at Eric, then pointed the gun at Clayton's head and fired. His body jerked and was still.

Eric saw Einfeld's gun lying on the floor and picked it up. He got shakily to his feet.

"Are you okay?" Lincoln asked him.

Eric nodded as he picked up the flashlight and turned it off. His hearing was returning. He looked carefully at Lincoln wondering how he could kill someone so easily. Where had he learned this ruthlessness. But Clayton had struck him viciously at the motel and was certainly a danger to them both at the moment.

"Let's go," Lincoln said, moving toward the door.

They stepped outside, then Lincoln turned back inside. He bent over, coughed and seemed to have trouble breathing.

"What's wrong, Lincoln?" Eric stepped beside him, fearing he had been shot.

"Goddamn asthma," Lincoln muttered. He took a small inhaler from his pocket and pressed it to his mouth. "I'll be fine in a minute."

Eric went outside again. The Mercedes was still parked at the end of the path that led to the cottage, but one wheel was off the edge of the road, the headlights pointing at an odd angle. He watched as Jon got slowly out of the car, his hands on top of his head. He couldn't see Liselle with the glare of the headlights but she must be there somewhere. He began to walk cautiously toward the car. He was breathing hard and realized he was shaking. He wondered what Liselle would do now.

Eric watched as Jon stepped clear of the car and came around to the front, standing in the light. Liselle emerged from the darkness and moved toward him. Jon dropped his arms and then quickly put them back on the top of his head. He must have recognized Liselle.

He heard her say something but couldn't make out the words. He was about thirty feet away from them now. Jon turned, leaned over and put his hands on the hood of the car in the classic police search stance. Liselle moved in behind him and reached toward him.

Jon moved incredibly fast. He lashed back with his foot striking Liselle a glancing blow on her leg. He rolled to one side, sweeping his arm in an arc that caught her on the shoulder and sent her spinning to the ground. Then he stood up and almost leisurely pulled out a gun and pointed it at her as she lay on the ground. He said something to her and then laughed.

Eric dropped to one knee and bracing his arm, gripped Einfeld's gun tightly. It was a large heavy gun. He aimed it at the centre of Jon's chest but it was shaking and he couldn't keep it aimed there. He watched in horror as Jon raised his gun and aimed it at Liselle. He took a deep breath and slowly exhaled.

CHAPTER ONE HUNDRED AND ONE

Thursday, May 11, 1989 Faro, Portugal

Liselle lay on the ground her right thigh numb, her right shoulder starting to throb. Stupid, she thought, utterly stupid. She knew Jon was well trained and still she had gotten too close. She was tired but that was no excuse. There was never an excuse for a fatal error. She looked up at Jon standing above her aiming his gun almost casually but unwaveringly at her. He must have recognized her when he got out of the car in spite of the light camouflage paint on her face and the black jumpsuit and hood. The shock value of revealing her identity was gone.

"Jon?" she asked. "Jon Falken? What the hell are you doing here?"

"More to the point, my dear," Jon said with heavy sarcasm. "What are you doing here?"

"I was tracking Eric O'Neill."

"Yes," Jon said. "You were masquerading as his wife, if I'm not mistaken."

"What are you talking about?"

"It doesn't matter now, Liselle," Jon said. "You knew who I was when I got out of the car, so your show of surprise, while touching, is not very convincing."

"I was behind you, Jon," Liselle said. "I couldn't see you."

Jon laughed and slowly raised the gun. Liselle watched. A head shot, she thought as she saw where the gun was pointing. At least it would be fast. Suddenly, Jon was hurled back onto the hood of the car, the sound of a gunshot fading as he slid slowly down and crumpled in a heap in front of the grill. Liselle raised herself shakily on her left arm and looked toward the direction the shot must have come from. Eric walked slowly out of the darkness, a gun dangling from his right hand. His mouth was slightly open, a look of utter horror on his face.

A second figure emerged from the darkness behind Eric. It was Lincoln Carswell, also holding a gun. She had heard a shot from the cottage a few moments earlier. Einfeld was dead and she knew her second shot had hit Clayton but was not sure how badly he had been wounded. Either Eric or Lincoln had shot him again. She crawled over to Jon. He lay unmoving on the ground. She checked for a pulse in his throat. Nothing. She checked the wound. A small entry hole on the left front side of his chest but a huge exit hole on the right back. Hollow point ammunition, she thought, massive damage from one shot. Eric had literally blown his heart out. She got gingerly to her feet and turned to Eric.

"Is he dead?" he asked, his voice a whisper.

Liselle nodded. "Yes."

Wordlessly, Eric handed her the gun. She looked at it, US Army issue, 45 calibre. That explained the hole in Jon. She looked at Eric. He was breathing deeply and evenly, obviously forcing himself to calm down. Good, she thought, at least he's not going into shock.

"Thank you," Eric said. "You saved my Life." He looked at her carefully. "That sounds like something from an old Lone Ranger movie, but I mean it."

"Thank you, too, Eric. You saved mine."

"Good evening, Lincoln," Liselle said as he came to stand beside Eric.

He looked carefully at her. "You look familiar," he said.

"No, I don't," Liselle said. "I am no one you have ever met and no one you ever want to meet."

Lincoln nodded. "Right." He looked down at Jon.

Eric walked around to the driver's door of the car and turned off the lights, plunging the quiet hillside into darkness. "What now?" he asked as he came back to stand beside her.

"Now I have to make a phone call and get this cleaned up." She turned to Lincoln. "None of this ever happened, Lincoln. You were never here. If you speak of this to anyone it will almost certainly be fatal. These people are utterly ruthless. Do you understand me?"

Lincoln stared at her and nodded. "Yes, I believe you. I was never here."

"Good," Liselle said. "Can you drive the Mercedes back to Faro?"

"Okay."

"Leave it in the parking lot of the Algarve Terrace Restaurant. I believe your rental car is there."

"Yes, it is, but how did you know that?"

"You followed Jon Falken to the restaurant, correct?"

"Yes," Lincoln replied.

"So did I. I saw you parked there before I came out here."

Lincoln nodded.

"I'll have someone pick up the Mercedes at the Algarve and return it." She paused. "I'm not sure what you're planning to do after you get your car but don't go near Marianne Falken."

Lincoln looked at her in surprise. "I guess that makes sense, doesn't it?"

"It does," Liselle said. "I'm not judging you, I'm just trying to keep you alive. You can continue your romance when you both get home."

"Can I phone?"

"No," Liselle said. "She will find out about Jon through official channels, which is how it should happen. You don't need to have any connection to the death of her husband."

"Good point," Lincoln said. He turned to Eric and held out his hand. "I still don't know what the hell all this was about and I don't want to know."

"I don't really know either, Lincoln," Eric replied, shaking his hand firmly. "Best of luck."

"Thank you," he replied. "You, too."

As she watched Lincoln turn the Mercedes around and drive off, she suddenly felt exhausted. She leaned against Eric and felt his arm slip around her shoulders.

"Now are you going to tell me who you are?" Eric asked.

"Are you going to disappear for a while like a good hunted man?"

Eric tightened his arm around her for a moment. "Yes," he said. "I guess I am."

"Let's walk back to Jurgen's cottage," Liselle said, slipping her hand into his. "I'll tell you what I can. My father was a French Jew, my mother was Vietnamese. My father was a soldier and met my mother while he was posted in French Indo China, which became more famous later as Vietnam. I spent time in

Israel, got connected to their intelligence service and eventually became a full blown Mossad agent, which is what I am now. I also got to know some old French people. Some of them had been collaborators who worked with the Germans during World War II, something Mossad thought might be useful in tracking down war criminals."

They arrived at the cottage door. "Wait out here," Liselle said. She pulled a small flashlight from a pocket in her jump suit. She shone it around the cottage. Einfeld lay where he had fallen. Clayton was on his back, shot in the forehead. That was the gunshot she had heard. Jurgen was still slumped forward in his chair. She lifted the receiver off the wall phone and dialled.

A few minutes later she walked out the door and rejoined Eric. He was looking toward the ocean as she slipped her hand into his. She was doing this to be reassuring but also to try to get some sense of how he was handling the events of the last short while. She felt him squeeze her hand lightly. He wasn't shaking and seemed calm but she knew she would have to watch him carefully.

"Is it over now?" he asked.

"Our part is," she replied. "Except for disappearing."

"Disappearing is beginning to sound more attractive all the time. I did it for a couple of years while I was sailing. It was a good time in my life." He paused for a moment. "But I'm not sure I want to do it alone this time."

Liselle smiled and wondered if that were an invitation, but now was not the time to talk about it. "Are you ready to leave?"

"Yes," Eric said.

"Give me your wallet and your passport. You can keep the money."

Eric pulled the bills out of the wallet and stuck them in his slack's pocket. He retrieved his passport and handed the two of them to Liselle. She turned and went back into the cottage, returning a moment later. "Say goodbye to Eric O'Neill."

He looked down at her and then out at the lights sparkling on the shore below them. She saw him look up at the clearing sky. A few stars were peeking through the clouds. "Goodbye, Eric O'Neill," he whispered.

Hand in hand they started to walk down the hill towards where Liselle had parked her car. "Finish your story," Eric said.

"About ten years ago my father was killed in Paris," Liselle was silent for a few steps. "He was assassinated. It seems someone believed he was collaborating with Palestinian terrorists. He wasn't. It later turned out that the information was wrong."

"I'm sorry," Eric said.

"He was completely innocent, an utterly honourable man," Liselle said. "He was assassinated by my employers, the Mossad."

They walked in silence for a moment. "But you're still working for them?"

"Yes," Liselle said. "They don't know that I found out who killed my father."

"You're certain?"

"Completely certain," Liselle said. "So setting you free is a small atonement for their assassination of my father." Liselle was silent for a few steps. "Besides," she said lightly. "I like you."

"Thank you," Eric said. "I like you, too. But how are you going to explain all of this to your employers?"

"Who was the old man you met with in Surrey?"

"He claimed he was Martin Bormann."

"Really?" Liselle halted, still holding Eric's hand. She was stunned. "What did you think?"

"He was very convincing. I think he really was Martin Bormann."

"My God," Liselle whispered. "They thought he was just an old Nazi, maybe just an old German."

"Maybe he was, but I think he was Bormann."

"Who is the woman you met with tonight?"

Eric hesitated. "I don't know for sure," he said. "I thought she might have been my mother but she claimed she didn't have any children. She said she might be able to get me more information if I paid her $10,000 US. I told her I wasn't interested."

"Why not?"

"I'm sick and tired of this whole mess."

In the faint light she looked at Eric carefully. She was fairly sure he was not telling her the truth. "My employers think that you, or Jon, or Lincoln is the son of Eva Braun and Adolf Hitler."

Eric looked down at her. "What?" he asked incredulously.

Liselle watched his face. He seemed surprised but she couldn't be sure.

"You have to be kidding me. This is nonsense."

She nodded. "Perhaps you're right. But it doesn't change what the Mossad believes."

"So what are you going to tell them?"

She thought for a moment. "That Jon Falken was the son they were looking for and that you and Lincoln are false leads."

"So does that mean I don't have to disappear?"

"It means that my employers may or may not believe me so you still have to disappear."

"I don't understand."

She stopped and turned to face Eric. "Listen carefully. You just told me that you don't know who the old woman was. I have chosen to believe you. You said the idea that Eva Braun and Adolf Hitler are your parents is nonsense. I have chosen to accept that, too, although I don't believe you are telling me everything that you know. My employers are among the most skilled interrogators in the world. They will not believe anything you tell them, and trust me, you don't want to have them interrogate you."

Eric stared at her for a moment. "Thank you," he whispered.

She looked up at him and wondered. Eric O'Neill was a caring decent man who had risked his personal safety to retrieve her purse in Ireland. She had enjoyed a gentle romantic interlude with him there. He was frightened but he still had dredged up the courage to shoot Jon Falken and save her life. Could he really be Adolf Hitler's son? Eva's child? She shook her head. "You're welcome," she said. "Like you, I just don't care anymore."

"What about Lincoln?"

"They're pretty well convinced that he has nothing to do with any of this. He just got caught up in it by accident."

Eric nodded. "So I will disappear."

"Officially, you will die in a fire. Jurgen's cottage will burn down later tonight."

"If you give your employers the briefcase that Bormann gave to me would this help? Tell them you got if from Jon."

"That would help a lot," she said. "Where is it?"

"In the Mercedes," he said.

They stopped beside a small Fiat. Eric had not seen it before. Liselle got behind the wheel and they drove up the narrow unpaved road to the highway, carefully avoiding Jon's body, inert at the edge of the road.

In Faro, she drove the small car down a narrow street and turned into a courtyard. She switched it off and got out. She watched Eric get slowly out of the other side. "Come on," she said. "We have a new place to stay."

"What about the old one? What about my stuff?"

"You are about to be reborn, Eric. You don't need your old stuff."

He nodded and followed her across the small courtyard and up the stairs. She opened the door, drew her gun and entered the apartment carefully, gesturing for Eric to wait at the door. She returned a moment later and smiled up at him. "I made one stupid mistake tonight. That was one too many," she said. "Come in. Make yourself at home. There's a bottle of Jamieson's on the kitchen counter, a bottle of water in the refrigerator. Make us a drink. I'm going to shower."

She went into the bedroom and got out of her clothes. She heard Eric moving in the kitchen. She would still have to watch him carefully to make sure he didn't have a delayed reaction to the violence he had been through. She turned on the shower, adjusted the water and stepped in. She stood under the heavy stream and felt the cleansing force of it. She soaped her face, scrubbing off the light camouflage paint she had applied earlier and soaped her hair, too lazy to hunt for shampoo.

She heard the click of the latch on the shower door as Eric stepped in behind her and smiled as she felt his hardness against her back and his hands sliding up over her breasts. She squirmed back against him. Eric had just moved into the first stages of rebirth.

EPILOGUE

Wednesday, January 30, 1990 Philadelphia, Pennsylvania

Lincoln Carswell saw Marianne Falken across the crowded gallery, her striking red hair covered in a fashionable white silk scarf. She was wearing a pair of lightly tinted glasses and was chatting to a couple of other women. Tonight's gallery opening was the first major public event she had attended since Jon had been killed in Portugal the previous May.

Lincoln saw Allen Jensen coming quickly toward him, a few drops of champagne foaming over the brim of his glass. Allen was the owner, and as he billed himself, the "curator", of the Liberty Gallery. He loved a Lincoln Carswell show. They were not only the most popular events at the gallery, but the most profitable.

"Lincoln," he said, arriving breathless at his side. "Dear man. You simply must allow me to sell Woman on a Boat."

Lincoln laughed. "I told you it was a display piece."

"But what a piece. I have had offers you could retire on."

"I don't want to retire."

"But what are you going to do with it?"

"Keep it," Lincoln replied.

"Who is the woman?" Jensen asked.

Lincoln smiled. He had been asked this question a dozen times this evening. "She's a composite."

"A composite?"

Jensen knew very well what a composite was but he explained it anyway. "I find a boat, a woman's face, a body, decide on a costume, create a group of on-lookers, and the other elements of the painting and then put them all together in one. Virtually all of my works are composites. You know that."

Jensen looked at him. "I do know that. I just don't believe you."

Lincoln shrugged and smiled. Marianne's hair was covered tonight to disguise the most obvious similarity. Her dress was black as befitted a widow still adjusting to the loss of her husband and it was uncharacteristically chaste, concealing the voluptuousness of her figure. There was no cleavage, no slash up the side of her skirt, no curve-hugging lines.

Less than a year ago he had not known her, now they were lovers, living together sometimes, separately at other times, planning a future together. He had suggested that she not come this evening but she had insisted on being present at the unveiling of her portrait. She wanted to gauge the reaction of those seeing it for the first time. There was a risk that she would be recognized but she was willing to take it, and as she pointed out, if someone recognized her as the subject, did it really matter?

Allen Jensen was speaking to him again but he had only been aware of the voice, not of what he said. "Sorry, Allen," Lincoln said. "I missed that."

"I said I see your patron is here?"

"My patron?"

"The recently widowed Mrs. Jon Falken."

"Why would you call her my patron?"

"She bought one of your paintings at the last show."

"So she did," Lincoln said. "I'm not sure that makes her my patron, although repeat customers are always welcome."

"Indeed."

"If you'll excuse me, Allen, I'm going to wander around a bit."

"Of course," Allen replied. "But think about Woman on a Boat. There is serious interest being shown in it."

"People always want what they can't have," Lincoln said. He smiled at Allen and wandered into the crowd.

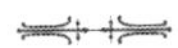

Marianne Falken saw Lincoln walk away from Allen Jensen, dressed as he always was for a gallery opening, in a tuxedo with a white dinner jacket, black bow tie and black cummerbund. He had told her the colours for the evening were in the paintings.

She was still outwardly the grieving widow, but inwardly she was in love. Lincoln was the most beautiful thing that had ever happened to her. Jon's death had saddened her. The years of companionship and friendship, even though it was an uneasy situation, had developed a closeness between them. However, after the initial shock, the overwhelming sensation she had experienced in Portugal when the police had arrived to tell her of her husband's death, was one of relief. She wondered why she didn't feel guilt over this reaction but she didn't. She wondered if her relief was related to her feelings for Lincoln. It was hard to sort that out, but basically it was a relief to not have Jon in her life anymore, regardless of what else was going on. Prior to Jon's death, she had also made the decision to leave him when they returned to Harrisburg, so some of the relief she felt at his death was what she would have felt after their divorce.

The circumstances of Jon's death remained a mystery. After their brief argument, following dinner at the Algarve

Terrace, Jon had remained behind with Clark Einfeld and Steven Clayton. They were to meet with someone, perhaps a potential supporter of his upcoming political campaign, or so he had implied. That was the last time he had been seen alive. His body was found on a deserted country road, outside the small Portugese coastal city of Faro. He had died from a single gunshot wound to the heart. No sign of Einfeld or Clayton had been discovered.

Everyone agreed that it was a surprising and unfortunate demise for an American war hero and a sad ending to a promising political career. Officially, his death was an unsolved homicide, still under investigation in Portugal. However, Marianne knew of Jon's affairs, and thought the more likely explanation was that he had gone to find a hooker and was simply the victim of a mugging.

A waiter wandered by and she lifted a full champagne flute from his tray and took a sip.

"What do you think, Mrs. Falken?" Allen Jensen had come up behind her.

"It's very nice, dry and properly chilled," she replied.

"Thank you," Allen said. "But I was referring to the show."

"I know," Marianne said.

"And . . .?"

"'American Diversity' is a good title for it. There's a large range of subjects."

Allen waved down a waiter and took a glass of champagne for himself. "I believe you bought one of the paintings at the last exhibition."

"I did."

"Have you chosen a favourite this time?"

"Not yet."

"What do you think of 'Woman on a Boat'?" Allen asked.

"It's lovely, but I didn't know he did portraits."

"Why did you call it a portrait?"

"Because the central focus of the painting is a person. I thought those were usually called portraits."

"Lincoln says it's a composite."

Marianne looked at her portrait across the room, wondering if Allen Jensen was teasing her. "Since he painted it, I guess he should know."

"Indeed he should," Allen said.

Lincoln lay on the bed watching Marianne. His white dinner jacket was tossed over a chair, the bow tie loosened, the black patent shoes kicked off.

She pirouetted in front of him. "How was my disguise?" she asked. "Do you think we really fooled anyone?"

"I think we fooled a lot of people but not Allen. He's fairly shrewd."

"I think he was at least suspicious."

"He was," Lincoln said. "But after the show is over and Woman on a Boat is back here, it will be difficult to remember exactly what the woman looked like."

Marianne walked over to the bed and turned her back to Lincoln. "Unzip me."

"My pleasure," he replied, pulling the long zipper down. "Your skin is flawless." He ran a finger tip down the middle of her back.

She stepped away and turned to face him letting the dress slide down her body to collect in a heap around her feet. She was naked except for the white scarf in her hair.

Lincoln gasped in surprise. "You were naked all evening?"

"Of course not," she said. "I was wearing a dress."

She reached up and loosened the white scarf and shook her hair. It fell in waves almost to her shoulders. She let the scarf float slowly down in front of her. She smiled at him. "Are you wearing your tuxedo to bed?"

Lincoln shook his head.

"Stand up and I'll help you out of it."

Wednesday, January 30, 1990 Auckland, New Zealand

Eric Shore leaned out as a small gust of wind hit the sail on the dinghy. It obediently healed over and as he eased the jib, it straightened up. He was getting used to the new name, and as far as he could tell, was adjusting well to his new life.

"Well, done," he said glancing aft to the tiller. "You're learning quickly."

"I've got a good teacher."

Eric laughed. It was a good day to be on a small boat, wheeling around Auckland harbour. His new boat, a forty eight footer christened "Rapture" was moored in the Royal New Zealand Yacht Squadron a couple of miles across the bay. But the way to learn to sail, to feel the wind, to read the ruffles on the water, to learn how a boat responded, was on a dinghy, not a large keel boat. And today was a good day to learn, the winds were light, shifty and occasionally gusty, all good tools, and his student was learning quickly. This was the third day they had been out since she had arrived a week ago.

"Let's try a jibe," he said. "Do you remember that one?"

"Is that the one where the wind goes behind us when we turn?"

"You've got it."

"And that's the one I have to be careful of the boom swinging over."

"That's the one."

"Okay. Here we go."

Eric began to move across to the other side of the boat. He felt the wind shift as the boat turned and ducked his head almost quickly enough. The boom slammed over, clipping him a glancing blow above his forehead, knocking him to the floor of the dinghy.

"Are you all right?"

Eric sat up and crawled up on the other side of the boat. "I'm fine," he said. "Just clumsy. I forget how fast little boats turn. And besides, you had a wind shift just as you started into it."

"You're bleeding.,"

"Where?" Eric asked, reaching up to touch the side of his head where the aluminum spar had struck him. He looked at his hand. His finger tips were bloody.

"You found it."

"Yeah, I did," Eric said. "Shall we head back to Rapture?"

"I need your electric razor, Eric. I'll have to shave a bit of your hair off to get at the cut but it doesn't look deep."

Eric stood up and went below. In the bathroom he picked up his rechargeable electric razor and went back up the companionway. "This should do the trick." He handed it to her.

"Thanks."

Her hands were gentle as they pulled the hair back, probed around the cut and shaved the hair away. "It's nice to have a doctor on board, Laura," Eric said. "But I hope I don't need your skills very often."

"Me too," Laura said. "Hold still." She handed him the razor. "How did you get the first scar?"

"I think I was born with it."

She looked carefully. "Could be. It's been there a long time."

Eric thought about the nameless doctor in Bavaria, almost certainly long dead by now, and wondered if it was worth explaining to Laura. He decided it wasn't.

"In any case, I don't recall getting hit on the head before." He felt Laura probing in a different spot. "What are you doing now?"

"Having a look at your other scar. Maybe you had a prefrontal lobotomy that I don't know about."

"That would explain a lot of things, wouldn't it."

"Maybe." Laura said. She probed for a moment more. "I'm not sure, Eric, but if I had to guess I would say it was a forceps scar."

"What's that?"

"You were entering the world a little too slowly and the doctor grabbed your head with a pair of pliers and pulled you out."

"Pliers?"

"Special ones designed to fit a baby's head. Called forceps."

Eric shrugged. "No evident brain damage?" he asked.

"Only your weird behaviour."

The chardonnay was icy cold as they sat cuddled in a corner of the cockpit watching the sun set. It was a beautiful warm summer evening. Seagulls wheeled around overhead, calling to each other. "Thank you for coming with me, Laura."

"Thank you for asking," she said. "I only had to wait for thirty years."

"Thirty two and a half years,"Eric said.

"Really that long?"

"Really," Eric said. "We graduated in June 1957, I went to Toronto, you went to Vancouver."

"I know."

Eric felt her tense a Little. She always did whenever the subject of Vancouver came up, and the separation that had led him to find another woman, the one he had eventually married. "So from June 1957 to January 1990 is thirty two and a half years." They were silent. Eric took a sip of his wine. "Can we talk about that period in our lives some time, if we're going to spend our life together now?"

Laura nodded. "If you want to," she said. "But can you tell me about what you did in Europe last year, too?"

"If you want to know."

"I want to know everything about you," Laura said. "No secrets. I have thirty two and a half years of catching up to do."

"No secrets," Eric said. He thought about this for a moment. Perhaps a slightly sanitized version would have to do. "Okay," he said. "Here's the short version. You know about my mysterious biological parents and my origins in Germany. When I went to Europe, I ran into some people who tried to kill me because they believed I am the son of Adolf Hitler."

"Are you serious?" Laura sat up and looked at him. "You can't be?"

"I am serious, Laura," Eric said. "They really believed that."

"And are you?"

"Adolf Hitler's son?"

"Yes."

"I don't know," he said. "I met a woman who was probably my mother but who isn't saying anything about it. She just looked at me with such longing in her eyes that I knew if I wasn't her son that she wished I were. Yet, she claimed she had not had any children. I wondered if she were Eva Braun."

"Hitler's mistress?" Laura said incredulously. "Why do you think that?"

"Hitler's wife, actually, although they weren't married when I was born and I doubt he ever knew he had a son, if he did," Eric said. But I think it was her because she was the right age, because later I looked up every picture I could find of her and she was the right height, build, same facial features. I am fairly confident that is who she was." He smiled and snuggled her against him. "And also because she told me she was Eva Braun."

Laura sat up and stared at Eric. "And do you believe her?"

"No way to know for certain, just a feeling." Eric paused and thought about her, beautiful, elegant, 77 years old now if she really was Eva Braun. But what did it matter?

"So what now?"

"Nothing," Eric said. "I've gone as far down that road as I want to go, as far as I am going to go. I'm just glad it's all over, that I don't have to deal with it or even think about it anymore. I just want it to stay gone."

"Gone?"

"If by some accident of history and biology, I am the child of Adolf Hitler and Eva Braun, then I am the only one. And I didn't have any children so the line is dead." He was silent for a moment. "Now, enough of that, tell me about your time in Vancouver."

Laura leaned back against him and snuggled under his arm. She took a long drink of her chardonnay. "Eric," she said softly. "I have to tell you this and I'm sorry. Do you remember the weekend at the end of July, the summer we graduated from high school, the weekend when I came back from Vancouver to get my stuff?"

"Yes, of course I do," Eric said. "We made love on the beach at Delta, with all the mosquitos and we didn't even notice the bites." He chuckled. "I scratched for days."

Laura was still against him. "And you wore a condom."

"Like always."

"It didn't work."

"What?" Eric sat bolt upright, spilling his wine over the cockpit floor. "What do you mean it didn't work?"

"I mean I got pregnant."

"And you didn't tell me?"

"I didn't find out until the beginning of November, you remember how sporadic my periods were? How we always worried? By the time I found out, you were settled in Toronto. I had the letter written to you to tell you when a letter arrived from you telling me that you had met Deirdre and were going steady with her." She stared into Eric's eyes. "I cried for days and then ripped up the letter."

Eric put his hands on her shoulders, tears were running down his cheeks. "Why in God's name didn't you tell me anyway?"

"Because I didn't want you that way," Laura said, drawing Eric to her. "I didn't want you giving up university in Toronto, abandoning your new life and coming back to Portage to marry the poor but bright little German girl that you had knocked up."

"So what happened?"

"Our son was born on April 20, 1958."

Made in the USA
San Bernardino, CA
12 April 2017